LEAR'S DAUGHTERS

DAW Fantasy Novels by
MARJORIE B. KELLOGG

THE DRAGON QUARTET

VOLUME ONE:
The Book of Earth
The Book of Water

VOLUME TWO:
The Book of Fire
The Book of Air

LEAR'S DAUGHTERS

MARJORIE B. KELLOGG

WITH WILLIAM B. ROSSOW

DAW BOOKS, INC.

DONALD A. WOLLHEIM, FOUNDER
375 Hudson Street, New York, NY 10014
ELIZABETH R. WOLLHEIM
SHEILA E. GILBERT
PUBLISHERS
http://www.dawbooks.com

First Printing, February 2009

1   2   3   4   5   6   7   8   9

ACKNOWLEDGMENTS

The authors would like to thank the following for generously sharing, in the past and present, their time and expertise:

Jane Ira Bloom	Karen Haas
Brian Brock	Olenka Hubickyi
Antonia D. Bryan	Jarvis P. Kellogg
Vicky Davis	Dorothy Koehler
Claire S. Derway	Marvin B. Koehler
Susan Dworkin	Barbara Newman
Lisbeth Firmin	Dr. Katalin Roth
Eric Golanty	

Thanks also to our agent, Joshua Bilmes.

Always thanks to Lynne Kemen.

And very special thanks to Sheila Gilbert, who bought us twice.

For WILLIAM SHAKESPEARE,
who would have been unsurprised by this tale . . .

" . . . Therefore the winds, piping to us in vain,
As in revenge, have suck'd up from the sea
Contagious fogs; which, falling in the land,
Have every pelting river made so proud
That they have overborne their continents:
The ox hath therefore stretch'd his yoke in vain,
The ploughman lost his sweat; and the green corn
Hath rotted ere his youth attain'd a beard:
The fold stands empty in the drowned field,
And crows are fatted with the murrain flock;
The nine men's morris is fill'd up with mud;
And the quaint mazes in the wanton green,
For lack of tread, are undistinguishable:
The human mortals want their winter here:
No night is now with hymn or carol blest:
Therefore the moon, the governess of floods,
Pale in her anger, washes all the air,
That rheumatic diseases do abound:
And through this distemperature we see
The seasons alter: hoary-headed frosts
Fall in the fresh lap of the crimson rose;
And on old hyem's chin and icy crown
An odorous chaplet of sweet summer buds
Is, as in mockery, set: the spring, the summer,
The childing autumn, angry winter, change
Their wonted liveries; and the maz'd world,
By their increase, now knows not which is which . . ."

—*A Midsummer Night's Dream, Act II, sc. i*

BOOK ONE

DELUGE

" . . . rain, wind, thunder, fire, are my daughters . . ."
—*King Lear*, Act III, sc. ii

1.

THE LITTLE MAN huddled high among the storm-bound cliffs, a young man, within the dark and weathered skin of an ancient. He sat cross-legged, alert in his cramped stone shelter, his slim body hooded and swaddled in a nest of furs and wool. The narrow door leaked cold light from a white and swirling sky. Fine snow blew in to pile in the folds of his blankets.

His head inclined as if listening. His breath rimed the rough rock with frost. One brown hand smoothed a strip of tooled leather against his thigh. He adjusted two edges between thumb and forefinger, eased the leather onto his knee, and resumed his sewing.

The wind moaned at the open doorway. The gales pounding the curve of his shelter had long ago buried the trail threading down the cliffs. Beyond his shallow ledge, the land vanished into storm. The tempest enclosed him in a roaring chaos of cold and white, ordered only by the deft logic of his bone needle: hover, like a ravenous hawk, swoop to the resisting leather, pierce and pull up, thread taut, to hover and swoop again, in time with the soft swell of his breathing.

Between one stitch and the next, the wind clamor died.

The little man's glance flicked up and outward, probing the sudden silence.

A cry came from a distance above, so faint even in the utter stillness that it might have been imagined. The bone needle froze in its downward swoop until the cry came again, repeated now from nearer by. The little man nodded, and unthreaded his needle. With disciplined haste, he folded it into the soft leather, and then into a pouch sewn to the inner layer of his woolens. His ringleted hair grazed the domed ceiling as he gathered his blankets into a larger pack. He slung it low across his back, then glanced around the shelter, patting at his chest with an absent frown. His fingers burrowed among leather and wool to squeeze a carved blue stone strung on a knotted thong.

He blinked, an anxious tic, then pulled on gloves, hugged his furs about him, and crawled into the open.

The snow fell gently now. The blind whiteness had coalesced into a landscape. The little man surveyed the towering curve of cliffs. To either side, they rose sharply into mountains, range after range of silver-white crags fading into the whiter distance. A long stride from the door of his shelter, the ledge fell away in a sheer, dizzying drop. Out on the plain below, a tall silvery cone rose through the snow cover. The little man's gaze lingered on it, noting no change since his last reconnaissance. Past the object's oddly symmetrical bulk, the white plain stretched away to hide beneath a lowering cloud cover.

The shrill cry and its echo came again. When a third and closer call took up the relay, the little man answered, and heard his trilled reply carried back, voice by voice, up into the frozen mountains behind. With a grimmer nod, he fastened his furred hood, cinched the wrists of his leather mittens, and pivoted down the icy trail.

He moved cautiously at first, easing the cramp out of unused muscles, searching the drifts for hidden dangers, but working at last into a fast, stiff-legged lope that sent up sprays of powder with every falling leap. Arms flung wide, he banked into his turns, racing along angled ledges where spires of bare rock broke through the ice and snow. At each hairpin switchback, he leaped and swerved, leaped and swerved, building up speed in a controlled fall down the mountainside. Along the lower reaches, the drifts drew up about him, slowing his progress. He plowed through ungracefully, furs and eyebrows crusting with white. His breath puffed out tiny clouds. His arms flapped like tired wings.

Lower still, the deep snow pack hardened under its own massive weight. The trail closed over to form a tunnel that dropped through drifts compacted into solid ice. A ghost of daylight filtered in to guide the runner's way, dimming with each descending step. Near the base of the cliffs, stone ledges pierced the floor to warm the icy gleam with glimmers of rose. The little man ran an urgent slalom around every twist and obstacle, slowing only when the tunnel leveled out.

Then, where a second passage met at right angles to the first, he skidded to a stop.

This tunnel was larger, more rigidly square. Yellow sand cut the slickness of its floor. A hard white glow reflected along its walls from around a distant turn. The little man hesitated at the intersection, catching his breath. He kicked at tusks of ice shattered along the bottom of the walls. Someone had cleared headroom among the icicles crowding the ceiling, someone much taller than he. He stared up the smaller tunnel. Its round, cool greenness slunk into watery dark as it curved back toward the cliffs at an upward slant. He sighed, pressed his jaw with a balled fist, and turned into the harsher light. The square tunnel widened after the first corner, then straightened like a ruled line. The little man took up a reluctant jog, his footsteps sending up a chattering cascade of echoes. After a long flat stretch, the tunnel took a final right-angle turn and dead-ended in a wall of ice.

The little man halted. The end of a large cylinder poked incongruously through the hard translucent surface. Its silvery, perfect arc was three times his height. Its open mouth exuded warmth and bright light. He squinted into it and shoved back his hood. Less than twenty paces away, bodies moved in a confusion of whiteness. Voices rose in unfamiliar syllables, murmurs mixed with strident tones. The little man lingered in shadow and reflected light, half-blinded, hopeful of invisibility, then cupped reluctant hands to his mouth. By the time his bellowed message had echoed the length of the cylinder, he had whirled around and was gone.

**FTL HAWKING Exploration of Byrnham Cluster
(UWSA/ConPlex Exp. 23)
Star System PT 6 (KO, 3 p?)**

(continued)

of a large terrestrial planet for stragetic mineral potential and possible evidence of ETI artifacts by landing science team for nine
month period.

(2) Astronomical study of Pop. II late sequence stellar system
from supporting (in-orbit) SCR BOSTON, with focus on composition of primary and nearby stars.

B. Expedition complement

  B.1. Ship Complement

    B.1.1. System Carrier - research
    SCR BOSTON   UWSA O36A3
        Configured for: 1 Lander, 6 planetary orbiting
        satellites, 4 message drones.

    B.1.2. Lander - research
    LR 14   UWSA 0014C2

  B.2. Crew Complement)

    B.2.1. Ship Crew

Captain Maxim B. Newman	(Commander, SCR)
Commander Weng Tsi Hua	(Commander, LR: Landing)
Lt. Commander Jen Wilson	(Master Pilot, SCR)
Lt. Veronica McPherson	(Pilot, LR: Landing)
Lt. Bea Suntori	(CRI Specialist)
En. Ro L. Gobajev	(Propulsion Engineer)
En. Josei Pilades	(Engineer/Medical Mate)

    B.2.2   Science team

Dr. Taylor Danforth	(Ch. Sci., Planetology, Landing)
Dr. Jorge Sundqvist	(Asst. Ch. Sci., Astronomy)
Dr. Susannah James	(Exobiology, Landing)
Dr. Megan Levy	(Anthropology, Landing)
Mr. Stavros Ibiá	(Linguistics, Landing)

    B.2.3.   ConPlex Team

Dr. Emil Clausen	(VP, Expl. & Dev., ConPlex, Landing)
Dr. Rye Hobart	(Remote Sensing, ConPlex)

C. Star System PT 6 Schedule

    The schedule covers the following mission phases: Star system en-
try, planetary orbit entry, pre-landing orbital surveys, landing and subse-

UWSA Form No. A6210

2

INSIDE THE WARM WHITE SPACE, two women glanced up from the work table to stare at the mirrored entryway.

"Who was that?"

"Was it Liphar?" The overhead lights flashed off a pair of gold-rimmed eyeglasses.

The girl in the recliner, the only one in uniform, tossed aside her reader and stretched lazily. "Some one of them yelling and running about, like usual."

The woman in glasses shut down her sketcher, raked back graying curls, and rubbed her nose in disgust. "A little more respect for the locals, if you please, Lieutenant."

"Meg. She's teasing," murmured the third woman, as she opened a plastic sample bag and spread its woody contents across the white tabletop. She felt her own impatience rise and willed it down again. "Ronnie, don't start, okay?"

Megan Levy lifted martyred eyes to the landscape of scorched metal lowering above their heads like a storm cloud. "There's one in every expedition . . ."

"You should hope you get one as good as me!" the young officer shot back.

Susannah followed Megan's upward gaze. Perhaps a more neutral topic could be found up there?

The underbelly of their landing craft now formed the ceiling of their work space, which was also their mess and sleeping quarters. It was heat-bruised, sand-scoured, grimed with soot and condensation, crisscrossed with the accordion piping and looping cables of contingency living. All but two equipment bays dangled open, their contents plundered or replaced with decreasing care as the long weeks wore on. Scattered stacks of steel canisters and storage crates hinted at a once-orderly partitioning of space now devolved into haphazard division, seasoned with equal dollops of temper, bullying, and political maneuvering.

"Y'know, they built the last of this model twenty years ago, before I was born, even." The girl flopped around in her recliner. "What'd you guys do to get stuck with this mission?"

Susannah glanced over, mildly curious. "Why? Did you . . . do something?"

"Sure. Punched out a paying passenger who got too free with his hands."

"You'd think that would be . . ." Susannah began, then thought better of it.

Megan sniffed. "People are trying to work here, McPherson."

"Yeah? How much observing-the-natives do you get done, hiding out down here all the time?"

"I'm working *now*."

Susannah raised hazmat-gloved palms. "Please! Both of you! It's bad enough in here as it is." She was sure Megan hadn't opted for the standard corrective eye surgery precisely to be able to shoot steely glares at her students over an edge of glinting metal, as she was currently glaring at McPherson.

"I *am* working." Megan resettled the sketcher on her lap and fiddled guiltily with its touch pad. "I'm just not getting anything done."

"Ah, cabin fever."

"Cure that, Doc," McPherson chirped. "You'd be a gazillionaire."

"I'll get right on it." And, indeed, it was taking its toll. Susannah noted how wan they all looked in the unforgiving electric glare. Megan's decades-of-fieldwork tan had faded to wrinkled beige. Her own pale skin was practically translucent. Doggedly, she brushed aside crushed twigs and sand to set out a withered specimen for study. As calm returned to the work space, she found herself listening, not for the pilot and the anthropologist to resume their daily battle, but to the ambient sounds of the Underbelly. The quiet hum of electronics and HVAC, the fathomless creaking of the ice wall surrounding them, the subtle clicking of the force field holding back that crushing weight. The mix was different somehow, in an indefinable way that made her uneasy, like a symphony with one instrument out of tune. Susannah wondered what the runner in the tunnel had been trying to tell them. "It probably wasn't Liphar."

"No. He tends to hang around when he comes down this far." Megan pushed the sketcher aside again and pretended to examine a stray thorn from Susannah's samples.

"Gloves," Susannah warned. Megan withdrew her hand briskly.

"Long enough to cadge a meal, most times," McPherson commented.

"We can spare a little food, for goodness sake!"

"A little?"

Susannah sighed. "It's an opportunity for study, Ronnie—his digestive system being so compatible with our own? More evidence in support of the Seeding Theory. It's not the case with every humanoid population we've come across, you know."

"Most of them," countered Megan. "But actually, I believe young Liphar considers our cuisine to be sadly limited."

"Well, he ain't lying," McPherson drawled from the depths of her chair.

Megan gave this rare point of agreement a sour nod.

"We were never promised a four-star galley," Susannah reminded them.

McPherson flexed one trim leg and then the other, fluffing her short cap of blonde hair. "Don't tell Emil. You'll hurt his feelings."

"As if he had any," Megan retorted.

"Not even Emil can do much with freeze-dried soy cake." Susannah grasped her specimen gingerly to prevent its sharp contours from piercing her gloves, and positioned it on the scanner plate. So far, every sample her native contacts had dug out of the ice for her seemed to be armed and venomous.

"But the Sawls' diet is just as limited as ours." Megan mused. "More so. How they survive on what's available on this planet is a miracle of dietary coping strategies."

"How we survive back home is miracle enough," Susannah said.

"You call that survival?"

"I said 'survive,' not 'thrive.' Why do you think I chose *exobiology*?"

"Wow." McPherson sat up. "I get it now. You both *volunteered*."

"Of course," said Susannah.

Megan smiled darkly. "That should've been your punishment: Earth duty."

McPherson sobered. "Jeez. I suppose it could've been. Yeah, I get why you'd want to be away from there. A week downside was bad enough!" She shook her head. "But why not stop along the route and provision up, y'know—with *real* stuff? In flight school, they say the food's better the farther you get from Sol. No such luck on this ice ball."

"Extra ports of call weren't exactly in our budget," Megan noted. "Nor were fresh vegetables."

Susannah reached for another change of subject. "If I understand him right, Liphar's real concern isn't the food, it's the packaging. It bothers him that we use something once and throw it away. I haven't yet been able to make the function of the recycling unit clear to him, and Stavros refuses to try."

"Stav feels the science is too advanced." Megan slid into that earnest professorial tone that always made Susannah want to run screaming from the room, even though she'd never dream of actually doing so. "He doesn't want to poison the native ideosphere before we get it fully recorded."

McPherson let out a hoot. "The what?"

"The body of ideas and symbols, of concepts that are particular to the Sawls."

"The idiot sphere, you mean."

Susannah cleared her throat significantly and turned over the specimen on the scanner. "Meg, look at the spore cases on this leaf. It's structured a lot like our *Equisetum,* but what would a water plant be doing in this frozen desert?"

"It got lied to, just like us," McPherson grouched.

Megan leaned forward. "Wait. Did he actually say that?"

"Who?" Susannah touched the fone nestled above her ear. "CRI, while you're analyzing the new samples, remember to scan for trehalose."

"Trehalose," replied the computer. "Certainly, Dr. James."

"Did Liphar really say that about the waste? It's a sophisticated notion for a low-tech society like this one."

"Is it? Well, maybe I'm projecting. He didn't say it in so many words."

"To quote our mad linguist: 'The Sawls are a subtle people.' "

Susannah rolled her eyes. "Or maybe just diplomatic."

"Professional moochers." McPherson flicked invisible dust from the space service uniform that fit her short athletic body like a second, bright-white skin.

"When you were Liphar's age," Susannah chided, "I'll bet you were doing likewise at the Academy cafeteria."

McPherson brushed the silver figure eight on her collar. "He's not as young as he looks, Stav says. And by his age, I'd graduated and won my first commission. I was buying other folks their lunch!"

"You might keep in mind," intoned Megan, "that food is a time-honored medium for social exchange, here on Fiix as well as throughout the galaxy. Food is a potent symbol of trust and hospitality that crosses all cultures. Certainly it is at home, during the current crisis, but also on many of the smaller colonies, those harsher worlds where subsistence is marginal, highly intricate food-based etiquettes have evolved."

"Trust? Where you come from, folks'll kill you for your breakfast."

"Where I come from is forty feet under water."

"Whatever." McPherson waved a leg dismissively. "Save your lectures for the classroom, Megs. The real world works differently."

"And what part of the 'real world' have you ever lived in, spacer brat?"

"Enough!" Susannah yelped.

McPherson snatched up her discarded reader and turned her back.

Listening to the quiet electronic beeps and Megan's irate mutterings, Susannah realized what was different about the sound in the Underbelly. For the six weeks since their arrival, weeks that were beginning to seem like an eternity, the storm-strummed vibration of the Lander's shell had hummed a constant accompaniment to the crew's sleeps and squabbles. Now she had to strain to hear it—in fact, she wasn't sure she could hear it at all. "Listen to how quiet it is."

Megan awoke from some icebound reverie of her own. "Yes. I guess it is."

Susannah stroked fingers through her straight dark hair—too long, too dark, her men always said, for one claiming to be a pure-blooded English-woman—and readjusted the plastic clasp at her neck, unable to restrain the anxious gesture. She took the surrounding force field for granted, as they all did. But if she set training aside and gave in to instinct, it was hard to put faith in the impenetrability of an invisible wall powered only by a slim beam of energy whose source in the Orbiter might as well be a million miles away rather than several thousand. The ice seemed the more immediate power, manifest and active, pressing relentlessly inward against the Shield, ever threatening the precious space carved out by the heat of the Lander's descent engines. "I wonder what he wanted."

"What who wanted?"

"Whoever that was at the tunnel just now."

"Yes, that was odd. Not like the Sawls to run around yelling."

McPherson thumbed off her reader. "Aw, Meg, be real. On the noise scale, they're about a nine. All jammed into their little holes up there, yammering a mile a minute."

"They don't yell at me," snapped Megan.

"Please! Can't you two work out your mother-daughter conflict elsewhere?"

"Mother, my ass!" bellowed McPherson. "My mother captained the *Orion* for twelve years! The fuckin' *Orion*. You couldn't get a better ship in those days!"

"Too bad she's not on this trip!" Megan muttered. "We could use a grown-up with some actual experience!"

"WHAT?" McPherson sprang up from her chair. "You think it was a picnic landing us in shit like this? Snow up to the retros, a river of melting ice, when the surveys all said it would be seventy and sunny, easy beans? Or that gale-force wind that blew up out of fuckin' nowhere just as I was setting us down, nearly mashed us against those cliffs?"

"Oh, congratulations. And by the way, you got those Sleds fixed up yet?"

McPherson cocked an arm and threw her reader like a fastball. As Megan ducked, the hard-edged missile whizzed past and slammed into a curtain closing off a corner of the work space. A moment later, the curtain was drawn aside. A tall, white-haired woman surveyed them with stern equanimity.

"Uh-oh." The young pilot clambered out of her recliner, and came smartly to attention.

3

THE RUNNER IN the tunnel slowed as the grade steepened and the green darkness drew around him. His lungs sucked cold air in short hard gasps. His gait grew sloppy. His brown face dampened with exertion. He loosened the fastenings of his furs so that the heavy layers flopped about him like sodden sails. He gripped the thong of his blue amulet between bared teeth to ease its banging against his chest. At a narrow turn, he tripped on a thrusting tongue of rock, slithered clumsily along the slick floor, then struggled up and pushed still harder up the slope.

Ahead, smoother ledges of rock broke through the ice, climbing in low wide tiers like steps. The icicled ceiling lifted gradually, and pale gray light washed in to ease the gloom. At the top of the grade, the tunnel ended in an archway, drifted with snow. The runner staggered into a tall circular well, formed of neatly fitted blocks of ice, open to the high, white sky. In the center stood a sturdy pinnacle of rock, its blunt summit pierced by a hole as big as the runner's head. On the far side, a second, wider arch broke the ice wall to admit a flight of stone steps. Above loomed the sheer, snow-swept face of the cliff.

The runner stumbled across the well, fighting waist-deep powder, and gained the bottom step. But there he faltered, sinking to his knees in the snow, letting the slow flakes melt on his steaming cheeks. Without pausing for breath, he threw back his head and hollered into the cliff face. His hoarse cry ricocheted upward, amplified to a roar by the curve of the well.

The echoes died into silence. The runner curled into himself, panting in the snow. Then a single voice answered, and a hooded face peered out from a ledge high above. The runner leaned back, squinting up the cliff face. He signaled frantically. A hundred feet higher, where the steep zigzag of steps split to climb in opposing directions, another ledge filled suddenly with inquiring faces. Embroidered sleeves flapped, fingers pointed. Now the runner could hear them calling to him all at once. He waved again and bellowed louder, querulous in his exhaustion. On the lower ledge, the single face withdrew and rewarded him with the slap-slap of feet hurrying toward him down the stairs.

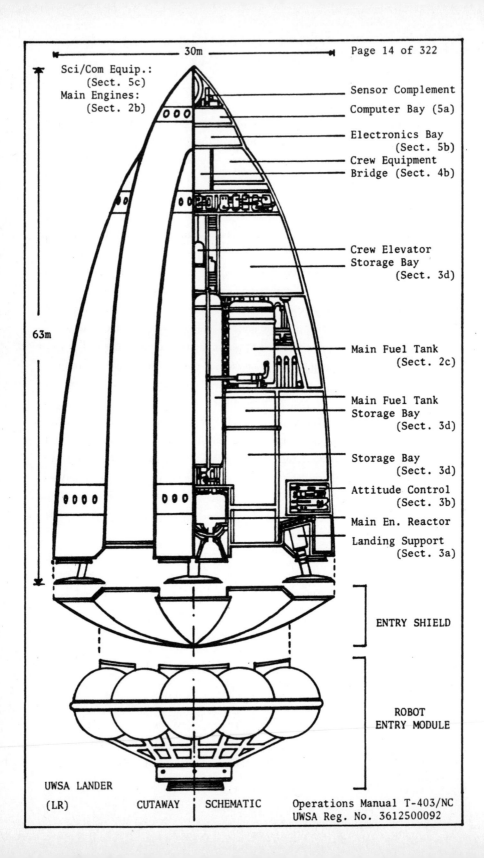

30m

63m

Sci/Com Equip.:
(Sect. 5c)
Main Engines:
(Sect. 2b)

Sensor Complement

Computer Bay (5a)

Electronics Bay
(Sect. 5b)

Crew Equipment

Bridge (Sect. 4b)

Crew Elevator
Storage Bay
(Sect. 3d)

Main Fuel Tank
(Sect. 2c)

Main Fuel Tank
Storage Bay
(Sect. 3d)

Storage Bay
(Sect. 3d)

Attitude Control
(Sect. 3b)

Main En. Reactor

Landing Support
(Sect. 3a)

ENTRY SHIELD

ROBOT
ENTRY MODULE

UWSA LANDER

(LR)   CUTAWAY   SCHEMATIC   Operations Manual T-403/NC
                                    UWSA Reg. No. 3612500092

4

"AND THE PLANETOLOGIST stands alone," the black man muttered.

The cubicle was low-ceilinged, a narrow pie wedge atop the starboard engine, tucked inside the Lander's curving shell. In the multicolored glow of a wall display, Taylor Danforth hunched over a remote keypad, his long legs cramped into the cranny below the brief shelf that served as a desk. One hand cradled his forehead while the other worked fitfully at the small of his back. After dinner, he decided, he'd call on McPherson's capable little hands for a massage. He was certain he'd never been so uncomfortable ever in his life. On most expeditions, he'd have a full lab to work in, but this old landing vehicle was too small. He'd had more room where he'd first set up in the Underbelly, but the constant chatter and bickering soon drove him back upstairs.

"Run that by once more, CRI."

The central display cleared and flicked back to life as the data appeared in neat blocks. Danforth studied it, glanced aside at the dimensional wind vector map floating above the holo-pad, then back at the figures in front of him.

"Jeezus. As if things weren't bad enough already . . ." His head wagged in disbelief and denial. "The heat flux profile's building way too fast. CRI, forget the cross sections. Give me the hemispherics on holo. Let's try it station by station, just the raw numbers."

"Time period?" The computer's voice was thin and scratchy. Recently, undertones of strained patience had crept in. CRI's model was designed to evolve according to the situation, but Danforth found electronic moodiness archaic and irritating. He wondered when he'd have to start saying please and thank you.

"Just the last five ship days, local conditions first."

The holographic vectors vanished, to be replaced by a slowly revolving black-and-white image of a cloud-draped sphere. A broad cut of clear sky crossed the planet's equatorial regions on a diagonal running northwest to southeast, like a sash on a decorated war hero. In the northern hemisphere, gray patches of ocean poked through scattered breaks in the clouds. The geographical features not hidden by clouds were whitened to indistinction by the heavy snow cover—except in one area.

Danforth leaned back in his chair, as if putting distance between him and the floating image might improve his view. "Damn. Look at that sucker."

A circular upthrust of mountains in the southern hemisphere remained oddly free of both snow and clouds. Between these southern mountains and the clear equatorial band, the holograph was incomplete in several sectors, so that the image was of a partial sphere, a planet missing square chunks of its anatomy.

"How am I supposed to make sense of this with so many stations crapping out on me! Useless secondhand junk!"

Fresh data blinked into the center display. "Home station L-Alpha. Position, Lander. 24.09 degrees north latitude, 31.66 degrees east longitude. Activated ship's day 119, Landing plus one . . ."

Danforth stirred restlessly. Maybe he should've sent some eager postdoc on this trip instead. Should've stayed on Gamma, working out the issues with his latest wife, the one he actually wanted to keep. He didn't like being in the field, never had. Always messy and inconvenient. Still, he had to do it, now and then, if only to keep up his lead at the cutting edge. Besides, he wanted *his* face to be the one beaming out from that first triumphant web release. "Spare me the calendar, CRI. Just give me the readings. Display the six-week averages alongside . . . please."

Ranks of data built at the center. A second listing began to the left. Danforth was reminded of building blocks: a wall of data, virtual in name but currently as opaque to him as actual concrete. Another thing he didn't like much—being mystified.

"Include surface radiation with each listing." He left off massaging his forehead and ran a few numbers on his keypad. "Six weeks' average temp, minus eighteen C., and look at it now. Skyrocketing. Never mind. Store that for later and move on. Wait. Fuck, shit, piss! Those high winds are back again."

"Excuse me, Dr. Danforth, but Mr. Ibiá is requesting immediate clearance."

"Tell him I'm busy."

"I have done so, but Mr. Ibiá insists that it's urgent."

Danforth's fingers hovered over the keypad as he thought through a revised calculation. Ibiá was the last thing he needed right now. "Tell him you couldn't raise me."

"I am sorry, Dr. Danforth, but I already told him you were in your lab. He seems very concerned to speak with someone in the Lander. Anyone."

"Patch him through to the Underbelly. Tell him I'm in the head. I don't want to talk to him. He makes me crazy. On to L-Beta."

"Is that an order?"

"Don't get sullen with me, CRI. L-Beta?"

"Weather station L-Beta." The computer's tone was noticeably clipped. "Position, 25.18 north, 32.46 . . ."

"Just the readings, damnit!"

When the new figures slammed into the display, Danforth was glad there was no one around to witness his response. Being caught with your jaw hanging open never did your reputation any good. He entered his notes in silence, starting to feel a bit sorry for himself. Not that he was the sort to court easy answers—no satisfaction in that. But this was sizing up to be a much bigger—and weirder—challenge than he'd bargained for.

When the probe data first came in to his university lab on Alpha Centauri Gamma, Danforth had worked hard to keep the lid on it. He'd even kept on an incompetent programmer, in case she'd spread the word if she got fired. It was, after all, the discovery of a lifetime—a globular cluster with Population II stars actually within starship range, offering a close-up look at a type of planetary evolution no one had been able to touch before: planets near a star going off the Main Sequence. Weirder still, one of those planets had shown distinct signs of life, where none should be possible. Danforth had little interest in alien populations, but the existence of anything alive on this rock pointed to something so unusual that only in his worst moments did he long for the company of scientific equals to discuss his problems with—having colleagues around would also mean having to share credit for a unique discovery.

So it wasn't his enforced solitude that had him rattled. Not at all. Rather, it was the sinking feeling that with each new numeral chattering past on his displays, a correlation between theory and observation was sliding farther and farther from his grasp.

Danforth smoothed down the long sleeves of his gray ship's issue sweats, adjusting the fastenings at his wrists. He took some comfort from the fact that a peevish temper at least kept him trim. He wouldn't go home soft and sloppy, unlike others in the landing party he could mention. He resettled himself at his keypad with a sour sigh. "CRI, update the vector map every five. Where in hell is that south wind getting all its energy?"

5

E.D 44–15:48

IN THE UNDERBELLY, the newcomer let the silence add dignity to her entrance, a dignity of age and bearing only slightly undercut by the VR net draped over one shoulder. "Lieutenant McPherson, Dr. Levy: I am sure you are both aware of how well sound carries in these denser atmospheres. I see no need for raised voices to make ourselves heard."

"Yes, Commander," McPherson murmured.

Megan shook her head ruefully. "Sorry, Weng. It's just that . . ."

"Yes, Dr. Levy?"

"Well, the usual, that's all."

"Ah. The usual." The Lander's captain moved to peer over Susannah's shoulder. Her pristine white uniform hung loosely, contriving to make her thin frame seem full and graceful. She sucked in a parched cheek and poked at a sprig of dried blossoms. "Any progress with the Fiixian flora, Dr. James?"

"Gloves, Commander!" Susannah followed her warning with an apologetic smile. "I'm grabbing every scrap and twig I can talk them out of, but without being able to get out into the field myself . . . well, it's all pretty much of a mystery, so I'm actually grateful for the extra time we've had here."

Weng's nod mixed faint amusement with skepticism. "You may be the only one, Dr. James." She stood a moment longer, then, as if struck by a sudden thought, turned and retreated to the relative seclusion of her corner, drawing the curtain behind her.

There was a beat of chastened silence, broken only by the ominous creaking of the surrounding ice. Then McPherson threw herself back into her recliner with a fierce whisper. "Even when she's listening, she's not really listening!"

"Don't kid yourself," Megan murmured. "She hears everything. She'd just *rather* it was all music."

"I prefer Bach to arguments myself." Susannah brushed grit from the scanner plate and laid out another leaf for study. She thought she heard a low distant rumble, more felt than heard, like the passing of an underground train, through the soles of her feet and through her fingertips as they rested on the smooth tabletop.

"The wind's come up again," she noted, though it didn't sound like the wind at all.

"Is it dinnertime yet?" Megan asked.

"I was up in the Caves earlier, to pick up these latest samples," Susannah deflected casually. "It's not so cold in the Meeting Hall as it has been."

"What, you're on my case now, too?" Megan's jaw tightened. "It's not the cold. I'd be up there right now, but Stavros is having one of his manic days. He's got all the com relays set up just where *he* needs them, like they're his personal property!"

"Requisition a power cell, then upload from the nearest cave mouth."

"Too much running in and out, and I need field access to the Library while I'm recording. Plus Stav's insisting it's too risky to put our backups on line! I mean, really! What idiot made him the Communications Officer?"

"Speak to Weng about it."

"He's got Weng in his pocket. I have a better idea. *You* speak to Stavros."

The corners of Susannah's mouth twitched. "I have no magic power over the man."

"So you say, but somehow you always get cave-side com when you need it."

"My reputation isn't as threatening as yours." Susannah conjured up patience she did not really feel. "Meg, he's just insecure."

"How can anyone that rich be insecure?"

"It's family money, and I gather he's not exactly in their good graces. Being stubborn is his defense. If you approach him obliquely, he's less likely to dig his feet in."

"He's off the charts," McPherson offered cheerfully. "Shut up in a damp old cave all day, with that hardware piled up around him like a fort. A total obsessive crazy."

"He's spent his whole life away at school," Susannah countered. "He doesn't know how to do anything else. Besides, a brand-new alien language on his first time out? Most people only dream they'll get so lucky. He's busy proving he can do it right."

She disliked feeling compelled to defend their most difficult colleague. Dealing with Stavros Ibiá was always a messy, ungainly business that left you more challenged than satisfied. His sheltered adolescence as a university wunderkind had not prepared the young linguist for the intimate politics of a small scientific expedition. But Susannah admired his unjaded commitment, not just to getting his work done, but to the ideal of the work, to the mystery and wonder of language. Still, as Megan often pointed out, however profound his gift for word theory, Ibiá had not yet learned to moderate his behavior like an adult. Just as well he spent most of his time up in the Caves, out of everyone's hair.

"Meg, you remember how it was. Your first planet is like your first love—it hits you the hardest. You think you'll never care as much about another world, or ever see the first as just one more in the string of worlds you'll study during a lifetime."

Megan grunted. "True enough. But there's not enough equipment for him to act like he's the only one who needs it."

"What's his excuse this time?"

"He's recording some major event in the Meeting Hall: music, tale chanting, dancing, you know, the works." At her friend's slow look, Megan waggled both palms defensively. "Yes, yes! All the more reason I should be up there, too! And yes, I could share the com the way he has it set up. But I don't know . . . I go up, I come back, I look at what I've got . . . and some days, it just seems like masturbation." Her bemused frown darkened, and she leaned forward, drawing her palms together as if in prayer. "Susannah, you'll agree . . . I *have* been working, very hard . . . until recently. Six weeks I've been trekking up there, listening, watching, recording. I have a book and a half's worth of observations already."

"Well, that's got to be good."

"No, it isn't. I can't . . . see its shape." Megan sat back abruptly. "I mean, it just *can't* be as straightforward as it seems in those caves. It *can't* be so pedestrian. My publishers will have my head in return for their, well, not-so-fat advance!"

"The flora's certainly not straightforward," Susannah offered. "And once Stavros gets the language sorted out . . ."

"That's my point! Nothing's ever simple and obvious. I know that, but I can't find the key. Like when I called Liphar's thinking 'sophisticated'—I meant 'modern,' really. I mean, it *looks* straightforward, like a grade-school text: your storybook pretechnical society, handcraft-oriented, the usual priestly caste, the elaborate guild organization, what we'd call medieval in the old Earth sense, minus the feudal system. But I can't . . . how can I describe this?" She paused, her gaze raking the confines of the Underbelly as if the surrounding ice might offer up an answer. "This is it: there's no *innocence* in their eyes. Like when you see a child on the street with a hundred-year-old face? The Sawls are . . . worldly? No, jaded. Blasé. Nothing seems to surprise them, even us, dropping on them out of the sky. All my observations say primitive, but my instincts keep yelling, 'old, old!' Yet they're resourceful and, god knows, energetic, so if their culture is so old, what's kept them from developing further?"

"Severely limited resources?"

"Well, sure, that's the standard answer, but . . ." Megan dropped chin to chest in an exasperated slump. "You know . . . deep down, I can't help thinking that the real problem is *me*. That it's been too long since I've worked with a *living* xenoculture. Too long in the classroom, too many excavations and dry artifacts. Old bones. A little shard of pottery. A well-preserved petroglyph. Inanimate objects." She pushed her glasses back on her head to massage the bridge of her nose. "A stone hide-scraper isn't going to mislead you intentionally by disguising itself as, oh, say, a water bowl. I mean, what in hell did I think I was doing, so late in life, schlepping all the way out here for the sake of one more book nobody'll read!"

Susannah dimmed her scanner. "Meg. Stop. This is nonsense. The Min Kodeh are very much alive and your study of them is considered a classic . . . as well as a best seller."

"That was years ago, when people still read books every now and then. Now the only reason people read about other worlds is if they want to move there!" Megan sighed, and her frown softened. "Besides, the Min Kodeh made sense to me."

"But the Min are far less Terran than the Sawls."

"Maybe that's the problem. So close and yet so far?"

"The Sawls will make sense to you. Just give it time."

A soft snore floated over from McPherson's recliner. Megan's scowl returned.

"Here. Look." Susannah dug among her sample bags and laid out two desiccated cuttings. One was bulbous and spiny, the other curled and delicate like a fern. "I'm just as mystified as you are. Normally, I wouldn't even classify these two in the same subphylum, but Stavros swears that the Sawls use the same word for both of them. Are they the same? Who's right? Only time will tell."

"Time is useless if you can't even concentrate!" Megan's dark mood had moved beyond easy consolation. "All this cold and snow and being cooped up all the time . . . !"

"The snow will stop." Susannah presented the sad, dry fern-thing as if it were a candle in the darkness. "This is the best proof we have that the sun will come out. There will be a spring."

But privately, and as the expedition's Medical Officer, she worried far more than she let on, about all of the landing party. It would be different if they'd been prepared for such arctic conditions. If the weather didn't ease soon, their productivity and their sanity would be frayed to the breaking point, along with their tempers and community relations.

Again, she heard it come and go, that odd, deep rumbling that didn't sound like the wind. It seemed to go on longer this time.

"Man on deck!" McPherson called out, startling them so that the table shuddered.

Susannah sat back, heart thudding. "Work seems to end earlier every day."

In the opening of the main hatch, neatly creased trouser legs appeared, and a man dropped gracefully to the ground. The fall of over three meters made landing upright a rather showy feat for someone his age, even in the lower gravity of Fiix.

Susannah glanced over. "Did I mention, Emil? That crash refresher course in emergency field medicine was rather basic—and mostly, I do research."

"There *is* an elevator." Megan nodded mordantly toward the central shaft that housed the Lander's magnetic lift.

Emil Clausen grinned, and his skin netted with the fine wrinkles of a permanent tan. He'd kept his color over the weeks since the landing. Susannah suspected a melanin stash, and wondered what other drugs the corporate prospector kept locked away in his stateroom—quarters that on any other mission would have belonged to the Lander's Captain. Paler tones encircled Clausen's sea-blue eyes, where sun goggles had marked him with an owlish expression.

He tugged his crisp sportsman's clothing into place. "Light I bring to your dull day, good ladies. Relief to your ennui!"

McPherson let her yawn stretch into a cheer.

Clausen sketched a bow. "Monsieur Emil, *le plus grand chef des dix-neuf mondes,* will prepare a feast for your evening delectation!"

"What did you fleece them out of this time?" Megan muttered.

As her friend shifted her chair around to face the enemy head-on, Susannah gave full attention to the large twig forming a scaly brown S against the white tabletop. It was Megan's folly and inspiration to be always tilting at windmills.

"My dear Dr. Levy, I merely offered an appropriate exchange. Your little Sawls are well versed in the intricacies of commerce." Clausen wandered over, hands tucked into the pockets of his true-leather vest. "I'd noticed that your friend Liphar was particularly enamored of a certain implement in my possession. It seems that, in his priestly studies, this bright young fellow has learned how to write."

"That old pen of yours!" McPherson crowed. "You fobbed off that lousy pen on him!"

"A *fountain* pen, McP! A rare and valuable antique. Like Dr. Levy and myself."

"Speak for yourself, Emil." But Megan's hand strayed consciously to her hair. "And how will Liphar like his deal when this antique ceases to write?"

Susannah patted her arm. "Meg, the Sawls are literate. They make ink. No reason why it shouldn't work just as well as Terran ink."

"Probably better, being closer to the source." Clausen pouted theatrically. "I was greatly fond of that pen, Megan. Nondisposable! It's seen me through the doldrums of nine expeditions. I even showed the little fellow how to clean and refill it."

McPherson bounced at his elbow. "So what'd you get for it?"

Clausen's eyes rose in comic ecstasy. "The dear boy talked that terrifying mother of his out of a brace of those pheasanty birds she raises up there in a black pit where no self-respecting bird should even venture."

"Whoo-hoo!"

"Sounds delicious," Susannah agreed.

"Those birds are raised specially for high ceremonial occasions," Megan countered.

"Are they? Well, that's your arena, not mine. But if that's the case, the least we can do is savor them with some high ceremony of our own."

Susannah abandoned all hope of working and began to pack her specimens into neatly labeled plastic envelopes. "Fresh meat, Meg! Come on! You'll enjoy it as much as we will. Besides, Liphar'll run that pen down to one of his craftsy older siblings and they'll get a whole work cycle's entertainment out of trying to reproduce it. That cousin of his in the Glassblowers Guild will probably have a fine line of glass pens available in the Market Hall in no time."

Clausen considered. "Maybe I should negotiate a percentage."

"Paid in foodstuffs, of course," Susannah grinned.

"Of course. Trade and barter, according to the local system."

Megan drummed her fingers, dangerously close to another tantrum. "Official policy is quite explicit in these matters, Emil. We are forbidden to interfere with alien technologies in any way."

"Megan, it's a pen, not a starship!"

"It's not the pen, it's the principle!"

"Oh. Principles." Clausen raised a satirical eyebrow. "Does this mean you won't be joining us for dinner?"

Megan pounded the table, rounding on Susannah. "You want to know why the Min Kodeh were so special? Or why I've had so little experience with *living* extraterrestrial cultures? It's guys like this, with their fast ships and their greed and their big corporate money—they're always there first, hauling in their military and their machinery, digging up the place until there's nothing left but slag heaps, malls, and mining saloons! Not enough they did it to Earth! Now they're off to wreck every planet in the galaxy!"

McPherson slid into the depths of her recliner with a groan.

"Mmmm." Susannah wished Megan wouldn't consider her an automatic ally in these confrontations with the expedition's true power heavyweight.

"Well?!?"

"Well, I think that's a little black-and-white."

"You'll be sorry, you'll see!" Megan leveled an accusing finger into Clausen's come-at-me grin. "His work is in direct conflict with ours, Susannah. He's not here to study, he's here to search and destroy. His presence on a First Contact expedition is a travesty, an affront to the scientific integrity of the mission!"

"As well as the prime factor in its funding," said Clausen dryly.

Susannah's gaze fixed tartly on her friend. "I'm a scientist, not a politician, and to me that means I collect and observe, and do a little doctoring when I'm needed. I do not legislate morality."

Megan threw up her hands in disgust. "Glib! *Glib!*"

Clausen relaxed against a landing strut. His placid smile said the debate was an old and tired one which he'd won many times, on many worlds, mostly by waiting it out. "Civilization moves in one direction, Meg—forward. Face it, just our being here, the seven of us in our shiny metal ship, interferes with the Sawls' technology. Before my first mine is sunk, even before my claim is staked, those busy little folk have a brand-new view of their universe, simply because we appeared in it, out of the heavens. That one event will change them more than any number of mines and machines. It has to. They may be primitive, but they don't appear to be stupid."

Megan shoved back her chair and stalked away from the table. Clausen shrugged, then spotted Susannah's sample bags. Eyes lighting, he dragged over a crate to pick through the discarded cuttings.

"Gloves, Emil."

"Nonsense." He crushed one leaf against a callused palm to give it a hopeful sniff.

Susannah could not help smiling. In pursuit of haute cuisine, Clausen was at his most Gallic and charming. She sorted through her sample bags and passed him one. "These are the local culinary herbs. What are you looking for?"

"Would you believe rosemary?" He poked around inside the bag, then sat back, dusting disappointment from his hands. "Oh, and by the way, everyone . . . it's stopped snowing."

McPherson bolted upright. "What?"

"What?" Four strides brought Megan back from her high dudgeon.

Susannah spread arms wide in disbelief. "Of course! That's why it was so quiet! Emil, how could you! You stand there ten minutes rapturing about pheasants when it's *stopped snowing?*"

"One-track mind. Sorry."

McPherson threw herself out of her chair with a victory yell and dashed behind a pile of crates. Drawers and lockers crashed open and shut. "Where's my therm-suit? Anybody seen my therm-suit?"

Clausen turned his smug grin on Susannah, but her attention slid past him toward the entry tunnel.

"Liphar! Hello! Come on in!"

The young Sawl stood breathless, cast in dark miniature against the mirrored arc of the giant cylinder. His smile was tentative. One hand clutched a blue leather bag tied to a thong around his neck. The hood of his thick outer garment was tossed hastily back. His woolen tunic had twisted around his childlike body as he ran. He struggled to unbind his arms, then shoved his thick ringlets out of his face with the hope of making himself presentable.

"Liphar! Speak of the devil!" Clausen boomed. "How's the publishing biz?"

"How, pleezhe?"

"Have you written the Great Sawlian Novel yet, my boy?"

Susannah sent Clausen a disapproving glance as the young Sawl's brown eyes mournfully sought her aid. She hoped the prospector's condescension was less obvious to Liphar than it was to everyone else. She'd heard he had ties to some minor European royal house, which might account for the worst excesses of his behavior.

"Never mind, then," Clausen chuckled. "Did you at least bring my birds?"

Liphar's hands flew out as he recalled the real purpose of his visit. "No bird now! No!" With a yelp, he ran to the table, grabbed Susannah's field pack and thrust it at her. Simultaneously, he snatched at her sample bags and pulled frantically at her sleeve. His small pointed features ran through an entire vocabulary of distress. Susannah stood openmouthed as he continued to tug at her. Slowly, she began to stow the bags in her pack. Liphar nodded eagerly, as one would to encourage a child.

"Maybe someone's sick up there," Megan suggested.

"But they have healers of their own, don't they, Meg?" Susannah chewed her lip. "Maybe it's Stavros? Liphar, I'll come right up. Just let me get my medikit."

Liphar pondered this until it made sense, then shook his head so violently that his long brown curls whipped against his cheeks. "No Stavros!" He pointed a finger at each of them in rapid succession. "You, you, you, you. All very danger!" Galvanized, he ran about the work space, slapping at the crates and furniture. "This, this, this all thing, out! You, out!" He gathered up gear and clothing from the ground, including the discarded rubbish lying nearby, and tossed it all in the direction of the entrance. When two or three armloads failed to spur his stunned audience into action, he halted, panting, to stare at them over the heap of clutter, his eyes begging for their instant comprehension. When they still did not react, he dove back to the table to shove a load into Megan's arms, then recommenced the frantic stuffing of Susannah's pack, railing all the while at high volume.

Finally, Susannah grabbed at him. "Liphar. Liphar! Slow down!" She pinned his hands gently to the table. "What do you need? Please explain slowly."

McPherson reappeared from behind the crate wall, shrugging on her white therm-suit. "What's with him?"

"It's a mystery," drawled Clausen.

"I'd say he wants us to pack up and leave," Megan offered.

McPherson pressed tight the fastenings on her therm-suit. "And go where, with ten meters of snow on the ground and the ship encased in ice?"

"Where is damn Stavros when we need him to translate?"

Susannah looked thoughtful. "There is one difference between now and any other point in the last six weeks: it's stopped snowing."

The mention of snow set off another of Liphar's violent noddings. His face promising patience, he pried himself loose. Immediately, his hands began sketching vast dramas in the air. "Okay. Snow stop, yes? Okay. Now, you hear." His brown palms rose and fell like cresting waves. "Snow gone, big water come—oh, so much!" His arms stretched wide, then rushed together until his fingers grappled madly with each other. "*Han chauk!* Big fight come, no good! Danger!" His tongue clicked sharply under furrowed brows.

"This is weird," commented McPherson.

"Liphar, who's going to fight?" Susannah pursued.

The young Sawl moaned, his hands fainting in frustration. "*O rek! O malaka rek! Han chauk!*"

"Rek," Susannah repeated softly.

"Rek," said Megan. "Isn't that . . ."

Susannah nodded. "You know, this does fit with Stavros' interpretation of the friezes."

Clausen fished out a silver penknife and began to clean his nails.

"Will somebody clue me in?" McPherson demanded. "What's this rak?"

"Rek," Megan corrected primly. "The gods. He's saying the gods are going to war."

"So that means he's got to throw us out of here?"

"Is there some problem I should be informed about?" Weng Tsi-Hua asked from the entry to her curtained cubicle.

"Possibly," Megan answered. "Liphar seems to feel we're in some kind of danger."

"From the *gods,*" McPherson giggled, then remembered. "It's stopped snowing, Commander!"

Susannah studied the little Sawl. His concern seemed so sincere. " 'Big water,' he says. According to Stavros, the Sawls believe that when the gods go to war, the weather turns bad. Is that right, Meg?"

"That's *Stav's* interpretation, yes."

Clausen chuckled. "Worry not, my friends. CRI's latest data promise sun and fun. Fortunately for our peace of mind, our ship's computer is not in the habit of consulting the local deities."

"Good enough for me!" McPherson fastened her cuffs. "I'm heading out!"

"I think Liphar would prefer if we *all* did," noted Susannah.

"Go on, Commander," said Clausen. "I'll stay with the ship. I have business with Taylor upstairs."

Weng nodded. "Certainly we could all do with some fresh air and exercise."

In the disorganized scurry for boots and therm-suits, Susannah kept an eye on Liphar as he danced impatiently at the tunnel mouth. She could dismiss his frantic concern as mere superstition—as the others, even Megan, had already. Or she could ask, as Stavros would: does the youngster know something we don't?

For instance: if the snow had stopped, what in hell was all that rumbling?

6

OUTSIDE, THE COLD land waited. The snow-swept cliffs loomed over the smothered plain. The mountains behind bore their oppressive burden, snow layered on ice layered on snow. The stillness was like an intake of breath.

Then, when it seemed as if existence itself had seized up and come to a halt, the dull cloud cover shuddered. Pale worms of light edged across the stubborn gray. Fissures opened, billows swelled and churned, a ponderous machine gathering momentum.

The frigid air softened. A spear of light dazzled the cliff tops with pink and amber. A breeze sprang up, nosing at the clouds, opening patches of turquoise sky, sending the billows into quickening retreat. A low red sun poked through the last shreds of haze. Brilliant orange washed the white cliffs with the colors of fire. At the scarp's eastern tip, a solitary spire of rock blazed like a red-and-white sentinel. Below, the vast rolling plain glittered as the snow softened under a warm southerly wind.

The cave mouths erupted with activity.

From the rows of dark recesses high up on the cliff, Sawls poured out into the sudden sun. Eyes slitted against the light, they tested the wind and hefted a battery of wooden hand tools. Long lines moved out briskly along the ledges that connected the four levels of caves. Some headed upward toward the very top of the scarp, some hurried downward, armed with brush brooms and wooden picks to clear the snow and ice from the buried steps and trails. Their chatter carried on the wind, high and urgent, mingling with the starting phrases of a work-chant, begun at the top of the cliff and relayed down the lines of workers to the bottom. The rhythm was brisk, the tune melodic. At each cave mouth, a small group remained to scour the entry ledge and sing out an antiphonal chorus.

One woman, taller than the rest, thin and hard, set her crew to work, then leaned her pick against the snow-drifted rock to shed a heavy leather outer garment. She listened, her seamed face set in a frown, as the wind's desert yowl delivered the dull thunder of avalanches from the southern mountain range. Her upper lip gleamed with moisture. She blotted her forehead on a knitted sleeve, her frown deepening as she scanned the greenish sky, nostrils flared. She thrust an arm forward, then shoved back her sleeve and bent the arm at the elbow, lining it up to measure the height of the crimson sun ball hugging the western horizon. Turning northward, she stared for a long time across the plain, straining to the limits of her vision. The distant wave of mountains was blurred by clouds of steam rising off melting snowfields, tinged sunset pink and amber.

Finally, her wary glance rested on the thick cone shape on the plain below, its broad base sunk in thirty feet of snow and ice. The pointed nose was level with where she stood, at the second tier of caves, though it was farther away than she could throw the smallest stone. The late sun glinted dully on its scoured smoothness, broken here and there with patches of a more reflective surface. Her eyes flicked eastward to the sentinel spire of red rock now shedding its damp blanket of white, then back again. The crooked arm went up again to measure: height, width. The woman muttered to herself, her mouth tight. The Visitors' cave was bigger than she'd realized.

The man swinging his pick beside her stopped to join her at the trail's edge. He nodded toward the thing on the plain, offering a speculative comment. She shook her head in reply. He nudged her elbow, spread his palms, then held up four fingers. The woman sniffed, considering. The man dug into a hidden pocket and hauled forth a fistful of small white stones, flat and smooth from long handling. He counted, put a few away, held the others out to her. She shook her head, grinning faintly, held up six fingers. The man chuckled, dug again, and returned one more stone to his palm. This time, she nodded in agreement. She reached for her pick but did not immediately raise it. For a moment more, she and her companion regarded the towering shape in silence. Then, exchanging brief, dubious glances, they returned to their work.

From the foot of the cliffs came the sound of water running beneath the snow.

ICARUS, Vol. 341, No. 4, 78 - 103   292 - 2067

UNUSUAL TERRESTRIAL PLANET IN BYRNHAM CLUSTER

J. Sundqvist   (MIT, Sol)
T. Danforth   (UW, A.Cent. G)
T. Riley   (MIT, Sol)
O.D. Bryan   (MIT, Sol)

Received 023-2065, accepted 002-2067

A KO subgiant system in Byrnham's Cluster was visited by UWSA Deep Probe 6 to investigate a large (radius = 8300 km) terrestrial planet with a massive (surface pressure > 2 bars) oxygen bearing atmosphere, discovered by previous survey probe. Analysis of flyby remote sensing confirms a low-density (3.1 uncompressed) and slow (40 day period) retrograde rotation. Surface geological features are consistent with past volcanism and significant erosion in extreme desert conditions. Results suggest a surface mineralogy dominated by light metals, especially Al/K silicates.

INTRODUCTION

Brynham's Cluster has been the subject of intense study for many years because of the opportunity to observe Pop. II systems first hand (see reviews, Gilbert et al., 2029; Wolf and Akai, 2051). Terrestrial planets, formed mostly of refractories, metals and silicates, are most interesting because of the expected low abundance of heavier metals in Pop. II systems. We discuss in this paper observations and model studies of an unusually large terrestrial planet in a system visited by UWSA Deep Probe 6. In particular, several interesting surface mineralogies can occur in the absence of the heavier metals that usually form the major ore minerals in the crusts of Pop. I planets. Lack of iron, in particular, increases the importance of magnesium and potassium in ore-forming rocks. However, the role of the rarer (in Pop. I systems), lighter metals in the formation of the old volcanic terrains seen in flyby imagery is particularly crucial in determining the char-

7

"DISPLAY THE MOISTURE flux alongside, CRI." Danforth sucked his cheek irritably. He missed his lab on Gamma, but even that favorite AI might not have an answer to this conundrum. "Bottomed out. Damn! Next?"

"Station L-Delta. Posit—"

His hand swung and stopped millimeters above his keypad. "L-Delt's been dysfunctional for two weeks! What's up with you?"

The curl of displays went dead. The holographic sphere blinked out. The planetologist fumed in the dark. After a pause like a sigh, the sphere popped back into glowing, revolving life, and the displays lit with columns of data.

"L-Epsilon," CRI continued stolidly.

Further protest would be a waste of his already flagging energy. Danforth scanned the figures, and then again. His shoulders drew up around his neck as if to deny their natural broadness and thus perhaps avoid some part of the burden currently weighing on them. Soon, he told himself. Soon he'd see a path through this befuddlement, a logical train of thought that would lead him to clarity and finally, understanding. That's how it went in science, right? It's what had drawn him to it in the first place. "Okay. Is L-Ep showing any sign of sensor malfunction? Its temp reading hasn't moved a degree in seventy-two hours."

"Any malfunction would be noted with the data," CRI returned. "This new activity is highly localized. However, I *am* registering sharp temp increases from the stations farther west."

The door of the cubicle slid open noisily.

"I'm busy," Danforth growled without turning.

"Taylor, pull your nose away from your instruments and take a look outside!"

Danforth sighed. He couldn't really tell the prospector to take a hike.

Clausen touched the light pad by the door. The room remained in semi-darkness. "Your lights are broken."

"Yep."

Clausen kicked aside a discarded meal tray. "I'm serious. Take a look."

"I'm perfectly aware of what's going on. Zero to seventy in eight-six minutes."

"Excellent acceleration for an old car," grinned the prospector.

"Makes no damn sense."

"Forget it! The sun's out, Tay . . . the *sun,* which you haven't seen since you arrived on this planet, which is going to set in another sixteen hours and which will then not reappear for another two weeks. Up in the Caves, the natives are restless. You can almost hear the drums beating."

Danforth eyed his visitor darkly.

"All you're doing here is making yourself cranky."

"And you've something better in mind for me?" Danforth arched his long back and stretched. He'd never choose to be buddies with a man like Clausen, but the man was the only other hard scientist around and an intellectual equal. He'd made pals of worse guys when the need was on. And maybe it *was* time for a break. "Okay, I'll bite: is there something new in the radar imaging? Intimations of pay dirt?"

"That's better." Clausen dipped his head to study the tiny planet revolving on the holo-pad. "I have some promising sites located. Resolution's only decent, at about fourteen meters, but it beats all that blank white in the photo survey. The altimetry and gravity anomaly data seem to correlate interestingly with a few of them. I'll show you when we get back."

"Back from where?"

"Outside." He edged around Danforth's seated bulk to crank open the metal shutters covering the cubicle's single port. They squealed softly on their pivots.

"Oil," CRI muttered as sunlight flooded the tiny space. Bright amber bars slashed high across the smudged gray walls, picking out craterlike dents and graffiti consisting largely of numbers and scrawled Greek letters. Danforth gazed at the liquid warmth as if it were an alien invader. "Oil," the computer repeated.

"Regular use," Clausen corrected. "And, CRI—the paint's chipping on your keypad."

"Mr. Clausen, there is no paint on my keypad."

"Figure of speech, CRI. Like 'oil.' A thing of the past. Full of subtle *human* connotations."

The machine remained silent.

"The proper response to that remark is 'Up yours, Clausen.' "

"That would be the *human* response, I believe," said CRI.

"*Touché!* You're learning, my girl!"

Danforth was not in the mood for levity. He slouched away from the invading sunlight to stretch his legs through the open door. "It really isn't fair."

"Fair? What's fair? Don't believe I know that word." Clausen leaned against the wall, arms folded, grinning with eyelids at half-mast, like a lizard sunning on a rock.

"Oh, come on! Fair is arriving at a planet and finding some correlation between projections based on the probe data and what the climate actually turns out to be. You have a different definition? Fair is when preliminary modeling offers some success in forecasting." Danforth waved dismissively at the displays. "The data is totally inconsistent with our model runs. If I'd wanted weird weather, I could have taken the Hansen Chair at Boulder. They were recruiting me hard."

"Sure they were, sure they were. But were you really going to ask that gorgeous young wife of yours to set up housekeeping on Earth?"

No. Of course not. Never that. Gamma was a man-made environment, but at least it was new and clean and relatively safe. The hydroponics and farm domes produced enough so no one starved. And there was room on Gamma. All the Sol colonies—Mars, the Moon—were filling to capacity, but few of Earth's billions could afford FTL passage to the Centauri system. It was a place you could imagine having children.

His barb having struck home, Clausen could be generous. "Look, Tay—relax. The probe wasn't in system long enough to record an entire seasonal cycle. We didn't think it would matter."

"The damn probe lied!"

"Why, Taylor. How quaint and anthropomorphic. And you object to my small attempts to civilize our back-model queen of circuitry."

"Ecch. The only ship's AI in the Colonies with an entire unit devoted to cultural trivia." Danforth shook his head in disgust. "How can you take this so casually? You want a profitable lithium operation on this planet. According to the probe . . ."

"Tay, we've been over this . . ."

". . . there should be no ten meters of snow in the first place!"

". . . and over, and over . . ."

"And now look at it!" Danforth was used to being listened to, even by people nominally his superiors, and he'd damn well keep at it till he'd finished. "I spend six weeks chasing whatever indeterminable's been keeping the temp down and the humidity up, and just when I think I've got it psyched, the damn temp shoots up, the moisture bottoms out, and we've got a major thaw on our hands! Not a hint of it in my long-range data! I mean, maybe you could expect behavior like this from a compromised system, or from a broken one like Earth's, but the surveys here looked stable—you know, predictable." Even as Danforth spread his palms in exasperation, he worried that he was exposing himself recklessly, that he shouldn't admit his confusion and disbelief, especially to Emil Clausen. But he couldn't help himself. "And how can it happen so *fast?* The heat's even coming from the wrong direction!"

Clausen shrugged. "Snow happens. Thaws, too. Assume an unusually harsh winter."

"Gods, Emil, don't you care about anything except what goes on *under* the ground?

Clausen's tongue flicked, a lizard grin. "Only if it gets in the way of my prospecting."

"Sure, we could dismiss this as winter and spring—if we could expect true seasons here. But you know better." Danforth pulled himself upright in his chair, ticking off items on his fingers. "Axial tilt of a mere eight degrees, 281-day orbit nearly circular with the planet right now as close to her sun as her orbit allows, massive atmosphere, slow rotation . . ."

". . . moderate greenhouse effect," Clausen recited tiredly. "Short distance from a cool star heating up to go red giant, blah, blah, blah . . ."

"All right!" Danforth roared. "I get it. You're bored with weather. Well, fuck you—I am, too!" He swiveled back to face the displays. "But look at that! Even with this planet's month-long day, the winds should keep the surface temp from varying so widely! Perihelion was thirty-six hours ago. My model says the global average should be 115 degrees, high summer in the desert, but here we are, socked in for six weeks under ten meters of snow! So much for the rational method!"

"Taylor, are you even listening?" Clausen's blunt thumbs beat a rhythm against the tooled leather of his vest. Through the port shutters, the topaz sky glared hot and cloudless. "It *is* high summer in the desert. Look outside!"

But Danforth needed someone to yell at, so Clausen was elected. "I didn't come here to do fucking weather, anyway! The atmospheric model should have been the easy part! I put my career in hock for this mission. They didn't like me leaving Gamma for so long, but after that probe data came back, I promised them the funding would pour in as soon as we could announce!" When Clausen wouldn't rise to his bait, Danforth shut his eyes and surrendered to gloom. "Meanwhile, I can't even get a simple forecast model working, much less a general circulation. And forget the macro stuff, like a full climate model or atmospheric and planetary evolution theories, the real *publishable* material."

The prospector pushed away from the wall, tugging at invisible cuffs and cackling like a mischievous dwarf. "CRI, take a letter. It seems our boy Taylor needs cheering up. How does this sound . . . ?

> *"A half a league inside the Coal Sack,*
> *Byrnham's Cluster lies . . .*
> *Clouds of dust and gas obscuring*
> *Taylor's Nobel Prize."*

Danforth's look was sour. "Dust and gas are not the problem, but sure, mock away, Emil. Your reputation was made long ago. All you've got at stake here is money."

"All?"

He regretted the slip. "I know, I know. No money, no expedition. My acceptance speech will include properly abject thanks to you and ConPlex. Don't lecture me, Emil."

The easy grin fell away. "A lecture for a lecture, my boy. You put my career in hock as well on this one." Clausen took advantage of the bigger man's seated position to stare down at him. "In my biz, you're only as good as your last strike, and hey, there are closer worlds than this to go looking for lithium. I had a list."

"A very short one!" Danforth countered. "Not so many rocky planets out there, it turns out, and on all the ones nearer by, ConPlex would be sharing mineral rights three, four ways. The rush is on, now that the new process has proved commercially viable."

"Thirty-three percent of a sure thing beats hell out of a hundred percent of nothing."

Danforth scowled. "There's lithium here. The system's history says so."

"But in what quantity? How pure? How accessible? Will the energy boys buy it at a higher price than it costs us to get it to them?"

"We're talking potentially a thirty percent jump in energy capture and conversion efficiency. Earth is strangling. The lights are going out. Of course they'll buy!"

The prospector contrived to look dubious.

"Risks are your business, Emil. You cross-checked the data in my proposal yourself! This is a fucking huge planet! When you strike, you'll strike big!" Clausen's unblinking snake-stare forced Danforth to glance away. "What, are you getting cold feet?"

The prospector raised a warning finger. "Never. Just reminding you of your . . . of *our* position here. One month into the job, I've usually made my strike, staked the claim, and ordered the equipment droned in. The Company is going to wonder what's taking me so long, and was I crazy to advise them to buy a whole research mission for some academic hotshot, on the strength of a theory."

"It's here. I know it's here."

"Like you knew the climate'd be ideal for mining?"

"Off my back, man! We share the profits, we also share the rap."

"My point precisely."

At a loss, Danforth retreated into disdain. "The biggest mining conglomerate in the Colonies can afford to fund a little pure science now and then."

"We do, we do. Our Public Relations Department insists on it. Do you think we'd have crazy Ibiá and Her Majesty of the Left along otherwise? But we don't often back it up by rerouting our newest and best FTL ship, which could be making billions for us elsewhere." Clausen gripped Danforth's shoulder. "You think 'pure' is something like 'fair,' pal? If so, I have bad news for you. Pure science went extinct years ago. This is a deal we have, Tay. You get your science, we get our lithium. This is not take-a-researcher-to-lunch."

He backed off finally, and smiled. "Of course, if you should happen upon a Nobel along the way of doing business, ConPlex—and I—will happily bathe in the reflected glory. But keep your priorities straight, for your own sake."

"Didn't I make major sacrifices for economy?" Danforth gestured resentfully around the crowded cubicle, at the tangles of cable snaking about his feet, at the holo-pad in its off-the-shelf rack. "Not exactly state-of-the-art, this crap!"

Clausen's sigh was mild. "What an ungrateful wretch you are, Tay."

"Me? How often have I listened to you bitch about having to spend six weeks doing nothing but polish your goddamned hand-sewn multimillion-dollar climbing boots! With a few more bucks, we'd both have full teams and a Lander capable of more than one lousy round trip. You'd be relaxing in the relative comfort of the Orbiter!"

"I'm surprised you don't blame the *weather* on ConPlex's funding level. Well, if I can't browbeat you out of your gloom, Taylor, let me try something else." Clausen dug deep in a pocket, producing a chunk of pale pinkish rock, which he held up like a prize. "So, tell me—how's your practical geology?"

8

E.D 44–16:39

A MODICUM OF DISCIPLINE at last prevailed in the Underbelly, despite all trends to the contrary. Liphar danced in and out of the cylinder, and McPherson fairly vibrated with impatience. But she stood stolidly beside her commanding officer as they waited for Megan to pull herself together and get suited up for the outside.

Her own therm-suit zipped tight, Susannah neatened up after Liphar's outburst. A moment had come during the long trip out from Earth when she'd realized that if she didn't try to keep peace among the landing party, no one would. Weng's authority extended only to the physical safety of ship and passengers, and the Commander took this as a directive not to meddle elsewhere. Susannah would have preferred to stay out of the battling altogether, but her determined neutrality inevitably cast her as mediator. Peacekeeping was now so integral to her shipboard identity that, seeing a chance to defuse yet another ongoing issue, Susannah asked McPherson, "By the way, what is this problem with the Sleds that Meg keeps bugging you about?"

The pilot eyed her so suspiciously that Susannah laughed.

"Hey, this is me asking. No politics. I'd really like to know. I'll need to use them myself for field surveys."

"Are you certified?"

"To fly them? No, but I'll need to be. I was counting on you to teach me."

"Well, then." The pilot straightened, hands clasped behind her back in unconscious mimic of the Commander's posture. "It's not like a thing you can really solve, you know?" She jerked her head toward the two shrouded hulks parked on the far side of the Underbelly. "It's a joke these things ever got to be called Sleds in the first place. Ain't worth a damn in the snow. They're designed for the desert."

"Well, we weren't expecting snow."

"Yeah, but any equipment should be tested to its limits. Problem is, on Earth, the only snow left is at elevations these babies can't do anyway. I mean, they fly okay, but they're basically a ground vehicle."

Susannah eyed A-Sled sympathetically. Its tarp had partly slid off, exposing the vulnerable open cockpit. Clothing decorated the windscreen. A wrinkled foil blanket lay in a comfortable nest along one of the triangular wings. The pilot's seat was strewn with loose wiring and eating utensils. A deserted mug lounged on the control console.

"There's no real power in 'em," McPherson explained. "Not against these winds. I tried 'em out when I was Earth-side for the provisioning. Scary! Still, a little customizing can work wonders. I'm an okay mechanic, so I thought I'd try working 'em up some, long as I'm stuck down here. Didn't get too far."

"Never mind. You'll have more cause to get to it now."

"But less time," McPherson returned.

Megan joined them at last, closing the wrist tabs on her therm-suit and shouldering a light field pack. Liphar bolted down the cylinder's length, and Weng turned to follow. She set a brisk pace as they crossed through the force field and headed up the long ice corridor to the Caves.

The still frigid air of the tunnel misted their breath. Susannah tuned up the temperature control on her therm-suit, but noticed that the antiskid grit on the floor was darkening with moisture. The icy walls, recently cold enough to grab a layer of skin off a bared fingertip, were slicked with a layer of melt. Weng slowed once they left the section of tunnel modified by the landing party and began the upward climb through tighter confines and over rougher terrain. Liphar trotted ahead, soon out of sight, but quickly ran back to urge them all to greater speed.

Coming out into the open well at the bottom of the cliffs, they stopped to catch their breath. A Sawl work party gathered around the tall stone in the center, cheering on a pair of young women as they scaled the spire, each with the end of a stout rope tied around the waist. The ropes looped down to the snowy ground, then back up again, up the cliff face to vanish over a protruding ledge. Susannah slipped on sun goggles to follow the ropes' rising path, and spotted Stavros Ibiá two ledges above, in heated discussion with a tall and angular Sawl. She recognized the woman as the Master Ranger, head of the guild responsible for all issues relating to security, travel, scouting, and, apparently, clearing away the weeks of snow and ice.

She nudged Megan and pointed. "Look who's taking on Aguidran."

"Good luck to him."

Liphar saw Ibiá, grinned, and took off up the stairs.

Anyone unfamiliar with Ibiá might not so easily pick him out from the crowd milling around him on the ledge. He was about the Master Ranger's height and as lean and wiry as any Sawl. When he was in the Caves, Ibiá wore Sawl clothing at all times, and let his thick black hair do whatever it wanted to. But Susannah knew there'd be no mistaking him if he turned their way, even under his many days' worth of soot and stubble. Stavros Ibiá was blessed with the face of a dark Caravaggio angel, all sharp planes and lucent skin and shadowed eyes—ironical, as he was nothing of the sort. So often, that classical beauty was creased by a scowl of disapproval, or even outrage. Susannah had once noted that if Ibiá weren't so beautiful, he'd be a complete embarrassment. Megan had looked perplexed, and began to reel off his many academic firsts and accomplishments. Susannah had smiled and said, "Never mind."

Rested, the women tackled the stairs, buffeted by troops of busy Sawls hurrying past, up and down. At the first tier of caves, they were out of the shadow of the well, and found room to stand aside and bask a bit in the warmth of the alien sun, to breathe in the sharp, clean air. Susannah inhaled deeply and greedily, until she was on the verge of hyperventilating. She sorted through the myriad of scents—wool and rope and leather and unwashed Sawl—and finally settled on one that might be the smell of the air itself. She marveled that unpolluted air should have a scent all its own, a small wonder perhaps but one that the billions back on Earth, lost in forests of scrubbers and carbon uptake towers, would never experience.

Weng and McPherson seemed to hardly notice the miracles of open air and good weather. They fell immediately into a discussion about freeing up the Lander from its prison of ice. Susannah's glance was drawn back to the upper ledge where Ibiá was still dogging the Master Ranger's steps, begging, pleading, reasoning. Aguidran seemed too busy with the cleanup operation to pay him the slightest attention. Ibiá's body language was as assumed as the Sawlish he'd picked up so quickly. It took its cues from the Sawls around him, a mercurial mix of impetuosity and obsequiousness, and at the moment, almost desperate. She saw in his impulsive gestures the needy, neglected boy he must have been. Considering her own fond if unspectacular upbringing, Susannah pitied him. Poor little rich boy. Who was Stavros Ibiá when he was not impersonating the subject of his study? She wasn't sure Ibiá himself knew the answer.

"He wants something from her, that's for sure," Megan observed.

"Badly. And it doesn't look like he's getting it."

Liphar gained the upper ledge and joined the melee. He grabbed Ibiá by the tail of his woven Sawl tunic and dragged him to the edge, proudly pointing down to where the women stood watching. Ibiá looked briefly relieved. He waved, but the gesture was curt, impatient rather than welcoming, as if they were one less thing he had to worry about. He took a bit longer to praise Liphar for accomplishing what was obviously an assigned mission, then turned back to his pursuit of Aguidran.

Susannah grew bored with spying on the linguist's machinations, whatever they were, and restless with the confines of the ledge and the cave mouth. She wanted to be out and about. The full length of the second tier had been swept clean of snow and debris. She had her day pack with her. She could walk along the ledge all the way to the steps that ascended the cliff past the farthest grouping of inhabited caves. From there, she could make a try for the cliff top. Back home, when the smog count was low enough, she'd hiked the hills around the relocated university complex at Ben Nevis—a field biologist had to keep fit, after all. And she was long overdue for some real exercise.

She patted Megan's shoulder as the older woman found a rocky perch to settle on, then mimed a salute at Weng's stiff back. "Enjoy the sun. I'm going for a walk."

She passed Liphar, heading up the stairs, and repeated this announcement with a cheerful wave. But he turned on his heel and scrambled after her.

"No, no, no! Not go, you!" His pinched frown was a complaint: he'd just brought her to a place of safety, and here she was, running off again!

Susannah pointed. "I'm just going up there. It's a perfect day for it!"

"No good! Very danger!"

"Liphar, I'm a good climber. I'll be fine." She patted him as she had patted Megan, but he would not be put off so easily. "Okay, then you'll just have to come with me."

To her surprise, he agreed.

9

E.D. 44–16:56

THE PROSPECTOR STROKED THE PINK ROCK fondly with his thumb. "Know what this is?"

Danforth felt distinctly manipulated. "I bet you can't wait to tell me."

"You should spend more time in the field, Tay. You've been staring at your numbers so long, all you can do is whine like a little old lady."

"So leave. You won't have to listen."

"Fresh air would do your disposition wonders." Clausen tossed the rock in a loop and caught it neatly. "Well, it's granite. I brought it to cheer you up. Pegmatites similar to this are a source of recoverable deposits of lepidolite. Lepidolite is a respectable lithium ore. Not as pure as we want, but a hopeful sign, certainly."

Danforth was wary now. "And your point is . . ."

"Taylor, I found this in the Caves, just inside the Fourth Entrance, practically lying on the ground. Imagine what I might find up there, deep inside those cliffs, if the clever little buggers didn't manage to sidetrack me every time I think I'm getting past the first maze of caverns. I swear they've tunneled in far deeper than they'd like us to think!"

"You show me this *after* you rake me over the coals? You are one bona fide sonofabitch, Emil."

"And don't you forget it."

Danforth ran a hand over his tight curls. "I'm the one who should have stayed with the Orbiter."

"Six weeks in parking orbit is your idea of fun? They're eating each other alive up there these days."

Just your sort of party, Danforth wanted to say, but didn't. "At least they've got a pool and a gym! Besides, spacers are used to it. Look at Weng. She's happy as a clam spending her days jacked in, taking up valuable computer time with her so-called compositions."

Clausen considered. "Weng's music is actually quite interesting. If I understand her correctly, she's exploring the use of game theory as a compositional rubric."

"Nothing new."

"You wouldn't say that if you heard the results. Music of the spheres and all that. Ask CRI to play some back for you sometime." Clausen's stubby hands toyed with his hunk of rock. He held it up to the amber light flooding through the port. Minute specks glinted in tiny ragged crannies, sharp as the gleam of anticipation in the prospector's eye. "So. You ready to go out looking for some more of this?"

"Sure. You bet." Danforth swiveled back to his console. "As soon as I . . ."

"Now."

"I don't think so."

"I'm quite serious, Tay."

"Are you planning to walk? It'll take more time than we have till sunset to dig out one of the Sleds."

"Not really." Clausen placed the rock on the keypad, between Danforth's outstretched hands. "Because, one, the snow is melting faster than you could ever imagine, and two, the way B-Sled's positioned down there . . ." He paused, one forefinger straightened toward the floor. "If we drop the force field, we can use the hot air from the Sled fans to melt an exit ramp up through the ice."

"Drop the field? What if the ice is unstable? It could all collapse and crush everything in the Underbelly. And every*one*. Too risky. Even for you, I'd have thought."

"It'll take weeks for ice that thick to melt. The Shield'll be down for ten minutes max. Besides, everyone down there is heading up to the Caves." Clausen shrugged. "My, my. I never took you for gutless, Tay."

"I'm too busy to go joyriding." It was not Danforth's idea of field study. He was supposed to stay in the lab, crunching numbers, while others did the joyriding. He pushed the rock aside. "Get McPherson. She's into risking life and limb. I've got new data pouring in every nanosecond. CRI, back to work."

"Ah, Taylor. You do wear on an old man's patience."

"I want to run a standard case, check the model's functioning: Earth 1997 and 2067."

"And you will force me to say it, won't you?"

The prospector's sulky tone roused Danforth's interest. "Say what?"

"That you have something I need."

"Me? Gutless Danforth? Surely not."

"Don't pout, Tay. It's so boring." Clausen turned toward the console. "CRI, local wind speeds, please."

"Variable. Gusting from eighteen to thirty-five meters per second."

"Thirty-six to seventy mph," Danforth noted. "Nasty."

"And I am required to remind you," CRI continued, "that although the manufacturer's safety limit for the Sleds in this atmospheric density is twenty-five meters per second, Commander Weng insists on a limit of twenty."

"Thank you, CRI." Clausen reached over Danforth's arm to press the computer's privacy key.

"Hey!" Danforth eyed him sidelong. "Ah, I get it. You haven't checked this out with Weng."

The prospector grinned.

"And where is our good Commander at the moment?"

"Inside the Caves. Incommunicado."

"Something wrong with her fone?"

"Out of relay range, apparently."

"Well? What's stopping you?"

"I prefer to walk the safe side of legal whenever possible." Clausen pursed his lips, eyes half-lidded once again. "And, due to certain technicalities in the chain of command, I need proper authorization in order to instruct CRI to lower the shield. With the Commander *in absentia,* you can make that authorization."

"Hmmm." Danforth stretched his legs and braced his feet against the pockmarked wall. Weng's insistent, stiff-necked propriety rankled him. Already, it had led to disagreements, which, as Commander of the landing vehicle, Weng usually won. Yet it was *his* expedition, serving *his* project. Weng would be a long step closer to retirement, if not for him. He decided there might be some fun in this crazed notion after all. "You're right. I can."

"It's a minor insubordination compared to the ones you'd like to commit."

"But . . . that's one hell of a wind out there."

"I've seen worse conditions."

"You'll pilot?"

"You think I'd trust *you* at the stick?"

"I'm not happy about letting down the shield." Danforth played out his pause, then abruptly drew in his long legs and rose. "But since you force me to see the reason of your ways . . . as Chief Scientist and Expeditionary Leader, and in the Commander's absence, I hereby authorize this use of expeditionary equipment." As he stood, the cubicle became too small to hold him. He swung an air punch, narrowly missing the shorter man's ear. "Okay! Let's get on it, before she comes back!"

A shout echoed down the outer corridor. "Danforth!"

The two men groaned in unison. Any lingering antagonism faded with the arrival of a far greater irritant. Out in the hallway, the magnetic lift rattled as it bumped up the Lander's central shaft.

"Danforth!"

Clausen put a finger to his lips, glanced right and left. The corridor deadended a few paces to the left of the cubicle. The right-hand corridor led to the lift.

"No escape," Danforth muttered.

"Danforth, where the hell . . . !" The cage jerked to level with the floor. The safety grating slammed aside with a screech and a crash. Stavros Ibiá whirled out of the lift, glaring at the pair watching him from the other end of the corridor. "I've been trying to reach you for hours!"

Emil Clausen shook his head. What a spectacle this Ibiá made of himself. Dirty, unkempt, clothes flying about. His mare's nest of dark hair hadn't seen a comb in days. His rough Sawl tunic fit poorly across the shoulders, and the sleeves had been lengthened in a different color. Clausen thought that someone—like Weng—should order the linguist into uniform and a decent haircut. He didn't approve of Danforth's perennial gray gym wear either, but at least it was neat and clean, and the look suited him. In an earlier colonial era, Ibiá would have been disciplined for setting a bad example for the natives.

"Now what's the matter?" the prospector asked reasonably as Ibiá pulled up, breathless, in front of them.

The young man turned his fury on Danforth. "Since when do you refuse emergency calls?"

"I've been busy with a few emergencies of my own, Ibiá. What's up?"

Clausen stood a bit aside. His objections to the linguist were mainly aesthetic, the welfare of local populations not being high on his list of priorities. Still, Ibiá had proved to be the wild card in his calculations. The usual pre-expedition snooping had assured him the boy was brilliant, that his new translation programs represented a unique approach to computer linguistics. Yes, there were reports of depression and instability, but Clausen had signed off on the nomination anyway. He'd had business dealings with the boy's uncle, and besides, the occasional nutcase could have a useful destabilizing effect on any de facto power structure that might form up during the expedition to challenge the company's interests.

But maybe Ibiá wasn't quite crazy enough. There was a steadiness of purpose about him that, despite his seeming vulnerability and eccentric demeanor, made it harder to dismiss him entirely. Plus, Danforth was particularly ripe for Ibiá's goading. Did the planetologist fear that success unorthodoxly achieved might undervalue his own more conventional methods? In any case, he rose to Ibiá's bait every time. Clausen usually found profit in encouraging personal rivalries, but this was becoming inconvenient. Danforth, the older and far better established, just would not relax into his seniority. In humbler moments, Clausen doubted that even his own diplomatic skills could effect a resolution between two men who had loathed each other from the first day out.

"You've cost us valuable time already!" Ibiá took a breath, shoving damp hair from his eyes. Delaying tactics, Clausen noted. The boy had a bomb to drop, and not a clue of how to do it gracefully. "Look, we've got to evacuate the Lander. All of us, all the equipment, up to the Caves! Everything we can carry!"

Predictably, Danforth sneered.

"This is real, Taylor. We have to get out as soon as possible. We're sitting ducks down here on the plain. We could lose everything. The priests say . . ."

Danforth folded his arms across his broad chest. "Ah, the priests. Uh-huh."

Ibiá glanced away, refusing to look up to the man simply because he was taller. "Listen to me for once, okay? They say a big storm's coming. Wind, rain, flooding. They're making serious preparations up there, and they've warned us to do the same." His dark eyes flicked past both men toward the open port and the green sky beyond.

Clausen felt the boy's resentment wash over him like heat. What did this kid expect? If you show up looking like that, of course credibility will be a problem.

Ibiá pulled himself together and tried again. "Look, I've talked the guild masters into finding us shelter in the Caves. They'd never sacrifice precious space if it wasn't a true crisis!"

"Huh. And you actually thought I'd buy this nonsense?"

Ibiá switched tactics, speaking too calmly now, as if trying to talk a moron out of doing himself harm. "Taylor, you don't know that it's nonsense. This is *their* world. You'll grant that they know it a bit better than you do."

Clausen judged it time to intervene. Coddling these bright youngsters in the University cocoon was bad policy. All those safe walls and decent meals. They came out prideful but disabled. Then there was Ibiá's family background as well. Clausen nearly laughed aloud. The kid had had all the advantages his own mother always claimed he (and she) deserved. "He has a point, Tay. I share your distaste for all that smoke and sweat and dubious sanitation up there, but they do seem to be engaging in some rather extensive hatch-battening. And weren't we just heading out for a look?"

"There is no storm coming." Danforth ducked back into the cubicle and thumbed on the audio link. "CRI, display all current weather data from the local stations, up on Six and Seven, then give me an updated short-range forecast on Eight and Nine, long-range on Ten. And restore hemispherics to holo." Then he reached back, grabbed Ibiá by his mismatched sleeve and dragged him through the doorway. His instinctive response to a tantrum was to produce one of his own. Clausen almost told him to back off, but Danforth had already shoved Ibiá up to the display wall. "Show me! Show me any indication of this monsoon you're predicting!"

"*I'm* not predicting it, the Sawls are!"

"Look at the data! Warm wind out of the southwest, bone-dry, temperatures up, pressure steadying . . . or are pictures easier for you?" Danforth fiddled needlessly with the holo-pad's controls. "See? Not a cloud in the entire hemisphere. Where is this storm, Ibiá? Where?"

"What about the thaw? That didn't show up in your data, did it?"

Danforth's mouth tightened. "It . . ."

"The Sawls knew about it." Ibiá was visibly edgy within the confines of the cubicle. "The moment the snow stopped, they started preparing for the thaw, before the sun came out, before the wind! Because the priests told them!"

Danforth shrugged. "Coincidence."

"No!" Ibiá retreated toward the corridor, his breathing low and rapid, like a cornered animal. But he wasn't giving up. He rounded on Clausen instead. "Okay, then: you. Checked your seismometers lately?"

The prospector nodded, a hint of respect complicating his placid smile. "And?"

"Avalanches, my dear Stavros, as you are obviously aware."

Danforth stared. "Thanks for telling me. Where?"

"All over the place. Haven't you heard the rumbling?"

Ibiá's grin was sudden and manic. "See? One morning you're frozen solid and by noon you've got a plague of avalanches! Anything could happen, so why not a monsoon? The point is, Danforth, you *don't know!*"

"Avalanches are not unusual in a thaw," the planetologist began.

Stavros knew he would lose control before he actually did. But as always, it was too late to do anything but taste the familiar dry regret and wonder if he would ever learn to catch himself in time. He knew his colleagues thought him messy and self-indulgent. He didn't mind, because he knew he was right about most things, so eventually they would be forced to listen. But none of them should ever know how close to the abyss such moments actually brought him. Eccentric? Unpredictable? Acceptable, if he proved his worth. But out of control? The end of his career.

He brushed past Clausen heedlessly, throat tightening, voice rising to a squawk. "All right, don't listen to me! I don't give a shit! Your own fault if you get washed into oblivion!" He put a hand to the wall for balance, but the emptiness of the corridor was not enough relief. He couldn't escape the shame of his own ranting. "Stay here if you like and the hell with you, but as Communications Officer, I'm ordering every piece of equipment moved up to the Caves. Effective immediately!" He sucked deeply for air. The wall was hard against his sweating back. "That includes this installation as well!"

"You have no authority over my equipment!"

"Check again, Taylor. It's all according to regs." Nauseated, Stavros bolted for the lift. "I hope you're a terrific swimmer!"

"You'll need Weng's permission, damn you!"

"Already got it!"

The gate crashed and the lift descended.

Danforth swore, slammed his chair against the cubicle wall, then whirled on Clausen. "You just going to stand there?"

The prospector raised a mild eyebrow. "The odds are always against you when you tangle with a lunatic."

"How's ConPlex gonna like its stuff being dragged off into the bowels of the earth?"

"Most of our equipment is quite at home in the bowels of the earth. We *are* a mining company, after all."

"Thanks for nothing!" Danforth shoved the chair against the other wall. "You're supposed to be on *my* side!"

"Look, Tay, it's of little import *where* our equipment is as long as we have the use of it. Let him move it about if it keeps him occupied. Besides, it'll give us a good excuse to hang around the Caves, maybe slip in farther while they're not looking."

"The little shit could have me off-line for hours!"

"Fine. Let him. We have fifteen-and-one-half hours of light left, and most of that will be dusk."

"I can't do my work in those filthy holes! It's cold and dark, and I won't let the asshole get away with it!"

"He already has. Now, shall we get on with our own business? B-Sled?"

Danforth braced both arms against his work shelf and glared possessively at his equipment. "Too late for that now. People'll be crawling all over the ship, with Ibiá on the loose."

"No problem. We make it look like we're helping move the goods, then snatch the Sled right out from under his nose."

Danforth let go of his rage slowly, as the possibilities at last took hold of him. He let out a long breath, straightened. "I hate this, but okay, you're on. We'll do it. What else have I got to do with my time?"

Clausen let out a quieter breath of his own. "Good man."

"Stupid sonofabitch probably won't even notice."

"Oh . . . I think he'll notice."

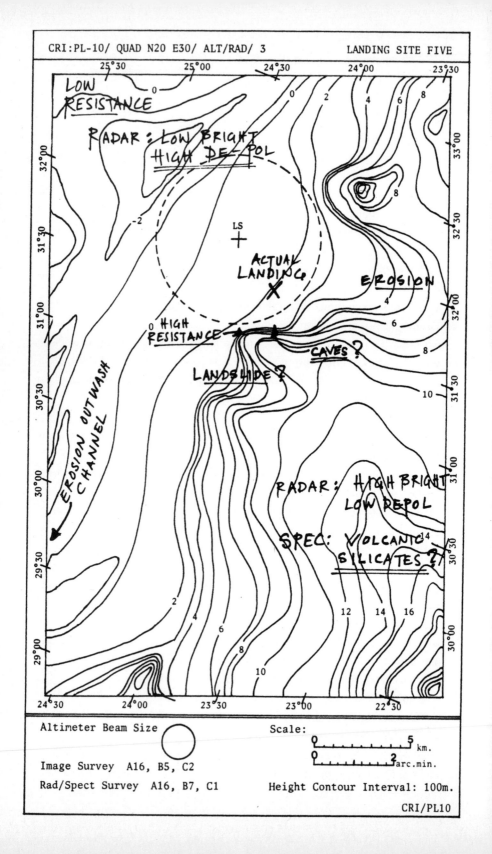

10

SUSANNAH HAULED UP into the shade of a pinnacle of red rock, and dumped her pack in an inglorious heap. A hot wind from the south whipped damp hair across her eyes as she struggled to appear less breathless than she felt. She glanced back along the trail. Liphar's methodical plodding up the rugged scarp had made her dance with impatience, but now, as he neared the top, she saw he was barely winded. She'd rushed the early part of the climb and exhausted herself. Plus, she'd allowed her sample bags to languish at the bottom of her pack. Just six weeks of forced inactivity and already she'd gone slack and soft. She was ashamed of herself.

Ah, but the joy of being out in the open at last! The very reason she'd applied for this lower-paying expedition, to be *away* from crowds and stale air and the tight spaces of her parents' house, and especially from Earth's constant aura of crisis and doom. Oh, and okay—from her messy divorce. This sudden thaw was like a release from prison.

The thought of her parents distracted her. She owed them a post in the next message drone sent back to Earth. Her quiet, normal parents, so confused by the current state of their world, by their daughter's eagerness to "desert" the crisis at home (never mind her marriage or her medical career), so convinced that the right solution was simply for everyone to buckle down and "pull up their socks," whatever that meant. Her mother still tried to keep a tiny garden, where nothing but the toughest weeds survived.

I'll write them soon, she told herself.

Susannah mopped her brow with a dirtied white sleeve. Her therm-suit was not cooling as it should. It might need servicing, after its long weeks in storage. She loosened collar and cuffs, but the wind was hot and brought little relief. Staring up at the rock spindle looming overhead, she guessed it was close to forty meters tall. It was deep red-orange, a perfect match for the sun ball hovering oblate at the horizon. It narrowed in stages as it rose: a giant's table leg, turned on the lathe of the wind. She'd seen similar formations in the Monument Valley theme park back home. According to Stavros Ibiá, the Sawls called it "the old king." But he offered this translation as tentative, since the Sawls did not seem to have kings, or anything like a king. Besides, the spindle's wind-smoothed summit was more reminiscent of a balding head than a crown—a more minor chess piece, a lonely pawn set out on this precipitous rock to await its part in an unknown gambit.

She circled the base. On the shaded side, the cracks and crannies were still packed with ice. Her boot soles slipped in meltwater sluicing across the terraced rock. She scrambled clumsily until she found a secure perch, where she could lean back against the massive shaft and give vent to a euphoric sigh. What a thrill! What a privilege! To gaze down on a new planet from such Olympian heights! So rare and precious, these fresh worlds, uncrowded and unpolluted—at least for the term of a normal field assignment. In full awareness that all optimism was unfounded, Susannah maintained her faith in a universe vast enough to provide an endless supply of such treasures.

Liphar arrived and assured himself of her well-being. But he would not settle and relax. His dark eyes constantly scanned the horizon, reminding Susannah of an old-time sailor, searching for a distant landfall. Between thumb and forefinger, he worried an azure bead worn on a braided thong about his wrist. Malachite, Emil had said. It was a lovely piece, carved in the shape of a trefoiled blossom, which Susannah took as a good sign for the botanical sector of her survey. Many Sawls wore such talismans. Megan was sure their purpose was more than decorative, and certainly, this bead's oiled patina suggested a very long history of pressure from nervous fingers.

Susannah studied the young man. How strange to think that, after six weeks, she'd not yet seen these people in actual sunlight. Unlike many primitive societies, there was nothing gaudy about the Sawls. With his nut-brown skin, his thick brown curls, his layers of plain clothing in shades of brown and ocher and rust, Liphar matched the colors of the landscape emerging so rapidly from under its blanket of snow.

Long past time to get to work. She studied her muddied palms for serious cuts and scrapes, but made no move for her pack. The warmth, the sun, were like a drug she couldn't get enough of. Liphar left off his sky watch long enough to extract a cloth bundle from under his tunic. He unwrapped a round loaf, divided it neatly, returned one half to his pocket and split the other between them.

Susannah clapped her hands in delight. He was so resourceful. Somewhere during their trudge up the stairs, he'd managed to pick up supplies.

"Okay. Eat first, gather samples later." She munched the coarse brown bread, again grateful for compatible digestive systems. It was after 19:00 by the ship's clock, and she had missed supper. How stupid, not to bring food along, or even water. She'd been drawn much farther away by the pleasures of sun and air than she'd ever intended. She touched the fone clipped to the shoulder patch of her therm-suit.

"Susannah here, CRI. Mark my location, please, and take a look around." She twisted left and right to test the fone's visual range. "Can you see okay?"

"Transmission is clear, Dr. James."

"I made it all the way up to the White Pawn, except it's red now, with the snow gone. What's my altitude?"

"326 meters above base camp."

"Phew! My legs feel like it's three thousand."

"As Medical Officer, Dr. James, it would be prudent for you to observe your own prescribed regimen of daily exercise."

"Thank you, CRI. But be glad that, as Computer, you will never have to know how boring calisthenics and weights are. How much time have I got till sunset?"

"Approximately ten hours. Was it necessary to go so far alone?"

"I'm not alone. Liphar's here. He wouldn't let me go without him. And there'll be a few hours of light after sundown, right, with this planet's long day-night cycle?"

"I would suggest a timely return to base, Dr. James."

Susannah removed the clasp from her long hair and shook it free. "No use scolding me, CRI. This view is worth every agonized muscle I'll complain about tomorrow. The sky is a sheet of polished jade and the air is all red and gold and smells like, well, freedom! Oh, and guess what! I spotted something like a lizard on the way up, or at least, a tail disappearing under a rock. Definitely a living creature! Liphar was not happy when I tried to hunt it down, so I let it pass. Not much else moving about up here so far—disappointing, but maybe on the way down. By the way, will you check my suit readings? The thermostat's acting up. I'm sweating like a pig."

"I register that. There has been intermittent static on that signal. If the problem cannot be solved here in the Orbiter, I suggest you unzip."

"How practical." She did not add, *for a computer,* not wanting to hurt the AI's feelings, as mysterious as they were. As the hot wind ballooned into her suit, Susannah giggled like a child. "Okay, save to accompany visuals: the mountains to the south are still in deep winter. As you can see, they're very forbidding-looking. The plain is hillier than it seemed under all that snow, very broken up with canyons and arroyos, which are mostly still choked with ice. It's mud-and-sand-colored, yellowish, but this red light and the steam rising off the ice make it look like the whole plain's on fire. Totally spectacular! The northeastern mountains are just a blur through the steam, but there's the Lander clearly off to the left, down in the shadow of the cliffs where the snow hasn't melted yet. Liphar's folk are very busy along the cliff top."

"Busy at what?"

"Can you speak up? The wind's drowning you out. It's getting gusty up here now."

"What are they doing?"

"Oh. I'll give you a look over the edge, if I don't get blown off."

Susannah knelt on the wet rock and crawled forward as far as she dared. Below the wind-torn edge of the precipice, wide ledges descended stepwise toward the rugged plateau that topped the cliffs. At the western end of the scarp, scores of dark figures bustled about among the snow and rocks. "Mostly they're moving big stone slabs around with cranes and levers. Liphar couldn't quite make it clear to me when I asked him before. Something about water running into the Caves, or water *not* running into the Caves. Meg and Stavros are down there. Between them, they should be able to figure it out—if you can get them to agree on an interpretation."

"Dr. Levy is recording from one of the cave mouths. A religious ritual, I believe. The priests have become very active since the weather changed."

"So Meg's finally got herself back in gear. Excellent news! What else is going on down there?" The answering delay suggested that the computer was pondering a dilemma not easily dealt with in mathematical terms. Susannah retreated from the edge and sat back on her heels. "Is there a problem, CRI?"

"Mr. Ibiá cannot locate the Commander. He's insisting we conduct a search." CRI paused. "He seems more than usually disturbed."

"Can't find Weng? I don't blame him. She's turned off her fone?"

"Apparently so."

"You can't even pick up her locator beacon?" Susannah frowned. Perhaps the Old Lady *had* been on the ground too long. "She must be in the Caves. Hiding behind all that rock."

"No doubt she is, Dr. James. You know how the Commander enjoys her own company. After serving with her for thirty-nine ship's years, I have learned that she will be found when she wishes to be found. I am not concerned."

Susannah's frown deepened. Even CRI, most loyal of AIs, was well aware that wandering off unannounced could be misinterpreted. Of course, Weng was still sharp as a tack, but she *was* beyond retirement age, and there were plenty of young bloods at the Academy jockeying for a command.

"What concerns me more is that the force field has been turned off. Dr. Danforth and Mr. Clausen appear to be trying to dig out around the Lander."

"Really? The Shield is down? Is that wise, with all this melting ice?"

"Dr. Danforth issued the order, in the Commander's absence."

"How convenient. That one doesn't waste any time taking over, does he?" Momentarily, Susannah considered suspicion, then chided herself. This sudden freedom was luring them all into hasty decisions. "Well, I hope Taylor knows what he's doing."

"Is Liphar still with you?" asked CRI.

Susannah chuckled. "Oh, yes. Poor boy kept begging me to turn back. Now he's staring at the sky and shaking his head. Perhaps my mad dash to the hills has taken him from his proper duties."

She'd spoken lightly, but felt a guilty start. As a priest in training, should Liphar be attending the cave mouth rituals with his fellow apprentices? She glanced over at him, a restless sentinel at the base of the Red Pawn. How embarrassing that she had no idea what his proper duties were. Very soon after their arrival, Liphar had attached himself to the landing party, following Meg and Stavros around when they visited the Caves, venturing almost daily down to the Underbelly. What she'd originally assumed to be childish curiosity now appeared to be a dogged determination to make the alien visitors his personal research project. Susannah suspected Liphar had learned a great deal more about Terrans than they had about him.

But Terrans were not Liphar's present concern. His tense gaze fixed on the dark crenellation of mountains far across the rugged plain to the northeast.

If there'd been room enough on the precipice, he'd be pacing. Instead, he spun his malachite bead in impatient circles around his wrist, now and then breaking into muttered song.

"I'm sure it's windier up here than when we arrived," Susannah told the computer. "Cooler, too, or maybe my suit's working again. I'll finish my report, then we'll head down, so listen up. It's really barren. The rock is worn and brittle, like an old man's teeth. Not much that looks like vegetation, though I did find some dead bushes on the way up, very thick-stemmed and squat. Too desiccated for me to tell much right off, but a desert type, I'd guess. I'll get samples on the way down." She unclipped her fone and curled it into her palm. "CRI, can you hear me all right? The wind's come up all of a sudden."

"There is a lot of background noise. Can you find a lee shelter?"

"Not up here. Maybe farther down. Hold on a moment. Liphar, what the . . . ?"

The young Sawl had scurried to her side. He grabbed her sleeve to turn her about and jabbed a finger toward the far-off mountain range.

"Oh, my!"

A moment before, there had been jade-green sky and the sunlit amber peaks shimmering through the rising steam. Now the green horizon was being smothered by the black domes of a cloud wall. Susannah squinted into the distance, not trusting her eyes. But the mirage swelled as she stared at it. The far mountains were disgorging a storm.

"CRI . . . do you have weather readings to the northeast?"

Beside her, Liphar shook out the heavy oiled-leather poncho he'd packed up the long, hot climb—she had kidded him mercilessly when he begged it off a passerby on the stairs. Now he threw it over his head and laced it tightly at his throat.

"I have no readings to the northeast," CRI replied. "Loss of signal from both those stations occurred six minutes ago. I am still trying to determine the cause. Mr. Ibiá did mention a native storm prediction just recently."

"Well, I don't need instruments or a priest to tell me there's a humdinger on its way. Take a look." She did a quick 360 to give the computer a view of the full horizon. "CRI, it's amazing! I've never seen a storm move so fast! Patch me through to Megan, quick! This could be Liphar's 'big water' after all!"

No doubt any longer that the temperature was dropping. Sweat that hadn't had a chance to dry ran in chill rivulets down her back. Susannah zipped up and tucked her long hair under her collar. The rising gusts yanked it free. She shook a resentful fist and tucked it in more tightly.

Liphar groaned in disapproval. *"Ph'nar khem!"*

"O rek, Liphar?" Susannah called over the howling wind. She pointed at the storm as it streaked toward the lowering sun. "O rek?"

His whole body shuddered, as if the words alone were threatening. He bounded to the head of the downward trail, then turned back to find Susannah still gaping at the onrushing clouds. His yelp was audible over the wind.

Susannah's fone spat static. She cupped it again. "Meg? Meg? Can you hear me?"

Megan's reply was scratchy. "You'd better get in. It's chaos down here!"

"There's a storm coming! I can see it up here, and it's moving like it's on fast forward! Both CRI and Liphar want me out of here, so I can't record it, but if you get up to a high cave mouth, you probably could."

Liphar ran back to drag her bodily toward the trail. Taking a last backward look out over the plain, Susannah stopped short. She shook Liphar off abruptly. "HEY! I just saw a Sled take off from the Lander, I swear I did! Meg, can you hear me?"

Megan's reply was broken up by static. The only words Susannah could make out were "trouble" and "interference."

"Meg? CRI? Anybody? Some fool's taken a Sled out!" Her voice cracked. "Call them back! You can't see it down there, but there's a huge storm coming!"

CRI cut in suddenly, barely intelligible through the increasing noise. "Conditions . . . abnormal . . . advise immediate . . . turn to . . . ander."

The fone went dead.

Susannah tapped at it with a muddy fingernail. "CRI? CRI?"

Nothing. The chill she felt now had little to do with temperature. From the moment she'd boarded ConPlex's new FTL ship *Hawking,* she had never been out of contact with her assigned Orbiter's computer. She had no idea what to do. She shook the tiny com unit as if it were a balky windup toy. Someone had taken a Sled out! Couldn't they see what was happening? She held the fone close to her mouth. Maybe that would help. "Meg? CRI? MEG? If you can still hear me, I'm coming in!"

When it remained inert, she shoved it into a tabbed pocket and snatched up her pack.

Liphar waited in jitters at the trail head. His eyes darted back and forth between Susannah and the approaching cloud bank. She sensed him weighing the potential of anger as a goad. She'd never seen him angry, and was tempted to find further cause for delay. But the academic value of such study faded in the face of the young man's obvious fright. This wasn't about getting wet, or some other minor inconvenience. Liphar was terrified by this storm. As it swept closer and closer, his loud urgings collapsed into inarticulate whining. Soon he would lose resolve for anything but flight, as panic overcame even his dedication to her safety. She'd be left alone on the mountaintop, which would be a unique experience, but likely not a good one. She gave in and hurried to join him.

The cloud line billowed across the sky like pirate sails ripped loose from their stays, fat and black, red-bellied with dying sunlight. The plain glowed orange, a painter's image of hell. Steam from the melting ice was pressed low into the canyons by the wind, where it lay like coiled entrails. As the cloud bank swept overhead, the Red Pawn turned the color of dried blood. Then the first raindrops hit, and the rock precipice ran red like an opened wound.

Susannah curled an arm around Liphar's narrow shoulders. Was it the storm's unnatural speed that made him credit it with such lethal intent? "It's weird, but it's only weather."

But the young Sawl was beyond comfort. *"O rek! Gisti! Gisti!"* He pulled loose and took off down the darkening trail.

Susannah trotted after him, pondering his unreasoning terror. This word "gisti" was key. Stavros said it encompassed both weather and concepts of deity, but he hadn't yet been able to define the precise relationship. Nor could he settle on a Terran word that fully matched its apparent complexities. *The gods' weather?* Or *godlike weather?* Susannah tended to side with Occam, even in matters of linguistic theory. Thus "weather gods" seemed the simplest answer. Megan agreed, from an anthropological standpoint, but Stavros insisted that language was devious in ways that the physical world could never be. It was Stavros who had first stated that the Sawls were a subtle people.

The cloud billows screamed past overhead, reaching for the lowering sun. Liphar leaped down the trail, gesturing wildly to speed Susannah along. The Red Pawn disappeared behind a rim of wet rock. The air turned bilious and ruddy, and the details of the treacherous terrain vanished into the shadow of the rocks. Then the scattered raindrops exploded into a downpour that increased in ferocity with every downward step. Susannah was forced to slow down. How could the sky hold so much water and still leave air enough to breathe? Liphar was barely visible through the sheeting rain. She felt again the chill of panic, but she was moving as fast as she dared. She checked her suit pockets, then her pack for gloves. She came up empty-handed. A march of ragged boulders rose out of the dimness as suddenly as specters. The trail circumvented them sharply, then sliced downward, nearly vertical and awash with muddy water.

A gray-umber darkness overtook them as the storm swallowed up the sun. The rain lashed at Susannah's eyes. She settled her pack on her back, then reached to fasten her suit hood, but the abrupt motion put her out of balance. Pebbles rolled beneath her feet. She fell skidding down the gravel-washed path, across razor edges of rock, past the fleeing Liphar. He grabbed for her, but could not break her fall. He let go just as her greater weight would have dragged him after her. She slid hard into a granite outcropping, edging the trail as if by miracle, just as it switchbacked past a deep cleft in the mountainside. Susannah huddled against the rock in shock until Liphar scrambled down to haul her to her feet. He briefly checked for injury but pushed on downward without further pause.

Susannah was too numb to protest. The therm-suit's tough skin had protected her body, but her bare hands and face were scraped raw. She touched her cheek, and the dim light showed a darkness on her palm. Her doctor's training told her these were only surface wounds, but the sight of her own blood welling up so freely frightened her unreasonably. She tore her gaze from the dark cleft and the vision of herself lying shattered on the icy rock fifty meters below, and tried not to cling to Liphar like a dream-waked child. When she could hear the wind and rain over the pounding of her heart, she cursed her foolhardiness. Rule #1 of planetary exploration: only a complete understanding of a world can render it harmless, no matter how benign its outward appearance. And she hadn't even bothered to bring gloves! She, who was never without them!

I know better than this! Nonetheless, I go charging off into the hills like some giddy schoolgirl. Idiot! If I had listened to Liphar . . .

And now it seemed perfectly obvious. Liphar had known the weather was due to turn bad. That's why he'd been so reluctant to make the climb. He'd known to pack a rain poncho up a hot mountain trail, no matter that it was a perfect, cloudless day.

But how could he know? Surely it was just his habitual caution at work.

She felt confused, dizzy, as she hurried along behind him with chastened concentration. Now she observed him scrupulously: when he slowed, where he looked, where he put each foot. She took note of each protruding rock he used for balance. The wind rose into swirling gusts that forced her to a crouch. She could see only a few meters ahead, but Liphar sped along as if he could walk the trail blind. He led her around two steep switchbacks to where the trail cut through a tumble of stone rubble clogging the upper end of a canyon. The wind howled among the boulders. Susannah found herself stumbling. Blood washed down the rock wherever she reached for support, and fire bloomed in her palms. She wondered how much blood she was losing. She was tiring too rapidly.

They struggled free of the boulder pile. Ahead, the path dropped sharply toward the canyon floor. Here Liphar hesitated. The bottom was invisible behind a curtain of rain. The roar of wind and falling water echoed a demon's chorus within the canyon walls. The young Sawl stood in anxious indecision, listening, as his hands worked tirelessly at his azure bead.

Suddenly he turned aside, onto a ledge that snaked high along the wall, below the canyon's rim. Susannah clambered up after him, wondering why he chose this path against the easier route across the canyon floor. The ledge was narrow, too narrow for a Terran to negotiate without a struggle. It was littered with rock debris and split here and there by the same thick root she had noticed on the upward climb. Liphar raced ahead, then waited for her to catch up, pointing out a line of handholds chipped into the crumbling rock. When he was sure she understood, he raced ahead again. Susannah had to scramble along half-bent to make use of the Sawl-height handholds. Her fingers were stiff and cold. She blessed the imperviousness of her therm-suit, but wished again for the protection of its gloves. With her eyes focused on the trail, she nearly slammed into Liphar, who had halted again, blinking into the rain.

Peering around him, she saw that the ledge ended abruptly where a side wash broke through the rim in a fresh jumble of collapsed strata. A roar of water echoed down the walls in a directionless bombardment as if born of the air itself. Liphar rocked on the balls of his feet and stared up the wash. It was wide and forbiddingly steep. Its smoothly rounded stones reminded Susannah of the cascading rivers of rock in Japanese gardens. Liphar beckoned her close to him.

"Go much quick, you!" His hands slashed swift straight motions across the wash to where the ledge picked up again. "Most quick! I go one time, next you go!"

Susannah nodded. His continuing anxiety puzzled her. Surely they were past the worst, being off the top of the scarp? But Liphar clutched his bead, his thin cheeks sucked in with doubt. Suddenly, he slipped the thong off his wrist and pressed the bead into Susannah's hand.

"*Khem khe!*" he declared and sprang away. She watched him jump down into the wash and fly from rock to rock, his feet barely touching one before he was on to the next. His poncho flapped around him like a sail, his skinny arms outstretched like unfeathered wings. He did not look back until he'd gained the other side and hauled himself up onto the ledge, panting. Quickly, he waved her on.

Susannah climbed down into the wash. She could not move as he had done, or as fast. Her booted feet slipped on the smooth wet rock. She fell once, caught herself, fell again and cried out as the rock smashed into her shoulder. She pulled herself to her knees, tucked the talisman into a pocket and began to crawl, using hands, feet, elbows, whatever helped to move her along. In the middle of the wash, she glanced up to orient herself. Liphar was gesturing with renewed urgency from the ledge. His eyes met hers, but a telling bias in his stance made her look sidelong, up the broad rubbled wash.

What she saw near stopped her heart.

A man-high wall of water thundered toward her. Deep in its muddy boil, stones ground and clattered like dragon's teeth.

Time slowed. The roar and clatter faded. The giant wave bowed gracefully into its downward rush, garlanded with a delicate wreath of bloody froth. Vast boulders danced and turned inside its curl, an endless freefall, slow as the movement of continents.

Liphar's high scream broke the spell. Susannah sucked in wind and spray, and launched herself across the wash in a frantic scramble for her life.

11

THE LANDER SAT LIFELESS, shuddering in the storm.

Stavros Ibiá set his emergency lantern on the corridor floor and gave the looted cubicle a final survey. He dragged a palm across his damp brow, then wiped both hands on his once-white fatigue pants. He hated to admit it, but he missed the comfortable cycling hum of the air system. When the power link with the Orbiter went down—his guess was the winds had smashed the receiving antennas up on the nose—Weng had brought the backup cells on line. But their only remaining energy source must be conserved, so moments ago, he'd unplugged them and sent them up to the safety of the Caves. Soon, he would follow.

We're on our own now. Thrown back on our own resources. Just like the Sawls.

It shouldn't be so satisfying. Lives were at stake. People would suffer. And no sign yet of Clausen and Danforth. If they hadn't found shelter, they might already have paid the full price for their folly. Still, it was thrilling. His life so far had been soft, too soft—in the family compound, at the University—while the Earth's billions labored and sickened and starved outside the gates. Removed from that privilege, he could finally test his own sufficiency, his true mettle. It was both harder and easier than he had expected.

He ran through a mental catalog of the salvaged equipment: items meant to be portable; others he'd spent ten sleepless hours cannibalizing; others he must leave behind. The power loss was manageable for now. When the storm passed, he'd get the emergency solar up and running. But having the com link down was like losing a limb. His fone was his right arm. He was accustomed—they all were—to CRI providing data, communication, structure, everything. He struggled to picture each emptied niche and cabin, but exhaustion blurred the images and numbers in his inadequately human mind.

He did regret that Danforth was not around to witness the rape of his precious instruments. Or better still, to be forced to admit that the Sawls had predicted the abrupt weather change with absolute and uncanny accuracy. Perhaps, during those last moments before B-Sled had lost its own power link and crashed in the storm, as Stavros was sure it had, perhaps *then* Taylor had harbored a brief suspicion, an inkling at least, that he should have set aside his habitual contempt and listened.

Stavros hoped he had, then was shamed by his own pettiness. An eye for an eye, the Old Testament demanded. But he did not wish to be ruled by the bias of antiquity.

The glare of the lantern stung his tired eyes. He left it in the corridor and moved into the darkened emptiness of the cubicle. The sounds of the last stages of the evacuation, the general clatter and human voices, the rattle of cartwheels, floated up the central service shaft, softened by distance. The rain beat a hard staccato on the outer hull, percussive, regular.

Like a Sawl work chant. Stavros pondered a possible connection.

In the hard lantern light slicing through the doorway, the cubicle's gray walls confronted him balefully. He read reproof in their smudges and stains, resentment at being deserted, left behind to brave the storm alone.

You're not prepared for this, he told himself. First time out of the cocoon. Who are you to take other people's lives in your hands?

But in his heart, he wanted it: the drama and the responsibility. He drank deeply from the clay jug dangling at his waist. The water was sweet relief from the heat of the Lander's upper levels. He felt it drop to his stomach and spread its chill down into his groin. Exciting, as the storm was exciting, and the smoothly coordinated evacuation of the Lander, due mainly to his success with the Master Ranger. She had given him her people to carry it out. The taste of crisis was as real and pungent as the acrid smoke from the cook fires burning in the Underbelly. An adventure myth come alive, all he had dreamed of in his dormitory in the Pyrenees, with its climate control and its spectacular views. Stavros was stunned by the power of these atavistic joys and, innocent of their dark allure, surrendered to them with a lover's trembling helplessness.

He took another step into the room, resisting the impulse to search its shadowed corners. In this space, he was an intruder. Danforth's presence lurked invisibly.

For the loss of Emil Clausen, he felt not a moment's regret. In fact, they'd all be better off, and Earth would be, too. Stavros had little faith in the salvation-of-the-world claims for the new lithium-based solar collector that had caused ConPlex to fund this expedition. Any additional power it might provide would go to the rich and privileged while the rest of the Earth went on burning coal and biomass and killing the planet. Stavros was in full agreement with Megan Levy on this point: the prospector and his company were a menace to all life-supporting worlds. University gossip made ConPlex specifically responsible for the loss or adulteration of at least five alien languages before Terran linguists had the chance to document them properly. Stavros had struggled hard with his conscience before accepting a post on a ConPlex-funded expedition. The probe data had suggested minimal humanoid habitation, possibly a civilization already gone by—not enough to rouse the interest of an experienced hand. Besides, ConPlex wasn't paying a Big Deal's premium. They didn't want this planet "discovered." But even a wunderkind couldn't afford to turn down a good first assignment, especially a potential First Contact. Stavros knew he'd got lucky when Fortune delivered the Sawls.

His quarrel with Taylor Danforth was mostly a clash of personalities, but it was hard not to feel challenged by the man's deep reputation. Measuring himself against the older scientist's confidence and expertise, Stavros found himself wanting, and thus compelled to sniff out Danforth's weaknesses and worry them like a terrier. Now this seemed a lot like adolescent posturing. He wished it were easier to write the planetologist off, but not even Danforth, for all his arrogance, deserved to die in the rain on some alien mountainside.

He rattled a stray clamp against the shelf of a stripped utility rack. He was uneasy about leaving the racks behind, but they were too tall to fit into the lift cage, and there was no time to disassemble them or drop them down the shaft one by one.

Taylor gone.

"Taylor . . . dead." He made himself say it, and the reality of it settled around him at last, like a chill fog. "Susannah missing."

This was even harder. McPherson had brought him that dark news. Events were spinning out of control too fast. Stavros snatched up the little clamp and surprised himself by stuffing it into his pants pocket.

Out in the corridor, two sweating Sawls grunted over the last of Danforth's holo equipment. The lift cage was packed tight. Their comradely debate over where to add to the load was escalating into an argument. Stavros heard the fear in their voices. They were not happy being away from the Caves in such weather.

Ropes as thick as his wrist ran up the forty-meter shaft. At the bottom, a giant wooden winch substituted for the dead lift system, a Sawl machine hauled down from the Caves to meet the emergency. Storm gusts howled about in the Underbelly, spiraling upward to rock the cage until it banged against its shaft. The hum of the magnetic lift had given way to the groaning music of rope on timber. In the cubicle, the gale circled him, tugging at his hair. Stavros was taken by a vision of ancient ships and storms at sea. He clenched his eyes in dizziness. He pressed his forehead to the cool alloy of the racks to settle the nausea, grasping for balance within the confusion of sound.

Not now, not now.

He was there again, near the edge, perilously near—relishing the anticipation of terror, recalling the shame and self-loathing each time it overtook him. He shook his head, a lunge for clarity, but was distracted by a slap-slap rhythm like the flap of a window shade on a windy evening, and then it was too late. Sound billowed around him, carried him to the precipice. He was too exhausted to resist, and why bother, when it was so much more interesting to slide over the edge. The rain drummed against the Lander's shell, and he heard the ocean's roar and the snap of storm-lashed sails. The singsong shouts of the winch haulers echoed up the lift shaft, and he was salt-drenched, hauling at shredded rigging with the men on his crew. Far below, the big machine moaned in its labors—brave wood straining at the upper limits of its strength, his ship's hull breasting the waves. His body rocked to the taut hum of the ropes, with the creak of canvas and timber. Ecstasy sang in him like a siren.

Like all his moments of transport, it seemed to last forever but did not. It crested and diminished, and he was released to drift unmoored. Reaching for a mast of pain to lash himself to, Stavros slammed his fist against the doorframe, once, twice, yet still swayed off-balance as the great ship beneath him rolled into a wave. His bare feet gripped for weathered planking. Another bash of his fist and his mind at last agreed that the deck he stood on was the smooth metal and plastic of a twenty-first-century vessel. But the fright in the faces of the two Sawls at the lift cage told him that this particular motion was not imagined. A toolbox slid off the top of the pile and crashed to the floor.

Forty meters down, the winch crew abruptly fell silent.

A cracking like the cry of a rent glacier echoed up the shaft. The Lander shuddered.

Stavros sprang toward the lift. He pushed the two Sawls stumbling into the cage, tossed them the emergency lamp, then grabbed the top rail of the safety gate. He swung up to wedge himself in on top of the load, against the ceiling grate. The huge knots attaching the lift to the winch system creaked right above his head. The cage bucked, dropped precipitately and stopped short with a jolt. The updrafts whistled like police sirens. The Sawls hung on with eyes shut tight.

The lift steadied. Stavros reclaimed his light and yelled down the shaft for the winch crew to lower away. A chorus of warnings shot upward as the Lander swayed again. The laden cage slammed against the shaftway as the Lander settled at a tilt. Stavros renewed his bellowed pleas, waving the lantern like a beacon. He heard McPherson's shout below; painfully, the cage edged downward, screeching along the side of the shaft. Stavros managed a relieved grin, to comfort his terrified companions on the lift. He raised the light at the entrance to each floor they passed on the way down, flashing the beam into darkened corners and calling out, making sure no one had been left behind.

E.D. 45–10:10

Megan Levy waited at the easternmost cave mouth, nearest to the trail that Susannah had taken up the cliff face. Outside, rain slammed across the steps and ledges. Raw gusts swirled in to snatch at her out of the creeping twilight. Megan backed farther into the shelter of the cave. The long slow Fiixian night had begun.

"Where *are* they?" she moaned helplessly.

Ten hours since she'd lost contact, and she could only pace and worry. A few more hours, and the darkness would be complete. It would not be light again for several weeks.

"Stupid. Stupid!" she grumbled.

But then, Susannah's foolishness paled in the face of what Danforth and Clausen had done. Had everyone taken leave of their senses? Or was it like it had been at home, when the super-storms first ravaged the East Coast and no one took them seriously? Megan massaged her wrists. The cold damp had awakened her arthritis.

Farther up the tunnel, a Sawl woman sat cross-legged at the foot of the stone stairs. She wore a knitted shawl over rough wool trousers and tunic. Even in the gloom, the soft drape shone as blue as the water of a summer lake. A thick knotted fringe bordered it like a darker shoreline. The woman worked from a ball of brown yarn, turning her needles into the light of a blown-glass oil lamp set beside her knee. The lamp's chimney was faceted, reflecting the light as a cut jewel would, aesthetic rather than practical. The woman held her knitting close to the glass while tiny prisms danced and sparkled along the walls, and the tunnel remained mostly in darkness.

How did she see to work in so little light? Susannah had often remarked how excellent Sawl eyesight seemed to be. Perhaps it was because they spent so much time in dark places. Or maybe it was just good genes.

Megan paced in and out of the shifting light, stiff with standing. The Sawl woman's name was Tyril, and Clausen would have said that her real duty was to keep Megan from straying too far into the Caves. No matter. Megan was grateful for her quiet presence, uncurious but sympathetic. She hoped this one might be a friend. After six weeks, she still knew none of the Sawls personally, except Liphar, if one can ever be said to know a shadow well. Only Ibiá could remark that a friend had said thus and so, and mean Sawl as often as Terran. More often than not, as he spent less and less time with his Terran colleagues.

"They do keep their distance, these Sawls," she'd remarked to Susannah recently.

"They're waiting until they know us, know what we are. Can you blame them?"

But Megan wondered if appearing unconcerned by the presence of visitors who said they came from another world was actually a way of denying that world's existence.

Whatever reluctance it was that barred the Terrans full access to Sawl lives and living places, it had been put aside willingly in a crisis. The Sawls had found space for the visitors in the already crowded Caves and worked hard to salvage huge loads of equipment with no purpose or value to themselves.

Megan was moved by their generosity. She wouldn't enjoy being descended upon by a pack of strangers, poking, prodding, recording, demanding explanations for this and that. Her intrusion was just as presumptuous as Clausen's, really. But she consoled herself that it was surely less harmful.

She studied Tyril's face. The same fine-boned angularity that seemed delicate in the Sawl men shaped the women's faces with strength. The mouth was wide and firm, yet sensuous. The nose was a straight line that met heavy arched brows promising a seriousness of mind. Tyril sat very still. But for the flick of her bone needles, she might have been carved from fine brown marble. Megan thought her very beautiful. The men were as well, but more in the way that a child is beautiful: sexless and unripe. But that was a personal bias.

Her gaze strayed up the wall to the niche above Tyril's head, the cave entry's only hint of decoration. It was shallow and long, and crowded with tiny clay statuettes. Their outlines were barely visible in the dim light, but Megan knew from her own research pix that the entryway friezes contained mostly grotesques: stocky little gnomes with smoothly misshapen limbs, or wraithlike stick figures full of ribs and elbows. Little nightmares of anguish or deformity, bent, twisted, dwarfed—each an embodiment, perhaps, of a specific agony. The figures were painted in rich polychrome, the hues deepened with the gloss of age. The hundred tiny eyes glittered with shards of black glass.

Behind them, two larger figures loomed out of the background stone. The clay grotesques bent toward them in a gesture of mass obeisance. In the odd dancing light, the little statues seemed to be dancing, too. *Danse Macabre.* Megan shivered and turned her back on them.

Commander Weng came down the inner stairs, moving with the silence that was her habit and gift. "No sign of them as yet, Dr. Levy?"

Megan shook her head dispiritedly.

Weng was accompanied by a grandmotherly Sawl bearing a steaming jug and a small stack of clay drinking bowls. A sweet scent of boiled herbs invaded the tunnel's damp. Tyril smiled but continued with her knitting.

Weng poured pale green tea, setting the bowls by Tyril's side. "Mr. Ibiá has managed to explain the situation to that tall woman who never speaks."

"Aguidran? The master of the Ranger Guild?"

Weng nodded gravely. "She is willing to mount a search, even after nightfall, but most of her workers are still occupied down at the Lander."

Megan stared into the howling gray at the tunnel mouth. "There's still some light left. We should be out there searching for them ourselves."

"Foolish and inefficient, Dr. Levy. An indulgence of survivor guilt that will profit us little. I've already had to resort to strict orders to keep Lieutenant McPherson from rushing out there herself."

Megan shrugged. "You know how she feels about Taylor."

"The Ranger woman is far better suited to directing a search in her own terrain. Besides, Dr. Danforth is a married man." Weng turned to leave, then paused and said over her shoulder, not unkindly, "Food is being laid out in the Meeting Hall, Dr. Levy, if you could see fit to leave off your vigil for a spell."

Men like Taylor, Megan mused, were only married when they were at home. "Thanks, Commander. I'll keep it in mind."

"As you wish." Weng remounted the steps as quietly as she had come, followed by her equally silent Sawl escort.

Tyril laid aside her knitting and unfolded a cloth bundle of bread and cold cheese pie. Megan accepted a bowl of the hot tea and a chunk of bread. She would have delighted in the cheese pie, but was unwilling to break her penance entirely. Weng's remark about survivor's guilt had been well placed.

Megan sipped her tea, smiled awkwardly at Tyril, and continued to pace.

E.D. 45–10:12

With a final screech and fall, the lift cage jarred to the ground. Stavros and his Sawl companions jumped off as efficient hands snatched the cargo to safety. The winch crew locked their machine and swarmed up over the cage to release their ropes. Stavros gave himself a moment to stop shaking. Other than getting caught in the occasional food riot back home, this might be the first time his life had truly been in danger.

The Underbelly was in an uproar. Shouts and chanting and the clatter of loading and carrying competed with the throb and yowl of the storm. The air was chill at ground level, and smelled of soot and wet wool and the strong herb tea brewing on the cook fires.

The partitions had been dismantled and the crates repacked with stuff to be taken up to the Caves. A few smaller boxes were still scattered about, half filled. Two hastily strung emergency lights swung overhead, casting mobile shadows across the milling crowd. Stavros was relieved to find the entry cylinder still firmly encased in ice, though the ice enclosing the perimeter had already pulled back alarmingly. Between the heat shield overhead and the top surface of the surrounding ice, a band of leaden twilight had appeared. Rain sluiced onto the Underbelly floor. The ice dike was melting into a circle of blunt teeth, with tongues of dirty froth from outside licking up into the spaces between. Moisture seeped through in several places. Stavros eyed it with foreboding. A lot of water behind that ice. It had to hold a while longer. The cylinder was a bottleneck and traffic through it was slow, but it and the tunnel beyond were their only escape route.

He shouted to McPherson through the cook smoke and bedlam. She finished lashing a plastic crate to a Sawl hand truck and sent its owner on his way with a quick pat. Stavros thought she looked tired, strained, but enviably in control. The crowd eddied around her as she made her way toward him like a small freighter steaming up current.

Behind him, the winch crew gained the top of the lift cage and picked frantically at the knots tying it to their machine. A young girl called out, and passed up a lantern with a jug of water. Stavros eyed the wide-open shaft and the central hatch. No manual closing. Without power, he'd have to leave them that way.

A woman backed into him with a cart full of Clausen's seismic equipment. Stavros considered telling her to leave it behind. But no, he'd just have to answer for the loss of ConPlex property. Besides, who knew what they'd need in the days to come? He helped jockey the cart about. As the woman dragged it toward the tunnel, the wheels bumped sharply along the ground.

"Look at that!" He pointed as McPherson joined him. During their landing, the descent engines had seared through several meters of snow and ice and fused the top layer of sandy soil into flawless glass: a flat floor perfect for setting up base camp under the Lander's belly. Now that perfect floor had developed cracks and slants.

McPherson shrugged and nodded. She was pure and uncomplicated in her refusal to bother herself with problems she could do nothing to solve. Stavros admired that. While he faced crises torn between terror and exultation, McPherson just got on with business. Maybe that's what you became, when you lived your life with only a thin metal skin between you and the vacuum of space.

"We're cleaned out upstairs." He had to shout over the din, striving to echo her efficient solidity. "Any sign of Liphar and Susannah?"

This merited a passing scowl. "No. Not the Sled, either."

Her anxiety didn't slow her down—why should his? "More to go down here?"

"Nothing much we need. 'Cept her." The pilot's blue eyes blinked in frustration. At the perimeter, fresh freeze blocked a Sled-sized hole in the ice wall. Beside it, the remaining Sled waited like a beached whale. Stray clothing still decorated its windscreen: a damp lab coat, a lone thermal sock. "How're we gonna get her outta here?"

Stavros had given up on the Sled and should have known that McPherson would not. But Weng had directed him to recover only what he could *safely*. "We're not."

"What?"

"We're not!" His irritation flared so suddenly that he wondered why he'd thought he had any taste for command. In his imagination, he was never faced with this constant questioning of his authority.

"No way! We got two crewmen to rescue!"

"Three," he reminded her.

"You wanna tour this damn planet on your feet?"

Stavros jabbed a finger at the wrinkled floor, at the melting ice wall. "I'm thinking about now, Ron, and how we'd better get ourselves and all these people out of here! They're our responsibility, too!"

With a cheer, the winch crew loosed the big knots and hauled the ropes free of the cage. A woman called to the others to clear the shaftway. The weathered cross-timbers of the winch towered over her as she bent her back to the crank handle.

"Where's Weng?" Counting heads, Stavros sought calm in the steady rhythm of the crank.

"Up in the Caves, keeping tabs on where they're stowing all our stuff. Stav, about the Sled, we could . . ."

"No. We can't. There isn't time." And then the winch and its crew took over his full attention. The ropes jerked up and rumbled through their pulleys high in the shaft head, then thundered into a heap at the bottom in a mist of hemp shreds. More hands grasped the crank and the big slatted drum began to roll, winding the rope around itself. The winch gleamed with a polish of hard use and age. It spoke to Stavros of time and of history. *I am a treasure,* it said. *I am the finest of my kind.*

It belonged to the Engineers Guild, and was constructed of thousands of small lengths of wood pegged together into stout beams. The wheels were a foot thick, five layers laminated at cross-grain to each other. Not a single nail or bolt had been used throughout the entire frame. Wooden dowel and a perfect fit alone held piece to piece, like the hull of an ancient galleon. The Sawls' response to a metals-poor environment was the creation of miracles with a nearly as inadequate supply of trees. Stavros lingered by the machine, stroking its oiled beams as if it were a faithful draft animal.

"Just think what they'd accomplish if they had more iron available to them."

The crew scrambled over each other to pull fat stone wedges out from under the wheels, then braced themselves to roll the winch toward the exit.

McPherson grabbed his arm. "They're taking it away?"

A shuddering crack rang out, like a long volley of pistol shot. The glassy floor vibrated. Stavros shook McPherson off and ran to help the winch crew.

"Stav, wait! We could use it to haul the Sled out! Shit, at least we gotta try!"

The ground wailed and shook again. The floor buckled under their feet. Black water shot up through the cracks. Now Stavros Ibiá paid dearly for his habit of hunting the thrills to be found at the edge of the mind's abyss. Terror and exultation battled, and terror won. The sudden cold and deadly gurgle around his bare ankles lanced a buried nightmare, of shattered ice floes and dark frigid seas. This time it was not romantic transport but panic that shattered his self-control.

"Out!" he shouted. "Everybody out!"

He whirled on the Sawl nearest him and pushed her toward the exit cylinder. Her bundle of plastic dishware went cascading across the floor. He turned to gesture wildly at McPherson. "Get them out! *Now!* This thing's gonna come right down on top of us!" He ran at a group of Sawls dividing a crate of tools into smaller loads. "Out! OUT!"

The Sawls stared at him, astonished.

McPherson charged after him. She planted her body firmly in his path, arms outstretched, and whacked him hard across the jaw.

He stopped, stunned. His eyes widened, then blinked as clarity returned.

McPherson saw him withdraw into himself. "Okay, I see the problem. Don't like it, but I see it, and you're right. We need to get these folks out of here. I ain't got the language, so if you crap out on me, we've had it." She eyed his naked, wet torso and feet. "And it wouldn't hurt you to get some proper clothes on before you catch your death."

Shaken, shivering, Stavros nodded, but could not make his tongue form the angular Sawlish syllables. The Sawls who had witnessed his meltdown glanced at each other and went back to work of their own accord. As cold water washed around their feet, and the towering alien hulk swayed above them, each resumed his burden and joined the orderly stream to the exit. The empty-handed picked up the nearest object they could manage, and everyone moved a little bit faster.

Have I become a liability?

Stavros was used to being a danger to himself, but not to others. On this world, in this situation, being out of control was neither thrilling nor romantic. It was potentially lethal. But no time now for self-recrimination. He would scourge himself later, in the privacy of the Caves.

McPherson shoved some clothing at him, his boots and woolen Sawl tunic. She watched him as he rolled up wet pant cuffs and pulled the boots onto his muddied feet.

"Serve you right if you get frostbite," she observed evenly.

"Not cold enough." He wrung water out of his tunic, then returned her measuring stare. "Leave me alone, Ron. I'm okay now."

"Better be." She gazed over his shoulder. "Crowd's backing up at the cylinder. You ready to go back to work?"

"I'm fine."

"Then let's do it. I wanna get outta this joint alive!"

E.D. 45–10:18

Megan banished her wilder visions of Susannah's body battered by the torrent and turned her anxiety inward. If she'd been properly on her game, she could have warned them. But she'd been too preoccupied with her fortress theory.

A strong theory, on the whole, but an incomplete one. She'd developed it to explain why the Sawls lived high up on the cliffs. There were lower, more accessible caves. Or, why the steep entry tunnels, with their long flights of steps up to the warren of living quarters deep in the rock? From the top of the inner stairs, the cave mouth was hidden from view. The draft flowed downward, musky with the odors of the caverns, and the rough-hewn walls were dry. Surely this was all about defense. Peoples choose inaccessible dwellings in order to protect themselves!

Then, during her vigil, she'd noticed the deep stone troughs on either side of the entryway. The probe data had predicted a desert planet, yet here were these serious rain gutters, obvious now that they were awash with water.

"Taylor did suggest climate," she told Tyril. "But I dismissed it as professional bias. Even Susannah couldn't shake me loose, pointing out your apparent lack of large predators. And then there's the gift you all seem to have for settling your differences peacefully," she added, as Tyril offered her a final corner of the cheese pie. "You have no armies, no uniforms, no police. There is the Guild Council, but the guilds mostly seem to discipline themselves. How do you do it, Tyril? We Terrans can barely keep the peace within a community of seven!"

Tyril offered a smile of commiseration, understanding no more than the pain in the other woman's tone. Megan felt a rush of warmth. Two women, separated by a vast cultural rift, yet joined in waiting, perhaps later in mourning? Megan rejected that nightmare and resumed her monologue.

"The Sawls have gone to a lot of trouble, said I, over what would appear to be a very long time to carve out these caves—what else but defense could drive such an effort? Well, it just didn't occur to me that the real enemy might be Nature. Instead, I invented a fierce past for you. When we fully grasp the language, I said, throwing the ball neatly into Stavros' court, we'll find such a history hidden in the legends of the Warring Gods." Megan paused, and sighed. "I had myself quite convinced."

She slouched back to the cave mouth to let the rain batter her face as punishment for her unscientific rush to judgment. "Susannah kept saying, 'Remember the pueblos.' Built above the spring high-water, shaded in summer, sheltered from wind, rain, and snow by the canyon walls, placed to catch the low winter sun . . ."

In the face of the gale, her chatter ran out of steam.

Did I say that the enemy might be only Nature? What more ancient and formidable enemy is there? Wind and water, heat and killing cold. We thought we'd conquered Nature back on Earth, but look how that serpent has turned round to bite us for our arrogance! No wonder the Sawls find their gods in the weather—better to endow the storm with intention than to face the realities of a chaotic and remorseless universe. . . .

Outside, the gray void was a shade darker than before. Megan turned back to Tyril, as even a one-sided conversation was less depressing than her private thoughts. But Tyril had set her knitting aside. Her head was cocked, listening, and suddenly, her face lit up.

A shadow appeared across the screen of mist at the cave mouth. Liphar staggered into the opening as if through a windblown curtain. His brown face was haggard, his clothing soaked through. He was plastered with mud from head to foot, the exact image of the clay grotesques crowding the wall niche. Megan refused to breathe until Susannah's hooded form struggled in after him. The pair scrambled up the tunnel like two drowning rats in a last effort to save themselves, fell stumbling past Megan as she was opening her mouth in relieved welcome, and collapsed at the foot of the stairs, choking and shivering.

Megan ran to kneel beside them. "Are you all right?"

Susannah nodded weakly, unable to speak. Tyril helped Liphar sit up and began to swab mud off his face with a corner of her shawl. Susannah dragged herself up to lean against the bottom step. She caught Liphar's eye and they gazed at each other with exhausted pride.

"We made it!"

"We thought you were dead!" Megan exclaimed.

Susannah fumbled to unsnap a mud-soaked pocket. She pulled out a blue talisman bead and raised it in victory, then handed it back to Liphar. Tyril nodded approvingly.

"Khem khe!" Liphar tapped proudly at his thin chest between attempts to wring mud and water out of his clothing. Still fighting for breath, he chattered compulsively, as if to tell the tale was to banish its terrors. Tyril listened with folded arms, now and then shaking her head with maternal sympathy.

"You look awful," Megan told Susannah. "Dry clothes, first. Can you walk?"

"Not just yet, I think." Susannah shuddered and sank back on the steps.

Mud dripped from her therm-suit. Her face and hands were streaked with blood.

"You're hurt," Megan declared.

"Nothing serious." Susannah sighed, a shivering intake of breath. "Oh, Meg, it's bad out there. Most of the way, the trail held up, but here and there . . . did you ever think it was trite when someone claimed they'd seen death staring them in the face?"

"That bad, huh?"

"That bad." They fell silent a moment, listening to Liphar's chatter. Tyril was trying unsuccessfully to get him out of his wet clothing, blotting at his cuts and scrapes, scolding softly. Finally she gave up and rose, laid a reassuring hand on Susannah's shoulder, and headed up the stairs. Liphar lay back on the cold stone and closed his eyes.

"Did you ever find Weng?" asked Susannah fuzzily.

"I didn't know she was lost."

"But CRI said . . . never mind."

"Right now, the Commander's seeing to the salvage of our gear before the floods carry it off to parts unknown. It's Taylor and Emil we can't find. One of the Sleds is missing."

"Yes!" Susannah jerked upright. "It took off! I saw it! I was up there where I could see the storm coming and I tried to warn CRI, but there was all this static and my fone went down."

"All of them. No com, no power. The whole system is down."

"But the Sled . . . you mean they didn't turn back? They're still out there in *this*?"

Megan nodded grimly. "Idiots. Pilot hubris. But we'll find them, soon as the weather lets up."

"But it's not going to let up! According to Liphar, it's going to get worse."

Megan peered into the roaring maw at the cave entry. "How much worse can it get?"

"Ask *him*. He seems to know these things well ahead of time!" Her head sagged to her knees. "Is the Lander . . . ?"

"Still there last time I looked. But the waters are rising."

Susannah's sag deepened. "Do we know why both links are down?"

"Weather. Storm damage. CRI said something about interference. Can't really tell till we get back out there and see what shape the Lander's in."

Megan fingered the small emergency pack on her belt, now powering her therm-suit. "Haven't used one of these in years."

Susannah held up her bloodied hands. "Well, we'll have her back when the rain stops. Till then, it'll be just like the good old days, when they dropped you in the bush with nothing but a canteen and matches. Some fun, eh?" She stretched, tried to sit up, and fell back with a groan. "I think my body's coming apart."

"Even I don't remember *those* good old days. Come on, I'll help you up the stairs."

"I must have lost a bit of blood." Susannah blinked, as if the rain still battered her eyes. "Hey—that network of ledges carved into every rock face around? Do you know they're *all* above flood level? Liphar and I would be dead without them."

Megan grasped her friend about her waist to support her up the stairs. "I know, I know. Remember the pueblos. . . ."

E.D. 45–10:26

The giant winch stuck at an angle to the entry cylinder, blocking the exit completely. The crowd's forward motion ceased. The stoutest set down their loads and shouldered in to lend their strength as the crew struggled to pivot the winch into a better position.

A single alto voice began a work chant. Its simple minor-keyed melody spread through the crowd like a fire in dry brush. The storm's shriek and moan was backgrounded to an atonal accompaniment. Stavros wished for a working fone, or at least his little pocket recorder. Like many Sawl ritual songs, this chant took the form of a three-part dialogue. Two of the voices were sung solo, with the responsibility passed from singer to singer. The third voice was a resounding choral answer to the first two. The language of the songs differed from spoken Sawlish, and Stavros suspected that an older version of their tongue was preserved in the ritual. He listened raptly as the melody rose and fell with the wind.

The winch rocked and creaked. Inch by inch, the vast rear wheels edged about until at last the chant broke into a cheer. The machine lurched and rolled ponderously into the cylinder. The crowd moved forward again.

He and McPherson made a last circuit of the Underbelly. Icy water bubbled up everywhere. Sodden rubble and clothing squished underfoot. The deserted cook fires hissed into ashes and smoke. McPherson stared at the remaining Sled for a long moment, then impulsively ran to sweep the junk from its windscreen. Then she turned on her heel and followed Stavros to the exit.

"Wait." He stopped, turning back. "The emergency lights."

She caught his sleeve. "It'll take too long."

"We'll need their batteries, if nothing else."

"That's what I said about the Sled."

He would not get her help with the lights. In memory of Danforth, she'd refuse him this last indulgence. As if in protest, the ground shifted again and rose in a prolonged quake. The lights swung and lashed about on their rope. The glassy floor began to separate like a spring ice floe. The Lander's support struts cried out in metal anguish. McPherson grabbed his elbow and yanked him into the cylinder.

The tube was empty by now. They ran down its silvered length into the drenching beyond. The ceiling of the ice tunnel had collapsed. The laden Sawls threaded a slow path through the ruins. Rain pelted in. Frigid slush puddled in the hollows. Above the ragged walls, the sky was disappearing into night. The Lander's sixty meters of metal loomed over the struggling caravan at an uneasy tilt. Stavros prayed again that the ice would hold just long enough.

McPherson pulled at his sleeve. The wind tore the words from her mouth before he could hear them. He blinked away rain to look where she pointed. Surf was breaking along the wall top, towering sprays foaming up into the twilit downpour, scattering into mist. Stavros put an ear to the ice and heard the roar of countless tons of rock and raging water beating against the other side.

The long caravan slowed again. Patient Sawls crowded the broken tunnel. Stavros shifted uneasily, feeling the walls close in, but the steady pressure of McPherson's hand at the small of his back helped him fight back the panic. But he couldn't dismiss the regret that so many Sawls were down here risking their lives at his request. He'd sought the Master Ranger's support because he needed it, but also to prove to his shipmates that he could get it, that he had . . . influence with the Sawls. He had asked, no, *pleaded,* that the winch be brought down. Yet, here it was, the main obstacle to their escape, and not a single Sawl looked to him in blame. How did one repay such generosity? How did one atone for such shortsighted ignorance and narcissism?

The crowd stirred into motion. Up ahead, the winch had stalled on the rocky incline at the base of the cliff. Once more, the work chant rose to drown out the storm. Stavros danced in place, adding his own whispered urgings to the chorus. Each small gain in elevation lifted them farther out of the path of the flood. The floor at last was solid ground and the ice walls were opening into a circle. The familiar cone of the ballast stone, with its pierced tip, loomed in the darkness, and beyond, the safety of the cliffs.

The Sawls strained and sang. The winch inched up the last steep slope and lumbered across the rock terrace to nudge against the ballast stone. Rain pelted down. Spray arched over the walls. Cascades of melt thundered from the upper reaches of the cliff, smashing onto the wide stone steps leading to the Caves.

The winch crew gathered at the stone. Thick strands of rope were looped through the hole at the tip, the short ends dragging on the wet rock. The long ends ran taut and true into blackness at the cliff top. The wind strummed at them madly. Stavros hoped Weng was up there listening to this wild music for Fiixian solo bass.

The crew loosed the ropes and made a lift harness for the winch. When the ends were secured and the knots double-checked, they joined the end of the line struggling up the steps. McPherson followed, dodging the avalanche of falling water. Stavros lingered on the bottom step. The great circular well was empty but for himself and the winch, waiting trussed and silent in the downpour. He turned away and went up the stairs, to where he could see over the ice wall. The Lander was a darker shadow against the deepening night. The surrounding snowpack had become a torrent. A thinning circle of ice around the Lander's base was all that held the flood at bay. A no-man's-land of angry water raged between Stavros Ibiá and his passage homeward.

Home. He pictured the concrete and razor wire walling in his family's farm and gardens, the armed guards patrolling the grounds, the bunkers provisioned against the major assaults. Home? He struggled to identify the emptiness that haunted him. Something he'd forgotten? Something he'd left behind? He shivered. His tunic was soaked through. The last Sawl was disappearing up the stairs.

Ah. That's it. My self-respect. He laughed, a rare surge of irony. Washed away in the storm.

He shivered again, and took the next flight at a gasping run. Halfway to the lowest cave mouth, he slowed to ease the spasm in his lungs, yet knew he must keep running, running. How else would he leave his humiliation and guilt behind? The winch rose past him, swaying in its sling like a slow pendulum. The cries of the crew slid down the rocks, faint and satisfied. Stavros drove himself upward, gasping, flight after flight, stumbling until his pant legs tore and his knees were raw. Small, strong hands pulled him up the last few steps into the shelter of an overhang. A blanket was draped over his wet shoulders. A steaming mug was thrust into his fist. His numbed fingers curled reflexively around the heat. He stood dazed with relief to be out of the punishing rain. His ears rang, and every limb trembled. He was conscious only of the rough wool of the blanket wrapping his cheek and the warmth spreading inward from his palms.

"That was very well done, Mr. Ibiá."

He was being spoken to. An answer would probably be expected.

"Was it?" He squinted about vaguely for McPherson, who knew better but he hoped would not give him away. The cave mouth swam into focus. All around him, Sawls busied themselves with the last of the rescued cargo. Oil lanterns flared from hollows in the rock. In the niche above his head, the hundred obsidian eyes of an entryway frieze winked lamplight at him.

Weng stood in front of him in spotless white, with eyes that might also have been obsidian. Her rank insignia was a glint of gold at her collar. "Very well done indeed. And you might like to know that Dr. James has rejoined us safely."

Relief curled his lips before he could bid the smile away. "And Liphar?"

"As well."

He shrugged the blanket closer and tried to stop shivering. "Danforth?"

"Not as yet."

He saw McPherson hunkered down at the side of the cave mouth, staring out into the storm. A Sawl blanket draped her shoulders. Her blonde hair was plastered to her head like a skullcap. Suddenly she stood.

"Look!" The blanket slid to the ground.

Stavros stumbled to her side, Weng close behind him. McPherson pointed to the dark spire of the Lander, as the diminished ring of ice groaned and crumbled, laying the Underbelly wide open to the flood. A triangle of paler gray swept out from underneath, lofted on the crest of a wave.

"There she goes!" McPherson wailed. "How are we gonna go after them now?"

Stavros recognized A-Sled as it tumbled past. The current tossed it like a toy boat, then swallowed it altogether. The Lander tilted crazily in the surge. For a moment, it seemed to bob in the water, a dark renegade berg loose among luminous brothers. It rocked back and forth, as if recalling a habit of equilibrium, then lurched up abruptly.

McPherson cried out, gripping Stavros' arm as if to keep from leaping to the rescue. Stavros hoped, wished for, imagined a miraculous burst of flame, and the valiant engine rising like the phoenix from the torrent. But it dropped and tipped to one side, falling impossibly slowly, until the tension must break that held it in this deliberate collapse. Then, astonishingly, it halted midway and settled, angled but still standing.

McPherson cheered. "Atta girl!"

Weng folded her arms in satisfaction, and actually smiled.

Stavros waited for the same bright hope to cheer his battered mood. The Lander was, after all, their lifeline. He should share their relief that escape from this alien planet might still be possible. But the spark of joy that flared in him had a very different origin.

What if it *wasn't* possible?

Stavros left them at the entryway. Confused and weary, he climbed the long stairs to lose himself in the firelit welcome of the Caves.

BOOK TWO

SHELTER

" 'Tis a naughty night to swim in."

King Lear, Act III, sc. iv

12

THE STORM SETTLED in with the night. The rain-dashed cliff sank into blackness, then awoke with a faint brave glow in each cave mouth as the Ranger Guild storm watch took up its stations. In small shelters to the side of every entry, an oil lamp was lit. The shelters were hive-shaped, their masonry clean and tight, but the doors stayed open to the weather. The watchers wrapped themselves in woolens and oiled leathers, hugged warm jugs of tea to their chests and settled in for endless hours, gazing into the wet darkness.

A tall woman in leather as dark as the storm waited in the lowest cave mouth while its first watch crawled into his shelter and lit his lamp. Water roiled in the gutters and roared off the edge to swell the flood raging below. The woman bent to exchange a word with the sentry, then laced her hood more tightly and vanished into the night. She carried no light, braving the dark and the storm on the exterior stairs, the shortest route between the caves. The wind snapped her leather poncho against the cliff as she strode up the steps, taking them two at a time without haste.

At the second entry, she crouched again by the door of the watch post. Her leathers glistened in the lamplight like the carapace of an insect. She spoke, listened, then nodded and moved on.

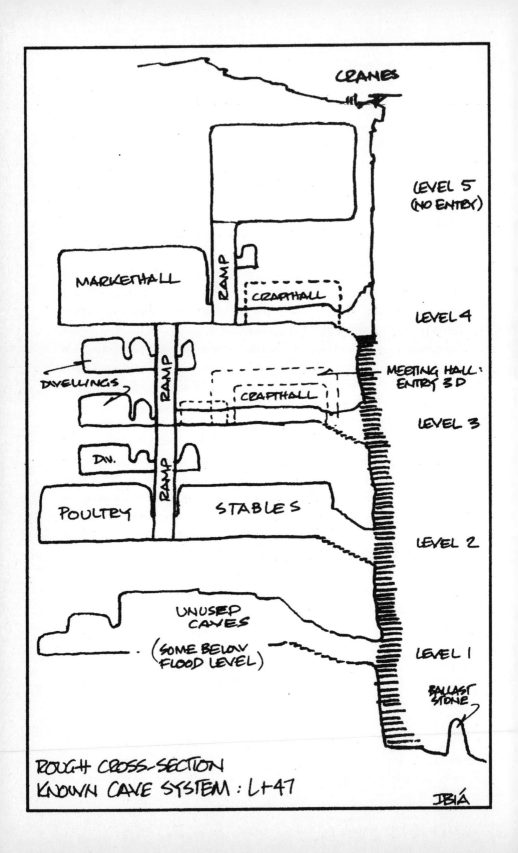

CRANES

LEVEL 5
(NO ENTRY)

MARKETHALL

RAMP

CRAFTHALL

LEVEL 4

RAMP

DWELLINGS

CRAFTHALL

MEETING HALL:
ENTRY 3 D

LEVEL 3

DW.

RAMP

POULTRY

STABLES

LEVEL 2

UNUSED
CAVES

(SOME BELOW
FLOOD LEVEL)

LEVEL 1

BALLAST
STONE

ROUGH CROSS-SECTION
KNOWN CAVE SYSTEM : L+47

JBIÁ

13

SUSANNAH'S STRENGTH GAVE out at the top of the steep entry stairs. "Can't make it, Meg, not without a rest."

Liphar stumbled up the last step and collapsed beside her, his final reserves burned out in chatter and worry.

"I'd go for help, but I don't want to leave you alone," Megan fussed.

"I'll be fine," Susannah murmured thickly. "Liphar's here."

Megan eyed the dazed and bleeding little Sawl. "He's hardly in any shape to . . . wait, someone's coming."

Tyril padded around the corner bearing a large bowl of hot water and strips of clean linen. The man behind her was a stranger. He was as thin as they all were, due to the limits of their diet, but tall, with the stoop-shouldered posture of one uneasy with looking down on the rest of his world. His gaze met Megan's at eye level, calm and measuring. She hovered in front of Susannah. But the man smiled reassuringly, and she found she could believe no ill of him.

He had a long, thoughtful face dominated by a wide mouth. He did not wear his hair in loose ringlets like most Sawls, but pulled back and knotted at the back of his neck with an air of maturity and precision. He wore a long linen tunic, unbelted, with many pockets. The soft unbleached fabric bore the ghosts of what Megan feared might be laundered bloodstains. He carried a lidded wicker basket slung from a canvas strap.

Tyril touched Megan's arm to ease her out of the stranger's way. To her own chagrin, Megan drew aside to let him pass.

He knelt between Susannah and Liphar. The younger Sawl greeted him with wan cheer, answering his murmured questions willingly. He uncovered his basket and took out a stoppered ceramic jug, then gestured to Tyril to bring the cloth and hot water. As he uncorked his jug and poured amber liquid into two small bowls, Megan settled herself opposite him, just in case.

The stranger put one bowl into Liphar's hands and, with his grave gaze full on her, offered the other to Megan, indicating that she should help Susannah to drink.

"I don't think . . ." Megan waved it away. "She shouldn't . . ."

"What is it?" Susannah stirred and struggled to sit upright. When she sagged back against Megan's knees, the Sawl raised a restraining hand, then held the bowl to her lips with such gentle solicitude that Megan had to agree it would be an insult to refuse him. Susannah took the smallest of sips, but it seemed to satisfy him.

"How do you know what he's feeding you?" Megan hissed. She had seen her fill of local witch doctors.

"It's just an herbal tea. What harm can it do?"

"You need more than tea—you're bleeding pretty badly."

"Still? You could go get my medikit."

Megan nodded but made no move as the Sawl fed Susannah another sip of tea, then wrung out a cloth over the steaming bowl and motioned that he would now wash the mud from her face.

"Really, it'd be a good idea. Antibiotics, antivirals, just to be sure."

"I don't want . . ."

"Meg, please. I'm sure I'm in good hands, but I want my stuff, too."

"All right, all right." Megan rose stiffly, easing Susannah's limp weight against the wall behind. "But it may take a while to find it; in all that mess coming up from the Lander. Are you . . . ?"

"Yes, I'm sure."

"Huh." Megan plodded off along the passage, followed by Tyril, her tireless shadow.

E.D. 45–10:37

Susannah winced as the stranger probed the deeper cuts for ground-in dirt and gravel. But the warm cloth was soft on her battered skin, and his touch comforted her with its care and skill. He was no brash inexperienced youth. Perhaps he was one of their healers and thus, in a way, her colleague. Susannah felt she owed him at least a show of trust, even if she insisted on the reinforcement of her own pharmacopoeia.

"Thank you," she said when he was done. Her tongue felt thick and lazy.

Liphar murmured something encouraging, and the Sawl healer—if that's what he was—nodded. He set the bloodied cloth aside. He poured hot water into a flat dish, tempering it with cold from another jug. He held it in his lap to wash her hands. The scent reminded her of mint and lemon, and of the herbs she was always trying to grow in the protection of her cubicle back in Scotland, but there was never enough sun. The balm tingled in her wounds but did not sting. When her hands were clean, the stranger presented the tea bowl again with such authority that Susannah drank deeply, even as she realized that more than simple warmth was seeping through her frozen limbs and dulling the ache in her bruised joints.

What has *he fed me?* She tried to ease the sudden thrill of fear by reminding herself that Liphar had taken the same concoction with no apparent harm. Doctors always make the worst patients. But she was weak, and beginning to float. She leaned back against the rough stone wall and smiled uncertainly at Liphar. He returned her a tired grin as the stranger rinsed out a clean cloth and went to work on him.

Some time later, a dream of motion woke her. She was on her back, cradled in a leather stretcher that creaked rhythmically to the step of bearers carrying her down a narrow, shadowed tunnel. She could not move or call out, but to her surprise, it was not an uncomfortable sensation. The Sawl stranger glided beside her, looming very tall in his rough linen smock. His fingers lightly clasped the pulse point on her wrist, and as she lay wrapped in the woolly cocoon of his mysterious sedative, she dreamed that warmth and calm radiated from his fingertips. Soothed, she listened to passing voices, to the bustle of people moving through the tight passageway, to the occasional rattle of cartwheels at tunnel intersections, as if listening to a symphony.

The stretcher tilted as they climbed a ramp. The tunnel walls opened away and vanished from her range of vision. Susannah could see only the ceiling, and what she saw convinced her that she must be dreaming, although she'd been quite sure that she was not. Instead of rough-hewn rock close above her head, she saw a lofty and graceful arch of amber stone. Pale light from invisible sources pooled along the smooth and shadowed curve. Her absence of fear interested her in the same languid way as the unlikely vaulting. She wondered again, with a more professional curiosity, what magic local ingredient the stranger had added to his herbal tea. A mild hallucinogen, no doubt, a common element of primitive medicine, able to transform the ordinary into the fantastical and help lend credence to the shaman's claims of mystical power.

The walls closed in again as they mounted another long incline. This passage wound a tight spiral and opened into an even taller corridor. Susannah distrusted any numbers counted in her present dream-state, but were they not a level higher than supposedly existed in the Caves? The bustle and cart noise increased, but voices were hushed, in a way that was somehow familiar. The pools of light on the ceiling were broader, closer together. The distant vaulting was finished to a high polish that emphasized the serpentine rose-and-lavender graining of the stone. If this was a drug-induced dream, it was a very detailed and pleasant one.

The stretcher bearers took a turn and passed through an archway. Susannah had a fleeting impression of elaborate carvings that made the friezes at the cave mouths look like the dabblings of an amateur, and then there was no ceiling at all, only blackness overhead and two long rows of hanging oil lamps. The air was dry, a refreshing mixture of cool and warm. It smelled exotic but again, familiar—of strange herbs cooking, of hot wax and steam and blood. Sounds were muted within the vast space but resonant with urgent comings and goings. Dimly, Susannah heard a baby crying.

Then the crying faded and she was among long tiers of shelves groaning with thick books and tall glass jars. Blue flames burned under steaming kettles. Liquids bubbled up in transparent flasks. Her grasp on reality stretched past breaking, Susannah gave herself up to the drug and its dreaming with an unresisting smile. Her drowsiness was overpowering. The stretcher came to rest on a smooth padded surface. A huge wheel-shaped lamp burned overhead. She heard soft orders being given, the clink of glassware, the rustle of clothing. The Sawl stranger leaned over her, and the lamplight haloed him in gold. He gazed down with the solemn, knowing smile of a da Vinci angel. He brushed a strand of damp hair from her face as if she were a child, and went away.

Susannah understood the familiarity at last. This was not a dream. Her injuries were more serious than she'd guessed. She'd lost consciousness, and time. A coma, perhaps, during the long trip home? But she was at the University hospital, and in the doctors' care, so all would be well. She fell asleep to the well-remembered sounds of a surgeon washing his hands.

14

IN THE MEETING hall, the huge wagon wheel chandeliers were dark. But orange firelight danced in a vast fireplace, flickering across the rough stone vaulting and into the shadowed corners. Stavros added yet another category to his list, stacked three crates together and pushed them against the nearest wall. He shivered, wondering what pneumonia felt like.

Good thing his system was still pumped full of antivirals and whatevers, the endless vaccinations required for living on Earth, never mind for ET travel. He hadn't slept in days—he'd lost track of how many. First, the Priest Guild's big ritual dance, then the deluge and the evacuation. Sounds of chanting and cracking ice still rang in his ears. If he relaxed, he'd collapse, so he kept his back to the temptations of the roaring blaze.

The great stone hearth was one of two that dominated the short ends of the long, rectangular hall. The sculpted mantel framed an opening twice the height of the average Sawl and wide enough for twenty to stand shoulder to shoulder within it. Above the mantel, a shallow bas-relief covered the entire wall with a crudely represented landscape of rugged mountains, in whose shadow a faceless crowd milled about, as if lost in a wilderness. A single giant figure strode among them, knocking them aside, even crushing them, with seeming unconcern. Over the unlit hearth at the other end, the composition of the carving was the same. But the background was a storm-tossed ocean.

In the warmth of the working hearth, scattered groups of Sawls lounged on the floor, their chatter subdued by exhaustion. Several had fallen asleep on stone benches carved into the angled sides of the fireplace. The slightly sour smell of hot Sawl beer cut through the smell of burning dung cakes. Someone called to Stavros to join them, but he shook his head with a gesture at the maze of crates and loose equipment piled up around him. His eyes watered and his lungs hurt and, more than anything, he wanted to sleep. But as he put the jumbled salvage in some sort of order, drawing up lists, making piles, deciding what could be stored in the Meeting Hall and what must go to their new living quarters, he could pretend to be putting himself and his life in order, and at the moment, he needed that very badly.

His shivering rendered his handwriting more illegible than usual. The Sawl quill was awkward in his hand, and he had to refresh the tip continually with ink. He longed for his keypad and his fone. His wool tunic clung with clammy insistence to his aching shoulders. It dripped on the minute scrawl of his inventory until the paper wrinkled and the ink ran. Stavros threw his makeshift clipboard down on a box, shed the tunic and continued his stacking and counting half-naked in his ship's pants, leaving muddy puddles on the floor as he moved about. He hefted a huge spool of nylon climbing rope and felt the muscles in his back rebel.

The raised voices reached him long before they entered the hall.

"But, Commander . . . !" McPherson dogged Weng's elbow. Two Sawl women followed a few paces behind. "How do we know there's even gonna *be* a break in the weather?"

"Venturing out there now on foot would almost certainly be fatal, Lieutenant. I cannot allow you to risk your life until we are sure there is no other option."

"But they could be dead by then!"

Weng crossed the hall to survey the piles of equipment. "The living quarters are a trifle dank, Mr. Ibiá. Not much in the way of amenities, but they will certainly do until the Lander is available to us again. Dr. Levy is getting them organized as best she can."

"You can fly it outta here just as good as I can!" McPherson exploded. "The launch sequence is practically automatic! You don't need me to do it!"

Weng turned to face her. "I think I am the best judge of that, Lieutenant."

McPherson glowered. "Yes, Commander."

"Our first order of business is an inventory of reserve power, and setting up the homing beacon." Weng returned her attention to Stavros with a nod toward the waiting Sawls. "I've located a site in an upper cave mouth that should be in line with almost anywhere they could have reached before the power went down. These ladies will help with the equipment if you have it sorted out, Mr. Ibiá."

Stavros handed over two neatly packed carryalls. Of course rescue should take priority—under normal circumstances. But he understood Weng's choice. He shoved a third tote into McPherson's arms with a look he hoped was sympathetic. She returned only a sullen glare. He guessed she was on the verge of tears, and did not want to see that. He needed McPherson to be an image of stability. He pushed her gently in the direction of the door, and was relieved when they were gone.

How quickly he'd gotten used to having the Caves and the Sawls nearly to himself, he mused. Like his private laboratory. His constant presence in the Caves and his gift for the language had allowed him by default to control his colleagues' access to the Sawls, a control he must somehow maintain—not for his own sake, but for the Sawls'. It would require a more conscious effort now, with the other Terrans moved in next door.

He sneezed and had nothing but the back of his hand to wipe his nose on. The chill in his feet was creeping into his knees. Life on Earth was certainly dangerous and unhealthy, yet for the privileged, such as the landing party, only rarely was it so raw and primitive. But the Sawls manage to survive here, Stavros told himself. We'll have to learn to live as they do. He'd come to Fiix wanting to do something Adventurous and Important, but now the fantasy element was fading fast. To his relief and surprise, he did not mourn its demise. The real-life adventure had its own unexpected rewards. Maybe, in fits and starts, he would end up doing something useful instead.

He moved on to the next unsorted heap of salvage. On top was a crate of loose items from Danforth's cubicle. Stavros sifted through photos, maps, and printed charts and pulled out a sheaf of bundled notes: pages of quick hand calculations torn out of notebooks, plus a few annotated data sheets.

Though the numbers meant nothing to him, Stavros could read the subtler signs, the languages of scale and the placement of marks on the page. Among other things, Danforth had been worried about the calibration of his instruments. He had spent hours hand-checking the accuracy of his incoming data, working his puzzlement out the old-fashioned way—on paper—keeping faith with his own brain when all else seemed to be in doubt. His struggle was eloquently expressed in the brutality of his cross outs and underlining, his incredulity weighting the pen as he resisted results he didn't want or expect, and certainly couldn't explain.

A scrawl at the bottom of one page read: "Cross-check all ground stations against orbital measurements." Another said: "Cloud-atmosphere interaction?

Run model with known data sets: Earth before and after peak warming. Yirkalla. Venus??"

The notes might be useful to someone in Danforth's home lab. Stavros tossed the pages back into the box as a pair of tired Sawls arrived with the last of the salvage, piled in a two-wheeled cart hauled by a small goatlike beast called a *hakra*. Its larger, more placid relations, the *hekkers,* made up the dairy herds housed in the lower caverns. Stavros helped unload bins of plastic eating utensils and bundles of sectioned eating trays. Underneath, he found a portable sonic cleaner from the Lander's galley. Artifacts from what already seemed a former life. He shut his eyes in a spasm of confusion.

"If we're going to live like the Sawls," he muttered, "why did I make them drag all this crap up here?

But he tapped the sonic indecisively. Perhaps it was not totally useless. Perhaps he could scavenge its power supply.

"Ibi!" Liphar raced the length of the hall, dragging a knitted blanket that wrapped him from neck to toe. He gathered it like a toga over one wrist. His long ringlets were caked with drying mud. "Ibi! Look for you! All everywhere!"

"You're back! You're okay?"

"Okay! Yes!"

Stavros cuffed the little Sawl gently and threw an arm around his shoulder, careful to avoid his bandaged chin. "Bad shit out there, Lifa?"

"Bad shit, Ibi!" Liphar's fists rolled and his teeth gnashed until Stavros laughed and pushed him aside. "*Na mena,* Ibi!" He assumed a hero's stance and beamed proudly. "*To sukahir le gin Susannah. To min!*"

Stavros's grin twisted. "Not *my* gin, Lifa. Not yet, at least. But I'm glad you saved her." He took up his clipboard and quill again. "You better go get cleaned up."

"Yes, yes. Come you, Ibi."

"Got work to do here."

"No, no, no." Liphar grabbed Stavros' wrist and rubbed it between his own warm hands. "Cold you. Be sick, ah? Very bad!" He glanced across the cavern toward the loungers around the fireplace. He lowered his voice. "Come you, Ibi."

"Where?"

Liphar put his palm to his mouth. "No say, you, ah?"

Intrigued, Stavros let himself be sworn to secrecy and lured away from his labors, which might prove worthless anyway. A left-hand turn in the outer corridor confirmed his hope: Liphar was leading him inward, toward a part of the Caves he'd never visited.

It was a matter of pride to Stavros Ibiá that he was allowed far deeper into the maze than any of his colleagues. He credited his skills as a linguist and his unorthodox ways. He could not wander freely, but as an unexpected stroke of luck, his constant guide and companion had taken a major shine to him, a happy matching of youthful temperaments. So, when the other Terrans were led a merry chase in order to confuse them into thinking they'd been everywhere in the Caves there was to go, doors opened to Stavros one by one. It seemed—though he knew Clausen, for one, suspected otherwise—that each cave mouth led up a flight of stairs to one or two large halls, occupied by the guilds or dedicated to a specific purpose, such as the Meeting Hall and Market Hall. A warren of corridors connected these to the adjacent living quarters. But each time Stavros thought he'd seen everything, Liphar would take him somewhere new, places that remained off limits to the rest of his colleagues. While Stavros went eagerly as far as Liphar would allow, he honored the Sawls' need for concealment, whatever it might be. Even he could only guess at how extensive these ancient burrowings might actually be.

So his anticipation rose as they hurried along the wide tunnel, past the carved and paneled doors of the Woodworkers' Hall. The paving stones were smooth but for two faint cart tracks, inbound and outbound, like everywhere in the Caves. Early on, Clausen had noted that the rock composing the cliffs was not at all soft, so if the Sawls needed to repave occasionally, they must have been using carts with the same wheelbase for hundreds of years.

Hundreds? No, thousands. It had to be. The language alone told Stavros that, never mind the laborious lengths of years required for a metals-poor civilization to carve away so much bedrock. But how many thousands?

Stavros had asked once how often the Stonemasons' Guild repaved the tunnels, hoping for a measure of societal age that did not rely on a shared standard of time. Liphar replied that though the masons' guild books contained such records, he'd have to find a guildsman idle enough to be willing to hunt up useless information. But Stavros was sure the masons wouldn't consider it useless.

Beyond the guildhall, they skirted a residential area. Solid doors were rare in the Caves, wood being too precious to waste on mere privacy. An embroidered fabric or tooled leather drape was considered sufficient. A far cry from, say, the multiple locks and bars on the doors in his graduate housing, even inside the University security cordon. Stavros shook his head at the memory, and that anything so relatively recent could already seem so remote. He wondered how Liphar might take in the concept of locks, but as this area's inhabitants were currently in the sleep part of their work cycle, he followed along silently. He waited until they were past the rows of darkened doorways before voicing the other concern that had been nagging him.

"Where did the Council put us, Lifa?"

Liphar read his subtext accurately. "New cave. Away. More good *wokind* home."

"You mean, better?" *Wokindu-moten* loosely translated as "heads-above-our-own." The Sawls had settled on a shortened version as a nickname for their uninvited visitors.

"Away," repeated Liphar.

Stavros nodded, satisfied. The Guild Council was way ahead of him. The new cave would put the Terrans where the Sawls could most easily keep an eye on them.

When Liphar turned right at an intersection, heading farther inward, Stavros was in unfamiliar territory. The corridor twisted and narrowed as they left the heavily traveled areas. They met no passersby and crossed no other tunnels for a long stretch. The floor was unpaved, the natural bedrock. The walls met the rough-chiseled ceiling in an imperfect curve, as if work was still being done here. There were the usual, regularly spaced lamp niches, but along this section, only every fourth oil lamp was lit.

Then they passed several intersections in a row, as if approaching a city behind the city. Liphar slowed, finally stopped altogether. He gave Stavros a long, uncertain look, gnawing at his fist in sudden indecision. So as not to have gone this far and be disappointed, Stavros gazed back and touched his open palm solemnly to his lips. His anxious guide nodded, put on a determined grimace, and made a quick turn into an unlit and previously invisible slit in the rock. Stavros followed more cautiously. The walls pinched so closely that single file and sideways were the only options. Stavros brushed sharp-edged stone inches above his head. He sneezed in the cold and dust. His exhaustion returned, dragging at his limbs, slowing his pace. And then, around a corner so tight that his bare shoulder scraped hard against the rock, amber light poured through a small archway. The air moistened perceptibly. A blessed warmth caressed his skin.

Liphar halted, staring ahead. "No say, you, ah? No say *wokind?*"

"I won't tell." Stavros raised a palm. "Ever."

Liphar shot him a nervous grin and a here-we-go shrug.

A crowd milled about beyond the bright opening. Stavros heard a good-natured commotion of talk and song and children at play. He longed for that warmth and rich golden light but held back, understanding suddenly that he would be intruding. But Liphar was past his own moment of doubt. He grasped Stavros firmly by the elbow and drew him through the archway.

The transition from dark to light, from cold to warm, was abrupt. They were at the top of a narrow flight of stairs, looking out over a vast golden cavern, as wide as three or four Meeting Halls and so long that the far end shimmered in an amber blur. Tall arched colonnades marched along the walls, framing white-tiled alcoves. The fluted columns were painted with colored glazes that gleamed in the light of countless chandeliers of porcelain and glass. Above the chandeliers floated a maze of fat white pipes and a haze of steam. The pipes were as big around as a man's shoulders and utterly seamless—not a single joint, except where a pipe angled to vanish into the damp shiny tile of a side wall.

Stavros let out a long breath of astonishment. Below, in the golden brightness, lay a neat grid of broad shallow pools, lined with multicolored tile. The huge space echoed with the splash and tinkle of water and the hiss of escaping steam. In the warm mist off the surface of the pools, Sawls lounged about everywhere, young and old, dressed and undressed, all those who had chilled and dirtied and exhausted themselves evacuating the Lander, chatting as they washed and soaked, or gathering at the gaming tables in the alcoves. Children played tag around the columns and ran laughing in and out of the water.

Still speechless, Stavros struggled to fit this vista into his previous understanding of Sawl technology. Pipes, steam, pressurized hot water, a vast system centralized around a single heat source? Had to be—no heat source was visible in the cavern. But after six weeks in dark, rough-walled caves, this bright, clean symmetry was the most disorienting of all: the sharp corners of the tile and the golden glow of the lamplight on the hard white glaze. It shook Stavros badly. Even he had been so wrong, so misled.

Liphar urged him forward, down the narrow stairs. A sweet-scented heat welcomed them, but the vast space grew still as his guide dragged him insistently downward. The crowds turned to stare up at them. Even the children left off their games, cowed by the resonant silence. Stavros agreed—his intrusion on their nakedness was inexcusable. He felt accused by the sharp breasts of the women, the rounded bellies and the parched limbs, the chests of the men so thin he could have counted every rib. Beside them, he was obscenely soft and well-fed. He pulled against Liphar's grip in genteel panic, wishing to be invisible or to have never come.

But it was too late to undo his intrusion, and Liphar held to his decision stubbornly. He hauled Stavros into the midst of the astonished bathers, toward the steam and the water. The crowd parted for them, then closed behind in a solid wall. For an instant, the very first since his arrival, Stavros feared for his life. What if this secret was too great to trust *any* Terran with?

At the edge of the nearest pool, Liphar halted. Having brought matters this far by his own hand, he now seemed to be waiting for a sign from the others. Stavros felt dirty and oversized, as pale as a grub and a little bit frightened. He stood up straight, smoothing back his wild hair and pressing wrinkles from his filthy trousers, to be less of a disgrace at his young friend's side.

Debate whispered through the crowd. Several older Sawls whom Stavros knew to be guild masters fell into a stiff ideological argument. But the crowd murmured around them, and the murmur rose into what sounded like approval. Liphar nudged Stavros and grinned. Tentatively, Stavros returned the grin, and as if that was all they'd been waiting for, the tension in the cavern gave way to spontaneous cheering and laughter. All at once, everyone wanted to welcome him. Acquaintances and friends who had hung back pushed forward to touch his hand and introduce other friends and families. The children charged about in circles. Wild with relief, Liphar rained little pats of celebration on Stavros' back. Stavros smiled until his cheeks were tired, greeted those he knew and many more that he didn't. Over and over, he thanked them for their help with the salvage of the equipment. The Sawlish words seemed to roll out of his unconscious, neither grammatical or precise, but with a fluidity that astonished him.

Meanwhile, he struggled to right his capsized understanding of Sawl society.

Each newly noted detail amazed him further. From along the edges of the pool came the telltale sucking sounds of a circulating water system. The floor was solid glass embedded with a grid of pipes. It warmed the soles of his feet.

He had assumed that the Sawl habit of concealment expressed arcane tribal and social taboos. Now he had a glimpse of what they were *really* hiding.

If they were capable of this, what other surprises might be waiting?

Not for a second did Stavros think to rush back and inform his colleagues of this discovery. He was sworn to secrecy. But, in conspiring to this concealment, he was headed straight into the heart of the dangerous no-man's-land of divided loyalties on whose outskirts he'd been lingering for six weeks.

He would deal with that later. For now all that mattered was the heady rush of the Sawls' approval. He watched as Liphar unwound his toga-like drape and tossed it aside to ease his slim brown body into the pool with a long sigh of pleasure. Stavros fumbled with the tabbed fastening at his waist. His pants were damp, grimy, and totally synthetic. Ship's issue. Plastic rivets at the seams. His body revealed would be pale and hairy.

He'd never felt more alien in his life.

Waiting in the pool, Liphar mistook his hesitation for an attack of modesty. The little Sawl laughed and let loose a side-arm swing that sent hot water cascading into Stavros' face. He coughed and blinked and tore open the tab.

He thought he'd made hard choices before, steering the course of his life and career. But most of that was doing what was expected of any exceptionally bright young man, so were those really choices? Nothing as profound as this one.

As his pants slid down across his buttocks, over his thighs, past his knees, he passed through a terrifying eternity. On one side of it he felt utterly exposed and alone. On the other, he stepped out of the muddy huddle of his ship's clothing with a sense of release that exploded into laughter.

To Stavros, it was miraculous. As miraculous as the clear hot water washing around him as he slid into the pool, as warmth and community brought tingling new life to his frigid limbs, to his uncertain soul.

How long since he had laughed so truly and so well?

15

SUSANNAH WOKE UP coughing, on a pad of blankets in front of a smoking fire. It took a moment to get her bearings, another moment to realize she was still on Fiix, still in the Caves. Well, this was not unexpected. So it had been a dream after all. On the far side of the fire, Megan blew into the reluctant coals, swearing softly. Though it hurt her ribs, Susannah couldn't help but laugh.

"I used to be good at this stuff, would you believe?" Megan pushed dung cakes at the flames as if feeding a wild animal, then sat back on her heels. "How do you feel?"

Susannah stretched cautiously. To her surprise, her body did not cry out in protest. "Pretty good. The bruises are tender, of course, but . . ." Her hands were immobilized by thick linen dressings. "How long have I been out?"

"Not long—eight, ten hours."

"Is that all? Whew. Whatever that guy gave me, it sure worked." Susannah sat up slowly. "I dreamed I was back home when I was up there . . . among other things."

"Up where?"

"Wherever he took me."

Megan shrugged, poking again at the fire. "Dream on, girl. Two of them brought you down here on a stretcher not so long after I left you in the tunnel. You've been sleeping like a baby ever since."

"No. Really?" Susannah lay back, confused. "But I distinctly remember . . . oh, well." She peered into the darkness surrounding the fire. "So, where are we?"

"Welcome to our new quarters." Megan gestured grandly around. "McPherson and I have dubbed it the Black Hole. Weng, of course, refuses to sink to our level, but then, she's still insisting it's only temporary."

"Is it still raining?"

"Oh, yes." Megan nodded grimly. "Like home on a winter's day."

"Any sign of . . . ?"

"No."

"I gather the power's still down?"

"And the com."

Susannah sucked her cheek, glancing about pensively. "Sure is dark in here."

"Oh. Sorry." Megan turned up the oil lamp at her side. "Conserving fuel, you know, just like the old days. By the way, your medikit's there, beside you."

"Thanks." Susannah slid the slim metal case onto her lap, but didn't open it.

The light revealed a good-sized cavern, longer than it was wide, with a lowish uneven ceiling. The walls were crudely finished but for a section near the front, where smooth stone met flat floor and the beginnings of a lamp niche echoed the curl of the entry arch. A jumble of familiar crates and equipment were stacked along one side.

"This is a new cave," Megan waved at a pile of stone rubble shoved hastily into a back corner. "Part of the 'western expansion,' says Tyril. She'll get her cousin the brickmaker to fix us up a proper fire pit, and Weng's worked out a plan for using the crate lids to create sleeping platforms in back. This lying on stone is hell on *my* old bones."

"I see they've left us alone."

"In here, yes. But venture two paces down the outer corridor and there's someone right at your side. It's going to be hard on the Sawls, with us up here all the time. They'll have to work shifts."

"They *have* been keeping track of us, haven't they—like Emil says."

"Of course. I would, too, if I were them."

"Why should they think we'd mean them any harm?"

Megan gazed at her, bemused. "Susannah, I swear, sometimes I ask myself, can she really be that naive? It's like with Clausen, you . . ."

"I what? He's smart and charming and able, and I like the man, no matter what he does for a living."

"But he *is* what he does."

"Don't start, Meg, okay? I feel good but not that good. Besides, how can you argue with a new way to mass-produce clean energy?"

"If it'll actually do that. Folks back home are so desperate, they'll leap on anything that even sounds like a solution, no matter the cost." Megan returned her attention to the still-smoking fire. "Emil doesn't even care if it works, so long as they buy his lithium."

Responding to this would only get her in deeper. After a while, Susannah murmured, "Maybe I could talk Tyril or Liphar into taking me up there again."

Meg raised an eyebrow.

"Okay, sure, it was dream-*like,* but I know I went somewhere!" Susannah sat upright. "Somewhere like . . . well, like a hospital ward. I swear! I wasn't *that* out of it!"

"If you say so."

"I need to get back there! Meet the healers. I could help out, learn about Sawl medicine!" She squinted vaguely into the darkness. "I remember . . . he had amazing hands."

A light bobbed in the narrow entry tunnel. Weng called a polite "thank you" to someone out in the corridor, then snapped off her lamp and made her way slowly to the fire. She sat down on a nearby crate, tucking loose strands of hair back into her silver bun. Belatedly, she noticed Susannah.

"Ah. Dr. James. A relief to have you back among the living."

Susannah smiled with professional concern. "None too soon, I see. You look exhausted, Commander. Are you neglecting that regimen I gave you?"

Weng forced her back into a straighter line. "I keep up as best I can, Dr. James, given the situation." She seemed to drift for a moment, then gave a small sigh. "Lieutenant McPherson has disobeyed my orders."

Megan clucked her tongue. "She went out by herself?"

"No. At least not that. Aguidran was more successful at restraining her than I was. She has gone with the Ranger Guild search party."

"One of us should be out there with them," Megan offered reasonably.

"I had planned, as soon as we're settled in here . . . if we still had our second Sled . . ." Weng fell silent for a moment. "But of course, you're right, Dr. Levy. Ship's regulations are not always appropriate to the situation on the ground."

Susannah hugged her knees. "What do the Sawls say about the weather?"

"What can they say?"

"What might be next? Liphar knew this storm was coming, long before I spotted it."

Megan exchanged a sober glance with Weng. "Well, that's the thing—they won't say. All sorts of strong opinions on most subjects, but about the storm, they just look at you and shake their heads."

"Huh." Susannah settled her chin on her knees. "Going to be a long night."

16

E.D. 51–14:21

EIGHT SHIVERING PRIESTS stood in a circle inside the overhang of the cliff face.

"These folk will put up with anything to talk about the weather."

Megan liked the ring of this statement, and scrawled it into her newly hatched notebook. Readers at home would identify with being at the mercy of a hostile climate, and no law said she had to be cheerful about the discomforts of the field. She'd always found a certain energy in the act of complaining. But here, in the damp and the darkness, the oblivion of sleep became more alluring day by day, and the only defense against slipping back into her recent lethargy was to invoke a strict schedule of study. Megan had done so and was much the better for it. As a happy by-product, it reinforced the fading distinctions of Terran day and night, morning and afternoon, on duty or off duty—concepts without reality in the depths of the rock. It did not help that, by the Fiixian cycle, it was not yet midnight, or that the Sawls lived around the clock. Their three revolving shifts divided an approximately thirty-hour day: there was no downtime in the Caves.

At this particular moment, afternoon by Earth schedule, the storm was at a singularly vicious peak. The priests had gathered at the narrowest, most protected of the cave mouths, but cold rain and wind still hammered in from the darkness. Megan had ventured onto the open ledge upon arrival, aiming for a reassuring glimpse of the landing vehicle, but had retreated immediately. The stone floor was drenched and the gutters roaring. She had to drape her foil blanket around her shoulders in a tent to keep her notes and sketches dry. The lamp flame swayed in its niche and her crude stick figures leaped and stuttered like an antique film. She thought with longing of the inner caverns and the warmth of her bedroll, but bent dutifully back to her work.

She thought these priests a ragtag bunch, in their damp layers of brown knits and woolens. Only two of the eight seemed to have given any thought to dressing as might befit a priest: they'd thrown long, sleeveless robes over their warm clothing. One wore hers open, the other laced his casually at the neck. At least the embroidery on front and back was formal and colorful, reproducing the Priest Guild's seal: a red-and-orange flame suspended over blue-lavender waves, encircled in green and brown.

Despite their unregimented aspect, Megan had learned that the Priest Guild held a central focus in Sawl society, no doubt because matters of weather fell particularly under their jurisdiction and, as she had noted, the Sawls were obsessed with the weather.

She could hardly blame them. She was becoming obsessed with it herself, as were the other Terrans, when not hiding ostrich-like inside their work. Stavros was collecting a weather language and mythology. McPherson faced the weather daily with the Ranger Guild's search parties, keeping Danforth alive in her mind long after the others had given up hope. Susannah pondered new theories of climate versus evolution. But the situation was particularly hard on Weng, who had all the responsibility and no work to keep her busy. Once she was sure that the antennas linking them to the Orbiter were gone, she'd left the homing beacon running and buried herself in her music.

Megan's attention returned to the priests as their murmured discussion careened suddenly into heated debate. The young apprentices hovered, listening in. One held a lamp at the end of a supple pole to light the center of the circle. Megan sketched the gentle curve of the pole, then held the pad away from her to assess the result. Susannah filled her own sketchbooks with speed and intimidating skill. Her studies of the Sawl dairy beasts were worth hanging on the wall. But even Megan's own inexpert hand convinced her that, at times, the pad is mightier than the screen. She missed her computerized sketcher, but there was great satisfaction in the editorial quality of line that a human hand could produce. She erased the curve and drew it again, more accurately.

Tyril, her faithful shadow, sat absorbed in her perpetual knitting. Megan had wanted to be closer to the priestly huddle, for a better view of the mysteries inside, but Tyril had persuaded her to leave them some private distance. Tyril never ordered or insisted, but somehow always got her way.

Now, as Megan sketched, Tyril looked over her shoulder occasionally to nod and smile encouragingly as the work on the page progressed.

Megan drew in the lamp at the end of its pole, and began on the circle of backs bent in earnest consultation. She drew knitted shawls and scarves and heavy cloaks and overtunics. The nodding, murmuring heads were rounded by woolen caps, some with long flaps that hung down like hound's ears. She heard nothing ritualistic emanating from that huddle, nothing like prayer, no chanting or singing. The debate rose and fell. Every few minutes, one of the younger priests pulled away to creep out onto the ledge. The wind threatened to topple her into the abyss as she strained her ears and eyes outward. What could the woman hope to see in such total blackness? Each time, she returned to the circle frowning and thoughtful, her long curls swinging as heavily as the rain-wet hem of her cloak. A few moments later, she was away again, pacing toward the edge.

When she did, an opening was left in the circle, and Megan could see fat books changing hands inside the huddle. Books, an anthropologist's dream: yellowed sheets pressed between slats of wood, bindings sewn of cloth and cracked leather, parchment and vellum crammed with faded writings. An apprentice waited with additional volumes, swathed in pale suede. The drape was embroidered with the guild seal, the flame and the wave, but nothing further. Apparently, the Sawls had no habit of meaningless decoration.

Megan eyed the books hungrily. Her interpretation of Sawl society had taken a new turn the day she had learned about the guild libraries. Sawl literature was still oral, but like good proto-bureaucrats, they were compulsive record keepers. Megan longed to hold just one of those books in her own hands. You didn't have to be able to read a book to glean a depth of information from it. But the Sawls were protective of their records. Tyril had made it quite clear through sign and scattered words that these were sacred books of a very great age: surely *Mee-gan* would not wish to risk of harming such treasures? Megan did not see the priests handling the books with any particular care, but Tyril had bartered with a trip to her own guildhall, where the records pertaining to the proud craft of weaving would surely be of equal interest. As no such offer had been made before, Megan acquiesced.

She thought of her old friends, the Min Kodeh. They were miraculous weavers, too. Maybe she should forget the weather-as-religion stuff and concentrate on the Sawls as craftsmen. An artsy feel-good book, with lots of pictures. It would be much easier, and sell better, too. By far.

She wrenched her concentration back to the priests. She'd been trying to determine a hierarchy within the group, but they tended all to speak at once, flipping through several books at a time to point out this reference or that. If one voice soared over the rest, its owner won a moment's domination, but then fast talking was required to get the point across before it was lost in the hubbub of discussion and the roar of the storm.

Megan did spy one odd detail as she squinted at a book more closely: the palms of the priest holding it were utterly smooth, almost shiny, as if layered with scar tissue. Peering into the circle, she saw that all the priests' palms were similarly smooth, while those of the apprentices were not. Curious, she peered at Tyril's hands: nothing unusual beyond her weaver's calluses. Megan made a note to look into this further.

The debate raged on. A few of the apprentices clustered around an older boy as he counted out a pocketful of thin stone disks, dividing them equally among his companions. Megan had a few of those disks in her own pocket. They were one of at least three unofficial currencies employed in the Caves. The official currency was Trade and Barter. Megan had traded a resealable plastic bag for her handful of disks. The trader was inordinately pleased with the deal, but Susannah had piqued her about it good-humoredly.

"If Emil can go around handing out pens, one little plastic bag won't change the course of Sawl history."

Tyril glanced up, and Megan realized she'd spoken aloud. Perhaps Susannah's gentle accusation still stung. But at least her trade had been for the purpose of study, not to pamper her palate!

The thought of Clausen depressed her further. It was easy money that he'd eventually lose his life to one of the planets he was routinely raping. Men like Clausen did not die in bed. Megan could appreciate the poetic justice, but the actuality saddened her. For one thing, it brought her up against the question that disturbed the sleep of all the surviving landing party. For each of them, for their own reasons, this expedition was a chance to get away from Earth. But what if they couldn't go back?

She turned her gaze to the roiling darkness outside.

Is this it? Are we to be stranded on this dreary world for the rest of whatever?

No way to know, until the night ended and the floodwaters abated. The Lander might still be functional, and if not, it might be repaired—if there was enough time. Time was the real concern. According to the overall mission plan, there were still seven Earth-months before the Orbiter must leave Fiixian space and rendezvous with the mother ship *Hawking* for the return jumps to Earth. If time was too short, or the Lander was dead, so was the possibility of the landing party's ever seeing Earth again.

No one would come for them, especially with Clausen gone. They were too few, and the trip too expensive. Many more important things to worry about back home.

Of course, one might ask why anyone would *want* to go back to a place where simply taking a breath was hazardous to one's health. Where food was scarce, and the habitable land was rapidly vanishing beneath rising and polluted seas. Where only the rich or talented lived a life that could be considered worth living. Where solutions to the crisis were increasingly elusive.

Why? Because home is a habit that's hard to break. And hope springs eternal.

Even mine, Megan admitted, with a melancholy sigh. There's always a possibility: the right world leader, the right scientific breakthrough . . .

A series of hollow thuds drew her mind back to the cave mouth. The books were being shut, and passed to the apprentices to be rewrapped in their protective finery for return to the guild library. The priests had ended their debate, and as one, turned a final gaze on the storm, exuding a grim mood of frustration and foreboding.

Megan closed her notebook and stuck the pencil behind her ear. Whatever the original intent of this gathering, it had not satisfied its participants, and she wasn't sure if she'd learned much herself. She stood up with effort and stretched her stiffened legs. The wind invaded the folds of her blanket and set her shivering again. Tyril stowed her knitting in a waist pouch and wrapped her own thick shawl more tightly around her shoulders.

"Coold," she ventured.

"Cold," Megan agreed, and led the way up the stairs.

17

SUSANNAH DUCKED HER head and squeezed the heavy water bag into the narrow entry corridor. Warm air and a bit of light from the interior cavern strayed along the rock walls. She sniffed, analyzing the separate odors. She could not scent out each individual, as the Sawls claimed to be able to, but the smells generated by specific activities were easy enough to identify. She smelled lamp oil and burning dung, the ever-present background odors of the Caves, together with the barn smell of the straw matting that softened the stone floors in the domestic spaces—another sign that spring would show up eventually, or at least, had done so in the past. Was the straw wild, she wondered, or cultivated? There were cooking smells as well: the flat odor of soy stew, the metallic tang of instant coffee substitute, plus the characteristic hot-paper scent of Megan studying her drawings too close to the fire. Struggling with the waterskin, Susannah emerged into the cavern breathless. She lugged it to the newly bricked-in fire pit and let it down heavily.

"Any word from the Outside?"

"Not back yet." Megan drew a red circle on the top sketch in her pile, then reached over the fire to stir a ceramic pot with a long-handled wooden spoon. "Every day for a week, she's out there in this! Comes back looking worse than you did."

"At least one of us hasn't given up on them."

"At least she can tell us the Lander's still there. How goes the search for the witch doctors?"

"Now, Meg . . ."

"Oh, I only say that to annoy Stavros. They patched you up just fine. I've always had a secret faith in homespun medicines."

Susannah frowned at the rapidly healing skin on her wrists. "I'm beginning to think going through Stav is not the best way to send a message around here."

"Finally, you notice?"

"He's too preoccupied with his own quest to help with anyone else's."

"You could read it that way." Megan pursed her lips. "Or you could say he's worse than usual since we moved into the Caves."

"Locating him is hard enough." Susannah gave an uneasy shrug. "Then when I ask what the words are for 'doctor' or 'hospital,' he says he doesn't know."

Megan eyed her. "Are you pissed off yet?"

Susannah grinned reluctantly. "Almost."

"Flirt with him a little. That'll change his tune fast enough."

"I doubt it." Actually, it might, but Susannah worried about what else it might do. Of course he was attractive, but so young and . . .well, just too much of a handful.

Megan sipped at a stained coffee mug. "You haven't practiced in a while, right?"

"Practiced?"

'Medicine."

"Oh, that. I thought you meant flirting."

"Did you?"

"Not really. Okay, I haven't been a working doctor for four years. But I was for nine years before, so you're safe with me. Don't worry."

"What I meant was, why?"

"Hum. Such big questions!" Susannah tended to avoid confessionals. But if this woman wasn't her friend, so far from Earth and her former life, who was? "The truth?"

"Always."

Susannah laughed, feeling awkward. "It was the business part. I hated not being able to treat just anyone—anyone who needed me. And there were so many who did."

"Corporate medicine." Megan nodded. "And now?"

"It's different here. It's like it should be, or at least, I hope that's what I'll find, if I ever get to talk to the healers. But what are you up to?"

Megan sorted through a handful of sketches, laid a few out on the notebook, and moved her oil lamp closer. "Trying to put the entry friezes into some kind of order."

"Chronological?" Susannah bent in for a look.

"No, more according to reappearing themes and characters."

"You mean, like the Giant Twins?" Susannah smiled at their nickname for the towering figures always paired in the friezes.

"Indeed. Unenlightening so far, but you gotta start somewhere." Megan looked up. "Well, well. Look who's here."

Stavros slipped in at the entrance and padded barefoot across the mats. His greeting to both women was a sidelong glance and a nod. He held a metal ship's wrench in one hand and a complication of ceramic tubing in the other. He wore ship's issue over his tunic and his fingers were black with grease. "Any sign of McPherson?"

"Not yet." Megan ladled stew into a clay bowl. "You better not let the Commander see you using that shirt as a rag."

Stavros gathered his shirttail and wiped at the threaded end of the tubing. "Ron promised she'd help me with this."

"What is it?" Susannah asked.

"Running water. Or it will be." He pointed into the darkness by the doorway. Ceramic pipes hung in leather fittings, bolted with scavenged hardware to the rock wall.

"Hot and cold?"

Megan chortled. "What do you think this is, the Ritz?"

Stavros frowned. "It's cold and it's gravity fed from the cisterns up top, but it's . . . um, the best we can do, and better than lugging water all the way from the central well." He held his handful up to the lamplight. "See how clean the cast is? Virtually seamless. The Sawls have a genius for ceramics. You couldn't find workmanship like this anywhere on Earth." He pointed to where the pipes ran along one wall toward the rear of the cavern. "They're sealed off now, but when I attach this, it'll break the seal and we'll have running water!"

"Or so the theory goes," Megan muttered into her bowl.

Stavros eyed her. "How can you stand to eat that stuff?"

Her mouth was full of soybean stew. She lowered her spoon and swallowed. "It's what we have. Didn't used to bother you before you went native on us." She looked to Susannah. "Wait till he gets one of those expeditions where you have to wear a breather and analyze everything before you touch it."

"I've never done one of those either." Susannah stirred the fire with a long metal spike she'd found lying on the mats. Too late, she recognized it as a piton borrowed from Clausen's climbing gear. She set it aside. "Listen. About this weather . . . is anybody besides me getting the impression that it's worse than usual?"

Megan balanced her bowl on her knee, a mild gleam coming into her eye.

"We really haven't been here long enough to know what usual is," Stavros replied.

"But I mean, what do the Sawls have to say about it?" Susannah pursued.

Stavros glanced around the high-domed cave as if searching for someone to call him away on urgent business.

Megan smirked. "Yes, Stav. What *do* they say?"

"Okay, okay. They say it's worse than usual."

"They're in a fret because their predictions are going wrong," stated Megan with an assured wave of her spoon.

"No, that's not it. They haven't been making any."

Megan turned to Susannah. "The only way to get information out of him—state an opinion he can't bear not to correct. But here's what I've seen for myself: the priests gather every twenty-nine and a quarter hours. I've timed them. Each time it's a different cave mouth—probably they're making sure the whole population knows they're on the job—and they look out at the storm and confer at length, and then . . ."

"Then no prediction." Stavros tumbled into the debate despite himself. "If the weather was due to change, they'd make a prediction. It's the lack of change they're concerned about, not whether they're right or wrong."

Megan gave a dubious snort. "Another chicken-or-the-egg dispute."

"No, again." Stavros gestured widely with his wrench and nearly lost his balance. "Change is long overdue, they say. The Food Guild is getting worried about their supplies. Rationing procedures were announced last cycle."

"All the more reason to eat the food we brought with us," murmured Megan serenely, dipping her spoon into her bowl.

"Is it really as bad as that?" Susannah asked. "Even if the dry supplies run low, there're still the dairy herds—their milk, butter, and cheese—and the fowl. And the mushroom cellars."

Megan looked to Stavros, her spoon halfway to her mouth. "If the priests aren't making predictions, what's keeping the gamblers so busy?"

"That is a side issue, Megan."

She shrugged. "So that's where we disagree."

"Gamblers?" asked Susannah.

Megan tossed a nod in Susannah's direction. "She's hopelessly naive, but we love her anyway, right?"

Stavros gave a dark growl, snatched up Megan's lantern and stalked away from the fire, wrench and faucet clenched tightly in hand. He set the lantern down where the water pipes angled into a square stone trough, and began making a lot of noise.

Susannah cocked her head at Megan. "Explain?"

"Well, it all started when I dared to suggest that the Sawl priests have no special gift for weather prediction, beyond your usual rural body of empirical knowledge. For instance, the farmer's almanacs common in agricultural societies."

"Seems reasonable."

Megan set down her bowl and spoon. "So I said, what they do have is a great gift for observation. They're objective, they record assiduously, they apply the proper data when a known circumstance recurs. But to listen to Stavros, you'd think there was . . . I don't know . . . *magic* involved!"

"Intuition!" Stavros roared from the far end of the cavern. The racket of the wrench increased.

"Get back here and present your case yourself, then!" Megan listed toward Susannah, stage-whispering. "The lad has become a total literalist. Now it's all about 'absolute meaning'—'I deal with the words, one by one.' That sort of university crap." Megan tucked her legs up under her and hitched closer to the fire. "It's like this: you ask a Sawl how he knew it was going to rain. First he says, because the priests said so. But then he adds that it was obvious anyway because the hot winds—you recall we had hot winds for about an hour?—the hot winds are the battle fires of Lagri, and Valla Ired always responds with the same strategic defense, that is, by throwing an ocean at him."

"Lagri and Valla Ired?"

"The Giant Twins."

"Ah. And the storm is the ocean? Rather poetical, don't you think?"

"Exactly! But Stav goes, 'Yes, yes, and then what do they do?', as if there are actual gods out there trying to brain each other with tsunamis and thunderbolts!" Megan threw her hands into the air. "He's reading metaphor as reality!"

"And your interpretation?"

Megan spread her palms. "We've seen it on a dozen different worlds, including our own. Lagri and Valla Ired are the sort of god constructs that primitives have always invented to explain natural phenomena. As for this business of predictions, look at the evidence. The Ranger Guild has this great system of lookouts and couriers providing round-the-clock vigilance. So, when the earliest signs of a change appear, too faint for our Earth-urban senses to detect, the rangers note them, relay them, report them to the priests, who base their prediction on their study of the collected lore of generations of devoted weather watchers. It's brilliant, but it's not magic. Even the priests don't pretend it's magic. You should see them hot and heavy over their books out there in the cave entries!" Megan dusted her hands together as if the issue was closed. "They wouldn't be such inveterate gamblers if they thought they were always going to be right . . . right?"

"I guess," replied Susannah, still puzzled about the gambling.

Stavros paced in out of the shadow and hunkered down across the fire pit, wiping his hands on his shirttail. Susannah saw the flames' bright image in his eyes and for a moment wondered if Megan was right to question his sanity. He fished brusquely among Megan's drawings, selected one with color, and passed it across to Susannah.

The figures dubbed the Giant Twins faced each other on the page with great formality, as if in ritual preparation for hand-to-hand combat. One was thick and helmeted, with finlike protrusions curling up from rump and shoulders. It was terra-cotta-colored, with traces of polychrome on its squarish visor. The other figure was smoothly contoured, carved in a cool white stone shot with green and lavender.

But Susannah found no particular message in them. "Ferocious, aren't they."

"Do you know what *Lagri* means?"

"No, I don't." She considered Megan's earlier advice, thought what the hell, and conjured her most sincere oh-do-enlighten-me look.

He looked caught off guard, then mistrustful, but he came around the fire anyway and crouched behind her. He reached over her arm and laid a finger on the head of the red figure. "It means 'drought,' as best as I can tell." His fingertip eased along the serrations of the brighter fins, a gesture so like a caress that, for a moment, Susannah's thoughts veered off in surprising directions. "These are flames. See?" He withdrew his arm. "The white one is Valla Ired. That means 'ocean bottom.' " He stood and gazed at her. "Interesting?"

Susannah was more interested in the novelty of her own distraction. "All the gods' names have literal meanings, then?"

He moved away, toward the shadows. "Goddesses, actually, and there are only the two. You've seen the Priest Guild's insignia, with the flame and the wave? It stands for them: Lagri, the flame, and Valla, the wave. The Sisters, they call them."

Susannah peered at the fiercely combatant figures. "Sisters? Some family."

"The Sawls' views on sibling rivalry might be very interesting," Megan agreed.

"But . . . two goddesses? Isn't that a peculiar number?"

"It is. The Sawls appear to be ditheistic, a first in my experience."

"There is a third persona," ventured Stavros, with less confidence.

Megan twisted in his direction. "What makes you say that?"

He was trying out a new idea. Susannah felt his tension like heat radiating out of the darkness. The deeper he got into his subject, the crankier and more defensive he became, as if sure that no one could care to listen, but unable to stop himself from telling them anyway.

"You'll see her if you look," he said. "She's there all the time, but only as a victim, never as a deity. Often she appears as a multitude, especially in the biggest friezes, like those in the Meeting Hall."

Megan peered at her sketches again, searching. "But who is she?"

"I don't know yet. There doesn't seem to be a dedicated name for her." Suddenly, he was back at the fire. "Listen! We all have our own methods of getting at the truth. The only way I can approach a total understanding of a language is by setting aside all, I mean *all,* personal or cultural preconceptions. I must try to see this world the way the Sawls see it. It's how I work! I learn to think the way they do." He glanced away, his frown as fierce as the sister deities, then fixed Susannah with a challenging stare. "If the Sawls say the rains come out of Valla Ired's arsenal, then for now, so do I."

Susannah eased back on one elbow, retreating from his intensity, from whatever it was he was really asking of her. "This is a methodological skirmish."

It was Megan's turn to resist. "Wrong! When you throw objective distance to the winds like he does, you sell the Sawls short. Because magic and superstition is a kind of literary exercise for them. It's poetry and metaphor, like the superstitions *we* still give lip service to. The Sawls know the weather is just the weather, but personifying it with names and histories promotes a richer understanding of their place in the world. Mythologies impose a human order on Nature's chaos. They make damn good stories, too, and the Sawls adore telling stories." She shook a finger at Stavros as if he were one of her students. "Did the ancient Greeks, your own half-ancestors, actually believe that the pictures they saw among the stars were the physical bodies of their gods and heroes?"

Susannah chuckled softly, but Stavros would not let it end so easily. "The ancient Greeks *knew* that gods walked the earth."

Megan glanced at Susannah. "See what I mean?"

"Now, wait." Susannah sat up, brushing her long hair behind her. "Aren't you both getting at the same thing? That the Sawls have developed a psychic defense to cope with the weather that goes hand in hand with their physical defense?"

"Maybe," Megan allowed.

"No," said Stavros. But behind his stubborn gaze, Susannah saw a young man striving for credibility and understanding. "Megan assumes the Sawls have the same relationship to superstition as she does. But there's a gulf of difference between believing and *knowing*." He rose and stood for a moment as if daring them to continue the debate, then slouched back toward the easier company of his pipes and sink. He moved the lantern to a shallow ledge above the stone trough and bent over to rub grease into the pipe threads. He fitted the faucet into place and rotated it cautiously. "Should have water any minute."

Susannah smiled, mostly to herself, and stretched her legs in front of her, brushing straw splinters from her therm-suit. She fed another dung cake into the fire. "So what's all this about gambling, Meg?"

Megan's gesture would have been familiar to her Jewish grandmother. "These people will gamble over anything!" She tossed a covert glance into the shadows. "But their real passion is gambling over the weather. Sure, they hold ceremonies and they carve their gods—that is, goddesses—into every surface available, but they don't *pray*. Instead, they invoke their luck. The traditional greeting, 'Rhe khem,' means 'Your luck.' The appropriate response, 'Khem rhe,' means 'Luck to you.' "

"But luck can also mean good fortune, as in 'Be fortunate,' or 'Be well.' That's a kind of prayer."

Megan shook her head. "It's the element of chance, of the random occurrence. That's what's important here. I mean, how devout can they be? They've got pools, odds, the whole nine yards, Vegas without the glitz. Wagers are laid whenever the priests promise an official prediction. Goods change hands at the drop of a hat around here!"

Susannah's grin was fond. "You actually sound shocked, Meg. I thought I was the innocent one."

"I suppose I am a bit shocked, but . . ." Megan rolled her eyes in satisfaction. "Not half so much as Stavros is. He's got the Sawls so romanticized, he can't even consider the possibility of a nation of gamesters. Here's the best part: guess who holds the bets."

"Do tell."

"Now this is no idle gossip," Megan reproved.

"Lay it on me."

"The priests' apprentices."

"Really?"

Megan nodded. "They note the stakes when the bets are laid, then settle with the winners when the priests send them around to announce the predictions. Not only is this gambling sanctioned by the priesthood, it's administered by them as well."

"I'm confused. They bet on the prediction or on the actual weather?"

"Both! All Sawls know enough weather lore to make educated guesses based on the reported signs. So they bet on what the prediction will be, then there's another round of betting on the final outcome, how the weather actually turns out."

Susannah let the first giggle escape her. "Do the 'prentices take commissions?"

"We've got a trickle here!" Stavros yelled from the sink.

"Tips," confided Megan, unable to hold on to her frown.

Susannah's giggle burst into a belly laugh. "Liphar!"

Megan's nod was more of a wobble.

"Our good friend Liphar," Susannah guffawed, "is a numbers runner!"

Megan gave in and howled along with her, as a coughing gurgle echoed from the dark end of the cavern.

"Water!" Stavros exulted, "It works!"

"What's so funny?" McPherson limped out of the dark entry up to the fire pit, kicked a blanket closer to the flame and dropped onto it like a stone. Her therm-suit dripped wet ocher mud onto the matting. Her round face was pale but for the high color of exertion spotting her cheeks. "Who's a numbers runner?"

Their manic cheer died abruptly, but Susannah obligingly explained.

The pilot shrugged. "Oh, yeah? Glad someone's clearing a profit around here."

Stavros shut down the faucet and brought the lantern over to the fire. With unusual gentleness, he said, "Never mind, Ron. Just keep thinking of the fortune ConPlex is paying into your account back home."

"Won't do me no good if I'm stuck *here* till hell freezes over."

"Did you run across Weng on your way in?" asked Megan.

McPherson shook her head.

"Where does she *go* when she's not here?" Susannah marveled.

Megan waved a hand. "The realm of the abstract. She'll be in soon enough. The Commander always shows up for meals."

McPherson peered in the direction of the stew pot. "Hope you left me some."

"What's it like out there?" asked Stavros.

"Same old shit. Black as pitch and blowin' like hell." McPherson rubbed her eyes with muddied fingers. "For this, I coulda taken Earth duty."

"Only another week until dawn," Susannah offered.

The others just looked at her.

Megan searched out a clean bowl and ladled out stew. Juice dripped hissing into the coals as she passed it over to McPherson. "No sign of them, eh?"

"Sign? Shit." The pilot dug into the stew without looking up. "We could walk right by 'em in this crap and never know it. Same goes for A-Sled."

Stavros dropped down beside the lantern. "The Master Ranger doesn't think there's much point prolonging the search," he told Susannah. "She doesn't want to risk her people out there day in and day out for nothing."

"It's not nothing!" McPherson threw down her half-empty bowl. It spun around, splattering stew, and clattered into the fire pit. Leaping up, she bolted the length of the cavern to the sleeping platform, yanked aside a partition, and snapped it shut behind her.

"Nice work, Ibiá," growled Megan.

"She should forget the damn Sled for a few days and get some sleep!"

"It's not the Sled," Susannah said softly. "It's Taylor. Besides, there *is* still hope. Emil was a veteran pilot, and the Sleds are provisioned for at least a couple of weeks."

"They're gone," Stavros stated. "And even if they weren't, Taylor's not likely to give her the time of day. Did you see his wife?"

Megan gave him a sour look. "You're working real hard at being a creep today."

"Meg, they are gone." He spread his palms like the most reasonable of men. "Why is everybody pretending otherwise? Two weeks out in the open, in *this*? We're wasting precious resources running after dead men!"

Susannah picked McPherson's bowl from the embers. "Stav, could you not do this now?"

"If not now, when?" He stood, his indignation barely restrained. "We should be digging in, maximizing what we have left! We need McPherson *here,* not out on a wild goose chase! We need to conserve the power cell feeding that damned beacon! When the hell are the rest of you going to realize we've got our *own* survival to worry about?"

"We know that. It's just . . ."

"You know it! You all know it! But you don't *accept* it." He turned away brusquely, but his stalk toward the entryway looked more like an escape. "We are gonna be here a while!"

Megan stared after him but could only shake her head.

Susannah studied her fingers and the even regiments of colored thread marching across the weave of her blanket. The dung fire crackled, its coals crumbling into ash. "He'll be sorry as soon as he's calmed down."

Megan stirred to add more fuel to the dying fire. "And he's right, though I hate to admit it. Leave it to youth to be so unsentimental."

"McPherson is younger than he is."

"McPherson is in love."

"Ummm." Susannah sucked her cheek pensively. "The hard thing about Stav is that he's always at his least reasonable when he's right."

SONG # 13 - WORK CHANT (Valla)

Recorded L+41 (ED 41) 16:47
Sung by: Tunnel maintenance crew, Entry 6
CRI: file # 386-49C/Sawlsong
Translation: Liphar to CRI/Ibiá
Notes: Antiphonal - 1,4,6,7 - single voices alternating
To Do:　CRI: compare with Lagri song 5 - same chorus?
　　　　SI/Liphar: REFINE TENSES

EDO VALLA DULVALLA-NI JELA
When Valla comes (down?) from Dul Valla

MAR-RI-EH KE-DO	(Chorus)
?	SI: rhyming gibberish?

MAR-RI-EH KE-DO
?

EDO VALLA NHE JUON SIVELA	SI: note dipthong
When Valla her (?) puts on)	*(ritual clothing? armor?)*

MAR-RI-EH KE-DO
?

E LAGRI NHE CHEKE	
Then Lagri her Sister	SI: note formal form

NANIN-NHO O LEKH
Answers the challenge (asking?)

MAR-RI-EH KE-DO	SI: Maur-rei?
(?)	

SRI DEMRA

SRI DEMRA

SRI DEMRA JEO
We are the weak

18

STAVROS REGRETTED THAT he must go empty-handed into the Priest Hall, but if he wished to make it a habit, he must observe its requirements. Not even his quill and notebook. Abandoned at the columned entrance: the battered canvas pack he'd carried like an identity card for his entire university career, his dead fone tucked into a side pocket.

It was not, Liphar assured him, that any threat was seen in the little talisman that talked, which had grown silent of late anyway. His subtle eye roll implied that priests—and even apprentice priests—lived elbow to elbow with mysteries equally as unfathomable. But tradition did dictate that everything but the body and its coverings be left behind upon entering the place of priestly studies.

Once inside the hallowed portal, Stavros was forced to discard another expectation. The Priest Hall occupied a prime location in the Caves, on a level with and one entry to the east of the great central Market Hall. He'd anticipated a cavern equally as vast, with lofty, shadowed vaulting and a forest of sturdy trefoil piers. He'd expected, he realized later, a Gothic cathedral.

Instead, Liphar ushered him with great excitement and ceremony into a smoky warren bustling with comings and goings, humming with the sounds of lecture and debate. The low-ceilinged space was more like a Romanesque crypt, though considerably more lively. It did offer a forest of piers: a dozen long rows of columns, each as wide as a man's arm span and set much closer together than their great girth and the low vaulting would seem to require. On each shaft, a small oil lamp burned in an eye-level niche. Straw matting rustled underfoot as they threaded among the fat stone cylinders and the clots of priests and student priests who sat cross-legged in debate, clasping mugs of hot tea and musty books, waving chunks of orange bread to emphasize a favorite point. They could as easily have been discussing the price of hekker milk.

Stavros wondered when he would discover some concrete trace of mysticism in the Sawl religion. He said *when,* not if, as his instincts insisted that the Sawls' relationship to their goddesses was not so pragmatic as Megan proposed. But his only real evidence so far lay in the weather mythos pervading every aspect of Sawl life and language. When being honest with himself, he knew it was not simple mysticism he was after, but a possibility of actual power. His imagination longed for proof that the Sawl priests were more than skilled guessers, that they could actually foretell the vagaries of the Fiixian climate by means of a magical relationship with the cosmos.

But this could never be discussed aloud, not with his colleagues, or even with Liphar. And as he peered about the Priest Hall, he could see he was unlikely to find magic here. This was not a place of worship or even meditation. With a sinking heart, he recognized the stolid aura of academia drifting among the pillars with the lamp smoke. He felt both at home and in revolt. At any moment, his old semiotics professor might come wheeling out from behind a nearby column. He laughed aloud to relieve a creeping panic, and several apprentices glanced up from their studies to stare at him as he passed. Liphar turned back to admonish him with a vaudevillian frown.

Ahead, a seated gathering blocked their path. A trio of priests was conducting a highly vocal seminar with several dozen older students. Liphar turned aside, but their entrance had already caused a lull in the intense debate. Stavros wished he were shorter and slimmer. Sawl clothing would never be enough to allow him to pass among the Sawls unnoticed.

Liphar urged him onward with impatient beckonings. They approached a long side wall, a tapestry of muted color behind the darker silhouettes of the columns. As they moved closer, Stavros could see that the rock was honeycombed high up into the vaulting, and the niches crammed with wrapped parcels of every conceivable size and description. Tall wooden ladders accessed the higher stacks.

Stavros gazed through the dim smoky light at the rows and rows of leather- and cloth-shrouded bundles. He knew those wrappings. The wave-and-flame seal of the Priest Guild decorated every one.

The Priest Guild Library, he thought with satisfaction. Megan would kill to see this.

Liphar waited at his elbow, savoring his awe.

"How many, Lifa?"

Liphar considered his ten fingers, struggling with the newness of Terran numbers. "Hunderd hunderd," he guessed, then splayed both palms in the Sawlish shrug.

"Are they very old?"

The young Sawl shook his curls in indignation. "Ibi! Give best care, we!"

Stavros grinned apologetically. ET linguistics theory warned that concepts of age might be tricky to communicate, time being among the most relative of phenomena. The Sawl astronomical year was roughly equivalent to 281 Earth days, roughly two thirds of a Terran year, and the Sawls did not use it as a significant time marker. Instead, they measured long time periods in generations. Stavros had not yet been able to determine the formal duration of a generation, as he and Liphar still lacked a common yardstick. He was left with only the more physical markers of age to point to, which inevitably led Liphar to misunderstand "old" as meaning "damaged" or "disabled." Stavros collected such near misses. His favorite character in all literature was Mrs. Malaprop, though this was a secret that would die with him. These glancing errors were not only funny, they taught lessons about the relationship of language and perception. Liphar seemed to appreciate this as well, since nothing could start him giggling faster than Stavros attempting to choose, from a battery of at least a dozen separate words meaning "rain," the one word that properly described a particular kind of rain falling at a particular moment. Stavros' senses were not yet tuned to the fine distinctions that a Sawl naturally applied to an issue as critical as the weather.

He moved closer to the wall of swaddled volumes to inspect a particularly fading wrapping. He drank in the musty smell of aged leather, momentarily sunk in regret. Libraries, already an endangered species in his boyhood, had been his favorite place of refuge. But so many were being lost, to the flooding, to a lack of funding, to riot and vandalism, or simply disinterest. Stavros sighed, and Liphar mistook his melancholy. He pointed at the bundle but did not touch it.

"Make new very soon, we." He cycled his hands one around the other, carefully enshrouding an invisible treasure. "New itra."

"Itra?" Stavros repeated the gesture. When Liphar nodded, Stavros added the word to his list, wondering how many times this particular ancient text had been rebound, and new wrappings made for it. He noted interesting variations in the wave-and-flame designs between the older and newer itras.

He would happily have lingered, forgetting his requested audience with the Master Priest. But Liphar tugged anxiously at his sleeve. This time, his palm was to his mouth, bidding silence.

They followed the last row of columns into the deepest corner of the cavern. Stavros heard the voice long before he could see the speaker: a woman who clearly did not care if her lecture disturbed any nearby gathering. Free space surrounded her group, as if others had moved off out of range. They slipped into the outer edge of the gathering and settled on the floor among the listeners.

"Kav Ashimmel." Liphar nodded at the speaker.

Stavros sat cross-legged on the matting with his back against a column. Now his un-Sawlish height allowed him an excellent view. Kav Ashimmel was a brusque and stocky priest with graying curls. She wore her vestments neatly fastened from hem to embroidered collar, but the long wide sleeves of her undertunic were rolled up to her elbows to allow for the greatest possible freedom of gesture. The smooth blank palms of her hands shone like silk in the lamplight. She paced as she spoke, and seemed occasionally to slip into a private distraction, out of which she broke with renewed vigor for her argument.

Stavros ached for CRI and his translation software. This was far more complex than your everyday conversational Sawlish, more so than most of the tale chants he had begun to make sense of. The cadences of Ashimmel's presentation suggested an almost Talmudic disputation on the interpretation of a certain piece of text. He was familiar with much of the vocabulary, as it had to do with the goddesses and the weather. But her tenses left him in a muddle, and now and then she would pause and repeat a long and carefully articulated phrase that he found totally incomprehensible. It didn't sound like quite the same language.

A corrupt form? Stavros thought that unlikely. A more formal form, for ritual use?

He leaned close to Liphar. "Lifa, what's she saying now?"

Liphar's eyes widened in distress. His palm flew to his open mouth.

Stavros drew in his shoulders and nodded his promise to be silent. He heard Lagri's name then, and soon after, Ashimmel growled the name of the sister-goddess, Valla Ired. A rustle breathed through the gathering as the listeners rubbed their talisman beads.

Stavros had noted that as the storm continued into the second half of the long Fiixian night, most Sawls avoided speaking Valla's name, for fear it might add to her strength. Many wore smaller red clay beads alongside the usual green malachite, and Kav Ashimmel was now using words from a vocabulary that Liphar was just beginning to teach him: the terms used to describe the various climatic weapons used by the goddesses to fight the *arrah,* the weather war. The word *"arrah"* was itself ambiguous. It did not seem to mean war per se, but rather "struggle" or perhaps "wrestling," which is what Liphar mimed to define its meaning. It might even simply mean "game." One thing *arrah* did seem to imply was the condition of endlessness, not as in "eternal," Stavros decided, but as in "for-goddamn-bloody-ever."

Kav Ashimmel again intoned her untranslatable bit of text, but this time, Stavros heard within it familiar syllables, a phrase that might have been *"atoph phenar."* Liphar often used this phrase to explain to Stavros what would happen if one of the Sisters ever defeated the other. Stavros had loosely translated it as "stillness of death," but however large his margin of error, he knew it meant bad news.

With this final repetition, Ashimmel ended her lecture. She surveyed her audience warningly, raking her sober glance back and forth until it met Stavros' unflinching Terran gaze. Her eyes narrowed, then moved on, until she had made contact with each and every listener. Then she dismissed them with a brisk exhortation, waited solemnly as they rose and filed away, then stalked forward to confront Stavros with her arms folded.

Liphar remained seated, looking cowed. Stavros elected to follow suit. Standing, he'd be forced to look down on this imperious priest. Ashimmel stared for a moment, then barked a question at Liphar. The young Sawl answered at length. Stavros heard his own name mentioned with that of Kav Daven, whom Liphar called the Tale Singer. Kav Daven was the one Stavros really wanted to see. Within the Priest Guild, Daven was Lore Master, the formal keeper of myth and ritual. He was also extremely *old* (as in "disabled"), and thus secluded, like a precious treasure. Ashimmel, as Guild Master, dispensed or withheld permission for any audience with Kav Daven.

But Liphar had implied that, frail as he was, Kav Daven very much maintained a will of his own. And this was a cause for gossip, apparently, as the same iron will that kept him moving and breathing at such an advanced age also encouraged him to prolong his refusal to choose a permanent apprentice. The entire Priest Guild agreed that it was long past time for young blood to begin training in the ancient complications of the ritual lore, eventually to succeed the old priest, who surely would not live forever, however iron his will, or his constitution. In addition, there was some myth or prophecy linking the choosing of this apprentice with the eventual fate of the planet, which Liphar did not seem to credit fully, and would not go into detail about. He only noted that many candidates had been offered, but Kav Daven would smile and nod and turn away each hopeful apprentice as unsuitable for this reason or that. Stavros contemplated the rationality of this gesture. Perhaps it was simply an old man's way of clinging stubbornly to life.

Ashimmel asked another curt question. This one Stavros understood. It caused him to glance up at her in surprise.

The wokind appeared in snow, she had declared to Liphar. *What proof does this one offer that he is not some new weapon of Valla Ired?*

Liphar drew himself up respectfully and offered that there was no proof the Wokind were not sent by Lagri to weaken Valla Ired at a time when she seemed to hold the planet in a death grip.

As humbly as he could, Stavros returned Kav Ashimmel's stare. "I am human, Kav. Kho sue epele, as yourself."

Ashimmel looked interested at the sound of her language on the alien's tongue. She stared a moment longer, then nodded abruptly and stalked away, her sandals flapping authoritatively through the forest of pillars.

Liphar let out a sigh and sprawled a little easier on the matting.

"Will she let me see him, Lifa?"

Liphar opened his palms. "Kav Daven say yes, say no. If he want, you come."

But how will he ever know if he wants it, worried Stavros, with a tough old soldier like Ashimmel standing in my way?

It was time to be out of there. Liphar scrambled up eagerly beside him.

"*O cilmillar,* Ibi?"

Stavros laughed. The young man was coming to know him too well. "Okay, Lifa, you're on. What better way to forget your troubles, eh? Yes! To the Baths!"

19

MEGAN'S OIL LANTERN disappeared into the entry passage. Susannah felt her way in darkness, avoiding the drip from the new water pipes just above her head. The entry needed widening, and the access tunnel linking their sector with the rest of the Caves was rough-hewn, its darkness unrelieved by oil lamps. When the Sawls had offered the Black Hole as a refuge, their apologies for its unfinished state had included the eager assurance that it lacked only a generation or so until completion.

Tyril was waiting with a second lantern as they emerged into the outer tunnel.

Megan greeted her cheerfully. "What's on the tourist agenda today?"

Tyril's calm smile was tinged with promise.

"Ah-ha!" Megan rubbed her palms together in anticipation.

"What are all these strips?" asked Susannah.

"Strips?" Megan raised her lantern. The sharp-edged rock around the mouth of the entryway was hung with many long bits of cloth. She moved the lamp closer. Even in the dim light, the colors of the cloth showed clearly: sun-bright yellows and flaming oranges, smoldering vermilion and strong, deep reds. Susannah drew one strip gently through her hand. The fabric was soft and fine. It had several small terra-cotta beads worked into a knot tied at the end.

"Decoration? Not likely, with these folks." Megan turned to Tyril. "What's this about, Tyr?"

A careful blankness came into Tyril's manner, her habit when she didn't seem to want to understand what was being said to her. Her brown eyes lowered briefly, flicking to the array of color and back to Megan.

Like a smooth lake rippled by disturbance from below, thought Susannah. She balanced one of the beads on her palm. "For khem? Is it for khem?"

Tyril nodded, too eagerly. *"Lagri embriha. Nho arma Lagri."*

"Ah, right." Megan stroked the bright streamers. "These are Lagri's associated colors. The colors of the Flame. But I hadn't noticed them decorating doorways before."

"Something special for us?" offered Susannah.

"Perhaps." Megan lowered the lamp thoughtfully as Tyril moved on ahead. "But why should we be in particular need of Lagri's attention?"

"And why just Lagri? Why not the other sister as well?"

"You weren't listening to Stav's lecture. Rainstorms are part of Valla's weaponry, so as you can imagine, she's very unpopular at the moment." Megan fell into a pondering silence, and Susannah left her in peace while she tried to replay the relevant conversation. She'd been too aware of the man at the time to pay much attention to what he'd been saying.

The tunnel opened into a wider thoroughfare with a high barrel-vaulted ceiling. The smooth floor dipped toward the center, where generations of Sawls had walked a path into the stone. Large oil lamps with decorated bases glowed in regularly spaced niches, bringing the sculpted walls to life. Here, the rock appeared to be woven, in a herringbone like fine basket weaving. Further on, a thousand tiny scorings dipped and swelled with the contours of the wall, like the furrows of a wheat field.

"Living rock," Susannah murmured, as she trailed a hand across age-softened stone that seemed to breathe in time with the slow flicker of Megan's lantern.

The big tunnel became brighter and more crowded as they went along. Guildsmen bustled by with big baskets strapped to their backs. Cartwheels rattled up ahead. Tyril doused her lantern, and signaled that Megan should do the same.

"Everyone's up and about." Megan emerged from her ponder. "This'll be the second shift, or actually, the second just heading home to eat and the third going to work."

"It's a sensible solution," Susannah noted. "Think how much more crowded the Caves would feel if they all lived on the same schedule. Earth could learn from the Sawls' example."

"Many cities already do. Aren't enough beds to go around. As for me, I miss the old middle-of-the-night lull. Used to get my best thinking done then."

Passersby smiled pleasantly or waved but did not stop to chat. A slim man wearing the sign of the Weaver Guild paced beside Tyril for a brief and murmured exchange, then sped off down a side tunnel. The congestion of people and carts thickened. They maneuvered around a slow-moving two-wheeler laden with grain bags, hauled by a bright-eyed cart hakra the size of a large sheepdog. Its fleshy, callused hooves made no sound on the stone floor.

"I must go down and visit the dairy stables," Susannah reminded herself. "Liphar rushed us right through there, back when."

Megan chuckled. "He doesn't much like those critters, I think."

"Well, they're huge! But very gentle. I could run DNA, when we get CRI back."

They passed through a residential area, where children played a Sawl version of tag at the crossings, or gathered against the walls, engrossed in games where brightly colored stone counters were passed back and forth. One boy hunkered over a huge pile of stones, sporting a victorious grin.

Susannah nudged Megan. "Even the children are gamblers."

Down each smaller side corridor, five or six dwelling caverns opened onto a common tunnel. Old men leaned in their doorways, calling across the corridor to each other. Householders swept up the cycle's deposit of straw and manure to dump into bins at the corners. A father called his children in to wash. Balls and small curly-haired animals tumbled underfoot amid shouts and laughter. The sounds and smells of cooking drifted down the side streets. The stares as the Terrans passed were brief or covert. There was no longer the pregnant hush that used to follow them wherever they went in the Caves.

Amid still-increasing traffic and bustle, they entered the Market Hall. Though they'd been here many times, the women could not help but stop and gaze about. It was as wide as an old urban boulevard on Earth, vast enough to dispel any sense of enclosure. But its arching vaults sharpened and magnified the clamor of voices, groaning axles, and wheels clattering on stone. The racket was overwhelming.

"I always feel at home in the Market Hall. Reminds me of New York." A distant look came into Megan's eyes. "Were you ever there?"

Susannah shook her head. "I thought about taking one of those Last Chance tours, but we had our own issues across the Pond. After they built the University Complex in the Highlands, I was a student volunteer from Cambridge, helping with the move."

"Tours. Hmmm. Maybe that's the solution. Make this planet one of those luxury eco-destinations. Might keep ConPlex from digging it up down to the bedrock."

"Oh, Meg . . ."

"I'm kidding, of course. Well, maybe I'm not. It's desperate, but it's a thought."

To either side, the Market Hall was a honeycomb of two-and three-storied shops clinging to the high cavern walls. Cloth awnings and banners hung from upper windows; signs painted above on the naked rock proclaimed product and proprietor in colored pictures and spiky lettering. Oil lamps flared from giant spoked rings suspended from the vaulting, lighting mountains of wares spread out on tables and carts. The open-fronted shops were bright with lamp glare, showing off shelves of glassware and ceramics, handwoven cloth, bright embroidery, paper and leather goods, wooden tools and painted toys. The raw materials were also offered: bulk wool and yarns, dyes, hides, select woods, clay, stones, and the strong plant fibers used for rope and straw matting and wickerwork.

"There's never any food for sale," noted Susannah.

"Food distribution is carefully regulated."

"At home, too, but nonetheless, you still have to shell out for it." Susannah gestured at the multicolored tapestry of goods. "Maybe this is how they satisfy their commercial yearnings, so they can practice classic Marxism where the food is concerned."

Megan nodded. "When the survival of a society is at stake, communal food stores feed the greatest number most fairly, and allow for the kind of long-range supply planning needed to make it all last. What's impressive is how little corruption there seems to be within the Food Guild." She shrugged ruefully. "Perhaps all that gambling helps satisfy those commercial yearnings as well."

Tyril urged them onward, into the midst of the bustle. Shoppers crowded in with baskets and carts, exchanging greetings and news and comments about the merchandise, but Susannah saw very little buying going on. The proprietors lounged in the doorways of the various guild shops. They gossiped and listened to the reed-and-pipes of the street musicians, and watched dolefully as the shoppers fingered their wares and moved on. Some essentials were being purchased—a new wooden bowl or a wicker back-basket to replace one falling apart at the seams.

"The buyers are in a cautious mood," Susannah commented.

Rations of the local green-amber beer were being distributed from the Food Guild's tentlike kiosks, spaced regularly among the stores. It was sour and low in alcoholic content. Among the Terrans, only Stavros found it worth the trouble. Among the shoppers, it was going like hotcakes.

"Cautious, but cheerful," Megan replied.

At the far end, the Market Hall broadened further into a vast interior plaza, which opened overhead into a shaft that sliced upward through the many residential levels of the Caves, all the way to the top of the cliffs. A system of deflectors and baffles drew out the stale, smoke-laden air without letting in the rain or snow.

In the center of the plaza, a deep stone well gave up crystal water into a long stone trough. Animal and Sawl alike lined up to drink from the cold green sparkle. The air was rich with the smells of beast and manure. Tyril led the two women through the jam of carts and wagons. A priests' apprentice stood in the center of a group of men wearing the Wheelwrights' Guild seal. His young face was sober as he collected a handful of bulging leather pouches.

Past the last jumble of shops and market goods, the central boulevard split: the right half dropped toward the next level down, the left climbed a wide ramp to the level above. Tyril turned upward, out of the hustle and noise. The incline was long and easy. At the top, she stood aside with an anticipatory smile.

"Here's the prize for our patience," murmured Megan. "New territory."

Susannah quickened her step.

They came into a dim space smelling of stone and wet clay. The air was fresh and cool. Then the walls opened up around them, and Susannah sighed in delight and awe. "These spaces just keep getting bigger and better!"

Her every sense was compelled upward as wonder and architecture merged into a single experience. The hall's enormous loft gave an impression of narrowness, yet it was easily as wide as the base of the Terran Lander, stretching resolutely into blackness right and left. There was a sense of both lightness and light—in the faint shafts thrown low through open doorways, or in the glimmer of a high row of glass chandeliers marching into the darkened distance overhead.

Tyril pointed upward. The chandeliers hung unlit but for a single lonely bluish flame that kept vigil in the center of each shimmering cluster of spheres. Susannah imagined a Sawlish festival graced by a thousand blazing galaxies of glass. Each chandelier was individually shaped and nearly as complex as a galaxy, like a froth of opalescent bubbles caught in flight.

A look of peace smoothed the last trace of uneasiness from Tyril's brown face. The marble floor was like a pond at twilight, a shining expanse of pale green and white and blue. As they moved across, Susannah picked out a repeating pattern of three interlocking circles, with each center circle missing some random section of its arc. The stone gleamed with the patina of age, as spotless as if recently damp-mopped.

Along both walls, a white marble wainscoting as tall as the average Sawl flared out into a bench. Tyril invited them to sit, where the high polish was worn away. The stone was warm to the touch, like skin. A sculpted geometric band finished the top of the wainscoting in a gentle roll.

Above that, the friezes began.

Susannah gaped upward at a vast wall of sculpture. It was broken into separate panels and levels, one above the other, mounting into the darkness beyond the chandeliers. The figures were life-sized or bigger. They sprang into motion as if born from the rock itself. With precisely imagined detail of expression and anatomy, they laughed and wept and danced and stumbled along the walls. They moved in families or in groups, never alone, muscles straining, faces vivid with momentary joy or anguish.

Here were stories to be read in stone. Some were easily made out, a simple telling of a domestic event: a particularly rich harvest, a contest of athletes, a gathering of musicians and dancing. Other sequences were more obscure, haunted by darker imagery, by violence and suffering, by outraged innocence.

"This must be Stav's 'multitude,' " Susannah murmured. "The third persona."

Megan nodded. "But I'm not sure I agree that all these crowd images depict a single character, or even a single idea. For instance, it could be how the Sawls think of themselves: not as individuals but always as a group."

Susannah peered more closely at the faces. Did she sense expectation beneath all that anger and bewilderment? "It looks like they're all waiting for something. Like a water rations line."

"You had those up in the Highlands?"

"Even there, mostly because we sent so much water elsewhere. But there's no lack of water here, lord knows, so what would you wait for on so grand a scale?"

"Traditionally? Salvation. Or a new round in the karmic cycle. If you're Christian, it could be judgment, along with some final disaster."

"And over there . . . the Sisters." In this grand hall, before these friezes, Susannah found she could no longer utter their lighthearted nickname. Besides, they were clearly not twins. Amid the dark chaos roiling across the wall, the tandem figures stalked, ever together, ever in conflict, always dominating the smaller figures of the multitudes. One was stocky and angular, the other sinuous as smoke. They fought without visible weapons, but the signs of unsettled weather shadowed them wherever they appeared: great billowing waters and towers of cloud carved in the rock, lightning scoring a ravaged stone landscape, fire, hail, wind, and ice. And through it all, the goddesses' eyes burned with a dim and malevolent fire that made Susannah shiver and long for the comfort of daylight.

Tyril roused them finally, and drew them down the hall. Farther on, a doubtful scaffold of lashed timbers climbed one wall. A rail-thin apprentice burrowed in the depths of a wicker basket, then tied a leather-wrapped object to a rope hanging from the upper level. He tugged on it gently. Atop the scaffold, a Sawl artisan was chalking a new design across a stretch of virgin rock. The scaffold quaked alarmingly as he moved about, leaning over to haul up the little bundle.

The apprentice grinned shyly as Tyril greeted him and went back to burrowing in the basket. A shadowy figure seated cross-legged on the bench along the opposite wall stirred as they approached.

"Hello," called Stavros quietly, without getting up. "Welcome to the Frieze Hall."

Susannah started. It was as if her thoughts had conjured him, although she had no time for that sort of magical thinking. He looked relaxed, very much at home, which he rarely was in any other place she might find him. He also seemed rather put out by their intrusion. Obviously not *his* first visit to this place. She wondered how long he'd known about this magnificent hall, but she couldn't find a way to ask that did not sound accusatory.

The scaffold shook again as the stonecutter set aside his chalk, rearranged his light, then reached for his wooden mallet. From the leather bundle, he took a stout little chisel, handling it as if it were a sacred object. Stavros rose from the bench and ambled out of the shadows to stand beside the women, gazing upward.

"Iron's as rare as diamonds here, remember." His expression shared some of the artisan's reverence for the rough-hewn sliver of black metal. "That chisel probably belonged to his great-great-grandfather, at least. Back in his guildhall, there'll be a record somewhere of all the different panels carved with this particular tool."

Megan nodded. "The tool's past deeds imbue it with good medicine, as an old friend of mine would say."

"Admirable, isn't it? So little metal available, yet they use it not to make weapons or currency but to tell their stories, record their myths, to explain themselves to the future."

"Very poetic, Ibiá," drawled Megan.

His jaw tightened. "Don't pretend you don't approve, Meg."

He directed their attention upward to the sculpted panel next to the artisan's sketch. Two familiar figures carried on with their endless battling. Touches of fading polychrome on hair and drapery hinted at an original brilliance of color, but now the natural pallor of the stone muted all but the Sisters' eyes.

"Lagri has the red eyes, of course," Stavros lectured. "And the lavender is always Valla, though sometimes she's blue."

"I've noticed," said Megan, "that most of the goddess figures have cabochon jewels, but in some that seem more recent, the eyes are faceted. Do you think that marks a change of taste or a technological advance?"

Susannah studied the wall more carefully. "Jewels? Precious stones? Not glass?"

"Well, I suppose they could be glass. . . ."

"Not glass," Stavros said. "The Sawls talk of shaping the eyes, not making them. So I'd guess the lavender is amethyst; semiprecious, at least on Earth. Or there are more exotic minerals that can produce a crystal that color. As for the reds, garnet has iron in it, which is rare on Fiix, so maybe they're ruby. And the blue could be sapphire."

Megan clucked her tongue. "Definitely not glass. Can you imagine what . . ." She glanced at Stavros then, and fell silent with sudden understanding.

Susannah was still peering at the dark sparkle above her head. "Well, we know who can tell us . . . oh." She paused, and looked down. "Could have told us."

"And now, we won't have to ask," breathed Stavros with relief.

Susannah frowned. "You shouldn't dismiss a man's death so easily!"

"I don't. But second to having him leave on his own, it's the best thing that could have happened for the Sawls and for this planet."

"Are you really that cold-blooded?"

"It's a question of priorities."

"I see." She let her gaze trail around the hall, down its vast length and up into its shadowed heights. She didn't expect Megan's support where Clausen was concerned, but the other issue affected them equally. "Just how long have you known about this place?"

He shrugged. "A while."

"A *long* while? Since before the storm?" She turned to face him, keenly aware that Megan was not joining in.

"Does it matter?"

"You told the Sawls not to let us in here, didn't you?"

He opened his mouth in automatic denial, then shook his head wearily as if opting for truth, however brutal and efficient. "You'd have preferred a diplomatic incident? Before we had half a chance to do what we came here for? You knew Clausen's attitude toward the No Interference Code! He'd have been up on a scaffold prying out eyes in a second!"

Susannah folded her arms. "And I used to think Emil was paranoid to insist that the Sawls controlled our access to the Caves."

"Clausen was a problem," Stavros insisted. "I couldn't risk him knowing."

"*You* couldn't risk! Meg, are you hearing this?"

"I'm listening," Megan replied neutrally. Unease resurfaced in Tyril's eyes.

"Where else haven't you let them take us?" Susannah pursued.

"Our welcome here is less secure than you think," Stavros defended. "We've been accepted so far because we've behaved ourselves!"

"I can't believe this! After all the times I've made excuses for . . ."

"What, for me? For my 'whacko' behavior?"

"Yes, damnit! For all the good it did me. Look, Stav, I'll assume you were looking out for our interests, and for the Sawls, but you cannot go making decisions on your own that affect the rest of us, and our ability to do our work!"

"Where does it say I have to share my own discoveries with the entire expedition?"

"Is it a competition now? We're supposed to be working *together*."

Megan at last stepped into the debate. "Stav, it's naive to think that Emil Clausen would have done anything so blatant. Taylor maybe, on hotheaded impulse, but not Emil. Not unless he was absolutely sure he could get away with it."

Stavros' chin jutted stubbornly. "Who could have stopped him but us? Who else knew what he was about?"

"You've got a point there."

"No, he doesn't," Susannah fumed. "The real point is, Stav, that you're interpreting each of us for the Sawls as if we were just bits of language. I am not a word. I'm more complicated and, yes, more willful than any word, and you might just be wrong about me. Can't you let the Sawls make up their *own* minds about us?"

Stavros scowled. "I did what I had to do."

A voice rose in complaint from the top of the scaffold. The apprentice stonecutter's mournful eyes begged for silence so that his master might concentrate.

Susannah lowered her voice, so that the words burst from her like quiet explosions. "Is *this* why I can't make contact with the healers?"

"No!" Stavros blurted unhappily. "Why would I warn them away from you?"

"Exactly what I'd like to know!" Susannah wondered how she could have ever felt drawn to this egomaniacal and irritating boy.

Tyril stirred, and Megan worked up a reassuring smile, tinged with irony at finding herself a willing arbiter, as the debate took on a decidedly personal tone. "Let me put it this way, Stav—if you're going to manipulate the Sawls' vision of us, remember we have no defense until we're as fluent in Sawlish as you are. By then, the damage could already be done. The best we can do is beg you to interpret with a clear head."

"You're preventing me from doing my work!" Susannah insisted.

Stavros shook his head, as if desperate for the right reply and unable to find it. Susannah waited for him to level a parting shot and then, as usual, flee before she had a chance to respond. Instead, he raked a hand through his ragged hair, muttered in Sawlish, and staged a pensive retreat down the long hall into darkness.

Susannah rubbed fiercely at her temples. If she followed him, would it be better or worse? "It's wrong, Meg. What he's doing is wrong!"

Megan took in a breath and let it out slowly. "Depends on your point of view."

"What?"

"What he's doing *is* best for the Sawls."

"No. I disagree."

"Really? Think about it. Aren't you just mad that he didn't let *you* in?"

"No, I . . . No." Susannah stilled her restless hands before they did her damage. "Well, I don't know. Okay. Maybe you're right. A little. And either way, it was stupid to lose my temper. It'll just make him more stubborn."

Megan grinned. "You call that losing your temper? Jeesh!"

"Will our knowing now make any difference, do you think? Will he let us in?"

"One can only hope."

A woody groan resounded through the hall, ending with a series of sharp cracks and a shout of alarm as the stonecutter's foot crashed through a rotting board. The uprights of the scaffold not supported by the wall bent outward, quivering like drawn longbows. The apprentice squealed as a length of planking tumbled to the floor. A narrow ladder snapped free and fell in a long graceful arc, narrowly missing Tyril as she yanked Megan out of range. The stonecutter scrambled for the wall-side uprights. He wrapped his arms and legs around a support and clambered down as fast as he could manage. His high platform of timbers tilted, spilling tools and chalk. A ceramic water jug smashed into dust at Susannah's feet. The apprentice dove under the creaking scaffold to snatch up the tools he had taken out of the basket. Fragments of rotten wood rained around his head. Susannah waved at him to run clear, but he grinned wildly and continued madly stuffing bits and pieces into the basket.

The scaffold quaked as an outside leg bent to its limit and snapped. The stonecutter leaped free from several times his height and landed moaning on the marble tiles. Susannah lunged for the unwitting apprentice but had the wind knocked out of her as an arm shot around her waist, jerked her away, and flung her clear of the falling timbers.

Breathless from his return sprint, Stavros whirled back for the apprentice just as a second upright gave way with a splintering crack. The boy shrieked, pushing and tugging at the heavy basket. The end of a thick plank struck his shoulder as he abandoned the basket and tried to scramble away. He staggered, looking confused. Stavros grabbed for him but had to shield his own head with his arms as the remains of the upper platform thundered down on top of them.

Tyril was into the wreckage instantly, heaving broken boards aside and shouting for help as the Terran women stood frozen in shock. A pile of splinters stirred and fell away as Stavros staggered to his feet and went to work beside Tyril. Susannah shook herself into motion. She dropped down at the side of the dazed stonecarver and took his hand. He was not a young man. His landing had jarred him badly. He winced with each breath but he was not in agony. When he came around enough to focus on the collapsed scaffold and the searchers frantic in the rubble, his eyes widened and he struggled to rise.

Susannah made him lie back. This would be no different from the Glasgow free clinic she'd moonlighted in until her sponsors called a halt. Gently, she began to probe for broken bones.

"Is he all right?" demanded Megan at her side.

"Shaken up, a few cracked ribs, I'd say . . . a bad ankle here, maybe a sprain, probably a fracture. What about the boy?"

Megan looked over her shoulder. "They're just getting to him now . . . Oh, my god."

Susannah continued her examination. "Meg, I'm going to need water and . . ."

"Susannah!" Stavros' shout was shrill. "Get over here!"

Tyril sped past, away, at a dead run. Megan looked faint.

Susannah grabbed her arm. "Find this man some water. And don't let him move!" Then she rose and looked behind her.

The apprentice boy lay spread-eagled in a splash of blood. Stavros had stripped off his tunic and was pressing it in an awkward bundle to the boy's thigh. His hands were dark and shiny. The blood had soaked through the fabric already. Two deep gashes on the boy's shoulder and forehead ran red onto the pale stone floor. His left arm was crooked at an awful angle. He lay limp as a broken doll.

"Keep up the pressure." Susannah knelt at Stavros' side. "How bad is it under there?"

"Open from groin to knee. Like with a carving knife."

"Let's hope it's shallow. Okay. I need you to take that cloth away and tear it into strips as fast as you can."

"Are you sure?"

She was glad for his calm. She was going to need it. "Yes, I'm sure."

"Whenever you're ready, then."

She opened her pocket knife. "Ready."

Stavros pulled away the reddening bundle. Blood welled up from a ragged slash as long as his arm. Torn fabric twisted with turned-back flaps of skin as if the child's leg had been split open by a plow. Susannah sliced at the blood-drenched pant leg, wrenched aside the fabric, then quickly folded the loose skin and muscle back into the wound. She grabbed up the strips as fast as Stavros could tear them and wrapped the thigh as tightly as possible. Her fingers slippery with blood, she ripped the end of a final strip, tied a quick knot and began a second layer.

"It's slowing a little," she said. "The femoral's intact. When you're done tearing, wrap the head wound just like I'm doing here. Did Tyril go for help?"

"I hope so." Stavros brushed blood-damp hair from the boy's forehead and then from his own. A slow trickle stained his cheek. He laid a strip of his tunic across the boy's forehead.

"He'll need fluids." Susannah reached to cut shredded wool away from the shoulder wound. "You'll have to explain to them about transfusing so they don't think we're hurting him, and then . . . oh, god, we'll need to test for the right blood type!" As she bound the shoulder, her hand brushed a hard-edged object pinned under the boy's body. She yanked it free and found herself holding the stonecutter's chisel. Its long flat blade was shiny with blood. She tossed it aside with far less reverence than the stonecutter would have used. "Metal has a way of becoming a weapon all of its own accord."

She knotted the bandage and sat back on her heels. "Now we've got to get him down where I can treat him properly. The old man, too. Meg . . . ?" She turned to see Megan standing aside as two sturdy Sawl women shifted the stonecutter onto a leather stretcher. "No! You shouldn't move him! Wait!"

Then she saw the woman waiting with a second stretcher. Next to her stood a tall linen-smocked Sawl with tied-back curls and a dignified stoop. His intent gaze was fixed on Susannah.

She knew him instantly, and smiled with relief and welcome. When he did not smile back, she felt bereft. But, of course—he might view her with suspicion, or as an intruder on his rightful turf. Time was of the essence, but at least she should offer him due respect. She leaned away from the injured boy and gestured for the man to come and look.

"Is this your healer?" murmured Stavros.

Susannah nodded, watching anxiously as the man knelt beside the boy. His brown hands were large and long-fingered but delicately built. They explored and probed deftly, traveling the length of the boy's limp body without haste, seeming often to hover just above the skin. She was surprised to note that his eyes were closed, his thin handsome face slack with concentration.

After a moment, he looked across at Susannah and nodded, as if in approval. When he spoke, his voice was soft and light.

"He thanks us for our efforts on the boy's behalf," Stavros translated.

"Ask his name!" said Susannah in a rush. "Tell him I'm a . . . a healer, too. I can save this boy's life, but we have to get to it quickly! The boy needs blood, and I'll have to test for blood type, but if we take him down to our cave immediately, I can get him anesthetized and sew him up properly. And, Stav, I beg you . . . for once, tell it to him straight."

The Sawl listened, his long head politely inclined.

But Stavros stared at her, then drew back and replied coolly, "If you want to work with this guy, you'd better not insult him. You have to let him treat the kid himself."

"What? But he's . . . the boy is . . ."

"I mean it, Susannah."

"But can he treat injuries this serious?"

"Do you know he can't?"

"But I have drugs. I have painkillers and antiseptics . . ."

"Do you know he doesn't?"

"Stavros, stop! You're doing it again! Are we going to sit here arguing principles while the boy dies on us?"

"No, we're not. We're going to get out of this man's way so he can do his job." Stavros grasped her wrist, pulling her firmly aside. "I wouldn't make it look like a struggle, if I were you. It's not likely to impress him." He nodded to the healer, who waved over the woman with the second stretcher.

Susannah looked to Megan, aghast. "But . . . !"

Megan shrugged and shook her head. "Stav's right. It's not our place."

Helpless, Susannah watched the two Sawls ease the broken body onto the leather sling. Stavros loosed his grip on her wrist as the stretcher was raised. He spoke rapidly to the tall Sawl, who listened as he supported one end of the stretcher. His reply was brief and then he was off with the wounded boy, hurrying down the dark Frieze Hall. When Susannah made a move to follow, Stavros held her back.

"He'll let us know how it goes."

Susannah snatched her wrist away.

"I conveyed your request," he said. "About working with him. He said he'd think about it. After he's taken care of the boy."

The rage that she'd held back earlier pushed out now between clenched teeth. "You can stick to your purism about the No Interference Code when there's a child's life at stake? Both of you? There is something wrong with you people!"

"Oh, so are you going to be around here forever to supply the knowledge and technology he lacks?" Stavros returned. "Or do you just want to dazzle with a few miracle cures and split, leaving guys like him feeling inadequate?"

"And forever dissatisfied," murmured Megan.

"I wouldn't . . . !" Susannah glanced away, as rage and frustration brought unwelcome tears. "All right! I'm damned if I do, and damned if I don't. I accept it, but I do not agree with it! Be it on your conscience if the boy dies!" She was appalled at them, but even more, she was appalled at herself: she had bargained with a boy's life to gain the access she sought.

But she was going to let it happen anyway. It might bring her to the healers.

20

E.D. 57–14:45

WHEN HE'D SLUICED the boy's blood off himself in a cleansing niche, Stavros exhausted his frustration by swimming laps for twenty minutes, while Liphar soaked in the shallows and looked on in disbelief. The pools in the Baths were ill suited to aggressive swimming. Steaming water roiled over the tiled edges and washed across the glass floor. A pair of elderly Sawls at the next pool glanced up in mild irritation and began to wring out their piles of clean laundry all over again.

At last, Stavros hauled himself up panting beside Liphar. "Out of shape."

A fleeting memory seized him, of the swim team at boarding school, of a rare camaraderie reminiscent of his hours here with Liphar. Away from the pool, he'd had few close friends. Friendship was risky—what if you got on with a guy whose parents' enclave was feuding with yours? Or if their business crashed and burned, and suddenly they'd be wanting to send him your way for visits all the time. Was it significant that he chose to spend so much of his time with a near-child? Certainly Megan would find it so, and now, Susannah—who was not likely to forgive him anytime soon.

He'd handled himself badly in the Frieze Hall, he knew it. But he'd only done—and said—what he thought was right. But he did it with a bludgeon instead of a feather. It was the old problem. What good was having the moral advantage, when you lacked the appropriate finesse and self-control?

They soaked for a while in silence. Liphar let his toes float up and stared at the fat white pipes suspended high above like tubular clouds. He watched the occasional droplet of condensation take the long fall into the pool.

Stavros studied the other bathers. They might bring a sign of how the apprentice boy was doing. The golden cavern was crowded as always, but the mood was subdued. A relative of the injured stonecutter described the accident to her fellow guildsmen in vivid secondhand detail, but the clatter of the stones across the gaming tables was louder than her anxious murmur. Even the children had withdrawn to the farthest corners to play their quietest games. Stavros saw many families enter the Baths, wash themselves and their clothing, and leave without the usual socializing.

"Kav Ashimmel still refuses to give us an answer?" he ventured at last.

Liphar grunted his assent.

"Has she some particular reason for keeping me from seeing the old Kav?"

The young Sawl's shoulders hunched as he drew his knees up to his thin chest and hugged them. The green water sloshed gently. *"O rek,"* he muttered. *"Gisti."*

"I know she said that, but I don't get it, Lifa. Why should she think the Wokind have anything to do with Valla Ired?"

Liphar glanced about anxiously. His fingers toyed with the amulet on his wrist. *"O wokind kurm arma . . ."* His voice dropped to a whisper. *"Valla Ired."*

"What?" Stavros exclaimed. "We're helping her?"

Liphar edged closer, pulled in a long breath and launched into an explanation so rapid and mumbled that Stavros had to make him slow down to catch even half of it. What he did understand stunned him.

"Wait. She actually thinks the storm's gone on so long because the Wokind have come to help Valla? Why would we want to do that? We've already lost two people to the storm, and nearly lost a third."

Liphar squirmed miserably as if he didn't want to be identified with the suspicions he was passing on, but wouldn't mind hearing them disproved. "Not like it, you . . ."

"Try me."

"Okay. *Wokind* help Valla, then all Sawl gone. *Wokind* all here."

Stavros was horrified. "Who put that idea into their heads?"

But he knew the answer. *I did. With my warnings about Clausen and Danforth.* He dropped his head into his hands. Talk about a backfire. He had sown seeds of territoriality and distrust to save the Sawls from what he saw as their own too-generous nature. But some of the ground had proved fertile indeed! So much for the purity of his Noninterference. Now what? The best he could do was to try to squelch the weed before it ran rampant. "Lifa, please. We don't want you gone! Clausen might have, but he was killed by Valla's own storm! You are the reason we came here, to learn about you, from you. And then we'll go away, back where we came from. Do you believe me?"

Liphar spread his palms mournfully. "Not important, I."

Stavros turned on one knee to face him. "It's not true, what Ashimmel says, I swear! With Clausen gone, Fiix will come to no harm at Terran hands." He held out a flattened palm. "My own life on it."

Only after he'd said the words did he realize how completely he meant them. If they ever made it back to Earth, he'd somehow have to discourage ConPlex from sending a follow-up expedition. And now he thought he could count on Megan's help in writing the appropriate report.

Liphar solemnly covered the offered palm with his own. *"Embriha Lagri,"* he intoned. Then he sat back, elbows against the tile, and looked at least momentarily relieved.

Stavros matched the young Sawl's relaxed posture, but his mind was racing. *Okay, it's true. I can't do this alone anymore.* He had to get the others involved. Susannah was right: isolation bred too much misunderstanding.

Yet his resolution wavered. His self-assumed role of champion of the Sawls could not be shed between one bit of insight and another. Even if Megan Levy could be trusted to keep the Sawls' best interests at heart, could Susannah be likewise? What about Weng or McPherson? He stirred the water with limp fingers, then cupped his hand to feel the heat run out of it slowly. Like he'd seen the lifeblood flowing from the apprentice boy's thigh. Like the heart and soul could be drained out of an entire planet.

"Lifa," he said finally, "I need your help. First, can you think of a way that we—the Wokind—can make a show of support for Lagri, to ease Kav Ashimmel's suspicions? Second—and this is probably harder—would you dare to speak to Kav Daven for me yourself?"

Liphar's shoulders rose like a clamp around his neck and a shiver escaped him. But he turned a wan smile in his friend's direction. "I try, Ibi. I try."

21

E.D. 60–13:16

SUSANNAH SULKED, BUT scolded herself for it, so she was relieved to be able to snatch a real moment of concentration and solitude.

As was usual in the middle of the Terran "day," the Black Hole was deserted. Weng had retreated to her secret ivory tower and the company of her now handwritten scores. Now that the search had been suspended, McPherson left each morning after breakfast to take up her daily vigil at the highest cave mouth, where she passed the hours filling a notebook with a letter to her mother, on whichever ship or station she commanded at the moment. Interesting that McPherson hadn't bragged about it, at least not within Susannah's hearing. Was it a lesser posting? Either way, the letter was shown to no one. Meanwhile, Megan had gone off hours ago with Tyril to the Weaver Hall, and Stavros hadn't been seen in three days.

Susannah raised the wick of her oil lamp to a scandalously wasteful height and reviewed an updated list. She was amazed by the variety of edibles the Sawls managed to produce in the virtual darkness of the Caves. This list covered only the fungi.

No surprise that fungi were a staple here, given the Sawls' cave-dwelling habit. But the range of shape, texture, and taste was remarkable. Some were grown in a compost that was nearly a hundred percent aged hakra manure. Other varieties grew on rotted wood or in moist sand, some on the dampened naked rock. The slim translucent bells like Indian Pipe were Susannah's favorite so far, but she also liked the tiny spherical mil, and the giant cushion mushroom, whose thick broiled slices tasted like Terran chicken.

Susannah smirked. Why are all indescribable tastes said to be just like chicken?

The guildsmen in the mushroom caves had warmed to her interest in their craft. At least someone has, she mused bitterly. Her new wicker sample basket overflowed with multicolored fungi.

All very interesting, but . . . did the boy live or die? Why wouldn't someone tell her?

It was like a thorn in her brain, painful and persistent, so reminiscent of being barred from her Glasgow clinic. But shaking her head was unlikely to dislodge it. Instead, she chose a morel-like cone, fished a scalpel out of her medikit and sliced the fungus neatly in half. She laid the rough-skinned sections out on her sketchbook and settled in to draw.

Meanwhile, she sifted through possible explanations for the amazing variety. There was no such range of dark-growing edible fungi on Earth, or any planet that she knew of. It could be an evolutionary response to the long Fiixian night, or it could be that the Sawls were unsurpassed hybridists. The same questions could be asked about the several dozen breeds of fowl, or the various small mammals that were raised for food in the Caves, or the schools of pale slow-moving fish bred in unlit pools at the back of the stable level. Or the fact that all Sawls seemed gifted with 20/20 vision.

Astonishing, really. She outlined a warty cone shape on the page.

A soft cough from near the entryway made Susannah's hand jerk, marring the precision of her curve. Her light-blinded eyes picked out a pale figure suspended in darkness. He carried no light, but his height and gentle stoop identified him immediately. A thrill coursed through her. How long he had been standing there in the shadows, watching?

She swallowed skittishly and laid aside her pencil. Her smile this time was wary. But if she had finally caught his interest, she was determined to make the best of the occasion. Did he speak any English? Probably not. She beckoned him in with all the respect she could conjure.

The healer nodded, and like a teacher observing a pupil's homework, he came to peer over her shoulder at her sketchbook. He murmured encouragingly, then crouched beside her and, without preamble, picked up her pencil. He studied it, set it down, felt the texture of the paper, tested its thickness between a slim thumb and forefinger. Susannah felt herself being sized up by way of her equipment. Then he reached for the scalpel.

This he held up to the lamplight, letting the high flame flash on the mirrored steel. As Susannah watched anxiously, he laid his thumb to the blade with professional caution. She saw knowledge in his eyes, and interest, but nothing like envy, though he clearly understood what he had in his hand.

He kept the scalpel with him as he settled across from her on the matting, the lantern between them. He had left his stained smock behind for this visit. His soft gray tunic and pants were worn long and loose, falling in straight lines from his shoulders. He held the scalpel delicately by both ends, his elbows propped up on his rather bony knees. He regarded her over its shining length.

"*Kho jeu Ogo Dul-ni, Ghirra min,*" he offered gravely.

An introduction. Susannah knew enough Sawlish to understand that. So his name was Ghirra, but there was an unusual prefix, "Ogo Dul." The Sawls called their cave city Dul Elesi, and each took the name as an accepted prefix to their own. This Ghirra either followed a different custom or was from somewhere else.

Somewhere else? The thought of other settlements hadn't yet occurred to her, or as far as she knew, to anyone else. But of course there must be other settlements on a planet as big as this. And "Ogo Dul" had a familiar ring to it. She was sure the Master Ranger used a prefix something like that. She hadn't thought to wonder about that either.

She struggled through her reply. "Kho jeu James-ni, Susannah min."

It didn't quite correspond, but she felt she couldn't very well give her last name as "Earth." She knew her accent was atrocious, but Ghirra's gracious nod showed that he had understood well enough.

"Zuzhanna," he repeated with satisfaction. His gaze measured both the scalpel in his hand and her response to his holding it. Did he expect her to be possessive of it? Or was this a challenge of some sort—a gentle, probing one, consistent with his manner?

Susannah considered her own assessment of the Sawls to be the most generous, more so even than Stavros, who she felt glorified their primitive purity well beyond what was flattering. But now she sensed the need for some quick reassessing, or this intelligent Sawl was going to be two steps ahead of her all the way and eventually would tire of waiting for her lower expectations to catch up with the reality. If only they could dispense with the introductory formalities, which would have to be awkward, without a common language between them. She wished Stavros was there, and then was glad he was not.

Because maybe we do have a language in common. . . .

She barely considered what she was about to do, except to wonder how she'd explain it to Megan. Grabbing up her medikit, she set it open on the floor in front of him. The Sawl healer looked at it, looked at her, then began to lift the instruments out one by one and lay them in a careful row along the matting. He studied each one as if it was telling its secrets to him in words they both understood.

Susannah kissed the No Interference Code good-bye, with only mild regret.

22

E.D. 60–13:20

THE WEAVER HALL was low and wide, divided by four rows of sturdy wooden looms, ten in each row. Megan ushered Commander Weng along the row ahead of her, lagging behind for a closer look. The machines' workings and construction were similar to old Terran looms, though not as refined (she was obscurely happy to note) as the great bronze looms developed by her friends the Min Kodeh.

Large bowled lamps hung above each workstation. As they followed Tyril between the rows, Weng pointed out that every single loom was in use. The weavers chatted and sang, trading jokes and gossip across the rows. The looms clacked and eighty small hands flew back and forth among the colored threads. The noise was deafening. Still, Megan was sure the chatter had dulled just slightly as they entered the cavern.

Wooden racks along the outside walls sprouted endless fat spools and long looping skeins of yarn. Bolts of finished cloth lay piled according to color and the weight of the weave. Tyril encouraged them to feel the smooth texture of the fabric and admire the tight regularity of the threads. She showed them her own loom, where she was working on a length of yellow wool as soft as cashmere. An apprentice in the next station wove with a thicker thread, like a heavy, reddish cotton. He glanced uneasily over his shoulder at the Terran women, and the patient journeyman who was showing him how to introduce a second color into the weave rapped his head lightly to return his attention to the work.

"Did you notice?" Megan whispered to Weng. "They're only using Lagri's colors. Or am I seeing signs now where there are none?"

Beyond the ranks of looms, intricately colored hangings curtained off a portion of the hall. Narrow strips of every possible weave, material, and color had been sewn together in a giant sampler of the guild's craft. Megan's anticipation built as Tyril led them through a slit in the drape. In previous visits to the Hall, she had not been allowed this far. Inside, a long wooden table sat crosswise in the space. Behind it, taut rope netting slung between thick posts supported the several hundred volumes of guild records.

Tyril gestured the women to a bench at the table, then chose a volume. She hauled it down from its woven shelf and laid it open on the table. It looked old but not ancient. Its parchment leaves were caught between stiff leather covers and sewn with a waxed string. The pages were crowded with spiky Sawlish lettering written in many differing hands: names, numbers, unintelligible notations. Tyril leafed through gently, then found the page she wanted. She ran a finger down the lines and stopped near the bottom.

"*Na,*" she announced proudly. "*O kemma-ip khe.*"

"Ah! Her eight-mother." Megan grinned, then explained to Weng. "We've been working on generational terminologies. All the guilds keep very exact membership records, you see." She leaned over the page myopically. "Dul Elesegar-ni-Suri-min," she read haltingly.

Tyril clapped her hands in delighted approval. "*Suri,*" she nodded. "*O kemma-ip.*"

"Dul Elesegar is an older form of the cave name Dul Elesi. Eight-mother is a grandmother seven generations removed," said Megan. "Great-great-great, etc. They record matrilineally within the guilds. The women are encouraged, though not forced, to carry on the mother's craft. The sons are encouraged to train out in a craft of their choice. Marriages are required to cross guild lines, however. There aren't many sexual taboos here, it seems, but that one is strictly enforced. I guess it helps prevent inbreeding."

Weng calculated briefly. "Two hundred years. Earth years, that is."

"And Earth generations. A generation seems to be a little longer here, in real time."

Tyril flipped two more pages, searched and pointed out another entry. The ink on this page had browned slightly but still read strong and clear.

"O kemma-seph," she said.

"Fifteen-mother," said Megan.

"Three hundred twenty-five," offered Weng. "More or less."

Tyril left the book open on the table and returned to the shelves for another, older volume. This one was bound between thin planks of dry wood. Its leather lashings creaked as she slowly levered it open. She turned these yellowed pages with extreme care. Her finger hovered over but did not touch an entry that preceded a short list. *"O kemma-lef sephip khe."*

"No . . ." Megan's eyes widened.

Tyril nodded emphatically.

"It seems she's saying her forty-eighth."

"That's over twelve hundred years," said Weng with admiration.

"Not possible. I must be getting the numbers wrong."

"Of course it's possible," Weng replied sternly. "I can follow my own lineage back that far."

Megan stared at her.

"Well, eleven hundred and fifty years," Weng conceded. "Nearly that far."

Megan gestured abruptly at the crowded shelves. "But look how many still older books there are!"

"Yes," smiled Weng. "Isn't it wonderful?"

Guild membership figures are approximate only:

Dyers   (130)
  pigment, paint
  ink
  dyes, dyeing
Engineers   (300)
  winchcrew
  plumbing
  tunnel maint.
  excavation
Weavers   (180)
Glassmakers   (125)
Potters   (210)
  pottery
  brick, tile
Keth-Toph (250) ("LifeGuild":
  lamp oil   'Heat and Light')
  dung fuel
  candles
  soap
Woodworkers   (200)
  toolmakers
  coopers
  wheelwrights
  cabinetry
Stonecutters   (300)
Basketry   (215)
Rugmakers   (75)
Papermakers   (60)
Leatherworkers   (285)

PriestGuild   (100)
Rangers   (130)
  weatherwatch
  trail guides
  mapping
Physicians   (27)
  healers
  midwives
  nursing
  herbalists
FoodGuild   (750) ?
  agricultural:
    mushroomers
    seedsmen: seed
              fertilizer
  husbandry:
    fisheries
    fowl
    small mammals
    herdsmen: dairy
                draft
  brewers
  breadmakers
  curers & smokers
  picklers & preservers
  icekeepers
  storesmen
  distributors
approx. 3357 working members

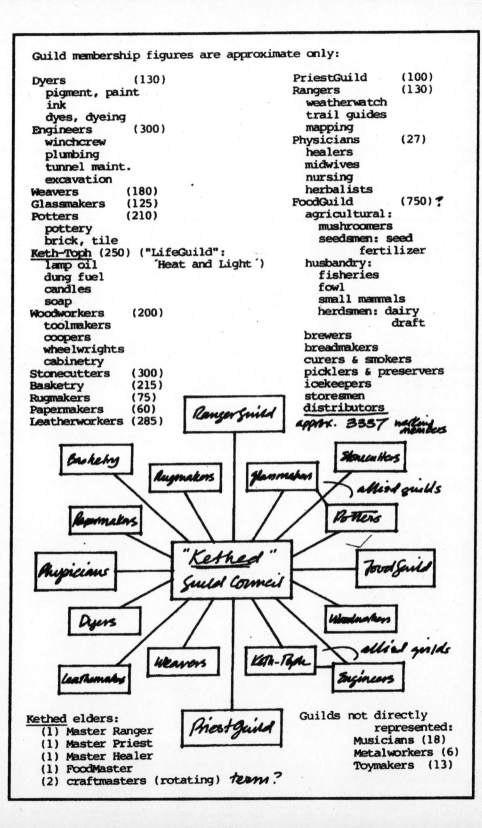

Kethed elders:
  (1) Master Ranger
  (1) Master Priest
  (1) Master Healer
  (1) FoodMaster
  (2) craftmasters (rotating) teams?

Guilds not directly
            represented:
Musicians (18)
Metalworkers (6)
Toymakers (13)

23

W HEN SUSANNAH HAD shown the healer through the entirety of her medikit, he nodded silent thanks, rose, and left her with nothing but questions. Susannah chewed her lip, wondering what else she could have done to win him over.

But the next day, as she was inventorying the root crops on offer in the Market Hall, a young woman in a white linen smock touched her arm respectfully and led her uplevel, where everything she'd finally dismissed as a fever dream turned out to be true.

The tall healer met them beside the elaborately carved entry arch, wiping his hands on a scrap of damp cloth. Behind him, just as she remembered, double rows of huge wagon-wheel oil lamps receded into a vast darkness scented with herbs. He handed off the cloth to Susannah's escort as she whispered past him into the echoing gloom of the hall.

"*Rhe khem,* Zuzhanna," the healer offered.

"Khem rhe, Keth-shim Ghirra." She completed the ritual greeting, hoping to appear more assured than she felt. Tyril had identified this man as the master of the Healers Guild, so addressing him by his proper title surely couldn't hurt.

He inclined his head, indicating that she should follow him, and it was like walking back into her dream: the rows of beds—thick pallets, really, laid out on low brick platforms; the murmur of voices, some soothing, some tight with pain; the odors of blood and birth and death. She was in a hospital ward, no doubt about it. In an instant, Susannah felt right at home.

The Master Healer proceeded past several rows of occupied beds, where children coughed and old women slept, or sat up gossiping with their neighbors. He was unhurried, letting her take in the details. Then he turned, and crouched beside a particular pallet, looking up to observe her reaction. With a shock of joy, Susannah recognized the stonemason's apprentice, propped against a triangular backrest. Their arrival stirred him from a doze, but he smiled wanly as the Master Healer laid a hand to his forehead and two fingers to his thin wrist. His head was bandaged, and when the healer questioned him gently, the boy's replies were barely audible. Susannah could tell he was sedated against the pain, but he was coherent and plainly on the mend. She peered over the Master Healer's shoulder as eagerly as a first-year intern while he unwrapped and checked the horrible gash on the boy's thigh. She knew it was wrong to expect the worst, but she couldn't suppress a faint, glad breath of surprise when the wound was revealed, clean and neatly sutured, showing no sign of infection.

The Master Healer sat back on his heels, as if inviting her comment and advice. Susannah only smiled and nodded, sensing that same ambiguity with which he had held her gaze over the blade of her scalpel: modesty and grace, spiced with a darker hint of prideful challenge. But then, what good doctor does not possess at least a modicum of arrogance?

When he turned back to rewrap the wound with a fresh bandage, her smile twisted toward something more rueful. Apparently, that needed reassessment had progressed without her conscious effort. She was already thinking of this man as a doctor, a full-fledged medical colleague. There was so much she wanted to ask him.

The boy slipped off to sleep again. As the Master Healer rose, a young man in white materialized with a steaming bowl and fresh hand towels. Rinsing his hands, the healer glanced Susannah's way, lifting a brow in question.

Hoping she understood him correctly, Susannah nodded eagerly. Hot water and linen was brought to her then, and a long linen smock, so that she could properly accompany the doctor on his daily rounds.

24

THE LANTERN CLINKED loudly as Stavros set it down on the sleeping platform. He wondered how seriously he was going to regret this.

He bent low to whisper. "Susannah!" He leaned closer to her ear. "Susannah!"

She stirred, deep in sleep. In the lamplight, with dark hair framing pale, lucent skin, he thought her as lovely as a Renaissance madonna, at rest but not yet at peace, her lidded eyes mobile with waiting energy. He nearly reached to smooth a wisp of hair from her cheek, then caught himself abruptly and nudged her shoulder instead. "Susannah!"

She jolted upright in her sleeping cocoon and blinked at him. "You are in my bedroom," she remarked with convincing clarity.

He pulled back on his heels. "Hey, it's mine, too. I mean . . ." Then he realized she was not really seeing him. "Susannah, wake up! You have to come with me!"

His urgency woke her reflexes. "Is someone hurt?'

"Shhh! No. There's something you've got to see, right now! Wake Meg while I get my stuff together."

"Stav, it's . . . what time *is* it?"

"Who cares? You won't want to miss this! And it's important that we be there."

Susannah slumped groggily.

"Look, I know you think . . ." His voice trailed off as she finally came awake enough to really look at him.

"I think what?"

He wished she'd see he was trying to apologize, but was too impatient to really work at it. "Never mind. Meet me by the fire."

"Put on coffee while you're at it."

He slipped away, leaving her in blackness. Susannah peered sleepily around the canvas partition to watch his lantern bob from sink to fire pit. She unzipped her cocoon and dragged herself across the dark platform as quietly as she could to jostle the huddle that was usually Megan.

Megan woke quickly, coming to full alert. "What is it now?"

"Shhh! It's Stavros. He's having an event."

When they joined him at the fire pit, he held out hot mugs to both of them. Susannah smelled shipboard Nescaf. Normally he would have made the bitter Sawlian equivalent and looked down his nose when they refused to share it. She nudged Megan loudly. "Watch out. He's trying to be nice to us."

But Megan grasped the mug gratefully. "Why are we being quiet?"

Stavros shrugged. "The others need their sleep."

"And I don't?" Megan downed a third of her coffee in one long gulp. "Never mind. I've been looking for you, Ibiá. I need you to look at some of this stuff from the Weaver Guild archives. I hadn't counted on five AM to be the time for it, but the implications are amazing, really."

"Later, later."

"I'd rather sooner, but . . . okay. What's so important right now?"

Stavros looked smug. "Only the Dance of Origins, that's all. What you might call the Sawl Genesis." He kept his voice low, but his body practically quivered with excitement. "The key to their entire racial history might be found in this one tale chant!"

"Whoa, slow down," said Megan. "Who and where? When is patently obvious."

"Things here don't always work on our schedule." Fidgeting, he leaned against the white battery packs stacked at his side. "The who is Kav Daven, the Lore and Ritual Master of the Priest Guild. Where is somewhere near the Frieze Hall. Liphar's coming to escort us. The old priest just announced he'd perform this chant, out of the blue. Liphar's been working on him, and finally he got permission for me not only to be there but to record it."

"Behind Ashimmel's back," Megan guessed.

He nodded. "She's refused to let me see him at all."

"Won't she be there?"

"Maybe. But if I get there first, she can't throw me out. But I need both of you there, too." Stavros shot Megan one of his rare half-grins. "To preserve my objectivity."

"I wouldn't miss it for the world," returned Megan dryly. "If only to make sure you don't totally misinterpret this 'Sawl Genesis.' If I know you, you'll take it as literally as the Old Testament version so often has been."

He was too excited to bother rising to her taunt. "And there's another thing: our being there will be seen as a sign of support for Lagri."

"Is that good?" asked Susannah.

"At this point, I'd say it was necessary."

"Then why so hush-hush?" Megan asked. "Why not bring Weng and McPherson?"

"The Kav is a very old man," said Stavros quickly. "I didn't want to throw too much at him all at once."

Megan eyed him speculatively. "Unh-huh."

Stavros turned away and busied himself, shoving battery cables, recorder, and keypad into his worn backpack. The slap of leather on stone announced Liphar at the entryway.

"Remarkable, isn't it?" Susannah yawned. "Eight hundred and ninety-nine hours in their day and they still manage to be on time."

The young Sawl trotted up to the fire pit. *"Khem, Ibi."* He patted the battery packs with a proprietary air, then crouched beside Susannah. *"Rhe khem, Zuzhannah."*

"Khem rhe, Liphar."

"Not see, you," he complained. *"Keth-shim* Ghirra keep you alla time uplevel."

Megan agreed. "Lucky if we see you for meals the last few days."

Susannah smiled happily. "Doctor's hours. But the Physicians Hall is only one level up, Meg. Now that it's not off limits, you should pay us a visit."

"One level up, but all the way at the other end of the cliff."

"Nice hot water in Physicians'. The Master Healer has his own supply." Susannah sipped her coffee, puzzled by the sharp look that Stavros gave her. "You know, I'd forgotten how much I love plain old-fashioned doctoring. Working with Guildmaster Ghirra may turn me into an herbalist yet."

"I be alla time with Ibi now, you know?" said Liphar proudly.

"No, I didn't."

He let out a huge chuckle. "Easy work. I talk, maybe sing. He listen." His tongue clicked and his fingers danced through a passable imitation of Stavros intent at his keypad. "Later, maybe, he talk, I listen, ah?"

"How does Kav Ashimmel feel about this? Aren't you missing out on your training?" Susannah wondered if he'd also removed himself from the apparently profitable weather racket. Or was he still taking bets on the side? When Stavros translated, Liphar grinned and waved a dismissive hand. Susannah thought it an oddly Terran gesture.

"He was spending most of his time with you anyway," Megan remarked.

Stavros nodded. "But now Kav Ashimmel has officially released him from his guild duties. She's finally realized she needs someone fluent in Terran as badly as we need to be fluent in Sawl."

If the others heard this as a reproof, neither allowed him the satisfaction of a response. He stood, slinging his rucksack over one shoulder, and picked up a battery pack. "Is Kav Daven ready for us, Lifa?" He patted the aggressively white plastic case. "Are you sure he understands about all this?"

"Ready, yes." Liphar scooted over to heft the other battery. With his arm extended under the weight, the case swung low to the ground, but he refused to be relieved of it.

Stavros nodded toward the entryway. "Shall we?"

The Market Hall was quiet. In the lighted shop doorways, Sawls gathered in murmured conversations that fell silent as the Terrans approached and picked up again when they'd passed by. When the expedition had first arrived, these pauses expressed wonder and uncertainty. Now Susannah detected something darker, a louder, more directed grumble. She recalled Stavros' warning about the tenuousness of their welcome in the Caves. She'd put it from her mind up in the Physicians Hall, which was its own little kingdom, a protected environment isolated from the daily life—and politics—of the Caves by people's natural aversion to illness. Besides, the Master Healer was proving to be unusually curious about things Terran.

But what would the Sawls do to us, she mused, if they decided they don't want us around?

Crossing the open plaza, passing by the groups around the well, she felt too many eyes on her. Not exactly hostile but still, the friendly curiosity she had come to expect had definitely faded. She was glad to climb the long ramp to the Frieze Hall and leave the restless crowd behind.

At the Frieze Hall entry, Liphar set down his case. His eagerness momentarily in check, he let out a peaceful sigh and let the quiet settle around them.

"It's this reverence that draws him to the priesthood," Susannah murmured.

Megan scoffed, sotto voce. "Priest *Guild*. Around here, it's a craft, like weaving or glassmaking."

Susannah eyed her sideways. "Ah, but he didn't choose weaving or glassmaking, now, did he?"

Megan shrugged. "Point reluctantly conceded."

Liphar picked up the case again. He looked to Stavros. "Ready?"

"Ready."

They trooped down the hall, the whisper of their footsteps echoing from wall to wall. The wreckage of the fallen scaffold was gone without a trace. The marble floor gleamed.

"Is the boy still on the mend?" Megan asked.

Susannah nodded. "He might even be going home soon." Several thoughts later, she added, "Meg, if I'm ever that presumptuous again, slap me, okay?"

"If you'll remember you asked for it."

Passing down the vast length of the Frieze Hall, they met no one but the stone multitudes thronging the walls. At last, Liphar halted beside a tall doorway. To either side, carved flames of ruddy marble licked around portal columns as thick as oak trees. A pair of paneled wooden doors filled the arch. Their heavy pulls were shaped like tongues of flame rising from the familiar trefoil of interlocking circles.

"Ironwork," Megan noted. "The first decorative use of metal I've seen here."

"Functional," Stavros countered. "You couldn't open the doors without them."

Liphar edged forward and knocked respectfully on the oiled wood. After only a moment, a smaller section of one giant door swung open silently. A golden-skinned child appeared, bathed in ruddy light, motioning them inward.

Stepping through the doorway, Susannah recoiled as the fierce glare beat at her eyes.

Fire!

The child was a wavering silhouette retreating into the roaring heart of the inferno. Susannah held her breath, lest the heat sear her lungs. She braced for screams and the horror of burning flesh.

"I could use some help setting up," Stavros murmured as he moved briskly past into the fire, all dark efficiency against the brilliant red.

Susannah forced her eyes to focus. The room was not in flames. The fire was confined to the center, in a large, circular hearth of glazed brick. The floor surrounding the hearth was laid with the same brick, and from it, six concentric brick tiers rose to form a horseshoe-shaped amphitheater, the open side facing the doors. The glossy brick reflected and magnified the fire-light, tossing it up the rise of the tiers and around the curving wall. Overhead, the wall curled into a plastered dome, and wall and dome vanished behind a painted illusion of flames. They began low, as sinuous tongues with bright yellow cores and sinister outlines, then raged through gold and orange and vermilion to scarlet at the apex of the dome. In the high center of the vault, they flickered into sooted crimson around a well-used smoke hole.

The sharp scent of burning dung offered a calming familiarity. Susannah let out her held breath. "What is this place?"

"A Story Hall, I'm guessing," Megan offered.

"What's that?"

"Where the myths of the goddesses are told and celebrated. A chapel, of sorts." Megan peered around the great, flame-heated circle of brick. "This one's for Lagri, I'm willing to bet."

The central fire lit up the faces of several apprentice priests occupying an upper tier. But the amphitheater was nearly empty, except for a few families with wide-eyed children and a scattering of elderly men and women.

Susannah's throat was as parched as if the flames were real. "But . . . if this event is so special, where is everybody?"

"Would you expect the world to show up for a reading of the Book of Genesis?"

Susannah had to admit she probably would not.

Still dragging his battery pack, Liphar shooed them hastily toward places off to one side, beside Stavros on the lowest tier. Only when Susannah was seated, facing the central hearth, did she notice the old man sitting alone on the far side of the fire.

Like the other spectators, he seemed to be waiting. His hands rested lightly on his knees. His brown garments fell around him like a layer of autumn leaves. His head was shriveled and hairless but for the silver stubble dusting his sunken cheeks. His back was ramrod-straight, which seemed like a miracle to Susannah who thought that she had never seen an older human being, certainly not one who could still sit upright. The tawny child who had greeted them now crouched at his knee. Her hand lay lightly over his as if, should she remove its feathery restraint, the old man would be swept up by the fire's draft to swirl into the sooty vent piercing the dome, and be set free with the smoke.

"What an interesting old man," Susannah whispered.

Stavros glanced, snorted quietly, and began unlatching his cases. "That's Kav Daven. The girl is one of his great-granddaughters."

Susannah stared. This ancient was going to chant and dance?

"So, this is Lagri's Hall?" Megan inquired, *sotto voce*.

He nodded, as if it were obvious.

"Does Valla Ired have a hall as well?"

"Do *not* say that name in here," Stavros hissed. Liphar threw a shocked glance over his shoulder as he struggled with the fasteners on his own case. In a lower voice, Stavros added, "Hers is at the other end of the Frieze Hall."

"What's that one like?" Susannah imagined it as dank as this one was dry.

"It's been locked up tight since we've been here—the only locked door in the Caves, far as I know." Stavros passed Susannah the male ends of several cables. "They won't set foot in it, not until Lagri shows signs of a comeback."

"The Sawls feel it's best to promote an even balance," added Megan.

"And performing this tale chant is a pitch for Lagri?"

"Performing it *here*," he replied.

"It's what the Sawls would call hedging their bets," Megan needled. "Have you heard what happens if V— if the other one wins?"

Susannah looked to Stavros.

"Total devastation. The world will drown." He said it as if reciting known fact. "The Sawls call it Phena Cilm: The Wet Death." He rested his keypad on his thigh and leaned over to plug it into the translator's slim casing.

"I can certainly sympathize with that anxiety." Susannah pictured the flood that had nearly meant her own wet death.

"If Lagri wins, it's Phena Nar, death by fire. The Two Deaths."

Megan raised her eyes to the flaming dome and sang softly, "Lord said a fire not a flood next time . . ."

Stavros' jaw twitched, but he took the jacks Susannah had been holding uselessly and fitted them into the battery pack. "You mentioned sensing a general anxiety about the weather? Well, the specter of a Wet Death is in everyone's mind, because all the signs indicate that Lagri's losing ground more rapidly and for a longer period than usual. Worse thing is, some think our arrival here has something to do with it, and that's the real reason I hauled you out in the middle of the night."

"Is this like a prayer to Lagri, then?"

"More like an homage, a show of support. The Sawls don't pray, exactly. The Sisters aren't going to listen to that sort of thing."

"Ah." A vague prickle chilled Susannah's reflexive chuckle. The fiery magic of the hall and the still presence of the frail old man lent credibility to the linguist's utter conviction. Envying Megan's easy skepticism, Susannah retreated to the safety of scientific objectivity. "Has it ever happened before, one goddess winning? I mean, is there any historical basis for the legend?"

Stavros shot Megan a give-me-a-chance glance, and Susannah prepared herself for another bit of disputed information. He set his keypad aside. "We know that the five thousand or so in the Caves don't represent the total Sawl population on Fiix, but Liphar has given me estimates for the other settlements, and even allowing for a large margin of error and the various social structures that prevent inbreeding, the figures seem abnormally small for so large a world, even one whose star is showing its age." He looked to Megan, who nodded her agreement thus far. "So I asked Liphar why that was the case, and he said that every hundred and thirty generations, more or less, a near victory for one of the Sisters wipes out most of the population."

Susannah raised an eyebrow at Megan, who shrugged reluctantly. "That *is* what he said, actually. I was there."

"He also implied," Stavros continued, "that a hundred and thirty generations is usually the time it takes for the population to build up again to excess levels."

"An interesting correlation," agreed Megan.

"Excess for what?" asked Susannah, unable to fathom such a possibility on Fiix.

"That's not quite clear," admitted Stavros. "More people than they can feed, I guess. Liphar just says too many people." He tipped his head toward the ancient priest, who still sat as if unaware of their, or any, presence. "So you can believe Kav Daven will be pouring everything he's got into this performance."

He beckoned Liphar over and strapped a smaller power pack around the Sawl's narrow waist. Liphar bent to let him fasten the scanner band around his forehead, stealing a sidelong glance at Susannah to be sure that she noticed how expert he looked. Finally, Stavros powered up the translator. "Our silence will tell him we're set up."

Megan and Susannah settled themselves. Liphar moved a few paces out onto the brick floor and dropped to one knee, facing the central hearth. For long unmoving minutes, the brilliant room was a place out of time, silent but for the fire's snap and spit. Around the edges of the coals, spent dung crumbled into ash. The flames sank into blue and lavender, and the hall darkened until the dome pressed in like a midnight fog. When the old priest moved, Susannah started. It was ever so slight, just the raising of a hand, but in such mesmerizing stillness, it had the power of a shout.

The hand lifted from the knee, a bird of bones floating independent of the body. Its smoothly scarred palm gleamed in the firelight. The girl stood quickly and crossed to the big double doors. She barred them with a beam that seemed too heavy for her to lift, then padded to the hearth. Digging her hands into the peripheral ash, she raked great chalky mounds onto the brick floor. With practiced sweeps, she spread the ash in a thick even layer, forming a perfect disk. She stood back, scrutinizing her work, then retreated to the far side of the fire and nestled down beside a stack of dung cakes. Her delicate face was solemn as she fed several cakes into the sunken coals. She leaned and blew gently into the glow. The fire sputtered. A miasma of black smoke billowed toward the dome, but as the flames rekindled, Kav Daven rose.

Stavros hovered over his translator and keypad like a concert soloist awaiting his cue. Liphar adjusted the scanner harness across his brow.

The old priest's rising was liquid, a flowing of spirit from one molecule of flesh into the next, boneless and unmuscled, as if gravity disdained to drag on so insubstantial a mass. He did not acknowledge his visitors, but glided across the glossy brick to the disk of ash. Its whiteness vibrated against the ceramic orange. He circled it without noticing it, his bare feet tracing its circumference with intimate familiarity. He seemed to hardly move his arm, yet from some concealment produced a long tapering reed, which he brandished at the fire. The gesture was both an introduction and the conducting of an opening cadence, a rise and fall that took its tempo from the reaching flames.

The girl fed in more fuel, and the blaze rose higher. Kav Daven began to dance a subtle crooked minuet around the disk of ashes. He hummed tunelessly and his bony shoulder dipped toward the fire, then toward the center of the ash, then back again. The tip of the reed and the silken folds of his garments flirted with the leaping heat as if his floating body could provide the bridge to bring back fire to lifeless ash.

His hum slipped into a murmur. Syllables came and went like whispers. Stavros touched his keys, impatient, enrapt, then held back, chewing his lip. His breath came short and tight.

The old priest stilled, but for the tip of his long reed, which drew every eye as he dropped it to the disk to draw in the white ash. In the center he raked the outline of a human figure. He lifted the reed and resumed his circling. Then, in a conversational, almost wheedling tone, he began the tale, like a neighbor relating the local gossip.

Stavros bent to the translator's display. The old man illustrated his account with floating one-handed mime and a widening spiral of tiny scratchings in the ash. Eyes glued to the intermittent flow of text, Stavros waved Liphar in for a close-up.

The words came slowly. There were frequent gaps. Severed from CRI's master brain and library, the translator could only stagger along like a cripple. Still, Susannah was impressed as she and Megan crowded in to peer at the screen. Stavros' word-substitution program managed to almost mimic a vast data cruncher like CRI.

His hands touched down to work over a phrase the machine could not immediately translate. "He's using words I've never heard before. It's always the priests . . ."

"Priests often have a secret or ritual language," Megan reminded quietly.

Stavros grunted, his fingers flying, and the thought was lost as the translation picked up after a lengthy gap.

In the very earliest generations, the display read, *before the five great (destructions) (deaths) (?)* . . . The translator added its own question mark to indicate dissatisfaction with both possible meanings. All word choices but the preferred one were put in parentheses . . . *the great (large) king (parent) ruled the land (planet) (world). The king was wise and skilled in the ways of (power) (weather) (?), and the kingdom prospered without sickness (war) (destruction) (darkness) for one thousand generations.*

"King?" said Megan.

"One thousand?" exclaimed Susannah.

"Sssh!" said Stavros.

Kav Daven paused to draw three new figures in the ash, in careful detail. Those on either side were looking away from the one in the middle, who was smaller than the other two. Across the fire, the silent girl added more dung cakes.

The translator continued: *The king had three beautiful children (daughters). The three were as one to the king. The eldest was tall and white (cold) with eyes of shining ice. The youngest was dark with eyes of fire. The middle child was mild and practical (craft-skilled). The middle child was* . . . Here the translator registered a complete blank, but as Stavros watched Kav Daven dig parallel furrows in the ash, he revised the data. . . . *a farmer.*

There was a soft knock at the double doors. The girl glanced up, frowning slightly. A sharper rapping followed, and voices could be heard through the thick wooden panels. The apprentices on the back tier murmured, but Kav Daven ignored the disturbance, and no one made a move to answer the knock.

The translator pursued its stumbling interpretation: *Though the middle child was weakest, she was much loved by the king, and the king charged her stronger siblings (sisters) with her protection* . . .

The knocking at the door had ceased. Kav Daven withdrew into himself, cringing before the fire. Suddenly he sprang up, then danced aside to rail and slash his reed at the space where he had been. His shout echoed around the dome like erupting thunder. His body seemed to shed decades with every whirling step. Keeping pace with him, the girl threw dung cakes at the fire as if slinging stones. The flames roared and reached for the ceiling. Water trickling down the smoke hole lent a rhythmic hiss of annihilation. The translator stuttered as the girl took up a thin staccato chant that underscored the priest's wailing with tones of imminent threat. Liphar, still bearing the scanner, chanted with her under his breath.

Stavros' fingers hovered, touched down, hovered again. Lost to the rhythm of the chanting, his body moved to Kav Daven's movement. His lips tried to form the words as the old priest sang them.

And then it happened, read the display, *that the war (darkness) arrived (neared) and the king grew old (ripe) (dark). Not the healers or the priests could save (heal) him/her.* The translator showed a sudden confusion about gender. *The king divided the land among his three children, and bade the two stronger siblings to protect the weaker. But when the king died (darkened), the world fell into strife. The eldest child and the youngest child were blinded by the warring (darkness) and disobeyed (forgot) the king's charge to them. They grew dissatisfied (bored) and battled (wrestled) (gamed) . . .*

Stavros shot a sudden finger toward the display. "That's 'arrah' there, the verb form. You see the ambiguity?"

. . . for control of the whole kingdom (world). Their battleground (arena) (gaming board) was the lands of the middle child. War (darkness) settled over the world. The war (game) had begun.

Kav Daven halted and for the first time looked straight at his audience. Susannah ground her fingernails against the hard brick to steady her surprise. The old priest's pupils were milky white.

"He's blind!" breathed Megan.

The girl's chant rose like an animal howl, then ceased midnote. The priest's opaque eyes commanded even the taking of a breath. Behind him, the fire wheezed and sighed. Stavros raised his head from the display, eager for the next line. The priest's whole body swiveled until he faced Stavros directly. Stavros started, then met the old man's stare, as if there was no other choice. Kav Daven lowered his reed and after a frozen pause, he offered a dazzling smile that crinkled his sightless eyes with elfin humor and showed a mouth full of strong yellow teeth.

Then brief as a bird shadow, the smile was gone. His years settled over him again. He turned away and shuffled across the brick, scuffing a trail through his pictures so carefully drawn in the ash. His right leg dragged a little behind. The girl went to his side and helped him to sit.

Megan's spent sigh was echoed by the Sawls on the upper tiers. Liphar remained kneeling on the brick, his shoulders slumped. He gazed at the old priest as if searching out his future in the old man's image. Even the fire seemed to recognize a culmination, and sank down exhausted. The inferno dimmed. The hall became a round room painted with flame. Stavros did not move.

"Why doesn't she fight back, the middle one?" Megan asked reasonably.

Susannah smiled and shook her head, moved to silence by the performer's magic and the shock of his sudden vanishing smile.

Liphar stirred and came over to kneel at Stavros' side. "Ibi?" he whispered. "*Tel khem,* Ibi!"

Stavros turned to him, his jaw slack. "I sure hope so." With mechanical efficiency, he relieved Liphar of his headband, saved the recording and the preliminary translation, then pulled all the plugs. His posture was pensive and puzzled.

"It isn't exactly a creation myth, is it?" Megan began. "But this is interesting: all over the explored universe, it's always the *youngest* child who gets ganged up on in the legends. Significant?"

"Why isn't it a creation myth?" asked Susannah.

"There's nothing about creation in it."

"You mean, no void or firmaments?"

"No creator."

"What about the king?"

"Creators don't usually grow old and die," Meg reminded her.

Stavros made a noise of distracted protest, then seemed surprised when both women turned to him expectantly. "What? Oh . . . well, you saw that the translator's unclear on that point. About what happened to the king. If it was a king." His reply was more than usually disjointed, though he was struggling hard to appear collected. "He grew old *or* ripe *or* dark. I think we can exclude 'ripe' as a possibility for now." He unbuckled the power pack from Liphar's back and handed it to him to put away in its case.

"Perhaps he simply left," Megan proposed. "Not an unfamiliar variation, the god who creates a world, then splits."

"A sorry excuse for a god," Susannah murmured.

"But he was 'skilled in the ways of power' . . . or 'weather,' " mused Stavros, regaining his focus. "You recognize the warring siblings, of course."

"Fire-eyed Lagri," said Susannah.

"And she of the lavender ice." He rolled the words in his mouth like a lyric.

"The middle child must be your unnamed multitude, then." Megan sighed. "Truthfully, I'd hoped for more. It's like a piece of mythical reporting, really, without much moral comment."

"Oh, I think the part about the sisters betraying the father's charge implies moral censure," said Susannah.

"Betrayed or *forgot,*" reminded Stavros.

Susannah frowned. "How could you forget such a thing?"

"There is an interesting sense of the original trouble coming from the outside," noted Megan. "Even before the king died, war or darkness fell on the land—am I remembering it right?"

"Let me refine the translation." Stavros stroked the little box musingly. "There must be a frieze somewhere to match it. That'll help answer some questions. Meg, about this idea of a separate ritual language . . . I'm beginning to think there is a kind of language within a language here—" He was interrupted by the return of the knocker at the doors. This time, the appeal was more insistent. The apprentice priests chatting on the back tier fell silent. The girl left Kav Daven's side and whispered across the brick to draw back the heavy beam. The doors flew open.

Kav Ashimmel waited in the archway, with a retinue of priests behind her. An unfamiliar gray-white light crept past the threshold to etch Ashimmel with a pallid halo that left her face in shadow. Liphar gasped, then sprang to his feet and dashed past Ashimmel and the priests crowding the doorway to stand out in the middle of the Frieze Hall, staring straight up. The same pale light caressed his face, which slowly broke into a joyful grin.

Stavros rose, setting aside his keypad. "My god. Oh, my god. He did it."

"What? What is it?" asked Susannah.

Shouts and singing rang in the farther corridors. The other watchers on the tiers gathered themselves and their children and surged down and across the floor, sweeping the Terrans along with them. They joined Liphar in the middle of the patterned floor, where the blue-and-green–tile circles were waking to new life. Everyone looked up.

The hovering darkness above the chandeliers had transformed into a realm of light.

"What is it?" Susannah asked again. "Where's it coming from?"

Stavros pointed. "From the clerestory, below the vaulting."

"No, I mean . . ." Still she could not comprehend.

"It's the dawn."

Liphar dropped his eyes from the new light to send an awe-filled stare through the flame-carved archway, past the silent Ashimmel, whose message was demonstrating itself, past the astonished little girl, over the embers lowering on the brick and straight into the heart of an old man's blind smile.

"It's dawn," Stavros repeated. "And the sky is clear. That's *sun* light!"

Beside them, Liphar exulted softly. *"Embriha Lagri!"*

BOOK THREE

EXODUS

"Thou, Nature, art my goddess . . ."
—*King Lear*, Act I, sc. ii

25

THE JUBILANT SAWLS gathered up Kav Ashimmel and her retinue and whisked them off down the Frieze Hall in a burst of cheers and laughter. Liphar danced around the astonished Terrans like an excited pup. He snatched at Stavros as the linguist spun back to grab the equipment waiting in the Story Hall, hard white against the fiery brick.

"No, no! Later, that. Come now, Ibi! Come all you!" He turned and sped after the others. The emptied Frieze Hall echoed with the rumble of distant celebration. Stavros seemed dazed. He gave his cases a bewildered glance and bolted after Liphar.

Megan gazed silently upward, into the unexpected light.

Susannah touched her elbow. "We could see it better from outside."

They hurried down the long hall past the rows of glowering friezes. Susannah honored Megan's slower pace, but the urge to be racing with the others was strong. She heard singing now, and the marble floor vibrated like a drumskin with the passage of thousands through the tunnels below.

"The dawn! I can't believe it!" She wished for Megan to hurry, to be younger, lighter.

"It had to come sometime."

"Yes, yes. If we'd kept an eye on the clock, it wouldn't have been such a surprise." But a demon in Susannah's brain was considering the possibility that they had just witnessed a true feat of priestly weather magic. *Is logic really this fragile?*

"Coincidence," she muttered aloud.

"No way." Megan was not supposed to have heard. "That old priest was out checking the signs. He knew dawn was coming, and the signs told him the weather was going to break. Why else would he decide to start his per-formance in the middle of the night?"

"Probably wasn't the middle of the night for him."

"I'm telling you, he arranged the whole thing."

The Sisters glared down at them from a frieze that rose the full height of the hall. Stavros and Liphar were distant shadows fliting in and out of dim pools of light, flying toward the ramp head. Susannah's stride lengthened unconsciously.

"A setup. What a nicely rational explanation. Why didn't I think of that?" She found herself dancing in place, to slow her pace. "But why would he need to do that?"

Megan chuckled, as if Susannah's innocence were the quaintest thing imaginable. "To convince *us,* for one thing! Impress the Wokind with a show of power. And do us a favor at the same time. If Ashimmel's been accusing us of being pawns of Valla Ired, Kav Daven can now claim to have brought us around. Liphar will be spreading this tale for many days to come, about how Kav Daven and the Wokind stood at the right hand of Lagri while she brought back the sun."

"But according to you, the Sawls don't really believe their myths."

"Well, they do and they don't. I exaggerate for emphasis."

"I'm sure they believe some of it. When Liphar and I were caught out in the storm, he wasn't invoking his gods for *my* benefit."

Megan scoffed. "Liphar's training to be a priest—what do you expect?" Then she slowed, considering. "Besides, how do you know he wasn't?"

Faint music and cheering floated up the ramp from the Market Hall. Susannah fidgeted. Often she pictured Megan as Sisyphus' rock. "Sometimes you just have to trust your instincts."

"Of course, there's some belief. The priests would have no power if there were no belief." Megan plodded along at the measured pace of her words. "Despite the apparent lack of a religious dogma, this society is structured around a religion: the weather. But what is the exact nature of that belief? Are the goddesses incarnate, as Stavros claims, or not? Do the priests have a hotline to them? Remember, the priesthood is effectively the police force in many primitive societies, using superstition to keep the people in line."

"But, here, the Guild Council holds the civil authority, not the priests."

"Well, then, a dual authority," amended Megan. "Church and State. Hearts and Minds, or in this case, Hearts and Bellies."

Ahead, Liphar suddenly reappeared, flickering through shafts of brilliance dropping from the clerestory. Susannah resisted the urge to grab Megan and run. "Weng claims Sawl society is structured like a ship's crew, with every Sawl doing his or her job in support of the whole. But she's also having trouble deciding who the captain is."

"Weng's viewpoint on that subject is hardly objective."

"It's as objective as any of ours."

Megan sniffed. "All I'm saying is that the levels of belief are more complex than Stavros would have it, with all his mystic cant about gods walking the earth. The Sawls are a pragmatic people."

And we keep laying down these reckless generalizations, Susannah mused uneasily. Liphar had stopped to wait for them in the shaft of light. On the walls, jeweled eyes glimmered like morning stars. She tensed against the chill that tickled the back of her neck. "I think Stavros also exaggerates, to fuel his argument, just like you."

"Not just like me," Megan insisted. "I ponder. Stavros acts. I question. Stavros accepts."

Susannah let the tired subject of Stavros' methods pass. "But about Kav Daven, though. If this was planned, his timing was impeccable."

Megan's shrug was confident. "That's why he's a successful priest."

They caught up with Liphar in the light of the clerestory. Stavros was nowhere in sight. The young Sawl beckoned them eagerly toward the ramp head, toward the shouts and singing below. Susannah felt as if the very air was in motion, drawing them down into the teeming mass of rejoicing Sawls.

"Come, you!" Liphar called, and danced away down the ramp.

But at the bottom, the women hesitated. The crowd flowed like a living river, fast and strong, across the market plaza. Many had come straight from their guild halls, with the clay drying on their hands or the dye still fresh on their leather aprons. Others wore whatever had come to hand when the joyous alarms woke them from a sound sleep. Children chased each other squealing through the throng. The youngest rode wide-eyed on their elders' shoulders. Grandmothers and grandfathers perched in the front of little two-carts, with fat canvas sacks jostling in the box behind them. The shaggy hakra hauled their loads with a jauntier step than usual, bright eyes eager, noses working.

"Exodus!" Susannah murmured.

Liphar waved, his guide duty done, and bounded off into the crowd. Megan was breathing hard. Like a swimmer, Susannah waited for the proper moment to plunge in. Once into that current of humanity, it would drag her irresistibly along. But there was no sign of hostility toward the Terrans now. Men and women called to them, laughing, gesturing them onward. Susannah took a step, and the current swept around her as gently and firmly as an arm laid about her waist. She grabbed Megan's hand to pull her along. They were carried around the wide plaza in a spiral. The new light of dawn filtered like dust down the huge ventilation shaft to touch the curls of two small children splashing in the stone water trough. The throng moved on toward the bright signs and lanterns of the Market Hall.

In the Market Hall, the shops stood empty. Both proprietors and custom- ers had gone ahead with the first wave. The signboards and painted banners swayed as if in a breeze, presiding over a wake of scattered gaming pieces, handcarts heaped with merchandise, deserted toys, and the occasional lonely broom parked hurriedly beside its pile of litter.

Susannah knew from the reproof in Megan's eye that she was grinning like a fool. Her attempts to explain her sudden giddiness were drowned out by boisterous singing all around them. Two songs were begun at once, and the singers faltered in laughter and began again, each choosing to sing what the others had started first. The singing was throaty and disorganizedly cheerful, and at times even it was lost under the cheering and chatter and rattle of cart- wheels as the throng swept along. Small bands of reed-and-pipers marched among the singers, their sweet shrillings offering a more disciplined music.

At an intersection, Susannah spotted three of the midwives, hurrying down from the Physicians Hall with their apprentices. The Head Midwife, Xifa, still wore her stained linen smock with its many pockets, baggy from use. The hardworking women's drawn faces were glazed with relief, as if the coming of the sun and the change of mood could effect some of the cures that they had been unable to. Behind them strode the Master Healer, who returned Susannah's victory salute with a wan smile and a wave.

"There's Ghirra," Susannah bellowed into Megan's ear, pointing him out as the crowd carried them by.

"Ah, yes." Megan craned her head with interest. "You don't forget a face like that."

Susannah laughed. "Yes. A lovely man, our Master Healer." She nudged Megan playfully. "Unattached, as far as I can tell."

"I remembering noticing how tall he was . . . is. For a Sawl, I mean."

"Like Aguidran, the Master Ranger. Ghirra's her twin brother." Susannah sidestepped a teenager pulling a cart laden with bulging sacks. "They're from the northeast, another settlement called Ogo Dul."

"Another settlement? Time to see some of those, yes? For comparison."

Susannah nodded. "They came here on a trading trip when they were babies and lost their parents in a mudslide. One of the herdsmen raised them."

"They've done all right for themselves here," observed Megan. "Both Masters of their guilds."

"Ghirra is a gifted healer."

Megan forbore from reminding her that, not so long ago, she'd argued strongly to keep him from his patient. "And Aguidran is a powerhouse. Quite a pair."

They overtook a lumbering high-wheeled wagon. It was stained berry-red, with clusters of white streamers tied to its corner posts. Megan peered through its slats as they passed. Inside, a leggy wooden device wound with leather strapping sat on top of another load of canvas sacks.

"Plow?" She caught at Susannah's sleeve and shouted over the din. "Plow!"

Susannah shrugged an inquiry. The noise swelled as the tunnel narrowed.

"I just realized . . ." Megan yelled.

Grinning, Susannah burlesqued deafness. The Sawls' joy was too contagious to dampen with endless serious discussion. She thrilled to the roar of a thousand voices echoing along the rock, to the pressure of moving bodies all around her. The reed-and-pipes urged her to hurry. She took a little skip, childlike, laughing.

Megan caught up to shout into her ear. "Don't you feel you should be carrying a rake or something?" She pointed at the ranks of poles sticking up from the crowd like a forest of porcupine quills. "That's what I just noticed."

"You're right. How odd!"

Everyone, no matter what age or guild affiliation, carried some sort of digging tool. Susannah saw rakes and harrows of all shapes and sizes, broad-bladed shovels and fat wooden picks, lashed to their handles with heavy oiled thongs. She saw even an occasional pitted iron hoe, carried reverently aloft like a relic.

"Now you can see how crowded the Caves would feel if they all worked on the same shift," she laughed.

"You wait," Megan pursued. "I'll bet this is no act of spontaneous celebration. I mean, when was the last time you took a plow to a party?"

Suddenly Susannah envied Stavros. Why shouldn't she lose herself impulsively in the crowd, as he had done? Why hold oneself immune from such contagious joy? At a moment like this, would science be any better served if she did? She let the human current carry her forward a little faster, turning to look at Megan, absorbed in her ponderings of priests and plows. The throng flowed around her like water around a rock. As she glanced up to see herself being left behind, Susannah waved guiltily but did not fight to slow her forward drift. Megan waved back and settled in to move along at her own pace.

Alone among the Sawls, Susannah felt lighter, relieved of sharing the burden of Megan's relentless sobriety. She fell in step with a young musician who shot her a friendly glance over her pipes. Her brightly colored guild tabard was slightly askew, donned in haste and never adjusted. The narrowing of the corridor compressed the crowd so that Susannah walked shoulder to shoulder with her. The hoarse singing coalesced into a more unified voice and a single song chant surfaced through the random cheering. Susannah swung her arms to the rhythm as the chant was repeated through verse after verse. Though she could not pick out the words, the melody soon became familiar. She began to hum along, to the piper's delight. She leaned toward Susannah and piped all the louder. Susannah reveled in it, for a moment, not caring where she was going or why.

The human river slowed to stream thickly down a wide spiral ramp. From joining passages, tributary flows swelled the river further. With a final curl, the ramp opened into the lowest level of caves still in use. The animal smells were damp and rich, and the lighting dim. The strong downdraft made the lamps flare and gutter in their niches. The main tunnel was low and wide, with barrel-vaulted corridors leading off to either side. The dairy herds bellowed from their stable caverns and the corridors bustled as the herdsmen led out huge, broad-shouldered beasts that strained against their halters, nostrils flared to the changed air.

Susannah started, pulling aside out of the throng. A new Fiixian creature! But no, these were the hjalk, the heavy draft animals. During his tour of the stable level, Liphar had shown no fondness for the hjalk, or for the somewhat less gigantic dairy beasts, the hekkers. He'd been disinclined to let Susannah observe either very closely. At the time, she'd assumed the hjalk to be over-sized members of the dairy herd. Now, in the open tunnel, they loomed far larger than when she'd glimpsed them stamping and steaming in their chill dark stalls. Each was several hands taller than the average hekker and much more muscular. Their bulky withers were level with their herdsmen's heads. Their coats were a mass of short tight curls that lengthened into a thick mane of golden ringlets around the neck.

Like a cross between a goat and a camel, thought Susannah. And maybe an elephant. But she'd used the goat-camel cross before, to describe the little hakra, and it could apply to the dairy beasts as well. In fact, except for the differences in size and musculature, the similarities between the three were remarkable: the same low rounded rump, the same high-boned shoulders, the same fleshy, horn-bottomed camel feet.

She studied the golden giants as the crowd jostled around her. A loaded two-cart moved into her line of sight. A little cart hakra stood side by side with a towering hjalk.

Hakra, hekker, hjalk . . . even the names sounded alike. More coincidence? The same basic morphology overlaid with evolved adaptations for specific function. But even assuming a directed breeding program, it would take many centuries to produce such a line. Was Sawl civilization old enough—far older than she'd assumed?

Susannah shook her head. *If I didn't know where I was, I'd congratulate these folks on some very efficient genetic engineering!*

She resolved to have a long chat with the herdsmen about their breeding practices, which she had clearly underestimated. More of that Terran arro-gance. But any chatting would have to wait until the Sawls got this celebrat-ing out of their systems. Meanwhile, she could check with Stavros about the apparent similarity of the names.

She backed away as an overexcited hjalk swerved its rump toward her. The herdsman at the beast's head laughed at her fright. He gestured to several of his apprentices, who threw down armloads of leather harness to slap the huge animal's behind or bounce their slight bodies against its giant shoulders. Finally, the harness was draped across its back and several squealing children were tossed up to dig their hands and feet into its golden curls. The hjalk settled down the moment it felt their weight, and rolled itself forward like a slow furry wave.

The herdsman let it go off on its own and, still laughing, dusted his hands on his tunic. His Food Guild insignia was faded behind layers of dander and golden hjalk hair. He shot a teasing grin at Susannah and dove into the nearest stable corridor to bring out another eager beast.

Susannah rejoined the throng. As they passed the dairy caverns, the hekkers lowed their complaints at being left behind. Squawkings and crowings echoed out of the poultry warrens. At last the cave mouth registered as a faint glow far ahead.

The inflowing draft was chilly but overlaid with a promise of warmth. Susannah gratefully inhaled the fresh and hopeful scent of wet earth. The rough walls brightened as the tunnel dipped toward the cave mouth. The pace slowed, and the laughter and singing stilled to a more businesslike excitement. Rake handles and cartwheels clanked against stone. An inexperienced hakra balked at the shallow steps, then compounded his offense by trying to descend them two at a time, his cart rattling behind him. Sawls scattered to either side until he finally halted at the bottom, looking confused and shamed.

This lowest cave mouth had a large open terrace and a deep overhang where it was still cool and in shadow. Guildsmen milled about, unhitching carts. The lighter ones were being carried down the long outer stairs by hand. The heavier loads were parked along the edge to be lowered by winch. The animals were set loose to negotiate the damp and precarious steps on their own. The triangular seal of the Engineers Guild was everywhere in evidence as they manned the winch ropes and loaded the pallets. Crowds filled the inner cavern and massed along the wide ledge outside the overhang. Brown-tunicked rangers directed traffic and kept the crowd moving down the stairs three abreast. A deep musical bellowing resounded from somewhere out on the cliffs.

After her experience in the storm, Susannah had learned to be wary of her reckless impulse toward open space. She sidelined herself from the throng to approach the light and air more cautiously, noting that the Sawls did not pause to exclaim over the ringing turquoise clarity of the sky or the salmon glow of the sun creeping over the distant mountains. They watched their footing on the slippery stairs, and if some bothered to look at the sky, it was in brief glances of assessment and speculation.

Susannah saw McPherson standing with Aguidran, and snaked between the stalled carts and bleating animals to join them. The Master Ranger was a giant by Sawl standards, taller than her twin Ghirra—perhaps because she never stooped—taller by two hands than Susannah, and rangy and brown as a weathered tree. Her thin body was cased in well-worked leathers cut more closely than the usual fashion in the Caves. She nodded a sober greeting as Susannah came smiling toward them, then returned to watching the procession move down the steps as if her will alone could prevent a dangerous stumble.

McPherson was buckling on a huge field pack. A fresh coil of Clausen's kevlar rope swung at her waist. Without comment, Susannah tightened the rear lacings and helped to adjust the load. Then she stood aside to watch the impossibly slow dawn reveal a devastated plain, all gullies and canyons choked with rock and yellow mud as far as her eyes could see. The tall needle shape of the Red Pawn rose into the greenish sky against the half-moon of sun. It echoed the blunter shape of the Terran vehicle stalled on the plain below. The Lander waited bravely at its incongruous tilt, reflecting a glimmer of pink dawn from its scoured nose.

"What a mess!" Susannah's giddiness deflated rapidly. "Did we get our com back?"

"Nah. I knew it wasn't just the storm. Looks like the wind got the omni. If we're lucky, we'll still have the high gain for the uplink—Stav's in trying to raise CRI on the main line now. But I'm pretty sure it's a no-go." Her hand knifed the air in a neat diagonal pointed toward the Lander, so firmly settled in the mud. "The array housing in the nose was sheared right off. The big dish probably wound up in the next county."

Susannah had stopped wearing her dead fone a week ago. She watched McPherson zip up the front of her therm-suit. The suit was no longer remotely white, after two weeks of venturing out into the storm. "You're going out again?"

McPherson's cherub face hardened as she prepared to defend yet another hopeless foray into the treacherous sodden hills. "First decent search weather we've had."

Susannah tried not to sound disapproving. "Let's hope it stays that way."

"Aguidran's coming with me."

"Ah, good." Susannah backed against the rock wall to make room for a giant hjalk as it lumbered past. She trailed a hand through the beast's golden curls and found them surprisingly soft. She also felt what was not so visible: beneath the thick ringlets, the animal was bone-thin. Food rationing must extend to the herds as well, she realized. "So you and Aguidran have finally come to terms?"

The pilot drew her shoulders together in a hopeful shrug. "Yeah. It'll be just the two of us out there, since they can't spare any more hands from the planting. But that's okay—we'll move faster that way."

"Planting?" Susannah stared at the devastation of mud below.

McPherson gestured at the crowd armed with its tools and the carts loaded with bulging sacks. "Whadda you think this is all about?"

"Well, I thought . . . a coming-of-dawn celebration? No? Wow. They don't waste any time, do they?"

"Smart," nodded McPherson.

At the far end of the ledge, an engineer apprentice swung out on a set of winch ropes, using his weight as an anchor while his guildsmen positioned a load. The taut ropes hummed, dark against the brightening sky.

"How long will you be out?" asked Susannah.

"Long as it takes," McPherson drawled with a hint of her old mischief. She swaggered a step or two. "No more than two Earth-weeks, actually, what Aguidran calls ten throws. That's all we got supplies for, and she tells me we can't live off the land."

"Not unless you learn to eat mud." Susannah heard a new respect when McPherson spoke of the Master Ranger. Perhaps the pilot had found herself a role model. "That ground will need a week of drying out before anything will grow properly."

"It's not that. She says anything growing out there is poisonous."

"Really?" Susannah wanted to hear more, but decided to ask Ghirra instead. His answers were willing and precise, even if they didn't always seem to make scientific sense. Like planting, for instance. Planting *now*?

The winch ropes sang. A shadow crossed her face, falling from above to cast its elongated plow shape on the sunlit wall behind her. The tossing of good seed into a plain of mud struck Susannah as movingly optimistic. Devastation and fertility, death and birth, loss and renewal: the ancient dichotomies. She pictured the wrecked Sled lying bright and broken on some muddy rockslide with new green shoots poking up around it, and regarded McPherson more gently. "I hope you're prepared for what you might find out there."

McPherson set her jaw again. "You think I'm a baby, don't you?"

"What? No, I . . ."

"I gotta know I did my best. If they're dead, they're dead. But we need that Sled."

"Even what might be left of it?"

"Even that."

Susannah shuffled a booted foot against the rock. The subject was closed. They let a detailed attention to the winch operations cover the silence, so full of their private thoughts.

Then McPherson focused on the crowds still streaming out of the shadowed overhang. "Shit, here comes the Commander. Gotta get outa here or she'll want me to climb right up into the nose and fix the damn antenna with my bare hands and her silver chopsticks."

"If you did, CRI's scanners could find the Sled in no time." But Susannah understood that this was not the real issue.

"Let Stav do it! He can scavenge parts as good as I can." McPherson was already moving away. "Besides, if they're mobile, they'd be back by now, so even if CRI did find 'em, somebody'd have to go out there on foot to bring 'em in."

"But you don't even know which way they went."

"I know where we haven't looked yet!" McPherson touched the fone clipped to her pocket. "I'm hooked in, 'case we do get back on-line. So, um . . . you call me, eh?" She adjusted her pack again and nudged the Master Ranger's arm. Aguidran took a last quick look around, then led the way up the stairs toward the top of the cliff.

"Rhe khem," Susannah called after them. Interesting that the phrase should so readily leap to mind. She hadn't for a second considered going with them, yet absurdly, she felt left behind. It would take more than the two of them to bring the bodies back. And what if, in all unlikelihood, a doctor was needed?

She shivered. The air was still cool. She contemplated going back into the Caves to find Stavros, but no translation query was worth being cooped up inside again, not yet. Too much like being at home. How sad that weather was proving to be the Enemy here as well. She leaned against the slowly warming rock, basking while the touch of Fiix's sun was still gentle. She would need dark-lenses when the sun rose to its full height later in the week.

"That is," she murmured, "If the weather holds. . . ."

Stavros raced along an inner corridor, slowing only in the unlit newer sections of tunnel where the floor was still rough. He smashed his bare feet against invisible ridges of rock, but didn't think to turn back for a lantern or shoes. The nearest light station was way back in the main corridor. He continued his plunge into darkness with hands outstretched.

Liphar's exultant cry echoed in his brain. *Embriha Lagri!*

"Even if the dish is gone," he muttered into the empty dark, "the omni might still be working. No power maybe, but at least we could get the com link back up."

Embriha Lagri!

When the tunnel narrowed, he guided himself with fingers to the wall. The blackness was suffocating, arousing phantom dreams of night drowning, or being caught outside the gates. A worm of panic stirred in his gut. But this was old reflex, a habit he refused to indulge any longer. He knew he was safe. He was in the Caves.

Then why was he in such an immortal hurry?

Embriha Lagri!

The phrase would not leave him alone. Stavros shoved it aside until there was time to deal with its full implications.

His fingers found an end to the rough wall, and beyond, the narrow entry to the Black Hole. He ducked instinctively as he turned in. The darkness ahead took on a reddish cast. Someone, Weng or McPherson, had left the fire burning when abruptly called out to the dawn. The coals were ruby, nearly spent. He crossed to the fire pit and placed several dung cakes in a careful pyramid around the brightest coals, blew gently and waited, blew again, squinting impatiently into the shadows. As the embers flared, he was rewarded with a glimmer of ceramic and glass on the edge of the rear sleeping platform.

The lamp was one of the largest sizes the potters made. Stavros found flint and tinder in a recess below the handle. He struck a spark into the tinder and lit the wick, a recently learned local skill that gave him uncommon satisfaction, then carried the lamp to the nest of crates where he'd set up a com link, plus keypad and displays, all useless since the storm began. It was Danforth's equipment, but Stavros was sure the planetologist was in no condition to care. He rested the lamp on a crate, plugged the emergency battery to the link, and perched on a smaller crate as he powered up the receiver.

When the display glowed, he spoke CRI's call code and held his breath.

Nothing. The ready sign glared back at him unchanged. He should have checked the relays on the way in.

He tried again, on the keypad this time. But his fingers trembled.

Still no reply.

He put the call on repeater and sat back to wait, while he pondered what to do with the anticlimax that was seeping through him like a soporific.

"Okay, the main antenna's out," he explained to the darkness around him. "And the omni's down as well. If the parts are still there, should be easy enough to fix."

The oil lamp flickered. He jerked as if out of sleep. He'd been staring at the display, mesmerized by its refusal to respond. Meanwhile, Liphar's voice still whispered its ecstatic refrain.

Embriha Lagri!

Stavros shook himself and shut down the link. CRI would pick up the homing beacon and know that someone was still alive down here. This would have to do until he got the antennas up and running again. As he reached for the lamp, his arm dislodged a stack of paper from the top of the crate. Damp scraps fluttered in the lamplight. Stavros stooped and came up with more of Danforth's handwritten notes. "Venus model run outputs nominal Venus data," he read, followed by a list headed "Possible Tinkering." Venus, again. Why was Danforth so concerned with Venus all the way out here on Fiix? Stavros held the sheet up to the lamp to decipher a scribble in a bottom corner. Danforth's frustration snarled at him from the page.

"Explore possibility of small-scale dynamic instability mode—probe data resolution too low?" And: "more detailed measurements!!" Finally, more purposefully: "CRI: new wind data. Increase resolution of model to check for possible instability mode."

Stavros neatened the papers and replaced them on top of the crate. His hand lingered in a kind of benediction. He knew now that he missed the energy Danforth had brought to their group, and to his own thinking. It should have been just Clausen. He turned away from the silent com link, taking the lamp to light his way.

He hurried along the outer corridor, running up a mental inventory of materials he'd need to repair the antennas. When he reached a lighted tunnel crossing, he blew out the lamp and left it at the light station, a long stone shelf with a row of similar, waiting lamps. The intersection, normally a jam of two-carts and pedestrians, stretched wide and empty. The echoes of his footsteps returned along the vaulting, then died away into an unprecedented silence. Not a whisper of sound but his own.

The Caves were deserted, and he was alone in them.

*   *   *

"Susannah!"

She started guiltily. She'd been daydreaming in the sun.

But here was Megan, waving from beside a two-cart bumping down the inner stairs. Weng followed at her usual stately pace, her white ship's uniform bright against the shadowed walls. A man from the Paper Guild paused ahead of them to take a child up on his back. Megan climbed around them, automatically offering her arm to Weng. The old spacer put out her hand so as not to refuse the kindness but negotiated the obstacle on her own, while her eyes sought out the tilted cone shape of the Lander with the concentration of the single-minded.

Susannah smiled. How very Weng.

"Hedonist!" Megan joined Susannah in the weak sunlight. Raising a hand to shade her brow, she squinted over the tortured plain. "Mud soup! How are they going to plant anything in that?"

"I'm adopting a wait-and-see attitude. By the way, the com is still down."

"So Weng said. She's been checking the caveside relays. What's that booming noise?"

Susannah had forgotten the basso howl from the top of the cliffs. "Horns. Big wooden horns that the priests are blowing. You can see them if you look up right from the edge."

Megan glanced uncertainly over the precipice. "Later."

Susannah nodded to Weng. "Good morning, Commander."

Weng suspended her long-distance inspection of the Lander long enough to be civil. "Ah, Dr. James," she replied, as if Susannah were a pleasant intrusion on deeper, more important thoughts. Megan's eyes were still slitted, but Weng did not seem at all bothered by the pale glare. "I suppose one must indeed call it morning, for that is the sun rising, even though one has just recently finished lunch."

"Lunch?" Susannah looked to Megan. "Were we that long in the Story Hall?"

"Did I see our young pilot with you just now?" Weng asked.

"Um-hum. Want me to go after her?"

Weng folded her hands at her waist, her eyes straying back toward the metal cone glinting on the plain. "No, I think not. Off into the hills again, is she?"

Susannah nodded briskly.

"No need to look guilty, Dr. James. A pilot needs her vehicle, and so do we."

Susannah's nod was gentler. This pilot needed her man.

"Better she be out there finding it," Weng concluded, "than pining around here underfoot. I can make a preliminary damage assessment on my own."

Megan moved away from the edge as a loaded winch pallet swung too close for her comfort. "I hope she's selective about what she brings back."

Weng toyed with the adjustment of her braid-trimmed cuff. "You surprise me, Dr. Levy. Mr. Clausen is such a cultured gentleman. I'd have thought you would find each other quite congenial." Only the slightest deepening of the soft lines around the officer's chin betrayed her.

Susannah giggled. *Weng, you old fox!*

Megan grinned outright. "Yep. Just my type. And no threat to your authority, either, right?"

"My authority was not endangered, Dr. Levy. Besides, any crew is a threat to a captain's authority if they're worth their salt."

"Very noble and archaic," Megan countered, "but Clausen was hardly your ordinary crewman."

"But, like Dr. Danforth, he was crucial to our mission."

Susannah wondered if the turn of the Commander's tone was to remind Megan that she too was officially "crew." Hopefully, Weng would not get started on the subject of The Mission. Music and The Mission were the Commander's own sister-deities, and the latter particularly encouraged her to indulge in a knee-jerk rhetoric that Susannah found embarrassing in an otherwise admirable figure.

"We are one machine," Weng continued, "not self-sufficient parts. If we have lost some of our parts, we cannot go home a success."

"I know, I know. Damn it, Weng, you brought it up." Megan sulked, having been encouraged to vent her loathing of Clausen, then taken to task for it.

Susannah suspected that Weng's real sore point had been the questioning of her hold on the captaincy. She pulled herself up from her slouch. "You're headed down to the Lander, Commander?"

"I was, indeed." Weng accepted the diversion gracefully. She could slide easily from leadership to companionship, as her expression of both was equally formal. The Commander's fabled calm was not true relaxation but a collected and controlled vigilance. The square of her shoulders directed their gaze over the ledge. "The sun may be shining again, but we are in far from an optimum situation. There is considerable question about the possibility of getting ourselves aloft again."

"We'll come along, then." Megan made a halfhearted attempt to make up for her diplomatic blunder. "The Sawls'll put us to work in the mud otherwise."

Weng nodded graciously.

The Old Lady. Susannah was proud of her. In the sunlight, the Commander looked more nearly her true age, information privileged only to the ship's computer and, of course, the ship's doctor. *Yes, Weng, I know. But I'm not telling.* Besides, she had skin like fine Chinese silk. Untouched by worldly weather for most of her years.

How odd that she had never until now seen Weng in natural light, except, of course, starlight, that faint supernatural light that bathed the Orbiter's bridge during night watch, when all but the running lights were down. Susannah could not keep her eyes from drifting upward. It seemed so long ago. *I wonder how they all are up there?*

"Dr. James?"

"Coming, Commander."

He'd never been alone in the Caves before.

The realization stopped Stavros short while he considered the ramifications. Free run. He could go where he liked. Either the Sawls had forgotten about him in the heat of their celebrating, or they had decided to trust him at last.

Because I was there . . . ?

Embriha Lagri!

Stalled in the deserted intersection, Stavros lost his battle with the notion that had been yammering at him, demanding his attention.

He did it. Kav Daven changed the weather.

No, that wasn't quite right.

His dance changed the weather . . . by lending power to Lagri.

Impossible, of course. But hadn't he seen it with his own eyes?

No. Coincidence.

But was it? His knees wobbled. He tottered over to the stone bench at the light station and dropped onto it, his head in his hands.

It had been easy, up until now, to play at his game of belief. He was well-practiced, from a solitary youth filled with holos and fantasy games. Later, it proved a useful tool in his work, a technique for which he'd developed the philosophical defense he used so successfully to goad more orthodox colleagues like Megan Levy. It could be vertiginous there, along the edges of belief. It encouraged the unstable behavior that tripped him up and marred his scholarly reputation. The empathetic gift that made him a superior linguist left him vulnerable to the belief systems of his study subjects. But he'd learned ways of dealing with that. He played games of logic and semiotics with their symbolisms while pretending to accept, and coexisted easily with the supernatural because he let it remain ever unrealized in his mind. He preached the leap of faith, and always turned back at that very last step. He'd never truly gone over the edge.

But Kav Daven's dance and the clear dawn that followed asked for more than abstract belief. More than belief put on like a suit of local clothing.

Actual belief?

His head sank deeper into his hands. What exactly had he seen? An old priest did a dance and the sun came out. Why even consider cause and effect?

A soft moan escaped him as Kav Daven's brilliant blind smile arose unbidden in his mind's eye. Stavros had not really understood the potential of true belief until now. He had not known that it could wrap itself around your soul and take you unwilling prisoner.

There was nothing abstract about the Sawls' belief. To believe with them, he must accept the existence of the sister-goddesses, not as spirits, not as disembodied energies, not even as icons of an intellectual faith, the sort that rational societies tended to evolve. Nor were they mere mortal representations of a deity, like a prophet or a pharaoh.

He must accept them as actual beings of incomprehensible power.

Lagri and Valla Ired. Goddesses incarnate.

How ironic that his mind balked so firmly at a concept that his neo-Christian grandparents had accepted without question. But their acceptance had been required long after the supposed fact of that particular incarnation, when time and faith had pulled a veil over history and there was no longer a physical body around to muddy the waters of their mysticism. The Sawl goddesses still walked the planet, and made war on a daily basis.

Stavros recalled his reckless statement to Megan of conviction on the part of his ancient Greek ancestors. His laugh came out as a strangled sigh.

Knowledge and Belief, Ibiá. Your own argument.

He could not yet accept the *knowing*.

In the leap of faith, he was stalled midway. He suspected he'd seen a miracle occur, but was unable to accept the faith-based explanation. What definition and degree of deity could he persuade his rational brain to swallow? The less rational brain and the good old unconscious would travel willingly down any path, but past experience suggested that an inner split would be hard on his sanity.

The thought of it made Stavros break into a cold sweat.

For another issue was in play here. There wasn't just his own sanity or well-being to worry about. There were the Sawls. Surely he would risk a tumble into the abyss of belief rather than lose the trust that even playing at belief had helped establish with them. If *actual* belief threatened his balance, it might also make him a truer interpreter of both the language and the culture. But losing their trust would render him useless.

Stavros saw the old priest's smile again: a very *knowing* smile, directed straight at him, as if it was the old priest doing the interpreting. He rocked a little on the cool stone, then raised his head and stood. His weakness had passed.

I don't need to resolve this all right now, he told himself, and felt comforted. Yet he hesitated. He had intended to head for the cave mouth, for the outside and the sun and other people, but was unable to make a start. The silence and the emptiness urged him in another direction. It drew him inward and down, toward the center of the rock.

All right, then. A compromise. The antenna repairs could wait a while longer. He'd go up to the Story Hall to retrieve his translator and battery packs. A pragmatic choice, and purposeful enough to get him moving again.

But at the back of his brain, the litany continued.

Embriha Lagri!

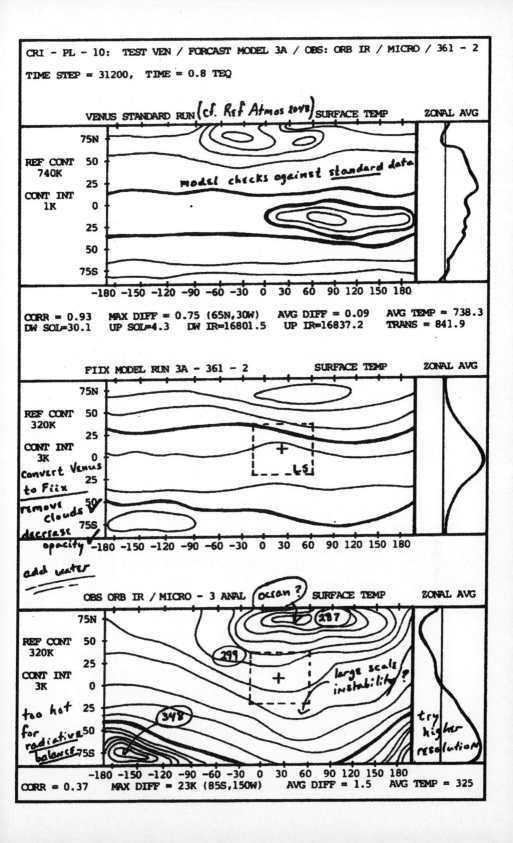

26

SUSANNAH SWORE AS she sank into mud up to her knees. "How clever of me, volunteering to lead the way."

The mud was cold, resisting each step with obscene sucking noises. It clung to her boots in thickening layers. Walking was like negotiating on some larger creature's feet. Behind her, Weng lifted both white trouser legs as if protecting the hem of a skirt, and steered Megan clear of the sinkhole.

Beyond the rock terraces at the base of the cliffs, the plain was rock-strewn and as treacherous as a swamp. Fast-flowing rivulets snaked between mud puddles as big as ponds. Susannah searched out a path across what remained of the high ground, but even the shallowest slopes were slippery, and the steeper ones perilous. She led her party down a long hill sideways and stopped to shake off her extra burden of mud. Megan sighed and lowered herself to a handy boulder.

Weng gazed into the distance like a sea captain on the forward deck. "Mr. Ibiá tells me the Sawls name this plain the Dop Arek, or the Gaming Board."

"The *Goddesses'* Gaming Board," Susannah added.

Megan pointed. "Look back at the cliff face."

It was their first chance to see the whole run of the scarp unobstructed by either snow or floodwaters. Even from a quarter mile away, the towering drop still filled their view. The white rock shimmered a glorious amber in the dawn light, but the lower reaches wore a ragged smear of ocher two stories high.

Megan calculated. "What do you figure? Eight to ten meters of water, at its highest?"

Weng nodded. "Or more."

Susannah only shivered.

The rising sun threw the cave openings into deep relief against the brilliance of the rock. Four long rows pierced the sheerest section of cliff, joined by a herringbone of ledges and stairs. She counted twelve openings per level, spaced more or less regularly.

"Back home," Susannah observed, "there used to be a bird called a bank swallow. It nested in holes dug into banks of earth. The old field photos look a lot like this cliff face, in miniature, of course. And a lot less regular."

Megan squinted through blue sun lenses. "I hadn't realized that the main stairs actually lead to the second level of entries. Those lowest openings are below the high water mark, but I don't recall any flurry about flooded caves. So there must be tunnels beneath the stables that are abandoned now. Flood levels could be rising over the years."

"I would be cautious, Dr. Levy, about applying Earth-typical explanations to random events here."

"Hardly random. The Sawls read the signs. They knew the flood was coming."

Susannah was tired of petty squabbling. "I bet there weren't even the beginnings of natural caves here. Some ancestral Sawls searched out a suitable cliff and went to work. Imagine how long they must have been at it, with their primitive tools!"

"On Earth, apparently, such caves would have collapsed long ago." Megan said. "Taylor suggested their stability might be due to the lack of tectonic activity."

"Emil did say the Sawls must be great natural engineers—like beavers."

Megan shook her head. "Sounds like something he'd say."

"Let us not speak ill . . ." Weng intoned quietly.

Susannah had actually forgotten, at least for a moment. Chastened, she gazed away across the flooded plain and said a quick atheist's prayer for the lost.

At the base of the cliff, on the broad, flat ledges raised above the mud, the Food Guild had sluiced away the rock and silt to set up a virtual city of tent canopies and cook fires. Wagons and two-carts were being unloaded and hauled off to one side. Loosed from their tack, the little hakra ventured to the edge of the mud to sniff the breezes. The hjalk stood patiently while their own harness was put on.

Finally Megan announced herself rested, and they continued up to the top of a ridge skirting a ragged gully. Thick yellow water oozed through the choke of boulders at the bottom. Susannah peered hopefully over the edge, scanning the shallows for signs of life, even though after two-and-a-half weeks of rain, it'd be a miracle if anything survived.

"You'd have to run high or burrow deep to make it on Fiix," she murmured.

The yellow mud did not smell like the earth she knew. She was surprised, when she rubbed it between her fingers, to find it rich with organic matter. She'd expected a sandy desert soil, with fewer organics. Plus, organics turned Earth's soils dark.

They clambered in and out of a narrow wash, gained another rise, and at last the Lander loomed before them. Weng's head mirrored its tilt as she began a true assessment of the damage, and of their chances for a ride back to Earth.

"Our very own Tower of Pisa." Susannah tossed Megan a weak grin, while both of them waited for Weng to say all was well. But of course, she did not.

"From here, it appears that the entire antenna array has been ripped off the nose."

"And carried who knows where by the flood," Susannah added. "But it looks like the ice dam protected our gallant ship from the very worst, wouldn't you say, Commander?"

"As well as its slightly elevated position. Let us hope the same for the interior."

The wash took an oxbow turn and ran straight under the Lander's belly. The number-three landing strut was sunk in the streambed, with a mare's nest of rocks and vegetable matter tangled in its trusswork. All four struts and a good four meters of the hull above were dented and battered. Drying mud hung in thick, rough slabs, like a dead skin being sloughed off. A shallow, muddy trench ringed the entire craft like a moat, an artifact of the ice wall created by the force field. The only way across was through it, and Weng did not hesitate. She hiked up her trouser legs and forged across, and the others could do nothing less than follow.

It was chilly and dank in the Underbelly, and it looked like a war zone. The ceiling clearance toward strut number one was reduced to less than a meter, due to the tilt and the ragged piles of debris. To feel useful, Susannah took a sharp stone to the mottled yellow coating on strut two, but could only chip away what had already cracked loose. Mud caked the Lander's pummeled underside as well. A man-sized equipment cover dangled by a single hinge. The two small storage bays had been ripped open, their contents stolen by the flood. Overhead, the main hatch gaped as wide as it had when the power died, almost within reach.

"Maybe it's not so bad inside," Susannah said, to fill the despairing silence.

Weng stood in mud ankle-deep beneath the opening and studied its hovering darkness. "We will need a rope."

Susannah craned her neck. It was hard to tell how far the mud and water had risen into the hatch. Weng's main concern would be for the precious ascent engines, but their status could hardly be determined by staring into their pocked and muddied exhaust cones. Susannah searched for something positive to say. "Perhaps the Woodworkers—or the Engineers Guild—would build us a ladder."

Weng glanced her way, her back a little straighter than a moment before. "Of course. I will arrange for it right away."

As she turned to start the half-mile trek back to the cliffs, a tired groan from Megan halted her briefly. "Do stay and enjoy the air, Dr. Levy. I'll see myself home."

When Weng had gone, the two women exchanged sober looks.

"Whatever she saw up there," Megan said, "She didn't like it."

Susannah nodded, gazing up at their only ticket back to Earth. "But we've got time. And a mission to complete before we have to worry about it."

27

E.D. 64–11:53

STAVROS PADDED THROUGH the Frieze Hall looking neither right nor left. When he noticed he was shunning the light pooled beneath the chandeliers, he also saw that he was scudding along on the balls of his feet, a sort of hurried tiptoe.

No one's here . . . who am I avoiding?

But sparkling at the edge of his glance was the red-and-lavender fire of the Sisters' jeweled eyes, and his involuntary shudder warned him: belief was creeping up of its own accord.

He drew up, breathless, at the open doors of the Story Hall. The old priest had gone, to rest or to celebrate. The fire was ash. The room was dark but for a cool, steady glow from somewhere in the upper tiers. Stavros slipped in and found his battery packs and rucksack waiting in a neat line just inside the door, not as he had left them, scattered in his surprise, but as some meticulous Sawl had placed them, ready for his return. He was ashamed to have worried about leaving them untended.

He carried the larger cases into the outer hall. Returning for his pack, he glanced about for the source of the odd glow. He expected a hidden window or a light shaft in the dome, but instead spotted a faint spear of light on the back wall, level with the highest tier. Curious, he climbed up for a closer look.

In the wall opposite the great wooden doors, a thin flame burned in an arched niche. It had escaped notice while the tiled room was ablaze with reflected firelight. An oil lamp, he assumed. But the flame was the wrong color.

The niche was tall and narrow, a semicircle set with a mosaic of tiny lozenge-shaped tiles, like a beaded lizard skin: glossy crimson, salmon, vermilion, and garnet. Black inlaid script marched in bands around the curve. Stavros made out Lagri's name, though the lettering did not exactly match the Sawl alphabet he was learning, and some of the tiles were chipped or missing. There were hairline cracks in the grout and webs of minute fracture in the glaze, much like the ancient pots in the museums remaining on Earth.

This niche must be very old, then. The letters excited him with their differences. Then he turned his attention to the flame itself.

The shelf was tiled in concentric rings. The outside ring was deep wine red, with the colors moving inward through red and orange. The central ring was a raised ceramic collar glazed in golden yellow and set with blood-red cabochon stones. The collar enclosed a small hole, from which sprang the flame. It was slim and blue. It burned clean and hot without a trace of soot. Leaning in close, Stavros heard a gentle hissing.

He stared at the flame, then stepped back to explore the tiled surfaces to the side and below the niche for a seam or a hinge, anything that would indicate a hidden vessel, a refillable reservoir. He found nothing. The flame apparently burned on its own.

More important, what would burn with such a flame? He knew and did not know. That is, if he were back on Earth, he would know it as a gas flame. But here? How could the Sawls, without metal or industry, harness a flammable gas?

He thought of the steaming, pressurized water in the Bath Hall, and beat his palm against his skull. Even knowing how wondrous that was, he had accepted it rather than dig further to learn how it was accomplished. What about the warm air circulating throughout the entire cave system? He'd explained that away as collective body heat. What about the hot water flowing freely in the Physicians Hall? He realized now that he could make up quite a list of things that he'd left unquestioned, things that would offer new revelations about the Sawls' capabilities. Things that had nothing to do with magic or weather. He could delve into these purely technical mysteries without worrying about issues of sanity or belief.

Galvanized by curiosity and relief, he scrambled down the tiers to root around in his pack. Pictures first. He untangled the video band to fit it around his head, then came up slowly, sucking his cheek.

No. There was a reason he'd avoided exploring these mysteries.

If he recorded this innocent blue flame, it became hard data that could then be discovered by others. And the others could not know, not even Susannah and Megan, because such news might cause a sensation. He could picture the journal abstracts already: "Stone age exoculture turns up advanced technology." The gold rush would be on.

Secrets again, Ibiá?

But it had to be. He had not actually promised Susannah that he wouldn't keep secrets, aware as he was that secrecy was his only weapon. And sure, Megan meant well, warning him not to become involved. But she'd seen many planets in her lifetime, so preserving any particular one was less of a priority for her. Also, it seemed that her long experience of failure with preservation efforts had jaded her into habits of protest without committed action.

It was bad enough that companies like ConPlex might be allowed to chew up the planet rock by rock and transplant the population to some barren moon not of their choosing. Even worse, somehow, was the possibility that everything unique and genuine that was the Sawls—their industrious fatalistic cheer, their rich mytho-history, their generosity and ingenuity, their *soul*—might be lost, absorbed into the common culture, if the rest of the galaxy decided to take notice, for one reason or another, of the planet Fiix. Stavros was not sure he could just stand aside if either happened, but now he knew for sure that he would do nothing to encourage it.

Weng would call it mutiny and have his hide. His crooked smile belied his awareness that he'd just made another of those turning-point decisions. Thus are the lines drawn, he mused, and fatal choices made.

But Stavros took up this new loyalty as easily as he shouldered his ruck-sack and prepared to leave. Outside in the empty Frieze Hall, Liphar was calling his name.

28

E.D. 64–13.10

A SOFT WIND SPRANG up as Weng retraced the rugged path through the mud and rocks. Susannah sniffed at it warily, reminded of the hot desert blast that had foretold the earlier disastrous thaw. She tried to calculate how long it would take to run the return distance to the Caves. Once, proximity to the Lander would have meant safety, even escape. And it might again, if it could be returned to working order. For now, it was a vulnerable metal shell parked on an open plain. For now, true safety was in the Caves.

She moved out from under the Lander's oppressive shadow, needing the comfort of the sun. She splashed through the shallow moat and walked to the top of the nearby rise. From there she had a nearly full panorama. Facing south, to her right, muddy hillocks and ravines led to the flat rock terraces beneath the cliffs. Ahead of her to the east, more mud and hillocks, and the cliff curling around to meet the steep scarp dominated by the Red Pawn. To her left, the vast ravaged expanse of the Dop Arek, with its saw-toothed edging of distant mountains. It was a barren, rugged landscape, devoid of softness or life. It was beautiful in its way, but now Susannah saw it as a threat.

Megan struggled up behind her. "Look what they're doing!"

"What? Where?" She was eager for a distraction.

The wide stone stairs were deserted. Gray smoke curled up from a dozen cook fires among the forest of newly erected tents. The harnessing of the hjalk continued, but a long procession of people and carts and animals was descending from the rock flats to fan out into the ravines, with digging tools shouldered like weapons. Susannah clambered up on a boulder for a better view.

One arm of the procession moved along the bottom of the wash that eventually ran under the Lander. At the head, a wizened Food Guildsman walked in intense consultation with two engineers, who simultaneously waved directions to the those behind them. They divided into work details and attacked the sides of the gully with rakes and hoes, shoveling the yellow mud into semicircular terraces echoing the contour of the rise. Four giant hjalk hauled flatbed wagons along the streambed. Stones pulled out of the mud were tossed down into the gully to be sorted by a horde of stonecutter apprentices and stacked on the flatbeds according to size. When a wagon was full, its hjalk drew it back up the gully to where the terracing began. There, a detail of journeymen wearing the Stonecutters' hammer-and-chisel seal raised a low stone dike to contain the bottom terrace. Fat earthworks edged the higher tiers. As each terrace was carved out and flattened, the runoff water was gathered by the earthwork, until a series of narrow stepped ponds lined the gully sides.

From the top of her boulder, Susannah could see the same process being carried out in every nearby gully or ravine. The terraces took shape with astonishing speed. The largest were nearly an acre square, though most were smaller, as the contours of the land dictated. Every available inch of ground was being shaped and put to use.

The mood of wild celebration had dissipated. The party transforming the gully nearest to the Lander worked with a concentration that was almost grim. The foreman from the Engineers Guild tramped about in the mud offering advice and encouragement to workers too intent on their task to really listen. The elderly Food Guildsman paced the top of the slope with his lips set tight. Occasionally, he halted to study the sky, with particular attention to the northeastern horizon.

The two women settled in to observe, admiring the care and speed of the work. When both sides of the gully had been terraced for several hundred yards, the work detail took a break. They passed around the water jugs, shed a layer or two of clothing and moved on to carve up the next section of waterlogged slope.

Susannah chewed her lip pensively. "Terracing is normally used where water is scarce, to keep it from running off. Here, you'd think they'd *want* it to run off."

The wall-building teams now climbed to the top of the finished terraces. Working down the tiers under the watchful eye of the engineer foreman, they opened a shallow sluice in each earthwork. A small amount of the water collected in each terrace ran off onto the level below.

"Equalizing the water level," Megan noted.

The finished terraces did not stand vacant for long. More hjalk appeared along the ridge, each hauling a double-shared wooden plow. A young herdsman sat high on each beast's burly shoulders, feet twined in the curly mane. They urged their mounts into the top terraces, driving them back and forth through the shin-deep mud and water. When one terrace was plowed, a digger was on hand to help lift the heavy blades and rollers over the earthwork and onto the next level.

"Gods, they're efficient," Susannah exclaimed.

"It's more than efficiency. I'd say they're in one hell of a hurry."

Susannah put the Sawls' uncanny nose for weather alongside the fact that the old Food Guildsman kept staring at the sky. Her nerves were on edge, and here it was, not even true dawn yet. The oblate salmon sun still rested between the peaks of the eastern mountains, as if gathering its strength for an exact moment of parting from the horizon. *This sun is not a friendly color,* she decided. Or maybe it was just that there was too much color, like a bad painter's attempt at a sunrise. The orangy pink was acidic, and the sky around it had a lime-green tinge that progressed through aqua and turquoise to azure at the zenith. It deepened again where the western sky met the sharp white profile of the cliffs in severe tones of malachite. "And why would they be in a hurry?"

"Only by our standards. You see, whatever it is, Sawls do it faster than we would. So, to us, it looks like hurrying when, actually, it's their natural pace of existence."

"Even though their day is longer and you'd think they'd work slower?" Susannah conjured a laugh, and felt better for it. "Is this Levy's Law of Special Relativity?"

Megan looked wounded. "I'm serious."

"Well, I have noticed that their metabolisms run hotter than ours, but . . . Oh, my. Look who's here!"

The hjalk and their plows had moved on to the next sector of terraces. The mud stood in furrows that just broke the surface of the water. A long-haired dairy hekker had just topped the rise. A solitary figure perched on a pad of blankets strapped to its back.

"Kav Daven!" Megan breathed.

The old priest sat erect and smiling on his barrel-chested mount. In the sunlight, he seemed to have gained substance. Susannah no longer worried that he might shatter like crystal in the slightest breeze. He stared straight ahead as the hekker plodded along the ridge. His bald head was slightly cocked, as if he was listening to the ground. Behind him strode the tawny child from the Story Hall. She led a double line of younger children, all trying unsuccessfully to appear adult and solemn.

At the first flight of terraces, Kav Daven raised his hand and the hekker stopped. The animal was as thin and gray as the old man himself, hardly tall enough to be a proper mount, but with a willing softness to its eye. Its long coat was plastered to its ribs in muddied strands. The kav's bony legs hung long at its sides, toes skimming the water.

The tawny girl came to stand at the animal's head. At a sign from the priest, she led it down into the highest terrace. Kav Daven carried a big sack slung from hip to shoulder, bulging with shifting weight. He dipped in, drew forth a handful of something small and reddish, which he raised to the sky in salute. Then, with a sweeping gesture, he cast his handful into the mud. The line of children began a high-pitched hum.

"What's he got there," Megan asked.

"But . . . he can't!" Susannah stammered. "Not yet!"

"What is it?"

"Seeds, of course! He's planting!"

The girl twined a hand in the hekker's shaggy mane and led it up and down the field. The younger children followed in vee formation, humming their shrill monotone, stalking along the furrows like a flock of water birds. Kav Daven scattered the seed from side to side and sang out in a voice that seemed to fill the nearby plain. As the children answered, the rhythm of their chant mimicked the swing of his arm and the swish of their own feet as they pressed the seed into the mud.

Susannah slid off her boulder. "I have to see what they're planting. It's all going to rot in this waterlogged soil!" She scrambled down the wet bank into the gully and waded along the streambed.

'Maybe it's a water plant." Megan started after her. "Rice grows in water."

"It's the rice seedlings you plant in water, not the seeds. Besides, what about Taylor's 'desert climate'? Rice won't grow in a desert."

"Irrigation? From what they've done here, I'd guess they were capable of it."

"Irrigation still needs a reliable water source." But Susannah recalled the plant sample she'd been working on before the sudden thaw. She'd never completed the analysis, but superficially, it *was* structured like a water plant.

She climbed the opposite bank of the stream, dragging Megan up after her like a troublesome child. The old priest and his entourage had progressed to the next set of fields. Other workers moved along the ridges now, Food Guildsmen with lines of apprentices strung out behind them, to do the actual bulk of the sowing.

Susannah reached the first level of terraces. The water stood knee-deep and still. The furrows had been flattened by the children's feet. She crouched and plunged both hands into the mud. "Whew! Cold! And those poor children walking in it barefoot!" She scooped up a handful of silt and let the water drain out through her fingers, sifting the mud until she'd sorted out a dirty pile of seeds. She rinsed one in the water and held it up for Megan to see. It was chunky, triangular, and the size of her thumb pad.

"What does it remind you of?" She tilted her hand to catch the pale sunlight. Freed of its coating of yellow mud, the seed was pale magenta.

Megan took it in her own palm and poked it. "Kind of looks like big corn."

"Go to the head of the class." Susannah fished in her therm-suit pockets with a muddy hand. "Damn! Again! Forgot to come equipped. Not even an old sample bag with a hole in it. Oh well." She dropped the dirty seeds into her breast pocket, leaving smudged fingerprints on the flap. "It isn't corn, of course, but it might resemble it. We'll take a look under Ghirra's lenses in Physicians'. They're more powerful than my medikit scope, would you believe? If only we had CRI on line, she could do a full . . . well, we don't." She took the single pink triangle back from Megan and tried to break the seed coat with her thumbnail. "Sturdy little bugger."

"I don't recall eating any corn here," mused Megan.

"It's not corn. It's *like* corn." Susannah's impatience was mostly directed at herself. She rubbed her fingertips together, testing the soil texture. "It could be feed grain for the animals. Or perhaps it's only used after being ground into meal. I really should have done that full diet breakout. And I could have . . ." She shook her head in despair. "What *have* I been doing these past two weeks?"

"Practicing medicine, a perfectly valid pursuit," Megan replied. "I ought to have done the diet study myself. How long will it take the seed to come up?"

"Depends. On the temperature, on the moisture. Corn will sprout within a short week in the factory fields. On the homestead worlds, where it's more likely to be grown in something approaching natural conditions, it'll take longer, especially if it's wet or cold. Also, even our fastest GMOs need a solid six weeks to ripen. So, either the Sawls are very sure of good weather this time, or . . ." The sweep of her arm took in the rising sun, finally clear of the saw-toothed horizon, and then the terraces, a descending flight of mirrors reflecting the malachite sky and the sowers at their work. "This is all a magnificent gamble."

Megan grinned.

"Yes, I thought you'd like that. But think about it! They could be just taking a chance, hoping that the weather will hold. If they're wrong, this whole great effort will be wasted, washed out, blown away, frozen solid or whatever the next natural disaster is that this world has in store for us."

Megan's smile twisted ever so slightly. "So, no wonder they're hurrying."

29

E.D. 67–23:15

THRUST FROM HIS weeks of darkness, Stavros felt disoriented, afloat in liquid light.

It was like being born, an experience he was not altogether sure he'd enjoyed in the first place. His eyes watered. The cliff behind him was blindingly bright. The sun seemed too fat and too close. His familiar sun spent its days behind a thick layer of haze, while this alien sun's amber glare pressed through the open weave of the canopy above to lie like weight on his head and shoulders.

Liphar was to blame for this. His daily rounds to the Black Hole had discovered Stavros sunk in a drift of scrap paper and the effort of working out a translation by hand and brain alone. Even more insistent than usual, wielding vivid descriptions of the Planting being done and the Feast being laid, he'd dragged the resisting linguist out into the building heat of midmorning to join the celebration.

Stavros was not sure he liked sunshine. He'd spent little time in it back home. But his ancestors, both the Greek and the Portuguese, had flourished under Earth's sun, in the days when its light was more welcome and benign. This sun, being old, should be safer, though its bilious color made him doubt it.

It had been a three-day bout of manic concentration. He'd slept only in snatches. His brain was stunned by deep exhaustion, and still as cave-adjusted as his eyes. It was unprepared for sudden change. But the sun was working on him, bit by bit. He let himself bask a little, his muscles uncurling petal-like to the warmth, like a lizard on a rock. Fitting, he decided, for one who lives life as a cultural chameleon. Perhaps this sun would turn his skin as dark as the Sawls'. Stavros liked that idea.

He heard water . . . no, it was the soft lapping of the multicolored banners tied to the tent poles. When he dared to look up, a billowing ocean of canopies brightened the rock terraces as far as he could see. A thousand guy ropes laced with silken streamers. Lagri's colors, yellow and red and orange, and joyous crowds wrapped in rainbows, milling about in shadow and sunlight, against the malachite sky.

He sensed the approach of sensual overload. Reeling toward the edge, Stavros shut his eyes. The confusion was manageable if he restricted the incoming data. He concentrated on the knobby beige-and-gray wool of the rug beneath him, on the subtle twistings of the unbleached fibers.

They've hauled out every rug and cushion in the Caves, he decided.

A mug of iced herb tea sat beside him, one small berg still afloat. The pale clay sweated in the heat. Ice. Another Sawl wonder. He'd not known about the ice-storage caverns until now.

In his lap was a platter of food. He dimly recalled accepting it from a flushed and laughing cook's apprentice. The platter was a satiny wooden oval, with raised dividers like a Terran baby dish, but the size of a serving tray, wide enough to balance securely on his knees as he sat cross-legged. Stavros inspected its contents distantly, as if it were a museum display or a piece of conceptual art. He nudged a pile of boiled yellow roots. One toppled and jumped its wooden corral, rolling into a lump of white mash next to several thick chunks of dark orange bread. He twisted an experimental fingertip into the mash. It was lukewarm but tasted spicy, like a cooked radish, or a turnip with pepper in it. He recognized it as specially prepared kamad root. Comforted, he ate a little more.

Food was so very real.

He eased up the volume on his internal receptors and heard music, many instruments pursuing different muted melodies. Conversation hummed among the canopies, gossip and debate, broken by laughter and the clatter of dishes, by a child's excited giggle, and here and there by satisfied mutual silence. The softened tone of the chatter told him that the gathering was feeling well fed and mellow. Yet there was still the crisp bustle of the cook's apprentices, busing loaded trays from tent to tent, singing out the menu in endless mouthwatering stanzas.

Beyond the music and conversation, he heard shouts and cheers, then a groan of disappointment surging through the distant spectators. Stavros imagined fortunes in stone counters being swept to the winds like so much sea foam. But the Sawls did not possess fortunes, only their own handmade goods and the promise of services, many of which would be traded back and forth by the time this Planting Feast was over.

Stavros laughed softly. He hadn't dealt straight with Megan about the gambling. Any fool could see the Sawls were inveterate gamblers, that games of chance dominated substantial portions of their meager free time (and tokens) and that any issue open to question was fair game for a wager. Megan considered this a product of boredom, greed, and tradesmanship, but Stavros embraced it as a brave metaphor for the Sawls' battle for survival on a hostile planet. Their whole lives were a gamble . . . why shouldn't they make light of it if they could? But if he offered this interpretation publicly, Megan would call him a romantic and think she had won the argument.

The food and the cool tea steadied him. In addition to not sleeping for the last three days, he'd forgotten to eat regularly. His fear of overload ebbed. Probably it was safe now to admit words to the data flow, to let the nearby conversation be more than aural nonsense.

"When you were little and you saw programs on the vid about the Land of the Midnight Sun, didn't you want to go there right away to find out how the Scand kids knew when it was bedtime?"

That was Susannah, her voice husky with ease and memory. In his dreams, she had sounded like that, but never yet in life. He sensed a slippage inside him, another warning sign, but the light and the heat and the food had sapped his resistance. He tuned in to the sound of her, and the wash of pleasure was more profound than he'd expected. She'd been on his mind while he was deep in the Caves and she out with the Planting. He was forced to admit that he'd missed her.

There was a small clatter, as of wooden objects tipping over.

"Is that your move, Dr. Levy?" Weng's voice held subtle mischief, accompanying the clink of wooden objects being righted.

"Does it help to fondle the bishop like that?" Susannah asked.

Stavros pictured her stirring, perhaps lying back.

"I wish it did," replied Megan distractedly. Stavros heard a tentative clunk. "No, wait. There's got to be a better move than that."

"There are a number of them," offered Weng mildly.

It was an easy guess who was winning, but it might be worth watching. Stavros raised his head carefully. His eyes had stopped watering. He blinked and focused, then blinked again, sure he was hallucinating.

Weng and Megan each perched on red cushions as tall and stiff as little ottomans, Weng in white and Megan in some sort of loose desert camouflage. They looked for all the world like two colonial pashas at tea among the barbarians. A pile of yellow cushions between them supported the chessboard. Stavros hoped this dizzy vision might supply palm fans and dancing girls, but he could see that endgame was fast approaching. He pitied Megan as she sent her remaining rook halfway across the board.

"Liphar says the priests will dance later, in the fields." Megan swiveled sideways on her cushion. "He seemed particularly eager that we be there."

Stavros followed her gaze. Susannah reclined in a tumble of soft pillows at the corner of his own rug, closer than he'd realized. Her head lolled lazily. Her dark hair fanned out in graceful waves against the bright yellow, red, and orange of the pillow fabric. She'd shed her unwashed, useless therm-suit for a loose and colorful Sawl shift that she'd had no chance to lengthen. Stavros' discovery of her bared knees and ankles was as disturbing and arousing as it would have been to a Victorian gentleman. Worse still, the sudden summer seemed to encourage a sensuousness in this woman that he had known only in his fantasies. Gauzy shadows played across her cheek. She stretched luxuriantly among the pillows. The arch of her back and her body's unconscious preening tied knots in his gut. He had to look away.

He focused on the ruins of the chess game, on the hot green-blue sky, on the food drying out in his dish. He remembered the papers at his side and felt for them blindly, pages of rough hand translation and a few bad sketches from memory of the Dance of Origins. He planted them in front of his nose. The blind face of Kav Daven grinned at him from the top of the stack. His ardor cooled with the leaden weight of the secrets he held, in his hand and his heart. Susannah disapproved of his running interference between Clausen and the Sawls. How would she feel about the secrets he kept now?

Megan heard the crackle of his papers. "Put that work away, boy. Get over here and win this game for me!"

"I'm afraid it's too late for rescue," Weng offered with polite regret.

Megan sighed.

"Still working on the Dance of Origins?" Susannah asked lazily.

"Mmmm." Guilt and reawakening desire left him inarticulate.

"It might help to take a break, if you're having trouble."

"Might." He heard her rustling among her pillows again and imagined himself among them with her.

"But if you insist on ignoring the most glorious weather that ever was in the history of the universe, there is something I wanted to run by you."

Stavros glanced over with what he hoped would read as polite interest, and found he could not meet her gaze.

"Would you say that the words 'hakra,' 'hekker' and 'hjalk' are root-related in any way?" she asked.

Curiosity offered a welcome anchor. Stavros reviewed the words in his head, then cleared his throat, fully expecting his voice to be as dysfunctional as the rest of him. "Um. If similarity of sound were enough to go on, I'd say yes, but etymology tends to be less logical than that. Why do you ask?"

"Because the creatures' morphology is so similar, despite the very different body sizes. Yet within each type of beast, the range of size is minimal."

"I'll put a flag on it in the translator's glossary. Part of the program searches possible roots and derivations. What's your guess?"

Susannah sucked her cheek. "That they were all the same animal once."

He sat up. "Really?"

"Which would suggest that the Sawls have been fiendishly clever at breeding for desired characteristics, and for quite a long time. These are not short-generation animals, these sturdy beasts. It would take a while to get them the way you wanted them."

"Could they have evolved that way in the first place?"

"I suppose." But her mouth pursed dubiously. "I'll know more once we get a better sense of the planet's—and of the breeders'—history."

A young Sawl wheeled in under their canopy, balancing a steaming tray on one shoulder. His gray apron bore the ubiquitous double red-and-blue stripes of the Food Guild, topped by the thin yellow band of an apprentice cook. He greeted them cheerfully, spun the tray down and presented it first to the chess players, with a flourish.

Weng studied the food closely without appearing to, then pincered a small dumpling between delicate fingers. She rewarded the apprentice with a gracious nod and laid the dumpling beside the neat file of chessmen she had captured from Megan. Stavros decided that Weng's stern half-smile must be the sort they used to teach queens to make. Her children had children his age. He was grateful to be able to love and respect her without confusion.

Megan shook her head over the tray, but as the apprentice turned away, she snatched a fat pastry from the edge. Susannah roused herself to take the tray's inventory in her battered notebook. She pointed to a slice of baked casserole and asked what it was.

The little cook smiled proudly and reeled off a list of ingredients. Susannah made a few rapid scrawls but quickly foundered. "Stav? Translate, please?"

"Eggs, butter, three cheeses: kidri, voss and nahrin; those onionlike shoots, blue fungus, kamad root, you know, like a turnip, flat noodles, uh . . ." He still could not look her in the eye. This was a problem he'd not had before. He asked the Sawl to repeat the end of his list. "The rest are spices that I think you already have in your listings. And by the way, asking made him very happy. The recipe is one of his own that the Guild is allowing him to try out during the Feast."

Susannah scribbled frantically. "Kamad, noodles, spices . . . jeez, this writing by hand is slow!"

"I know." Stavros chose to read subtle rebuke into her remark. "I'm working on that. You heard one of the terracers found the main antenna out in a gully?" His uneasiness made him talk too fast, too brusquely for a relaxed and festive occasion. "Now that Planting's done, they'll help us haul it in, so I can get it back in shape and set up in a proper send-receive position on the ground. Plus, I'll have to cannibalize the electronics left in the nose, and that'll take a while."

She smiled a puzzled apology. "Stav, it's all right. I didn't mean . . ."

"Liphar mentioned an old metalsmith in Engineers' who might be able to help with the welds, if he can get his forge hot enough. He works mostly with high-temp ceramics, but he also does all the metals repairs in the Caves."

Susannah laid her notebook aside and took a square of kamad casserole onto her platter. The apprentice went away beaming. "It's all right, really. There's plenty of work I can do without a computer. I just get impatient sometimes. There are crucial tests I can't run while CRI is off-line."

Weng made a small agreeing noise that was not quite a grumble, and then looked embarrassed that she had let anything so inadvertent escape her.

Megan laughed. "I think the Commander misses her music. What is it now, Weng, two weeks' worth of compositions playing around in your head that you haven't been able to listen to yet?"

Weng's discomfort deepened. She arched a thin finger at the chessboard. "If CRI were on-line, Dr. Levy, you would not be required so often to let me lay your armies to waste."

Megan swiveled back to stare at the board. "Is that what's happening?"

Susannah chuckled. "Game theory has its practical applications, Commander?"

"An enlightening system of analysis, Dr. James."

Other visitors followed the fledgling cook. Tyril stopped by to show off her baby, a plump five-month-old girl. After the women had cooed over her and let her grasp their fingers, Tyril invited them to visit her family's canopy later, before the priests' dance ended the celebration. As she left, Weng's eyes followed the baby. She gave it a grandmotherly wave and went back to her chess game.

The Master Healer came along next, dressed still in his linen smock.

"*Rhe khem*, Suzhannah." He ducked under the canopy and folded his long legs beneath him on the rug.

"*Khem rhe*, Ghirra." She offered a mug of cold tea and made the introductions. Weng smiled. Megan became positively girlish. Stavros let his attention wander. The Sawl physician's soft voice and stooping, gentle carriage did nothing to detract from his dark good looks, and Stavros did not like the way his long-fingered surgeon's hands hovered around Susannah as he praised her skill in the infirmary. He brought no wife or companion visiting with him, and it was a blow to Stavros' pride that Ghirra was mastering English without an ounce of aid from the official Ship's Linguist and Communications Officer. Stavros sucked at his lukewarm tea and watched his neighbors.

Under the adjacent canopy, a large and jovial group had been raising their mugs in semimusical unison, emptying endless trays of food. Leather dyers, he guessed, looking at their hands. He recognized a woman who worked a stall in the Market Hall, trading exquisitely colored pouches and strapping. Now the more boisterous of this group rose and sauntered away to watch the games. Others drifted off to wander from canopy to canopy on the expected after-dinner rounds of socializing. A single couple remained, and as Stavros watched from the corner of his eye, they snuggled themselves among their pillows and began to make quiet love. Stavros nearly groaned aloud. Circumstances were conspiring to keep him from tranquillity. He decided it would be less painful to listen to Ghirra charming the ladies.

The Master Healer was discussing remedies for arthritis. As he detailed his preparations of certain herbs, Susannah lounged beside him, attentive to every word. Megan was enrapt. Even Weng seemed intrigued. Stavros retreated to the consolation of his translation. Perhaps it was time to look for an actual lover, and forget this frustrating fantasy.

But who? He could not imagine himself and McPherson together, but there were many Sawl women who were interesting and desirable. Taking a Sawl lover could be seen as a positive solution to his dilemma and a natural extension of his work, though that sort of thing was professionally frowned upon. The Sawls would have no objection. Their sexual taboos centered on avoiding inappropriate childbirth and inbreeding. Liphar had already nosed him in the direction of a lovely young weaver, though Stavros suspected excess generosity in that case, and that Liphar was interested in the girl himself.

He savored a moment of calm. Surely this on-and-off infatuation with Susannah could be blamed on a wrongly perceived lack of alternatives. He just hadn't done enough looking around. He could have an everyday life with a lover in the Caves, certainly a saner and more placid vision than the passion and drama that heated his dreams of Susannah. Stavros relaxed. He laid aside his paperwork, his decision made, and looked up to find Susannah watching him. His calm evaporated.

Her smile was warm and lazy. "You do realize you're making us all feel guilty, sitting in a corner working while we play."

"Stavros never learned to play," muttered Megan. "Deprived childhood."

Ghirra refilled their mugs from the tall misted pitcher he had brought with him. His brown eyes rested on Stavros for the first time. Stavros was unable to read their expression, so he nodded a greeting. It felt stilted and sullen.

"Check," said Weng.

"Again?"

"If you'd pay closer attention, Dr. Levy . . ."

"Surely Kav Daven's tale will keep till tomorrow," Susannah teased.

For a terrifying moment, he thought her smile acknowledged his confusion. *She knows!* It was probably the last thing he wanted, but still . . . and then she yawned and stretched and turned away as Ghirra asked a question in his gallant, halting English.

Stavros reclaimed his calm and sense of relief. Let the Master Healer's well-known curiosity for things Terran occupy Susannah's interest. This man was not yet ready.

"Mate," declared Weng without much satisfaction.

Megan slumped away from the board with a thankful sigh.

Weng gathered the venerable ebony-and-teak chessmen into a threadbare velvet pouch and tied it to her belt. "O-one-hundred. It's late." Above the open-weave tenting, the fat sun hovered halfway to zenith, still midmorning by the Fiixian clock.

Susannah smiled up at her fondly. "It's late, said the White Queen."

"That was the rabbit," Megan corrected.

"Ah."

"The White Rabbit. The guy with the pocket watch."

"I know, but . . ."

Stavros grinned into his paperwork. He, too, preferred Susannah's image of Weng as the looking-glass queen, with that wisp of hair straying from the silver bun at the back of her neck, happily insisting that nonsense made sense, that it could be late though the sun was still rising.

"I think I shall retire," Weng said. "Tomorrow, repair work must begin in earnest. We will start by checking all the joints and welds. With the hull sensors off-line, that may take some time."

Ghirra rose as she did, exhibiting a sensitive eye for Terran manners.

"Yeah, no more of this fartin' around!" Megan's passable imitation of McPherson's roughhouse drawl made Susannah giggle.

Weng straightened her spotless uniform as if camouflaging a shrug. "And, Mr. Ibiá, perhaps you might have com and power back up within the next few ship's days, now that the high gain has been located?"

Stavros blinked, picturing a tangle of flood-wracked metal. "Uhh, well . . . I'll do what I can, Commander."

"Excellent. If the lieutenant returns, I assume someone will inform me?"

"Of course, Commander," chorused the three civilians, like loyal ensigns.

Ghirra took the advantage to excuse himself also, murmuring of further social obligations. Megan gazed after him wistfully, as one gazes upon the unattainable, but said only, "I wonder if that stuff he was describing really works."

"Ghirra and his herbalists could give most pharmaceutical houses a run for their money, especially given how little they have to work with." Susannah took a long sip from her mug and settled back among her pillows.

Weng's departure removed a certain tension. In an easy silence, they watched her weave a stately path among the canopies, pausing to smile at children along the way. As she left the woven shadow for the open sun, she blazed white like a vision of angels. She headed down a wide dirt track, newly graded but already rutted from cartwheels. It wound among the still-muddy acres of field and the repeating tiers of mirrored terraces. A half-mile out, a side track would lead her to the Lander, where she had once again taken up residence, much to the chagrin of her crew. The Lander's scoured metallic solidity together with its improbable tilt made it look like a cutout pasted onto the background of plain and sky. Stavros thought it had never looked more alien.

"What do we think?" asked Susannah. "Will she make it home again?"

"It is a long walk in this heat," agreed Megan.

"Oh, Weng'll be fine. Tough old bird. I was talking about the Lander."

"Hard to say. Stav?"

"Hardly my area of expertise. But the engines look solid. We can run tests once we get the power up."

Megan stirred. "How long did McPherson say they'd be out?"

"Supplies for two Earthweeks, she said. More than a week left still."

"She won't come in before she has to," Stavros put in.

Megan stood, shaking out her legs with a groan. "Got to get me some of Ghirra's magic potion. I'm off to pay Tyril a return visit. Don't forget to go watch Liphar dance."

"We'll be there," Susannah replied.

Megan wandered off. Susannah lay back on her pillows with a contented sigh. The cries from the games had quietened. An old man snored several canopies away. Stavros watched Susannah covertly. Now would be the time. She was both beautiful and terrifying, lying in the dappling sun. But that was exactly the problem.

She turned on her pillows and regarded him slyly across the emptied stretch of carpet. He glanced away. Was she going get the drop on him, and steal his moment? In his fantasies, he was always the seducer, not the seduced. But she tilted her head, and the look in her eyes was coolly speculative.

"Are you happy here?" she asked.

He was startled out of his silence. "That's a weird question."

"And that is an evasion." She was always more direct in person than in his memory.

"Why do you ask?"

She sat up and shook her long hair behind her. "Because instinct tells me you're in no rush to get the antennas fixed."

He caught his breath. The sensation inside him was that of a well-oiled locking pin sliding into place. "You mean, do I want to stay here?"

"Well, for a while at least. I didn't mean forever." Then she leaned forward. "Forever? Is that it? Is that what you want, Stav?"

His attempt at a careless grin stiffened on his lips as vast chasms of possibility opened before him. He tried to sound incredulous. "Whatever gave you that idea?"

Susannah let silence and an appraising stare be her reply, weighing on him as heavily as the heat. Defiantly, he met her eyes and saw that he had suspected correctly the first time. She did know. She knew everything about him. His confusion, his desire, his guilty keeping of secrets, all of it was as clear to her as if he had shouted it out loud.

"Susannah . . ."

It was not at all the moment he had imagined, and now that it was here, her directness intimidated him far more than her beauty. His own romanticizing had centered on bodies and bed, neatly avoiding the painful if also delicious tension inevitable when two individuals attempt to share the same point in space and time.

When did this get so complicated?

"Susannah," he began again, and again fell silent. In the distance, from over the fields, he heard singing.

Susannah rose, smoothing her short robe, tightening its braided sash. "I'm going to walk some of this meal off." Her tone was not quite an invitation, nor yet a rejection. Perhaps she was merely gifting him with the solitude he so obviously needed, now that he'd failed to make his move. "It looks like the priests are starting their dance."

She passed close by him as she left, trailing her hand across the top of his head, letting his hair slip through her fingers like dark silk. He felt it as both a caress and a condescension, and jammed his eyes shut in pain and effort. It was all he could do to keep himself from grabbing at the billowing hem of her robe to pull her down beneath him. That would certainly settle it, one way or the other.

But he did not, and she said nothing more, only moved away beneath the rainbowed canopies, following Weng's path toward the new roadway. Stunned and miserable, Stavros crouched in the half-shadow. The singing drew him with its rising joyful cadence, but he could not move. He would not run after the woman like a sorry puppy.

All around him, a new bustle arose with the singing. There was a general stretching and moving toward the fields. The first deep notes of the ceremonial horns boomed from the cliff top.

"Aren't you going down?" Megan called from another world, across the scattering of carpets.

Stavros knew it would be childish to shrug.

"No one will say what it's about," she complained. "They just smile and say, 'Wait, see.' "

He'd let Megan be his escort, then. No lovelorn pursuit. Just two colleagues arriving to observe the local rituals. He scrambled up, packed his notes away, and slung his rucksack to his shoulder. As he joined Megan, he felt brisk and steady again.

At the edge of the rock ledges, they fell in with the long procession to the fields. In place of tools, many carried full mugs of beer. The woodworker next to Stavros munched a thick slice of kamad-root pie while his friends nudged him and joked about the size of his belly. They followed the new road as it dipped away from the base of the cliffs and wove across the tops of the flooded terraces. It curled past the Lander and headed outward. Weng's small footprints broke the thick mud at the turnoff. Stavros saw her standing in the shadow of the Underbelly, one hand shading her brow.

Megan pointed ahead. "I think they're gathering at the field the old priest planted."

"The Kav sowed the first seed because it was his song that gave Lagri the strength to drive back Valla Ired."

Megan threw him a sidelong glance and cleared her throat. "You might want to take it easy for a while with the I-believe-what-they-believe technique."

"C'mon, Meg. What else do you expect from me by now?"

"I mean, for your own sake. Getting too caught up in your field subject can be . . . well, dangerous personally. Not just professionally."

Sssk-chunk. Somewhere inside, another locking pin slid home. Stavros spread his arms in protest. "What did I say?"

"It's not what you said, it's how you said it, like it was all full of capital letters." When his pace quickened, she caught up with him. "Stav, it's not about objectivity or interpretation anymore. It's about being able to function, to keep yourself from . . ."

He stopped, faced her squarely. "From going off the deep end? Is that what you're getting at?" She did not flinch from his furious glare. This time she was not just playing out their habitual debate. Stavros shivered. Susannah reading him like a book was bad enough. Was he wearing *all* his most private torments on his sleeve? He took a breath, reaching for that elusive calm again. He should never have let Liphar lure him from the safety of the caves. "Meg, I know where the deep end is, don't worry. I've been there."

"I know."

"And I don't want to go back."

Now she did look away, with a dubious shrug. "Okay. If you say so."

Topping a rise, they spotted Susannah working her way back through the crowd, signaling frantically. "Hurry! Come see!" she cried, over the singing and the boom of the horns. She turned and dove back into the throng. Stavros edged through the joyful mob to the side of the road and broke into a run. Megan struggled after him gamely.

Farther down the slope, the procession backed up into a packed and sweating mass. When Stavros asked to be allowed through, no one seemed to mind.

Cheerful hands patted him, helped him along, while those at the edges of the throng balanced carefully to avoid stepping down into the planted terraces. Ahead, the road dropped into the bottom of a gully. Stavros saw Susannah head and shoulders above the others. He had to call three times before she heard him. She waved him forward, whirling away so quickly that he was left only with an image of eyes, wide in confusion and amazement. Then she dropped completely from view, as if she had knelt or fallen.

The singing snatched at his attention. Its throaty volume and tonal richness stirred him in ways he'd experienced only in the great cathedrals of Earth. How could he resist such a voicing of joy . . . and why should he? Where was the harm in celebrating with more than food and drink? The tightness in his chest wasn't due to fear. It was from fighting the natural impulse to exult, to laugh, to sing along without restraint.

Hands urged him gently forward. The throng thinned until gaps in the front rows revealed Kav Daven shin-deep in the middle of a water-filled terrace. The priest's bony arms were outstretched, his head thrown back in ecstatic benediction. Kav Ashimmel waited to one side, the hem of her embroidered tabard trailing its red and gold in the muddy water. Behind the Master Priest, the full complement of the Priest Guild, a hundred strong, were drawn up in rows ascending the flooded tiers, first the senior priests, then the journeymen. Higher still, along the ridge bounding the topmost terrace, the apprentices, Liphar among them, raised banners of triumphant yellow and red.

Susannah appeared at Stavros' side. "Can you believe it?"

He nodded, seeing only the bliss on Kav Daven's face.

She grabbed his sleeve and pulled him through the press of bodies to the front of the crowd. "I mean this. Look!"

He'd not noticed it yet, but in addition to water and priests, the terraces were full of bright yellow shoots. The tallest reached to Kav Daven's thigh and already, strong secondary leaves were uncurling from the stalk like the fronds of a fern.

"That seed went in less than four days ago! There wasn't a sign of life out here yesterday!" Susannah struggled to remain coherent. "These things shot up in a matter of hours!" She knelt on the earthen dike and cradled a slim leaf in wondering fingers. "I swear they've grown centimeters since I've been standing here!"

"Shhh!" he breathed.

Megan nosed in beside him. "What's all the . . . oh!"

"Quiet! Please! Not now!" Stavros' instinctive glance toward Kav Daven met the old priest's blind gaze directly. The impression of sight without seeing was stronger than ever. A touch of amusement seemed to curl the priest's withered lips.

Ashimmel ignored the noisy Terran outburst. She sent an acolyte scurrying up the terraces to the waiting ranks of apprentices. The ranks parted to clear a space along the ridge. Two dozen senior apprentices passed their banners to a neighbor and fell into formation, filling the space with three interlocking circles. The younger apprentices struck up a high-pitched rhythmic wail. When the dance began, the journeymen priests joined in a lower key. The circles broke and reformed, revolved and broke again.

Stavros had come to see Liphar dance, but Kav Daven held his gaze, and he would not insult the old priest by looking away. No matter that he was blind and had no right to know the difference. The chanting built a wall of sound around them. The flooded tier shimmered and seemed to fade behind a blaze of light. Stavros felt its heat wash across his cheek and a shudder run up his back. The priest was again perturbing reality in ways that defied understanding.

Then from the cliff top, the wooden horns blared a new and dissonant note. The uncanny light faded. The singing faltered, the dancers staggered, and silence descended. Kav Ashimmel looked dumbfounded and annoyed, but Kav Daven's amusement broadened into an elfin grin. He nodded slowly to Stavros as if sharing a private joke, then lifted a parched hand toward the cliff in an invitation to observe.

Stavros turned. At first he could see nothing unusual, just the amber brilliance of the rock and the green sky beyond. Splashes of red and gold glinted regularly along the scarp, where the nine teams of horn bearers manned their giant instruments.

The throng rumbled in confusion. Then a sharp-eyed young ranger whooped and pointed. Others saw now, and a chorus of victory yells swelled across the terraces. Stavros felt himself once again propelled through the crowd, toward the cliffs this time. Hands clapped his back. Faces grinned, congratulating.

Behind him Megan murmured, "Oh, my loving god."

At last he spotted it: stuttering motion along the top of the cliff between two of the horn emplacements. Smears of dull color against the sky, beginning a slow descent of the easternmost stair. He made out two figures, no, three—tall Aguidran unmistakable in the lead, the second in white nearly invisible against the pale hot rock. They carried, half-dragged, something dark between them. The third trailed a bit behind.

"It's Ronnie!" Susannah exclaimed. "She's found them!"

Stavros swore without thinking. And then swore again.

"And one of them's walking!" Megan noted.

He turned back to find Kav Daven still smiling. If anything, his smile had broadened, until it glowed, until it could swallow the entire plain. But Stavros returned a look of dread and disappointment, pleading silently with the old man.

Don't you understand this is the worst thing that could happen?

Megan muttered into his ear, "Just pray the live one is Danforth."

BOOK FOUR

CONSPIRACY

"Have more than thou showest,
Speak less than thou knowest . . ."

—*King Lear,* Act I, sc . iv

30

THE NOISY THRONG fell back at the entrance to the Frieze Hall, parting to let the stretcher bearers through. The Master Healer followed, already rolling up the long sleeves of his smock. With Megan muttering warnings in his ear, Stavros intercepted Susannah at the top of the ramp.

"We can't let him in there!"

"What? Don't be ridiculous!" Susannah pushed past him, breathless from her sprint to the Black Hole for her medikit.

"How can you keep him away?" Megan hissed. "It'll be worse if you make a scene."

A step behind them, Kav Ashimmel halted on the ramp and swung to face the crowd. She raised her arms for silence and launched into a ringing extempore speech claiming the return of the lost as a sign of the power of Lagri. But the long tails of her ceremonial tabard dripped mud onto the stone floor, and the din in the crowded tunnel abated only slightly as pockets of cheerful debate raged around wager-holders calling in bets.

Stavros dogged Susannah down the Frieze Hall as she hurried toward Physicians'. "Look, you don't understand . . ."

"It doesn't matter what I do or don't understand! A doctor can't refuse to treat an injured man."

"Treat him downstairs, or in the Lander!"

"When I tried to take that injured boy downstairs, you called me arrogant. Make up your mind!"

"This is not the same!"

"Physicians' is better equipped!"

"That's just it!! He'll see that, all the . . . ah, damn. Damn!"

She was past him, not listening. Stavros let her go and slumped onto the side-wall bench, his face tight with despair. Megan dropped dispiritedly beside him. Moments later, Liphar trotted up, looking busy and concerned. He stuffed a well-fingered strip of paper into a pouch under his mud-spattered ritual garb and a pencil into the thick of his curls. He glanced at Stavros, then at Megan, then back at Stavros. Clearly, he had something on his mind, but it could wait.

Megan was not so accommodating. "Are you going to tell me what you're so worried about?" When Stavros just stared at the floor, she sighed. "You've got to keep a lower profile if you want to slip something by them." She paused. "That *is* what you'd like to do, right?"

He stretched his legs out, staring at the wall opposite. "Too late now."

Liphar shifted his weight, patient but with one ear tuned to the transactions back at the ramp.

"Maybe it's not."

Stavros gave a soft snort of dismissal.

"You give up easy! For instance . . . I don't know what the deal is, but if the problem is Physicians' . . ." Megan's tone was like a foot inching out to test thin ice. "Say we went in there and simply contrived to keep him from noticing anything . . . unusual."

"Ummm," replied Stavros neutrally.

"Well, to begin with, what sort of unusual might that be?"

Down the hall, Ashimmel ended her speech with a flourish. She gathered her dignity and the small entourage that remained, and swept off down the ramp. The excitement was over, until the final news of life or death came out of Physicians'. A mild dispute arose among the wagerers at the ramp head as to whether the terms of a particular bet had been properly met. Liphar drifted back in that direction, easing the pencil out of his hair.

"Well?" prompted Megan.

Stavros stalled. He was in desperate need of an ally, but could he trust Megan to keep the sort of secrets he'd been holding? "Ashimmel is a fool to promulgate that interpretation."

"She's an opportunist. This'll raise her status in the Guild Council."

"But her approval could open up the whole cave system."

"Until the weather turns bad again. Then we'll be out on our ears. It was smart of you to go after Kav Daven. Shows some political acumen at least."

"That wasn't why . . ." But this he didn't want to explain. "Gee, thanks."

"Don't mention it." She glanced up as Weng hurried toward them with a bedraggled McPherson in tow. Megan pointed down the long hall. "To your left and up, Commander. We'll join you in a minute." When the two had gone, she pressed her advantage. "So what should I be looking for up there?"

Stavros decided he was out of options. "Little things. Like a pressurized hot-water system, like . . ." *Piped-in gas?* "You'll know when you see it."

Megan absorbed this information thoughtfully, and rose. "Okay, then. Let's go."

"You go. I've got to deal with Aguidran about getting the Sled hauled in. Didn't he say he'd made contact with CRI?"

"Sounded that way."

"So there's a functioning antenna out there. We get it, we'll have our com back."

"I thought distracting him was your main concern."

"It is, but . . . low profile, you know? I can't be trusted in there right now." He shot her a bitter glance. "I don't want to become any more of a liability than I apparently am already."

"Stav, I never said . . ."

"Just go. Be my eyes and ears, and do what you can."

So Megan went off, but not without a backward glance that promised she'd press him later for a fuller explanation.

"*Ph'nar khem.*" Liphar returned to unburden himself of the thought that had been bothering him. "Kav Ashimmel not smart say Lagri bring this."

"You said it." Stavros rubbed his brow, searching for a coherent plan of action. "What if we went before the full Guild Council?"

Liphar shook his head warningly. "Big voice of *Kethed,* Ashimmel. Bigger now."

"We could talk to the other guild heads first, in private." Stavros was asking the young apprentice to work behind his own guild master's back, but he could think of no other solution. Megan's remark about political acumen haunted him. She had a reputation for this sort of maneuvering, though he'd not noticed her keeping her own political profile particularly low. Of course, at the moment, she had nothing to hide.

"Then you go. Tell them there are things they need to know, before it's too late. That there are issues vital to the safety of the community, and that they should call a Kethed to decide what's best for all."

Liphar nodded unhappily, but Stavros knew he would follow through.

"We have to do *something*, Lifa. We had some respite, but the wolf is back at the door."

Was this what Megan meant by political acumen? Stavros was not sure. He squeezed the young Sawl's shoulder in guilt and gratitude, and sent him off. With an anxious glance in the direction of Physicians', he hurried away to find Aguidran.

31

E.D. 68–3:20

"MORE LIGHT HERE, if you can, Ghirra."
Susannah blotted her forehead on her sleeve, wishing for a good O.R. nurse, then found Ghirra's youngest apprentice at her elbow with a clean cloth. She let the boy pat her face thoroughly, then bent to inspect the last of the serious wounds. Ghirra reached up to adjust the reflector on the battery lamp Susannah had clipped to the hub of the oil chandelier. The big spoked wheel swayed on its stout rope and the hard glare of the Terran lamp flashed in and out of the darkened corners like a berserk searchlight. The anxious faces around the operating slab raised hands to shade their eyes.

Megan slipped in as a second apprentice brought a fresh bowl of the long absorbent fibers Ghirra used as a sponge. She put on a concerned and hopeful look, and took stock of the room. Ghirra's operating chamber was the smallest of the four caverns that made up Physicians Hall. It was tall and narrow, and the air was fresh. In the shadow of deep shelves cut into the rock, ranks of glass jars glinted in long neat rows. The patient lay on the central of three waist-high marble slabs.

Susannah glanced up, nodding Megan to a stone bench along one wall. "We'll be a while here." She gathered up a fiber sponge. The Master Healer steadied the swinging lamp, then leaned over the patient for a closer look. His surgical assistant Ampiar hovered nearby.

The wound was a near-critical puncture high on the right side. A shard of metal had cut deeply but at an angle that allowed it to just miss the lung. The shard had been removed in the field, but bone fragments from a shattered rib remained to fester. The tear had partly healed, but infection had set in. Susannah swabbed away the purulence with Ghirra's herbal disinfectant. She probed for the fragments, then applied an antiseptic from her own supplies. Ghirra shared a quiet glance with Ampiar and wrinkled his nose.

"Apologies, Guildmaster." Susannah was aware that the flat medicinal smell smothered the healthy pungence of his herbal infusion, but she wasn't taking any chances.

When the wound was cleaned, she set a small section of tubing in it to drain any excess fluids, and closed as neatly as she could. There would be a nasty scar, but the patient's entire body was hot and sandpaper-dry. There were more pressing considerations than cosmetics. She moved on immediately to a shallow gash needing only minor stitching. She cleaned it out, and as she reached for a suture, Ghirra's hand met hers halfway with the instrument already prepared.

"Thank you, Doctor," she remembered to say. As an intern, she had suffered through many months in chill operating rooms before she had learned to detect the gratitude that lay unvoiced behind the operating surgeon's mask.

Danforth stirred weakly under her hand.

"He's waking up!" McPherson hissed. Wan with exhaustion, she leaned against the stone table until the plastic sheet crackled. Ghirra frowned absently and spread the wrinkles smooth. Plastic seemed to intrigue him.

"Soon," Susannah soothed as she completed a stitch. "But not just yet. Don't worry. If the gas runs out, Ghirra has other ways to deal with pain."

At Danforth's head, Weng tipped the valve on the small field canister of nitrous oxide and set the mask to the patient's nose and mouth. "Still a quarter full."

"You won't improve Tay's chances by leaning all over him, McP," chided a cheerful voice from the next table, where Emil Clausen sat jauntily upright, legs swinging over the edge, calmly peeling back the emergency sealant from a small gash on his forearm. The white therm-suit he had donned three weeks earlier was mud-stained but intact, except for the sleeves, which had been cut away at the elbows and folded back in neat cuffs. A sandy gray beard furred the prospector's sunburned cheeks. He looked gaunt but healthy. Only the stout stick by his knee belied the suggestion that he'd walked home entirely under his own steam. On the slab beside him was a bulging leather knapsack.

The apprentice Dwingen brought a bowl of hot water and gestured shyly that he might wash out Clausen's wound. The prospector twisted away with a grimace, then caught himself and smiled at the boy. "Nothing personal, you understand."

"He doesn't speak English, Emil." Megan settled onto the hard cool bench.

"Then he must learn, my dear Megan, if he's to make his way in his new galactic life."

Megan shot back a glare of disapproval. His smug grin was really too much to bear right now. But she'd seen nothing in the room so far to worry Stavros. Ghirra's setup was clean and simple, and it would take a connoisseur to appreciate how skilled the Master Healer's long-fingered hands were, or how he and Susannah worked together with the smooth rhythm of doctors familiar with each other's techniques. What bothered Megan most was that Clausen had survived his ordeal with little more than fading bruises and a healing scab or two. Okay, there was the matter of a twisted ankle, swelling again now that he'd stayed off it for a while, but compared to Danforth, who'd been stretchered in delirious with fever and both legs in field splints, Clausen had got off scot-free. He seemed to possess more lives than a cat. Had the two men not been allies since before the expedition, Megan's habitually tender suspicions would have been mightily aroused.

"Who was driving?" she inquired sullenly.

"Yours truly." Clausen's dry look said he'd have allowed nothing else.

"What did you do, run the passenger side into a wall?"

"I was attempting an unpowered landing in a gale. It was better than the alternative." When he offered her his grin again, she glanced away to study the glass-stocked shelves.

Ghirra's operating chamber had clerestory windows like the Frieze Hall, so that a narrow band of amber sunlight fell from above onto the operating tables. Megan thought this a sweet if melodramatic gesture on the part of the builders, suggesting that the tables were especially favored by nature. A linen curtain divided the chamber from the outer cavern. Through a center split, Megan saw rows of pallets set on low platforms of glazed white brick. They were mostly empty now, as anyone well enough to crawl was downstairs celebrating. One old man reclined with his back to the curtain. In a far corner, a young mother nursed her newborn under the watchful eye of Head Midwife Xifa. Megan stretched her legs and turned her attention to the incomprehensible labels etched on jars filled with substances beyond her imagining. Her eyelids drooped. By her loose calculation, it was 3:20 in the morning, ship's time. She wondered how Susannah and especially old Weng remained so steady of hand on so little sleep.

Little Dwingen came toward her balancing a bowl heaped with bloodied linens. Megan drew in her legs to let him squeeze by. He passed through a narrow archway at the end of her bench. Megan peered casually around the corner. A white-smocked teenager tended a row of steaming ceramic cauldrons. Dwingen emptied his load into a deep sink, then turned a large brown wheel protruding from the wall above. Hot water flowed into the sink. Impressive, but Susannah had already mentioned that Physicians' had hot running water. Megan shrugged, but her attention was caught by the cauldrons and the tiny blue flames dancing beneath them.

Suddenly she was very much awake. Gas burners? This had to be what Stav couldn't bring himself to talk about out loud. Come to think of it, how did the water in the tap *get* so piping hot? Not what you'd expect of a so-called primitive people.

Megan estimated Clausen's line of sight. She was fairly sure he could not see through the archway from his slab. But if he decided to try walking about, she'd have to get imaginative. She stretched her legs to block the way again and left them there.

"Okay." Susannah completed a final stitch. "He's as clean and tight as I can get him." As she checked the drip taped to Danforth's arm, Ghirra laid two fingers on the wrist. After a moment, he gave a faint shake of his head.

"I know," said Susannah. "He's very weak. But the antibiotic ought to bring that fever down—that is, if your bugs are anything like our bugs."

"Buggs." Ghirra savored the final consonants as he spread his hands and let them hover over Danforth's head, then his chest, where he laid them lightly over the heart. "But if not, we try . . ."

"None of that stuff in the jars!" exploded McPherson.

Susannah shot the pilot something uncharacteristically like a glare, but the corners of Ghirra's wide mouth twitched to conceal a smile. Megan decided that the Master Healer picked up a lot more than he let anyone know.

"One more outburst, Lieutenant," said Weng, "and you're confined to quarters."

"Where you should be anyway," Megan chided. "You can barely see straight."

"I'm fine. I'm not leaving here until I know he's okay."

"Worry not, McP," said Clausen. "You'd be surprised at the useful little medicinals these primitives stumble upon sometimes."

Susannah's hand twitched on the lid of her portable autoclave. She let it down very carefully. "Almost as surprising as the emergency care some clumsy amateurs manage in the field."

Clausen chuckled wearily. "Did the best I could. He'd have died without it, you must admit."

"You did well, and we're all grateful," put in Weng sternly.

Clausen blinked at McPherson and grinned.

Susannah turned her back. Ghirra readjusted the battery lamp to light the full length of the slab, then nodded to Dwingen, who waited with a bowl of minted hot water and clean strips of linen. While Ampiar helped Susannah peel off her bloody surgical gloves, the Master Healer washed and dried his hands. Then, again, he let them hover over Danforth's body, his eyes closed. His long fingers barely skimmed the white over sheet. As he reached the right leg, just above the knee, his hands stilled.

Weng looked interested. Susannah watched unsurprised, as Ampiar fitted her with a clean pair of gloves. "Needs to be reset," she agreed. "The other's fractured below the knee but it seems to be healing. The alignment was undisturbed."

"Thanks to my expert splinting," Clausen reminded her.

"Of course," Susannah replied, with only the faintest show of sarcasm.

Ghirra's hands skimmed the left leg briefly and he nodded.

"What's he doing?" McPherson whispered.

Susannah's face softened. "His hands are . . . like sensors. He feels . . . well, abnormalities, like heat or . . . oh, if I could fully explain it, Ron, I'd try it myself."

McPherson's expression implied native mumbo-jumbo, but she held her peace.

Susannah folded back the over sheet to expose Danforth's legs. The right knee and thigh were scabbed and discolored. Carefully, she probed the kneecap.

Clausen slid himself along his table to the end nearest Megan's bench. "Tay'll be the worst sort of invalid if he wakes up," he confided. "Should have heard him out at the wreck, whining and complaining."

"Yeah, for shame," Meg growled. "Pain is such a lot of fun."

The prospector tilted his bullet head. "It wasn't the pain, it was the boredom. Do you take me for a sadist? I kept him well stoked up with the Sled's supply of painkillers. But he hated having to lie there while I was out scrabbling in the rain and dark. By the time dawn arrived, the fever'd gotten him." Clausen patted the leather knapsack at his side. "I hope he comes to long enough to find out he was right."

Megan had stopped listening, but the gloat in his voice alerted her. "Right about what?"

"It's here, just like he said it would be."

"It, Mr. Clausen?" inquired Weng without diverting her focus from the anesthesia.

The prospector grinned. "The lithium."

The word fell among them like a lead weight.

Here we go, thought Megan. The Sawls' eviction notice.

"It's what we came for, remember?"

"What *you* came for," Megan amended.

Clausen had expected a livelier reaction. He hauled the mud-caked pack up onto his lap and unbuckled a side flap. Several chunks of glittering rock tumbled out. He caught one up and held it overhead like a victory cup. "It's lepidolite. The real thing. A proper lithium ore. Pretty little sucker, eh?"

The rock was pale translucent lilac, like a summer dusk. Crystalline out-croppings of quartz alternated with flat plates of silvery mica. As Clausen twisted it in the light of the battery lamp, deeper hues of rose and lavender twinkled in veins along one side.

Interesting how bad news often feels like a physical blow. Megan thought of the sparkle-eyed goddesses in the Frieze Hall. Clausen wouldn't need those jewels, now that he'd found his own. And so, another world would fall to the miner's shovel, feeding the insatiable appetite of the failing Earth. The inevitability of the moment was both familiar and unbearable. Every time she went out into the field, she hoped that the prospectors would find nothing to interest them, and every time, they did. We used up everything we had, so now we poach the resources of others. Clausen would confidently call it progress. He was so sure of his right-by-might that the dissolution of entire cultures by his hand became a necessary part of that forward motion. Perhaps he also saw it as proof of his superiority, that he survived and they didn't.

Did it matter now what Clausen saw and what he didn't? The outcome was preordained. She should be the one to tell Stavros. Better he hear it from a sympathetic party than be forced to suffer Clausen's gloating. There would be enough of that in the days to come.

Clausen juggled the sparkling rock from palm to palm. "And I think it's a big strike. I have to get back out there with instruments, of course, before I make an official filing, but I located at least one good vein in the side of a ravine below our crash site. Pretty decent, for working in the dark!"

Weng was still intent on the operating table. "Excellent news, Mr. Clausen."

Clausen regarded her ramrod back with amusement. "Oh, you bet your ass it is, Commander! And by the way, how did our antique landing vehicle weather the storm?"

"I will be glad to have your opinion on that matter," Weng replied.

"Shhh!" hissed McPherson, and then groaned aloud as Susannah grasped Danforth's thigh top and bottom around the break and wrenched it into alignment.

Megan felt the crunch to the very roots of her teeth. It was too much. She rose swaying from the bench. "Excuse me," she mumbled and fled from the hall.

Ghirra stepped back from the operating table with a look of relief. But relief drained away to dismay as he saw the glittering rock held high in the prospector's hand.

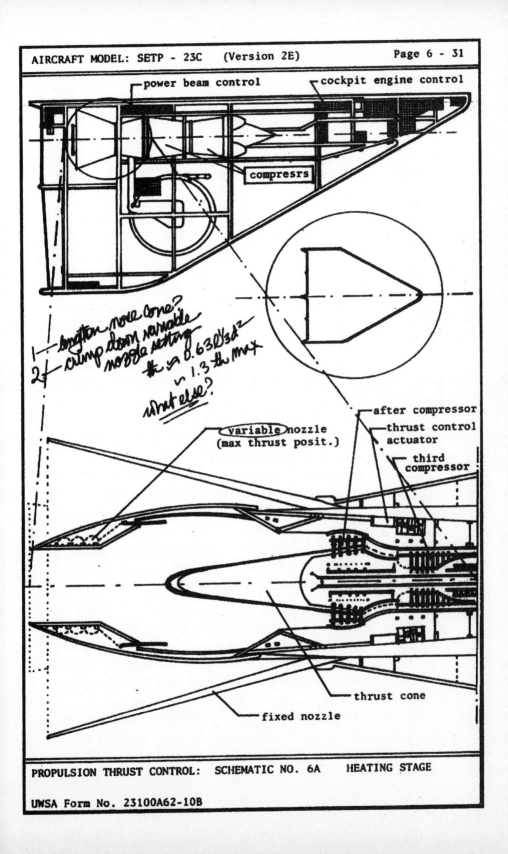

power beam control

cockpit engine control

compresrs

lengthen nose cone?
crimp down variable nozzle setting
$t_c \approx 0.63 \varrho^{1/3} d^2$
≈ 1.3 the max
what else?

variable nozzle
(max thrust posit.)

after compressor

thrust control
actuator

third
compressor

thrust cone

fixed nozzle

PROPULSION THRUST CONTROL: SCHEMATIC NO. 6A   HEATING STAGE

UWSA Form No. 23100A62-10B

32

A GUIDRAN MADE HER office at the head of a long wooden table at the far end of the Ranger Hall. It was the last clear space in the Hall, which otherwise resembled the cargo bay of an old sailing ship on its homeward voyage. Tall racks stuffed with gear hugged the walls. A hanging jungle of ropes and strapping brought the ceiling down to just above head height. Piles of sacking and fat wooden cabinets fought each other for floor space.

Stavros watched over her shoulder as the Master Ranger scrawled a hurried map of the wreck site: a small plateau surrounded by steep ravines and rockslides in the southern mountains, the Grigar.

Grigar. Stavros dissected the word reflexively. *Lagri-egar.* Lagri's Wall.

Aguidran sat back in her leather-bound chair to study her work. She was so tired from the return trek that her hands shook as she twisted her charcoal between her fingers, then drew a circle to indicate the downed Sled. She used a blank corner to detail the Sled itself. Clausen might have supplied a more technical assessment of the Sled's position and condition, but Stavros could not imagine putting himself close enough to ask.

Smug bastard. Smug as a sunning crocodile.

He beat his fist gently on the stout back of Aguidran's chair, and she looked up, frowning. He backed away, abashed, and began to pace instead. He pondered Megan's notion of low profile. Not being present could give as loud a signal as words. For instance, his absence from Physicians' at such a moment was sure to be noticed—by Weng, if not by Clausen.

No. He would notice. He'd want to know where his damn gear was stowed. Fuck 'im. I'll say I had to sleep sometime.

Aguidran growled privately and rubbed out a line to redraw it in a sharper curve. Her visual memory was keen and her hand practiced at conveying scale

and spatial relationships. But her diagram of the Sled suffered from her ignorance of the machinery. Stavros squinted sideways at the drawing, trying to
coax the rough charcoal lines into readable information. The stubby triangular
body of the vehicle was apparent enough. Despite its bent or perhaps missing
stabilizers and its crumpled tail fin, it seemed miraculously intact. Clausen
had managed a cleaner landing than should have been possible, given the
weather conditions. Stavros hated the man for being so relentlessly skilled.

A relay runner appeared at the table with several minutes' worth of verbal
messages and a rare written letter to deliver. Aguidran shoved her drawing
aside to listen to the runner's recitation and to dictate replies. She set the
letter aside. Something of a confidential nature, Stavros deduced. Otherwise
she'd have taken the usual advantage of the message runner's trained and
prodigious memory.

When he got her attention back again, Stavros persuaded her to try a rendering of the rear section of the Sled, and the all-important power and communications equipment in its transparent blister. Aguidran tried, but without
knowing the function of the intricate shapings of rod and mesh and wire, she
could not clearly delineate their form. The sketch rapidly degenerated into
a smudged-out study in abstract. Frustrated, Aguidran crumpled the rough
paper into a ball and lobbed it into the dead ashes in the fireplace behind her.
She gave Stavros a look that implied several cycles' worth of more pressing
matters that required her attention, so he relented, nodding his gratitude. He
picked up the site drawing, and Aguidran bent to sift through the mountain
of paperwork that had piled up while she was out on the search. Very likely,
she hadn't slept since her return.

He looked around for an out-of-the-way perch that was still within the
circle of light from the overhead wheel. Short backless benches with leather
pads were tucked against the long sides of the table. Stavros slid onto the
nearest vacant one, laying the drawing out to make sense of and memorize.
The benches next to him were occupied by three youngish guildsmen, no
longer apprentices but still required to put in time at copying and book-
keeping. Two more sat opposite, all five sharing a huge inkwell that squatted
in the center of the table like a glass sea urchin. One muttered to himself
as he counted. The girl next to Stavros chewed the end of her quill and
occasionally glanced around at the others as if measuring the extent of their
progress against her own. In the shadow of the inkwell sat five equal stacks
of flat stone counters.

Stavros wondered idly what the bet was. First to finish a page? First to finish ten pages? First to run into a snag and be forced to disturb the Master Ranger? He yawned. He was having difficulty concentrating. The trestled table drew his eye down its enormous length, out of the pool of lamplight, through the darkened jungle of equipment toward the cool glow of daylight that leaked up from the cave mouth to peek in at the entrance arch. The table was a double arm's reach wide. Its thick planks had been planed and sanded and oiled until the seams were visible only in an abrupt change of the grain. Stavros smoothed its golden surface with a reverent finger and recalled his love affair with the winch.

Perhaps I was a tree in a former life. . . .

He envisioned a guild meeting, with the hall alive with torch and firelight, every one of the guild's ninety-odd full members comfortably seated and the storage racks and ceiling hooks groaning with the load of apprentices eager to observe the goings-on and dream about the day when they could claim a ceremonial place at the table. Stavros considered it an honor to be allowed to sit at it at all.

A draft slipped down the long low cavern to lift the corners of his paper. It brought warm air and earth smells from the cave mouth, and the faint echoes of the continuing celebration at the foot of the cliffs.

Concentrate, Ibiá. Haul the Sled in, or salvage what you can?

A senior ranger came through the archway with a Food Guild clerk. They stepped around fat bundles of rope fiber and coils of half-twisted rope, and stopped at the table. The Food Guilder dropped a sheaf of mud-stained papers by Aguidran's hand and left. The ranger stood mopping his brow while his guild master dipped her pen to scratch a series of numbers into a cloth-bound ledger. Stavros left his bench to fish the sketch of the antennas out of the ashes. The arch of the fireplace was as tall as his forehead. He stepped back to study the finely carved mantel. From the center of a big frieze right above, the Sisters beckoned him with their jeweled eyes.

Not yet, he told them. I know what you want, but you haven't convinced me.

He turned his back and flattened the wrinkled paper against his thigh.

Okay. So Clausen had contacted CRI when the storm cleared, so the high gain must be down or he'd have powered up and tried to fly back to the Caves. Or maybe the damage was worse than Aguidran's sketch suggested. Stavros looked again at the site drawing. As the Master Ranger lacked his understanding of the machinery, he lacked her knowledge of the surrounding countryside. He would need more complete directions to the wreck. He gathered his courage and went back to Aguidran. She returned him a steely glare, but pointed to a boxy wooden cabinet halfway down the hall, hemmed in almost to disappearance by overflowing storage racks. She snapped a number, then turned away to let the waiting ranger finish his report.

Stavros went to the cabinet and pulled open its man-high double doors. The interior was divided into several hundred numbered pigeonholes. More than half of them contained what looked like slim rolls of fabric. Stavros located the right number, slid the roll from its cubicle, and carried it to the table. Loosing the faded ribbon ties at either end, he unrolled it gingerly and felt his pulse actually quicken. Spread out before him was a yellowing map, carefully inked on vellum and attached to a cloth backing, with flaps that folded in to protect the delicate edges. The backing had been neatly mended in several places. The map was so worn that the vellum had entirely lost its curl.

Thrilled, Stavros returned to the cabinet to ease several other rolls part-way from their slots. Judging from their varying colors and states of repair, they were of vastly differing ages, some dark and threadbare with use, others as fresh as if they had been inked the day before. He chose one of the oldest ones at random from the top row and brought it back to the table.

It lay as limp as silk in his hands. Carefully, he spread it flat. Two large circles greeted him, side by side, filled with various markings indicating features of terrain.

A world map? Could it be? And hemispherical at that.

According to history, it was not until the advent of spaceflight that the inhabitants of Earth truly believed that the apparently flat ground they walked on was in reality a section of arc. Stavros studied the double hemispheres again. Every area was complete in its detail. Particular attention had been paid to a slanted quasi-equatorial band, and two isolated points. One was low in the southern latitudes, circled by the squiggle marks of mountains, and the other centered within a vast body of water in the northeastern quadrant. Stavros thought it odd that he'd heard no tale chants or histories of intrepid Sawl explorers gathering this wealth of data. Had the mapmakers simply invented it? But more intriguing was the focus on those two widely separated points. Lagri was said to make her home in a mountainous desert far to the south, while Valla Ired, it was taught, lived in the great northern ocean.

Would they actually put that on a map: *This way to the god-home?* It was comical, and yet . . . the map was otherwise bland and understated, offering up those two markings as just another bit of fact. He would question Aguidran when she was rested, when she could find the time. He rolled the ancient document and replaced it in the cabinet, then went back to the map the Master Ranger had directed him to.

He found it cryptic in the extreme, being more at home with circuitry diagrams than cartographies. The double hemispheres had been easier to relate to—their conceptual layout was more or less familiar. This other was deliciously exotic. As the days progressed and he slipped closer to accepting Sawlian reality as his own, an object like this, with its obscure symbolisms and hen-scratch notations, would bring him up short, reminding him that he was living inside an alien culture. He studied the yellowing chart for a while, then gathered it up and brought it to the head of the table.

Aguidran took it from him brusquely and cleared a space among her layered papers. She called to an apprentice clambering noisily around in the storage racks. He set aside the keg he was struggling with, climbed down, and brought her a sheet of crinkly paper from a set of wide drawers beside the map cabinet. Aguidran smoothed the translucent paper over the map and traced out her route. Her dotted line started with several circles to mark the Caves, then wove through canyons and ravines and up into the mountains. She went back to ink in landmarks such as the Red Pawn and the Talche, a low range of knobby mountains directly east of the Caves. She drew a broad serrated oval to represent the Dop Arek, adding labels in her spiked Sawlish script. Next to the Cave circles, she wrote "Dul Elesi" with a final flourish. As an afterthought, she added a smaller circle for the Lander.

The Master Ranger's calligraphy had all the big-bellied curves that she did not, but Stavros was sure that such hinting at concealed softness was illusory. Her writing was clear and strong, far easier to decipher than the ancient crabbed markings on the original map, and each letter finished with a sharp serif or downturn that more than reinforced her outer image of grit and reliability. Aguidran regarded her work with amused pride, then flicked an impatient hand at Stavros, sat back and stretched.

Stavros went back to his bench. Having the route defined made the trip a reality. From McPherson's description, he estimated two days and some to get there, a day or so if he decided salvage was the only option, then the return. Five days, seven max, if they didn't run into more weather. Later, he'd get Aguidran or maybe the Engineers Guild to lend him enough men to bring back the rest of the vehicle. He laid the tracing on the table. Aguidran's route out had been circuitous, a searcher's route. It dipped south, then snaked east, following the contours of the mountain canyons. But the crash site was due southeast, so coming back, they'd cut straight across the high plateau bordering the Dop Arek, avoiding the rougher terrain they'd come through to the south.

Of course, Clausen was going to want to come along. The prospect filled Stavros with dread, but he could see no way around it. On the other hand, it did beat leaving the man behind to run rampant in the Caves. He'd want the Sled hauled in right away, but for that he was just going to have to wait. As Communications Officer, Stavros was bound by the priorities set by the ship's Commander.

The slap of running feet broke the hall's industrious silence. A young courier charged through the main arch, took a flying leap over the bundles of rope fiber, and sprinted the length of the hall to skid to a halt at her superior's elbow. She spilled her report breathlessly, and Stavros saw genuine surprise touch Aguidran's weathered face. She made the runner repeat her story more slowly, then shoved back her chair and strode muttering from the hall, trailing the excited courier behind her. The journeymen at the table noted their guild master's hurried exit with mild interest and returned to their work.

Stavros hastily folded his copy of the map and stowed it in his waistband. He took two long steps after Aguidran, then caught himself and ran back to return the old map to its numbered slot. In the outer corridor, he had to twist aside sharply to avoid slamming into Megan.

"What are you doing here? You're supposed to be . . ."

"I couldn't take it up there any better than you could. What's going on?"

"You shouldn't have left him alone!"

"He's got a bum ankle. He's not moving around much. Why's everybody running around all of a sudden?"

"I'm on my way to find out."

A small but noisy crowd had gathered at the cave mouth. Stavros counted half a dozen priests, Ashimmel, several of Aguidran's couriers, and the Master Ranger herself, listening with stern and tired eyes while they all tried to speak at once. Only Ashimmel remained aloof and silent, puffy-cheeked as if she'd been hauled out of bed. She hadn't even taken the time to don her embroidered regalia. Stavros thought she looked older, less substantial in her civilian tunic and pants. It was no mystery why priests throughout the inhabited worlds assumed some kind of fancy dress.

He took up an unobtrusive post near the entry. He'd nearly managed to isolate from the pandemonium the one phrase that seemed to be on everyone's lips when Aguidran hushed them with a hoarse bellow and elbowed her way onto the ledge. Ashimmel did likewise, standing with the Master Ranger but pointedly not beside her. The other priests drew up behind their guild master, and the crowd fell silent, waiting.

Puzzled, Stavros stared out across the plains. The ravaged Dop Arek stared balefully back. Below, the tent city still sported its bright streamers, like cheerful arms waving in the breeze while an army of Food Guild apprentices bustled about cleaning up. The planted terraces were now solid with waist-high yellow stalks, beginning to uncurl their segmented leaves. The larger open fields showed rows of amber spikes. The little vegetable plots stuck into the odd remaining spaces bristled with new growth. Even the far gullies and rises of the plain were softening under a pale lemon fuzz. The air was warm and fragrant, the sky a clear watery green shading toward azure overhead. The salmon sun was approaching zenith.

Stavros thought everything looked fine. What the hell were they staring at?

Finally, he understood. They were not looking. They were listening. Then Aguidran's head jerked up and swiveled to the northeast, toward the mountains that bounded the plain, which the Sawls called the Vallegar, or Valla's Wall. This time, Stavros heard it also, a low slow grumble in the distance.

Megan nosed in beside him. "So what is it?"

He nodded northeastward. "Thunder. Or something like it."

"Is that bad?"

"I doubt they'd make this much of a fuss if it meant a little summer shower."

Megan asked, only half-seriously, "Which Sister do we have to root for this time?"

"Rain coming would be Valla's territory."

The crowd stirred into motion as Aguidran issued brisk instructions to her couriers. One jogged back into the Caves. The others sped out along the stairs and ledges to alert the weather watch. Aguidran folded her leather-clad arms and turned to face Ashimmel.

Megan eased herself down the wall and sat hugging her knees. "Mmmmm.

The crops'll never survive the kind of rain they come up with around here."

Stavros crouched beside her. "And if that crop isn't harvested, we may all starve."

"Well . . ."

He nodded emphatically. "Liphar told me the last of the seed stores went into the ground this time. The previous harvest, before we arrived, wasn't good."

"Bad weather?"

"Correct."

"Sometimes I wonder if there's *good* weather left anywhere in the universe," Megan commented. "Rash, though, to use up all the seed,"

"It was either that or risk a harvest too small to feed everyone," he defended, as if it were his own harvest.

"They need seed banks. They need more land under cultivation."

"Fine, Meg, but then they'd have to not eat part of a harvest that barely feeds the population as it is, in order to save seed or have more for the expanded planting."

Megan rubbed her forehead. Her eyes were pink with exhaustion. "Susannah understands all this growing stuff better than we do. She was postdoc right when the shit really hit the fan for the farmers back home, when the climate started changing faster than anyone had predicted and not even the hybridizers could keep up—maybe she could help out the Sawls." She dragged both hands down across her eyes. "Speaking of which, there's plumbed gas in Physicians'. Is that what you thought I'd find?"

Stavros' mouth tightened. "Suspected it. I'd seen it . . . elsewhere."

"But you didn't see fit to tell us. Do you know where it comes from?"

He nudged her silent. Aguidran's conference with Ashimmel had flared into heated debate. Ashimmel was fully awake now, arms waving, gray curls flying as she stalked about inside the circle formed by her priests, with Aguidran at its center. Her tunic sleeves flapped like pinion feathers as she pointed alternately at the sky, then down at the planted fields. The Master Ranger stood her ground, talking right over the priest's harangue, ticking her arguments off on her fingers like so many items on a shopping list.

Stavros eavesdropped intently. "Something about going or not going," he translated. "Ashimmel insists on staying in case the storms return."

"Sounds logical," Megan ventured.

"Yes, but it isn't like Aguidran to be unreasonable. I can't quite understand where she means them to go, but it seems to involve a lot of people."

"A lot?"

Stavros frowned. "Like . . . everyone?"

"Everyone?"

He was as mystified as she. "It's as if it's what they'd normally do, but now Ashimmel doesn't think it's the right time."

"Everyone," repeated Megan. "Well, what they do, they do tend to do en masse."

The argument ended abruptly. Ashimmel looked dissatisfied. Aguidran moved away to squint fiercely at the Vallegar.

Stavros listened to the murmurs in the circle of priests. "Okay, they've agreed to wait a while, to see if anything comes of the thunder."

Finally, the Master Ranger turned on her heel and mounted the stone stairs into the caves. Ashimmel followed but only after discussion with the other priests, several of whom settled cross-legged at the edge, their gaze fixed on the northeastern horizon.

Stavros leaned back against the rock and felt a corner of the folded map bite into his hip. The Sled. The damned Sled. If it rained, the salvage mission was going to be a hell of a lot harder. Well, there was plenty he'd rather be doing anyway.

"And *now* can I have two seconds of your undivided attention?" demanded Megan.

He looked at her blankly. Between one moment and the next, he had forgotten she was there.

"Here's the bad news: Emil's found his lithium."

"What's the good news?"

"There isn't any."

He was glad to be sitting down. "Already? But how?"

"Leave it to Emil Clausen to go prospecting in the middle of a hurricane." Megan bowed her head. "He came back with big chunks of it in his knapsack."

"Actual lithium?"

"Some ore he seemed happy with."

"Shit."

"My thought precisely."

"Shit, shit, shit!" Stavros pressed his hands to his temples. Why was he so stunned? He'd known this would happen sooner or later. "What do we do now?

"I don't know."

"There's got to be . . ."

"Well, okay, I *have* been thinking. There is one thing . . ."

He looked up hopefully. She sounded so earnest. "What thing is that?"

"It's a really long shot." She shrugged. "But it has been done, once or twice."

"What has?"

"Getting a world declared closed to development."

"Really?" He'd paid little attention to such things in his former life on Earth.

"Like Urhazzhle, for instance, or the Double Moons."

"That's right! Luna Prima is a classic linguistic study!" He felt the hope well up in his eyes, then saw Megan retreat as if from too much light.

"In those cases, though, life signs had been detected long before the landing parties arrived. A friend of mine from the Bad Old Days . . ." She smiled ruefully. "He spearheaded the case for Urhazzhle. The lawyers got a head start on the commercial interests, for once. But both of those were advanced civilizations, thriving planet-wide, not like this." Her shoulders drooped. "Remember Feingold's Star, the fourth planet? Nah, you're too young. Well, ConPlex found something they wanted there, too, and they had an indigenous population of half a million moved to the next planet closer to the sun, where they promptly became wards of the corporation because the planet was too hot and dry for them to practice their traditional agriculture. In some corporate report I read later on, the rapid decline of that population plus their alcoholism and high crime rate was laid to the natives' 'failure to adapt appropriately.' Can you believe the gall and arrogance?"

She was trying to ease the blow, but instead she'd fueled a resurgence of optimism as Stavros pictured the Bath Hall in all its glory. "Wait. You mean, if the Sawls could be shown to be sufficiently *advanced*, we might . . . ?"

"I doubt gas and running water are enough to build a case, Stav. Fusion or spaceflight is more what the courts have in mind, being stuck into using themselves as the standard to judge by." She paused thoughtfully. "There was one world where the enormous size of the population won the case. I mean, there *are* environmental regulations and humanitarian laws on the books, but they're buried deep and repeatedly ignored, usually in the name of the world

238 Marjorie B. Kellogg

emergency, which of course has turned out to be just a fab opportunity for the Big Guys to make themselves even more billions! And doesn't the government look the other way, so they can belly up for their share? Don't save energy! Use more, use more!! Of course nothing gets done, and so we're in the mess that we're in!" Megan broke off her tirade to massage her eyes with consoling fingertips. "Besides, Stav, who knows what those regulations are, exactly, or how to research them at this distance or even what evidence would be sufficient to prompt legal action? We'd need a court injunction against ConPlex and a team of first-rate counsel." Out of gas and out of answers, she threw up her hands in angry despair. "Plus, you'll never guess who alone among us is the proud possessor of a law degree!"

Stavros didn't need to ask. "Son of a bitch."

"Uh-hunh."

They sat in silence, watching the equally silent priests. Stavros waited for his brain to stop ratcheting around the insides of his head. "Wouldn't CRI have that information in her library files?"

"If we could get to CRI."

Suddenly, the working antenna in the Sled assumed a crucial importance. "But we'd have to do our search in secret. Can't tip Clausen off until we're sure of our case."

"Damn straight. You'd have to file a protest before he gets his claim staked, if I remember correctly. Just to get the case heard."

"Jesus."

Megan shrugged. "I wasn't trying to offer you hope, so much as discussing the extent of the tragedy."

Stavros felt the map again, prodding sharply at his hip like a goad. "But he hasn't staked it yet? Not while he was in contact with CRI?"

"Said he needs to determine the extent of it first."

"What if I could keep him from doing that for a while?"

Megan chuckled bitterly. "Convince Emil Clausen to postpone 'Progress'?"

"Keep him from being *able* to do it, I mean." Stavros leaned forward, as an entire scenario opened up before him. "Meg, if the com link stays 'broken,' he can't report his claim. Meanwhile, we do our research. Is your lawyer friend still around? If we can pull together the rudiments of a case, we can put it to him. Send an FTL drone back to Earth with a message."

"We'd never get the legal wheels moving in time," resisted Megan, but she peered at him sideways. "How could you keep it broken?"

Stavros laughed softly. The salvage trip to the Sled had just switched from inconvenience to opportunity. Never mind if there was weather coming. His idea offered the Sawls a chance, so somehow he had to make it happen. He was past praying that Megan was really the one he could trust. She was, after all, the prospector's natural antagonist, and she'd just said *all* the right things. "Meg, I know it's five AM by your schedule and you're dead on your feet, but I'm making us some coffee, real Nescaf, and then I need you to talk this over with me real carefully. We've had our disputes, but basically we agree on the basic issues, the *moral* issues. So let me ask you this: if it turns out there's something legal we can do to save this world for the people who live in it, just how *ill*egal are you prepared to be in order to get those wheels in motion?"

Megan sighed, and he feared she was trying to decide how to turn him down most gently. But then a dreamy smile passed like a shadow across her face, some flicker of memory that caused her to look up at him with a younger woman's eyes.

"Stav," she murmured, "just because it's law, doesn't make it right."

BOOK FIVE

CARAVAN

"First let me talk with this philosopher.
What is the cause of thunder?"

—*King Lear*, Act III, sc. iv

33

SUSANNAH ASKED AMPIAR to prepare a bed in the ward, and stood back from the operating slab. Danforth's breathing was shallow but steady. As Weng packed up the anesthetic kit, McPherson hovered at Ghirra's elbow, taking in the expression of deep peace on the patient's ebony face.

"He looks dead," she mourned.

The Master Healer rumbled gently, a wordless negative.

McPherson stared up at him. "Well, he could still die, couldn't he?"

"Yes," Ghirra replied. "Always we can die, M'Furzon."

"Ah, a philosopher." Clausen yanked the last of the plastic sealant from his arm with a tight grunt of pain. The wound reopened and began to bleed. He clamped his hand over it and looked annoyed.

Ghirra noticed Clausen as if for the first time. He left Danforth and brought over fresh linen and a bowl of hot water. He eased aside the bulging knapsack as if it, too, might need his care, setting the water down at Clausen's side. Then he stood back and waited, as blood seeped through the prospector's fingers and dripped onto his white-clad thigh.

Clausen met his gaze. "Always a bright one in every bunch." He offered his bleeding arm. "You win, friend. I'm all yours."

Ampiar returned with a wheeled stretcher as Ghirra finished cleaning and wrapping Clausen's arm.

"This guy's not bad," the prospector noted to Susannah. "Good hands. You ought to take him on as a trainee."

"That's just what I'm hoping he'll do with me."

Ghirra summoned his burliest apprentices to shift Danforth's limp weight onto the stretcher. He held the linen curtain aside as Ampiar wheeled the patient into the ward. Susannah gathered up her instruments and checked

244 Marjorie B. Kellogg

the battery reading on the autoclave. Like much of her equipment, it would soon be useless, unless the power link was restored. Clausen slid down from his slab, supporting himself on his stick. Susannah felt a vague frisson as he peered through the arch at the end of the room, where apprentices stirred vast clay cauldrons with wooden poles, bathed in clouds of steam. Stav's anxiety must be rubbing off on her. But Clausen only shook his head and limped onward.

Weng lingered at the curtain, her attention drawn to a second opening just on the other side. It was low and narrow, nearly hidden in the drapery's stiff folds. She pointed. "Dr. James, I wonder if I might . . ."

"Oh, yes." Susannah was delighted. "Let me show you, Commander."

A faint light burned inside, a small oil lamp on a wooden table in the center of the room. The two women stood gazing into the shadows at tier after tier of polished wooden shelves sagging under the weight of enough books to fill an old Terran library.

"Ghirra's laboratory," said Susannah proudly.

Along one wall, the shelving gave way to a long waist-high counter. A confusion of glass glimmered in the darkness, cylinders and tubing and long-necked spheres, and tall jars with etched labels. Thick books lay open among the glimmer. Weng crossed to squint at the dimly lit pages. Columns of faded Sawl numerals marched across yellowed vellum, numbers and letters in vertical array, like mathematical formulae turned on their sides. She reached with careful fingers to turn a page. More numbers, some embedded within geometric figures: circles, triangles, six-and eight-sided polygons. She lifted the front half of the book to leaf through it gingerly. There was a long passage of text, then more numbers. Fastened to the third page and carefully bordered by silk bindings, was a brown-and-spotted fragment from a far older volume. Susannah saw a chart and notations, so precisely and regularly formed that it might have been a scrap of a printed page. The figures in the chart were again laid out in vertical columns, but in noticeable eight-part groupings.

Weng frowned at it gently. "Has the Master Healer told you anything about this?"

"Not really. Why?"

Weng turned her head to study it sideways, and frowned again. "It's odd, but . . ."

McPherson stuck her head in. "Why can't he be downstairs with the rest of us?"

"He can." Susannah moved toward the door. "When you can supply better round-the-clock nursing care than Ghirra can up here, and still manage the rest of your duties. Get some sleep, Ron. You need it!"

Weng returned the book to its original page, and followed her from the room.

Danforth lay on a clean pallet in the middle of the ward.

"Consider the Sled, McP, how we'll haul her back." Clausen hobbled around among the shining tiled pallets. "The distraction will do you good." He raised his face to the slice of sunlight streaming through the wide glass panes of the clerestory. Reflections illuminated the vaulted ceiling. The prospector rubbed his new-grown beard. "Nice room. I'd like to see what else they've been hiding up here."

"Our first priority is still power and com," Weng said. "And as soon as you've both had some rest, your assessment of the status of ascent engines would be useful. We can trust Dr. Danforth's recovery to Dr. James and to our friends here." She smiled graciously around, catching the Master Healer's eye. He dipped his head in return.

"The Sled's not in such bad shape." Clausen curled an arm around McPherson's shoulders. "I had her nearly to the ground before we lost power. A little tinkering, you'll have her in the air in no time."

She shrugged him away. "I was out there. I saw her. Needs a week in the shop."

"Could you two do this somewhere else?" Susannah glanced meaningfully at the unconscious Danforth.

"Yeah, like he's gonna hear anything!" McPherson fussed, but she turned to leave.

Clausen fell in step with her. "Her omni's working fine. We had com, once the weather cleared. The high gain's down but could be just shaken up. I didn't dare open the housing in all that rain. But—We get her back here, we'll have com at least."

"Emil!" Susannah called after him. "You ought to let me look at that ankle!"

"Forget it. I'm fine."

Ghirra smoothed the bed coverings, murmured briefly with Ampiar, then turned back toward the operating hall.

"I wonder, Guildmaster . . ." Weng began.

Ghirra slowed, inclining his head politely.

"I wonder if I might spend some time in your library?"

Ghirra smiled. "Lyberry?"

Weng indicated the narrow doorway with a wave. "*Books* are kept in a library."

"Ah," said Ghirra.

An old man in a multipocketed apron thrust himself through the operating room curtain, nearly colliding with Weng. He stared at her accusingly, then bustled off grumbling. Two apprentices followed breathlessly. They apologized to the Master Healer with big eyes and hurried after the muttering ancient.

Susannah shook her head. "I'm sorry, Ghirra. It's me he's angry with. I asked earlier for some cussip to soak Emil's foot. That's Ard," she explained to Weng. "The Head Herbalist. I don't know how Ghirra puts up with him!"

"*Cussip.* I will get," Ghirra offered.

"He said something about the weather and growled at me."

Ghirra threw a questioning glance at Ard's back, but then nodded to Weng. "Welcome you my . . . lyberry, Commandur."

"Thank you, Guildmaster. I will take you up on that. And perhaps you would care to visit mine, in the Lander? It is not as extensive as yours, but you might find one or two things of interest. I don't believe you have been down to our Lander yet."

"I will come," Ghirra assured her.

"Excellent. Then I will be off. Dr. James, I hope you will get some rest as well?"

"Certainly, Commander. As soon as I finish here." Susannah joined Ampiar at the patient's bedside and put a hand to his hot papery skin. "Still burning up."

Ampiar gave a worried nod.

"Well, I've done all I can. But he's strong. I'll check in later."

She returned to the operating hall to finish cleaning up, and found Ghirra beside Clausen's pack. He had a chunk of the frosty lavender rock balanced cautiously on his palm, as if it were a holy relic or a snake that might bite him. She'd seen him approach a shattered limb with greater equanimity.

"What's the matter, Ghirra?"

He looked up, searching her face. Clausen and McPherson retreated down the hall, noisily debating the condition of the Sled and plotting their next move.

"What?" she asked again, more quietly.

He tilted his palm slightly. The rock flashed star-specks of lamplight. "What does he with this?"

Susannah opened her mouth to give the easy answer, then realized how loaded that answer would be. He might as well have asked what was inside Pandora's Box. She felt a stab of resentment. Why should *she* have to explain the prospector's intentions? That nasty job belonged to someone official: Weng, or Clausen himself. But what a melange of half-truths it would be. No real answer at all, and Ghirra deserved better than that.

But how do you tell someone, *"They're going to strip-mine your planet."*?

It wouldn't be the entire planet, of course, only what was commercially viable. Susannah had seen strip-mined worlds before. Some of the mining companies even terraformed when they were done, usually due to the demands of the Terran colonies that sprang up around most off-world mines and stayed on to expand and thrive. Susannah pictured one of those colonies and found herself fighting back tears.

"He wants to dig it up." Her voice came out flat and hard. Perhaps the notion would strike Ghirra as mere offworld eccentricity and the confrontation could be postponed.

"Why?" he pursued. Clearly, the thought was not inconceivable.

"He says it's lithium. He wants it . . . some . . . to take away with him." That he had proved her a coward, even unwittingly, made her angrier still.

"Lithy-um."

"To study, you know? Emil studies rocks, like I study plants." That at least was not a lie. She mimed her field microscope and wished herself a thousand light-years away.

Clausen's voice floated in from the hallway. "If we can get enough of these little guys on it with some good rope, we can haul it over the . . ."

Ghirra nodded thoughtfully and laid the chunk among its brethren. Then he reconsidered and picked up a smaller one which he wrapped in a square clean cloth and slipped into his pocket. He said nothing further as he helped gather up the used instruments and linens. But Susannah sensed dissatisfaction in him, smoldering on a slow burn.

Maybe not so unwittingly, she decided. He has an ear for the truth, this quiet man, and he knows I have not given it to him. Half-truths, just like Emil would do.

This was precisely why she made sure never to get too committed to her subjects in the field. Except this time, she realized. Her nearness to tears probably meant it was already too late. If only Clausen had come back empty-handed! But that was postponing the inevitable. Susannah pondered ways to phrase the prospector's mission, to make it seem less dire in its consequences, and so allow her to tell the truth, yet disassociate herself from it. She failed.

For now, she would deal with the issue by ignoring it.

"Taylor's a strong one." She followed Ghirra into the hot room to dump her armload of soiled linen into the long stone sink. "If we can get that fever down, he'll be fine."

"Yes," Ghirra agreed coolly. "*Nhe khem.* He has luck."

"No, he has us." She tried smiling at him. "Two good doctors."

He returned her smile, but a polite distance had settled into his eyes. He loosed the tie that held back his long curls and turned away, calling for his apprentice Dwingen, who came running, eager for a task. Ghirra bent and murmured briefly in his ear. The child nodded and sped off toward the outer corridor. Susannah tagged after the Master Healer when he headed toward the ward. Already, she felt banished from the fraternity that had been her solace in the face of the growing possibility that she'd never see her home again.

But it was childish to expect trust and commitment where it wasn't being offered in return. As she laid out clean linens on the slabs, Susannah watched the Master Healer deftly remove the obsidian-flake blade, one of his own, from her scalpel. He squinted at it and set it aside in a bowl with other used blades. These would be passed along to various craft halls that required a sharp but no longer surgical edge. The metal clamps and handles he placed in a ceramic basket pierced with triangular holes that would fit on top of one of the steaming cauldrons in the hot room.

He did nothing without purpose, nothing without good reason. Susannah knew she was missing some connection here. Did his intuition about being fed half-truths really explain this much awkwardness over a few chunks of rock?

34

STAVROS TROTTED TOWARD the Priest Hall. The coffee recently shared with Megan had grabbed his nervous system and was running with it, but his heart's anticipatory pounding spoke of adrenaline as well as caffeine. He had gained an ally in his secret battle to protect the Sawls. An ally and the rudiments of a plan.

He saw Liphar in the corridor ahead, standing outside the Priest Hall entrance in a huddle of debate with four fellow apprentices. Stavros heard none of the usual excited chatter, only a hiss of urgent whispering. He grinned and waved as Liphar glanced up. Liphar did not grin back. As Stavros drew up beside him, the young man leaped on him, hushing him as he tried to speak. Half pushing, half dragging, Liphar herded him away from the huddle, away from the Priest Hall, down the corridor and through the open double doors of the Woodworkers Hall.

"Lifa! What the . . . !"

Two surprised guildsmen drew back from the doorway, nearly dropping the large crate they were carrying. Liphar's apology was inaudible over the racket of sawing and hammering from inside the hall. He hauled Stavros past a stack of crates. Sawdust and wood shavings covered the stone floor. Several apprentices pushed at the rubble with brooms, only to have their neat piles scattered by the busy feet of the journeymen. Racks of rough milled planks lined the walls. Stavros sucked deeply at the sweet heady scent of fresh-cut wood. The central row of worktables was buried in a mountain of crating, most already well used and being repaired. Bright new wooden pegging or replaced slats showed hard white against the darker aged wood.

Liphar put on an unconvincing grin, which he threw at any guildsman who bothered to look up at his sudden appearance. Woodworkers' was one of three or four guildhalls with two entrances, so they were accustomed to being used as a shortcut between two main corridors. But finally, as Liphar snaked a rapid path among the stacks of finished crates, Stavros let his weight drag the smaller man to a halt.

"Okay, enough. Lifa, what's going on up here?"

"Hssst! Hssst!" Liphar's feet slipped in the sawdust as he yanked Stavros onward. "Ibi! Please, come you!"

At the far end of the hall, a second set of carved double doors yawned open. Crates were piled just inside and out in the corridor. A senior woodworker with a list stood among a bustle of apprentices, directing the movement of crates from one stack to another, matching up the individual guild seals burned into the side of each crate. In the corridor, a handful of glassmakers loaded their guild's refurbished crates onto a big hjalk-drawn wagon. Stavros had never seen a hjalk in the upper caverns. But then, he'd never seen Woodworkers' in quite such an uproar either.

Liphar ducked around the crates and out the door. He sped past the wagon with a backward glance to assure himself that Stavros was there, jogging gamely after him.

Opposite Woodworkers' was the entrance to Keth-Toph, the grab bag, all-important guild whose name literally meant "Life Guild." Stavros had nicknamed it more prosaically: "Heat and Light." Liphar slowed at the open doorway, glanced up and down the corridor, and ducked inside. Stavros shrugged and followed.

Keth-Toph was an island of calm compared to Woodworkers'. From a tiny deserted antechamber that served as the local light station, Liphar led the way through a maze of narrow shelf-lined caverns. The shelves were stocked with boxes of brown soap and tallow candles, bundles of lamp-wick, ceramic lamp bowls, and glass chimneys. Comfortable items, Stavros thought. Practical. If people were willing to live this simply back home, we could stop raping other planets one by one to feed Earth's energy appetite. Of course, Earth's legions of poor already lived simply, or worse. But he wasn't naive enough to imagine that the rich and powerful would willingly give up the lifestyle whose excesses and heedlessness had caused the crisis in the first place. A crisis, he decided, that would never be resolved, certainly not in his lifetime.

Even here, he could see that supplies, as basic as they were, were dwindling. One long cavern held row after row of tall graceful jars for lamp oil.

Less than a quarter of them bore the wax seal indicating a full load. A larger cavern off to one side was pitch-dark but reeked of dried dung cakes. They passed through a small messy workshop for the repair of lamps, also deserted, and came into the central guild hall, a large circular cavern dominated by the traditional broad table with numerous backless stools for guild meetings. In a gesture worthy of the eccentricity for which Keth-Toph was known, a single-bowled oil lamp hung over each and every stool. Against the wall, a ring of giant cauldrons, encrusted with use, hung over soot-blackened fire pits. The hall was empty and the fires cold, but Stavros could imagine the stench and heat in the Round Hall during the dark-time rendering of fat for soap and candle making.

Liphar finally came to rest, leaning against the great central table under one of the three oil lamps that remained lit.

Stavros folded his arms, breathing heavily. "Well?" he demanded laughingly.

But the young Sawl was not playing games. He shook his head and began to pace.

"Okay, Lifa, what's going on? What's all the secrecy, and what's with the crates in Woodworkers'? I see a lot of preparation, and I hear talk of going somewhere."

"Anu!" exclaimed the Sawl unhappily.

"Anu" referred both to the giant wooden priest-horns and to the thunder whose sound they imitated. Thunder was said to be the war horns of the goddesses, blowing the challenge, the call to battle. But the priest-horns were reserved for ritual use.

"Thunder?" Stavros replied. "Yes, I heard it."

"Sisterfight maybe, too soon!"

"Lifa, the thunder was very far away."

Liphar was not consoled. "Ashimmel, Aguidran, very worried, very mad both!"

"At each other." Stavros tried a smile.

"Aguidran want go. Ashimmel say no, bad *khem* go now!"

"Go where?"

"Ogo Dul," replied Liphar as if it were obvious. As he read Stavros' confusion, he stopped pacing and spread his arms wide. "Big Market Hall. Go there, we. Make trade always."

"Ah! Now?" Bits of observation and information finally added up. "So that's what all the crates are for! But it sounded like Aguidran was saying everyone goes."

Liphar nodded. "All go."

Stavros couldn't quite get his head around it. "Every single *everyone*?"

"Okay, some too old, too sick. Some stay with crop." With a touch of his old mischief, Liphar added, "No good stay here, Ibi. Many beautiful lady in Ogo Dul."

Stavros grinned, but his brain still balked at the idea of five thousand men, women, and children trekking off simultaneously, like an army on the march, in search of markets and mates. The logistics were staggering. But suddenly, it became a magnificent idea, as he saw it as the perfect cover for a salvage operation he needed to carry out in secret. Yet again, it could be a disaster: if the entire population deserted, who would keep Clausen from invading the Caves unchallenged?

"What about the Kethed?" he remembered. "Did you talk to the guild masters?"

"Did." Liphar's anxious frown returned. He lowered his voice even in the deserted hall. "No *Kethed* now. Maybe after come back Ogo Dul. No guild master want hear bad *khem* now." He pushed himself off from the table and began to pace again. "*Anu* bad *khem,* Clausen bad *khem,* Ashimmel say no go Ogo Dul. Guild master all say *need* go, say need trade very bad, no food, no stuff. Food Guild big mess, not know if go trade food, if stay here keep crop. All guild master very worried, no listen Ashimmel, no listen bad *khem.* Big mess, Ibi! Big mess! Too soon now, *anu!*"

Stavros' head swam with the complexities of politics. "You mean you told the guild masters they should leave some cave-watchers behind, but meanwhile, we have to keep Ashimmel thinking all Terrans are terrific or she'll use us as the excuse to call off the trip? So who do we go to, to both keep the Caves protected *and* go to Ogo Dul?"

Liphar peered into the shadows, as if Ashimmel herself might be listening from behind one of the giant black cauldrons. "Must talk Aguidran, you."

"She's not going to want to hear about any bad khem either."

Liphar squirmed visibly. "Listen you, Ibi. Aguidran not same. Guild masters see only food and trade. Ashimmel hear *anu,* bad *khem,* only want stay in Caves. Aguidran not same. Aguidran hear *anu,* get mad." He hesitated, then whispered, "Aguidran get mad *Rek.*"

"Mad at the Sisters?" Stavros worked hard to hide a smile. He liked the image of the weathered Master Ranger howling her rage at the heavens.

Liphar frowned but added, "Aguidran not think *Wokind* come by *Valla Ired*."

Stavros thought he had it figured out: Aguidran wanted the trade trip but was unlikely to link (as Ashimmel surely would) the "bad luck" of Clausen to the premature return of bad weather. It was unlikely she'd ever linked (as Ashimmel had) the recent retreat of Valla Ired to the Terrans' show of support in the Story Hall. The Master Ranger saw the Terran issue as independent from the weather issues. And she had the ear and support of the craft guild heads.

Stavros looked at Liphar with new respect. Despite the accompanying anxiety, he was willing to balance priestly convictions with a sensitive nose for pragmatic considerations. Stavros knew his next question would cause further anxiety, but he'd ask it anyway, meanwhile absorbing another lesson in his crash course in political maneuvering: one can always rationalize using one's friends for the sake of the Cause.

"Will you talk to Aguidran with me?"

Liphar had foreseen the request and had already decided. He nodded miserably. "What will Ashimmel do if she finds out you're working behind her back?"

"Very mad, she." He would not elaborate, and Stavros was relieved to discover a limit to the discomfort he was willing to impose.

"Then let's get it over with," he said gently.

They slipped out of Keth-Toph. Liphar did not want to use the exterior route to the Ranger Hall for fear of running into a weather-watching priest on the stairs or in the cave mouths. They took the inward corridor instead and cut through a busy domestic sector. The narrow streets of the living quarters were jammed with any two-cart not already winched to ground for the planting. Families had turned their caves inside out, deciding what to pack and what to leave behind. A few carts waited already packed, among piles of household goods that would have to be carried down to carts below.

Stavros eyed the size of the piles. "Lifa, how *long* is this trade trip?"

"Go light-time, stay trade some dark-time, come back dark-time, light-time."

Stavros calculated, came up with about an Earth-month. "Long time." He was going to have to rethink the salvage trip yet again.

Leaving the living quarters, they came upon a group of Food Guilders arguing furiously about the wisdom of going ahead with the trade trip. They still wore the aprons stained while preparing the Planting Feast. They looked hot and tired, and confused by their own impassioned choosing of sides. Liphar hurried past with averted eyes and whipped gratefully around the next corner.

At the entry to the Ranger Hall, the Master Healer's diminutive apprentice Dwingen stood chewing a finger and fretting. He asked hopefully if they'd seen the Master Ranger or knew where she was. When Liphar shrugged, the boy returned his finger to his mouth and then asked if they agreed the best thing he could do was return right away to Physicians' and tell his guild master that Aguidran was nowhere to be found.

Liphar offered a grown-up nod, and the boy looked grateful and sped off. The older apprentice hesitated at the tall arched entry.

Stavros said, "We might as well wait for her inside."

"Stav! *Stav!*"

Startled, he turned. Liphar ducked into the archway. Megan hurried toward them.

"You'd better come down," she called, "before Emil and Aguidran tear each other limb from limb."

35

E.D. 68–9:44

TAYLOR DANFORTH WOKE with the abruptness of one shuddering free of a long drifting sleep. His eyes and head hurt. His hearing seemed preternaturally sharp. The incessant hellish drumming of the rain had ceased, the endless rain battering the hull of the broken Sled. Just before waking, he'd had the sensation of hands resting on his forehead, soothing, like his mother's hands. He could not move his head, but he could see well enough and move his eyes. Amber sunlight hung in the air above, exciting the little dust motes into their frenetic dance. He watched them for a while, thinking about the sunlight and what it meant, and wondering if his arm would be there if he tried to raise it.

He tried to call out, but his voice still slept. His jaw worked. He was a fish gasping for air. He could manage only an inarticulate gargle. And there were the hands again, soothing, calming his panic.

He told himself he'd had worse dreams than this. Up past the motes in their shaft of light, a huge wooden wheel floated in shadow. Glints of sun reflected off glass and glazed ceramic. Beyond that, stone vaulting and darkness. He had no idea where he was.

He swallowed. "Hello?" he croaked.

He was rewarded by an instant answering rustle. The hands withdrew their gentle pressure from his brow. He was not sure if he'd imagined them and the comfort they brought.

"Wait!" He discovered his arms, enveloped in tubes and bandages.

"You wake, Taylor Danforth," said a quiet voice.

A man appeared from behind to crouch beside his bed and press cool fingers to his wrist. Against the pale beige of his collarless smock, the man's skin was dark, nearly as dark as his own. The man stood, and rolled the IV stand out of Danforth's line of sight. His long ringleted brown hair was gathered into a tie at the back of his neck. He looked tall and thin leaning over the bed.

"Who're you?" Danforth's sudden wakefulness was slipping away.

The brown man smiled as he crouched again at Danforth's side. "I am Ghirra Ogo Dul. I am a doctor."

Danforth closed his eyes in relief. "I was sure I was gonna die out there!" He marshaled his drifting awareness. With effort, he could turn his head. "Don't know you, do I? Did they send a rescue crew down from the Orbiter?"

The brown man considered for a moment. "No," he replied finally.

Danforth tried to place the man's odd accent. "You from one of the other ships?" Even this impossibility seemed minor compared to the miracle of being alive. For a moment he was lost to a memory of pain and despair in endless cold and hammering rain. Then he saw other white smocks hovering at the periphery of his vision. The Orbiter's sick bay? No, he would recognize that. His drifting stopped abruptly. A hospital?

"Am I offworld?" he demanded in a waking panic. "Did they send me *home*?"

The man restrained him as he struggled to sit, laying one hand firmly across his brow, the other alongside his jaw. Danforth's lethargy returned, deep and inviting.

"You must rest, Taylor Danforth." The man beckoned one of the white smocks to him, a woman with brown skin like his own. He murmured briefly and sent her away. Danforth clung to a few familiar syllables. "Susannah? Is she here? Am I still on Fiix?"

"*Phiix*, yes, you are," the man soothed.

Danforth felt the hands again as the man returned to the head of his bed. Cool fingers rested lightly on his temples and at the hinges of his jaw, radiating comfort and languor. There might have been a sound: wind or the soft trill of a flute.

"Then who are you?" he repeated thickly, closing his eyes against the confusion.

"I am a doctor," the man replied, and Danforth slept.

36

E.D. 68–9:56

MEGAN POINTED. "THEY'RE down there. He wants the Sled made first priority."

"So he can get out there and get to work. What's Weng say?"

"She seems to be lying low. Aguidran is our main line of defense right now."

"I'll see what I can do."

Megan stayed in the cave mouth to watch from a distance. Squint-eyed against the sunlight, Stavros slipped out into the confusion of goods and people inching down the long stairs. He took cover among a detail of apprentices loaded down with bales of cloth stamped with the red sigil of the Weaver Guild. The rough outer wrappings smelled of musty straw. Clinging to their shadow, Stavros glanced back up the steps. Liphar was lost in the bustle, having stopped to share the load of an elderly rug maker.

Above, the cave mouths yawned darkly. The winches tossed rising and falling shadows across the pale rock. No sign of Ashimmel, but Priest Guild watchers were stationed at half a dozen entries, eyes fixed on the skies while a Fiixian year's worth of hard labor in the craft halls journeyed toward the cliff bottom. An emptied pallet rose past where Stavros stood, while crates of pottery and glass dropped to either side in careful tandem. All five of the cliff-top winches were in service to speed the loading. Surely the caravan would go ahead, by default. Not even Ashimmel could halt this powerful a momentum.

Progress down the stairs was slow. The weaver apprentices struggled with their bales. Stavros peered into the seethe of activity at the cliff bottom. The tent city had been dismantled and whisked into storage. The rock terrace was crammed with half-loaded wagons, from single-family two-carts to the twenty giant red-and-blue Food Guild wagons. Off the far edge of the flat, the waiting hjalk milled in the sun, their fleshy hooves buried in the cooling mud. The flooded fields and terraces gleamed like a vast shattered mirror. Food Guilders bent solicitously among the yellow stalks. The water was merely ankle-deep now, and the tallest crops were uncurling broad fleshy leaves.

Halfway to the bottom, Stavros picked out the dapper figure of the prospector, face-to-face with the Master Ranger: she leaning against a tall-sided wagon, her arms negligently folded across her leather-clad chest, he doing the talking, with his bullet head set at its most amiable angle. McPherson hovered uncertainly in between.

Stavros briefly considered retreat. He'd played roles all his life, but always ones he'd chosen. Doubt assailed him as he approached this first skirmish in his newest one. Lives other than his own were at stake this time, and he'd only rehearsed on the fly with Liphar and Megan. Would the prospector suspect? Seeing Clausen and Aguidran subtly arrayed for conflict brought home how suddenly the battle lines were being drawn, without—he hoped—Clausen's awareness. The struggle must be kept *sub rosa* for as long as possible. With luck, the first Clausen would know of it was when he tried to stake his claim, only to discover that a legal action had already been filed. Stavros must play his scene with calm and confidence, as cold-bloodedly as Clausen would in his place.

The congestion on the stairs eased as four slow-moving basket makers finally reached the bottom, balancing wobbling stacks of their most intricately woven wares. From his concealment behind the cloth bales, Stavros saw Aguidran shrug and glance significantly at the sky. Clausen's answering gesture to

McPherson was abrupt enough to reveal impatience. The two looked about as refreshed as could be expected from a scant five hours sleep, the pilot in clean whites, Clausen in neatly pressed tans, leaning on his rough crutch as if it were a gentleman's walking stick.

Stavros hit the bottom step and sidled through the crowd.

"So where is our Ship's Linguist when I need him?"

"Right here, Emil." Stavros took a deep breath and moved into the open.

The prospector swiveled gracefully. His sunburn was already deepening to a healthy tan. His new beard had been scrupulously trimmed to the same brusque length as his sandy hair. One raised brow took in Stavros' bare feet, blousy linen pants, and long ropy vest tied across a naked chest.

"Stavros, my boy! Missed you at my triumphal homecoming. Feared you'd been washed away with the flood!"

"Sorry. It's a busy time, with all this: the Planting, the packing." Stavros noted Aguidran's baleful look and did his best to affect innocence. Liphar's fist nudging the small of his back fortified him somewhat. "Is there a problem here?"

Clausen smiled. "This gentlelady and I seem to be having some trouble making ourselves understood."

"Usually she gets me just fine," McPherson complained.

Stavros bit back a smirk. Aguidran could forget she spoke Sawlish if it suited her purpose. Clausen's oily charm seemed a bit burned around the edges. Probably he'd resorted to it only after being thwarted in his presumption that the Master Ranger could be ramrodded. As this was roughly equivalent to charging into a force field, Stavros wished he'd sneaked up earlier to witness the collision. Was it possible Clausen had met his match?

"What do you want her to understand?"

Liphar moved away to chat with Aguidran. His part in the plan was to convince her to play along until they had a chance to properly explain themselves.

"Very simple," Clausen replied. "I need as many of her men as it takes to haul B-Sled back for repairs."

Stavros kept his nod carefully neutral. "I'll see what I can do."

He approached Aguidran with elaborate courtesy, and the most rapid Sawlish he could muster. It would help his pose as the crucial go-between if he appeared more fluent than he really was. Meanwhile, as he slid into the role more easily than he'd anticipated, he found himself enjoying a bit of a power rush. More of a buzz than the heady responsibility he'd felt during the evacuation of the Lander, and which had nearly betrayed him. This was about control, of people and situations. In the past, he'd had enough trouble controlling *himself*. Now, he actually had the prospector at a disadvantage.

Aguidran's eyes slitted in response to his obsequious formality. Her reply was terse and equally rapid.

Stavros breathed a private sigh of relief. "Doesn't look good for now, Emil. She's already way behind schedule from going out after you and Taylor. She has to get the trade caravan on the road as soon as possible in order to reach Ogo Dul by darkfall." He reached for a collegial tone. "It's a major undertaking for her, you understand, packing up the entire population and all the market goods, supervising the provisioning. She just can't spare any-one right now."

"The entire population." Clausen's expression remained patient. "All right, I'll bite. What or where is Ogo Dul?"

Hoping to sound unastonished by information that was still very recent news to him as well, Stavros replied, "A city on Dul Valla, the great ocean to the north. She says it's ten throws—that's a local unit of both time and dis-tance, equivalent, as far as I can gather, to about twenty kilometers of travel in a thirty-hour cycle. So, about two hundred kilometers away, somewhat less than thirteen of our days' travel."

Clausen nodded tightly. "One way."

"You mean there's *cities* out there?" McPherson broke in.

"A number of them." Stavros implied a sort of brotherly reproof he could not direct at Clausen. "On a world this big, it would be unusual if this tiny settlement were the only population."

"This is interesting news," said the prospector darkly. "I would have expected actual cities to have shown up in my remote sensing data."

"Not cities as we think of cities." Stavros gestured upward, at the cave openings. "Would Dul Elesi have shown up as a settlement? Particularly under thirty feet of snow?"

Clausen pursed his lips. "And what is the population of this Ogo Dul?"

When asked, Aguidran shook her head unhelpfully. Liphar piped up with a suggestion that sounded like a guess.

"They don't keep track of such things." But in his mind's eye, Stavros saw the volumes of extensively detailed records that swelled the library of each and every guildhall. Just the beginning of the lie. "Liphar says the tunnels of Ogo Dul spread through many miles of the coastal cliffs. His population guess is several hundred thousand at least."

"And how many other such . . . settlements are there?"

Stavros let this require a more extensive consultation, and Aguidran's answer surprised him. A mere stretching of the truth would be sufficiently impressive. "In the most livable zone, the equatorial regions, there's a settlement every ten throws in any direction. Widely but evenly scattered. She says there's word of hardy pockets of population to the north and south of the zone, but she can't vouch for them herself." Stavros pictured the world map in the cabinet of the Ranger Hall and wondered if Aguidran was telling *him* the truth. Certainly somebody had at one time had very detailed information about the northern and southern regions, in order to draw so complete a map.

Clausen nodded calmly, leaning on his stick. "And again, the reason for the trip?"

"To trade in Ogo Dul."

"And this requires the entire population? Not very efficient."

Stavros shrugged helplessly. "That's the way they've always done it."

"Of course. We wouldn't want to upset tradition." Clausen stroked his beard with a cupped palm. "Well. Perhaps once she's done organizing this . . . caravan?"

McPherson scuffed the mud-caked layered rock with the white toe of a clean boot, as if she knew the answer to that question already.

"The problem is, most of her rangers have duties with the caravan en route." Stavros pumped meek apology into his tone. "But give me a minute. Maybe with Liphar's help, I can make her understand the, um . . . urgency."

He drew Liphar and Aguidran aside, finally able to explain to the Master Ranger that he needed to visit the wreck first, in secret, to get to the omni before Clausen did, to stall the repair of Sled, com, and power for as long as possible. He didn't have time for details, asking mainly for her cooperation until he could explain himself more fully. Clausen waited, sharing a things-we-have-to-go-through glance with McPherson. His only sign of impatience was his free hand twitching at his side, worrying the seams of his trim, real-canvas slacks. This is too easy, Stavros thought. What if he understands every word? But that was impossible. Or was it?

Aguidran listened impassively. When he was done, she rubbed her nose thoughtfully and growled a curt order to meet in the Ranger Hall at the start of the next shift.

Stavros turned back to Clausen. "She says she'll think about it."

"And how long might that take?"

Aguidran saved him from having to feed the prospector another answer he didn't want. She shoved off from the side of the wagon and stalked away through the maze of wheels and crates and bundles, scattering low-voiced orders right and left.

Stavros called up apology again. "I think I can let you know first thing in the morning, ship's time. Let her get this mess sorted out and we'll try her again later. They need this trade trip badly, so there's a lot of pressure. You heard there's been thunder up in the northeastern mountains?"

"Heard it myself. Are they afraid of a little weather?"

Stavros wanted to shake the man and yell, there's no such thing as a *little* weather on this world! But that would never do. "Aguidran'll do the best she can for you. Didn't she risk her life and those of her guildsmen, going out to search for you guys in the middle of the storm?"

"So I've heard." The prospector offered a neutral smile, and Stavros caught his breath as a vision of crocodile jaws opening to rows of needle teeth shivered his imagination. It terrified him. He struggled for composure as Clausen continued, "Well, I'm a patient man. In the interim, McP and I can give some effort to the Lander's high-gain dish. At least they saw fit to haul that wreck in before they got too busy." He turned to McPherson. "Time we got us some power back, eh? I, for one, could use a hot shower." He grasped his cane, and when he looked at Stavros again, his eyes did not match his smile. "You won't mind, I presume, since you've found so little time to work on it yourself?"

"Be my guest." But Stavros felt thrown on the defensive and could not help adding, "You're going to need a welder."

"Shouldn't be a problem," called the prospector as he limped away with McPherson in close tow.

Stavros scowled. The man managed to swagger even with a cane. And it'd be just like the sonofabitch to have a cutting torch hidden in his overpriced pocket.

Beside him, Liphar muttered the first unprintable comment Stavros had ever heard him make about his offworld visitors.

"You said a mouthful," Stavros agreed. "You think we convinced him? With that guy, you can't ever tell."

Thunder rumbled beyond the plain, so faint it sounded like distant waves. Stavros caught Liphar's shoulder, his balance wavering as the tension of the moment ebbed. "Let's grab a few hours' sleep before we get much further into this. *Then* we go explain ourselves to Aguidran."

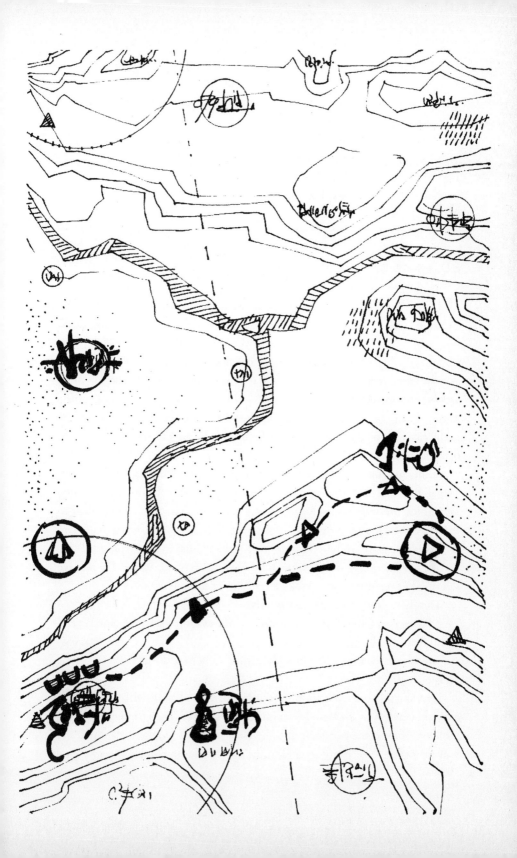

37

E.D. 68–16:22

THUNDER WAS GROWLING above the Dop Arek in earnest by the time Ghirra's runner found Susannah, in the shade of a giant Food Guild wagon stating her case for going with the caravan to a pensive Weng. The wagon's freshly painted wheels, red rims with blue spokes, stood as high as their shoulders. The wagon itself was nearly four meters to the top of its arching canopy. At its rear, four Food Guilders struggled to find space for a last load of grain sacks, grumbling in their frustration but distracted by the oddly discrete pockets of green-black cloud gathering in the no-longer-so-distant northeast.

While Susannah offered her argument with quiet and reasoned intensity, Megan hovered in the background, pretending to study the intricate pinning system for the wagon's removable wooden canopy. She restricted herself to an occasional comment or grunt of support. It would be better for the "plan" if she did not seem to have too urgent a stake in Susannah's request.

"It's a chance to travel, Commander," Susannah was insisting. "In relative safety. We'd be insane not to take advantage of the opportunity!"

"Derelict," Megan elaborated lamely.

A Physicians Guild runner trotted into the wagon's shadow, panting and damp from the heat.

"Invaluable data on population dynamics . . . a look at the flora and fauna on the way!"

The courier was loath to interrupt but brimmed both with his message and with anxiety as the thunder rumbled louder in the background. The Food Guilders shoved the last sack into the back of the wagon and slammed the rear gate shut. One came around to the side with a thin stick. He squeezed behind Susannah and Weng to check the water level in the huge wooden kegs lashed to the belly of the wagon.

"Who knows how long it'll take Ronnie and Emil to have a Sled running again?" Susannah pursued, while the courier fidgeted. "Or what if they can't? It might be our only chance to expand the zone of inquiry."

Weng dipped her silver head. "All you say makes perfect sense, Dr. James. My concern is that expeditionary personnel and resources not be spread too thinly while we are still in a state of emergency."

"Meg and I can't help fix the com or the Sled. If the population departs, Meg's left with nothing but her notes. If I go, I can finally begin my biological survey."

"Her primary mission objective," Megan added, hoping she hadn't hit the word "mission" with too heavy a hand.

"And we wouldn't be using expedition resources," said Susannah.

Megan patted the red-and-blue-striped side of the towering wagon. "Tyril says two or three more people aren't going to overburden the Food Guild's resources."

"Two or *three?*" Weng inquired.

Megan shrugged. "Figures approximate."

A particularly loud boom of thunder, like a distant cannon, spurred the waiting courier to dart into Susannah's line of sight and signal impatiently. He delivered his message in such a rush that only its general sense was intelligible.

"Okay?" he concluded, with what seemed to be every Sawl's first and favorite word of English. When she nodded, he waved and ran off.

"Ghirra wants me upstairs, stat. I hope nothing's gone wrong with Taylor. Will you give it some thought, Commander?"

"Indeed, Dr. James. In fact, I'll come up with you and consider on the way."

"Let's all go." Out of the wagon's shadow, Megan had a better view of the several acres' worth of other wagons and carts. The packing had slowed as guildsmen gathered in nervous groups to observe the rumbling activity over the plain. She heard the clink of stone counters and the murmur of wagers being placed.

"Now that's really odd," she remarked.

As Susannah and Weng turned back to look, a single clot of darkness detached itself from the lumpy bank of cloud hugging the saw-toothed profile of the far-off Vallegar. With surprising speed, the cloud scudded southward over the Dop Arek, growling thunder and spitting tiny forks of lightning. A breath of heat ruffled the back of Megan's neck. Halfway across the plain, the cloud seemed to lose substance and momentum. Within seconds, it had dissipated. The Sawl watchers cheered, invoking Lagri's name and passing their counters back and forth. The hot south wind died, but sprang up again as a second cloud detached itself and a third, each seeming to reach a little farther across the plain before dissolving.

The Terrans watched openmouthed.

"Small wonder they ascribe intent to the weather," Megan exclaimed. "I'd like to hear Taylor's explanation for that!"

"Hopefully he will live to give us one. We'd best get upstairs."

The Master Healer was not in Physicians'. Ampiar stood by Danforth's bed, her sober face touched by sunlight from the clerestory as she gazed down at him with quiet satisfaction. The planetologist looked very limp and still.

Susannah hurried to his side, laid a hand to his skin, then quickly checked his pulse and put her head to his chest. "Oh, my. He was so cool, I thought . . ." She wrung her hands in a gesture of amazed gratitude. "It's impossible, but the fever's broken. Already. He should regain consciousness any time now."

"Congratulations, Dr. James."

Susannah shook her head. "Just like Ghirra, to take care of the problem, and then send for me."

"The intemperate herbalist Ard is worth his keep."

"Yes." Susannah smoothed Danforth's wrist in bemused wonder. "But mostly it's Ghirra himself. I never believed in the laying on of hands until I watched him work. There's no ceremony or ritual—he's very casual about it—and I'm sure it's the patients' total faith in him that helps them heal. But why would that work for Taylor? He's never even met Ghirra." She fell silent, frowning.

"It's a mystery," quipped Megan, uneasy with the idea.

Weng pursed her thin lips. "Faith is a strange thing, Dr. James. Often we find it where we least expect it."

"I suppose, Commander, I suppose." But her frown remained.

38

AGUIDRAN STOOD AT the cold hearth of the Ranger Hall, arms braced against the high carved mantel. Head thrown back as if in pain, she stared up at the frieze marching across the wall. Stavros halted by the head of the long table, reluctant to intrude on a moment either of pure exhaustion or private angst. He held Liphar back, though at the other end of the hall, guildsmen came and went noisily, stowing equipment into canvas packs, lifting down coils of rope and masses of leather harness from name-plated pegs. Senior journeymen edged among them, checking lists of provisions and personnel assignments.

At length, the Master Ranger turned to regard them. Stavros thought he heard a quickly repressed sigh. She pushed away from the mantel and came toward them.

"*O rek,*" she muttered, shaking her head in disgust.

"*Gisti.*" Liphar looked awed that her unusual candor was addressed to him, a mere apprentice, but he was clearly disapproving of her tone. He slid his blue-green amulet back and forth on the thong around his wrist, his brow furrowed.

"Anu?" Stavros decided that the Master Ranger was more concerned about the thunder than she wished the priests to know.

Liphar nodded. "Remember, I say too soon Valla? Big trouble she come now. Now, Lagri too weak. Bad for us. No food, no go Ogo Dul."

Aguidran turned aside as a guildsman trotted up with a question. Stavros recalled what previously Liphar had spoken about easily, but now refused to discuss: the too rapid return of one Sister to strength after a defeat was taken as a sign of that Sister's power rising toward domination of the other, a situation that historically brought famine and devastation to the human population.

"Can the Food Guild trade for provisions at Ogo Dul?"

"Yes. There they grow . . ." Liphar bladed one hand and sent it on repeating S-curves through the air. "Big. In water."

"Fish?"

"Phish, yes. More bigger phish."

Stavros looked forward to the idea. The fish grown in the deep cave pools of Dul Elesi were no doubt nourishing, but they were tiny and bland, worse even than the factory fish he knew from home. But as he understood it, Ogo Dul was on an ocean, and that might provide something a lot more interesting.

"But, Ibi, if Valla too strong here, she more strong there, you see?"

Ogo Dul was closer to Valla's territory, then. No hope for the battle being locally contained.

Aguidran sent the guildsman off with a growled word of encouragement. She stalked to the head of the table, dragged her chair back and sat, gesturing them sharply to join her. Stavros slid onto a bench and laid his hands palm down on the golden wood.

Here the defense enters its first plea. Better make it good, Ibiá.

But it turned out to be unnecessary to remind the Master Ranger that Clausen's movements must be restricted. The image that Stavros had given Liphar to warn the guild heads—of the prospector scaling the walls of the Frieze Hall to pry the jewels from the Sisters' eyes—had been a potent one. Plus, one direct encounter with Clausen had been enough to arouse Aguidran's enmity. She was contemptuous of Ashimmel's self-serving nonchalance regarding the Visitors. The tall Master Ranger did not use the Terrans' cave nickname "Wokind"—"heads-above-our-own"—for the obvious reason. She assured Stavros that her own guild would keep Clausen under surveillance. What little had been revealed to the other Visitors in the presumed safety of Clausen's absence would now be covertly guarded. And she would bring pressure to bear on the other guild heads in the Kethed, to see that a home guard was authorized, drawn from all the guilds. Those who stayed behind must seem to be a random selection of the population.

So Stavros could go after the working antenna on the Sled without fear of disaster in the Caves. But he needed Aguidran's advice about the route, provisions, and equipment, and most important, her compliance in his cover story. He needed her to lie for him, not only to other Terrans but to any Sawl, such as Ashimmel, who might through ignorance or for political reasons give the plan away.

First he had to explain the significance of the object he sought so desperately, and why he needed to obtain it without the others knowing. He'd never felt more professionally inadequate as he searched for words to express the concepts of the Sled and long-range communications in nontechnical metaphor.

Then he recalled a long rambling session with Liphar in the Bath Hall, when he had worked himself up to a peak of intimacy and confessed his otherworldly origins. The anticlimax had been shattering. The young Sawl had accepted Stavros' descriptions of Earth and his flight across the light-years with unperturbed interest, as if it were one of his own tale-chants. The linguist's disappointment had soon faded to amusement: if the goddesses walk the world and play games with the wind, what was so remarkable about spaceflight? Magic is magic is magic.

Liphar had been equally unsurprised to hear that the Wokind came from the sky, for hadn't the ranger sentinels seen the Lander descend with their own eyes? He was far from associating such skyward origins with divinity, as the ancestral Catholic in Stavros had feared. The sister-goddesses of Fiix did not live in the insubstantial heavens but on the good solid ground, where any worthy deity belonged.

So, instead, Stavros offered the Master Ranger a straightforward description of the Orbiter, explaining that the object he required from the wreck would allow him to talk with the people on this other "lander" in the sky without actually going there. Liphar received this information with his usual acceptance, but Stavros thought that Aguidran regarded him with some skepticism. Still, she let it pass as he moved on to the real issue, that Clausen must be kept from communicating with this other ship even though he himself was clamoring to do so. He had no idea how to explain why the Orbiter could instantly communicate with Fiix by using the antenna, but could *not* communicate with the even stranger, far-off place he called Earth. How could he make the exact nature of the danger clear, when a true understanding required knowledge of faster-than-light travel, and of the bureaucratic workings of an interstellar civilization from one who was clearly dubious that it existed in the first place? How could he explain to the Master Ranger what the word "lithium" meant?

Stymied by the limits of language, Stavros was shaping his hands into a lump that might resemble a rock, the rock that Clausen wanted and would do anything to get, when he saw Aguidran glance up and smile. It was a small smile, very tired, but it brought to her brown face the softness he had sworn could never be there. It dazzled him.

He turned to find the Master Healer striding toward them through the stacked-up packs and piles of supplies and equipment.

Ah, thought Stavros disgustedly. *It's the smiling ladies' man.*

But Ghirra was not smiling. His linen smock flapped like a cloak around his tall frame. His brown hair, loosed from its usual tie, stood out from his long face in a mane of curls. Aguidran rose to meet him, an arm outstretched to grasp the hand he offered. He carried a small bundle which he set on the table with some ceremony. He'd bent to undo its cloth wrappings when he recognized Stavros through the screen of his Sawlish clothing, having taken him for another guildsman. The healer straightened, let his hand sweep up the still-wrapped bundle as he drew his sister aside. Aguidran listened to his hurried murmur, her own smile fading. When he was done, she leveled at Stavros a long and speculative gaze.

Stavros stared back in confusion. What had he done now?

Ghirra awaited his twin's response, his handsome face grim as he eyed Stavros guardedly.

He doesn't like me much either, Stavros noted with creeping satisfaction. He pushed this counterproductive thought from his mind as Aguidran guided her brother back to the table with a firm hand. She slipped the cloth bundle from his grasp, set it back on the table, and flicked a corner of the fabric to reveal a triangle of sparkling lavender rock.

Stavros sensed the familiar slippage inside his head. His imagination running amok again? He gripped the hard edge of the table, seeking reality reinforcement. No, he wasn't imagining it. It was really there, a rock, right in front of him, when he'd just now been struggling so hard to describe a rock. But not just any rock. A rock of exactly this color and crystalline formation. It had to be. Lithium.

Liphar stirred beside him, molding a gasp into words. *"Guar rek!"*

Aguidran nodded gravely.

The rock was as Megan had described it: pale, coolly glittering against the soft fabric and polished wood, very beautiful. The Master Healer must have lifted it from Clausen's field pack. But why bring it here?

Stavros glanced up to find Ghirra studying him with the same intense speculation that Aguidran had pinned him with a moment earlier. He was like a moth on a specimen board. He returned Ghirra's scrutiny purely out of self-defense.

Apart, he had seen brother and sister as opposite extremes: stern, stiff Aguidran who was never heard to laugh, and handsome Ghirra, always with a smile and a gentle word for the world. But together, it seemed as if they drew in toward some invisible center to mirror each other more exactly. Ghirra, taking on some of his sister's hard-edged gravity, came to share the power of her presence. Stavros was forced to reconsider, to take him seriously, and wonder how he could not have done so before. Why had he not, as Susannah had requested, gone up to the Physicians Hall to observe the Master Healer at work? She'd wanted help discussing an ambiguous topic: what she called Ghirra's "laying on of hands." Stavros had scoffed.

Because you're a jealous fool. Or rather, jealous and a fool. . . .

Stavros waited, half resentful, half abashed. Finally Ghirra picked up the triangle of rock. With a long reach across the table, he set it down between the linguist's fists.

"Do you know what this is?" he demanded softly.

The precision of his wording unsettled Stavros further. Only days ago, Ghirra's English had been broken. "I think . . . it's a lithium ore."

"Lithy-um. Yes. She said this."

Liphar touched a hesitant finger to the rock. *"Guar rek,"* he murmured lovingly.

"Guar rek?" Stavros had not heard the phrase before.

But Liphar was lost in his contemplation of the rock. He cupped both hands around it protectively, smiling into its crystalline facets.

"This is old words," said Ghirra with gentle dismissal. "Priest words. Now we say '*gorrel.*' "

"Gorrel? But that means . . ." It meant "food." "Gorrel rek" then meant "food of the goddesses." Instinct said here was a mystery ripe for revealing. "Old words?"

"The priest words," Ghirra repeated, and this time Stavros heard the phrase differently, as a true descriptive rather than a dismissive. "They are from long time past."

Priest words. The reason he couldn't always follow Ashimmel's tirades? A root language, perhaps—preserved like Latin through the priesthood, bearing the same distorted resemblance to the modern tongue as Latin did, only less so. The "old words" must be very old indeed. The seemingly alien and untranslatable words embedded in many of the songs and rituals had led Stavros to suspect as much, but no one before Ghirra, not even Liphar, the priest-in-training, had been either willing or able to confirm his theory. His estimation of the Master Healer rose another notch.

" 'Guar' means 'food'? The rock is the goddesses' food? I don't understand."

Ghirra sucked his lean cheek, clearly seeking an improved translation. "Sister Bread," he offered at last. His shoulders hunched loosely and dropped. "Old words."

Liphar's nervous fingers had returned to telling the malachite bead on his wrist, but his concentration remained with the rock. Stavros reined in his excitement. Old words! If he could keep the information coming, at some point it would begin to make sense. A key to all those untranslatables could be a key to the origins of the Sawl mytho-history.

"I'd like to know more about the 'old words,' Guildmaster. Can you enlighten me?"

Ghirra straightened away from the table and came around to straddle the end of Stavros' bench. So close, he was a substantial presence. He commanded attention. And though the healer was as lean as any Sawl, Stavros could imagine him, like his sister, as a physical strength to contend with. Stavros half turned to face him, sharply aware of Liphar at his back and Aguidran leaning against the table with folded arms. He was trapped, and not a little uneasy. He slid a hand along the edge of the bench to nudge against Liphar's thigh.

Liphar glanced up, distracted from the rock by the sudden silence. "Ibi . . ."

The Master Ranger hushed him brusquely.

Ghirra reached, wrapped the rock in his lithe surgeon's fingers and held it up for emphasis. "What does he with this?"

Stavros swallowed, relaxed. Ghirra's manner implied less a threat than a moral imperative to tell the truth. "You mean Clausen?"

"Clauzen, yes. Why does he want this?" The Master Healer set the rock down on the bench between them and sat back a little, folding his arms in an exact reflection of his sister behind him. "You know this?"

Stavros met the healer's fierce gaze, then dropped his chin to his chest in a spasm of relief. *Set personal prejudice aside, Ibiá. You can make this man understand.*

"Yes, I know. I was just trying to explain to Aguidran. . . ."

"Explain to me."

At last, a chance that the full implications of his news would be understood. But elation warred with dread of the moment when those implications took hold in the healer's consciousness. Stavros anticipated reproach and horror and rage. He nodded weakly and plunged in. "That rock, the substance in that rock, the lithium, is very valuable . . . important . . . where I come from. We don't have any left there, but we need it for our . . . industry, to make . . . power." This would be a difficult concept to get across, the generation of a kind of energy you didn't light with a tinder. Stavros fell back on ideas they'd be familiar with. "To light our lamps and heat our water and . . . other things. Here on Fiix, there's supposed to be a lot of lithium. Danforth's probe . . . his, ah, studies told him so, from the distance of my home world." He paused. Ghirra was listening intently, nodding encouragement. His expression told Stavros nothing of what he understood and what he did not.

Stavros sighed, a release of long-stored tension. "Emil Clausen works for a company—that's sort of like a guild—a group of powerful men. They sent him here to dig up all this rock and take it home with him. Because they need it so badly there, it will make both him and his company a great deal of profit."

"You say, all." The healer refused himself the laziness of incredulity.

"Every ounce and gram he can get his hands on." His next sigh was more like a sob, or a dam breaking, as the words spilled out unconsidered. "And he won't go after it with a wooden pick and shovel. He'll bring in huge machines that can extract every last molecule of lithium and anything else he happens to want from this planet's crust, and the parts they don't dig up, they'll use as a trash heap or a spaceport or a parking lot—"

Ghirra raised a hand. "Please. I do not understand this."

Stavros took a breath but could not slow or stop himself, not until he was purged of the burden of this dreadful knowledge. He swung his leg over the bench and stood, as if being in motion might help shake loose the horror. "Imagine your land all torn up, the whole Dop Arek shredded for as far as you could walk in a hundred cycles. Imagine mountains of rubble, the growing fields reduced to dust, the air unbreathable, watercourses rerouted, polluted. Imagine noisy, dirty shantytowns and unplanned cities springing up like fungi around the mining pits. Imagine the disease, Guildmaster, with all that crowding and bad sanitation. You won't recognize this world when Clausen gets through with it. He'll make it unlivable, unproductive. He may even try to round you up like a herd of hekkers and pack the whole population off to some other planet!" Stavros found himself facing Aguidran, one arm raised toward the invisible sky. "Which is why we can't allow him to tell anyone out there that he's made his lithium strike on Fiix!"

The Master Ranger regarded him impassively.

"He would not do this in his own Caves," Ghirra murmured from the bench.

Stavros laughed harshly, pacing again. "It's already been done. Long ago, by those before him. There's nothing left on Earth except more people than you can imagine, all choking to death on filthy air in megacities built from the resources of other planets."

Ghirra was struggling with an understanding. "Suzhannah say to me one time about a box. This box has words inside. Knowing."

"Knowledge," Stavros corrected reflexively, and stopped pacing. What vast connective leap had the healer just made? "The box is an artificial intelligence. A machine that thinks. We call it a computer. One of *our* old words."

"Also she say the box . . . the computer . . . it talk. It talk words to friends far away." Ghirra waited for agreement, then added, "But the . . . computer does not talk now."

"That's right. It's broken, from the storm."

"Clauzen cannot talk to these far friends now."

Stavros blinked, but no, it was not some blind hope feeding him illusions. He had heard the healer correctly. First Megan, now this remarkable Sawl, in the same day. Allies were appearing out of nowhere just when Clausen seemed to own all the artillery. He wanted to shout for joy and relief but contented himself with matching Ghirra's slow, intelligent smile. "No. He can't. And we have to make sure it stays broken until we can figure out a way to stop him permanently. I was trying to work that out with Aguidran." Finally he gave voice to his astonishment, hoping it would be taken as a compliment. "Guildmaster, what made you suspicious? About the rock, I mean, and Clausen? How did you *know*?"

Ghirra picked up the rock and weighed it on his palm. "I know nothing. But this rock . . . I see Clauzen want it, very much." He rotated his hand and the chunk of ore flashed lamplight. He glanced up at Aguidran as if seeking her approval of what he was about to say. "But also *we* need the Sister Bread."

"Yes," breathed Liphar, who had been listening with increasing confusion and dismay. He recited a line of what might have been a prayer, if the Sawls had prayers.

Stavros translated on the fly. " 'The Sisters gave to us, ah . . . before the wars . . . their bread, that we might live, ah . . . survive'?" He looked to Ghirra for confirmation. "Is that right? What does it mean? How can a rock be bread? Why do *you* need lithium?"

"That is many questions, Stavros Ibiá." Ghirra rose from the bench, looking pensive. "Suzhannah would not say about this."

"You asked her?"

"Yes." Ghirra was studying him again.

So, Susannah was still determined not to get involved. He had been right to keep all this from her.

"She has orders not to talk about it," he lied.

"Ah. And you do not?"

"I do." Stavros shrugged. "We all do, but . . ." The truth was, no one had thought such orders were necessary. He felt the sudden pressure of time. How long would he be able to keep his campaign against ConPlex a secret, and what would Clausen do to him if he found out? "Look, Guildmaster—you don't have to tell me why you need the lithium if you don't trust me with the knowledge. It's enough to know you need it. It means there's more at stake than I even suspected."

"Why only you?" Ghirra asked.

"What?"

"Why only you know this must not be?"

"Not only me. Megan knew before I did. She's seen this happen on other worlds. She was against Clausen and his company from the beginning. And we'll bring some of the others around in time. But meanwhile . . ." His urgency pushed him onward, past all the answers he wanted, all the questions he was dying to ask. "If you'll hear me out, we have a plan. . . ."

39

"TAYLOR, I'LL PUT YOU in a walking cast when you're ready for one, and not before! Do you want to limp like Quasimodo for the rest of your life?"

"Hell, no!" Danforth winced and fretted as Susannah changed the dressings on his wounds. A bowl of herbal infusion steeped fragrantly beside the pallet. Its thin curl of steam rose into the shaft of sunlight warming his bound and splinted legs. "But I'd do better down in the Lander. I have work to do. And I hate all these locals running around doing who knows what to me."

"You have 'these locals' to thank for being here at all!"

"Okay. I'm grateful. Now get me the hell out!"

"*In* the Lander is not currently an option. The lift's not working, and you won't be climbing ladders for a while." Susannah began to pack her bandaging supplies away in a lidded basket.

Danforth's big hands grabbed hers and held them tightly. "Susannah, for the love of god, I really am grateful but I'm going nuts up here in this stone hole! I feel like I've died!"

"You nearly did."

"Okay. But I'm alive now, and I need to get *out* of here!"

Susannah laughed. "Taylor, we did miss you around here. Our impatience quotient has foundered drastically while you were gone."

He shoved her hands away. "Okay. Go ahead. Torture me. Sabotage my bloody career!" He struggled against the nest of sacking that supported his back. "CRI's down, I can't read shit in this lousy light, I haven't the vaguest idea what's going on outside . . . !" He tried to sit up, gasped, and eased himself down, tight with sudden agony. "Whew."

"Tay. Please. Go easy. In addition to breaking both legs, you nearly lost a lung."

Danforth clamped his eyes shut in frustration, but lay quiet as Susannah finished packing. "He does have fine hands, that healer man."

"I know. And Ampiar thinks you're the worst spoiled thing to cross this threshold in many a cycle . . . but also the loveliest."

"How nice." Danforth sighed. "So how long, do you think?"

Susannah heard the real despair in his voice. "You'll be on your back for a while yet. There's no hot water or facilities at the landing site, but . . . all right, you don't need twenty-four-hour care now that the fever and infections are gone. I'll speak to Ghirra about moving you. Question is, where?"

"Outside. I've got to be outside."

"Well, the Commander has reestablished base camp under the Lander. But I don't know how she'd feel about you being around to distract Ronnie into playing nursemaid." She gave his dark cheek a motherly pat and fastened the lid on her supply basket. "But I'll see what I can do."

Danforth gripped her arm. "Wait! Is it still clear out there? No clouds?"

She smoothed the blanket with her free hand. "Some clouds, coming and going." His lids were finally looking weighty, and she did not want to tell him the exact nature of the clouds' coming and going, for fear he would demand to be taken outside immediately.

"Ronnie said there'd been some reports of thunderstorms?"

"Thunder, very far away across the plain. No storms."

"Yet." His shoulders relaxed and his breathing slowed as he slipped toward sleep. "You know, I had a lot of think time out there in the torture can, before the fever got me . . ."

"In the what?"

Danforth's jaw tightened, even as his eyes slid shut. "Close quarters with the boss man. It wasn't pleasant. But it showed me I've got to hit the problem of this place from a whole new angle. *Tabula rasa.*"

"I know what you mean," she agreed.

"Patterns. Gotta look for existing patterns. Stop worrying about what it *should* be. There's something missing from the model, some process, maybe unique, that I should have been looking for instead of trying to force it all into some known shape."

"Sounds right." Susannah eased her arm free as his hold relaxed. She stood, gathering up basket and bowl and the dirtied dressings.

"Wait . . ." Danforth murmured sleepily. "Did you happen to notice what direction the wind was coming from?"

She smiled at the big man lying as quiescent as a child. "No, Tay, I didn't. Around here, you'd best ask a ranger or a priest for that kind of information."

This unanswerable seemed at last to drag him into sleep.

As Susannah headed for the hot room with her bowl and basket, Weng called from the entry to Ghirra's lab. "Something to show you, when you get a minute, Dr. James."

"Be right with you, Commander."

She found little Dwingen in the hot room and put the sterilization of her equipment into his charge. In the lab, Weng stood in the middle of the floor, gazing up at the crowded bookshelves and stroking her chin as if she were a bearded old man.

Susannah slumped into Ghirra's padded chair with a dramatic sigh. "Well, Emil was right about the kind of invalid Tay's going to be. Can you deal with him down at the Lander, do you think? He can't stand being left alone with nothing to occupy him."

"Bring him down, by all means, if he's well enough," Weng murmured abstractedly.

Weng was always at her most amenable when the majority of her brain was off in the higher reaches of contemplation. A good time to take advantage. "Have you had a chance to think about our request to go with the trade caravan, Commander?"

Weng pointed up at the rows of dark volumes. "Do you have any idea what's in all these books?"

"Yes. Those are the Birth Records."

"Ah. Every birth is written down, then?"

"According to Ghirra, yes. And I've seen Xifa entering new births. It's practically the first thing she does as soon as she's sure the mother and child are delivered safely. It's not exactly eugenics, but they are very careful to avoid inbreeding."

"Yes, I recall Dr. Levy mentioning that." Weng's black eyes narrowed. "I wonder how far back these records go."

"Ghirra claims, all the way."

"All the way to what?"

"To the beginning of their recorded history, I guess."

"That could be a very long time, Dr. James. Tyril's Weaver Guild records barely scratch the surface at twelve hundred Earth-years, by my rough calculation."

"Goodness." Susannah was ashamed to admit she had not given the matter of the Sawls' age much serious thought. "Twelve hundred . . . ?"

Weng tapped the spine of an ancient leathery volume. "If we could determine what constituted a generation, we would have only to count backward. Indications are that this is a very old civilization, Dr. James, far older than we at first assumed. And here's a remarkable coincidence for you to ponder."

She lifted a heavy book from among the flasks and jars on the back counter, and brought it to the table. She set it in front of Susannah, open to an obscure diagram, then laid sheets of her own notes beside it. "When I first saw this drawing, something about it struck me as familiar, though of course it isn't anything I could have seen before. But the thought kept coming back to me, and I did a few scribbles, and finally it came to me: it's partly grouped in eights, you see? Twos and sixes. And notice this." She turned the old book sideways. "Do you see?"

Susannah shook her head, mystified.

Weng sifted through her own notes, extracted a sheet and laid it on top of the stack. "What about this? Is this familiar to you?"

"Of course. That's a periodic table."

"Excellent. Now if you remove this block containing the rare earths from the middle and place them down here, as is sometimes done . . ."

Susannah reconstructed the table in her mind's eye. "Oh, my goodness."

Weng gave her best Cheshire Cat smile. "It was the eights that got me. You know that the rules of atomic structure dictate a return to a similarly structured atom every eight elements. And . . ." She let a fingertip glide reverently down the ancient scrap of page. "If we consider the elemental family structures to be oriented this way, the space that has been left could be a diagrammatic pause for the transition metals, etc., starting with number twenty-one, and so on. This peculiarity here could analogue the horns that hydrogen and helium create in our own table."

Susannah's own curiosity quickened. She'd never seen Weng so eager and excited.

"But, Dr. James, most remarkable of all: remember that this restructuring of our own periodic table still contains the full range of noble gases, which in the history of our science were not discovered until after the advent of absorption-line spectroscopy and the analysis of stellar spectra.

"Now, the question I must immediately put to our Master Healer is this: if this aged Sawlish diagram does indeed represent the families of the elements, when and through what method was it assembled? Dr. James, it preserves the same number of slots as our most updated table, *plus a few more!*"

Susannah allowed a healthy skepticism to slow her astonishment. "Spectroscopy and periodic tables require a more precise grasp of atomic theory than I would have expected here, even of Ghirra."

"Have you ever asked?"

"Well, no, but . . ." She spread her hands, taking in the low-tech accommodations of the Master Healer's lab. "Commander, are you sure about this?"

"Not in the least, but the coincidence is seductive, is it not?" Weng stood back, arms folded and black eyes glittering. "Consider the implications, Dr. James! The most recent additions to our own table are no longer found in nature. They had to be manufactured for proof of their existence."

"Manufactured?" Susannah shook her head. "Sorry, Commander, you just ran past my credibility limit. But try it out on Taylor—he's ripe for anything, I think."

"You worry for my sanity, Doctor?"

"Don't be silly. But I do worry about what boredom and frustration can lure us into. I have enough trouble fighting off the various local implications of the paranormal, between the seemingly sentient weather and Ghirra's, shall we say, less traditional methods of healing. Now you're going to have me thinking my wild ideas about genetically engineered plants and animals might have some basis in possibility."

"Is there anything that doesn't, Dr. James?"

Susannah laughed. "Mind games, Commander. Shame on you."

Weng's raised eyebrow was like a faint shrug of disappointment. "Well, then, I shall keep my games to myself, until further proof presents itself. And so, Dr. James, that brings me to your request. Go with the caravan, by all means. Observe carefully. Discover everything you can. But I hope you will keep an open mind."

"For the sake of *my* sanity, Commander?"

Weng said nothing, only smiled again, so privately amused that Susannah would have been hardly surprised if the Old Lady did fade away, leaving only her smile behind.

40

THE BIG YELLOW INFIRMARY WAGON gave shade enough for ten. As little Dwingen and another physicians' apprentice, Phea, looked on amazed, Susannah hauled pillows and blankets and wicker boxes out of the back for the third time, in preparation for packing it all back in some new way that would allow everything to fit.

"A Sawlian periodic table?" murmured Megan dubiously from her seat beside the rear wheel. She polished her little field compass on her shirt, opened it to watch the needle maintain its sure hold on Fiixian north, toward the Vallegar. Hemmed in by the tall canopied wagons and the bustle of people and hakra carts, she could not see the mountains or the cloud banks slouching about their summits like a street gang massing for a riot. The sky above the white cliffs remained unclouded turquoise.

"A very up-to-date one, at that," Susannah replied. "Well, she admitted it was a long shot, but she was so entranced by the idea, she said yes to the caravan without a fuss."

"But not without her reasons, I'm sure. Did she suggest keeping an eye out for anything in particular?"

" 'Discover anything you can,' she said." Greedily, Susannah considered the empty field cot, a hekker-skin stretcher with a folding wooden frame. It was lashed along one side of the wagon, and because it was open, taking up a great deal of room. But the first of Ghirra's instructions had been to reserve sufficient space for the transport of serious injuries. Dwingen and Phea fidgeted in the sun, waiting for their assistance to be required. Though she was Dwingen's senior, Phea was a short and solid child, and equally as wide-eyed. Susannah folded the cot experimentally, then opened it again. "I'll tell you the first thing I intend to discover, and that's how to mend this awkwardness with Ghirra over Emil's rocks. Was it some sort of taboo I stumbled on, do you think?"

Megan pursed her lips and shrugged.

"You're not interested in taboos? What kind of anthropologist are you?"

"Cautious." Long and subtle thunder tumbled over the plain. "You know, this word 'arrah' we've been blithely using to denote 'weather' doesn't really mean that at all. It means 'struggle.' There is no word for weather, or climate, or anything that neutral."

"Goodness. Sounds like you and Stavros are finally consulting like colleagues."

"Umm. Yes. I guess so."

"About time." Susannah grabbed up a basket full of linen. "Almost the first thing we learned here was that the Sawls don't think of weather as a natural phenomenon."

"True, but have you really thought about what effect that has on them, seeing themselves as pawns in the midst of an eternally ongoing war? There's nothing they can do to end it, as they see it, not good works or prayer or sacrifice, none of the traditional offerings." Megan stretched ostrichlike to listen without rising as the thunder died into the uproar of the packing and loading. "Tyril assured me quite calmly the other day that the arrah would end when the 'darkness' lifted from the Sisters' eyes, and until then, the best the Sawls can do is try to keep one Sister from winning. What 'darkness'? says I. *The* darkness, she replies, as if I had asked a Baptist, what Satan?"

Susannah put down the linens and dragged her own medikit out from between the legs of the lashed-in cot. "There's not much talk of the goddesses up in Physicians'."

"Probably because they're said to have no interest in the fate of the individual. Their only power over life and death is through the havoc they wreak with the climate." Megan blotted her cheeks and neck with a moist square of cloth. "Speaking of which . . . you know it's going to be hot as blazes out on the plain."

"Oh, yes." Susannah yanked at a heavy wooden box until Dwingen could bear it no longer and leaped in to grab a corner. Phea followed eagerly, and Susannah left them to struggle the box into the dust while she concentrated on the problem of the wagon. It had looked gigantic when empty, as cheerful as a sunflower in its fresh yellow paint. It was long and narrow, rather like a Conestoga in construction but for its hard bentwood canopy and its lack of metal underpinnings. It was larger than any of the other guild wagons except for the Food Guild's twenty red-and-blue giants. Like those, it had been winched down from the Caves in three pieces, and would require double teams of hjalk to haul it fully loaded.

Sweaty and dust-coated, she was despairing of ever getting it fully loaded, when Phea touched her arm. Politely, the apprentice pointed under the big wagon, which rode high off the ground to make room for an ingenious suspension system made of leather and oiled hardwood. Susannah looked, then groaned. Above the rear axle was a large shelf with several tough woven straps attached. Earlier, against Dwingen's meekly proffered objections, she had buried three odd-sized wooden boxes at the bottom of the load. They contained the store of dried herbs that Master Herbalist Ard was sending both for use and trade, and Susannah had wanted to be sure they were safely stowed. Suddenly it was obvious that the boxes had been built specifically to fit on the secure but easily accessed shelf in the undercarriage.

Ghirra had not demurred when she offered to oversee the packing, even though Xifa and Ampiar were in charge of supplying the trip. Susannah pouted ruefully. Another of the Master Healer's subtle lessons for pushy offworlders.But she'd made the offer only to please him, trying to win back his confidence, so badly eroded by the issue of the rocks. Perhaps the point had been reached in the Terrans' relations with the Sawls when the initial goodwill of both sides had been exhausted, and cultural differences were being felt as obstacles rather than novelties. With a little extra diplomatic effort, Susannah was sure, the difficulties could be worked through, but she felt sad and isolated, and now doubly irritated with herself for botching the loading of the wagon.

It was only a minor relief that at a nearby wagon, an aging potter was suffering a similar dilemma. He, however, had the good humor to offer a wager to the apprentices assisting him. Susannah overheard him swear that space would never be found for every last bowl and tankard. One eager girl eyed the stack of straw-wrapped pots waiting to be packed and accepted the bet with a cunning grin.

With a sigh, Susannah set Phea and Dwingen to digging out the herb boxes. Megan chuckled hugely, looped the braided lanyard of her compass around her neck, and rose. Thunder kettledrummed across the plain, and the guildsmen at the Potters' wagon stopped their work to glance over their shoulders at the sky.

"I suppose it's possible," said Susannah, "that Aguidran'll get the whole population packed up and still have to call it off at the last minute." She searched the sky for clouds and found not a one.

"That's what Ashimmel's pushing for," Megan agreed. "Look at her down there with Ti Niamar, like a fly buzzing in his ear, poor old guy. She's been at him for hours."

Between the lines of half-loaded wagons, Susannah saw the Master Priest pacing beside the elderly Master of the Food Guild. One hand solicitously supported his elbow, though the old man's step was agile. The other gestured sharply in the direction of the cloud-shrouded Vallegar. Ti Niamar's round face was prune-dark, wrinkled with equal parts worry and irritation. He looked ready to tell Ashimmel to just leave him alone.

"She figures as goes the Food Guild, so goes the rest of the Kethed," Megan continued. "If she can get him scared enough that Valla might sneak by Lagri's defenses with a storm that'll devastate the crop, she'll swing him to her side. She's already won over the Papermakers and Keth-Toph."

"But neither of them really need the trading in Ogo Dul. Their products are made and consumed at home."

"Precisely."

Susannah noticed how carefully the guildsmen working at their wagons watched the pair, gathering when they'd passed by to murmur and shake their heads. The old potter sent one of his apprentices scrambling to the top of his wagon's canopy, where she perched as a lookout on the activities of the cloud bank now barely visible across the plain. Among the smaller wagons down along the lines, families halted their packing as the two guild masters approached, only to begin again as soon as they'd passed.

Beyond the cluster of family wagons, a few brightly colored festival pavilions remained, nestled against the rock of the cliff. As Ashimmel and Ti Niamar turned to pace back down the line, they interrupted their conference to nod courteously to Weng, who was observing the commotion of wagons and goods from the canopies' filtered shade. Weng returned their greeting, then resumed her own intense conversation with someone in clean ship's whites, whose face was in shadow, back to the brilliant sun. Judging from the incline of her head, Weng was engaged in being gracious.

Susannah squinted into the shadow. "Well, I'll . . . Meg! Look who's back in uniform!"

Megan chortled knowingly. "He's trying to convince her that going to Ogo Dul is more vital to his official mission than fixing power and com."

Susannah found herself staring. The Sawl clothing Stavros had assumed so many weeks ago had obscured the shape of his body. He faced away from her, the close-fitting Terran shirt and pants clinging damply to his skin. His dark hair was wet, slicked behind his ears, newly clipped closer to regulation length but as if without benefit of a mirror. On the trip out, Susannah had dismissed Stavros Ibiá as a bright but irritating boy, amusing to tease but in need of protection. And probably Megan was right about him having a bit of a crush on her. But she had to admit, he cleaned up well. She couldn't help but notice the trim white triangle formed between shoulder and hip, and the gloriously affecting line of his back. She sucked her lip. Were the sun and heat going to her head?

The potter's apprentice atop her guild wagon called down a report, followed immediately by a crack of thunder loud and lengthy enough to briefly still the hubbub of the pack up, as every Sawl on the rock flats glanced over his or her shoulder, shuddered, and went back to work with newly frantic energy.

"Getting closer," Megan commented.

Susannah shook herself loose from her rediscovery of the ship's linguist and renewed her assault on the infirmary wagon. She shoved at a stack of boxes next to the field cot, so hard that a pile of blankets cascaded onto her head. Dwingen succumbed to a fit of giggles which Phea could not manage to discourage.

"The Sawls call it Valla's Ice," Megan continued.

Unaccountably annoyed, Susannah shoved the tangled heap into Megan's arms. "Shut up and fold these, will you? Make them small." She gestured in surrender and stood aside while the two apprentices jumped in to finish the packing themselves.

"The thunder, I mean." Megan settled on a crate, hauling a blanket onto her lap. "Because it sounds like an avalanche."

"Did you mention spectral Dutchmen with giant bowling balls?" Susannah muttered, as Stavros' sun-bright image teased at her mind's eye.

Megan made a slow fold and smoothed it flat as if to press the blanket into miniature. "You don't trade mythologies with these folk—they're liable to take you literally. They'd end up sure our thunder's made differently from their thunder."

"Maybe it is." Susannah felt snappish, and forced herself to smile. "So you've given up on holding out for metaphor versus belief?"

Megan nodded glumly. "Stav is right, much as I hate to admit it. The Sawls believe their goddesses are real. Actual physical beings."

Susannah smiled again. "Perhaps they are."

The anthropologist made a wry face. "Wouldn't that just show us all."

They heard another profundo rumble that could have been a legion of cartwheels groaning across the stone terrace. This time work came to a true halt. Aguidran appeared, flanked by her two most senior guildsmen, strolling down the line of wagons as if nothing in the world were on her mind other than the pleasant sunny day and the proper ordering of the wagons for the trek. She gave the inside of the yellow wagon a cursory inspection, growled briefly at Phea and Dwingen, and moved on, picking up speed so that she and her aides contrived to reach the bottom of the cliff stairs just as several elder craftsmen from the allied guilds of Weavers, Leatherworkers, and Basketry openly confronted a retinue of priests who had descended from the cave mouths to broadcast their latest dire warnings. Debate flared into open argument, but was quickly snuffed by the Master Ranger's barked reminder that guildsmen's wagons needed attending to if the caravan was to depart on schedule. Ashimmel stalked out of the press, having deserted Ti Niamar the moment she heard raised voices, only to find the argument dispersed before she could make use of it. Ranger and priest flicked dismissive glances at one another and went off in opposite directions. As if on cue, an entire phalanx of rangers gathered to work up and down the long lines of carts and wagons, checking the loads, tugging at ropes and harness, kneeling to inspect wheels and axles, the mountings of running lanterns, and water supplies.

"And there you see the traditional division of Church and State." Megan turned back to her lapful of blankets. "Though not your traditional spiritual versus temporal, since both priest and craftsman in this society consider their bailiwicks to be totally temporal, here and now."

Susannah had watched the argument with some surprise. "But I thought they had that division nicely worked out."

Megan shook her head. "Recently they've begun to air their differences in public. The cracks always show most during times of crisis."

Under the canopies, Stavros finished his discussion with Weng and stepped out into the sunlight. The flash of white caught Susannah's eye. She studied him as he walked her way, his attention on the scattered tendrils of debate drifting through the crowd at the bottom of the stairs. He listened as he walked, frowning slightly as if the flare-up was an intrusion on some other train of thought. His step was purposeful but, for Stavros, oddly unhurried. He carried himself with a taut confidence that Susannah had not seen in him before. His energy was collected, instead of spinning off like sparks from a flywheel.

When he glanced around to find her watching him, his first impulse toward a smile was damped immediately by awkwardness, and he retreated behind his usual misunderstood whiz-kid glower. He allowed her a nod and dropped his eyes as he approached.

"It's all fixed with the Commander," he announced to Megan.

"At what price?" she asked, still folding blankets.

Absurdly, Susannah felt rejected. In the space of a second, the man had become a boy again. *Did I do that?* she wondered.

"She wants Danforth's equipment moved down to the Lander, on battery power." Stavros replied with only mild disgust. "He wants to be able to keep his eyes on the sky, since he hasn't got CRI to do it for him."

Megan smirked. "Never trust a weatherman who refuses to look out the window."

"Taylor is not a weatherman." Susannah was surprised how defensive she sounded.

"Closest thing we have at the moment, next to Ashimmel and her cronies." Megan turned back to Stavros. "Will that leave you the equipment you need?"

"All stowed away," he replied casually. "It's not much, but I'll manage."

"Are you bringing relays along?" Susannah asked, mostly to force entry into a conversation that did not seem to include her. "In case they get the com back on-line?"

"We don't have enough to span the distance. What we need is a few more satellites in the air, but . . ." He rubbed thumb and two fingers together. "ConPlex was too cheap for that. All I'm taking is my translator and its power packs."

Megan glanced from one to the other, about to say something, deciding finally on silence. She bent her head and reached for the last blanket. Stavros stood with his hands on his hips, as if uncomfortable being there but not yet willing to leave.

"Has Clausen stopped yelling yet?" Megan asked eventually.

Something's going on here, Susannah realized. She was missing every-thing but the innuendo. From her self-assigned position as neutral observer, she'd acquired a nose for the currents of alliance and coalition, rather like a magnetic field detector. But it was unclear yet where the poles were in this particular alignment.

"Clausen doesn't know yet," said Stavros. "He's busy fussing with the trashed high gain. I told Weng he thinks we should all dump our own jobs to help him, but she agreed that until a Sled's recovered and repaired, a wagon train is as good a way as any to explore the planet. It's fully in line with the Mission."

Megan finished with the last blanket. "Is Emil making any progress?"

Susannah was sure she read smugness in Stavros' shrug.

"The antenna's almost okay as is for com, but he's got to bring the elec-tronics down from the nose. And for power, well, that could take a while." His glance flicked toward her and away, and she recalled accusing him of purposefully delaying the repair of the link. Now she saw defiance in his response instead of guilt. The implication piqued her.

"So it must have been to encourage the Commander's dedication to Mis-sion that you reported to her looking like an Academy recruiting poster." She took the folded blankets from Megan and stood with them hugged to her chest. For reasons she was not entirely proud of, she let her gaze be frankly appraising. "I believe you even shaved."

She'd wanted his attention, and she got it.

He looked startled. His hand strayed unconsciously to his jaw. "Yah," he admitted with an embarrassed half-grin. "Guess it must have worked, eh?" For a moment, the boy slid away and the man stared out at her with a look as intimate and hungry as a hand slipped between her thighs. Then it was gone, and the boy returned, as he caught himself and backed off, moving away from her, aware of having been discovered. "Gotta find Aguidran," he muttered and stalked off down the line of wagons.

Susannah dropped her gaze to the ground, sure she must be blushing. She turned to the wagon with her load of blankets and began shoving them into every available crevice.

Megan tipped her crate back against the wagon and shook her head. "Susannah, Susannah. Why don't you just go to bed with the lad instead of torturing him this way?"

"Oh, Meg, don't be . . ."

"Take him or let him go. The boy's in pain."

"Pain? Come on." Susannah gave up the obligatory protest. "You think so, really?"

"How many times have I told you?"

"Just never took it seriously. I mean, it's not exactly cradle robbing, but . . . well, I thought he'd be a lot to handle, being the way he is, and you know, that stuff always gets in the way of the work. . . ."

"But?"

"Well . . ." Susannah stowed a final blanket. "Doesn't he seem different to you?"

"Different? How so?"

"I don't know . . . not like he was."

"When?"

"Before." She waved her arms about as if she could frighten off this new dilemma.

"How wonderfully articulate."

"I just don't *know*." Susannah's shoulders hunched, then let go. "Hell, maybe I should."

"Well, if you do," Megan offered more soberly, "don't expect it to be casual with him. Life is not a game to Stavros."

Susannah nodded. Every instinct told her to run like hell from this complication. And yet, he did seem interested, and here she was, suffering from the recent chill among the fraternity of physicians. It would be . . . comforting. But would it be fair to him?

In the distance, thunder cracked and built into a rolling boil that finished with a dying basso flourish. The priests at the bottom of the stairs formed a circle on the dusty rock and began a low-voiced chant.

"I think," said Susannah, "that I'd better give this long and careful thought."

"Don't think about it for too long."

"Why?" Susannah laughed, but Megan's serious eyes stopped her. "Come on, Meg, time's the one thing we have plenty of here on Fiix."

"Don't count on it. The Sawls wouldn't. Why should you?"

41

STAVROS SEARCHED DOWN one line of wagons, then doubled back along another, heading for the stairs. He put Susannah from his mind with an ease that was at last becoming practiced. The plan and its various unresolved details dominated his thoughts. He was impatient to be on his way to B-Sled, committed in action as well as in words. He wondered if a few light questions to Weng on the subject of extraterrestrial development legalities would attract her undue attention.

She was gone when he reached the pavilions at the stair bottom. A ranger group leader was bundling up the poles. The canopies lay folded on the rock, ready to be stowed in heavy canvas bags. Stavros chatted with the group leader, a youngish maternal woman, especially cheerful for a ranger, and secured the aid of two of her guildsmen for the hauling down of Danforth's equipment. Better not to bother the Master Ranger with such minute details. He helped the woman tie up the awkward bundles, then stood with her on the bottom step, where the planted terraces were visible over the sea of multicolored wagon tops. The thunder was in retreat for the moment. A haze of damp heat hung over the flooded fields.

The ranger pointed across the wide Dop Arek to the cloud bank hugging the Vallegar and spoke about Valla's habits of battle strategy and what Lagri might be expected to do in response. She discussed each Sister's arsenal as familiarly as if she had the care of it herself. She described Valla's Water Soldiers in precise detail, and allowed that Lagri's counterforce of fire was one of the best defenses but was difficult to maneuver on the attack. Stavros took note of the greater tendency among the rangers to use this battlefield vocabulary when speaking of the Arrah. The priestly vocabulary more often emphasized the formal, gaming aspect of the conflict, though its imagery was no less aggressive.

On his way up the stairs, he met Ghirra, in his best gray linens, descending ahead of the four burly Sawls stretchering Danforth out into fresh air and sunlight. Stavros leaned against the cliff to let the stretcher pass.

"Weng's letting me go," he murmured as the Master Healer paused beside him. Ghirra nodded, careful eyes on his patient.

Danforth gazed up at Stavros as the stretcher went by. "Hey there, Ibiá. Someone throwing you a party?"

Stavros brushed his spanking clean whites. "It's your homecoming, Danforth."

His brusqueness left him shamed. The planetologist was painfully thinner, weaker. His handsome ebony face seemed hollowed and a bit haunted. Stavros called to the stretcher bearers to wait and descended the steps to Danforth's side. "I'm bringing your stuff down now," he offered more gently. "Go easy on the batteries, okay?"

They shared a silence made awkward by the acrimony of their past confrontations. Danforth glanced away first.

"Ibiá, I . . ."

Thunder rumbled. Danforth's head swiveled toward the sound. The stretcher bearers cast worried looks up at Ghirra, who gestured them onward.

"No, wait!" Danforth struggled against the webbing binding him to the stretcher, searching for the source of the thunder. "Hold it! Ibiá, get them to stop!"

Stavros looked to Ghirra, who nodded. The bearers unfolded the stretcher legs and set it down across two wide steps.

"Untie these damn straps!" Danforth demanded. "I can't see a thing!"

Ghirra came down the steps to calm him.

"I've got to see!"

Ghirra loosed the restraining chest straps so that Stavros could help the big man sit up. As they moved him, Danforth's knuckles whitened, grasping the stretcher rails.

Feeling him go rigid, Stavros put his hostility aside. "Easy, now."

"Damn!" Danforth wheezed. "Doesn't get easier!"

"You try too much, Taylor." Ghirra pressed both hands to Danforth's temples. "You must sleep more to heal."

"Doc, I got too much to do!" But his grip relaxed, and he raised a more collected gaze to the distant Vallegar. The lurking cloud bank had retreated, though the thunder remained. "Ibiá, are my eyes going with the rest of my damned body, or is the sky out there clear as a baby's ass?"

"It is right now."

"And what's that yellow fuzz all over everything?"

"Vegetation," replied Stavros. "Cultivated on the terraces out there, wild on the plain. A shipweek ago, the ground was waterlogged mud. Now the crops are shoulder-high in the fields. The wild species seem to grow considerably slower."

But Danforth was new to the phenomenon of near-instant growth. He stared at the fields in wonder. "One shipweek! Christ!"

"Oh, no," the linguist corrected. "Lagri and Valla Ired."

He shared a glance with the Master Healer, helped him ease Danforth down again, and continued up the stairs.

Later, he rode the winch pallet loaded with Danforth's equipment. He dropped past the long stone flights, clinging to the ropes as the pallet swayed with the speed of its descent. The steps were again impassable, as the herdsmen led out the dairy herd. They nosed cautiously out of the cave mouths into the light, blinking, five or six hundred rangy long-haired beasts, crowding along in ragged double file. Their hornless heads were lowered, intent on the steps. They needed no encouragement to stick close to the cliff side of the stair. At the bottom, a group of herdsmen urged the leaders off the last wide steps where they proposed to halt for a leisurely look around. Apprentices yelled and shoved to hustle them off to join their larger cousins in the muddy flat at the end of the rock terrace.

Stavros clucked at the stolid hekkers as he slid past them. The herd was to be part of his cover. Traditionally, Ghirra had explained, they accompanied the caravan for the first two throws across the Dop Arek, following a more southern route than would lead straight to Ogo Dul, so that in the middle of the third throw, the herd could be turned aside and driven up into the foothills of the eastern mountains, the Talche, to graze those more edible pastures until the caravan collected them on its return trip.

More edible? Stavros set the question aside to pass along to Susannah later, when there was more time for random investigation.

The plan was, while the caravan lay camped and—he hoped—sleeping soundly during the rest period before that third throw, for him to vanish with Liphar into those hills, from there making their way through the

Talche to the site of the disabled Sled. It was a longer route than the obvious one, but it provided the advantages of surprise and a substantial head start. Only after the dairy herd was settled in their new pastures would Aguidran send back a small number of her rangers to help Clausen haul in the Sled for repairs.

The winch bucked, swung precipitously toward the cliff, but slowed and swung back short of impact. Stavros barely noticed, preoccupied with his plan. It sounded viable, as far as it went. What would happen after he'd stolen the antenna and its crucial electronics was the thing most in question. He was not schooled in law or lawyer's rhetoric, yet he would be on his own when he reestablished contact with CRI. Megan insisted that she would be a physical burden to him, that going underground as he must required being able to move fast, on the spur of the moment. She would go to Ogo Dul and return to remain as his mole in the enemy camp. He would have to do the research himself, in hiding, without benefit of her long experience in such matters. He must patch together the skeleton of an argument convincing enough to lure her people's advocate into taking the case. Finally, he must fox CRI into sending an FTL drone to Earth in secret with his message. From there, they could only hope that the lawyer would be won over enough to begin proceedings immediately, so that when Clausen did file his claim—Stavros knew he could not hold off that inevitability forever—he would run smack into an already full-blown court case.

As he played through his alternative scenarios for the hundredth time, the pallet touched ground with a gentle shudder. A borrowed hakra two-cart waited, along with his volunteer help, two young ranger apprentices whom he did not know. He wondered whose household goods now lay in the dust until the return of their conveyance. The apprentices helped load the equipment, then set off ahead of the shaggy little hakra to guide it along the road to the Lander.

Stavros followed, with a backward glance at the continuing pandemonium of the pack-up. While the last of the hekkers began their ungraceful clatter down the stairs, the bulk of the herd still milled about among the wagons, kicking up dust clouds and resisting the best efforts of the herdsmen to get them moving toward the mudflat. The big hjalk were being led up to be put into their traces, team after team, pushing a path through the dust and the lowing hekkers and the swarms of little hakra carts. The winches rose and fell with last-minute bundles of goods for already overstuffed wagons. Children darted back and forth among the beasts and vehicles with armloads of clothing and utensils.

Along the edge of the rock flat, their bright red-and-blue reflecting in the watery mirrors of the nearby terraces, the twenty Food Guild wagons waited in an impressive line, fully packed and ready. Ti Niamar huddled with his senior guildsmen and Aguidran at the head of the line. At the back of the last wagon, two older women wearing the guild's red-and-blue stripes lounged against the big wheels, playing stones.

At the top of the path, Stavros let the ranger apprentices go ahead with the cart. He stood in the still heat, tugging at his damp shirt, already anxious for a chance to shed the close Terran clothing. There were carts and wagons as far as his eye could see, at least a hundred large hjalk-drawn wagons, and six or seven times that number of smaller hakra carts and wagons, nearly five thousand men, women, and children on the move together. What a glorious madness! If he had been able to observe this process beforehand, the evacuation of the Lander would have seemed merely efficient instead of miraculous. Stavros saluted the ambitious spirit of the venture, then braced himself to face the base camp at the Lander, where he had not set foot since before the storm.

Ocher dust billowed from under the cartwheels ahead as the already drying road dipped down through the plantings. In the mirrored fields, sheaths of fernlike fronds were thickening into stout fleshy clusters. Behind the terrace earthworks, the tall yellow stalks sank muscular roots into mud topped by several inches of warming water. Broad furry leaves shaded the path where it narrowed, the lower foliage shading from yellow to amber and orange between bright lemon-colored veins. Food Guildsmen hurried barefoot between the rows, peering into the fat leaf whorls, scattering dried manure from sacks slung across their chests.

The road narrowed at the turnoff to the Lander site. The wheels of the hakra cart just fit between the earthworks hemming in the path. Stavros brushed leaf stalks aside as he passed, and glanced up through the foliage to see the Lander towering above him. He hadn't been back here since the evacuation. He felt like a runaway, caught and forced to return to a home he no longer wished to claim.

The Lander rested in a barren circular clearing, surrounded by a velvet yellow wall of vegetation. The mangled high-gain dish lay between two of the landing struts, five meters of mud-splashed metal, half in, half out of the cooling shade of the Underbelly. Stavros gave it a sidelong inspection, as if it were old news, though this was as close to it as he had been since the Engineers Guild had found it and hauled it in. Sections of its golden mesh and several of its umbrella ribs had been ripped away during its tumble in the flood. Other ribs had been bent like hairpins, their mesh interstices shredded and hanging loose like dead skin.

McPherson glanced up at the rattle of cartwheels and freed one hand from the rib she was straightening, long enough to wave. Clausen crouched in the sun near the center of the dish, in a pie slice between two barren ribs, contemplating the stump of the sheared-off central post, apparently all that remained of the receiver mounting. He stood to watch Stavros approach, his expression unreadable behind his mirrored sunglasses.

Stavros was relieved to see the Master Healer seated beside Danforth in the shadowed Underbelly. A small section of the space had been again partitioned into private quarters, using crates and storage lockers brought back down from the Caves. But Danforth's bed had been set up beside the third landing strut, where he could watch the sky and still be shaded from the ferocious sun. An arrangement of blankets and bundled tarps allowed him to sit up, propped against the trusswork of the strut.

Stavros halted the ranger apprentices beside the cart and eased into the shadow. Table-sized crates were pulled up around the bed, already littered with flood-stained graphs and backup data sheets. Danforth seemed diminished, his dark skin almost pale against the thick stack of tarps, but he was busily sorting old photos into piles laid out around him on the bed. Weng sat to one side, taking careful notes as Danforth read off time and location from the bottom of each photo. Stavros noted that the Master Healer, seated at Danforth's shoulder, sheltered a photo in his lap, turning it this way and that for study, rubbing the limp plastic between two fingers. Stavros was glad he hadn't thrown all that seemingly useless documentation away.

"The mass cloud movement seems to be diagonal," Danforth was pointing out. He tipped a photo at an oblique angle, then grabbed up a second and a third to match them side by side like a fan of cards. "Northeast to southwest? Bearing no relation to the planet's rotational poles . . . okay . . . well . . ." He nodded to Weng. "Put a flag on Sequence L-Beta 374-29 through 34."

He tossed the photos aside to greet the arrival of his equipment with a mixture of impatience and relief. Weng looked merely relieved. She unobtrusively dropped her hand to shake out an attack of writer's cramp, and

Stavros decided that playing secretary to her second-in-command, no matter how much she favored him or the work he had come to do, was not her idea of the first order of the Captaincy. But her usual groundside pastime did require a computer. Stavros regretted that his private purpose required her to remain without her music for a while longer. Meanwhile, the Commander apparently welcomed any task that put idle time to good use.

"Over here, over here," Danforth urged the cart drivers. Grimacing from the sudden movement, he gestured to the crates nearest his bedside. "Ibiá, pull those over closer. Lay that stuff out on the ground—no, wait, I need that box! Hand it over here."

"He's already back in stride, I see," Stavros murmured to Weng as he unlatched the cover on a portable mini-terminal. Directing the ranger apprentices in quiet Sawlish, he felt like the repairman from the native quarter, called into fix the colonists' holo-set.

"At last! Toys to calm our restless invalid!" Clausen strolled in out of the sun and stood with his hands in his pockets, curling an avuncular grin beneath his mirrored lenses. Stavros saw the Master Healer withdraw into himself. He turned his own back as if absorbed by the arranging of equipment.

"No fresh data until we get CRI up again," Clausen continued. "A shame really, but there's what, six weeks of backlog for you to play with?" He leaned against the landing strut at Danforth's side.

"It was all coming in too damned fast," Danforth admitted peevishly. "And kept changing on me. Without CRI, I can't run the high-resolution models, but the simpler ones will run on this little box. I can do some tinkering with the input, see what it takes to match the weather patterns we're actually observing. That should tell me whether I'm right about there being a whole term missing from the big model." He looked to Weng. "Our mystery factor."

Weng nodded and Clausen clucked sympathetically, but his silvered eyes focused on Stavros' unresponsive back. "Taylor, don't you feel honored that our Ship's Linguist has taken time from his very important work to do you this favor?"

Stavros ignored him. Danforth, for whatever private reason, let the opportunity for a dig go by. Clausen stretched his grin and winked at Weng. "This's more time than he's given so far to fixing the link, am I right, Commander?"

"I was made Com Officer by default." Stavros straightened with an armload of battery packs to power the unit. "I didn't volunteer for the job."

He made an elaborate business of plugging in the emergency power, testing Danforth's unusual silence. The planetologist's glance was carefully neutral. Stavros realized it was time to stop thinking of Clausen and Danforth as a single entity. Their relationship had shifted during their long night out in the storm. Stavros allowed Danforth a moment of honest empathy. Two weeks in the dark with Clausen had surely been no picnic, especially if you were already in pain and disabled.

"Tut," admonished the prospector. "Was I complaining? The Lander seems to be in passable condition. I'll need something to keep busy with until the Sled comes in. By the way, Stav, I hear you're joining the exodus."

Stavros waited. Would it be more mockery or an ultimatum?

"Mr. Ibiá asked my permission and I gave it," Weng interceded coolly. "After all, Mr. Clausen, you are the person most experienced with the electronics of the link. It seemed most efficient to let Mr. Ibiá get on with his real work."

Clausen was all patient understanding. "Whatever you think is right, and of course I'm flattered. As a boy, I loved being up to my elbows in chips and wiring. But there's also the matter of securing help to recover the Sled."

"I believe Mr. Ibiá has already arranged that."

"I did the best I could for you with Aguidran, and here's the deal." Stavros fitted the last jack and flipped the toggle on the battery pack. His drying hair kept falling in his face. He shoved it back, making it a gesture of impatience. How second nature the dissembling had already become. Even better, Ghirra chose this moment to rise and wander around to Clausen's side to play the responsible healer checking the progress of all his patients' wounds. Only the precariousness of the situation kept Stavros from laughing. "I got her to agree to send back the extra contingent of rangers assigned to the dairy herd, once the herdsmen have them settled in the summer pastures. That should be as many as a dozen rangers, and they should be able to make it back within, oh, five shipdays after the caravan leaves, which will be very soon now, within the day."

Clausen did some fast calculating, distracted as he was by Ghirra's gentle but insistent ministrations. "By which time, it will be dusk again."

"Late afternoon," Stavros conceded. "You'll make it out to the Sled by nightfall easily enough, maybe even get it ready to be hauled out. The night will slow down your return, but the rangers work well in the dark, and maybe you can do some of your repairs along the way. As long as the weather holds, you should be okay."

The mirrored lenses stared at him as Clausen shook off Ghirra's hand with a sharp jerk. Stavros heard a soft mirthless chuckle. At first, he couldn't imagine where it had come from.

Danforth?

Then the prospector laughed also, and pulled off his sunglasses to rub his eyes with apparently amused exasperation. "Well, my boy, in that case I shall have to feel encouraged, shan't I?" He turned the friendliest of smiles on Ghirra, who waited like a concerned Samaritan at his side. "Are you done with me, honored doctor? I'm quite all right, as you can see, and I really must get back to work." As Ghirra stood aside, Clausen nodded a cheery adieu and strolled back into the sun.

Stavros hoped his gratitude read clearly in the look he gave the Master Healer.

Weng stirred. "While you have a moment, Guildmaster?" She drew Ghirra away to her worktable deeper in the Underbelly. Stavros sent his helpers on their way to return the borrowed cart, then fussed with the equipment setup, conscious of Danforth's steady quiet attention.

"Ibiá," said the planetologist finally. "I don't know what you're up to, but I've got one bit of advice for you out there."

Stavros met his glance and caught the disappearing remnant of a bitter grin.

"Take a hat. The hardest one you can find."

"I'll keep that in mind."

"See that you do."

"Mr. Ibiá, perhaps you could be of some help."

Stavros turned aside on his way through the shaded Underbelly, to join Weng and Ghirra at her crate-top workplace. She had hemmed her space in with tall storage lockers, creating a three-sided cubicle whose cramped dimensions and molded alloy walls recalled a shipboard cabin. A single folding camp chair faced into the cubicle, presenting a stubborn back to the hot sun and the dust and the velvet yellow foliage beyond the Lander's shadow.

Ghirra hovered at the cubicle opening, avoiding the angular space.

Removed from his own frame of reference and set against this aggressively Terran background, he seemed thinner, browner, smaller, yet so much richer and more complicated. He had dressed carefully for his first visit to the Lander: clean, neat, and composed. A gesture of respect, or a hint of vanity? Stavros sensed his entire data set for the Master Healer reordering yet again. He noted a certain fragility of expression in Ghirra's long, fine-boned face, visible only when the golden smile had retreated. He read it as a sign of hidden doubt, and longed to know the nature of the Master Healer's personal dilemma, instantly sure that there was one.

Doubt rose closer to Ghirra's surface as he attended politely to Weng's inquiries. He held an erasable scratch sheet in his hand, delicately, as if he would prefer to be without it but had no wish to offend the alien Commander.

"Mr. Ibiá," began Weng brightly. "I have asked the Guildmaster if he would explain in his own language what this is." She handed Stavros a second scratch sheet. A neatly drawn but obscure diagram dominated the page: joined columns filled with oddly distorted Sawlish characters. Jottings in Weng's hand decorated the borders of the sheet. She was clearly excited. "This is from his own library."

Stavros looked to Ghirra.

Ghirra spread his palms. "I cannot."

"Guild lore?" Stavros guessed. "Not to be revealed?"

Ghirra shook his head, a mixed gesture of pride and apology. "Physicians' keeps no secret. I cannot because I do not know it. It is from the very old books."

Stavros looked back to Weng. She had obviously received this answer already.

"Guildmaster, if you will?" She gently plucked the first sheet from Ghirra's fingers and passed it to Stavros.

He gave a grunt of puzzled recognition. "Periodic table?"

"Correct. Ours. Can you explain it to our Master Healer?"

Stavros struggled at it, lacking a major part of the appropriate vocabulary. Ghirra listened impassively, looking very like his stern sister as Stavros talked of the nature of matter, then launched into a basic outline of atomic theory. Hoping to settle on a viable word for "atom," he paused.

"*Imael*," supplied the Master Healer.

Stavros cocked his head at the uncommon diphthong.

"Old words," Ghirra added tightly. "This is a Priests' Truth, what you say." Then he delighted the linguist by continuing the explication on his own. It did not matter that his description was highly metaphorical, like a complex tale-chant. The theory contained within the poetry was essentially intact. Most significantly, the technical sort of specifics, such as the atom and its parts and characteristics, were all named in the ancient ritual language that Ghirra had called priest words.

When he'd finished, Stavros translated for Weng, who returned as broad a smile as he'd ever seen from her. But he sensed a certain bias in the Master Healer's recitation.

"A *priests'* truth?" he asked. "You do not believe this?"

Ghirra seemed to mull the matter over anew. "How do I believe what I do not see?"

The man has the soul of an empiricist, thought Stavros. No wonder he's contemptuous of the priests. He handed him the Terran periodic table. "Through this, you can see. It offers the truth of numbers."

Weng took the second sheet and offered it to Ghirra as well. "And through this. In your own tongue."

Stavros glanced at her, brow furrowing. "What do you mean?"

Weng passed the sheet to him instead. "Take a closer look, Mr. Ibiá."

He grasped at an impossible connection. "What? This?"

"I believe so. The more I study it, the surer I am."

"This is from the *very* old books, Ghirra?" Stavros pursued a notion that had to be delusional. "But you cannot read them?"

Ghirra's eyes were lost when he looked up from the two diagrams held side by side. *"Dho imme rek,"* he murmured helplessly.

Stavros felt the familiar awe that prickled him whenever he heard the Sisters sincerely invoked. He had unwittingly plumbed the bottom of the physician's anti-Priest Guild skepticism, and at last, touched belief. Unwilling belief, perhaps, or belief crying out for a more satisfactory explanation, but belief enough to cause Ghirra to stare at Weng with new eyes.

Stavros explained to Weng: "The ancient books come from the goddesses, he says."

"Toph-leta," Ghirra added faintly.

"Life-gifts," Stavros translated.

Weng noted the healer's now very evident disturbance, but she was not to be deflected. "I apologize if this causes you discomfort, Guildmaster. I merely seek confirmation of the idea that perhaps once, a very long time ago, your society was a different one." She chose her words carefully, avoiding all value judgments. "It is not unheard of that a civilization has once been more extensive, perhaps more mobile, perhaps lacking the raw materials necessary to spaceflight but with more time and interest for the pursuit of the sciences. That diagram, if it is what I conjecture, might be proof of this. Do you have history of such a time?"

"Science," said Ghirra softly. So the word was not unknown to him. Stavros supposed there must have been talk of science with Susannah in Physicians', though perhaps on a more pragmatic level. The healer seemed to recover his composure by a sudden effort of will. "No. No history. The Sisters only."

Weng pursed her lips, disappointed but not discouraged. "The veil of time is always thicker than we hope for."

"Weng! Come look at this," called Danforth from the confines of his bed.

Weng did not refuse the interruption. She slipped the diagrams from Ghirra's hands and laid them on her worktable. "Perhaps we will speak of this again, Guildmaster. I thank you for your time." She nodded to them both and glided away to answer Danforth's summons.

Stavros did not move. Ghirra was silent for a long time, head bowed. When he lifted his chin, his gaze was profoundly troubled, seeming to bore into Stavros' soul in search of an answer.

"Keth-shim Ghirra. Anything . . ." Stavros offered humbly and meant it.

Ghirra considered. "Yes. It is time." Having made his decision, he let a smile uncloud his face and warm it with anticipation. "Come, Stavros Ibiá. There is a thing I must show you."

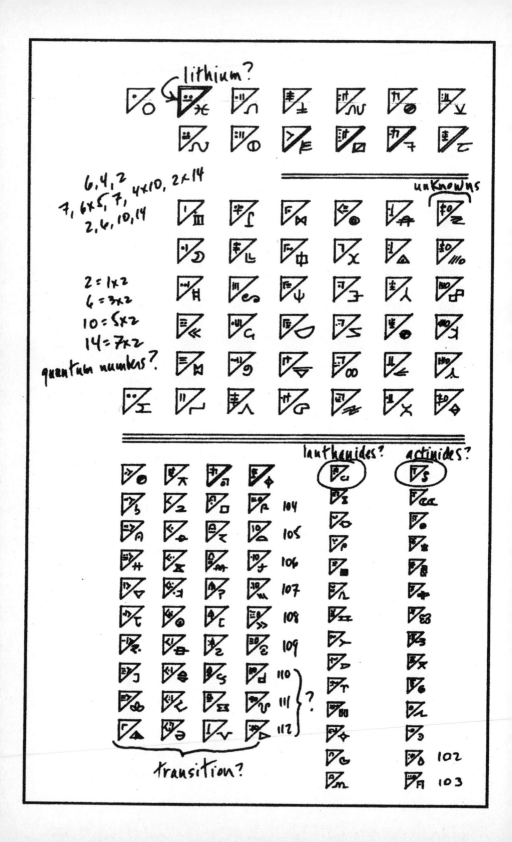

42

THE CLOUD BANK had returned to shroud the Vallegar in a massive fog as Stavros followed Ghirra up the stairs. The physician was in a hurry, his troubled manner transformed into determination that built with each step. When they passed Liphar coming down, breathless, pointing at the clouds, Ghirra barely slowed. Liphar called back to ask where they were going.

"Eles-Nol," Ghirra replied, in Aguidran's growl.

Liphar let out a strangled squawk. Stavros glanced back to find him slack-jawed and staring, while behind him, the clouds began to roil and darken.

"Guildmaster . . . ?" Stavros stumbled, heading upward, looking back.

"Tell him come."

At Stavros' signal, Liphar sprang to follow. Ghirra led them to the second level, then along the exterior ledges to the easternmost entry. The cave mouth was a small one and deserted. Ghirra hurried up the inner stairs and into the tunnels. Stavros gave up on his mental mapping and allowed himself to be led. The last time he'd gone blind into the maze behind the main tunnels, he'd ended up at the Bath Hall. He was encouraged by Liphar's nervous bird-dog twitch, as they paced along darkened empty corridors, to hope for something equally wonderful.

At length there was a door, a low wide wooden door set in a stretch of wall unbroken by other openings as far as he could see in either direction. A niche beside the door housed a light station, apparently not much in use, as its shelves were crowded with dusty, unlit lamps.

The thick, oiled planks of the door were carved in shallow relief, and strapped with curlicued bands of precious iron. The heavy barrel hinges were of hardened wood. Above the doorframe was the wave-and-flame motif of the Priest Guild. Ghirra lit a lamp and held it up to the door, lighting the top panel of carvings.

"It is the story when Valla forget . . ." He mimed a one-handed tying of a knot. "She forget tying the clouds on the Vallegar." On the next panel, the staunch figure of the goddess, long curls and garments flying, pursued a herd of amoebic shapes across fanglike mountain peaks.

Stavros was relieved to see a grin stretch Liphar's anxious face. So, not all the Sister Tales were deadly serious. "Valla can be forgetful, eh? . . . What happened?"

Ghirra consulted the door. "It's hard to explain."

Stavros started, hearing Susannah's intonation rendered exactly. One explanation for the Master Healer's rapid absorption of English, then: he was a superb mimic.

"I'll bet Lagri took full advantage of that."

Liphar laughed, pointing out the bottom panel. "That time much wager lost!"

Ghirra's smile was tolerant, but he had not come this far to revisit old legends. He checked the lamp's oil reservoir, passed it to Liphar and grasped the stout door handle. The huge door swung inward without a sound.

Inside was a small chamber. Stavros found it disturbingly reminiscent of a ship's air lock. A second, less decorative panel with practical wooden knobs confronted them, set in a faceless wall. Liphar cradled the lamp protectively, nodding his readiness as Ghirra reached for the inner door.

It opened with a whoosh that sucked at their eardrums. Beyond the opening, Stavros saw only darkness, heard the hollow moan of rushing air. He gave in to a delicious shiver. Here was a place of genuine storybook mystery, just the sort of thing to inspire his imagination. Plus, he was still sleep-deprived, and revved by Ghirra's solemn excitement. He would have to watch himself very carefully.

Liphar went first, with the lamp. The flame danced madly against the glass chimney like an imprisoned djinn. It lit up a brief landing, and a wide spiral stair that curled both up and downward from where they stood, wrapping around a giant bundle of vertical tubing: fat white pipes like in the Bath Hall, slimmer ones of glazed terra-cotta, and sheaves of still-thinner pipe, green-ishly translucent. All these ringed a dark inner shaftway whose height and diameter could only be hinted at by the howling insistence of the updraft.

Lamp in hand, Liphar trotted down the stairs. His earlier surprise at their destination had been subdued by eagerness to get there. Stavros followed more slowly, soon finding himself hugging the outer curve of the wall, wishing for handholds or a railing. The singing void of the inner shaftway was visible in long night-black gaps between the runs of pipe. Gaps you could tumble into. Their vertiginous presence roiled the pit of his stomach and crawled up his spine like a subsonic base line. Liphar was almost out of sight, and Ghirra behind him was a force pressing him downward, ever faster. He was more frightened than he ought to be, and for the first time since the evacuation of the Lander, the specter of panic rose to haunt him. Not here, not now, was his new mantra. He couldn't bear to disgrace himself before the Master Healer, whose opinion had begun to matter seriously to him. If only he could see better. Beyond the circle of the lamp, the stairway seemed to drop away in darkness. For all he knew, it did, at the very next step. Stavros put a hand to the wall for psychic anchoring, and discovered that it was extraordinarily smooth, like polished marble.

Or like glass. It glimmered in the lamplight, seamless, crackless, without bump or blemish. His fingers worshiped the perfection of its arc. No anchoring to be found there. Then he noticed the heat.

The updraft was not just warm, like the cozy body heat of the inner living quarters. It was hot. And dry. The impossibly flawless glass, enclosing them like a giant crystal tube, was feverish to the touch.

Stavros conjured a mammoth conflagration raging far below. He was on a descent into hell. This silliness at least brought the relief of a smile. But his excitement built as he followed Liphar, down, down and around in endless dizzy spirals, until the heat and his increasing giddiness and the rush of air lifting his damp hair awoke a seductive thrilling in him.

Because the truth was, he'd missed walking the edge, for so many days of keeping himself tightly wrapped, of driving himself without rest for the sake of his newfound purpose . . . to say nothing of preserving his dignity. But in this lovely, singing darkness, the responsibilities of the daylight lost substance. It became easy to forget why restraint was necessary, or even desirable. As always, the precipice drew him, as the siren voices of terror and exultation rose out of the night-black pit like old friends. The music of the updraft vibrated through his internal spaces. The darkness caressed. The mystery enveloped him. He was descending into it, step by dizzying step, with Liphar his Virgil, the flame held high to light the path to the heart of truth and revelation.

Stavros pushed free of the wall and laughed. Revelation! He must kneel in gratitude. But as his knees buckled, an arm caught him from behind, supported his fall and pressed a practiced hand to the back of his neck, forcing his head between his knees until the dizziness passed. A delicious, steady calm spread through him like a balm.

When he breathed evenly again, Ghirra eased him against the wall and tipped his chin into the lamplight, prying back an eyelid, brushing away his hair to feel his brow. Ghirra's palms resting at his temples seduced the panic from behind his eyes. Stavros groaned and struggled to sit upright, to shake off these hands with a life and energy of their own. He met the healer's gaze and could not bear its compassionate scrutiny. He let his head slump to his chest.

Ghirra read his shame accurately. "Sleep you need."

"I know."

Liphar knelt beside Stavros in concern.

"I'm okay, Lifa. Hopeless, but okay."

"You hear too well the voice inside," said Ghirra.

Stavros looked up. "The what?"

He'd learned long ago not to describe his moments of mania in terms of "voices"—that was the surest route to a court-ordered drug regimen. But often it *was* like someone else speaking in him, or like losing the self he knew to some other self, or often, selves.

Ghirra pressed both hands to his heart-center. "The voice that talks here."

Close but not quite. "Ah. Yes, perhaps. How did you know?"

Ghirra smiled. "It is my work, as the words are yours."

"The mind is your work, as well as the body?"

"How not? They are the same thing."

Stavros nodded, because it was easier than unburdening himself further, more expedient than starting a complex and touchy discussion on the stairs. But it was only postponed, he knew, and it would be one of many with this man.

"And I say sleep you need." Ghirra grasped his arm. "You walk now, yes?"

"Yes. My thanks, Keth-shim." Stavros eased himself to his feet. To have Ghirra treat his fit of imbalance as simple exhaustion was somehow stabilizing. "I'll be fine."

And of course he would be, until the next time he allowed his id to take him by storm. But perhaps there wouldn't be a next time. He *was* tired, but mostly of his own luxuriant self-indulgence. There was too much at stake now: Megan's plan, the Sawls' future. He should not presume to take on such responsibilities if he still needed a McPherson around to slap him out of panic, or a Ghirra to hold him back from the edge. Praying for restraint and strength of purpose, Stavros swore there would be no more indulgences. He urged Liphar onward and followed with a firmer step.

Moving downward, he counted stairs, and tiny landings where other levels and half-levels accessed the shaft. At major intersections, sections of the central pipe column bent away from the shaft, crossed over the stairs, and vanished into horizontal tunnels of their own. The black gaps open to the void widened.

He had no idea where he was. They had entered the shaft on the third level, the level of the Ranger Guild and the Meeting Hall. So far, they'd passed three major landings on the way down, corresponding to the second or stable level, the unused first level and beyond that . . . what? Now they were on a stretch of stair that had descended unbroken by any landings or openings for several turns around the shaft.

Stavros guessed they were well below plains level. They had to be.

And then, amazingly, there were others on the stair. Two old women came toiling upward in the heat, sharing a lamp and identical peaceful expressions. A young priest bounded past, a tiny lamp clutched in one hand, his wave-and-flame tabard bouncing against his chest. He panted a hurried greeting without breaking his ascent. As they continued downward, the roaring of the updraft lessened but the heat increased, until a deadening of the echoes announced the bottom of the shaft, and a cool cross draft floated past to refresh them.

Liphar stopped on the last step and raised the lamp. Overhead, the pipes angled out of the shaft to run along the ceiling of a tall corridor slanting still deeper into the rock. The base of the shaft was a broad circular depression. Stavros stepped into it to stare upward. The circle of pipes faded into darkness, but the configuration resonated with other, more familiar structures—the lift shaft of the Lander or the internal service columns in the high-rise architecture of Earth.

He offered the two Sawls a wondering shrug. "It's so big. So . . . perfectly round."

Ghirra waved him out of the shaft bottom with a laugh. "Wait, you."

He led the way down the tall ramping corridor. Heat radiated from the suspended piping but the cooler draft continued to whisper across their faces. In the bouncing lamplight, Stavros could see that, unlike the more rough-hewn excavations of the upper caves, this corridor had exact corners. Floor and walls and ceiling met at clean right angles. The surfaces were as smooth as the wall of the shaftway, not glass but a pale granular stone. The floor hollowed slightly toward the center of the corridor, a mark of ancient wear and the passage of countless footsteps. The walls bore shadings of darkness at the heights of hip and shoulder. Stavros let his fingers brush the staining as he walked.

"Old, old, old," he murmured. Weng's speculation had to be right: some other Sawls, some former technological giants, had built these corridors. What became of them? Could the Sawls have no memory of such a glorious past? Could it be, as Ghirra implied, that their true history was completely buried in myth, even while the technology it produced was still very much in use?

A gargle passed through the pipes overhead, some liquid message speeding uplevel. He felt no drips, heard no hiss of escaping steam. The joints were still clean and tight. After how many hundreds of years?

At last, there was light ahead. Ghirra extinguished the lamp, and deposited it at the light station at the end of the corridor, where a shaft of light leaked through a pair of towering double doors. One was ajar. Ghirra pulled it open and motioned Stavros in.

He entered a vast space suffused by a cool greenish glow. A vast space but not an empty one. Its monumental size could be grasped only from the number and enormity of the objects within it, which were cylinders at least fifteen meters high and six or seven wide, like mammoth Doric columns but too broad and closely spaced for their purpose to be simply support. Now Stavros understood what architecture the Priest Hall had attempted to mimic. As he moved in among them, dwarfed by their greenly transparent bulk, Stavros saw that their shine was actually the glint off of fine vertical ribbing. Light penetrated the furrowed surface until swallowed within the depths of the material. More glass. Stavros tapped the ribbed surface with a tentative knuckle.

"This is *Eles-Nol*," Ghirra announced with quiet ceremony.

"What is it?"

"First, you look." His arm swept the hall, then pointed upward.

A grid of slim pipes was suspended from the ceiling, joining the tops of the cylinders to the bundles of smaller pipe entering from the shaftway. Stavros traced the route from cylinder to corridor and back again. The fatter pipes, the terra-cotta and white, continued on between the rows of cylinders without connecting. Liphar danced impatiently at Stavros' side, but Ghirra restrained him, letting the linguist set his own pace of discovery. He led him around one immense base. On the far side, a slender glass pipe dropped down the face of the cylinder, nestled in the ribbing. It passed through a low tiled shelf set with a small ceramic valve. Embedded in the shelf was a glass disk with a tiny hole in its center. Ghirra reached under the shelf and drew out a hand-sized box. It was a more elaborate version of the wood-and-emery strikers carried in the base of every public oil lamp. The physician gently twisted a valve and put the striker to the glass disk. At his spark, a flame jumped up, hot yellow and orange. As Ghirra adjusted the valve, it settled into a pencil-thin blue spear. Liphar whispered a small priestly invocation and settled himself in front of the flame.

"Gas." Stavros took it all in, shaking his head slowly. "Storage tanks. Giant *glass* storage tanks." From this point on, nothing he might learn about the Sawls would amaze him. He reached down and passed a finger quickly through the flame, to feel the compact sear of its heat. "I saw this in the Story Hall."

"Yes. *Shallagri,*" Ghirra replied, none too reverently.

" 'The Breath of Lagri.' And you have it in Physicians' as well."

"And in the Story Hall of Valla. The priests say the small fire there is the light from her eyes." Ghirra stooped, adjusted the flame more to his liking. "But in Physicians', we use to make sterile. Also to cook the medicines." Practical uses, his half-smile implied.

"Natural gas?" Stavros could just imagine how thrilled Clausen would be. It made him queasy even to think about it.

"*Hjuon.* I do not know how you name it."

"Where does it come from?"

"It is there, in the *nol,* the rock. From the Goddesses, the priests say."

"And you say?"

Instead of answering, Ghirra laid a gentle hand on Liphar's shoulder to draw the young man from his contemplation of the flame. Liphar smiled as radiantly as if Lagri herself had been speaking to him. Ghirra closed the valve and the flame died. "Come. There is more."

He allowed Liphar the choice of path through the towering forest of cylinders. The air was still warm but not unpleasant. A faint continuous whispering filled the hall, like the sighing of a quiet sea at night. They passed several cylinders where the tiny gas flame burned in its glass disk. At each flame, a silent Sawl or two or three sat cross-legged, staring into the blue fire with the rapt concentration of deep meditation. Farther along, they met a trio of elderly priests walking along the rows, chatting quietly like monks in a cloister. They nodded a serene greeting and passed on. Liphar's nervous pace relaxed into calm elation. He led them proudly, without urgency, radiating a joy so true and earnest that Stavros could not help but envy him. Even Ghirra seemed to absorb a little bit of it. The green luminescence of the glass was restful, the soft warm air as comforting as sleep. Once, Stavros had stood in the last redwood grove at dawn. Not until this moment had he sensed a deeper, older peace.

Rounding the glimmering curve of a cylinder, they came to a series of wide steps leading down to an open stretch of floor. Here, the astounding dimensions of the hall could be more fully grasped. A half acre away, within a space the height of a five-story house, sat three more cylinders. They were larger than the others by half, forming a close triangle around a circular tiled platform. Laid into the stone floor in slabs of white marble was the three-ringed symbol from the floor of the Frieze Hall, arranged so that each cylinder sat within a ring. But here, the circles were unbroken.

Ghirra drew Stavros' attention to the tops of the cylinders. A halo of heavy white pipe hung above each domed summit, joined by the white pipes from the shaftway. The halo connected with the cylinder at several points around its perimeter. The smaller terra-cotta pipes ran directly to the cylinders' sides. From the apex of each cylinder's dome, a single greenish pipe rose and angled across the vast open plaza to join the network above the storage tanks.

At Ghirra's nod, Liphar led them down the stairs and across the plaza to the steeper steps of the circular platform. A horseshoe of pipes filled the space between the platform and the three cylinders, making connections with them here and there, then running off behind. From the the platform, a trio of railed wooden gangways ran over the horseshoe of piping, one to meet each cylinder. The smooth-milled ancient wood seemed worlds apart from the sleek tech of the glass and ceramic, yet in the confines of the giant cavern, curiously at home. Where gangways and cylinders joined, Stavros noted what might be handles on the glass, though no openings were apparent.

Liphar guided him up the steps as if bringing him into a Presence. Ghirra followed, but reluctantly, hands shoved into the pockets of his smock. A circular structure dominated the center of the platform. It was nearly two meters across, waist-high, like a drum of greenish glass, but topped with a clear glass dome. Through the thick transparency of the lid, Stavros saw a rosy lavender sparkle. Ghirra withdrew one hand from his pockets and placed a glittering triangular chunk of rock on top of the glass.

"Guar rek," whispered Stavros.

"Yes. The *true* Sister Bread." He drew Stavros away to the edge of the platform while Liphar pressed himself to the glass with reverent longing, his arms embracing the dome. "When he is made priest, he is allowed to feed the Goddesses. Now he cannot." Ghirra traced a finger across his palm. "His hands are, ah . . ."

The physician used a Sawlish word that Stavros had thought meant "free" but now considered amending. Unbound? Loose? Profane? His jaw tightened uneasily as he pictured the layers of scar tissue on Ashimmel's, on Kav Daven's palms, the heavy repeated scarring that scoured the palms of every full priest. He hadn't yet found proper occasion to ask what rite of passage the scarring represented. "Feed the Goddesses?"

Ghirra motioned with his thumb from the domed glass drum with its hidden amethyst treasure to the trio of cylinders, then out along the piping and across the plaza. The sequence was clear. The guar was placed into the cylinders by the priests, and the gas came out through the pipes.

"What's inside the cylinders?"

"The priests say, the Goddesses."

"Of course they do."

Here was a meshing of science and religion it would take a chemist to unravel. A reaction, obviously: lithium plus something equals a gas. But plus what? And what gas? CRI would have the answer in a nanosecond. And so would Clausen.

Ghirra had watched his amazement with evident satisfaction but Stavros sensed he was waiting for something more. For what? An explanation?

Stavros circled the platform, analyzing the system as a whole. "The gas comes from these cylinders. It's stored in those cylinders." He considered the fat white and terra-cotta pipes, recalling the heat in the shaftway. "There's upwelling hot air as a by-product, but also hot water, which is piped upstairs. And that comes from . . ." He looked back to the larger cylinders. "Ah. That's it. From the cooling system surrounding the reaction vessels inside the glass." He let out an explosive breath. "Wow."

Ghirra smiled, still waiting.

"And where does the lithium . . . the guar come from?"

"From the *nol*. Come." Ghirra retrieved his chunk of ore from the top of the glass dome. He headed down the steps of the platform and around the nearest cylinder. Behind the glassy bulk, the vast cavern ended in a wall pierced by three openings. Three arched tunnels led off into blackness.

"The nol," puzzled Stavros. "The rock . . . ah. The bedrock! You mean, mined from right under the cliffs?"

"Yes. The priests dig there, very deep." Ghirra balanced the ore in his hand. "But it is not like this. The *guar* from the *nol* burns."

Burns. A vague memory from grade-school chemistry returned to him: a tiny sliver of pure soft metal dropped in a beaker of water, with rather spectacular results. Pure? Probably it would have to be, or nearly so, to produce a worthwhile reaction in the cylinders. *Holy shit! Pure lithium!* A chuckle rose and died in his throat. Clausen might be sitting right on top of the biggest strike of all! But the irony was not amusing enough to keep his stomach from knotting with the implications of this discovery. If the prospector found his way down here, it was all over.

"It burns?" Stavros pictured Kav Daven's smooth palms with sudden understanding. "What, do the priests carry it bare-handed?"

Ghirra's brow creased with distaste.

"Why do they do that?"

"It is the way."

"But you disapprove." Of course he did. How could a healer with subtle magic in his own hands be expected to approve of so painful and disfiguring a practice?

The physician shrugged. "The priests' way. It is not my way. But it brings the *hjuon*, and the *hjuon* is our life."

Stavros nodded, and then again, as the full scope of Ghirra's statement finally sank in. Their *life*. Without this source of energy, of heat and hot water and even light, the Sawls would be reduced to the primitive existence that the Terrans first assumed. He recalled how the concept of power generation had seemed too advanced to explain Clausen's lust for lithium. "I'm standing in a power plant!" He spread his arms wide, spun around, taking in the wonder of it, overwhelmed at last into a cascade of laughter. "Ghirra, this is *astounding!* How long has it been here? Who *built* it?"

Had he asked this of Liphar, the reply would have been that the Goddesses made it and that would be the end of it. But, for Ghirra, an answer did not come so easily.

"It is here." The Master Healer traced a seam in the marble floor with the toe of his soft boot.

Stavros sucked his lip. Something was definitely being asked of him but he was going to have to nudge the man harder to get it out of him. "It's here? It just exists, like the books, from the Goddesses?" He paused, praying that his assessment of the Master Healer was correct. "That's not good enough, Ghirra. Not from you."

Ghirra pinned him with Aguidran's knife-edged stare. "You say?"

Stavros forced himself to take his next breath. "I say it's lazy thinking. It's . . . priests' thinking."

The physician slouched away abruptly, hands deep in the pockets of his smock. Stavros let him go, then came up beside him when he ran out of momentum.

"The priests do not like our idea." Ghirra's murmur carried intimations of heresy.

"*Our* idea?"

"My idea and Aguidran's." Ghirra lifted his gaze to the dark arches of the mine tunnels. "It is not . . . priest thinking."

"Will you tell me your idea?" When Ghirra remained silent, Stavros added, "My sponsors don't like my ideas either, or they sure as hell won't once they find out what they really are. Our plan to prevent Clausen's claim could put me away for the rest of my life. And if you're worried about Liphar, he won't hear a word of it from me."

Ghirra drew in a long breath. "It is not an answer."

"Ideas lead to answers."

"This gives only more mystery." He dealt out the words deliberately, in a safe and neutral tone. But a fierce glimmer rose in his eyes. "The First Books tell stories of the Creator who gave the Sisters from her womb. But

I know there is also knowledge in the old books, as your Commander say. And I think, maybe the books and *Eles-Nol,* all this was made by she who made the goddesses."

Stavros felt an echo of Weng's earlier disappointment, but only at first. The Master Healer made a habit of deceptively simple remarks, he was learning. "Wait. *Made* the goddesses? You mean, built them, like you make a building, or a machine?"

"Machine," repeated Ghirra, as if that thought were new to him.

"Are you thinking some race of super-techs built all this and then left it behind?"

The Master Healer looked cautiously blank, unsure whether his idea was being received or ridiculed.

"I mean," Stavros continued, "not a supernatural Creator or goddesses at all, but a human civilization with supremely developed science and technology that would be capable of all kinds of miracles. They could build any machine they'd want. They could control the natural processes. They could remake entire planets, move moons, harness suns!" He spun out the fantastical vision, enjoying it, until he met Ghirra's hungry, questing look. Then he felt ashamed, as the nature of the physician's heresy came clear to him. It wasn't the *existence* of the goddesses he questioned, but their *divinity*. Faith did not answer his questions, as it did Liphar's. Like any truly scientific thinker, Ghirra demanded a rational explanation for everything, even seemingly irrational phenomena.

"But that stuff's just fiction," Stavros said. "At least, so far."

"Fiction?"

"Dreams. Imaginings."

Ghirra's fierce gaze leveled on him. "You can do these things!"

"I . . . *what?*"

"You. You . . . *Wokind* can do these things!"

"No! I . . . we . . . listen, do you even understand what all those things are?"

Ghirra dismissed his own ignorance with a wave. "You say about miracles. It is a miracle that you come here!" He gestured sharply upward. "From the sky!"

Well, I'll be . . . someone finally noticed.

"Not a miracle, Ghirra. Technology. Science."

"*This* is science!" The healer spread his arms to the vast space around them, eyes alight with frustration. But just as quickly, he caught himself, with a hooded glance around and at the platform, where the young priest-to-be still rested in deep communion with the precious contents of the glass drum.

Stavros dropped his voice to match Ghirra's caution. "Of course it's science! One man's faith is often another man's science." He read the man's dilemma as the mirror of his own. While he plumbed his own soul for the possibility of true belief, Ghirra fought that same belief because it would not satisfy his questing intellect. "So, you think the goddesses are science, too?"

But the outburst had blown Ghirra off course. Even he was reluctant to talk heresy in the very heart of a priestly sanctum. He withdrew into a brooding silence while Stavros fidgeted awkwardly beside him, thinking how much easier any man's life would be if he could accept that gods were gods, and question no further. His own life, for instance, should he ever achieve such an acceptance. On the other hand, wasn't Ghirra offering a way to sidestep the whole dilemma? Incarnate, all-powerful goddesses required irrational belief, the leap of faith. But goddesses-as-science required only an explanation—difficult to discover, perhaps, but easier to believe in. By showing him Eles-Nol, by sharing his heresy, Ghirra had unwittingly shown Stavros a place where he could believe without the scary encumbrance of actual faith.

He touched the physician's elbow to lead him aside, out of sight of Liphar and the guar shrine. "Keth-shim Ghirra, I don't know how much of what I'm going to say will make sense to you now, but I'm going to try it anyway.

"Earth science, Earth technology, *my* technology, could do what's going on in this room. We might use other methods and materials, but we'd get it done. And, yes, that technology brought us here from Earth, which is farther away than either of us can truly comprehend. And, yes, it can store nearly infinite amounts of information and run the most lengthy and complex calculations and allow us to talk to each other at great distances.

"But there are many, many things it cannot do. For instance, all our most advanced science has failed to repair the wreck we've made of our home world. We made machines to do the things we wanted before we considered any of the consequences. But those consequences were deep and long, and now we survive only by raping the resources of other planets. If we could build machines that wage war with the weather as your goddesses apparently do, we'd have used them to fix our own biosphere. If Valla Ired and Lagri are products of some super-race's technology—and that idea had never occurred to me, so you're already way ahead of me there—but if they are, then that race is already the next thing to gods, or goddesses, anyway."

The Master Healer had turned away to stare off into a middle distance, but he listened intently.

Stavros came around to face him. "Ghirra, you wield healing powers in your own hands. Susannah talks of it, and now I've felt it myself. I can't explain it with the science I know, but does that make it miraculous?"

"Is not. It is only my learning."

"If you say so. But I'll wager you could teach me everything you know and I still wouldn't have your gift of healing. Anyway, after a certain point, science versus miracle becomes a matter of personal definition. You can dispute your goddesses' divinity without mourning its loss, as long as you can believe in the wonder of their accomplishments."

Ghirra shook his head. "No, Ibi, it is not only word meaning. In your Earth, maybe. Not here, where always we live or die by the Sisters' game. A hundred generations we struggle and grow, but one time Lagri weaken or Valla sleep and we are nothing again."

This was an unexpected diversion. "You believe in the myth of Devastation?"

"What is 'myth'?"

"Story. Legend. Fiction."

"You name it this?"

"You don't?"

"I see writing of it in the old books."

"Actual records?" Stavros absorbed the implications. "I'd like to see those books. Liphar talks of signs that a new devastation is coming."

"Yes. But the priests say only, this is the way. We can do nothing. They teach, accept this, until the Darkness passes." Ghirra tossed his head, anger rising in him again. His fist and his long curls slashed the air. "Accept! If there is sickness, I do not say 'accept!' I fight the sickness! Should I accept always the deaths? Our friends, our children? My mother and my father in the storm? Accept the ever struggle to put food and warmth in our caves? If the goddesses are as the priests say, we must accept. But if not . . ."

"If not what?"

Now the words rushed forth unguarded. "This *Eles-Nol*—the priests say it comes from the goddesses. I say, and you say also, it is *science*. It is tech . . .

technology. Why not the goddesses also? If what they give is science, they should be science also."

"I'm with you so far," Stavros encouraged.

"If this is so," Ghirra continued fervently, "we can ask, why does this science help us sometime and kill us sometime?"

"Well, it wouldn't be the first time. On Earth, science created all sorts of so-called wonders that turned lethal on us. You can't . . ."

"If it is machines," Ghirra interrupted, "it can be not-made, yes?"

"Not made? You mean, unmade? Taken apart?"

Ghirra was not happy with that meaning. "If the winch on the cliff top will not turn, the guildsmen say not 'accept.' They *un*make it to make it new again."

"They repair it." Stavros felt his heart start to pound. "Ah, Ghirra, what a wild-assed, outrageous, spectacular idea! To fix the gods! Earth has a long history of people struggling to change themselves to suit their gods: sacrifice, penitence, celibacy, charity, reform, good works, whatever it takes. But here stands a man who would change his gods to suit himself!" He beamed at the Master Healer and shook a fist at the distant ceiling. "Hear that, you Sister-ladies? Watch out!"

Ghirra shifted, moved away. "You laugh at my idea."

"No!" Stavros pursued him. "No. My life on it, Ghirra. Forgive me if it seemed that way. The idea fills me with joy. I . . ." He fumbled for the right word. "I exult in it, Keth-shim, and in you for thinking it!" Stavros decided to allow a different leap of faith, as much to offer solace and support as from any real proof. "From your books, Weng suspects an older, advanced civilization on Fiix. But it's not some other race she posits. It's you. The hints are there in the old words, which seem to contain technical names for all the parts of the atom. Your ancestors spoke that language, and if your idea *is* true, the super-race who made these god-machines was your ancestors. And even if you have only the leftovers of their technology, you've inherited all of their vision."

Ghirra took this in silently, staring at the floor, but Stavros thought he stood a little taller than he had a moment before. And it was true, it had to be! Because what better argument could there be for preserving Fiix from destruction and development? Suddenly, a clear and necessary path presented itself, and Stavros made a promise as mad and wild as the idea that prompted it.

"We'll find your goddesses, Keth-shim: man-made or divine. Whatever technology we can . . . or, I can . . . muster, we'll put it to use. You'll have an answer, and if we are able, a solution."

Ghirra's head sank into his shoulders, but after a moment, he began to laugh.

Stavros gave an embarrassed grin. "Okay, I guess that did sound pretty presumptuous. Especially from one who's just insisted he's incapable of miracles. We might be able to do it, though . . . with a little work. And a little Wokind science. Even if we're not the super-race you hoped we were."

Ghirra's nod said he expected nothing, but was ready for anything. "We will work this together."

"Then how can we fail?" Though he felt buoyed and victorious, Stavros resisted the urge to clap the Master Healer on the back, for the sake of both their dignities. Instead, he turned to gaze at Liphar, still rapt in his meditations. "Meanwhile, the wagons leave soon, and Lifa and I have a job to do out there."

Together, they walked back to the platform, and collected the priest-in-waiting from his reverent dreams of the day when he would be allowed to feed the goddesses.

43

E.D. 69–14:41

THE CRACK AND ROLL of thunder echoed up the tunnel from the cave mouth. The three separated by the entrance to the Meeting Hall, Ghirra to assure himself of the final readiness of the infirmary wagon, Liphar to prepare for the Leave-taking rituals, though the thunder made him tight-lipped with doubt.

Stavros headed for the Black Hole to pack the few necessities he could carry for the second, secret leg of his journey. He trotted through the dim corridors, eager to be moving at last, eager to prove his worth to the Sawls. The concreteness of his new purpose was exhilarating: find the goddesses! He found himself actually whistling as he rustled about the darkened sleeping platform, stowing away his less portable belongings, settling the load in his pack more to his liking.

Bright light slashed past his nose.

"You also work well in the dark?" Emil Clausen stood at the cavern entrance, a battery searchbeam in hand. He stepped in, flashing the beam into the hidden recesses, picked out the cold fire pit, the stone sink, the sleeping platform, the tiny oil lamp burning at Stavros' side. "Your neighbors said I might find you here. Obliging little folk."

He stopped at the fire pit, nosing a casual boot into its ash. "Quite a storm brewing out there, from the looks of it. Right up out of nowhere, like the last time."

Stavros fastened a final buckle on his field pack. "Taylor must be thrilled."

"He's positively seething. And he's not the only one. This wagon train of yours may never get off the ground."

"Of mine? Hardly."

"The one you are leaving with. Pardon my imperfect grammar."

Stavros slung the pack across his back and stood, abruptly tired of fencing. "What's on your mind, Emil?"

Clausen sighed, wandering deeper into the cavern. The lamp swung offhandedly at his side, but the beam slid deliberately from floor to sink to pipes and on around the wall. "I'm glad you asked. Because I'd like to work this out in a friendly fashion." He ceased his wandering, rested one real-suede boot on the sleeping platform and let his lamp beam settle at Stavros' feet. "What the hell happened while I was out there in the bush? I don't recall we had such adversary relations before that, you and I." His smile might have included a wink, had Stavros been looking at him. "No more than your usual with the rest of the world, that is."

Stavros crossed to the sink. He hadn't expected direct confrontation, not this soon. "What seems to be the problem?"

Clausen chuckled. "I could almost believe you don't know, Stav—so focused on your scholarly work and all. So, let me point out that you could be a little more accommodating to the rest of us here and there. I'll let the issue of the link go by. Weng's right. I'm best qualified to fix it. But when I ask for your help with the locals . . ."

"I've been doing the best I can."

"So you keep saying. But I know you can do better."

"I'm a linguist, Emil. Labor relations is not my job." At the sink, packing away razor and soap in a side pouch of his pack, Stavros heard the prospector come up behind him. The lamp flashed on the wall and steadied as it was set down on the floor. "Is this where I get the lecture about remembering the source of my funding?"

Clausen grabbed his arm, spun him around and threw his weight against his chest. Stavros was flung spread-eagled against the wall. The back of his head slammed into solid rock. Pack, razor, and soap clattered across the floor.

"Your job is what I fucking well say it is!" Clausen shoved a skilled arm against his throat, immobilizing him.

Stavros gurgled, the wind crushed from his lungs. His vision blurred.

The prospector raised a silver laser pistol, a small personal weapon of the sort expressly forbidden on board space-going vessels. "The truth is, you don't like me much. And you're doing everything in your power to get in my way."

Stavros sucked air dizzily. How could this have happened so fast? It was only yesterday that the conspiracy had taken shape. Cool metal kissed his temple. The arm across his throat pressed harder, making him much too aware of the fragility of his windpipe.

"Am I right, my boy?" Clausen's tone was paternal, while his forearm increased its grinding pressure.

"No!" Stavros choked out. Even to his own ears, his desperate lie sounded convincingly like terror. He struggled for a free breath, but the smaller man had him expertly pinned. He heard himself whine like a wounded animal. "You sonofabitch! Get your fucking hands off me!"

Clausen laughed and stepped back, releasing Stavros as easily and unpredictably as he had taken him prisoner. The little laser gun swung to level at Stavros' chest. "Well. That at least answers one of my questions."

Stavros sagged against the wall, gasping.

When no counterattack came, Clausen shrugged and lowered the pistol. "So tell me, son, what's your beef? Surely we can work this out. What have I done to offend our pet wunderkind, so wet behind the ears from the university?"

"Nothing." Stavros rolled along the wall and slumped against the sink, panting with shock and rage and humiliation. "Except right now you're being a real prick."

"I am wounded to the quick. Well, then . . . I have something you want, perhaps?"

"Nothing," rasped Stavros, this time truthfully. Clausen had money and power, and Stavros had always been sure he wanted none of that. But he saw now that this might have been due to not comprehending how little of either he possessed.

Clausen dragged over a three-legged Sawlish stool and sat, one leg crossed over the other, the laser resting comfortably on his knee. "You academics just don't seem to understand the realities. This is not fun and games, boy. I'm putting your career on notice. You get me?"

When Stavros held onto his sullen silence, Clausen shook his head. "It's as simple as the old cliché, Ibiá. I can make you or I can break you. So why make it the latter when the former would be so much more satisfying for both of us? Believe it or not, I get no kicks from having to shove you boys back in line."

Stavros hated the prospector for his calm, while he still fought for a measured breath. What price, what form of bribe would Clausen offer? He was almost curious enough to open negotiations. The cold lamplight splashed across the prospector's back, leaving his face in shadow as he sighed and uncrossed his legs. The pistol flashed a sharp glint of reflection into Stavros' eyes.

"And then, there are always those unfortunate accidents that occur on these uncharted worlds. . . ."

Stavros gathered the shreds of his self-possession and laughed. "Don't you think you've threatened me enough already?"

"Evidently not," replied the faceless voice. "Or in the midst of all the heavy breathing, did I miss your promise to get in line? You do know I've seen all this before, boy, these petty alliances with the locals. It's always some idealistic youngster like you who gets himself in over his head. You should take a tip from Megan Levy. You don't catch the old pros like her messing about, no matter how much they'd like to smear my ass from here to Centauri."

Stavros held himself very still, pinned by the searchbeam. His slightest move might surrender whole paragraphs of meaning to Clausen's canny hunter's instincts.

The prospector's shadow leaped against the wall as he rose. "I could put a bolt through your tiresome skull right now and be done with you, but there'd be some awkwardness to deal with." He stooped for the lamp, training the beam into Stavros' eyes. "And I prefer to think you're as bright as they say you are and you'll learn to value your future health as a working professional more than a few temporary local acquaintances." He paused. "Do I get the help I need?"

"You'll get it," Stavros growled, only to be rid of him. "Like I said you would."

The searchbeam held steady, then dropped. "Excellent thinking, son. Well, go on, then. Have a good trip, get out of my hair, but send those coolies back to me ASAP. ConPlex and I are delighted your work means so much to you, but don't let it get in the way of the real mission, eh?"

No bribe, then. No bribe at all. The offer was simply his life.

"Does the Commander know you smuggled an illegal weapon on board?" Stavros spat after him helplessly.

"Tut, tut. Smuggled?" Clausen balanced the pistol on his palm. "This little guy's classified as a tool, my boy, officially listed with the contents of my emergency kit. And you should be glad of it, since you yourself mentioned that I'd need a welder to repair the dish." He raised the shining gun and laid the stubby barrel alongside his nose. "You might be able to nail me for assault and battery, though you'd be hard put to offer convincing evidence. But illegal possession? Never. The Company doesn't want me running around unarmed." He switched off the lamp as he reached the doorway.

"Predators, you know," he whispered and ambled off into the darkness, laughing.

44

E.D. 69–16:12

MEGAN FOUND HIM still slumped against the sink, head sunk to his chest. The little oil lamp sputtered on the sleeping platform. In the sink, the faucet dripped into an overflowing stewpot.

"Aguidran says it's time, Stav. You all packed?" She had put on her last machine-pressed set of khaki field clothes. Her compass swung around her neck. "Stav?"

He didn't move.

"Stav?"

His head lifted, barely. "I just had a visit from Clausen."

"Yeah, he told me you were up here."

"Is he . . . ?"

"He went back down to the Lander."

"You're sure?"

"Ronnie grabbed him to talk about the antenna."

Stavros shifted, coughed. "Did he also tell you he'd slapped me up against the wall like I was nothing, like some ball of shit, and shoved a gun in my face?"

"Ah. So soon. A gun? Hmmm. Well, I'm not surprised."

Stavros glared at her. He pushed limply away from the sink to muddle about gathering up his pack and soap and the shattered pieces of his razor. He clutched it all to his chest, looking dazed, then sank in a dispirited heap on the steps of the sleeping platform. The pack tumbled from his grip as he dropped his head into his hands. "I couldn't stop him, Meg. He could've fucking killed me."

Megan went to sit beside him, slipping an arm around his back. His sweat-drenched shirt was cold against his skin. "Of course he could have. And would have, if he'd been feeling threatened enough." She rocked him for a moment. "How much does he know?"

Stavros muttered something inaudible, dragging his hands across his eyes. "He's not on to you yet. Mostly he's noticed me getting in his way more than he thinks I should."

Megan patted his shoulder as she drew her arm away. "It could have been a lot worse. He probably thinks a simple threat will scare you into line . . . it won't, will it?"

"Hell, no."

"Good lad." She sat back. "Weather's acting up again out there. Aguidran seems to want to go ahead anyway."

Stavros remained sunk in his gloom. "So goddamn helpless . . . !"

Megan leaned her elbows on her knees, matching his posture. "Look, Stav, I'm sorry. I thought you understood when you got into this that Emil is the real thing. He plays stakes in the gigabillions, and he plays them for keeps. What kind of a gun?"

"A little laser pistol."

"Ummm. Cute."

"That sonofabitch'll never get his fucking hands on me again."

Megan eyed him. "My goodness. You sound as if no one's ever knocked you around in your life."

"Not like this! Not with so little chance to fight back!" A door had been flung open, the walls of his former life blown away. How could he have believed he was powerless then? There'd always been his family, or the University, places where his talents were currency. But now . . . Stavros roused himself long enough to slam a fist helplessly into the air. "Sonofafuckingbitch! How could I let him get the jump on me so easily?"

"Whoa. Hold it. Keep that young blood of yours below the boiling point. You have to stay as cool as he is, or he'll have you. He'll have all of us. We're too few and too weak to risk giving ourselves away with impulsive action. We need you, Stav, and we need you calm and quiet and undercover. If you make this personal, your anger will be just another weapon in his very experienced hands."

Stavros pretended not to hear. "We should get rid of him. A little trip at the edge, a casual push, and . . . splat!"

"It could come to that with him, in self-defense. Are you ready to kill a man, Stav?"

"You got a better solution? That's what he'd do to me—or you—if nobody was around to notice!"

"I asked if you were ready to kill a man."

"I'm ready to stay alive! Shit, now who's the innocent?"

"Stav," she chided, "listen to me. You're rightfully pissed at the man for proving his power at your expense, but that's no excuse for suicidal vows of cold-blooded murder. He is, as they say, armed and dangerous. You are neither. So put away your bruised ego and remember who the real enemy is. If by some holy miracle you did manage to get Clausen before he got you, ConPlex would just send in another one like him, maybe two, once their attention was roused. Emil is basically a highly paid errand boy in the megacorporate universe. His power is localized, and he's smart enough to know it. That infernal confidence of his is based on accepting both where the real power lies and his place in its structure."

"Welcome to political science class," Stavros sneered.

"Know thy enemy as thyself—and never let it get personal."

He shook his head, relapsing into gloom. "The innocent and the professor . . . fine pair of conspirators we make. What the hell can we do against the likes of him?"

"Hey, I said calm down. I didn't say roll over and die." Megan nudged him playfully. "Listen, I've seen much worse than us going up against the biggies. How do you think revolutions get started? You can't give up on the legal approach just because you got messed around a little. Be warned: you're likely to get messed around a little more before this is over, but next time, you'll be ready for him. Adopting his methods is not the answer. The laws have been written to keep power like Clausen's in check, and sometimes—rarely, I admit, but *sometimes*—you can even make them stick."

"Meg, laws and revolution are a contradiction in terms."

"Not if what's revolutionary is to invoke the laws as they're written, or to ensure that they're enforced." She touched his chill arm. "Stav, don't jeopardize the Sawls' chances for the sake of personal pride."

"I won't! I get it! I'm not a child!"

Megan wondered. Still, the incident could be seen as fortuitous: Clausen had provided a naive and idealistic young man with a bloodless first blooding that left only his ego gasping for its life in the sand. Later, he would realize how lucky he'd been. But would Stavros learn self-discipline fast enough to save himself and their plan?

It was all mad, of course. After years of talk and no action, she had chosen this out-of-the-way planet to make a new stand and this volatile raging boy for her ally. Very bad practice. She was flexing muscles left too long unused, and was still unsure why she'd done it. Perhaps because she was no longer so young and innocent, and it might be her last chance to take action where it mattered.

And then, of course, there were the Sawls, day by day winding their spirit and their sore predicament around her heart.

It was too late to do anything but worry, pray their conspiracy was not breached, and that it was not as hopeless as it might seem. She gathered up Stavros' pack and shoved it onto his lap.

"On your feet, comrade. We've got a caravan to catch."

45

THE LIVING QUARTERS WERE DARK and the corridors deserted. Megan and Stavros met no one until they neared the Priest Hall, but the hubbub could be heard several tunnels away. Turning the corner, they found the corridor filled with apprentices, chattering excitedly as they helped each other into ceremonial tabards. The wave-and-flame sign of the Priest Guild glimmered on every proud chest. The chat, interspersed with wrangles over the assignment of various banners and flags, mostly concerned the threatening weather and the dubious wisdom of going ahead with the Leave-taking rituals.

Stavros was relieved to find Liphar absent. He was still shaken and angry, and Liphar would notice and be concerned. Edging through the busy crowd, he glanced inside the Hall. There was as much noisy milling confusion inside as out. The majority of the Priest Guild, convinced until the last minute that the ceremonies would not take place, now rushed to ready themselves. Mutters of thunder still rolled in from the nearby cave mouth, but they were drowned out by the interior din. As always, Stavros noted the unnatural gleaming smoothness of the priests' palms, but now he thought of the guar and the Master Healer's uneasy acceptance of the painful ritual that brought life and comfort to the Caves. He longed to tell Megan about the guar cavern and its power plant, but was stayed by the chill sense memory of Clausen's laser against his skin. Among the prospector's less formal credits was probably a master's degree in extracting information. For Megan's sake, he would keep new information to himself.

"The Priest Guild seems to have accepted the inevitable," Megan remarked as they sought a path through the mob of apprentices.

Stavros ducked to avoid a silken banner hoisted by a boy too small to control its weight. Just as they'd worked themselves free, Kav Ashimmel came striding down the corridor with her entourage scuttling along behind her. The apprentices stilled at their guild master's approach, then cheered when Ashimmel announced that the sky had cleared and the ceremonies could proceed. With a wave that seemed to imply responsibility for this change of fortune, the Master Priest proceeded into the Hall.

"Well, luck is with us," said Megan as they hurried toward the cave mouth. "I wasn't sure how we'd explain your disappearance if the caravan was called off."

"Or how I'd get to the Sled if the weather turned *really* bad."

A group of journeymen engineers crowded the entry, bustling around a tallish young apprentice dressed in white. They all talked at once as they fixed the folds of her tunic, fussed with the arrangement of her beribboned hair. The young woman's eyes shone while she patiently withstood their ministrations and advice. To one side, two guildsmen polished a large plaque painted with the guild's triangular seal.

As Stavros stepped from the shade of the overhang, he thought he heard thunder again. But the sun was hot on his forehead and the sky was a pure turquoise all the way to the Vallegar. One or two discrete spots of cloud still lurked about the sawtooth peaks. Stavros tried picturing them with heads and tails, lashed to the mountaintops as Valla had neglected to do in the tale carved on the entrance to Eles-Nol. The exhilarating sense of the Possible he'd felt among the giant shining cylinders had vanished, crushed by Emil Clausen's efficient arm. He was left with a reckless promise he could no longer conceive of being able to fulfill.

"It's the priest-horns." Megan thought his sober frown a response to the baying richocheting from the cliff tops. Below, dust rose in an ocher cloud as eight hundred wagons and carts jostled for their assigned positions in rows that stretched for a solid half kilometer along the cliff bottom. Farther to the east, the dairy herd nosed among the ravines where the newly sprouting vegetation softened the drying mud with a dense yellow carpet. Rimming the eastern horizon were the blunted mounds of the Talche, the Knees. As he and Megan started down the stairs, Stavros noticed two more little cloud scouts lingering there, as if reconnoitering the terrain. They moved even as he watched, sliding farther south, clinging to the profile of the lavender hills like low-flying aircraft.

Weird shit, he thought, and wondered why it had taken him so long to see it that way.

The Engineers guildsmen came clattering down behind them, surrounding them with excited greetings and swallowing them up in their midst, urging them to greater speed. The priest-horns ceased their random thundering and segued into a thrilling basso call that stilled the racket below and drew the population away from their last-minute frenzy. Everyone gathered on the rock terrace in front of the rows of wagons, leaving a wide strip of open ground between themselves and the cliff face. Stavros hurried along with the engineers, planning his observations of the coming ritual as a distraction from self-pitying gloom. He lost Megan in the throng at the bottom of the steps. He looked for Susannah or Weng, but if they were there, they were hidden in the confusion.

The ceremonial horns fell silent. The dust cloud settled about the wagons as the shouts and chatter and the rattle of harness died into an expectant hush. Stavros searched his pack, located the pocket recorder he'd preserved for just this sort of occasion, and eased himself with a journalist's presumption into the front ranks of the silent crowd. By now used to his polite but aggressive curiosity, the watchers parted to give him room. Crouching in the hot sun among the children and the elderly, he thumbed the little device to check its battery.

The cave mouths waited, black and empty against the sheer fall of sun-bright rock. Then the horns sounded again, first the westernmost, followed by the others in sequence toward the east. When all twelve were booming a single drawn-out chord, the caves overflowed amid a burst of song. Across the third level, twelve dark entries glittered, and with a swirl of color, twelve honor guards of apprentices carrying bright banners marched out of the shadowed mouths to begin the processional descent. A pair of musicians followed each cluster of banners, followed by a cohort of priests, all moving in single file to the beat of skin drums and the shrill of woodwinds.

The priests had donned their longest, whitest robes, simple long-sleeved shifts over which they wore soft tabards and shawls of earthy red. Unlike the apprentices, they bore no Priest Guild seals. Their hems and sleeves were embroidered in the colors of flame, the hot salmons and vermilions, the golden yellows and the crimsons that honored Lagri, whose dominance they hoped to encourage until the trade caravan had returned and the crop could be harvested. They poured into the sunlight in a blaze of finery, and behind them came another glowing rank of banners and the rest of the apprentices, dressed also in white. The younger ones carried triangular flags in Lagri's brightest colors. The older ones supported tall fringed standards, painted or sewn with picture tales of the goddess' past victories over her Sister-rival. Last came a master apprentice from each of the guilds. Their white tunics sparkled like sea foam as they moved to the staccato beat of the drums. Each carried a carved or painted plaque bearing the symbol of his guild. As they marched, they sang, priest and apprentice alike. A hundred voices joined as one brought the masses assembled at the cliff bottom to their feet to raise a throaty chant of exultation.

Stavros rose with them, surrendering his gloom to the crowd's contagious enthusiasm. But he remembered to clip the recorder to his waistband and set it on auto.

A stout figure in white appeared at the mouth of the highest cave. Even with the distance and the glare of the sun, Stavros recognized the redoubtable posture of Kav Ashimmel, putting on the kind of show for which she was famous—very likely the reason for her election as keth-shim of her guild. She gave no sign that she was anything but ecstatic about the forthcoming departure. She stood alone for a moment, arms spread with palms up as if humbly receiving the accolade of the throng. Then she bowed her head and moved toward the ledges to begin her stately descent.

Behind her came a line of open sedan chairs and litters carrying the members of the guilds too elderly or infirm to walk. Each was supported by a pair of strong white-clad apprentices from the elder's own guild. The litters were draped in white. The chairs bore white canopies and their side panels were decorated with carved polychromed friezework. The last and largest was a high-sided chair carried by two pairs of priests. The wave-and-flame seal gleamed on both side panels. The curved white canopy was tied with streamers that fluttered in a diaphanous curtain around the sides and back, in colors that honored both Valla Ired and Lagri. The Master of Lore and Ritual was nestled inside, as slight as a child in the huge chair's embrace. His blind smile lit up the inner shadow.

The procession zigzagged down the cliff face to the rhythm of the music and the joyous chanting of the crowd. At the bottom, the guild apprentices lined up facing the throng, the hundred priests and their apprentices behind them, banners and flags raised in a rainbowed wall at their backs. The freshly painted guild seals glistened in the sun. The elderly were set down next to the seal of their guild and their bearers retired into the ranks behind. When Kav Daven's chair had left the final step and was lowered lovingly to the ground, the horns on the cliff top sounded a final note, a long tumbling call that fell like water into silence as the chanting ceased within the space of a breath.

Stavros dropped a hand to his recorder, thumbed it off. Better to save the batteries. No chance it could capture the quality of that intent silence, filled with wind sighs and the flap of ribbons and banners, with the silken murmur of long priestly sleeves, with the lowing of the distant dairy herd and the wavelike rustle of the yellow stalks in the fields behind the wagons. In that silence, there was every sound but the non-sound of five thousand people waiting motionless, enrapt.

The sedan chair's ancient joints creaked as the Ritual Master inched his bony legs over the edge and climbed down into the sun. No one stepped forward to offer him support. He balanced a moment, smiling as if it were a game to relearn the art of existing upright. In the harsh sun, he seemed as insubstantial as pale smoke. He wore not the ceremonial white but his own soft brown layers, draping his body like wilted leaves. Seeing the Kav like this, Stavros could not blame the Priest Guild for pressing the old man to name his successor. What would become of the treasure trove of knowledge and lore tucked away inside his head if there was no one to pass it on to?

Kav Daven's shoulders slewed in a gentle arc as he oriented himself with the preternatural hearing of the blind. He took a few shuffling steps, then stopped and beamed at the crowd, as if he would follow this act with juggling or a few jokes. He took a few more steps, firmer now, advancing as far as the front ranks of children so that he could bend, an old tree swaying stiffly in the wind, to touch fingers with those sitting nearest him. The children murmured to him and softly called his name and there was no disapproving adult around to hush them except Stavros, who felt like a child himself, in awe of the old priest's mystery.

Kav Daven smiled again and shuffled back a step. Then, impossibly old and frail, he began to walk along the long line of enthralled watchers, a solitary brown figure moving through heat and dust and silence. Asking his blessing, the watchers knelt for his touch as he trudged by, so that his passing was like a slow wave receding across a sea of heads. Stavros thought of the recorder again, but knew he'd need no machine to recall this moment. His brain would retain the memory in all its vividness, quite possibly forever.

When the Ritual Master had passed by on his journey along the line, Stavros backed through the crowd and made his way through the press of smaller carts to climb the slatted side of the nearest wagon for a better view.

He spotted Liphar among the ranks of apprentices, not far from Ashimmel's retinue of senior priests, gathered in a semicircle around her. Liphar looked scrub-faced and solemn in his knee-length white tunic. His long brown curls had been combed and braided with red-and-orange ribbon. Feet braced, head high, he clasped the tall shaft of a triangular banner sewn with the wave-and-flame seal of the guild. The long orange point of the banner fluttered just above his head. The silky threads of the embroidery shone very blue and red in the brilliant sunlight.

From his higher vantage, Stavros saw the yellow mobile Infirmary in the middle of the front line of wagons. Megan had found a grandstand view, hunched in the driver's seat, scribbling in her notebook. McPherson perched beside her, whispering eagerly into her ear, laughing and pointing. Ghirra leaned beside the tall rear wheel, intent on the ceremony. Susannah watched from beside him. Danforth lay in his folding stretcher, propped up against the wheel rim. Weng stood to his left, slim and erect, her uniform outshining even the white of the priests' robes. Stavros savored the irony: his Terran colleagues, arrayed like a happy family. But Clausen was nowhere in evidence.

The thought was a dark cloud passing over the joy of the ceremony. From now on, Clausen's absence would always hold the threat of his arrival, until the grudge was repaid or the man himself was light-years removed, or dead. Stavros replayed his moment of humiliation, rehearsing all the things he could have done to the prospector if only he'd been able to free a hand, an arm, a leg, anything. And he would have done any or all, even with the cool steel of the laser pressed to his head, anything but suffer the awful impotence that Clausen had forced upon him, with hardly a visible effort.

Surely Megan was wrong to think that the personal bore no relation to the larger issue. ConPlex might be the ultimate power, but Clausen was here and the company was not. Local power is the only relevant power when one man threatens another with death. But the real lesson Stavros took from his personal violation was that Clausen would treat the Sawls with the same arrogance, the same casual violence. He would grind them under his heel without a thought. Just as the goddesses marched roughshod over the Sawls in their blind determination to subdue each other.

Stavros had a sudden gut comprehension of Ghirra's raging at the Sisters, which before had been merely intellectual. If it was possible to "believe" an emotion, Stavros was a true believer at last, as helpless in his rage as the Master Healer had been. It was the same rage, after all, the rage of the powerless against the powerful. Did Clausen see himself as godlike in his power over others? Stavros was sure the directors of ConPlex nurtured vast Olympian notions.

Remembering made him restive. What was to be done? He could not back away from his commitment to Ghirra, to the Sawls. He'd be left without purpose, an empty judas-shell. So he would throw himself against the rocks for their sakes, though it might do precious little good. He felt no resentment, only sadness that he'd made promises he could not fulfill.

Clinging to the side of the tall wagon seemed suddenly to be an unnecessarily conspicuous and vulnerable position. This was what being hunted would feel like. And he knew he would be, once he took action in earnest. He unclipped the recorder from his belt and replaced it in his pack, then eased down from the wagon. He could see over the heads of the seated crowd well enough, and feel protected by them.

He wandered close to the Infirmary wagon, past two wagons belonging to the Leatherworkers Guild. A bevy of apprentices perched on the curving canopies, whispering excitedly. The hjalk teams, bored with standing, bent their heads to watch him pass. Stavros found a vacant wheel to lean against, and returned his attention to the ceremony.

Incredibly, Kav Daven's pace had quickened as he progressed along the line. A glad tension built within the crowd as he neared the end. When he had a mere hundred meters left to travel, the tension became a sound, a low eager humming like a swarm of bees. Kav Daven covered the final distance in a miraculous swinging walk, his wilted-leaf clothing floating around him with a rhythmic life of its own. His stride was more a curious lope than the deliberate putting of one foot after the other. Every eye followed him, and the humming increased its pitch and volume.

He reached the end and stopped. From behind the lead wagon, Aguidran emerged. She was dressed in dark road leathers, but over them, she wore a white sleeveless robe with the Ranger Guild insignia embroidered on a wide soft collar. She approached the Ritual Master, made a formal bow of greeting, which he returned, then came to stand beside him. He raised his right arm, palm up, and offered it to the sky, the white cliffs, the wagons and lastly the waiting crowd.

When his salute was done, Aguidran extended a leather-bound arm. Kav Daven laid a feathery hand on her steady wrist, and the rising hum climaxed in joyous song. The crowd surged into motion. The old priest and his ranger escort started slowly back along the line of people and wagons. The priests and apprentices broke rank to fall in behind, banners and long robes flying. In their wake, the musicians started up several tunes at once, and the populace rose from the dusty rock to mob after them in cheerful, chanting disorder.

Stavros was once more swept up in a throng of celebrating Sawls, drawn away from the wagons as if caught in the current of a laughing stream. Hungry for the soothings of communal joy, he gave himself to the sensual rush of music and song. He drifted forward with the watery surging of the crowd, laughing with them, picking up snatches of the song, humming when he lost the words. He was enjoying his surrender when into the center of his vision came the mismatched pair, the ranger and the priest, approaching with measured step.

Caught in the riptide of song and elation, Stavros sensed the familiar signs, the slippage, the slight quaking of his reality. Not again. Not twice in one day. He shook his head, tried to back away. The oblivious crowd held him tight, and priest and ranger approached, now in an aura of misty brightness. Then bodies shifted, spaces opened, paths were cleared for some to move forward. Stavros joined them, dazed as a sleepwalker, grateful for a place among the others kneeling to receive Kav Daven's greeting. A silly impulse, perhaps, but what did he have to lose? Given the hopelessness of his endeavor, why not ask a blessing for it and for himself? Ghirra would disapprove of his giving in to the "voice inside," that self who needed support and recognition, but what if . . . ? Stavros knelt, dropped his pack to the ground, and bowed his head.

Kav Daven worked his way slowly along the line, touching fingers, greeting those he knew with soft words and laughter, but always moving on. Aguidran paced beside him patiently. When they reached the kneeling offworlder, the old priest stopped.

This was unexpected. He had stopped nowhere else along the line. Stavros dared not look up into those sightless eyes. Did the Kav think him presumptuous, perhaps sacrilegious, for placing himself among the petitioners? He saw feet, booted and sturdy—Aguidran's—and also Kav Daven's, gnarled and brown and bare, dusted with ocher, planted right in front of him. He heard murmurs, a grunted exclamation of surprise, a discussion and a rustling. Perhaps there were voices raised, he wasn't sure. They wouldn't understand the mixture of need and compulsion that had drawn him to his knees here. If the Kav could lend him just a little of his grit and serenity, Stavros could better help all of them. More feet appeared, women's feet in thin white sandals, a pair on either side of Kav Daven's. The booted feet withdrew. How odd that he could hear such quiet sounds through all the uproar. Then he realized that the singing had stopped.

The crowd shifted behind him.

"Ibi, what is this you do?"

Ghirra. Where did he come from? Stavros knew that voice at least.

"I must ask his blessing."

"Leave this, Ibi. It is not for you."

"I need . . ."

"No. It is not needed."

With the last ounce of will left to him, Stavros shook his head. The Master Healer sounded sad and angry. Why should the asking of a simple blessing disturb him so?

Someone growled in Sawlish: "Let him." Was it Aguidran?

"I will help, if you must do this thing. The pain I will help."

Do what thing? What pain? Stavros started, as cool fingers brushed aside his hair to rest against the nape of his neck. Thumb and finger slipped inside his collar to lie along his shoulder in a protective caress, almost sexual in its intimacy. He shivered, too lost to this inevitability of events to resist. It occurred to him at last that he'd set something in motion that he did not understand.

"The Kav accepts this asking. Give him your hands. He will say if it is not true."

Stavros put out his hands, confused by youthful memories of the altar rail.

The white-sandaled feet shuffled uneasily. Stavros waited, palms outstretched, through another muttered discussion and a volley of protest that was certainly Ashimmel's. A low singsong command brought abrupt silence. Stavros recognized the throaty diphthongs and ancient cadences. Old words. Priest Words. Kav Daven had spoken, in a voice both firm and smooth, a younger man's voice.

In the stillness and the beating heat of the sun, the old priest's silken palms enfolded his own, pressed them palm to palm, then gently opened them to form a bowl. The strength of the priest's hands was surprising, for they seemed to have no bones.

No. Not strength. Power. The same imponderable that had brought him to his knees in the dust. It was strange to be so acutely aware, of the Kav's soft hands, of the sun's heat, of the rustle of the white robes around him, of Ghirra's touch on his neck, so aware and yet so unable to act. So aware, and yet in such confusion.

The priest's hands cupped his own. The old man bent low. Stavros could feel the whisper of breath against his ear as Kav Daven spoke.

Do you will this calling?

Stavros heard the old words and the sense of them as if with two separate parts of his consciousness. His voice returned to him long enough to answer.

"No, Kav."

The sun was a weight on his head and back. Its light was thick and amber, like honey. What is happening? He was amazed at last.

Who wills it, then?

"Kav, I know not." This at least was true, though it frightened him to hear his voice replying as if it were someone else's.

Ghirra's fingers twitched against his skin, then steadied. There was a quiet stir behind, someone else approaching through the crowd. Aguidran's booted feet moved suddenly from behind Kav Daven and stepped to Stavros' left as Ghirra shifted right. He felt their strength as a single presence, brother and sister, protecting him.

From what?

He glanced up. A flash of silvered lenses in the crowd jolted him with unreasoned terror. Ghirra gripped his shoulder, steadying him as rage displaced his terror, rage that felt pure and clean, sharp as honed steel, a weapon to draw quick and fatal blood. But Clausen kept his distance, his slouch confident, his mocking smile suggesting he had come merely to observe the native antics.

A murmur from Kav Daven brought his focus back where it belonged. The shock of fear had cleared his head, reminding him that rage was a double-edged blade, as thirsty for his own blood as for Clausen's. Stavros set aside both fear and anger to concentrate on the old priest, and felt the compulsion ease. Kav Daven no longer appeared through a mist of awe. Stavros observed his own pale hands between an old man's knotted brown ones. No need to look anywhere else. He forgot Clausen for a time.

The Kav spoke again, and a Priest Guild journeyman in embroidered red and white came forward, holding a small cloth-swaddled bundle. The loose white wrappings masked the shape of the object inside, but to Ghirra's tight-lipped mutter, Stavros merely nodded. He had known what it must be the moment he saw it.

Guar. The rock that burns.

Stavros' entire being irised in on the singularity of the old priest's scarred palms.

Do you accept this calling?

"Tell him no," whispered Ghirra urgently. "You can still."

Stavros tried to answer the healer's sincere concern, but words deserted him.

"You understand this, Ibi, what he means?"

He could not move his head.

Do you accept?

How can I refuse?

Impossible to turn aside from a visitation of Power that swooped down from a place unimaginable to take without asking, to sweep him up unsuspecting like so much stardust? Part of him demanded understanding, while the rest bid joyful welcome to this cosmic manifestation, beside which Emil Clausen and ConPlex and all the mundane issues of money and politics were reduced to insignificance.

Kneeling with hands extended, the age-old supplicant's posture, Stavros was granted an instant of true knowledge. He saw himself with the harsh objectivity of distance: a romantic, silly young man on his knees, in the grip of the incomprehensible and afraid in his soul for his sanity. He thought of the Catholic saints and martyrs: was this how it was for them, no climax of faith at all but an accidental attack of terror and truth, a window opened to the abyss that only faith could close again?

His back arched as a wind rushed through him, ageless and immaterial.

"Ibi?" Ghirra's voice was strained.

A gasp of ecstasy and fear. The parts of himself, already imperfectly joined, were breaking up like a ship on the rocks, scattering timbers, sails, rigging, all.

Do you accept?

"You understand this, Ibi?"

"Yes!" He must silence the questioning, until there was only the wind, hurling the scraps of his being to the farthest corners of the universe. He was sorry that his physical body would remain behind. If this disintegration must be, he would prefer it to be total.

"Too weak," he murmured, failing.

Ghirra's fingers searched the side of his neck, checked the pulse point, then slid upward to probe beneath the curve of his jawbone. Already surrendering his reason, Stavros offered up his life as well to hands whose delicacy concealed strength enough to snap his neck with a single motion.

Kav Daven smiled. He leaned over and spat into Stavros' cupped hands, drawing his own hands along Stavros' palms, spreading the moisture. Then he turned to the bright-robed journeyman to receive the white cloth bundle. He let the wrappings fall open, and raised the chunk of guar in both hands for all to see.

The throng murmured: approval, confusion, dissent.

Silver-white metal flashed dully, enough like mirror to rouse a spark of will in Stavros' yielded consciousness. He remembered Clausen.

Rage boiled up like magma. Dizzy in its heat, Stavros thrust his cupped hands forward. With the sureness of the sighted, the blind priest transferred the guar and its wrappings to one palm, making a dome over it it with the other. With a deft twist, he rotated the palms, balled the white wrapping in one fist and closed the knobby fingers of the other around their silvery burden. His ancient face showed no change, no sign of pain. He slipped the white cloth between the brown layers of his clothing, then joined both hands around the guar and rested them lightly within the bowl of Stavros' palms. He bent lower, swaying on ancient legs, kissed Stavros on the brow, and opened his hands.

Stavros felt no impact as the guar dropped into his palms, but the moisture of the priest's saliva made the pain instantaneous, as excruciating as molten metal poured onto his skin. He shuddered. He would not be able to bear it, but a moment later, he knew he must, as Clausen moved into his line of sight, insinuating himself through the crowd. Something had stirred his interest.

He must not weaken. If he fainted, the rock would fall and be seen. He must deny himself oblivion a little longer. But the pain seared him to the heart as the guar, greedy for moisture, ate wormholes in his palms. His throat made noises he could not control.

Ghirra's fingers pressed hard into the curve of his jaw, no longer a caress but a businesslike probing that hurt almost as much as the corrosive guar. Stavros moaned in a delirium of agony. Then the pain eased, marginally, or his tolerance of it increased. Kav Daven's brown hands embraced his once more, squeezing gently so that the guar was imprisoned more tightly. Stavros was aware of nothing but a fiery locus in the center of both palms. But for the relieving pressure of the Master Healer's hand, he'd be screaming like an animal, begging for release.

But the pain itself was steadying, now that he could imagine enduring it. He was not so shipwrecked as he feared. What the Power had riven, the pain knit back together as Stavros discovered new depths of endurance. No mere physical pain could be as annihilating as that ancient, soul-sucking wind, or as Clausen's intended rape of Fiix. Hiding the guar was motive enough to recall his scattered parts and renege on his surrender.

There was movement to his right, a flash of silver, then an instant of scuffle. Ghirra's hand was torn from its grip with a speed and economy of movement that left Stavros no doubt who now stood behind him. The crowd backed off in surprise, giving room to Aguidran as she moved to restrain her brother. Stavros had no time to consider the simmering of his rage. Its heat was mild compared to the fire in his palms. He braced himself as his deadened nerves awoke, and clamped his hands still tighter about the source of his agony.

"You all right there, Stav?" Clausen demanded loudly.

Stavros held still, erect, silent. Rage hardened around him like a wall, with the pain at its center.

The prospector put a hand to his shoulder, bent closer, and hissed, "Open your hands, Ibiá. Let me see what you've got there."

Stavros made himself relax within the prospector's grip. He was on his own, without benefit of Ghirra's analgesic touch. Calm flooded him, cool as an evening breeze. He dared a smile, though it came with effort, and looked up to see it mirrored in the old priest's face. Stavros shivered, this time with joy. Not so helpless after all.

He let the anger crack and fall away, no longer needed. He'd never felt so whole, so in control as he did at this moment, giving his entire self willingly to the pain so that its secret might remain concealed. If this was the guar ritual that welcomed an apprentice into the priesthood, though the Master Healer considered it barbaric, Stavros thought he understood something of its purpose.

Clausen shifted, his knee pressing sharply into Stavros' back. It was no surprise when the sleek chill of the laser pistol slid like a metal snake to nestle behind his ear.

"Open them, boy. *Now.* No one will know any better when I say I was too late to stop these native pals of yours from making you a human sacrifice."

Stavros kept his smile focused on Kav Daven, who returned it as if there was nothing out of the ordinary, as if it was just the two of them beneath the hot amber sun. At last, he nodded. He laid his fingertips to the top of Stavros' rigid hands and broke their seal by gently uncrossing the thumbs. His smile widened as he spread the palms apart.

Stavros stared, as his rational universe turned inside out all over again.

The guar was gone.

And his palms were intact. No blood and stink and charring. No ghastly burns. The skin was as clear as if freshly scoured.

My god. A miracle.

But that could not be. Miracles were a proof of faith, and his faith was anything but proven.

Gasps and murmurs and exclamations of surprise rose all around him. Clausen's muttered oath filled his ear. He gazed down at his hands, held still in Kav Daven's grasp. They hurt as if the burns were real. Flexing his fingers sent agonizing shocks up both his arms. His other senses felt the burned tissue ooze and crack, but his eyes saw only clear olive skin.

"What does it mean?" he asked the old priest fearfully.

Kav Daven regarded him with satisfaction. His smile grew inward. He seemed to be smiling to himself alone as he drew his fingertips slowly across the linguist's uninjured palms. He nodded again, and drew his hands away. The ritual was complete. As he turned to go, Clausen was after the old man like silent lightning, imprisoning his fisted hands at the wrists.

Without thinking, Stavros launched himself at Clausen's back. But his legs would not hold him. Real or unreal, the ordeal had drained his strength. He stumbled. Ghirra caught him before he fell and held him back.

"Leave him alone!" Stavros snarled, struggling against Ghirra's restraint. The ghostly agony returned to sear his palms. He sagged back against the Master Healer, cradling his arms against his chest.

"Tut, Ibiá." Clausen gripped Kav Daven's scrawny wrists with surprising gentleness. "Hurt a blind old man? A coward's act. Do you think that ill of me?"

Firmly, as if dealing with a child, Clausen pried open the fingers of one and then the other of Kav Daven's hands. The old priest did not resist. He gave the prospector his jester's grin and proudly extended his hands, palm up.

Clausen seemed surprised. "Now you see it, now you don't," he muttered at the empty hands. He stared at the silky scar tissue for a long moment, stroking it once with a curious finger before he released the priest's hands and stood back. "A thousand pardons for doubting you, ancient sir." He offered the Kav a little bow.

"Aren't you going to beat him up?" Stavros growled.

Clausen scoffed. "If you think what I gave you was a beating, Ibiá, you don't know the meaning of the word."

He watched as Kav Daven turned away again, still smiling but losing strength. The old priest reached a frail arm toward Aguidran, who was instantly at his side. The Master Ranger shot Stavros a single piercing glance, then the pair resumed their interrupted march along the line toward the waiting sedan chair. Ashimmel followed, perturbed and solemn. The other priests and flag-bearing apprentices fell in behind her. They moved more slowly than before, for Kav Daven showed signs of fatigue and there were many left who wished to exchange greetings with him. The chant was raised again, with some confusion at first, but finding again its joyous intensity as the throng followed the priest and his escort, streaming past with only the occasional awed smile for Stavros or nod of support. The whole incident had happened very fast, and most of them had not seen enough of it to be amazed.

Clausen sighed, his hands in his pockets, one of which had swallowed the little laser gun. "Besides, that blind old man outfoxed me fair and square, and I have to admire that. We must treat the elderly with respect, Ibiá. They have seen so much in their lives. I hope there's someone tough as me around to admire me when I'm that age."

"You'll never live that long," snarled Stavros from the cage of Ghirra's arms. What the hell was the prospector going on about?

"Neither will you, at this rate. You'd better pray this traveling circus gets itself on the road while you still own your skin." Jiggling his pockets, he nodded in the direction of the wagons. "Ah. Here comes the Ladies' Auxiliary, to see to your welfare. What are you going to tell them, Ibiá?"

"That you bulled your way in when a high priest was showing us the honor of including me in a harmless ritual."

The silvered glasses flashed as Clausen shook his head wonderingly. "Perhaps I've misjudged your intelligence. Well, suit yourself. You've had ample warning." He shrugged and strolled off to lose himself in the crowd.

Ghirra released him, and Stavros slumped forward onto his knees. Odd that his body should feel so weak when he felt so strong inside. He held out his burning unmarred hands in wonder. "What does this mean?"

The Master Healer hauled him roughly to his feet. The rumbling growl from above must be the priest-horns resuming their call, but the crowd was slowing, halting, gathering in groups to stare apprehensively at the sky. Stavros tried to look, but Ghirra guided him abruptly away. Stavros' feet scuffed in the dust, his legs threatened to fold. He heard Megan's voice in the distance.

"Ghirra, what . . . ?"

The Master Healer dragged him into the shadow between two wagons and dropped him ungently onto a wicker crate. "How did you that?"

The physician's anger confused him. "Do? The guar . . ."

"That is not how it goes with a calling!"

"I did nothing . . . Ghirra, I . . . a calling to what?"

Ghirra folded his arms, bristly with suspicion. "You do not know this?"

"No, I . . ."

"A call to the Priest Hall."

"No, that's not right. How could . . . ?" Stavros absorbed the information slowly. "How should it go?"

"If true, the guar is held. A new priest. If not, the guar is dropped. Find a new guild. Both ways, is injury." Ghirra paced away, glancing between the wagons, tossing a black look at the sky as another booming roll shook the air.

That's not the horns. As Stavros looked up, a single dark cloud sped by overhead.

Ghirra came back, grasped one of his hands and turned it palm up for study. He drew his finger across as Kav Daven had done, but with far less satisfaction. Stavros winced. Ghirra's eyes narrowed. "This hurts, still?"

"Oh, yes. But not as much as before."

"The guar went . . . where?"

"I don't know."

Ghirra looked incredulous, but his roughness eased.

"The pain was real, Ghirra. I *felt* it! Even with your . . . help. Will you do that for Liphar when the time comes for him to hold the guar?"

"Yes, for all, when they are called. It is nerve damping." He used Susannah's diction but his own tone of professional dismissal. "Simple tricks. But none who hold the guar come like this. Not this. . . ." He explored the linguist's palm more gently, pressing the joints, stretching the clear skin as if willing it to show a crack, a sear, a blister, some sign other than obviously radiant health.

"Kav Daven didn't seem surprised," Stavros reflected vaguely.

"He makes some game, this Kav." Ghirra pushed the hand aside, murmuring deprecations about the Priest Guild.

"That's what Clausen said. But, Ghirra . . . something happened . . . something I don't understand."

"A trick." The physician buried his hands in the pockets of his smock and stood rocking gently on his heels. "If true, where is the science?"

"I don't know."

What "game" would the old priest play with an offworld stranger? It almost didn't matter. Stavros could not shed the conviction that he'd received the blessing he'd hoped for, that his purpose had been somehow sanctified. Besides, there was more than the disappearance of the guar to be explained, but he quailed at the prospect of articulating his cosmic visions of power and annihilation to a tough-minded realist like Ghirra. "Back on Earth, there are religious fanatics who can dance on burning coals with no apparent damage to the skin. And on Ba-hore, the fertility rites include flame-walking." He held out his palm with a feeble grin. "I'm small change compared to that."

Ghirra regarded him without humor. "Are you a religious fanatic?"

"Of course not." Stavros dropped the hand into his lap, into the protective curl of his other, so that the lingering phantom pain was centered in his body. "Though this sort of experience could make you one." He tried out a deflecting grin. "I don't know. Belief and knowledge again, Ghirra."

"Science or miracle," echoed the Sawl unhappily.

"Ghirra . . . say nothing of this."

"If you wish it. But all others will talk."

"Others don't know what you know." Unable to leave it at that, Stavros added, "But I need to tell you, I felt such . . . joy out there, despite the pain. I feel . . ."

"There you are!" Megan peered between the wagons.

". . . whole," Stavros finished lamely. The more he tried to express it in words, the more it began to sound like simply getting his shit together . . . finally.

"I am glad for you, Ibi."

And perhaps he was, but Stavros did not mistake compassion for acceptance. This incident had disturbed Ghirra deeply, and he was sure he'd hear more of it.

"There's one hell of a storm brewing out here again," Megan warned.

Susannah came into the shadow of the wagons. "What happened, Stav?

With their arrival, the aura of the inexplicable passed, leaving only its residue: the ghostly fires in his palms. He'd have to learn to use his hands all over again, as if they were a normal part of his body.

Susannah looked to Ghirra. "What was all that?"

"Nothing much," Stavros replied. "Just a little send-off ritual."

"The sun," Ghirra offered. "But he is better now."

Megan found a free crate to sit on. "A send-off ritual that includes Terrans?"

Stavros spread his hands in a Sawlish shrug. "Kav Daven's gesture to ecumenicism."

Thunder cracked overhead. Through the space between the wagons, Stavros saw shadows scudding across the bright face of the cliff.

"May have all been for nothing." Megan followed his glance. "Shall we get back out there to watch Ashimmel have the final word after all?"

Ghirra's concern had already shifted to the sky. He lingered long enough to see Stavros pull himself successfully to his feet. Megan followed him into the open. Susannah waited while Stavros tested his balance.

"The sun, indeed," she sniffed. "Are you sure you're all right?"

He was relieved to hear no pity in her voice. His physical strength was returning, even while the pain haunted his palms. "Yes, yes." He wished he could tell her why and what had happened and of the new strength he'd found. "Better than I've ever been."

Susannah laughed. "No need to exaggerate. I believe you."

She led the way to join Megan and Ghirra.

The chanting had stopped. The assembly had backed against the cliff face, to gain a clear view of the northeastern horizon over the wagon tops. Weng stood with Ghirra and Aguidran in the front ranks. Megan had found Tyril and was holding the baby while the weaver comforted a frightened older child. McPherson found help to carry Danforth up to join them. Seeing them together, Sawl and Terran, Stavros felt as possessive as a father. My people, he thought happily. Glancing higher, he spotted Clausen lounging on the cliff stairs. Spread out across the next flight up were no less than three of Aguidran's biggest rangers. Stavros grinned. How could he have thought he was in this all alone?

Shadows sped past as he crossed the dusty rock to Ghirra's side. When he turned to look over the plain, he realized once again that Clausen and his megacorp were only part of the survival problem.

Out there, Valla's forces had massed for the attack.

A towering cloud front advanced from the Vallegar, at the measured, inexorable pace of crack infantry. The clouds cut a straight line across the full eighty-kilometer width of the Dop Arek, stretching from the far western hills to the knobby Talche in the east. Along the leading edge marched a Himalayan range of thunderheads, their distant tops shining like golden helmets in the sun, their bottoms roiling brown and black and spitting lightning like a den of dragons. The dark plain beneath was shattered by the strobic flash of green and yellow.

"No rain out there," Stavros observed.

"She saves the water for her Sister," Ghirra replied tightly.

No mystery now about the physician's rage and despair. The wagons were hard-roofed and shuttered tight, as safe as it was possible to be outside the Caves. But the crops were not yet ripe. There'd be no hope for them in a storm. Still, it felt wrong to stand by and let destruction happen. Stavros had so recently learned that helplessness came from within as well as from without. "Shouldn't we *do* something?"

"What? Tell me what can be done!" Ghirra glowered at the approaching cloud bank. "The storm comes again. No trade in Ogo Dul. The food dies in the fields. We die in our Caves. You see how it is with these Sisters, Ibi?"

"I do. But it's not over yet."

"No," Ghirra agreed darkly. "Lagri waits her time."

The cloud scouts sped northward past the sun and into the approaching darkness, as if delivering their report. The front continued to advance. Stavros noticed Kav Daven's canopied sedan chair, out in the open between the crowd and the line of wagons. One bare, gnarled foot nosed through the curtain of ribbons.

High above the Dop Arek, the fast-moving little cloud puffs detached once more from the main front, this time scudding straight across the plain. Behind them, the thunderheads discharged a brilliant electrical display and a deafening roar of challenge. The sound hit the cliffs and rolled off in echoing crescendos as palpable as shock waves.

A warm breeze lifted Stavros' hair.

Ghirra straightened expectantly. "Now we will see it."

The breeze picked up, gusting at first, then steadying into an unnaturally even blow, like the wind from a giant fan. The temperature rose. Static sang like cicadas in the hot dry air. The assembled throng jostled with eagerness and dread, loving the anticipation of battle, fearing the outcome. Softly they invoked Lagri's name. Stavros heard wagers being exchanged.

The cloud scouts approached in a neat and widely spaced row, a cautious vanguard. They slowed as they neared the southern edge of the plain. Suddenly there was a wavering of the air around the easternmost scout. Like a desert mirage, it shimmered and vanished. The next in line quickly met a similar fate, and the next, while the others reversed themselves and fled back toward the main column.

The black cloud towers kept up their steady advance. The strange shimmering of the air spread east and west, parallel to the oncoming cloud and as high as the tallest thunderhead. The front was a dark distortion behind a plane of dancing air. The hot wind blew with its eerie consistency. Stavros shivered as the static played like fingers up and down his skin.

He pointed at the line wavering across the plain, so remininscent of the undulations of a force field. His brain ached to imagine the energy required for a field barrier eighty kilometers long. "What is it?"

"The fire," said Ghirra. "Lagri's *tshael*."

"Heat weapon." Stavros thought of Clausen's laser.

"Now Valla will answer."

A roil of motion erupted behind the shimmering curtain of heat. Lightning lit up the darkness in blinding shocks. Thunder cracked and rolled and shook the bedrock. The heat barrier glowed and rippled, sparks dancing along its curves. Steam billowed up along its length. A child began to wail in the rear of the throng. There was motion in Kav Daven's chair. The old priest was rising again from its shadowed depths.

He climbed out of the chair with agonizing slowness, balanced on unsteady legs, shuffled a few steps away from the chair, then straightened, facing the plain. He stood like a sentinel as the heat curtain glowed and billowed and the steam clouds mushroomed into a dense white fog suffused with light. Kav Daven began to dance.

He twisted and turned in the same boneless minuet that had accompanied his tale chant in Lagri's Story Hall. In a single voice, the populace raised a keening wail that sent chills up Stavros' spine and drowned out the boom of the thunder. In the diffuse flash and glow of the heat barrier, the veil of steam became a wall of light, brightening until it hurt to look at. Steam rolled overhead, obscuring the sky, dimming the sun, until the fog had the brighter glow.

As Kav Daven danced, the hot wind stilled and died. A heated deadly calm settled in against the cliff face. The crowd held a collective breath. Just as the tension became unbearable, a touch of chill brushed past, a cooling current of dampness from the direction of the plain. The white fog coalesced into a low-slung cloud cover that gathered about the cliff tops, and finally it began to rain, no violent torrent, no slashing downpour, but a soft warm springlike rain that tasted sweet on the tongue. It settled the ocher dust and brought a shine to the wagon canopies and the yellow leaves in the fields. The wall of light glistened like a million rainbows, and then the hot wind sprang up again in a sudden shuddering gust. The light wall broke into a rain of sparkles. The sun brightened. The white fog thinned and vanished. The towering front was gone. The sky above the wide Dop Arek was restored to singing turquoise clarity.

A murmur of awe and delight swept through the throng. Kav Daven lifted his brown hands to the last drops of gentle rain, then slowly shuffled back to his chair and hauled himself inside.

Celebration broke out along the rock flat. The priest-horns bellowed from the cliff top. The jubilant populace danced and cheered and congratulated each other for their narrow escape. Aguidran mobilized her rangers at once to hurry the final preparations for leave-taking. The guild masters rushed to see to the hanging of the guild seals on the sides of their lead wagons. Even Ashimmel looked relieved, and took it upon herself, in full regalia, to check the harness of all the teams pulling the Priest Guild wagons. The Terrans gathered in quiet astonishment around Danforth's stretcher as McPherson and Susannah tried to calm the apoplectic planetologist.

Truly, anything is possible, Stavros thought to himself. He grinned at Ghirra. "Slipped by that time, Guildmaster."

Ghirra nodded solemnly. "That time, yes. But next time . . . ?"

"Ibi!" Liphar was breathless at his elbow, fumbling his tall banner into the crook of his arm to snatch up Stavros' hand and stare at his palm with a mixture of doubt and reverence. "Ibi, a wonder!"

Ghirra only looked bemused, but Stavros threw an arm about the young man's shoulders. "Yes, Lifa, a wonder!"

He let him go and, on impulse, seized the brilliant orange banner sewn with the wave-and-flame, the Priest Guild symbol of the Warrior Sisters, and raised it high above the crowd. Pain flared to molten agony in his palms. The shaft of the banner hummed like a tuning fork within his grip. Amber light played among its folds. Fine embroidery glimmered. For a moment, the silken triangle outshone even the sun hanging swollen against the malachite sky.

Stavros felt a returning brush of power, soft and mysterious as a nightbird's wing, and was not afraid. The pain fueled his ecstatic roar of triumph.

"EMBRIHA LAGRI!!"

Along the cliff face, five thousand voices echoed his call.

And in the shadow of his chair, Kav Daven smiled.

BOOK SIX

HEAT

" 'Who's there, besides foul weather?'
'One minded like the weather, most unquietly.' "

—*King Lear*, Act II, sc. iv

46

E.D. 69–22:18

THE EXULTANT THRONG cheered. But among the ranks of the Priest Guild, the elders eyed the shining banner—and its bearer—uneasily, flicking glances in the direction of their guild master's frown.

"Always a flair for the dramatic, our Stavros," Megan commented. "Poor old Ashimmel can't decide whether to approve of him or not."

"What is he up to?" Susannah sensed challenge as well as celebration in Stav's raising of the Priest Guild banner.

"Getting the caravan off to a rousing start."

Susannah was unconvinced. It was odd enough that Kav Daven had drawn Stavros into his strange ceremony, without warning or formality, as if it were common practice to include offworlders. She struggled again with that creeping sense of exclusion. "He's really thrown away all objectivity."

"Which the rest of us would never think of doing, of course." Megan cocked a mildly satiric eyebrow.

Stavros lowered the banner then, as if made self-conscious by the drama of the moment. The crowd exploded into hubbub and bustle and a surging toward the wagons. At Kav Ashimmel's impatient signal, two white-robed apprentices lifted the Ritual Master's sedan chair as easily as if it were empty, and trotted it across the dusty terrace to the stairs. Kav Daven's milky blind eyes glimmered within its shadows. The elderly and infirm of all the guilds followed in their own chairs and litters, ascending to the Caves in a long and colorful line.

The other celebrants shed their finery where they stood. The winch ropes were loosed from their ballast. Standards and banners and neatly folded ceremonial robes were loaded onto pallets to be hoisted up the cliff. The Master Ranger strode among the wagons and carts, barking orders, receiving hurried reports from her guildsmen. Every so often, she glared up at the hot green sky, daring it to show a single threat of cloud.

Susannah and Megan caught some of the ranger's urgency, and pressed through the milling mass to the Infirmary wagon. They found Ampiar overseeing the harnessing of the double teams of hjalk. The huge golden beasts bore the sun's amber heat without complaint. At the rear of the wagon, the packing still progressed. Susannah made sure that her own medikit was not too deeply buried, then stood aside while the physician's apprentices scurried about tying lash lines and stuffing each remaining nook and cranny with last-minute items.

McPherson wandered up to watch. "Gonna be real quiet around here. Never thought I'd wish I was on a science mission."

Susannah smiled. "Want to come along?"

"Hah. Can you see that happening, after the hell Emil raised about Stav going? I bet the Commander ain't had a tongue-lashing like that since she was a cadet—with me and Tay right there, you know? She just stood there and took it."

"I'm sure she's heard lots worse in her time." Susannah exchanged a glance with Megan. "Not like Emil to throw his weight around in public, though."

Megan snorted. "Must have run out of his day's ration of oily charm."

McPherson scaled the high side of the wagon to wriggle into the padded driver's seat with the curiosity of a professional. "Well, we do need CRI back on-line and a working Sled. I hate you guys going out into the middle of nowhere with no connection to Base."

"Besides," Susannah added, "Someone's got to be around to nurse Taylor along."

"Hell, yes." McPherson pushed off her perch with a sprightly bound that turned into a suggestive cavort as she touched ground. "Well, see you guys. Hurry back!" She lingered to point out the line of litters climbing the cliff. "Who'll take care of all the oldies left up in the Caves?"

Megan draped her arms over the chest-high rim of the front wheel. "Liphar says a basic maintenance crew stays behind—a few priests and rangers for the weather watch and a bunch of Food Guild agriculturalists to keep an eye on the crop. It only looks like the whole world's on the move."

Susannah felt a twinge of doctor's concern. Megan looked heat-worn already, eager for the shade, perhaps reconsidering the wisdom of embarking on a month-long trek without the standard expedition amenities. Susannah was less concerned about herself or the Sawls, who were well used to hardship. But she hoped for the speedy repair of the com and power links. Gazing across the wide, rugged plain to the lavender mountains in the north and east, she worried about the kind of medicine she might have to practice out there, with little more than her own hands, a few drugs and herbs, and the Master Healer's intriguing skill set.

Ghirra arrived just then, with his own small caravan: on one side, Weng in her habitual white, her rank insignia glinting on her collar; on the other, little Dwingen struggled to match his guild master's long stride. Behind, four apprentices labored with Danforth in his leather stretcher. Stavros followed, a little apart and smiling inwardly, as if at some private thought.

The bearers set the stretcher down on its folding legs and shook the cramps out of their arms. Susannah thought of a black Gulliver among the Lilliputians. Being out and about had sapped his strength. McPherson hovered solicitously.

"Did you see all that?" Danforth demanded. "What did *you* see?"

Susannah checked his pulse and temperature, and adjusted her stance so that her shadow fell across his sweat-rimed face. "I hesitate to put it into words."

"So I wasn't seeing things."

"Not unless we all were."

Danforth breathed his thanks and let his eyes droop shut.

"So you see, Guildmaster," Weng was explaining to Ghirra, while one thin hand tucked wisps of silver hair back into her bun. "By our ship's clock, it is the end of a long day. It will be very hard on my people if your sister insists on a full twelve hours of travel."

The Master Healer's long, handsome head inclined in respectful sympathy. He had put on travel gear, his blousy cloth pants tucked calf-high into the tops of loose-fitting leather boots, softened at the ankles with long, hard wear. He looked taller and leaner without his linen physician's smock, his brown curls gathered at the nape of his neck. Like his sister, Susannah mused, even more than usual.

"The second and third work shifts haven't had their sleep round either, Commander," Stavros pointed out from his slight remove. "Had to make up the delay. Everyone's going to be tired."

"I think my sister asks only one half throw this time," Ghirra offered. "But already we are late. We must go many throws by darkfall."

"But so long as we're into night travel anyway in a week or so," Megan asked, "why not rest now and start refreshed?"

Ghirra smiled. "Rest *after* a Leave-taking, Meeghan?"

She grinned and shrugged, but Susannah sensed her embarrassment. Talking to Ghirra, it was easy to forget you were talking to a Sawl, until you indulged in some particularly Terran reasoning and received his oh-so-courteous but dismissive response.

Stavros looked on with uncharacteristic benevolence.

Like he has nothing to do with the rest of us Terrans. Susannah had seen that distanced look before. His face was still flushed with the excitement of the Leave-taking ceremony and his unexpected participation. His usual glower had transmuted into a kind of glow. When McPherson moved over to discuss a strategy of repair for the antenna, he replied with benign inattention without losing his odd, half-wondering smile.

A pair of rangers came by on a last-minute inspection tour, dressed in soft road leathers and boots, and wide-brimmed hats of waxed cane woven on a bent reed frame. With them was the Head Herdsman, a short, energetic woman with bared muscular arms and thick braids of auburn hair shot with silver. She bustled over to draw the Master Healer toward the front of the wagon for an explanation of the slight limp on one of the hjalk she had assigned to his teams.

Weng made a small shrugging gesture confined mostly to her chin. "I trust, Dr. James, that you three will fare well enough out there. Hopefully, this more settled weather will favor our repairs, so you will find us powered up on your return."

Susannah dug for the desert service hat that had languished for two months at the bottom of her field pack. "We'll need our hot-weather gear after all. See, Taylor, you weren't so off base as you thought."

The planetologist stirred from the fringes of a doze. "Even *more* than I thought," he mumbled, but did not elaborate. The stretcher bearers exchanged covert looks and shifted restlessly.

"Go on, take him down." Susannah nodded toward the Lander's tilted silver cone, looming a half-mile away. McPherson waved a cheerful farewell and sprinted after them. Weng followed at a more disciplined pace.

"You notice Emil hasn't condescended to offer a farewell," Megan observed, not without satisfaction.

Susannah shouldered her pack. "He'll work out his high dudgeon on the repairs. You'll see: one day we'll be trudging along out there and he'll come whizzing by in B-Sled, hot on the trail of a billion-euro lithium lode."

"Exactly what I'm afraid of."

A cry rang out from the distant head of the caravan. The lead wagons jolted into motion, a dark brown wagon with the carved seal of the Ranger Guild gleaming on its side, then the first of twenty giant red-and-blue Food Guild wagons that were interspersed throughout the train, next the Master Potter's wagon, and following, a graceful wagon from Woodworkers'. The rattle and creak of wheel and harness made a din accompanied by a spreading cloud of yellow dust. Ghirra reappeared at the side of the Infirmary wagon with the Head Midwife, Xifa. The two youngest apprentices danced around them like excited puppies. Smiling gravely, the Master Healer explained that little Dwingen was taking his first trade journey away from his family wagon.

Megan did not object to Ghirra's suggestion that she might prefer to ride. She hauled herself up into the driver's seat to settle beside Ampiar, who took up the reins. The double hjalk teams bent into their harness.

"I'll be up ahead with Liphar's family," Stavros announced. He gave Susannah his same odd smile and loped toward the head of the train.

Susannah watched him go. "What's *with* him?"

"He sees this all as a great adventure."

"But that's just it. You don't think it's peculiar? I mean, he actually looks happy."

47

E.D. 70–1:02

THE WIDE CART track led eastward along the stony ledge at the base of the cliffs. The long train of wagons and guildsmen moved at a snail's pace at first, carefully skirting the acres of planted fields where the new amber shoots reached skyward with such astonishing speed. The still-flooded terraces mirrored hard green sky between neat rows of slim yellow stalks unfolding their first true leaves.

Passing under the sentinel shadow of the tall rock spindle she had dubbed the Red Pawn, Susannah conjured visions of white-topped Conestogas sailing the ancient North American wilderness, and felt her excitement quicken. As the caravan rattled down a long, stony incline to the level of the plain, a gang of Food Guild apprentices began a song chant that spread down the line until the refrain was picked up by the herdsmen escorting the dairy herd through the dust clouds at the rear.

Beyond the Red Pawn, the cliffs veered to the right, as the mountains behind swung south to join the rugged Grigar Range, then curved around in a deep arc to fill the distant eastern horizon with the gentle foothills of the Talche, "the Knees." Ahead and due east, the plain opened up like a vast expanse of water. Far to the northeast waited the Vallegar, its sharp peaks a deeper, bluer green against the green sky.

Susannah took long, deep breaths, a reaction to the sudden sense of end-less space, after the long and confining weeks spent in the lamp-lit caves. The Dop Arek—the Goddesses' Gaming Board. The name seemed ominous, considering the violent nature of the sister-goddesses' games. The Sawls' eager forsaking of their sheltering caves for the open ground seemed reck-less at best, but it was the truest measure of how critical the trade mission was to their long-range survival. Ten throws, Ghirra said it would take, two weeks by the Terran clock, to reach Ogo Dul.

Progress was slow. The storm-ravaged ground was broken by deep ravines and still-damp washes. The big hjalk strained against the constant pull of the mud. Susannah's field boots and khakis were soon caked with drying ocher. The Master Ranger was forced into frequent detours around steep-sided gullies and arroyos choked with rock and flood debris. The detours often required further detours, seeming to lead the caravan ever farther away from their eastward route.

The noon air was windless and thick with humidity, as the hot sun sucked water from the sodden ground. The Dop Arek was utterly treeless, either by natural habit or, as Susannah judged from the twisted nests of unidentifiable vegetable matter clogging the ravines, due to the extreme violence of the flood. But despite all, new plant growth furred every surface that offered moisture and nourishment. Susannah broke out her gloves and a new pack of specimen bags, and eagerly began her biological survey.

She took her first samples along a section of visible roadway: delicate yel-low coils uncurling into fernlike bracts. They grew in soft spreading patches, the tallest reaching to her waist. On sandier ground, she found clusters of a broader, thicker leaf set in whorls about clusters of tiny scarlet flowers. She gathered several of differing maturity, intrigued by the early development of prominent seed pods. It was thirsty work, bending and cutting and hurrying to catch up with the Infirmary wagon as it repeatedly passed her by. After only two hours, the canteen on her belt was two-thirds empty. The hazmat gloves were heavy and hot. Her ship's-issue clothing, though designed for desert climates, was overly tailored and binding. Already, she missed a working therm-suit.

The golden-curled hjalk, as well as the hakra, their diminutive cousins, pulled their loads uncomplainingly, as if they required no rest or water to maintain their steady pace. Taking a break from the exertions of her survey, Susannah walked on the shade side of the Infirmary wagon. For many miles, she was haunted by the oddness of Stavros' parting smile. Finally, she set herself the more useful task of reviewing her knowledge of camels, reminded of them by the hjalks' broad fleshy feet, equally well suited to the rough mud of the Dop Arek as they would be to sand. She wondered if the hjalk and hakra stored water like the camel, or possessed the camel's incredible stamina.

Ahead of her, the Master Healer had fallen into a shambling gait as steady as the hjalks'. It was a practiced traveling pace that propelled him along with the least expenditure of effort. A ceramic jug rested in a sling across his back, but Susannah saw him uncork it only twice. The singing and chanting were more sporadic now, occasionally reinspired by the pipers who walked with the ranger wagons, playing the rhythm of the pace.

Megan remained in the wagon, at Ghirra's insistence. Dwingen currently occupied the other half of the driver's seat, while Ampiar took a turn on her feet with the rest of the medical staff. Dwingen was a frail but brilliant boy, Ghirra's favorite apprentice. She grinned up at him as he tried to look serious and in control with the great bundle of reins bulging out of his small hands to lie slack across the hjalks' backs. Fortunately for Dwingen, the hjalk knew better than he which way to go.

As the caravan wound down into a shallow valley, Susannah spotted new specimens for cutting and ran ahead armed with her sample bags. She took sprigs of low-lying scrub covered with minute yellow leaves that were thick and oblate, like tiny pea pods, and crisp with moisture when broken open. In the damp bottom of a wash, she discovered a scattering of waxy orange blossoms with sharp red spikes at the end of each petal.

The physician eyed her with increasing concern as she rushed about taking her samples. Eventually, he demanded assurance that she would not try to eat any of her cuttings or use them as herbs.

"Of course not! But, Ghirra, there must be all sorts of edible plants out here. With your own supplies so short, shouldn't you take advantage of any available foodstuffs?"

He flicked a warning finger at the bagged sprigs and leaves. "This is not food, Suzhanna. This make you sick."

"Which will?"

"All."

"All of them?" She gestured to include the distance to the horizon. "Every one?"

"Yes," he insisted. Beside him, sturdy Xifa added her nod of agreement.

This suggested very peculiar relationships within the Fiixian ecosystem. But, as with the cultivated crops, what astonished Susannah the most was the stupendous growth rate of all the native flora. Several shipdays earlier, the entire landscape had been a barren sea of mud and rubble. Now it was rich with plant life in full leaf and bloom, already showing signs of rapid seed development.

"The plants grow so fast!" she marveled to Ghirra from the Infirmary wagon's shadow, when the caravan finally halted at the bottom of a brush-lined sandy ravine for a rest and a mid-throw meal. Aguidran stalked by on her routine inspection tour, nodding to her brother as she passed. The Food Guild wagon nearest them bustled with the unloading of bread and cheeses and dried meats into wide baskets for distribution down the line.

"It is fast?" Ghirra was interested. "Do the plants grow much slowly in your caves?"

"Much slower." She turned a sample bag in her hands. Would his fertile mind be up to the notion of genetic engineering? "We're in a constant struggle to make them grow faster, to mature and fruit quickly, so that our very limited agricultural space can produce more harvests. The mechanism that allows such rapid growth would be well worth discovering."

"You must ask this of Ard when we come again to Dul Elesi."

The idea of asking anything at all of the irascible Head Herbalist was daunting. Susannah was glad he'd remained at home with his cave-grown medicinals and his freshly planted herb plots, sparing her the ordeal, for the time being at least.

Ghirra considered the question further. "I think it is that if the plants do not grow fast, they die before the seed comes to grow again after the rains."

"That's evolutionarily sound, for sure, but it's still amazing. If our computer was working, I'd cross-check her files, but I'd bet money that your plants, especially the cultivated varieties, grow faster than anything on record. It's positively uncanny."

His interest quickened. He tried out a word he had recently learned. "You name this growth *abnormal?*"

"Well, we'd call your weather abnormal, too." Susannah reached for chunks of bread and cheese as a Food Guilder offered his laden basket. "But growth rate is relative, isn't it—it depends on an organism's needs in a given situation. Who can judge what 'too fast' is, relative to the universe as a whole? Back home, we had a nicely balanced ecosystem, until we messed it up, and now we have to make our food sources do things they weren't evolved to do, in order to feed our billions."

"Do you feed them?"

"What?"

Ghirra cocked his head innocently. "Is there food enough?"

"No, not always." Susannah looked down. "Often, in fact . . . there isn't."

"Do they not die?"

"Of course they do. But we're doing the best we can to produce more food."

Ghirra frowned gently, as if it was clear to him that someone on Earth wasn't doing their job right. "This is too much people, then."

"Yes, it is. But you can't tell people they're not allowed to have children."

"When so many die, the lesson is learned."

He seemed so sure of this. And indeed, the Sawls seemed to have their population well under control. Intentional practice, or merely a result of the hostile climate? Susannah was glad when he turned his attention back to his meal. She had no personal reason to feel defensive: she was a responsible consumer, she was childless, and, arguably, her work added to the store of knowledge needed to improve living conditions. Still, Ghirra's questions seemed so . . . pointed, as if framed by some unspoken agenda. And she was fairly sure she knew *whose* agenda.

What had Stavros been telling him about life back home?

She leaned back against the tall rear wheel and nibbled her cheese, feeling fortunate that she was not, in fact, on Earth, but here in the clean, open air, pondering the mysterious details of her work. Megan dozed on a blanket beneath the front axle, snoring gently, too tired even to eat. A small stream wandering the flat ravine bottom played gentle music to accompany the meal. An insect, or something that sounded like an insect, buzzed out in the sunlight. Susannah looked for it, but it had passed too quickly.

"What means this word 'evolu-tion'?" asked the Master Healer suddenly.

Susannah sat up, marshaling her thoughts. Did any of this discussion come under the jurisdiction of the No Interference Code? When did intellectual notions become advanced technology? "You could say it means changing to suit a changing environment. An organism adapting itself in order to survive."

"And your or-ganims can do this change if they wish?"

She laughed gently. "Only over many thousands of years, Ghirra. It's not a thing you do consciously, like changing your clothes. For instance, in the analyses I ran of the dried plant specimens I was given during the snows, I found a substance very like the sugar trehalose, which some Earth organisms produce to allow them to survive drought. Trehalose replaces the water that maintains the spacing between molecules on the surfaces of cell membranes. Only a few Earth organisms manufacture it, but here on Fiix, every plant I've tested so far contains an analogue for it. This is a perfect example of evolu-tionary adaptation to a changeable environment." She recalled Danforth's pre-landing predictions of desert conditions, now confounded by the empirical evidence of two months of snow and rain. "Do you ever have long periods without much rain?"

Ghirra nodded as if this were grimly obvious. "When Lagri fights well her battles, the dry times is long, and the same is after a long *gist,* when the Sisters are tired and also their armies. It is very hot then, for many cycles."

"That sounds more like the desert Taylor expected to find here."

He continued quietly, as if even to speak of such things was to risk bringing them about. "But if a Sister wins in the *Arrah,* this is most bad of all. Many die then, in the Wet Death or the Death by Fire, and then will come *Atoph Phenar,* when the Sisters rest from sunrise to sunrise and the air does not move."

"The air doesn't move?" Susannah tried to imagine what he might mean by this. Weather had not often been a topic of discussion in the Physicians Hall. "And that's what you call a Great Devastation?"

"This is, yes."

"But so long as Valla Ired and Lagri are fighting, which is most of the time, you get this freakish weather? If Lagri's strong, it's hot and dry; if Valla, it's cold and wet." Susannah dusted crumbs off her hands and took up one of her sample bags. "I think you're right. It could account for the growth hormones being turned up off the scale." Tiny blunt thorns like ridges of little teeth poked at the resisting clear plastic in her hand. "On Earth, weather patterns are generally predictable by scientific means, so you know what'll happen ahead of time. Not as precisely as when the climate was healthier, but it's never freezing one morning and tropical by noon. That takes a day or so, at least."

"Your goddesses, perhaps, are kinder than ours," Ghirra murmured.

Megan was awake, and listening from under the wagon. "When is the weather worse, when the Sisters are fighting or when they're not?"

He pushed one flattened palm against the other. "When the strengths is same, this is best for us."

"The two in balance."

"Yes. This is the time of *Otoph*." He considered the Sawl word, nodding. "Balance is possible translation."

"Is it Otoph now?" asked Susannah.

Ghirra spread his hands. "It seems, but the signs . . ." He squinted furtively at the hot, green sky. "There are other signs."

He never seemed comfortable, speaking of the goddesses. Not like Liphar. But then Susannah felt the same discomfort when discussing the sister deities as if they were actual living beings—which, according to Stavros, the Sawls believed they were.

Ghirra sucked his cheek. "Ibi says you do not have these goddesses in your world. Perhaps you do not need the *Arrah* to move the air."

"You're saying the fighting's necessary, then?" Susannah asked.

An eagerness flared in his eyes and he dropped his voice again. "The priests do not teach this, but my sister shows me from her own guild books. The priests teach that the Darkness brought the fighting, which can end only when the Darkness goes."

Susannah awaited Megan's favorite question, "What Darkness?" which would lead to a discussion of the Sawls' lack of savior mythology and why they gambled over the weather instead of praying for it to change.

Instead, Megan leaned forward, her compass swinging loose around her neck like a talisman bead. "Do you think societies only have gods when they need them, Ghirra?"

Ghirra hesitated, as if caught by this thought.

"If a world has no gods . . ." Megan was hot on the trail of anthropological pay dirt. "Then who created it?"

"They who created all," the healer replied with only slightly more conviction than before. "If the night lanterns are worlds, as you say, the creators made these also."

"Valla Ired and Lagri are not creators?"

His expression was a mix of offense and amusement. "The First Books say the Sisters were born as we were." He found a sharp stone and scratched the familiar symbol of interlocking circles in the dirt. "They teach we are all three daughters of the creators."

"Not supreme beings, then, these Sisters," observed Megan.

"Meg, remember the Dance of Origins, how you complained that there wasn't a Prime Mover mentioned in it?"

The older woman nodded. "It's that father/king figure. Wait until I tell Stav. I'll bet he's found his Sawl Book of Genesis after all."

The rangers passed the starting call down the line and the caravan continued along the marshy ravine. The gravel bottom of the streambed offered a damp but firmer base for the wagon wheels than the choppy mud of the upper plains. An occasional lavender-pinkish streak showed among the striations of earth and rock, but the tall crumbling banks of the ravine were increasingly crowded with vegetation. Susannah was forced to be more selective in her sampling so as not to use up her supply of bags too early in the journey.

After the sixth hour of travel, Ghirra asked Dwingen to surrender his place on the wagon. Susannah was showing signs of wear. Instead, Megan offered to walk, and Susannah climbed into the high driver's seat without protest. The harsh din of wheel rattle and harness was amplified by the ravine walls into a rhythmic roar that made her dream of an ocean after a storm. Rocked by the sway of the wagon, Susannah dozed.

Later, the rhythm was broken by a jolt, and she woke clutching the worn leather of the seat. The ravine had deepened, curling back on itself like the coils of a snake. The streambed gravel was roughened by larger stones and the occasional boulder. The hjalk labored under their loads and the pace slowed as Aguidran sent a contingent of her rangers ahead to clear the worst of the obstacles left from the flood.

Susannah stretched and called to the girl apprentice Phea, who'd not yet had a turn in the shade of the wagon's yellow canopy. Phea climbed up gratefully, and Susannah grabbed her field pack to go clambering among the rocks for samples of a fleshy orange plant growing in spiny clusters, like a vegetable porcupine.

Overturning a stone by accident, she had her first confirmed sighting of local fauna: a long, whiplike body that slithered quickly away to hide under the next boulder. Briefly glimpsed, its eyes were yellow and bulging. The shape of its limbs seemed blurred, as if still forming themselves.

Amphibian, she guessed, like a frog tad. But the creature's movements and its smooth-scaled skin were more like a land animal's, a snake or a lizard. Instinctively, she grabbed for the disappearing tail.

"NO!" Ghirra barked, as hard-edged a syllable as she'd ever heard him utter. He raced across the gravel, but slowed in relief as he saw her straighten up empty-handed. "You must not touch these," he chided, as if to a child.

"Poisonous?"

He nodded. "Lagri's Messengers, they are called. Touching brings fire on the skin. If they bite, the fire is inside."

Abashed, she tucked her spiny cuttings into her pack and climbed down from the rocks. "I don't know what's the matter with me. I don't go grabbing at strange animals on Earth . . . of course, there are no strange animals on Earth anymore." She followed him back to the wagon. "Are there many poisonous creatures around?" She recognized his look of gentle perplexity. "Okay, I've said something you think is stupid."

"All are poisonous. It is for their safety. If not, the larger ones would eat them and they would be gone."

"If they're so poisonous, would that be bad?"

His puzzlement deepened. "You are a doctor, Suzhannah. Do you cut away your arm if it pains? All of the parts are necessary to the whole."

"Of course. Is this what the priests teach?" She was eager to disprove Megan's contention that Sawl religious views did not include a system of ethics.

"This is what I teach." He frowned at her gently, then excused himself and moved ahead to speak soothing words into the small ears of the hjalk as they struggled to haul the heavy wagon along the obstructed ravine.

Susannah tramped behind in silence, feeling rebuked without quite knowing why. The change in Ghirra's manner since the incident with Clausen's rocks was not so much distance as subtly implied moral superiority. It was all too reminiscent of a certain young linguist of her acquaintance. Perhaps she ought to have it out with Stavros after all.

The caravan rattled around a narrow, stony bend. Ahead, the leafy banks fell away and the ravine joined a wide sand wash, which then curved and dropped to meet a deep, flat-bottomed canyon. The far rock wall was steep and sharply corrugated, with layers of rose veined with ocher and white. A thin yellow river snaked across the canyon floor. A faint stir in the humid air cooled Susannah's damp cheek and set the dairy herd, straggling at the rear, to bellowing with unrestrained enthusiasm.

Tall lemon and amber grasses grew in the marshy areas between the river's tight curves. Where the water wound close to the steep eastern face, tumbles of rock were overgrown with thick palmate fronds and the bristles of tall stalks resembling giant aloe. A few hard-trunked succulents with long muscular roots clung stubbornly to the stone. They were mud-caked and scarred, but Susannah found them particularly beautiful. They were the first plants she'd seen that had lived through the recent storms.

Several dark oval creatures waddled tortoiselike into the water as the caravan halted along a gentle curl of the river. Susannah watched after them hungrily, taking quick snapshots in her mind for later translation into her sketchbook.

The herdsmen hurried to unhitch the teams. The freed hakra and hjalk were sent downstream to splash and roll among the dairy herd, under the watchful eye of rotating shifts of apprentices. Ti Niamar of the Food Guild trudged the length of the line, from one blue-and-red wagon to the next, hastening preparations for the cooking of the dinner meal. Water casks were unshipped. Fire pits were begun.

The first throw was over.

Susannah drained her canteen, no longer concerned if it ran empty, then kicked off her boots and walked to the water's edge. The stream was shallow and lazy, deeper along the inside of each bend where the current was cutting a more comfortable channel into the sand and the sparkling bottom was barely visible through several feet of golden water.

She rolled up her stained pant legs and waded in up to her calves, then crouched to dip water with cupped hands, splashing the sweat and grime from her face, letting a handful or two dribble down the back of her neck. The water was not cold, having traveled too many miles over hot sand to retain much of its mountain temperature. But it was cooling, and Susannah lingered in her crouch, face dripping, hands trailing in the gentle current, mind dazed from eight hours in the Fiixian sun.

"Thank the lord for state-of-the-art sun blocks." Megan padded across the sand to join her. "Aren't you going for a swim? It looks like everyone else is."

Susannah rose blinking from her reverie. For half a kilometer in either direction, while dust-caked rangers patrolled the banks, Sawls were shedding their clothes and hurrying for the water. Small children ran naked and squealing with delight. Infants barely learning to walk waddled intently after their siblings. Older children carried babies in harness on their backs. The adults were watchful but no less eager, and soon the riverbank teemed with brown naked bodies sinking gratefully into the stream. Even paunchy Ti Niamar and iron-haired Ashimmel forsook their duties long enough for a cooling thigh-high wade.

Megan and Susannah exchanged glances.

"When in Rome . . ." shrugged Megan.

The two women dropped their muddy clothes on the bank and threw themselves into the deepest part of the water. Susannah dove and came up for air refreshed and laughing.

On the bank, still in their sweat-stained trail gear, Ghirra and Aguidran walked along the row of wagons, deep in conversation.

48

E.D. 70–6:30

THE LANDER, RESTING at its incongruous tilt, was a clownish and surreal addition to the landscape of white rock and cultivated fields, backed by the solemn, majestic cliff. A clearing surrounded it, a barren no-man's-land separating alien metal from the burgeoning red-leafed fields. McPherson tuned out the dissonance, a fist pressed to her jaw in sober contemplation of the large dish antenna lying wounded in the mud, its battered spokes and torn golden mesh glinting with amber sunlight.

In the shade of the Underbelly, Emil Clausen wiped the blade of his oak-handled cleaver on a towel and surveyed the ingredients laid out on a horseshoe of crates, his improvised kitchen. "I assume we're all in an experimental mood tonight?"

He chose a handful of brown golf ball-sized spheres and set them on his cutting board. "Rock fungus," he explained to whoever was listening. "Should do nicely. And this . . ." He lifted a bunch of vermilion leaves sprouting from broad yellow stalks. "A trifle garish, perhaps, but when I smelled them cooking up in the Caves, I couldn't resist. Such a marvelous pungence. Still and all, Sawlian cuisine will attain no great heights without the introduction of a few crucial ingredients . . . like garlic."

"You mean you didn't bring your own?" Danforth shifted his cast-bound legs to the far side of his paper-littered bed. The orange sun, beginning its ever-so-slow descent, was invading his precious shade. He gasped softly as his right knee bumped the work table McPherson had rigged up out of one of the smaller hatch covers. The concavity of the hatch and its various shallow protuberances were minor inconveniences compared to everything else that was bothering Danforth.

"By the way," Clausen continued cheerfully, "I did a few basic field tests. The ore samples I brought back have an exceptionally high lithium content for plain old lepidolite."

"I'm glad for you," Danforth muttered.

"Thought you'd be pleased. But, I'm thinking, since lithium cools so late out of a melt, we can expect fairly pure veins, I'm going to wait the claim until I find one."

"Ummm. Say, Weng, have you got a moment?" Danforth pulled himself upright by his arms, the one part of his body that remained strong and whole. The thickly humid air was like weight in his lungs. His chest wound had begun to itch as it healed. He settled more comfortably against his pillows and spread a sequence of photos across his worktable. Weng came up to look over his shoulder. "Okay," he said. "Tell me what you think of this."

Clausen shrugged, expertly sectioning the spherical mushrooms. "Other breaking news: I've stumbled on a handy way to extort real food out of these little fellows."

Danforth drew a red diagonal line across the center of a hemispheric photo of the planet. "That storm activity was confined largely to this narrow band."

"Equatorial," Weng noted.

"More or less, but inclined, as you can see, northwest to southeast." He pointed to top and bottom of the planetary disk. "Here are the rotational poles. But the axis of symmetry for the recent activity runs this way, northeast to southwest, some twenty-eight degrees off the rotational poles."

Weng's nod managed to imply both encouragement and a vague disassociation with all matters of planets.

Clausen said, more loudly, "I simply hang around the Caves looking like I'm trying to get in without anyone noticing. The clever little buggers have psyched out my weakness: they know they can distract me with groceries."

Danforth glanced over his shoulder in annoyance. "And the wind direction is northeast to southwest and vice versa, moving in both directions along the axis of symmetry."

Weng said, "Ah?"

The planetologist's pencil beat a rhythm of frustration on the metal hatch cover. "Under *normal* circumstances, Commander, the winds should move west to east, zonally, and perpendicular to the rotational poles. A nice simple system. Not like this nonsense."

"Ah." Weng leaned in for a closer study of the photos.

"So every day . . ." Clausen scraped the chopped fungus into a plastic bowl. "Up I go. And every day, they trot out some new Sawlian delicacy to tempt me. Must keep them working overtime, with so few of them left at home." He left his horseshoe counter, rubbing his hands, and went to the edge of the shade to turn the four little carcasses browning on skewers above a glowing dung fire. He wagged his head in falsetto mimicry. "Oh me, oh my, what shall we put that nosy dude off with tomorrow?" He poked the fire. "They've even learned to surrender the goods uncooked. Food for the imagination as well as for the stomach." He straightened and called out into the sun, "What's the verdict, McP?"

McPherson returned an unintelligible reply from her crouch beside the broken dish.

At Danforth's worktable, Weng picked up a photo between delicate fingers to squint at the dateline, then placed it beside others in the same sequence.

"The snow clouds breaking up," said Danforth.

"Extraordinarily rapid change," she murmured. "But then, we saw that with our own eyes at the Leave-taking."

"Some anomaly due to extremes of heat and cold," he replied brusquely. "I'll get to that later. I'm still dealing with the data we had before we lost CRI. After I woke up, I promised myself I'd approach this problem from a completely different angle. Before, I kept blaming inexplicable data on inaccurate instruments. I'd lost confidence in my circulation model. But when I plugged in proven Venus data instead, it came out fine. So I started altering this term or that, tinkering with the Venus measurements, pushing them more toward the weird Fiixian data, but then the snow stopped and I . . ."

He riffled the corners of a mud-stained photo. "Well, whatever. I never got to finish that process, and I can't do any complicated model runs until we get CRI back."

Weng offered no comment. Danforth required only her patient, listening ear.

"So I'm thinking about it this way: A does not equal B. What does B lack to make it A? It lacks C. C is the term missing from the equation. It's not just poor data resolution or some minor imbalance. It's a whole term. Some sort of X-factor, some anomalous something. Some force that's unique to this planet and makes the weather behave the way it does. Something the probe instruments missed, so it never got into the model. That's what I have to look for now, the ad hoc that will make the model start churning out the right results."

"What are the possibilities?" Weng searched briefly for an empty crate, then slid a stack of papers aside and sat.

"Don't get him started," Clausen warned, testing the temperature of his skillet with a dampened finger. "I'll have to hold supper, and then it'll be cold, not to say ruined."

Danforth's jaw clenched, then relaxed. "I started with the snow data, since that's what's available. In that case, we had a classic winter warm-front situation: warm, moist air coming in from the northeast to meet cold, dry air from the southwest."

"And the moisture was precipitated out as snow," she offered.

Danforth nodded. "We'll make a forecaster out of you yet."

"Why do I get the feeling I'm being ignored?" Clausen complained.

"So far, so good, except it went all the way around the planet," Danforth persisted. "And on a slow rotater like Fiix, I expected large-scale wave motions, so any weather should be due to mechanical instabilities in the wind flow, not to temperature differences or these compact front phenomena."

Clausen cut a corner from a brick of white Sawl butter and dropped it into the skillet. "No one talks to the help around here? Doncha know good cooks are hard to come by?"

McPherson trotted in from the sun. "We can just set her upright for straight com, Emil. But it's gonna take some major welding to get her into shape to catch the power beam. What's for dinner?"

"Maybe you all don't get the point." Clausen lined up yellow leafstalks with the flat of his knife. "Which is that the Sawls are going to great lengths to keep me out of those caves. Obviously, they're hiding something."

"What?" McPherson wrinkled her nose at the bubbling skillet.

The prospector shrugged. "How do I know until I get in there to find out?"

"They let *me* in."

"Way in, McP. Way in. Beyond the beaten path."

"Oh."

"And why is that the point?" muttered Danforth irritably.

Clausen glanced up. "What?"

"I mean, what do you think is in there, for god's sake, dragons and treasure?"

Clausen stopped chopping. "Excuse me?"

"I mean, haven't we got more important things to worry about than what the goddamned natives might be hiding in their goddamned caves?"

"Hey, you guys . . ." McPherson protested.

Clausen looked down at the leaves neatly diced on the cutting slab and nudged them around with the sharp tip of his knife. "Forget it, Tay. Go back to work."

Weng's chin lifted in silent disapproval. McPherson took a step toward Danforth, then glanced back as the prospector returned to his food preparation in silence. She threw up her hands in exasperation.

"You guys . . ." she muttered, and stalked out into the heavy sunlight.

49

THE FOOD GUILDERS cut their swim short. While the other travelers lolled about in the shallows, debating the weather and trade strategies for Ogo Dul, the twenty red-and-blue wagons were turned inside out to produce dinner for five thousand hungry stomachs. A dozen emptied two-carts, their hakra still hitched and waiting patiently, were sent off to gather the drying flood debris, the thick root skeletons and the matted brush. Long cooking pits were dug in the sand in front of each hard-canopied Food Guild wagon. Huge fires were built. River water was set to boil in ceramic cauldrons that made the rough journey packed among the sacks of grain. Into the bubbling water went entire bags of reddish triangular seed. Baskets of crooked tubers were buried among the coals to roast. Flatbread dough was mixed and shaped and set to bake on rocks near the flames. Milk was brought up from the dairy herd to be churned.

Megan rested in the shadow of the Infirmary wagon, fluffing her gray curls dry after her swim. She watched Kav Ashimmel consult with her senior priests, legs still damp from their wading. The apprentices not still in the water hung close by for hints of a weather prediction. The Master Priest was an imposing figure even without her white robes and wave-and-flame tabard, but her stature was more political than spiritual.

The population was in a mellow mood, resting after their long day. Megan saw very few wagers laid as Ashimmel's conference dispersed and the apprentice priests wandered among the relaxing families and guild cliques with their lists and pouches.

Susannah joined her with a handful of plant specimens and her portable chemical analyzer. She sat cross-legged, her dark hair falling loose about her shoulders, shading her oval face. "Won't tell me much, but at least I'll get a jump on it."

Megan nodded. Sometimes she thought of Susannah as a lovely, earnest child. She was often self-righteous in the way of children. Which was why she couldn't be let in on the conspiracy. She was so sure that everything should be open and aboveboard, and that all parties were equal before the law.

"Seen Stav anywhere?" Susannah asked suddenly.

"No. Why?"

Susannah shrugged. "Just thinking about him."

"I'll tell him. He'll be delighted."

"Actually, I was going to take him to task for subverting our Master Healer."

"Pardon?"

"Spreading bad tales about life back home, I mean. It won't make Ghirra think any better of us."

Megan sat back, relieved. "No, I suppose not."

When the caravan had cooled and napped for a few hours, a long note from a wooden horn sent the loungers scurrying for their platters and utensils. Susannah packed up her samples and analyzer and woke Megan from her doze.

The apprentice Dwingen dug in the back of the wagon and produced a stack of oval eating trays. He presented one each to Susannah and Megan, then scampered off to join the long line piling up at the nearest Food Guild wagon. The queues were noisy, an encouragement to singing and wagering debates, but there was little impatience. The accepted order seemed to be that the children be served first and sent out of the line, so the adults could help themselves in relative calm.

Susannah and Megan hung back in the Infirmary wagon's shade until it seemed possible that the food might be gone if they didn't hurry. Food lines reminded them none too pleasantly of home. But there was food enough, and they carried well-laden trays back to the wagon. Phea giggled as Megan attacked her food with a spoon and fork retrieved from her field pack. The Sawls used fingers or made neat scoops out of strips of flatbread. Susannah found the hot grain mash to be bland but filling, and the pinkish flesh of the roasted tubers delicious. They drank the golden river water and fresh hekker milk brought around by a Food Guilder in jugs stacked high in a brightly painted two-cart. A grateful munching silence prevailed and Susannah observed privately that the only time the Sawls were truly quiet was when they were eating.

Ghirra and Aguidran joined them as they were finishing. The Master Ranger ate on her feet, leaning against the rear wheel, her eyes flicking constantly from her food to the river, down the line of wagons and diners, to the sky above the canyon walls. Ghirra sat cross-legged at her feet, eating with slow care.

Susannah was full of questions about food and eating. Ghirra's statement about the wild creatures being part of the whole and venom as a guard against extinction had set her thinking about ecological systems. She saw an odd duality within the Fiixian food chain.

"We eat what we grow only," Ghirra had said to her once, after the planting of the fields at Dul Elesi. She had taken this as an expression of his pride in the Sawls' self-sufficiency, but now she heard his words differently: "We eat only what we grow," became "we *can* only eat what we grow."

This restricted eating pattern was not a luxury born of abundance. The Sawls survived only by careful management of very limited food resources. From her own observations, Susannah knew that all scraps and leftovers were collected and mixed back into the hakra feed. Human and animal waste went back into the fields. There was no such thing as a trash dump in the Caves, only storage awaiting recycling.

And there was no Hunter Guild. The only flesh in the Sawl diet was from domestically raised animals and fish. According to Ghirra, humans never foraged among the wild plants, though the four-legged creatures could graze, if only in particular pastures, without ill effect. She would note specifically what the animals ate and did not eat, and from her samples, try to isolate potential toxins.

Susannah extended her inquiry past the realm of edibles. The leathers, wool, and skins used for clothing, bedding, parchment, boots, harness, and countless other articles were all derived from the domestic beasts. She had learned that every other planting cycle, a portion of the cultivated acres was given over to fiber plants for paper and a cotton-like thread. The fine linen used in Physicians Hall was traded for in Ogo Dul, as were the reeds and cane and rushes used for basketry.

She ate automatically, hardly tasting the sweet chewy tubers. Had Ghirra actually meant, "We *consume* only what we grow," as in "use" as well as "eat"? Could it be that the Sawls, except for the air they breathed and the water they drank, lived in their own entirely closed system, coexisting with but apart from the rest of the Fiixian ecology?

An odd arrangement. Choice or necessity? Philosophy or survival?

The Sawls' birth, death, and survival rates would have to be minutely well adjusted to their production capabilities in order to allow for such autonomy. If it was isolation by philosophy, say the ethics of a religion, were they never tempted—even forced—during the hardest of times to raid the resources existing outside their own system? They couldn't be, if these resources were truly unavailable to them by cause of natural defenses that they were unable to penetrate.

"Ghirra," she ventured at last, "there's something I don't understand."

But she stopped, confounded. There was so much she did not understand, too much, in fact, to be able to shape the questions she needed to ask. She recalled Megan's earlier tantrums over too much data and too little insight. At last she understood, several weeks too late. Taylor Danforth had questioned the validity of his data, Megan her own competence, but both had the right idea.

There was something odd going on here, something . . . special.

Ghirra awaited her question, a bread scoop full of grain mash poised between tray and mouth. The patience in his dark eyes could be interpreted as sympathy, but the easy interpretation no longer satisfied. Susannah could pinpoint exactly when she had lost confidence in her ability to read him accurately: Emil and his rocks.

So she smiled and shook her head. "It's not important."

"There's *lots* I don't understand," Megan chuckled, applying yet another lay of sunblock to her freckled skin.

Ghirra finished his mouthful, chewing thoughtfully.

Xifa and Ampiar excused themselves to go visiting down the line. Megan yawned up at the high, fat sun. "I have no idea what time it is, theirs or ours, but I'm turning in."

But before she could lay her blankets out under the wagon, Stavros arrived, his black hair sleek and wet, his dark eyes surveying them with restless interest. Liphar trailed along behind, curling a strip of bread to mop the last bits of mash from his tray. His wagering pouch bounced heavily on his hip. Stavros had shed his ship's whites for Sawl clothing and, like most of the Sawls, he was wearing very little, just the loose light-colored pants tied at the waist. His olive skin was already sun-darkened. Usually, he'd favored an air of secrecy, which Susannah considered a defensive tactic. But now he seemed bursting to share his secret, whatever it was.

He greeted Aguidran with a hint of ceremony. Susannah noticed a trace of deference in her curt nod, and Ghirra's smile held honest welcome. His arrival was like a bolt of energy shot into their languid circle. He settled between Ghirra and Megan as if he had great news to impart, yet he sat without speaking, legs pulled up to his chest, arms wrapped boyishly about his knees.

"Don't see how anyone'll get a good night's sleep in all this heat and sunlight," complained Megan idly, though she did not look particularly uncomfortable.

"Be grateful we still have light to see by," Stavros returned, and Susannah was perversely relieved to see a trace of his old glower.

"The night lanterns give light in the darkness," Ghirra offered. "I mean, Ibi, the *stars*."

Liphar's tray was finally scrubbed as clean as he could get it. He set it aside in the sand, unfastened the cloth pouch from his belt, then emptied its load of colored wood and stone disks into his lap and began to count them back into the sack. Only little Dwingen paid this much heed, eyeing the bright lapful enviously from his perch on the driver's seat. Finally, as if reminded of more childish playthings left at home, the boy asked Ghirra's permission to visit his family's campsite.

When he'd trotted off, taking Phea with him, Megan sighed and stretched her legs, as if some restraint had been lifted. Aguidran set her empty food tray on the lowered tailgate and hunkered down beside her brother, their shoulders nearly touching. Ghirra sketched absently in the sand. Stavros rested his head on his knees. Liphar counted busily under his breath. Somewhere nearby, a single piper blew a sweet melancholy air, joined by a few murmuring sleepy voices. The mood was relaxed and casual, yet to Susannah, the sensation of being odd man out became suddenly unbearable. She sat in the circle but apart from it, waiting for someone to tell her what was going on.

The silence stretched uncomfortably until Stavros lifted his head to gaze at her. His mouth softened, an almost-smile, self-contained and proud.

And then the moment was broken. Everyone moved simultaneously. Megan resumed the laying out of her bedroll. Aguidran rose, grasped her twin's shoulder with brief affection and departed to give orders to the weather watch. Stavros drew the healer into a discussion of the next day's route. The two of them sat side by side in identical postures, chatting like old cronies.

But Susannah knew she had witnessed a true moment, though she could not tell what it meant. She suspected, though, that however she tried to plot this five-way relationship, it would always take Stavros as its center. She pictured him among the cheering throng, raising the embroidered banner of the Priest Guild like a young warrior from another age, and she wondered again what he was up to. And if Megan was in on it, why didn't she share what she knew?

If there was some secret afoot, they did not trust her with it. The realization made Susannah defensive and instantly lonely. It was one thing to remain aloof and objective within the constant company of a shipload of colleagues, but out here in a wilderness inhabited by lethal flora and fauna as well as hostile weather, she needed to know she had friends around her.

But that was not it, not really. They would be there if she needed them. She simply felt bad being excluded, and yet, could not bring herself to confront them, perhaps force them to lie to her.

She waited until Megan had stretched out on her blankets and fallen asleep. Liphar finished counting and joined the two men in their discussion, which had fallen into Sawlish as it became more complicated. Susannah regretted that because Ghirra had acquired sufficient English so quickly, she'd let her learning of his language slide. She rose casually, making an elaborate show of combing out her long hair, and wandered around to the far side of the Infirmary wagon.

As soon as she was away from their sight, she struck out across the sand, heading south at random, along the river, having no purpose in mind but to escape that unspoken camaraderie that did not include her. She broke into a trot, her stride lengthening as the release of running on the hard-packed river sand took over. She passed wagon after wagon, each sporting its painted or carved guild plaques. She passed clusters of smaller, slat-sided wagons and the single-family two-carts with freshly laundered clothing drying on their traces. Some families relaxed in quiet conversation, the children digging in the sand or playing stones, but most had laid out their blankets and rugs and fallen into a well-deserved sleep.

Beyond the last wagon, she slowed to pass through the dairy herd, and, already out of breath and sweating in the humid afternoon sun, she continued walking after she had left the placid hekkers to continue their destruction of a certain variety of yellow brush growing up the side of the canyon.

So there was one place where the two food chains met. It was a small satisfaction, but she found totally separate ecosystems too neat for comfort.

The river slipped lazily around a wide bend. Out of sight of the caravan, away from the dust and noise and the constant jostling, Susannah's paranoia eased and she began to feel foolish that she had let it carry her even this far. As she was turning to go back, she noticed a section of the canyon wall ahead that had collapsed and spread itself in a jumble of ocher and white across half the canyon floor. The river curled languidly to one side of the obstruction, leaving some of itself behind in a deep pool held within the arms of the fallen rock. Clumps of the thick-trunked succulents sprang from between the boulders. The tallest leaned out over the pool to dip spiny amber leaves toward the water.

Susannah approached the bank, coveting the small shade of the golden trees across the water. She was hot again and sticky from her run. She wondered if Ghirra's rule about small creatures being dangerous extended to whatever might be living in the brown depths of the pool, then reflected that she and everyone else had already thrown themselves into the river without mishap. She stripped and waded in.

She felt cautiously among the sand and pebbles with her toes. When she stirred up nothing ferocious, she ducked into the water and swam a rapid nervous crawl across the pool to the rockfall. Nothing rose from the shadows to grab at her. She treaded water, holding on to a low, jutting ledge, then pushed off again to swim in slow, luxurious circles. The water cooled her as it slipped across her bare skin. The busy caravan was reduced to mere echoes sliding along the canyon walls, the hekkers bleating, a piper's sweet trill, parents calling their children to bed. Susannah's loneliness mellowed as she savored her first moment of true solitude in many months. The magnificence of the landscape was company enough, golden trees, towering walls of pink and amber rock. She lay back in the water and smiled up at the cloudless turquoise sky.

In that stillness, she heard approaching steps. She turned easily in the water to see Stavros picking his way slowly along the stream, intent on the ground as his bare feet chose a careful path among the broken stones.

Had she planned this all along? She made no move to retrieve her clothes.

He halted when he reached the pool's edge, and considered her for a moment in silence as she floated in the center, gazing back at him with as neutral a stare as she could muster. Finally, he loosened the tie at his waist with a quick gesture, let the soft trousers fall and stepped out of them. He dove and came up swimming, his body slicing neatly through the water, speeding past her as she floated expectantly, heading toward the rock pile and its welcoming trees. He pulled himself up on the rock ledge, dripping, as sleek as a water animal, and stretched flat on his stomach across the warm stone.

Isolated still, treading water in the middle of the pool, Susannah could not repress a crooked smile. Why was nothing ever simple, or ever as you imagine it would be?

She considered swimming back to shore and leaving him to bake in the sun alone. It would serve him right. But he was decidedly beautiful, naked on the rock like the unwitting, handsome shepherd from some Greek myth. She did not feel very much like the proverbial goddess and he was hardly unwitting, but she decided that the game between them had gone on long enough. She swam toward him and hoisted herself up to rest by her arms on the overhanging rock. Her eyes were level with the back of his head. The smooth muscles of his back were within easy reach. Susannah did not reach. She waited.

"The most remarkable thing happened to me," he muttered at last, his face turned into the rock. He raised his head to stare abstractedly at his open palm, stroking a forefinger across it in wonder. He looked at her then, seeming to discover her nearness, and reached to touch her cheek with some of the same wonder.

"You are so beautiful," he said.

When she smiled and did not back away, he moved impulsively, arching his body across the rock to catch her behind the neck and pull her mouth up to his.

"What has taken us so long?" she asked when they drew apart.

Stavros laid his head on her folded arms. "Will you come up on this rock with me?"

"Gladly," she replied, for her body could not have refused him.

Later, she stroked his drying hair. "What remarkable thing happened to you?"

But his answer was to kiss her with gentle passion. "You, I meant. Only you."

*   *   *

As Megan had predicted, Stavros was not to be a casual lover. During the next twelve hours of travel, he did not leave her side. He walked beside her in the sun, matching his stride to hers, helping her cut samples from the spined and needled plants along the way. He caught her hand and held it, until the damp heat or the roughness of the road forced them apart. When the caravan stopped for the mid-throw meal, he flopped down in the shade of the yellow wagon, and drew her into the crook of his arm while she laughed self-consciously and the others looked on like indulgent parents. Ghirra seemed oddly relieved and Liphar grinned as proudly as if he'd made the match himself.

Susannah was overwhelmed. Stavros seemed determined to focus on her with the same single-minded intensity he gave to his work. He said little, content to be with her, acknowledged as her lover. She thought it all a bit impulsive but, enormously flattered and instantly addicted to his impassioned lovemaking, she put it down to his youth, as she had his other excesses.

For the first part of the throw, the caravan pursued the winding canyon bottom, traveling upstream and more or less eastward toward the foothills of the Talche. After the mid-throw rest, the river narrowed as its bed was increasingly lined with rocks. The white spittle of rapids broke the surface as the current picked up speed. The canyon walls closed in around them until there was little more than a boulder-choked gorge ahead, thick with broad-leafed clusters and tangles of the yellow brush.

Aguidran turned the lead wagons into an upward-sloping dry wash, and with much urging and swearing and shouting, the lathered draft animals hauled the train of wagons back to plains level.

The Dop Arek was gentler here, the ground less ravaged by flooding. Soft brush-covered undulations flowed like waves into hills to the east. The old road appeared again, offering a decent surface over which they could at last make good time. The brush soon gave way to tall, sharp-edged grasses that bent before the wagon's passage like a mango-colored wheat field. The dairy herd as well as their drivers perked up at the sight of the hills and the rounded peaks of the Talche beyond them, but Stavros slipped his arm around Susannah's waist and pulled her close as they walked.

Aguidran pushed past the usual twelve-hour travel period in order to reach her intended campsite. Appearing suddenly out of the sea of orange grass was another river, broad and fast-moving but very shallow, full of sandbars and reddish reeds.

After dinner, Stavros led Susannah off to find a bed among the concealing grasses.

"When all this is over . . ." He waved an arm at the sky as they lay entwined on her blanket. The nearby clatter of the caravan was settling down for the sleep round.

Misunderstanding him, she said, "But I thought you liked it here."

He dropped his arm to stroke the curve of her belly. "Oh, I do. I do."

She fell asleep in his arms. Later, his kisses woke her. He smelled of strange grasses and desire. Sleepily, she pressed herself against him.

"I love you," he said.

She laughed softly, to lighten his mood.

"I do. Just remember that."

But when she woke hours later, she lay on an empty blanket. Stavros was gone.

"He'll steal the working antenna from the wrecked Sled, contact CRI in secret and send a message drone home before Clausen can file his claim." Megan was sympathetic but unrepentant. "We agreed I could tell you once he was on his way. He was afraid you'd try to talk him out of it."

Susannah stared at the ground. To her surprise, she missed him already.

"He didn't want a fight."

Susannah's voice was flat. "If you'd told me about all this before . . ."

Megan's shrug held no apology. "We just couldn't be sure how far you'd carry your insistence on neutrality. We thought you might turn us in, on the admittedly sound principle that politics has no place in the practice of science. But out here, we're safely out of contact, and by the time we get back to Dul Elesi, Emil'll have figured out what Stav's up to anyway, so the only additional risk in telling you is to me."

"And to Ghirra and Liphar and Aguidran . . ."

Megan raised an innocent brow and Susannah's anger blossomed.

"Come on, Meg. I may be untrustworthy as a conspirator, but I'm not stupid! My own work depends on good powers of observation!" She spun away, pacing in short spurts of frustration. It was unjust to be taken to task for loyalty to the ideal of objective observation. It did not mean that when the time came, she would not commit herself. "Meg, if I thought there was any legal way to stop ConPlex from ruining the planet . . ."

"Then my point is well taken. Our strategy is semi-legal at best, and that's only if everything works out the way we've planned. But, Susannah . . ." Megan's gesture embraced the Sawls and their caravan and everything it and they stood for. "Surely you can see the need!"

The fear that her outrage had buried dug its way free. "Emil will kill him."

Megan smiled mirthlessly. "Funny you should see that as quickly as I did. It took Stav having a laser put to his head to realize that possibility." She nodded as Susannah glanced up sharply. "Oh, yes, our man from ConPlex came armed. We're not safe in this either, you know. Or at least I'm not. You still have the choice."

Susannah's eyes stung with tears she did not want to shed. She was angry with Stavros for choosing his cause over her feelings . . . but would she have respected the opposite decision? She was angry that he'd left her so vulnerable—not just to Clausen, but to her own emotions. "It's not a real choice if you're forced into making it. I just wish he'd . . ." She stopped, then let the tears come, of loss and confusion.

And Megan mused soberly: what sure instincts the boy has, to bind each of us to him with a different chain.

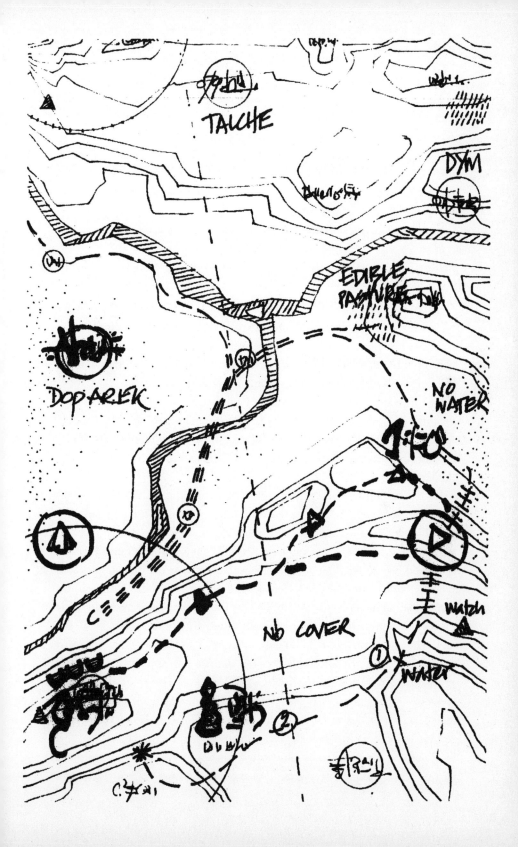

50

CLAUSEN BOUNDED UP the last flight of steps, ignoring the twinges in his ankle. Only pure dumb luck had kept him from breaking bones in the Sled wreck. He still thought of his body as the well-honed tool he'd made of it, but the reluctance of a mere sprain to heal forced another of those irritating reminders: he wasn't as young as he used to be.

He turned past the entry to the Food Guild's main storage cave and headed along the ledge toward the stable entry. It was one of the oldest caves. The opening was ragged, shaped like a wide mouth caught in an awkward smile. The old stone shelter for the weather watch hunched to one side like a single blunted tooth.

He paused in the shade of the overhang, seeming to brush dust from his impeccable khakis. No one waited on the inner stair, or hurried down to meet him with the usual armload of produce. Clausen adjusted the fit of his soft, fingerless suede gloves, pulled the straps tight around his tanned wrists. He flexed his left hand gingerly to assure himself that the tiny air-powered hypodermic lay comfortably in its sheath against the pad of his thumb. He lounged about, alert to the possibility that he was being watched. He made a show of standing back to study the guardian frieze in its high niche in the rock. The ancient frieze held no aura of mystery for him. He saw it as just one more artifact of a culture that did not impress him as particularly distinguished. He could admire the boldness of the carved representations of the goddesses, or the crude expressiveness of the many tiny figures lamenting at their feet, but he'd seen far better in his time. Even so, he would take a few crates worth with him when he left, to make up for the regrettable fact that Sawl pottery was both too sophisticated and too pragmatic to bring much of a price on the primitive arts black market. Clausen's already generous income was nicely supplemented by his connections with wealthy art patrons and dealers back home.

He edged toward the upward stair. His eyes skimmed the inner walls, tracing the smooth striations of the rock with the frustration of a compulsive reader who has been allowed only one book to read over and over. If the lithium strike on Fiix was as big as he expected it to be, he'd probably make it his last. Go out in a blaze of glory, and retire to the seclusion of his colony planet estates and the company of his priceless collection of orchids. Clausen was tired of waiting, waiting for the link to be fixed, waiting for the Sawl rangers to return and haul the broken Sled back to base, waiting to be able to begin the task he'd traveled two hundred and twenty parsecs to accomplish. But there were dangers in letting frustration sour into rage, so he channeled his pique into cooking, into tinkering with McPherson, into disputing subtle points of astrophysics with Weng. His single personal indulgence was to needle Danforth with relentless cheer, knowing the other's frustration to be as near the boiling point as his own. It was an amusing game, seeing who'd erupt first, though not that much of a contest. His own cool was legendary.

But what absorbed his truest concentration and effort was his quest to get past the Sawls and into the secret depths of their Caves.

The guardian frieze glared at him with unblinking obsidian eyes. He gave it a mocking salute and started up the inner stairs. To his disgust, a welcoming party awaited him at the top: two elderly women, bent and smiling, and a young man with a limp, well known to him by now, by name of Leb. Apparently, the fellow's leg had been crushed in a rockslide, so he supported himself with a knobby wooden cane. But Clausen noted that he moved with surprising agility when the need arose. He regarded the boy as his principal watchdog, and longed to kick away the cane to discover just how much of Leb it actually supported.

But he could not yet afford overt acts of hostility. He needed the Sawls' help to retrieve the Sled. He flexed his left hand once more and mounted the stone steps with a hearty greeting in the beginner's Sawlish that he'd finally decided it would be advantageous to acquire.

McPherson unloaded the last boulder into the appropriate pile. She slumped comically and let her tongue loll like a dog's. "Heavy sumbitch."

Beside their emptied two-cart, the three Food Guilders looked on with dubious curiosity.

"Thanks for the loan of the wagon." She did not add that it would have been even nicer if they'd offered to help shift the stones. She took a swig from her canteen and bent back to her task.

She hefted a square, flat rock and staggered gamely through the hot sun to an open area beside the Lander which she'd cleared of flood debris. Two neat circles of stakes stuck out of the ground like concentric teeth. McPherson set her rock down between the first pair of stakes. She stood back, satisfied with the fit, and went back for the next stone.

The three Sawls spread palms to one another. They pulled down the brims of their sun hats, reloaded their sacks of compost onto the cart and trundled off into the fields.

When she'd laid the first circle of stones, McPherson paused for breath, brushing sweat from her eyes. Her hair was quickly bleaching to near white from the constant sun, and her round face was turning golden brown. Danforth accused her of looking like a beach bum. McPherson, who'd met a beach once in her life, took this as a compliment.

She walked to the edge of the Lander's shade. "This is gonna work just fine, Commander."

Weng's charts rattled briefly as she leaned over to make a brief calculation on a crumpled data sheet. "Excellent news, Lieutenant."

"Next it's up into the nose to cannibalize the receivers and the beam converter." The wounded high-gain dish lay on its back, as useless as an upside-down tortoise. " 'Course, without the omni, we'll be in deep doo-doo if the Orbiter ain't still in geo-stat."

"She'll be there," Danforth rumbled from the depths of his own ruminations. "What, you think they'd go off joyriding?"

"Shit happens."

"Nah. Those guys'll be glued to their readouts till they hear from us again."

"Better be. I can get the angle pretty much right but this contraption won't have much of a search capability."

"You can adjust for signal strength once we pick up a trace."

"Calibration by rock," McPherson grumped as she headed back to the growing circle of stones.

"Captain Newman won't start worrying for another week or two," Weng observed. A top collar button unfastened was her only concession to the heat. She bent gracefully to a large transparent star chart that lay unrolled across a pair of waist-high crates. Sinuous red tracings wove like the parallel lines of a contour map around and among the dark blots of stars. Weng figured an angle, drew a faint slash tipped with a spidery arrow. She sat back, considering, then folded her pale hands across a stack of well-thumbed astronavigation manuals.

"Dr. Danforth," she began carefully. "Perhaps it is presumptuous of me, but I do wonder if enough weight has been given in our thinking to the astronomical situation of this system. I have been using the navigators' approach data to create a more complete and up-to-date map of this sector, and unless I am very much mistaken, the whole of Byrnham's Cluster is migrating slowly into the Coal Sack, in fact has been for some hundred-odd thousand years. It is even now approaching the regions of highest concentration of nebular materials."

Danforth looked up in wonder. This was the longest sustained sentence he'd heard out of Weng since boarding the *Hawking* as it looped past Centauri Gamma. He waited for her to make her point.

"Well, surely this could be expected to have some effect on the planet's climatic mechanisms?"

He nodded slowly. Usually, he'd have dismissed the idea as the red herring he was sure it was. But Weng had worked hard to derive it and he hadn't the heart left to dump on the woman, no matter that on the trip out and for the weeks after Landing, he'd welcomed each and every such chance. Must be the heat, sapping his resistance.

"It would affect the primary, over an enormous time scale," he temporized. "But it could hardly cause the freakish local variability we've observed planet-side. Unless . . ."

"Unless the primary itself has become variable," Weng finished for him.

Danforth rubbed his jaw thoughtfully. "Yah. Due to interaction with the increased concentrations of dust." He frowned. "No. Scale's still too big— maybe we'd see some effect over the course of several hundreds of days, but between one hour and the next? . . . Well, what the hell. Do we have any decent stellar output figures in that stuff you rescued?"

"Some." Weng fanned a stack of water-stained papers and spread them across the star chart. "For the twenty-two days of approach, between dropping out of jump and orbital insertion. The data since then are in CRI's files."

He saw she was not so pleased with this part of the evidence. "And . . . ?"

"The star's output seems steady over that period."

He shook his head. "With further data, we could tell better, but my guess is that collision with the Coal Sack will effect the situation only over a scale of tens of thousands of years. Let's agree, though, that the nebula is at least partly responsible for the current condition of the primary. If dust interaction is causing it to heat up, then the planet will also . . . well, we *can* be sure that the planet is not what it was before the collision began. Let me see the numbers on the dust concentration."

He stored the graphs he'd been toying with on his mini-terminal and did some hurried figuring. "It's little better than a guess when you have to do it practically by hand," he complained. "But following your first line of reasoning: before collision, the average planetary temperature could have been a nice comfy seventy degrees, probably fairly constant, due to the negligible axial tilt. A pretty nice place to live, in other words.

"Then, as the system rolls into the center of the nebula, the temps might be working themselves up to a potential average of one thirty to one fifty Fahrenheit, a not-so-nice place. All very interesting, but useless for the moment, since here we are, pretty much into the middle and the temps aren't even near those levels . . . though the probe data did lead me to expect at least one fifteen . . ." He gazed musingly at the screen. His own dilemma had resurfaced in Weng's figures. "This heat business, Weng . . . it *is* a fundamental conundrum. I tell you, there's heat missing from this system."

Weng's expression did not change. She traced a thin finger around the curlicues of braid on her white cuff and stubbornly pursued her own line of inquiry. "Accepting, then, that the Coal Sack has its effect only over the long run, would the climate here be expected to revert to normal once the passage through the nebula is complete?"

Danforth winced at the word "normal," which he'd recently exiled from his own vocabulary. He wondered what she was getting at. "Well, yes, if there's anything left of the atmosphere after another . . . how long did you figure?"

"Approximately eighty-five thousand years until the system exits the Coal Sack."

"Right. After eighty-five thousand years of heating and dust interaction . . . wait, come to think of it . . ." He slumped into his many pillows with a grimace. "A lot of my original assumptions about this star's evolution may be totally dog-faced if the nebula's interacting enough to make the star look older than it really is."

Weng was for once interested in the fate of planets. "Is the atmosphere really endangered?"

"Sure, if the star swells up enough."

"What has our average surface temperature been?"

"Hell, you're the one who's been reading the thermometer to me these days." Danforth was distracted by this new threat to his preliminary theorizing. "Locally, it's been around eighty degrees, but averages doesn't mean much when you leap from zero to seventy in an hour and a half, then back to forty in twenty minutes. Globally, it's been . . . Holy shit!" He sat up so suddenly that his chest wound protested with a lancing arc of fire that took his breath away.

Weng reached to steady him.

"No, I'm okay, I'm okay." He felt for his keypad, and though his face was tight with pain, he began tapping at it frantically. "Damn it, CRI, where are you when I need you!" He stared at the figures evolving on the screen. "*Global* averages, that's the key . . . well, I'll be . . . that heat's still here, all of it." He squinted out past the landing strut, through hard amber sunlight and dust, to the russet and gold wall of stalks and giant leaves ringing the clearing. "Somewhere."

Weng cleared her throat, prodding gently.

"I was stuck on the time averaging, the variability, but the *spatial* average is correct for the model!" Danforth hoisted a fist in emphasis until the pain stopped him. "I kept looking for the extra heat! But it's not missing. It's all here, only something's out there moving it around!"

Weng gazed at him in restrained surprise. "Something out there, Dr. Danforth?"

"I mean, some redistributing mechanism. The missing term to my equation, my X-factor." He glared at her to cover his embarrassment. "What'd you think I meant, some old guy with a wand?"

Weng pursed her lips noncommittally. "It strikes me that the Sawls would say very much the same thing: something's out there moving the weather around. But they've given that something names and personalities."

"Oh, no, you don't. Leave that goddess crap to Ibiá."

She let an impish smile surface. "My apologies, Dr. Danforth." She gathered up her lapful of papers. "I must concentrate now on extracting from the Master Healer's library a reasonable estimate of this civilization's age."

"You must?" Weng made the most bizarre connections sometimes, as if cause and effect followed different rules in her spacer's mind. But it was Danforth's new policy to remain open to every possibility, every path of inquiry.

"Well, just think," she replied. "If the collision with the Coal Sack has altered the planet's climate, imagine what it might have done to something as fragile as a human civilization on that planet. With worse to come, if the planet continues to heat up."

At the top of the steps, Clausen gave the old women his courtly half-bow. The ladies dipped their heads and giggled, rearranging the wrap of their shawls like young girls. The prospector inquired after their health in broken Sawlish and bent to admire the spotted eggs gathered in a basket on the stone floor. The young man Leb stood in the middle of the tunnel, leaning on his cane. He returned Clausen's smile pleasantly.

Chatting his way toward the limit of his language, Clausen backed up casually as if to include Leb within the circle of his attention. He draped his left arm genially around the boy's thin shoulders, palm down against the soft muscle behind the neck. Leb's shoulder twitched and his eyes flicked to Clausen, briefly puzzled. The prospector drew his arm away to accept the egg basket offering. Leb's knobby stick clattered to the floor. The boy sighed once, staggered to the wall, and collapsed. The women gasped and scurried to his aid. Clausen was beside them one minute, checking the boy's pulse. In the next, he was gone up the passageway, shouting back that he would bring help.

The steady clink of McPherson's wall building was as disrupting to Danforth's concentration as the heat. The reedy chanting from the fields was an annoying counterpoint: the home guard continuing its round-the-clock care of the precious food crops.

Muttering into the privacy of his pocket recorder, Danforth tried not to think about how much he would dearly love to be able to get up and pace about.

"Concentrating on the snow data. Normal circumstances that would give rise to such activity within the observed semi-equatorial band: One, winds blowing northeast to southwest and southwest to northeast, converging on the band. Two, strong heat flux away from the band. Three, strong moisture flux into the band.

"Now, at these low latitudes, we would expect the radiative heating of the surface, plus the small-scale dynamic heating of the atmosphere, to balance the large-scale dynamic cooling."

He let the recorder drop to his lap and sighed, rubbing his eyes. Sighing was not something Danforth had done much of in his life. Hopelessness had been alien until recently. He picked up the recorder with weary resolve.

"What we seem to have instead is strong radiative cooling plus large-scale dynamic cooling balancing the latent heating."

He paused again and let his attention wander, distracted by McPherson's bright shape moving about in the sun. The distant singing rose and fell. McPherson had achieved a fieldstone circle as high as her chest, offering a base for the high-gain antenna. She'd planned carefully: the wall tapered upward in neat overlapping tiers of pale, dusty rock. Danforth watched her set the first of the extra layers that would tilt the dish at its proper receiving angle. He admired her careful craftsmanship and the structure's apparent stability. He found her wisecracking persistence comforting. She was one of the things keeping him sane.

To the side of the clearing, several sun-hatted Food Guilders took a break from hauling water to observe the mysterious stone circle taking shape. They stood in the shade of their own tall crop, their chatter punctuated by the arm-waving, measuring gestures of a building crew assessing the problems of the site or the quality of a competitor's work.

McPherson's voice rang out. "Ain't you guys ever seen someone build a stone wall before?"

Danforth wrenched his attention back to his recording.

"In addition, the movement of the snow to the northeast, toward the great northern ocean, was observed throughout the entire band of activity. Thus, in relation to my X factor, we cannot assume spatial dependence only. Frontal movement indicates that the missing term is also time dependent, and is, we will assume for now, global in scale."

He took a breath and reached under his worktable to haul one useless leg into a more comfortable position. "Must-do's for when we finally get CRI back: detailed mapping of heat and water distributions, horizontal and vertical profiles." He touched the recorder to his lips pensively, then set it aside and lay back against his pillows.

"Right through the goddamn Coal Sack." Recalling the satirical doggerel that Clausen had used to wind him up those several weeks ago, Danforth closed his eyes and surrendered to his exhaustion and the heat.

Clausen jogged lightly through the stable caverns. He slowed at each turning or tunnel crossing, watching his footing carefully in the half-dark, hugging the walls, ready to leap back into shadow at the slightest sound.

He knew the layout of the stables. The Sawls had not bothered to curtail his explorations there. These caves, tall and wide, did not extend deeply into the rock. Clausen liked their smell of dry hay and manure, reminiscent of his own stable at home, the home he rarely saw. But he did not linger. He headed for the nearest ramp to the upper levels.

The ramp was empty, but pitch-dark. The pragmatic Sawls did not waste good lamp oil on unused corridors. The darkness heightened the sound of his own footsteps, even with the soft-soled shoes he had worn for stealth. He paused, weighing his minute flashbeam on his gloved palm along with the disadvantage of feeling his way in blackness versus that of giving his presence away with light. He stowed the beam in his pocket and put a hand to the wall, noting to himself that no deep-cave rock surface had a right to be so warm and dry.

Along the wide thoroughfare at the ramp top, one lamp in five had been left burning, their flames turned as low as possible. The rhythm of light and shadow was punctuated by the dark half-moon entrances to living enclaves. Farther on, the back entry to the Meeting Hall, impressive but again, familiar. Beyond that, more dwellings and other guildhall entries, Woodworkers' and Keth-Toph. Clausen had no fondness for wood or its related technologies, only for fine objects into which it had already been made, preferably long enough ago to add to the objects' value.

He glided to the right and slipped into the first tall archway he came to. He listened to the darkness, then palmed his light and nosed the beam around the room. Tall wooden rug looms lined the walls, each with its attendant well-worn bench and great wool skeins suspended above the frames like bunches of multicolored fruit. The storage racks for the finished rugs were picked clean but for one or two tightly bound rolls lingering like rejected suitors in the isolated upper reaches of the shelves. Not for the first time, he marveled at the apparently unsupported height and breadth of these inner caverns. But there was nothing for him here.

The prospector shrugged and turned down the outer corridor, dipping in and out of dwelling entries until he found what he had hoped for, a wider tunnel that did not dead-end in the usual trio or quartet of living caverns, but continued inward, sparsely lit but passable. Single-unit dwellings opened to either side. Bachelor quarters, he decided. His pace quickened. Unexplored territory at last, heading deeper into the rock.

He passed dwelling after dwelling, and side corridors and cul-de-sacs that led to multi-unit complexes. Ibiá was right after all: the Caves were like a small city. A good half mile of cliff face had been hollowed out into a giant apartment megalith. Even this deep inside, the air remained temperate and sweet-smelling. Clausen looked for vents and shaftways, and finding none, concluded from the constant slight draft against his face that the tunnels themselves comprised the ventilation system. From his first visit to the caves, he'd known what he'd not seen fit to pass on to his colleagues, particularly bleeding-heart Megan Levy: some of the tunnels were extremely ancient, easily tens of thousands of years old, yet none were natural formations. Clausen could not but respect the Sawls' determination, digging a city out of solid rock with what about amounted to their bare hands, due to the scarcity of proper tool-making metals. Idly, he speculated about the heights their civilization might have achieved, had they been gifted with the planetary resources he considered essential for bootstrapping a society out of its initial stone age.

A noise ahead alerted him. His inward-leading corridor ended at intersection with another, running perpendicular. Voices floated around the corner, raised in cheerful debate. Laughter was followed by a chorus of heavy groans, as if a weight was being lifted, unsuccessfully, for the groans broke off and the laughter increased. Clausen crept forward to peer around the corner. A large cart with a broken axle filled the passageway. Four sturdy Sawls milled about exchanging jocular repair suggestions. In the opposite direction, the intersecting tunnel ended after several hundred paces in a blank wall.

Clausen flattened against the rock, considering his next move. Almost simultaneously, he heard new voices approaching along his own corridor, and retreat became impossible. He swore softly, but rueful admiration curled his mouth. The Sawls had activated another of their seemingly endless repertoire of defense strategies. He eyed the unlit doorway of the nearest dwelling, but found that option unsatisfying. If discovered in hiding, his hand would be forced, and he was not yet ready for open warfare. He had yet to assure himself of allies among his own party.

Quickly, he stripped off the fingerless gloves, disengaged the tiny mechanism, then slid the needle and its heavy dose of tranquilizer into a slot in the butt of his laser pistol. He folded the gloves around the little gun and shoved the wad into his deepest pocket. He took what satisfaction he could from having gotten farther in this time than ever before. Then, laying on an expression of urgency, he launched himself into the open, calling for help.

51

E.D. 73–10:00

USANNAH DREW HER ANGER up around her like a wall. During the next throw, she adopted Ghirra's habit of walking silence. At mealtimes, she buried herself in notetaking, ate mechanically and withdrew into sleep as soon as the cleanup duties were done, or went off to other wagons to gather information for her population survey. She let observation become her obsession, as if a conscious retreat into empirical practice could save her from messier, more subjective considerations.

Was it not selfish for Stavros to make love to her when he knew he'd be leaving so abruptly? This wasn't love, it was lust. Still, he'd guessed right: if she'd known of his plan, she would have tried to talk him out of it. But her "determined neutrality," as Megan called it, was not prudishness. It was a learned defense against the same impulsive streak that had catapulted her into the sun after the snows, and nearly cost her life—as well as Liphar's. As she mistrusted this tendency in herself, she mistrusted it in others. Now she was angry at having been being dragged into a dangerous scheme she was not sure she approved of.

Megan watched and worried and speculated, spending time that should have gone into her own notes and observations. Ghirra left Susannah alone, waiting for her to come to terms with the situation and with herself.

Meanwhile, the landscape blossomed. The rapid growth cycle progressed into full flower. The roadside was a riot of color. Tender shoots and leaves broadened and thickened, soaking in and storing the now abundant water.

In the east loomed the Talche, oddly rounded little mountains with a friendly aspect, like ranks of golden buttocks. The dairy herd had turned aside midway in the third throw to climb the curvaceous grassy slopes into the lush foothills. Several senior herdsmen remained with the caravan, shepherding two dozen prize heifers to be bred in Ogo Dul. But relieved of the drag of five hundred ambling, loquacious beasts, the caravan made better progress, accomplishing for the first time the full twenty kilometers per throw that the term implied.

A contingent of rangers and two teams of hjalk went with the herd, to guard the placid dairy animals from the increasingly active wildlife on the road to their new pastures. Afterward, they'd return to Dul Elesi for the salvage of the Sled. As Megan explained it, while Susannah tried not to listen, the rangers would arrive at Dul Elesi about the time that Stavros and Liphar reached the site of the wreck, allowing the conspirators time for their own secret salvage project, while providing the help Clausen demanded.

The caravan followed a rough track winding among the crotches of the amber foothills. A stream accompanied them, lined with lithe river grasses. The wagons splashed across many clear, shallow rivulets rushing down from the hills to throw themselves into the silty, slower-moving water. Susannah saw entire herds of the shy tortoiselike creatures, and amphibious lizards cavorted like otters in the brown water. More than once, she spotted huge, spiked, toadish beasts that fired off basilisk glares at the human intruders from the safety of midstream boulders. They did not attack, but they did seem to be waiting for an excuse.

As well as shooting up and bursting into bloom, the flora diversified geometrically in the wetter foothills. Susannah did not have to pretend to be busy with her notebook and sample case, though sampling became increasingly difficult as the plants' natural defenses improved along with the growing conditions. The squat clusters of bristles that had dotted the Dop Arek grew into clumps of tall yellow swords, triangular and barbed in bright red, as thick as a man's thigh. The desert brush enlarged into misshapen trees, stubby trunks caught in a mare's nest of tubular branches that twisted and curved back on each other. The branches were jointed like fingers, brittle looking but resistant to every blade except Ghirra's obsidian flake scalpel.

Deeper into the hills, the air smelled sweet and damp. The cart track narrowed where huge trees reclined along the stream as if blown over at an earlier time, and content to take life lying down. They sent up rows of frail shoots like soldiers at attention along their fallen trunks. Tall, waving stands of amber-plumed succulents uncurled fernlike in the shallows, offering the travelers a feathery but welcome shade. Tangled root systems fringed the riverbank, competing for space with the razor-edged grasses and spreads of fleshy ground cover. Broad orange pads armed with crimson thorns sprouted lemon-colored blossoms iced with pollen, delicious looking, but apparently deadly.

Ghirra's insistence kept Susannah to the path. Beady eyes in the underbrush followed her movements along the verge. Shiny red leaves as big as dinner plates shuddered to the passage of heavy reptilian bodies beneath. Later, she would have to risk trapping a sample population of wild creatures, but now, for the Master Healer's peace of mind, she would concentrate on the flora. Her pique with Megan and Stavros did not extend to Ghirra. She could hardly expect him to be objective about the fate of his own planet.

During the fourth throw, the meandering stream showed a few stony rapids. The hillsides steepened. Craggy rock broke through the yellow topsoil, and the gentle river glen roughened into a deep gorge. The wagon wheels clattered over exposed stone ledges, descending with the river toward the northeastern reaches of the Dop Arek. Stretches of the pinkish plain below appeared in brief vistas over the canyon's crumbling rim, through gaps choked with soaring amber plumage.

Picking her way along the rocky path behind Ghirra, Megan noted an unusual restlessness in the Master Healer's gait—as if he was searching for something.

The air hung heavy and still, sluggish with moisture. Megan's trail clothes clung like a binding second skin. Ampiar plied her brakes skillfully, but the hjalk snorted and shook their manes, bracing their fleshy feet against the slanting ledges, shivering against the press of the wagon behind. Ghirra's restlessness was evidently shared. Xifa sent Phea and Dwingen to crowd behind the driver's seat, then walked beside the lead team of hjalk, soothing and petting them. Megan was unsurprised when several Priest Guild apprentices went running past, their high, urgent voices overlapping as they announced a weather alert.

Ghirra counted heads and called Susannah back to the wagon. Up and down the line, guildsmen checked the fastenings of harness and canopy stays, and watched the sky. Conversation swelled as wagering and debate spread from wagon to wagon.

"A little rain might be nice," Megan remarked as Susannah drew up breathless, stuffing her notebook and samples into her field pack.

"I don't know." Susannah peered at the still-cloudless green sky, and around the enclosing walls of the gorge. Her sullenness sank into something grimmer. "Not a good place to be. Flash floods nearly got me once before."

Aguidran apparently had the same thought. On the heels of the Priest Guild alert, a phalanx of rangers raced by, urging the drivers and the teams to maximum speed. Passengers piled out of the wagons to lighten the loads. The strongest lent their backs to push or pull. The brittle rock was treacherous underfoot. Thorny vegetation poked through the cracks to snatch at pant legs and the curly fetlocks of the hjalk. The beasts bent their broad high shoulders into the harness to haul valiantly against the stubborn drag of brush-bound wheels.

The clouds appeared suddenly. The hot sunlight flickered and dimmed. Fat cushions of mist with ominous mouse-colored bellies gathered overhead, jostling about like an expectant crowd.

Megan regarded them darkly. "Valla's army awaits her orders."

The Master Ranger halted the caravan and ordered the wagons drawn up against the side of the gorge farthest from the riverbed, where ledges and high piles of rock offered some shelter and escape. Rope coils sprouted like a plague of snakes as wagons and carts were lashed to everything available: rock, dead tree stumps, the rigid sword plants, anything solid enough to hold a line.

Aguidran appeared in person to direct the Infirmary wagon onto a stretch of particularly high ground, helping her brother to fasten it down as best they could. Ghirra sent Megan and his four apprentices to climb the rocks in search of a safe niche to ride out the approaching storm.

Megan did not argue. "I'm not so quick on my feet as you."

Susannah elected to stay on the canyon floor with the wagon and the others.

The clouds closed ranks abruptly, shutting out the sun. The ocher walls of the gorge darkened to dull shadow brown. Megan pulled herself onto a perch at the top of a rockslide. Xifa and Ampiar busied themselves in the rear of the wagon, checking the accessibility of supplies. Susannah stood with Ghirra as he soothed the anxious hjalk.

Silence settled over the gorge. No wind or thunder threatened. Ghirra stared at the leaden brown sky, his mouth set, his long fingers tapping a quick rhythm against his thigh. Megan could see him clearly from her perch. He looked not scared, but angry.

The first drops fell, huge and scattered, shooting up puffs of dust as they hit the dry rock. The ground was hardly wet when Megan was slammed back against a boulder by a sudden jarring of the air, like the shock wave from an explosion.

A spasm of cold turned the rime of dust and humidity on her skin to a chill sweat. The giant raindrops froze midair into a thunderous clattering of hail.

Below in the gorge, a mad scramble for shelter ensued. Many flattened themselves into the lee of the cliff or crowded beneath the overhanging ledges. Others dove under the wagons. The hjalk dropped their heads, skittering and wailing, unable to escape the merciless pounding of the ice.

Megan struggled further up her rockslide to curl into a ball beneath the brush clinging to the wall. The branches broke the fall of hail on her upper body, but left no protection for her legs. The ice balls were as big as eggs and hit with the force of a stone flung from the top of the gorge. Megan turned her face into the wall as a chorus of pain and confusion rose around her.

Strong hands pulled at her roughly. A wiry ranger, her hard-brimmed hat deflecting the hail, dragged Megan from her perch and hauled her down the rockslide through the battering of ice. She was shoved under the belly of the medical wagon, where Susannah huddled with the others.

Xifa passed over a blanket, easing Megan's shock with warm hands as she shivered in relief. The hail roared down around them, filling the cracks between the rocks, piling up in the gullies, bouncing and rolling beneath the wagon in chill cascades. Thick clots of ground fog congealed above the ice and spread to isolate each wagon in a blind cloud of mist and noise. Through the din came the sound of shredding wagon canopies and the squealing of the hjalk.

Megan did not see Ghirra anywhere. Beyond the sheltering curve of the wheel, the booted calves of the rangers and some brave bare legs raced among the tethered wagons, releasing the beasts from the prison of their harness. Their own four hjalk broke away one by one as their straps and buckles were loosed. When the last had bolted off, moaning in terror, Ghirra ducked and skidded under the wagon to hunch beside the left front wheel. His usually serene face was dark with outrage, as if he saw in the hailstorm not just ill luck or the vagaries of a capricious climate, but a genuine maliciousness, directed at innocents.

Megan was distracted from her own pain. She'd thought stoic resignation to be the typical Sawl attitude toward the lethal weather, the classic victim's acceptance of his lot. But Ghirra's rage was anything but accepting. She recalled then that his parents had died in a storm-triggered mudslide on a similar trading trip long ago. Unlikely that she'd hear him praising the sister-goddesses any time soon.

The wagon vibrated with the drumming of the hail. The still-warm ground ran with meltwater and grainy slush. A cold mist wrapped the canyon in a smoky shroud.

And then the roaring abruptly ceased. The silence left in its wake was almost as painful as the noise. A gust of wind swept through the gorge, stirring the fog into spiraling tendrils. The sky lightened.

The wail of a child broke the silence. Ghirra levered his lean body from under the wagon, squinted at the thinning clouds, listened for the all-clear signal. Xifa and Ampiar tumbled out after him to unpack the medical supplies. The four apprentices climbed down from their shelter, wide-eyed, checking each other for bruises and scrapes. Hjalk wandered dazed among the wagons. Rangers came and went, relaying damage and injury reports, their boot heels rattling the scattered ice like dice in a cup.

The sun shone hot again. Steam rose from the melting hail. Megan remembered the mist burning off a summer dawn on Lan Le, the world of the Min Kodeh, and wished for something as peaceable. The faint breeze was fresher and drier than it had been before the storm. Bringing a load of bandages from the wagon, Xifa paused, sniffed the air, then shook her head worriedly and went back for another load.

Susannah treated minor injuries for many hours without a break. Few had escaped some light cuts and scrapes in that first mad scramble for safety, and there was a lot of serious bruising from the hail. Ghirra set one broken arm and calmed the terrors of several messy broken noses, stroking them back into place like a sculptor working clay. Susannah and Ampiar wrapped sprains and swabbed and poulticed and bandaged wounds, while Megan and the apprentices tended the fires, and Xifa brewed and dispensed herbal painkillers and calmatives.

The material cost was higher. With the exception of the Infirmary wagon and the Food Guild's hard-topped giants, hardly a wagon was left with its canopy intact. Some, with tough double layers or a wicker under-structure, had suffered minor puncturing. The worst were totally shredded, and the goods inside battered by the ice.

The Potter guildsmen muttered and swore as they dug out the shards of countless jugs and bowls that had been packed uncrated to fill the excess spaces in their wagons. The Glassblowers gathered silently around the second of their three blue-painted wagons, afraid to look beneath the crumpled heap of torn, ice-damp canvas. Megan's friend Tyril claimed the Glassblowers of Dul Elesi were the finest of all the nearby settlements and a prime attraction at the Ogo Dul market. They'd show little profit this trip.

But the real victims of the hail were the animals. The hakra, being lithe and quick-minded, had generally taken care of themselves. More than one frightened Sawl had shared his shelter with a small, insistent beast. The little group of prize hekkers had their frantic herdsmen to search out trees or overhangs for their protection, and keep them from mindless panic.

The big hjalk had suffered greatly. They stood about on splayed legs, stunned and swaying. Ghirra set Dwingen to ferrying pots of infusion to the anxious herdsmen, to sponge the blood from the beasts' golden coats. Several of the older hjalk had been driven to their knees by the ice. They lay moaning while their drivers washed and petted them and tried to coax them to their feet.

Swabbing grit from her hundredth nasty scrape, Susannah found herself in tears. She was too busy to wonder much at this uncharacteristic display. She continued her cleaning and binding while the tears ran unchecked down her cheeks. She took comfort from the fact that she was not alone. The tears of the many hurt and confused let Susannah's go unremarked, except by Ghirra, who watched her covertly as he worked at her side.

When the line of injured had thinned at last, and the apprentices could give their attention to repacking the wagon, Aguidran appeared to ask her brother's advice in the case of a hjalk that had broken a leg in a frenzied attempt to climb the canyon wall.

Ghirra crouched beside a weeping little boy, bandaging his thorn-ripped arm, softly talking him into a smile. When Aguidran touched his shoulder, he barely raised his eyes. He asked a few murmured questions, then shook his head and went on with his work.

Aguidran's mouth tightened. She bent to her boot and drew out a razor-edged, eight-inch sliver of metal, mounted in a handle of age-dark bone. The blade was nearly two inches wide at the handle, narrowing toward the tip and wafer thin along the cutting edge from generations of sharpenings. It glittered darkly in the returned sunlight, a tapestry of ancient etch-marks and scourings. The butt of the handle bore the carved hallmark of the Ranger Guild.

The drawing of the shining metal caught everyone's attention, those who saw it and those others who heard the collective intake of breath. The child in Ghirra's arms shrank against him at the sight of it. Aguidran herself regarded it with respect tinged with distaste, though it rested in her hand with the ease of long familiarity.

None of the life-threatening events she'd experienced so far aroused Susannah's sense of mortality as profoundly as Aguidran's knife. It was the longest blade she'd seen on Fiix, and the first true weapon. Its impractical length, its slim profile, its demon edge, all declared without apology that it had been forged for one purpose alone, the taking of a life. Its efficiency and sophistication invoked a sudden vision of Emil Clausen.

"Ghirra, wait . . ." Susannah fumbled at the bottom of her medikit, dug out a syringe and laid it in his hand. Ghirra frowned at it. He knew its workings. She had schooled him in its use.

Aguidran shifted, gently slapping the long blade against her thigh.

Ghirra closed his fingers around the syringe, then handed it back. He nodded to Aguidran, who strode off down the line of wagons. A crowd had gathered around the stricken hjalk. As Aguidran shouldered her way through, a mournful chant was begun and soon spread along the entire caravan.

Susannah watched the Ranger kneel, then turned her head away, tears flowing again unbidden. The hjalk would not suffer, there would be meat at supper, nothing would go to waste, but still . . .

Ghirra said gravely, "The killing must not be ever easy."

"It should not, it should not," she agreed, shaking her head and weeping. She pictured Stavros caught in the sights of Clausen's gun. "But for some, it always will be."

52

HIS EYES WERE OPEN and alert to the pounding hail, but his mind dreamed of holding her in his arms. His empty hands remembered the pale silk of her skin. The pain he felt was physical. He could lay his palm against the place where it lived, deep in the soft tissue between heart and groin. But it was a different pain—his palms' faint, insistent heat—whose summons he must follow.

"Ibi." Liphar touched his knee gently.

"I know. It's time."

They crawled from under the low-hanging ledge, dusting dirt and crumbling twigs from their hair and clothing. Hailstones glistened like pearls on the wet, battered grass. Steam misted the landscape with a golden haze as the sun renewed its hot glare. Stavros found the mixed signals of debilitating summer heat and autumn-colored flora to be subtly disturbing to his body chemistry. But there were no seasons on Fiix, only weather.

Their young guide adjusted her pack and pointed across the brush-choked gully, where ground fog obscured their path. Edan was the Master Ranger's favorite protégée, as thin, hard and energetic as Aguidran herself, but with an overbearing arrogance that Aguidran had mastered long ago. She was a thorny companion but worth it, for the wild explosion of plant growth had, to Stavros' untrained eye, rendered Aguidran's map irrelevant. Despite all, Edan had found the Sled, the proverbial needle in the wilderness haystack. She'd kept them alive as well, the two tenderfoot adventurers, a University-bred offworlder and a skittish apprentice priest. Stavros was not sure which task had required the greater effort.

He squinted at the steep slope ahead as it faded in and out of the shifting fog. He'd sighted the Sled just before the hail, a bright sun-glint on a patch of white amid the tangles of reddish vegetation. The downed craft lay on its belly at the edge of a plateau backed by the northernmost scarps of the rugged Grigar, "Lagri's Wall." It was impossible from this distance to judge its condition, but probably the hail hadn't done it any good. Stavros hoped the super-hardened plastic bubble over the communications equipment had withstood the bombardment.

Edan and Liphar were not happy about the hail either. While the young ranger strode ahead into the waist-high fog to scout out the trail, Liphar studied the skies with genuine anxiety and a tinge of priestly officiousness. He muttered to himself about this sign and that, long after Stavros stopped listening. He worried the blue talisman bead on his wrist until his telling of its obscure rosary was no more than a reflex.

His complaint with the hail, Stavros finally understood, was not its abrupt violence and peril, but its size and abnormality. Normal, Liphar explained, for the current point in the Sisters' conflict, would be Valla Ired feinting with quick, light thrusts of rain, a mere flexing of muscles, good for the crops back home in Dul Elesi but not threatening enough to entice Lagri from the rest period gained by her recent successful skirmish.

Except Lagri was not resting. Instead, she had staged a vicious counterattack. Liphar sifted a handful of ice through his fingers to illustrate how Valla's soldiers froze in terror as they fell, and thus brought hurt to the ground, instead of moisture.

Edan called to them, impatient, already halfway down the slope. Liphar shouldered his pack resignedly and crunched away through the rising patches of steam and the melting hailstones to descend the brittle ledges of the fog-bottomed gully.

Stavros followed, adding Liphar's worries to the long list jostling around in his head. He'd done a lot of thinking since leaving Susannah asleep in the yellow grasses, a lot of thinking while they searched for the wrecked Sled. Walking away from the woman he'd just won had been hard, but as he lost himself in an alien wilderness with aliens his only company, he had the distinct sensation of relaxing into the arms of his destiny.

He meant nothing predetermined, nothing so melodramatic. Stavros did not believe in fate. But he did believe that for each individual, there is a given path. Such life courses are never obvious, but for the lucky few who stumble upon theirs by accident, there's no refusing it. And so, it becomes a kind of destiny.

What shape that destiny was to take, he wasn't sure. Part of it was to foil Clausen's claim and part was his promise to the Master Healer to discover the true nature of the sister-goddesses. And there was more, unknown as yet, or unrecognized, because at the center of the mystery sat the Ritual Master, Kav Daven, and the miracle of the guar.

As he had many times since the Leave-taking, Stavros replayed his miracle, while crashing along the bottom of the fog-wrapped gully. Though he was clawed by fang-sized thorns and tripped by tangled roots and undergrowth, the memory was as vivid, as present, as if it had happened moments before. He felt again the corrosive guar, the pure lithium from the bedrock. He suffered the agony of seared flesh and a lingering touch of the inexplicable Presence. He stared, again, at inexplicably unblemished skin.

Stavros had learned not to trust the evidence of his senses, which were so often too willing to be ruled by his imagination. True, such pain without mark or damage was strong evidence for mysticism. He could accept the miracle as proof of the goddesses' omnipotence. Or he could share Ghirra's conviction, that Kav Daven had played a very public trick, for some mysterious reason of his own.

Instead, he explored a third avenue: if something other than a freakish nature was at work in the Fiixian atmosphere, with the power of a god if not a god, could it be reasoned with? Had Kav Daven's ephemeral magic, the pure intensity of his faith, somehow touched this realm of Power when he danced the Tale of Origins or later at the Leave-taking—enough to shift the balance of strength from one Sister to another? Had Stavros himself, with the guar-fire searing his hands, felt that Power sing through him?

He stumbled, caught himself on an overhanging branch, jerked away a lacerated palm. The thick orange branch was armed with rows of needle teeth. Stavros saw his own bright blood well up from parallel punctures, already swelling and reddening. What the guar had not harmed, a simple plant had shredded with ease. He could only laugh.

A proper warning. He recalled the cold shock of Clausen's pistol against his skin. It could be fatal to exaggerate the import of his "miracle," even while the ghostly fire burned in his palms. Just imagine the recklessness it might inspire, should he take on delusions of immortality.

And he must remember what was really at stake. The deity of the goddesses, though an intriguing philosophical question, was not what mattered. Their *actuality* did. Science or magic, they must be proved to exist, to be real, in whatever form. Only then could they be used as an argument against the commercial development of the planet.

Liphar fussed over his bloodied hand. Edan trudged back through the brush to give it a quick glance, then waved them onward. She had nosed out a rocky access to the plateau using the scar of an old landslide, where the spiked and knife-edged vegetation found less encouragement to grow. They struggled upward with hands and knees as well as feet. Stavros left a trail of bloodstained boulders in his wake.

At the top, he sluiced water from his canteen across his palm and bound it with a strip of linen from one of Liphar's many pockets. The fog had dispersed, the hailstones melted into the spongy ground. Edan waded into the dense growth enveloping the Sled, and Stavros followed, wishing for a machete.

Even close up, it was impossible to assess the flier's true condition. Broad-leafed vines already obscured most of the delta-winged body, insinuating fuzzy tendrils across the crumpled nose. The cockpit had been neatly secured with a tarp, covering the seats and control panel: Clausen's precaution, which Stavros grudgingly admired. The open cargo hold showed signs of habitation, more tarps, some clothing hastily tossed inside. Beneath the tilting wing, the damp ground was still barren, packed down from the weight of bodies seeking shelter from the storm. Stavros crouched and peered into the pocket of dank shadow, imagining them stuck there together, Clausen agile and restless, Danforth crippled, fevered, eventually delirious.

He straightened with a shudder, and pushed through the grasping vines to the rear of the sled. The bent tail fin poked up through a tangle of prickers, looking much as Aguidran had drawn it. High on the upper curve of the hail-scarred hull was the transparent blister housing a high-gain grid, built to receive both the operating power beam transmitted from the Orbiter, and high data rate com for navigation. It could be removed in pieces but was too bulky to carry and more trouble to repair. Tucked along one side of the blister, however, was a slim metal fin: the omni-directional antenna, his potential link to CRI, to the legal files stored in her memory, and eventually, to the authorities back home.

Though his instinct was to call CRI immediately, his faith in McPherson's ingenuity stayed his hand. If she or Clausen had managed to fix the antenna at the Lander and were in contact with CRI already, the computer would give away both his position and his purpose before he had time to accomplish it.

He must do his salvage hastily and be away from the site by the time Clausen returned with the rangers to haul the Sled back to base.

He set his pack down on the hull. The omni's electronics were inside the blister. He would need the whole assembly. He had purloined a few items before he'd left with the caravan, the appropriate tools from the Lander's general repair kit. He'd taken a few other precautions as well, ones which would make him unpopular with the remaining crew of the Lander, even more so than he was already.

He beckoned to Liphar, his extra, clever pair of hands, then drew out his tools and set to work.

53

E.D. 74–23:10

WENG STOOD VIGIL at the edge of the clearing, in mute sympathy for the handful of Sawls striving to restore order to their battered fields. Sadly, the fastest growing of the plantings were the most damaged by the hail. The younger shoots were already drawing themselves upright on their own, but those closer to harvest were more brittle. The workers were splinting weakened and bent stalks, but entire rows had been snapped clean in two. The broad leaves hung limp on their stems like red-gold lace. In the terraces, the succulents wept from fist-sized punctures, their precious juices evaporating into the building heat.

The Sawls sang softly as they worked, and Weng's faint nods acknowledged the rhythm. Her family hadn't seen the inside of a planted field for many generations, but a lingering farmer's instinct had her debating an offer of assistance.

The drumming of hail on the Lander's hull had woken them out of restless, heat-drenched sleep. On the far side of the clearing, McPherson yanked the silver-film off the high-gain dish, cursing the damage sustained before she'd gathered her wits enough to race out and cover it.

Clausen joined her. "How'd she do?"

"Mother Nature sure ain't giving us much of a break." McPherson folded the tarp and tossed it to the ground. "Holes here and there. Could be worse, I guess. Could be like that." She jerked her thumb at the fields.

Clausen took in the frenzied activity as if he hadn't noticed it before. "Yes, I suppose this might seriously cut into their food supply."

"And ours, if we can't ever get ourselves outa here!"

"Tut, McP. Of course we'll get out of here." He checked his watch and then the sun, now beginning its low drift toward the horizon. "Our salvage help should have been here by now. Ibiá better be dealing straight with me on this."

"The storm could've held them up."

"Hail is a local phenomenon, McP. You spend too much time off planet."

"You're talking Earth standard. Who knows what it is here?" McPherson squinted across the damaged fields. "I was hoping some of those farmer guys would help me lift this thing into place. But I can't ask them now. I'll search up the cable we need first."

Up in the Black Hole, McPherson searched through the supplies not yet hauled down to the Lander. She found clothing, utensils, medicine, and some packaged food. She stumbled over the edge of the sleeping platform and smashed a small Sawl oil lamp to smithereens. She located the utility racks that had held the backup computer and electronics, the extra relays and several reels of cable. The racks were empty.

Puzzled, she flashed her battery lamp around the cavern. She knew there had been equipment left after Stavros brought down a load for Danforth's use. She sucked her cheek. Could he have taken it all down and stowed it in the Lander's upper levels while she was distracted with the dish? Possible, but unlikely.

She let the lamp beam droop. Without relays or cable, all her efforts to repair the dish would be useless. The power and com links would remain severed. There would be no words of reassurance from the Orbiter, no force field to restore climate control to the Underbelly, no hot water . . .

She fought an upwelling of dismay. "Emil'll kill me."

Worst of all, Danforth would get angrier and more depressed, as he did each day of no new data coming in, no master computer to help solve his mysteries.

She left the cave resignedly and went down to search the Lander.

*   *   *

"Sixteen feet?" said Clausen later. "That's all you could find?"

"Yah. Without relays, we need at least a hundred." McPherson planted her hands on her hips in unconscious imitation of the prospector's stance. "You think the Sawls might've taken the stuff?"

"What would they do with it, eat it?" Clausen's eyes narrowed as he contemplated mayhem. "No, I'd say this is Ibiá up to his tricks again."

"Why him?"

"You tell me, McP., you tell me." He regarded her owlishly. "But then, you're fortunate enough not to be afflicted with that particular sickness." When she gazed at him blankly, he chuckled. "The disease of idealism, McP."

"Oh. No, I guess not." McPherson frowned gently.

Clausen pondered for a moment, then shut his eyes convulsively. "That's it! The sled! The antennas on the Sled!"

Already moving, he grabbed her arm. McPherson held back against his sudden ferocity but he jerked her forward. "To hell with our native guides! We're wasting daylight. Round up your gear. We'll find the fucking Sled without them!"

54

E.D. 76–13:19

WITHIN A DAY'S JOURNEY to Dul Elesi, distinct trail signs had reappeared, old cairns and ranger blazes chipped into the sides of boulders. They'd been pushing hard. Stavros made Edan turn aside, to lead them across a stony rise where the harder surface would hide their tracks. The young ranger's sharp face was shadowed into obscurity by her wide-brimmed hat. She grumbled because it was her nature, but agreed that an unused route would be advisable.

Stavros squinted down the trail behind them. "I'd hate to run into them on their way out here to pick up the Sled. Clausen's sure to be with them."

Liphar nodded dutifully, absorbed in his own concerns.

The nearness of their goal renewed Stavros' flagging optimism. "Don't worry that hail to death, Lifa. We haven't seen a cloud in two whole cycles."

But the hail had upset Liphar badly. He used every excuse to point out that the heat was increasing steadily, even as the afternoon sun reddened and sank between the teeth of the mountains. He straggled along at the rear, his eyes on the salmon-stained sky, muttering and stumbling until Edan threatened to abandon him in the wilderness if he did not watch where he was going. Stavros silenced her with a rare stern glance. Though Liphar's unrelenting caution was exhausting, he was trained in the details of weather prediction. Stavros lent at least half an ear to his mumblings and insisted that Edan do likewise, as well as keep her sharper ranger's eyes open for the signs of a change.

As they trudged among the rocks and brambles, Stavros tried to pin Liphar to a specific prediction. But he tended to lapse into abstraction and priestly hyperbole when approaching the subject of the weather. He quoted the Priest Guild records and unraveled long histories, couched in the archaic language of the tale chants. Hearing the Old Words only made Stavros think of Kav Daven and the questions he longed to ask the old priest.

Meanwhile, Liphar muttered about impending Devastation. The signs were right, he said, as recorded in the oldest books. During the flood, he had feared a final victory for Valla. Now the building heat had him worried about Lagri's domination.

Stavros used the time to probe the specifics of the myth. If the sister-deities were actual physical beings—and Ghirra and the priests did agree on this point—then they must have shapes, sizes, places to live. Liphar's chants and legends were colorful but hopelessly metaphorical on the first two counts— Lagri was as tall as the mountains, Valla's veins ran with icy sea water. Lagri's voice was the desert wind. Valla Ired's white hair trailed for a hundred throws along the sea bottom. Stavros took it all with a grain of salt.

But oddly enough, the chants and songs and records were unanimous and clear on the issue of habitation. Lagri dwelled in a high-walled palace of rock that dominated the very heart of the southern desert, far beyond the three ranges of the Grigar. There, her sun fires burned perpetually and nothing mortal lived.

On request, Liphar recited the tale chant of the Building, when Lagri's parent sent a stupendous bolt to thrust up the desert rock. The rubble fell back to earth as a magnificent cave complex, vaster than a thousand settlements, with endlessly intertwining corridors and the finest carving, and great halls so high that the night lanterns drifted through the clerestories to light the goddess' solitary banquets, leaving the surrounding desert in darkness.

Valla, on the other hand, inhabited the bottom of the great northern ocean, called Dul Valla in her honor. This wonderful home was also created for her by the mysterious unnamed parent, in the same mighty gesture that housed her sister. Valla's halls were jewel-encrusted, and the giant barbed fishes kept watch when she went out to war with her sibling.

The desert and the ocean. Interesting. Stavros rappelled down the sheer face of a boulder, nearly losing his grip on the rope. Edan waited at the bottom, coiling her own rope and Liphar's, impatient to move on. It shouldn't be hard to check up on. He could have CRI search the remote sensing data, see if anything shows up in either of those places. Something concrete, something *real*.

At last, the bulbous spire of the Red Pawn appeared above the hillocks and rockslides. The travelers came down out of the mountains onto a stony plateau whose gradual slope fell away to form Dul Elesi's cliff. The plateau supported a rich garden of cacti and gorse, nothing tall enough to hide a man. But along the rubbled southern border was a scattering of hidden tunnels, entrances to the cave complex below and known only to the Ranger Guild, secrets passed down the generations as closely guarded guild lore.

Edan led them to a nearly invisible cleft masked by a jumbled rockfall and boasting the additional camouflage of a thicket of sword plants and brush. Though invisible from the cliff top, the site afforded a panoramic view. Handy, Stavros reflected, that a position advantageous for observing the weather served to detect approaching enemies of another sort as well.

He dug his small battery lamp from his pack and showed Edan how to use it. She rewarded him with a brief, delighted grin. He squeezed after her into the narrow cleft, realizing once he was in its cooler shadow how oppressive the heat outside had really become. He longed to linger in the relief, but the tunnel was too confined even to crouch. After hairpin right and left turns, it appeared to dead-end in a confusion of crevasses and burrowings.

Edan flashed the lamp around, enjoying the tight, directable focus of its beam. She let it linger on a random crevice, then twisted, inserted herself sideways into the wrinkled rock and vanished. Darkness descended. Stavros felt Liphar tug at the straps of his pack, urging it off his back, pulling him toward the wall. Then the pack was gone, Liphar's hands were gone, and Liphar's thin voice was calling him through the invisible crack.

Stavros turned sideways in the darkness and eased his body into the tiny crevice. Rough rock embraced him front and back. With his head askew, his chest presented the broadest obstacle to passage. Momentarily, he knew the horror of being pinned for life by the weight of a mountain. Then with a final skin-scraping wrench, he was delivered into the inner tunnel.

Liphar collapsed against a wall, mopping his sweat-drenched face with the hem of his tunic. Edan lowered herself to the floor in what passed for a willingness to rest.

Stavros crouched with his head sunk between his shoulders like a tired horse. But he could not sit idle for long. He stood wearily, orienting himself, then padded down the corridor to reach into a high niche in the wall. He hauled out a thick coil of cable, stashed there by ranger allies after the caravan left. Reclaiming his pack and lamp, he sat down on the stone floor to refit the whip antenna of the Sled's omni to a scavenged mount. With the antenna in hand, he squeezed back through the entry crevice, dragging cable behind him to the outer entrance. Outside in the heat again, he scaled the rockfall, careful to keep out of the line of sight from the cliff top. He tied the antenna in a high clump of brush, buried the cable with stones and dirt, and retreated into hiding.

He told Liphar and Edan they could go on to their home caves to clean up and rest, as long as they kept out of sight. Liphar looked hurt and Edan's sour smirk suggested that her guild master would have her head for dereliction of duty if she left him unchapperoned. Stavros was relieved. He had not relished the prospect of sudden solitude. He grinned at them, gathering the last dregs of his energy, hooked the cable coil over his shoulder, and headed down the tunnel, reeling out the line as he went. The two Sawls levered themselves to their feet and followed.

The passage was straight, low, and narrow. No concessions had been made to aesthetics in these secret diggings. The rock remained as ragged as the excavators had left it, many ages ago, though the tunnel widened at intervals into larger chambers as if to relieve the claustrophobia of too-long travel through a constricting tube of stone.

The coil of cable lightened rapidly. It had nearly played out when the tunnel widened once again. Here, instead of a single chamber, there were several, opening off a central hall. Stavros paused at a left-hand archway to let Edan go ahead of him with the lamp.

His equipment waited as he'd left it, a week before, set up on a wooden Sawl table, ready to go as soon as he made up the cables. He sent Liphar around the low, domed room to light oil lamps. A bedroll was revealed, a rough fire pit in one corner, stoneware jugs filled with water, boxes of pur-loined ship's rations, tools, utensils, clothing.

He was shaken by the sight of all the detailed preparations he'd made in his first blind rush into commitment. With Aguidran's help, he had planned the theft of the antenna very well. But he'd let the long-range consequences slide by largely unexplored. The rage from his humiliation at Clausen's hands and his heady new sense of mission had carried him this far when, in real-ity, it was mad recklessness to launch himself nearly single-handed against a corporate juggernaut like ConPlex. For now, he would be safe enough in his secret cave, while he did his research and framed his court case. Later, he would worry about consequences, when the message was sent and the die truly cast.

He thought of Susannah, and wished her with him, if only to help him forget for a while. And he thought of Kav Daven, nearby down-level but off-limits for now. Stavros could only guess how long this dark space and its associated caverns would be his home and his prison. He could not venture safely into the open until Clausen's hands were legally tied.

And perhaps not even then. Stavros suspected the prospector had a taste for revenge.

He slouched toward the table with a resigned sigh. Edan watched intently as he patched the antenna cable into the receiver brought from the Sled, the receiver into his scavenged mini-terminal, and the terminal into purloined battery packs. He wondered what end results she expected from their long trek through hail and thorns and heat. What a puzzle all these cables and keys and lights must present to one who'd never heard of domesticated electricity, never mind the entire rest of the electromagnetic universe.

He pulled up the waiting wooden bench, and sat down to activate the mini-terminal. When the ready light glowed, he poised his fingers over the keypad, then froze, tongue-tied at the final moment. He hadn't worked this part out yet.

Liphar eyed him with concern. Stavros pushed past his stage fright, and touched in CRI's call code, followed by his own. He put the call on repeat and waited.

Edan jumped as the computer's tinny voice filled the room. Stavros lunged for the volume slider and keyed in voice transmission. CRI must have kept a search circuit functioning round the clock.

"Don't shout, CRI, I'm here." Not the immortal words he'd imagined uttering, but they would have to do.

55

E.D. 76–18:03

A S THE HEAT MADE TRAVEL harder, Susannah spent less time sampling and more time just trudging along in the sun, deep in a muddle of thought. She started keeping a list. It contained nothing conclusive, but its illusion of cohesion was comforting: all her most burning quandaries neatly inscribed on the back page of her notebook, as if grouping them physically might also relate them causally.

As the list grew, she saw that new entries were often variations of questions she'd already noted earlier. The prime issues were settling out like salts in a solution.

Megan discovered the list at the end of a long cycle's march through the tall amber grasses of the northern Dop Arek. She'd picked up the notebook as if hungry for something other than her own notes to read, flipped through it, then stopped and held the last page up to the orange light of the lowering sun.

" 'Oddnesses'?"

Working with her portable analyzer, Susannah tossed her head diffidently. "Well, not each one so much, but maybe together . . ."

" 'Three beasts,' " read Megan.

"The hakra and the hjalk and the hekkers. I told you they seem remarkably similar, like specially tuned forms of the same animal."

"Generations of clever breeding."

Susannah nodded. "But still an astonishing achievement, to breed three out of one and so perfectly adapt each to its intended specialization."

"The Sawls have had a lot of time, judging from guild records."

"But I can't think of a Terran animal that breeders were able to work *all* the kinks out of before the genetic engineers were around to lend a hand. I'm going to do a DNA match as soon as I get done with my plant chemistry and can reprogram the box here. For instance, where are these animals' other relatives? We haven't seen a single wild herbivore, not a single wild *mammal* for that matter."

"Or birds. No birds, just those hideous flying lizards." Megan shuddered only half jokingly. "Have you asked Ghirra about this?"

Hammering resounded from the Weaver Guild wagon next door. A wheel-wright from the Woodworkers Guild had stopped by on his repair rounds. The weavers patching the shredded canopies broke off to help jack up the wagon and hold muttered debate over the significance of the heat and the long stretch without rain.

"Ghirra says such animals were not meant to run wild. Now what the hell does that mean?" Susannah understood his surface meaning, that wild animals were those who could survive in the hostile wilderness without man's care, being hard-skinned, spiny, sharp-toothed, poisonous, aggressive, and omnivorous. "I mean, did he intend the subtextual implications of that remark? When he said 'meant,' was he suggesting intention and creation, and if so, by whom?"

Megan offered the anthropological interpretation. "Maybe that mysterious Creator who bore both the goddesses and the Sawls. However much the rationalist he claims to be, Ghirra's still the product of a society steeped in religion. Next item . . . 'abnormal growth rate' . . . The domestic crops grow faster than the wild plants?"

"It does seem to be the case."

Megan continued reading. " 'Trehalose analogues' . . . 'poisonous'?"

"Yes. Doesn't it seem odd to you that *all* wild animals and most wild plants on Fiix should be poisonous?"

"All? Are you sure about that?"

"No, but Ghirra says . . . well, besides, it's the only excuse I can come up with for the split food chain."

"Ah ha. The very next item."

"I'm positing two separate ecosystems in operation here: the Sawls and their domestic plants and animals versus everything else. Normally, this would be an inelegant system, not making efficient use of the planet's resources. It would seem to work against survival, unless survival was what necessitated the split in the first place. Thus, I'd prefer it if all the wild animals do prove to be poisonous."

"Does evolution work that way? I mean, does it support the development of coexisting separate systems?"

Susannah shrugged. "On a local level, it's not impossible, but on a planetary scale? If this is a natural mechanism, it's unprecedented."

"*If* a natural . . . ? Now who's getting heavy with the subtext?"

"Well, I keep thinking about Weng's periodic table."

"Weng's so-called periodic table," Megan returned.

"She's only suggesting there were some people here once who knew things the Sawls don't know now. Not unreasonable."

"Ummm. So the three H's *might* have been engineered?"

"No . . . I don't know . . . well, maybe." Susannah threw up her hands. "But how? And perhaps it's only Terran bias that insists on that explanation. The real explanation's probably a natural one. I just can't imagine it within my particular frame of reference."

Undisturbed by further weather violence, the caravan settled into a routine: walking, eating, and sleeping deeply after long hours in the heat. The hail damage was repaired little by little, injuries healed, and the wagons inched across the open plain at a measured crawl, like the sun sinking slowly at their backs.

On the sixth throw, they picked up a little stream, shallow and sluggish, but the first fresh water since leaving the canyon of the hail. An unscheduled stop was made to refill the water kegs tied to the sides of the wagons. The brush-grown track ran parallel to the distant northern mountains, the Vallegar, Valla's Wall. In the east, the turquoise sky faded into pale ambered green as it dropped to the grassy horizon.

By the seventh throw, as the sun rested its salmon disk on the western limb, the stream had widened into a small sand-bottomed river. The caravan plodded through a hot, red dusk. The sharp grasses in Susannah's path were darkened by her long purple shadow.

She thought it a trick of the odd light that the plain no longer seemed to stretch ahead to infinity. But again, there was a restlessness building along the caravan that caused her to search the ruddy sky for sudden clouds. She was rewarded instead with the shrill music of the pipers striking an upbeat rhythm. The hjalk jostled and picked up their pace self-importantly, as if embarrassed to have been woken from a walking doze.

From the head of the train came scattered singing, weary but cheerful. Susannah saw the lead wagons turn abruptly aside and appear to fall off the edge of the horizon. Over the rattle of harness and cartwheels, she heard a steady roaring.

Ghirra smiled as she stopped short, staring in confusion. He took her arm and drew her forward to the edge, where she stood gaping like a tourist at Olympus Mons.

The plain simply ended. Half a kilometer below, it began again, as a low-land savannah that sloped gently toward a green arm of ocean curling around the eastern extreme of the Vallegar. The northern bay shore was sharply mountainous, broken by rugged fjords. The southern shore was too distant to be clearly seen in the red dusk. At the nearer, western end, a region of tall sea cliffs and steep-sided inlets sheltered a smaller, narrow cove.

Ghirra pointed. "Ogo Dul."

Susannah squinted into the dusky distance. She saw no bustling trade city on those wave-splashed cliffs, no sign of human habitation at all. The battered yellow canopy of the Infirmary wagon passed beneath, drawing her attention downward. A road nestled into the side of the stupendous drop, descending in eight long switchbacks. It was two wagon widths across and paved with worn octagonal stones. A knee-high stone curb ran along the drop-side edge of the road, broken here and there where dry slides of dirt and gravel had shoved across the pavement. The lead wagons, beginning the third switch-back, seemed cast in miniature, already far below.

Susannah looked for the source of the roaring. To the north of the road, the little river that had accompanied them for the last few throws fell in a single red-gold ribbon off the edge of the precipice. Several hundred meters down, it smashed into a ledge and rebounded in a cloud of ruddy mist to drop again, a fan of sparkling threads cascading into a wide pool at the shadowed base of the chasm. There were clumps of trees, a level meadow flanking the river where it flowed out of the pool to resume its seaward journey, and blossoms large enough to be visible at a distance as points of vermilion glowing in the yellow grass.

"Hell of a drop," murmured Susannah inadequately.

"Looks like Paradise down there," Megan remarked.

They missed the first sunset in two and a half weeks, by their ship's clock. The air cooled only slightly as they descended the long curl of road into premature evening and the fat red sun disappeared behind the chasm's rim.

"My ears just popped," Megan noted.

"And the humidity's back," Susannah added. She watched the lead wagons reach bottom and pull aside onto the grassy terrace beside the pool.

"Will Aguidran let us stop here?" Susannah asked.

Ghirra nodded at the russet mist. "This water we call *Imvalla*. Is a favored place."

"Imvalla?"

"Valla's Tears. She leave them here, all she have, for weeping of the beauty in this place . . . so the tale say. Now Valla never cry for the hurt she bring."

The air was warm in the poolside meadow, but a long collective swim in deep water and the absence of the punishing sun brought a festive air to the campsite.

Megan relaxed and stared contentedly at the distant hot gleam of sunset ocean. Ghirra rediscovered laughter, telling light stories of past trade trips. Even the laconic Master Ranger was persuaded to sip at a ration of sour beer, adding the occasional droll detail to her brother's recitations. At the twenty giant red-and-blue wagons, the Food Guilders sang as they cleaned up after the dinner meal. The terrors of the hail were, for the moment, forgotten.

Susannah rolled out her blanket in the red twilight. "It's easier without the sun, but how will we find our way in the dark?"

Ghirra smiled like a parent on Christmas eve. "You will know this, Suzhannah, when you wake."

Singing woke her, throaty and solemn. Shadows moved through warm dim light, and Susannah was confused, mistaking it for lingering dusk.

But the light was in the east. The ocean horizon glowed in secret anticipation. The waking caravan faced that way and sang its welcome.

Dawn already? Susannah's entire understanding of the lengthy Fiixian light-dark cycle was abruptly thrown into question.

And then the false dawn faded as the night sky's glowing magnificence, the densely packed star globule of Byrnham's Cluster, nosed above the horizon.

Its center, perched on the sparkling rim of the ocean, was a rosy fuzz as luminous as an aurora. As darkness fell, its halo became visible, a semicircle of pointillist light that dominated half the sky, thinning gradually toward the perimeter and ending quite suddenly against velvet black. There was no familiar background star field. A profusion of nearby stars, bright as planets, were scattered across the otherwise empty night, red, gold, white, and blue, like glimmering shells thrown up on the dark sands of a volcanic beach. Sooty tendrils of the surrounding black invaded the cluster's luminous arc. Susannah thought of dark, long-fingered hands grasping a glowing melon.

Ghirra crouched beside her, his expectant smile of the evening before made proud by her wondering delight. "Do you like these night lantern?"

She nodded, awestruck. "I've never seen anything more beautiful."

He pointed out a huge red giant of a star halfway out from the cluster center, then a hotter blue spark caught in a dark cloud wisp. "The Rangers. They watch the Darkness, red light for Lagri, blue light for Valla."

"The darkness?" She assumed he meant the night. But Ghirra traced a finger in the air, outlining the tendrils of nebular dust.

"There . . . you see this? The Darkness." He sat back on his heels pensively, then murmured, "Ibi say each night lantern is another world. Do you say this also?"

"Well, yes, of course. At least, maybe not a world that supports life, but lots of stars have planets, worlds, that is. Mine has eight, but people only live on three of them, plus a few of the larger moons."

"Mooon?" He wrapped his tongue around the syllable, making it two.

"You have no moons here. A moon is a smaller world that moves around a larger world."

Ghirra lowered himself to the damp grass beside her and sat like a small boy with his knees pulled up to his chin. "So many. So many world."

CART HAKRA

level 3,
entry 6
L + 51

two-cart
(PotterGuild)

MARE

→ 11.6 ←
cm.

note: <u>wide</u> color variation--
white, tan, brown, camel
rust, gray, spotted, pinto,
striped.

← 19.7 cm. →

~1.2 m.
(two distinct
sizes observed:
larger is
~1.6 m. tall.)

← 1.8 m. →

SAJ

56

"THE SALVAGE PARTY has finally left, with two hjalk teams. I wish Mr. Clausen had seen fit to wait for them." Weng set a Sawl oil lamp down on Danforth's worktable. "I thought you might appreciate some additional light."

Danforth stared over steepled fingers at the Cluster glowing above the dark silhouette of the Talche. "I don't know, Chief. Pretty good night for stargazing."

"The Cluster must have great spiritual significance for the Sawls. They sang in the fields when it rose."

"They sing all the time."

"Ah, but this time, they stopped work and sang. For a while, at least."

Danforth squinted into the shadowy stalks walling the clearing. "They're out there working in the dark? Don't they ever quit?"

"Their night is too long for work to stop every darkfall, Dr. Danforth. The salvage party didn't think twice about setting out in darkness."

Danforth made a small noise of disgust. "You think Ibiá is after the antenna?"

"I really couldn't say."

"Well, if he is, I hope he gets the hell out of there before Emil finds him at it."

Stavros shoved away from the makeshift console. CRI was relating a long horror story and would not be sidetracked.

The cavern was suffocating. The unrelenting heat outside was beginning to translate downward through the rock. His fingers were slippery on the keypad.

He stood, stretching the cramps out of his back, and went to the stone sink to splash water on his face. The water was gravity-fed from a cistern buried in the hill above his hiding place. It was tepid and tasted faintly of earth, but he gulped it gratefully and let it stream down his bared shoulders and chest. He hated the soiled, nervous smell of himself. He was going to risk a trip to the Baths later, down through the hidden back corridors, even if he had to overcome Edan's caution by force.

Once he'd reestablished contact with CRI, Stavros had plied the computer with a complicated fiction explaining the "temporary" absence of all his colleagues, and gone right to work, first to do the necessary fiddling to hide all record of his inquiry, from the Orbiter crew as well as from the landing party, when and if the com link was fixed. Then he set CRI to search her files for all regulatory legislation covering the operations of corporations exploiting extraterrestrial natural resources, with specific reference to mining companies.

It was soon clear that Megan had been right. A statutory scheme did exist, whereby the World Union claimed jurisdiction over the actions of corporations operating within the settled zone, including the extraterrestrial colonies.

The stated intention of this body of law was both to protect a legally staked claim, and to provide for circumstances where private claim rights might be overridden by a regulatory agency. However, specific determination of such circumstances rested with the agency involved. Stavros found reference to protection of preexisting populations or unique natural wonders, but the language seemed, to his linguist's ear, to be intentionally vague. Asking for a history of past cases, he discovered that removal of a population to a reservation or even off-planet entirely, had often come under the World Court's definition of protection.

"The law would seem to lay responsibility for compliance on the corporate entity," CRI pointed out, the nanosecond of signal delay due to distance adding an aura of hesitation. "And there is an admitted difficulty of enforcement over such great distances."

"And if they don't comply? Could the WU put the squeeze on them back home?"

CRI took a moment to review her files. "This has been done in one or two cases of blatant infraction or complaints by rival corporations. In cases where regulatory infractions are alleged by private individuals, such individuals must file an action with the World Court. In emergencies, where the allegations can be substantiated, injunctive relief may be sought."

This lawyer pal of Meg's better be a genius, Stavros thought glumly. "What constitutes 'substantiated'?"

"That is obviously for the Court to decide."

And then, operating out of some mysterious prime directive, CRI had begun to tell him horror stories.

Cautionary tales was a more accurate description. The data bank's supply seemed bottomless. Tales of extortion, blackmail, bribery, mayhem and murder murmured in his ears, all acts of vengeance called down by ConPlex and like entities on the heads of those who thought to defy the megacorporate will. Stavros wondered if this admonitory device was CRI's own invention or was somehow embedded in her programming, to steer a user away from ill-considered action. Either way, he cursed the programmers who had seen fit to design such stubbornness into a machine.

Two cycles of lost sleep later, he could almost filter the recitation out of his consciousness. CRI chattered on nonetheless, in her binary way, assuming his rapt attention and squandering his precious power supply. Stavros had turned off the audio several times, then on again, made anxious by the silence. Should the com link to the Lander come on-line, he needed to know it immediately, faster than CRI might think to inform him of it.

At the sink, he dried his face on a sweat-stained shirt and raked back his damp hair. He considered taking the time to hack at it with the clippers from his tool kit, but he liked the thought of letting it grow until he could tie it back as the Sawls so often did with their dangling curls, as Ghirra did, so that with his slight, elegant body and diffident stoop, he resembled an eighteenth-century dandy, lacking only a frock coat and lace.

Stavros left his hair alone. Turning from the sink, he tuned in on CRI's recitation. He judged the current tale to be in a windup phase. Would she start all over again once she ran out?

The thought appalled him. He paced toward the narrow entry arch, feeling caged. Liphar was stretched on his bedroll in front of the doorway, fast asleep. Stavros stared at him, considering escape, then slouched back to the terminal. He checked the time elapsed on his power cells, noted the oil level in his lamp, and resettled himself with a ragged sigh. He glanced up at the display, readying his notes.

While CRI lectured him on the folly of his ways, she was also searching the legal files for precedents that might help him build a case. The message sent to the lawyer could not be an inarticulate call for help. Such a person needed to be wooed, to be convinced that the case had merit. Most of the cases that CRI dredged up were further indication of how sporadic the enforcement of existing regulations was. But occasionally, there was something hopeful to add to his notes, inscribed in tiny space-saving letters in a small sketchbook he'd liberated from the ship's stores.

At the back of the same sketchbook, during the few breaks he allowed himself, he entered his personal notes. He worked on recalling the words that Kav Daven had spoken to him during his "miracle," the Old Words of the Priest Guild. He told himself he was building a vocabulary for the more complex ancestral tongue, with its hints of a technological bias. But, in truth, his search was for answers to the mystery of the Ritual Master himself, for clues to what the old priest wanted of him. As the hours of stifling heat and back-breaking concentration wore on, the events of the Leave-taking eased their grip on his imagination. This current grimy task was far from the heroic vision he'd conjured when he raised the Priest Guild's shining banner.

A new case entry appeared on the display. Stavros reached for his pen. *Halloran vs. Microdyne, 2067.* He waited, pen poised, while CRI's voice nudged at his flagging concentration.

". . . remains in prison at Lima, serving three consecutive life sentences." CRI's speaker hissed softly, and as he had during each and every pause over the last two cycles, Stavros prayed that she'd come to the end of her supply.

"*The New York Times,* Thursday, December 10, 2059: The disappearance of Gabrielle Roget has been . . ."

"CRI, I'll shut you down again." For reasons he was unable to comprehend without resorting to hopeless anthropomorphism, CRI did respond to threats of being cut off. But not this time.

". . . under investigation by the Department of Commerce, following allegations by several witnesses that . . ."

"This will do no good, CRI, though it's worse than any torture ConPlex will dream up."

"Mr. Ibiá, Captain Newman is very disturbed to have remained out of contact with the landing party for so long."

"I'm part of the landing party. You're in contact with me now."

"Mr. Ibiá, if you would allow me to patch you through to Captain Newman, I am certain he would be able to put all of your worries concerning the fate of the inhabitants of 2-PT 6 Fiix to rest in no time."

Stavros rested his forehead on his pen hand. "CRI, even you know better than that. Who do you think pays Captain Newman's salary? Now why don't you accept this as a challenging puzzle you'd love to help me solve? Have you no curiosity for the mysteries of legal linguistics, for the intricacies of the argument?" He blotted his damp upper lip against his equally damp arm. "CRI, the price of development here is just too high."

"Mr. Ibiá, it is my duty to inform you that . . ."

Stavros reached and cut her off. Impulsively, he shut down the whole system.

He sat in the silence, feeling the heat like a thickening of the air. The smell of his own body sickened him. He wondered where Edan was, prowling the tunnels in search of food or just outside the door, waiting to spring, should he so much as stir from hiding.

"Lifa!" He barked suddenly, and swiveled from the bench to shake the young Sawl awake. "Lifa, come on, get up! We're going to the Baths, and I'll fight like Lagri herself if Edan tries to stop me!"

57

E.D. 79–22:47

MEGAN ENVIED THE ILLUSION of precision that Susannah's list provided, but she couldn't work that way. By the time you're forty-seven, she mused as she swished through the dark meadow grasses in Ghirra's wake, you work the way you work.

She attempted lists on occasion, hoping her habits had become more fashionably reductive, but each soon evolved into mammoth run-on sentences. How could anything truly be as simple as a list, or even an outline? She also eschewed the geometric comforts of the graphs and charts relied on by her younger colleagues, who insisted that anthropology be pursued through statistical analysis, like any other hard science.

Intuitive connections were Megan's method, and so far, this had worked. Often before she had gathered what others would consider "adequate" data, the structure of a culture became visible to her. She visualized the process as an old-time photograph swimming up out of the developing fluid, while willingly admitting that her imagery was as antique as her methodology.

"That's why I was feeling so frustrated," she exclaimed to Susannah, her arms spread wide for silent emphasis. The overbearing magnificence of the night sky had the two women whispering as if in a place of worship. The light of the Cluster was, as Ghirra had promised, enough to see by—enough to keep from stumbling into holes or bumping into a neighbor or his wagon, but only just. "Like Taylor—lots of data, no connections."

"Was, past tense? You have the connections now? All I have is a bunch of items on the same piece of paper."

Megan's head bobbed, uncommitted to either a shrug or a nod. "Here and there. Bit by bit." She fixed her gaze on Ghirra's back. Walking in the half-dark was awkward. The ground was either deceptively close or too far away, and the stiff, sharp grasses snatched at the fabric of the Sawl pants she had taken to wearing, tripping her up or breaking her step.

Susannah paced alongside. "I sense you working yourself up to theoretical levels."

Megan blotted her brow on her bare forearm. The coming of darkness had barely lessened the heat, about which the Sawls were clearly apprehensive. "Well, I was thinking about survival."

"That's been on all our minds lately, I suspect."

"But we take survival too much for granted with respect to developing cultures. I mean, the pursuit of survival. We say: they work so hard to survive, or they must do thus and such in order to survive, as if the pursuit of survival were merely one more obstacle to the real business of culture, which is to get on with expansion and development."

"Isn't it?"

Watching Ghirra ahead, Megan wondered how much of their conversation he could hear, or more important, understand. "Usually we think of it as Emil does, that civilization only moves forward. But it could be considered a cultural bias to assume that expansion and development are civilization's only valid goal."

"If not expansion, then at least evolution? Change? Stasis equals extinction."

Megan chuckled. "Spoken from a biological bias. Perhaps humankind's horror of stasis is a race memory of aeons of evolve-or-get-eaten . . ."

"I think I shall shut up till I hear this theory."

"Not a theory. Not yet. But change is part of it, as a matter of fact." Megan paused to glance around as if checking classroom attendance. "Sometimes I find my connections in the patterns of change in a society, as reflected in their history or their myth or their artifacts over a period of time. But here, I sense a pattern of *no* change.

"Look at it. If the Sawl histories have any relation to fact, we have here a cycle of devastations, repeating for thousands of years, more or less regularly decimating the world population. So it builds up to a certain point of development and then, wham, back to where you started. The net result is no change. Stasis.

"Therefore, the very idea of progress, as you and I understand the word, has never entered the Sawls' vocabulary. For instance, do you ever hear the Food Guilders talk about developing a faster seed?"

Susannah laughed. "A *faster* seed? How much faster do you want?"

"It might be useful, given the climate. Well, how about a way to grow more food indoors, or improved farming methods so they could increase the acreage under tillage?"

"I haven't heard that kind of talk," Susannah admitted. "But they do have their hands full just getting anything to grow."

"There! You're assuming they'd do more *if they could*. Okay, try this: any guess how long it's been since the Engineers Guild built a new winch?"

"No, but I'll bet you can tell me to the minute."

"I asked. It's been the equivalent of two hundred years, if I understand their calendar right. And though they made a few improvements at the time, the new one was mostly an exact copy of one that had been in use for the previous three hundred and fifty-odd years. I have this through Ghirra from Aguidran, who thinks it would speed up the loading at caravan times if Engineers built another winch, but she hasn't been able to talk them into it. Another one, mind you, not even a *better* one!"

Ghirra heard his name and glanced around. Self-consciously, Megan dropped her voice. "The point is, the Sawls perfect, but they do not advance. Expansion and development are not part of their cultural imperative. Why is the population contained in such regularly spaced settlements? Why do we go to Ogo Dul to trade rather than to conquer? Not because the Sawls are so peaceable, as I used to think until I heard them arguing like banshees among themselves. It's because they don't even exhibit that most basic of developmental urges, to expand territorially. They divided the available resources up among themselves long ago and are content to keep it that way."

"Meg, it's all they can do to hold on to what they have. There's a big enough war going on over their heads, without them starting new ones among themselves."

"Again, you make the old excuse. But that's fine, because it brings us back to the issue of survival." Megan slowed to let the Master Healer move ahead, out of earshot. But somehow the space between them remained the same.

He's listening, she decided. Probably, he was always listening.

She continued more quietly. "It would be logical of course to suggest that the Sawls have stagnated due to the harshness of the climate and the lack of metallic resources, that their growth is stunted by the extremities of their world."

She felt a soft, insistent nudge against her shoulder blade, and stepped out of the path of the lead hjalk of the wagon behind her. She saw Ghirra also move slightly aside, but was too deeply into airing her theory out loud to stop the process.

"What if we turn our thinking end for end, and suggest that the stasis is not a *result* but a *goal*? A necessity. That the Sawls have survived *because* they haven't changed."

"Ummm," considered Susannah. "Blasphemy."

"I know. Antievolutionary claptrap! But hear me out." She tossed Susannah a sly grin. "Jews understand these things. Just lying low can be the better part of valor.

"Again, for instance: how about the Sawls' obsessive record keeping? Beyond the usual religious books, the priests' First Books of the goddesses, and their Second Books of purported history, there are all the guild ledgers, the reams of lore and records and instruction going back for hundreds of generations. There are the endless weather rolls, and the stories carved on every available surface, plus the whole oral tradition, the songs and chants, not to mention the family records and genealogies."

"And the Birth Records, and the crop inventories and the animal breeding charts," Susannah added.

"All this represents a high degree of literacy—and literary consciousness—for such a technically backward culture. Well, for a while, in the

Middle Ages and later, the Jewish people were doing just what these folks are doing: keeping the records, observing the old ways . . . and waiting." Megan's tone made this last word the solid core of her thesis.

"Waiting," Susannah repeated. "What for?"

"For an end to persecution, in the case of the Jews." replied Megan with unusual gentleness. "Here, for an end to the Sisters' fighting. The Sawls are waiting for peace."

"Meg, the entire galaxy is waiting for peace."

Megan shook her head stubbornly. "No. Everyone else, it's within the power of the participants to end the wars if they really want to. Not here. The Sawls are victims of a war they cannot participate in, beyond offering their prayers to the goddess who seems to be weakest at the time. And remember: they can't even hope for a victory to put an end to the struggle, because a victory of one side is what brings on a Devastation.

"They're lost in a cycle of hopelessness. The myth is quite specific on that count. Stavros found no ambiguities in his translation of that section of the Tale of Origins. The Sisters have been blinded by the Darkness and they will not see clearly again until the Darkness ends."

"And they fall into each other's arms," remarked Susannah.

Megan frowned at her. "More or less. Anyway, the Arrah will end. Why are you being so snide?"

Susannah ducked her head. "Sorry. It just smacked a bit of the Second Coming or something . . . do I detect a Judeo-Christian messianic bias here?"

"If so, it's yours," Megan returned. "There's not even a whisper of messiahs in this myth. It's far more pragmatic. The struggle will go on until the Darkness ends, or lifts or passes, whatever. Nothing will help it along, not prayer or good works or sacrifices, nothing but the passage of an unspecified length of time. *That's* why the business of this culture is survival, for the sake of that day when peace will be restored."

Susannah offered a chastened silence, and Megan walked on, chewing her lip. She gazed at Ghirra's gray silhouette, outlined by the glow of the Cluster and the black of its encircling smoke. "I tell you," she said finally, "if I had this damn climate to deal with, theirs is exactly the sort of myth I'd develop, as a weapon against self-hatred and despair. A society can't function if it feels responsible for so much random suffering."

"A culture in limbo," mused Susannah.

"Exactly. Seeing them that way answers a lot of my questions. It explains their dogged acceptance. Have you ever heard a Sawl rage against the injustice of his goddesses?"

As she said this, their eyes together flicked toward the Master Healer's back.

"Except for him," Megan whispered. "It also explains the lack of a coherent ethic tied to the religious teachings, because it shows that the Sawl religion is not an ethical system, it's a survival system. Behavioral ethics become irrelevant in religion if they're not believed to influence the response of a deity. If prayer and good works won't end the wars, then the only true moral imperative becomes survival, or I should say, survival *until*. The day-to-day issues of ethics and behavior are left to the guilds within each settlement to teach and administer. The Priest Guild deals with the long-term issue of surviving the wars, with the Rangers Guild as their active analogue. Aguidran and her guildsmen teach the practice of survival while Ashimmel teaches its philosophy. The ceremonial association of ranger and priest that puzzled me at the Leave-taking represents their dual guardianship over their people."

Her mouth dry from talking, Megan uncorked her canteen. The heat was like a weight on her brain. But there was one further thought to add. She swallowed and plunged ahead.

"The gambling: a classic reaction to despair. Gambling elevates the power of luck—*khem*—in their lives, which are denied free will. If the goddesses view them with such disdain, then so be it, life will be treated as an ironic game. What better response for the powerless? The philosophy of luck encourages two hopes: first, that it's your *luck* and not you that's at fault if you suffer, and two, that things might get suddenly better. You might win."

"The Darkness might end."

"Right."

Susannah pondered this. The caravan ahead was a long line of gray shapes receding into steamy night. "Stav would be scandalized."

"Often his response to my ideas."

"I mean, elevating gambling to such noble heights."

"Well, there's no one here getting rich off the losers. Plus it helps let off competitive steam. This society *must* work together to survive. In the long run, it's still share and share alike."

They trudged along some more, listening to the wagon wheels grind through the brittle grass. Beside them, the hjalk snorted wearily. In the driver's seat, little Phea crooned gentle encouragements. Somewhere in a wagon behind, a father sang to his fretful child. The pace music of the pipers seemed caught in a mournful key.

"You know what else he would say?" Susannah said finally. "He'd remind us once again that the goddesses are real to the Sawls. Not a colorful metaphor . . . no mere article of faith."

Now Megan was even more aware of Ghirra's rigid, listening posture. "Doesn't change my thinking one iota. Valla and Lagri could sit down to dinner with us and unless they agreed to give the Sawls a break, the theory still stands, with fact substituted for mythos. That's why I'm happy with it."

"Does this mean you're leaving yourself open for the possibility that they might?"

"What?"

"Sit down to dinner with us."

Megan exhaled ruefully. "It means I've decided to leave issues of faith and reality to the theologians, or to young linguists who care to act as theologians. As the poet said, 'There are more things 'twixt heaven and earth, Horatio . . .' "

Susannah sighed. "Amen to that."

Ghirra was silent through the mid-throw meal. He ate quickly with lowered head, then excused himself, claiming business with his sister. Megan watched him stride away through the dim starlight. Was the jerkiness of his step due to roughness of the ground or to anger?

"He was listening," she worried to Susannah.

"To every word."

"And understanding?"

"Stavros said Ghirra's intellect was awe-inspiring. That's a quote."

Megan shifted uneasily, setting her empty plate aside. "Even allowing for Stav's penchant for exaggeration . . . I have a feeling we'll hear about this sooner or later."

The Master Healer rejoined them at supper. He brought a lantern from the back of the wagon and set it lit in front of them. He bent the stiff grass into a mat beneath his long legs, then settled comfortably with his laden food tray balanced across his knees.

He smiled at the two women, who had ceased even pretending to eat the moment he sat down. "This was much interesting talk, Meeghan," he remarked without letting go of his smile.

"I thought you might have picked up a word or two," Megan returned lightly.

Susannah said nothing. The moment was rightfully his.

The healer turned his smile to her. "It is like, I think, when you lie on the stone and the doctors talk about how you are sick and how they will do for you."

Megan cleared her throat. "Ghirra, I didn't mean to offend. Only to understand."

"Yes." He drew out the final consonant into a hiss of resignation, yet his tone hinted at challenge, behind the veil of his smile. "You want knowing how I think with this?"

The two women leaned forward with an eager deference that made him laugh. His dark face relaxed. He set his food aside and leaned forward as well, his hands folded in a mimic of Megan's professorial air, his elbows resting on his knees. The yellow lamplight caught the occasional strand of silver in his curls.

"I think you understand this right, Meeghan, in many matter. Is true we wait many generation for the ending of the *Arrah*." He paused, then without a trace of resentment said, "For generation more than all Terran have lived on your world."

Susannah started at the word. Sawls rarely used "Terran," favoring their own "Wokind" instead. Ghirra's use of it seemed intended to emphasize his recognition of their differences.

"That old?" Megan prodded.

Ghirra nodded. "We count this, Ibi and me. I tell him a history, always he want knowing when this is. Not enough I say, long time past. He say . . ." Struggling against the limits of his English, he slipped into a passable imitation of Stavros' edgy tones. "He say, 'But when? When *exactly* this happen? How long? How many times?' I begin wondering that Terrans are so much worried with time. You take a short cycle, you need sleep very often, eat very often. Work must end at a time you say, not when is finish."

He sat back, as if remembering his meal cooling on the tray. He swallowed a spoonful of mashed kamad root. Megan took this cue and began eating with a restrained care that allowed her to keep her mouth full and her eyes glued to the Master Healer's face.

Ghirra tore his bread into chunks. "Now, I understand our time is not like your time. Also our animal and our plant and what you call 'weather.' Suzhannah say, the plant grow too fast, this be 'abnormal.' But Meeghan say, 'Sawl do not grow fast, and *this* be abnormal."

He ate another spoonful, using the moment to form his next sentence.

"What I say: thing be as they must to live, so this be not abnormal. Also I say, we do grow." He leaned forward again and Susannah was moved by the passion he managed to express within such calm, measured phrasing. "The winch you say about, Meeghan, is more good than the old winch." He tapped his chest in restrained emphasis. "I am a more good healer than my teacher. But Terran have not these Sister hold you back. You grow so fast, it seem like Sawl stand still."

Listening with creeping shame, Susannah heard Emil Clausen's bored voice repeating its lesson in her head: "*. . . these little brown folk have a brand-new view of their universe simply because we appeared in it . . .*" He was right to scoff at the noninterference regulations. The only true noninterference was to stay away.

"Meeghan, your talk of accepting is correct. The priests teach this. They say this last until the Darkness end. They mean this is, yes, a . . ." He quoted Megan neatly. "A weapon against despair. For me, there is no comfort. Not ever.

"But same as you learn and watch and ask your question, I learn also. I learn that a box can have word and knowing inside. I learn about other world that have no Sister. I learn how what Ibi call 'impatience' is not wrong, when Aguidran and me ask our question about these Sister. I learn that accepting is not the only way of men.

"So I feel more angry at these Sister from this learning, but I am happy at it." He regarded them both seriously, then offered a smile taut with irony. "For me, Meeghan, this learning is a faster growing."

58

THE LIGHT WAS DIM in the Bath Hall. Four of the pools had been drained. The water was low in the remaining two, and a faint soap scum floated about the tiled edges.

Stavros did not care. He tossed his pants aside at the nearest pool and dropped into the waiter's tepid embrace with a grateful sigh. Liphar dunked, washed himself hurriedly, then sat with his legs dangling over the edge, watching over his shoulder for Edan, still clearly astonished that they had managed to elude her. Stavros swam the length of the pool and back, rolling his body around and around like a playful seal.

"Lifa!" he challenged, "If she comes, we'll just throw her in! She could use it!"

Liphar grinned, but nervously.

Stavros dove and surfaced, scattering water with an exuberant shake of his head. Then he noticed a small group of bathers at the shallow end of the second undrained pool. His legs drifted down and found bottom as he floated motionless in surprise.

Kav Daven hunched naked on the green tiled corner steps, his knobby thin legs soaking in the water. Two other elderly priests sat nearby in weary conversation. At Kav Daven's side, his child companion wrung out wet cloths to drape on his bent head and shoulders.

Stavros climbed slowly out of his pool. He had never met the ancient Ritual Master outside of a ceremonial context. At those times, he'd felt that the frail body barely contained that vibrant spirit with its aura of power and magic. Now he saw how tenuous the old priest's grip on life really was, how his withered skeleton was sadly burdened by the heat, how surely he was failing. Stavros had a moment of reluctant sympathy for Kav Ashimmel, understanding why she had to press Kav Daven to designate an heir to his office. If he died without training an apprentice, ritual knowledge that he alone possessed might be lost to the guild forever. But still the old man resisted, stubbornly refusing all the candidates offered so far. Perhaps he had this young girl, his constant caregiver, in mind but hadn't yet told anyone.

What was he waiting for? Did he think he could go on forever? Stavros was ready to believe it possible, to believe anything possible, remembering the miracle of the guar. He motioned Liphar to join him. The dim fire in his palms, almost forgotten over the past cycles of concentrated brain work, flared anew as he padded across the tile.

The other priests eyed his approach with neutral wariness, but the blind Ritual Master seemed entirely unaware. His bony shoulders drew up high around his neck as he sang an almost silent chant, faintly rocking. His small attendant looked away from Stavros and laid a damp cloth across Kav Daven's back.

Stavros crouched tentatively at his side. "Kav . . . ?"

The old man ceased rocking. He sat up straighter and a smile lit his gaunt, papery face. *"Raellil,"* he said, liquid syllables but distinct, spoken softly as if in welcome.

Stavros did not recognize the word. He glanced at Liphar.

"Old Words," the priest-to-be mouthed apologetically.

Stavros stored the word in his memory. This wasn't the time to debate appropriate translations. He had so many questions, pounding at his mind like a crowd outside a door. "Lifa, please, tell him I need to understand what happened at the Leave-taking."

Liphar's look was reproving, as if miracles were not meant to be questioned. Still, he bent respectfully and spoke beside Kav Daven's ear.

The Ritual Master nodded and smiled, but continued to murmur his unintelligible music. Stavros began to suspect that this long-awaited personal audience was not going to be the clarifier of mysteries he had dreamed it would be.

"Ask him about the guar, Lifa. Why didn't it burn my hands like it burns everyone else's?"

Liphar tried again, his thin mouth set in protest.

Kav Daven's smile widened, but he still stared blindly ahead, his head marking the rhythm of his chant.

"Kav, please . . ." Stavros guessed the priest was testing him. He needed to ask these questions himself. He worked it out carefully before he asked: *Is there a way to talk to the goddesses? If one wished to reason with them, how would one go about it?*

And this time, an answer came, but in whispered Old Words, sounds like water, or fabric falling in silken folds. Stavros heard the word "raellil" fall softly among them. He looked to Liphar questioningly.

"This Kav say you have this answer."

"What?"

"Yes. But only, you not see this yet."

That's for sure, Stavros thought, sitting back on his heels. The old man continued to chant and sway.

"What is 'raellil,' Lifa?"

"This is like me, the learning one, that bring the words around."

"The guild messengers, you mean? The apprentices?"

"Yes. Like me. I am *raellil*." Liphar tapped his chest, and then glanced up abruptly, past Stavros, toward the entrance to the hall. Stavros let his head droop, knowing what the young man saw.

"She found us already, did she? Aguidran trained that girl too well."

He leaned toward Kav Daven, opening his palms in offering though the blind man could not see them. "When I find these answers you say I have, I will ask you, Kav, if I have them truly."

Edan strode angrily across the hall, and he rose regretfully, leaving the old priest to his private litany.

59

E.D. 82–9:16

THE DESCENT ACROSS the grassy savannah took far longer than Susannah had guessed from atop Imvalla's dizzying precipice. The succession of gently rolling meadows was treeless, though not so arid as the upper plain. The grass grew tall and even, like a field of wheat, and stretched as featureless in the gray half-light as an ocean before dawn.

The caravan followed Imvalla's winding river for two full throws. During meal stops, lanterns glimmered along the line of wagons, like bright beads between the flickering jewels of the cook fires. With darkfall, the wild creatures grew bolder. The rangers patrolled constantly, guiding stragglers closer to their wagons, keeping up the pace. During sleep rounds, though there was never a breath of wind, the grasses rustled out past the light of the lanterns. Once Susannah woke to the cries of a terrified hakra and the pounding of the rangers' feet as they raced to its rescue. Visiting at dinnertime, Aguidran watched the darkness restlessly, muttering about the continuing heat.

Ahead of them always was the glow of the Cluster, a cloud-wrapped beacon that inspired their constant wonder. Susannah remarked that it felt like marching into the maw of a smoking inferno. She drew her long hair back and fought a comb through its mats. She felt sticky and dirty and longed for a bath, but Aguidran would allow no river swimming in the darkness. "We could use a poet on this expedition," she ventured more seriously. "Or a painter."

"I know what you're thinking," Megan replied, "but it wouldn't do a bit of good. Beauty is a sentiment these days, not a value. Beauty alone wouldn't move the Court an inch, even if Stav could muster enough poetical eloquence to bring tears to the judges' eyes. I'm hoping he'll surprise us with the instincts of a crackerjack lawyer. . . ."

"He's got CRI for a research assistant. That should help." Susannah smiled at the image: Stavros struggling through the baroque jungles of legal precedent under CRI's machine-patient tutelage. And picturing him, she wanted him with a fierceness that startled her. She'd been right, then, not to let herself dwell on him and the danger he'd put himself in. At times, certain things just did not bear thinking about.

Early in the third throw past Imvalla, faint firefly sparkles sprang to life across the savannah in the direction of Ogo Dul. A ragged cheer rose among the wagons. The hjalk pricked up their ears and snuffled.

"The welcome lamp." Ghirra grinned with relief. "Our cook fire tell we come."

He ruffled Dwingen's hair as the boy trudged beside him. The child's thin face was taut from fighting exhaustion and the heat, but he perked up at his guild master's touch and walked a little straighter.

Sweating rangers trotted past with orders for lanterns to be lit. A faint stirring of the heat-laden air brought a tang of salt and the growling sigh of distant surf. Travel-weary guildsmen revived enough to discuss market strategy.

The meager pinpricks of light ahead offered Susannah no sign of a city. The steep fjords to the north towered darkly against a darker sky. The broken sickle shape of the ocean bay tossed back a glimmering reflection of the Cluster.

"How will the people of Ogo Dul react to offworld visitors?" she asked Ghirra.

"They will think as most here, that your 'other world' mean a Cave more far than they have knowing."

"You mean, just another settlement here, but very distant?"

"Yes. They will think this, and no one will say them no."

"Stay undercover, he's saying." Megan tugged at her Sawlish pants. "Shouldn't be hard, tanned now and dressed for the part."

"But why?"

"The sign is not good to bring strangeness here," said Ghirra.

"Ashimmel was ready once before to blame Valla's strength on us," Megan reminded her. "No point taking that chance again."

Ghirra nodded gravely. "I am glad you see this, Meeghan."

The lights of Ogo Dul did not seem to grow bigger and brighter as they neared. Susannah waited to see the gaily lit windows of a bustling town at night. When the running lights of the lead wagons began to thread among those isolated sparkles, she realized that their seeming distance was a deception of the darkness. The sparkles were indeed just lamps, as Ghirra had said: small lanterns suspended on poles stuck into the sandy ground.

The poles were set several hundred paces apart in a broad snaking curve. They picked out a road worn through the grass to a base of fine sand that shone white in the starlight. A few pale streamers rustled at the base of each lamp as the wagons passed by. At the end of the curve, free-moving lights bobbed among the larger flames of a double row of stationary torches. Beyond the torches lay a velvet darkness.

Susannah was forewarned by her experience at the precipice, and sure enough, when the lead wagon reached the last pair of torches, its running lights set like tiny moons as it passed over an invisible edge. Chanting and music rose up past the descending wagon. A faint glow from below caught on its torn and mended canopy as it disappeared. Again, the Master Healer led his visitors to the rim, this time to gaze down on Ogo Dul.

Where the torches ended, the white sand road swerved to drop along the side of a deep ravine. The incline was steep and neatly paved, walled on the drop-side by a shoulder-high stone balustrade. The railing was an arm's span wide and carved of thickly veined and polished marble. The balusters were thinner slabs cut in the design of the three interlocking circles. Dark water filled the ravine far below.

A dozen pairs of bridges spanned the seawater canyon, joining five tiers of shops and dwellings hollowed out of the solid rock. Each tier was fronted by a lamplit portico of finely detailed columns and arches. The inner walls were pierced by half-moon doorways and round windows glazed with colored glass. The interlocking circle design was repeated in the portico railings and along the low walls of the bridges. The salt smell was sharp, and the wave sigh magnified by the reflecting rock, growling a bass accompaniment to the chatter of the crowds that filled the tiers and flowed across the bridges beneath strings of swaying lanterns.

"This is Trader's Finger," Ghirra announced, then considered his own fingers, outstretched in a star. "No. How do you call the finger of a plant?"

"A leaf? A twig?" supplied Megan. "No, a branch."

"A branch. Trader's Branch, it is." He gestured into the darkness toward the glimmering ocean bay. "Along here, there is many cut into the cliff. This is each a branch, and the large branch has also small branch. They come by tunnel through the rock, like Dul Elesi. Or if Valla allow, you travel by *chresin*." He pointed down at the black water. Narrow boats with lanterns at stern and bow poled back and forth between the rows of floating docks lining the water's edge. "By *chresin* is more fun."

"You were born here," Susannah recalled.

"It's like Venice was," murmured Megan, "before the sea swallowed it."

Ghirra's smile clouded. "In Potter's Branch, we live. Very big, with many small branch. When we come back first time, I go with my sister to discover which cave is ours, but we cannot. Too many, too much the same."

"No other family?" asked Megan.

"My three-father is too old to go that time, but he is dead when I come back to Ogo Dul. The other, all dead in the mud, and many other not my family. My sister and I have luck that time. The mud fall little on us."

He allowed the lantern-jeweled boats far below a long moment of study, then shook off his melancholy with a self-scolding laugh. "This is old remembering, not for now. Much here to see that is not sad. I will show you." He smiled brightly to prove the return of a cheerful mood. "We will go by *chresin*."

They descended on the heels of the dawdling dairy herd. The incline was paved with rounded oblongs like cobblestones to secure good footing, but the young hekkers chose to snort and shy about and give the herdsmen needless anxiety until they were on level ground once more, swinging their heads about in bovine curiosity as they waded through the crowds thronging the noisy columned street.

The portico was several wagons wide, from its pierced marble railing to its smoothly polished inner wall, like a winding, covered boulevard. The columns were as thick as a man's torso and skinned with shallow carvings that told the histories of the goddesses in spiraling panels.

Susannah peered into the brightly lit shops that honeycombed the inner wall, where the guildsmen of Ogo Dul bustled about, chatting a patron toward a choice, moving goods around and restocking shelves in preparation for the new influx of customers. The street was hot and stuffy, though open to the air along one side. She stuck close to Ghirra, avoiding the brighter lights, but no one paid two Terran women in Sawl clothing any unusual notice. Megan's skin was naturally darker than Susannah's, and after two and a half weeks in a punishing sun, she was the very image of a sturdy Sawl matron. Like Ghirra and Aguidran, the ocean folk of Ogo Dul were generally taller and broader of frame than their cousins from Dul Elesi. And though Susannah had never seen a Sawl who could be considered anything but thin, the heat and the constant walking had slimmed Megan considerably, and hardened them both.

"We'll fit right in," murmured Megan. "As long as we don't open our mouths."

"Too bad we haven't anything to trade." Susannah's eye was already caught by the colorful clothing brightening the shop windows.

The columned street wound this way and that, conforming to the natural shape of the ravine, which soon opened out to admit a narrow side branch. The portico wrapped around into the branch and a wide bridge carried the major traffic across the cut. A muffled racket of snorts and bleats and conversational lowing rose out of the side branch. Here, the herdsmen turned the hekkers aside with good-natured whistles and shoves. Ghirra led his companions across the bridge, where the rich animal smell of five tiers of stabling joined the pervasive tang of salt air and iodine.

They caught up with the end of the caravan, stalled on the far side of the bridge in a jumble of wagons and two-carts and tired families. The street was wide enough for the wagons to be drawn up tight to the inner wall and still leave passageway along the outside. In place of the shops were suites of smaller rooms to serve as temporary dwellings and trade stalls. Susannah poked her head into one where a single lamp burned in a corner niche. The arrangement was familiar from the dwelling spaces of Dul Elesi: a stone sink with ceramic piping, a raised hearth surrounding a sunken fire pit, a neatly swept stone floor, and no furniture or decoration.

Easing through the noise and jumble, they found the Infirmary wagon, its dented yellow canopy nearly grazing the vaulted ceiling. Xifa explained the delay as a problem with the assignment of quarters, since there were more of them than on past trips. She noted that the crowd was unusually impatient and disagreeable in the heat and congestion, while Susannah pondered questions of population growth and the straining of psychological as well as biological resources.

The Food Guild began passing out sour beer rations by hand-to-hand relay, unable to squeeze their little delivery two-carts through the press. Ghirra disappeared into the sweating throng and returned a while later with a tray piled with bread ends and bits of cheese, all that could be managed until the Food Guild maneuvered their big wagons into the larger halls intended for their use.

Megan was grateful enough for stale bread and cheese. "Is it always this bad?"

Ghirra laughed, sipping his beer, and repeated the query to Xifa and Ampiar as if it were a modest sort of joke. Xifa joined his laugh, but Ampiar nodded darkly.

"Not so much heat, before," Ghirra admitted. "And this time, we are too many."

Just when Megan thought that the last molecule of hot salty air had been exhaled as waste, the crush eased. Proper quarters were found, with much doubling up among related families. The carts and wagons were parked in formation against the wall.

The medical staff was assigned two large adjoining rooms on the second tier. The wagon was driven down and unloaded, and the larger room was quickly converted into a mini-infirmary, to deal with the sickness and minor injuries already accumulated during the confusion of the arrival.

Hours later the Food Guild brought them dinner, lukewarm and soggy, but no one stopped to eat. The elderly in particular were finding the unrelenting heat a difficulty, and parents were still turning up with wailing infants and snuffling older siblings. It was an endless parade of mostly psychosomatic complaints. Susannah thought this peculiar, but kept at her soothing and doctoring until Ghirra at last took pity, gently removed the cloth and bowl of herbal disinfectant from her trembling hands, and sent her off the other room to sleep. Megan had long since found a spot to unroll her bed.

The smaller room was close and humid. The single window was draped with a torn tunic to muffle the noise from the street. Dwingen and Phea had crowded into the rear with the older apprentices. Megan lay at their feet, head to the wall. Susannah laid out her bedroll beside her and collapsed.

She woke later to the soft clink of a lantern being set down nearby. Ghirra rolled out his pad, pulled off his loose shirt and made a pillow of it. He lay down on his back with a tired sigh, taking a moment of contemplative stillness before dousing the lantern.

Susannah feigned sleep, watching him through lidded eyes. When someone is unaware of being observed, often they offer the clearest clues to who they are. *Where does Ghirra go in his head?* she wondered.

His face was delicately orchestrated, a harmony of elements tuned like a fine instrument, color and line flowing together without one feature standing out, except perhaps his wide gentle mouth, mostly because it so often smiled. Less often of late, Susannah reflected.

Age had hardly lined his brown skin, but for the weary crinkles at the corners of his eyes. She guessed him to be over forty in Earth years. He looked ten years younger.

He turned his head, reaching to turn down the lamp, and found her watching him.

Susannah raised herself up on one elbow. "You look exhausted. What a night! Did they keep coming in at that rate?"

Ghirra mirrored her pose. "Not so long. But my sister need my talking with the Priest Guild and the *Kethed* and the *Kethed* of Ogo Dul."

"What's the matter? Ashimmel up on her high horse again?"

He gave a soft chuckle that turned into a yawn. "Suzhannah, you must talk English at least to me."

"What? Oh, a horse? It's like a . . . never mind. What's Ashimmel's problem?"

"The word come not good from other far settlement. The Priest Guild worry it be so hot everywhere. The Food Guild worry for the planting. All say, go back soon."

"Early, you mean? Poor Aguidran, always getting caught in the middle."

Ghirra shook his head. "Now, she worry also, talking to her guild from more south on Dul Valla. Everywhere it is not good."

"Aguidran agreeing with the priests? Hunh." Surprising that this small bit of information should have the power to chill her so. Susannah had come to rest total confidence in the Master Ranger's judgment. "We'll go back early, then?"

"Yes." He rubbed his eyes, holding back another yawn. "When the Food Guild wagon is full for the return, and the broken part is made again. This is two, three cycle." He managed a regretful smile. "This is small time for you to see Ogo Dul."

"And you promised me a chresin ride," she teased.

His laugh was a hoarse tired whisper. He leaned to blow out the lamp. "This promise I keep, Suzhannah."

Susannah lay in the stuffy darkness, listening first to his breathing as it evened into sleep, then to the sounds of the alien city, the muted lapping of the sea canals three tiers below, the cries of the boatmen ferrying across the dark water, the steady murmur from the upper tier as the traders got underway a half cycle early to make up for time that would be lost to a premature departure.

She decided that if Aguidran was worried, then so was she, and she fell asleep to dream fitfully of broiling on the slow spit of the planet's unnatural heat.

60

"   . . . SUIT WAS BROUGHT by the heirs of Michael J. Halloran . . ."

Stavros muttered as he wrote, but a glance at the display stopped him cold. The case involved ConPlex, and among the names listed by the complainants was one Emil Friedrich Clausen. It was like dropping anchor after a long drift at sea. A chill of humiliation and fear dispelled the dreamy aura of recent cycles. The threat of Clausen and ConPlex became real again.

He asked CRI for press reports on the Halloran incident. They were scanty, suspiciously inconclusive. Halloran had been the staff anthropologist on a ConPlex-funded expedition into the Perseus sector. He had advised a hold on mining activities to allow for the exploration and cataloging of extensive ruins on a small world that ConPlex later developed as a colossal source of titanium. When Halloran died in a landslide, his heirs sued for negligence. The prospector on the expedition was Emil Clausen. Stavros was sure poor Halloran had been good and dead well before this convenient landslide had occurred.

Noises in the outer hall spooked him. He sprang up, knocking over his bench, and shrank into the darkness at the back of the room.

Liphar pattered around the corner. He halted in dismay at the sight of the deserted console, the toppled bench, and the single oil lamp burning low. Feeling foolish, Stavros moved back into the light.

"Ibi!" Liphar was clearly on edge himself.

Edan appeared silently in the arch behind him. They came brimming with what looked to be bad news.

"Clazzan," Edan hissed.

"What? Here? Now?"

Liphar nodded. "He come with Furzon, from the Grigar."

Stavros breathed a little easier. Not *here*. Not in the Caves. Not yet.

"Very mad, him."

"I'll bet," said Stavros grimly. "He's down at the Lander? Have they got the Sled?"

"Come after soon, they say."

Stavros pressed his eyes shut. Now Clausen knew, if not all, then certainly enough. A desperate urge to run expanded like a bubble inside his chest. The cavern was hot and dark and close, too much like a trap. Only the knowledge that it was hotter outside than in sobered him out of a touch of the old panic.

"Our grace time has ended," he murmured. "The battle begins in earnest."

Back to work. Activity would distract him from his creeping sense of helplessness in the face of the corporate juggernaut that Clausen represented. For one thing, fear played right into the prospector's hand. For another, here on Fiix, Clausen was only one man, however skilled, well-armed, and ruthless he might be.

He asked Edan to post an all-cycle watch on the Lander. He described the big dish antenna, emphasizing the need to observe and report all changes in it carefully, so that he could assess the progress toward reestablishing the link. He also asked for a tail on Clausen. Edan threw him one of her looks, mixing a growing deference with an edgy reminder that he was not her real boss. Then she turned and strode off down the tunnel.

Stavros began to pace. Liphar watched with solemn concern while the linguist wore out his burst of adrenalin.

"Gotta get the case together now! Gotta send the damn thing out, fast! You hear that, CRI? Clausen's back from the hills! You know, the man who pays for your juice?"

But this was petty and mean, his panic speaking. CRI was designed to be all things to all users. It was unfair to accuse her of taking sides.

"Shall I expect to hear from Mr. Clausen shortly, then?" the computer asked.

"Maybe so." To himself, he muttered, "But by the goddesses, I hope not!'

Weng and Danforth were asleep when Clausen stormed into the Underbelly, dragging an exhausted McPherson in tow. He shoved her in the direction of the Commander's curtained cubicle. Bleary-eyed, she stood outside the curtain, knocking on the piled-up crates and calling softly, glaring sidelong at Clausen as he shook Danforth roughly until the planetologist stirred, grumbling, out of deep, sweated sleep.

Weng drew the curtain aside dazedly. "What . . . ah, Lieutenant. You're back." Blinking into the glare of Clausen's searchbeam, she looked pale and unusually disheveled. She wrapped her wrinkled silk robe more tightly around her.

McPherson sagged against the crates. "It's Stavros, Commander . . ."

Weng stiffened. "Injured?"

McPherson frowned, confused. "No, he's . . ."

"The omni's missing from the Sled." Clausen stood with his laden pack slung across one shoulder, awaiting Weng's response.

"During the storm . . . ?"

"Removed, Weng, as with tools. Along with its box." He advanced on Weng's worktable, swept her precisely ordered papers to the floor with a vehement arm, and swung his pack into the cleared space. "Ibiá's stolen it, as I suspected. McP, bring in that other gear." Set up on end, his searchbeam became a small tower of work light. He began to unload bits of wiring and circuitry from the pack's side pockets, spreading them out on the table.

McPherson hesitated, looking to Weng for a cue. Weng's chin lifted, then settled stubbornly. But she nodded stiffly, and the pilot retreated into the darkness.

Danforth struggled to sit up in bed. He exchanged a groggily covert glance with Weng over the prospector's back. "What the hell's going on?"

"The kid's not as clever as he thinks." Clausen lifted a fistful of circuitry from the pack's center pocket. He set it down carefully and smiled at it as if it were a newly won prize. "He left too much behind. Hook this up to the dish and we'll be in business."

"Receiver?" Danforth could not restrain his interest.

"Better than what's left in the nose. Low data rate for sure, we'll see how she does. And a converter for the power beam, as long as we can get the dish shaped right."

Weng bent to retrieve her papers from the ground. She held them to her chest for a moment, watching Clausen fuss over his trophy. "What makes you so confident of Mr. Ibiá's responsibility in this matter?"

Clausen glanced up with a feral grin. "Experience, Commander. Plus a little gift I have for knowing who's on my ass. You need that in my business."

Weng stared back at him silently, tucking a strand of silver hair back into her disordered bun.

"What I can't figure is why," said McPherson, returning with a second bulging pack and two coils of cable.

"Why, indeed! You all should be on my side! I'm the one who came here to make things better back on Earth! You all just wanted to get away from it for a while!" Clausen snatched the pack from McPherson's listless grasp. "Fuck it. Doesn't matter why. We have ourselves a saboteur, and the only thing that matters is stopping him."

On a calmer, cooler evening, Clausen's grimace might have seemed unnaturally fevered, but Danforth found it exactly in tune with the sweltering, suffocating dark.

"Gotta find him first." McPherson slumped onto a crate.

"No. First we beat him to it, whatever it is."

Weng seemed to discover anew the clutter of papers clasped in her arms. "Get some rest, Lieutenant," she said with pointed kindness.

"No way," countered Clausen. "I need her artful little fingers right here."

"Mr. Clausen, such tired fingers can hardly be artful."

Clausen leaned over his assortment of parts. "We're both tired, Weng. What do you think this is, kindergarten, we should all go take a nap?"

"I think it is an expedition of which I am still in command."

Clausen's eyes flicked up from his work, a reflex checking for the weapon he considered to be the only possible backup for such bravado. He smiled mockingly at Weng's empty hands.

"And I will not allow this chronic mistreatment of my crew," she continued. "Lieutenant, you have your orders."

"Yes, ma'am!" McPherson saluted and escaped, offering Danforth a pat of greeting as she slipped past him into a farther corner of the Underbelly.

Weng approached her appropriated worktable and collected her papers into a single thick sheaf. "Now, Mr. Clausen. If you will grant me the favor of allowing me to get dressed, I myself will assist you with this assembly."

Clausen closed down his heavy-lidded stare with a satirical shrug. "I would welcome your assistance, Commander."

Weng neatened the stack of papers, gathering it to her like a shield, and retired behind her curtain. Clausen went to work, his stubby fingers probing the central chunk of circuitry with careful confidence. Danforth watched from his bed.

"Crazy motherfucker," he commented finally. "Probably hasn't a clue what he's getting himself into."

"Taking on ConPlex is never wise," Clausen agreed.

"Actually, I meant taking you on. I notice it hasn't occurred to you that he may be aiming this at me."

"Out of what . . . professional jealousy?" Clausen chuckled. "Dream on." He held a small bit of plastic up to his lamp for closer study. "You 'pure science' types have such grand ideas about your place in the scheme of things."

"Lucky for me, I have you around to ride herd on my illusions. I'm grateful, Emil, I truly am." Danforth kept his tone light, hoping that in the darkness, the prospector would miss the ambivalence twisting his face even as he labored to erase it from his voice.

He wanted com and power restored as desperately as he wanted to stand up and walk again, but his dismay at the disappearance of the omni was tempered with curiosity and a touch of reluctant admiration. What was in Ibiá's mind to drive him into open sabotage? It was too easy to dismiss his actions as merely crazy. There had to be more to it.

Did Ibiá realize, so fresh from the womb of the university, that this single gesture of defiance could earn him a permanent exile? He might find a safe port in the Colonies and work enough to keep himself fed, but Earth belonged to the corporations, and as Clausen had said, crossing them was never wise, or healthy.

But that, Danforth decided, was Ibiá's problem.

"Send the drone out as soon as I complete transmission of the text."

Stavros yawned convulsively. He should not have turned his nose up at the instant coffee when raiding the ship's stores in preparation for his siege. The equivalent Sawlish brew, even in Liphar's long-simmered version, did not pack the same caffeine wallop. He shook his head, blinking at the scribbled and madly annotated mess of his notes and the hopefully more coherent message in the display.

He'd given up trying to perfect the legal case himself, once he knew of Clausen's premature return. It seemed, finally, that legal language was beyond even a linguist's interpretation, and he was rapidly running out of both time and battery power.

In the end, he opted for a straightforward description of Fiix and its inhabitants, including an outline of ConPlex's intentions as he understood them. He ended the statement with a desperate plea for help. He would have to leave the lawyering to the lawyers, and hope that Megan was right that there was at least one lawyer left with morality enough to read his report with indignation and outrage, plus a willingness to take on the case. It was frustrating and anticlimactic to have struggled this far only to be forced to hand over his efforts into some distant stranger's hands. He could not repress a nagging sense of futility.

Too little, too late, too small, too weak . . . He had to take more immediate action.

Once again, thoughts of murdering Clausen milled about in his brain. How could he even manage it? He had no weapon, and Clausen had already proven to be his superior in hand-to-hand.

The next transmission completed, Stavros sat back.

"You are requesting a court injunction against ConPlex?" The computer sounded incredulous.

"The message is top priority and to be decoded only upon proper voice-print identification of the recipient."

"Authorization?"

Was that resentment he heard? He was forcing CRI to bow to the imperatives of her basic programming. No matter if the computer's ephemeral sentience preferred otherwise, his instructions must be obeyed. "My authorization. As Communications Officer, I am authorizing the sending of a priority FTL message drone."

"Without Captain Newman's prior knowledge or approval?"

"Yes, CRI. I *do* have that authority."

"Of course, Mr. Ibiá."

"Signal me when the drone is off."

Stavros laid his head among his scattered papers. "Officer . . ." he muttered, yawning.

How far removed by time and distance his *official* responsibility to Earth and her authorities seemed now. The formal rank had been illusory anyway, a fiction in his mind or at best, a game. Until now, when it became real in a way he could never have predicted, at its most useful when it meant the least to him, a tool against all it stood for.

He argued the case in his mind. Could the lawyer really know, never having set foot on Fiix, never having talked to a Sawl or watched the Sisters battle from the safety of a cave mouth? In the waking dream of his exhaustion, Valla Ired and Lagri appeared in court as witnesses for the complainants.

He sat up suddenly. "CRI!"

"Mr. Ibiá?"

"There's something else! I want you to run through the remote sensing data to see if you pick up any geographical features of interest in either the desert highlands in the southern hemisphere, or the northern ocean."

CRI was silent a moment, as if puzzling over this sudden shift of inquiry. "What sort of interest? Could you be more specific, Mr. Ibiá?"

"No." He was reluctant to admit the purpose of his request. "It's a long shot, and I don't know exactly what I'm looking for. Anything anomalous, I guess."

"I will run a search, Mr. Ibiá, though I might suggest that you consult with Dr. Danforth . . . or is this inquiry also to be entered in a coded file?"

"No, leave it open."

It'll do as a cover, he thought, as his eyes drooped. Besides, Danforth might have something useful to offer.

"I'll wait for your callback. But make it quick. The cells are almost down."

"Yes, Mr. Ibiá."

The heat made him overpoweringly drowsy. "CRI?"

"Yes?"

"Thanks."

The computer did not reply.

61

E.D. 84–3:57

MEGAN SLOUCHED IN the doorway of the empty infirmary. "This leaving early is a disaster. All my craft guild contacts are too busy at the market to help me gain access to the local records."

"Too busy to get sick, too. Peace at last!" Susannah transcribed figures from her analyzer's tiny screen and slipped in a new blood sample. "What about Tyril?"

"She doesn't understand the need for a broadened database. She claims I won't learn anything here that I can't learn back in Dul Elesi. She says it's the same wherever you go, just listen to the chants."

"Surely she understands the difference between myth and actual history?"

"Nothing sure about it," Megan replied. "All this doomsday talk going around is no exercise in metaphor. She did tell me one interesting thing: all the known settlements on Fiix are the same age—or so she claims, and as if this was nothing unusual."

"Every one?"

"So she says. What brought it up was my remarking on the lack of dialect differences between Dul Elesi and Ogo Dul. Stav would tell us that geographically isolated settlements tend to develop distinct linguistic traits. Look at tiny Papua, New Guinea: before joining the modern world, it supported hundreds of different dialects."

"Your point is, the Sawls aren't so isolated?"

"Or haven't *always* been isolated . . . keeping in mind Weng's theory about a former, more advanced civilization."

Ghirra came yawning from the inner room. He noted with relief the wrinkled but empty field cots, and padded up to look over Susannah's shoulder at the glowing numbers on the analyzer screen.

"Got quiet at last." She smiled up at him. "Xifa said to let you sleep."

"What is this you do now?"

"Blood and tissue analysis, for my population survey. I asked anyone who came in to be treated if they'd mind a few extra tests. Well, actually, sometimes it was simpler not to ask, just do the tests."

"I'm trying to drag her along on my tour of the market," Megan complained. "All she wants to do is work, work, work."

Susannah laughed. "Not true. Now that Ghirra's up, I declare myself off duty." She glanced at the Master Healer. "If that's all right?"

"This is my insis-tence, Suzhannah."

Megan unearthed a tiny camera from her pack.

"Where'd you get that old thing?" Susannah marveled.

"I've had it forever—in the field, there's always a time when you want self-sufficient equipment. My version of Clausen's contraband, you might say. Only a lot less lethal. I've been saving it for a moment of true need."

She took her images unobtrusively and hid the slim, silver rectangle in the folds of her sash.

The market was in full sway. In the visitors' sector, the goods of Dul Elesi were laid out across four brightly lit tiers: soft rugs and knobby woven wools, dyed leathers and embroidered bolts of linen, delicate eating and sewing implements of bone and wood, polished buttons and flutes, sturdy unbleached papers with lacy edges, inks and hand-colored picture books. Even the potters had managed, despite the hail damage, to mount an impressive showing of their richly glazed stoneware. The glassblowers looked on with saddened pride as the remains of their own depleted wares sold as fast as they could uncrate them for display.

The congestion along the columned streets thickened to near immovability as the craftsmen of Ogo Dul jammed in to finger and compare, bringing samples from their shops, offering their openings in the intricate game of bargaining. The street lanterns flared above the crowds with a daylight brightness that reinforced the sweated excitement of the market, reducing the dark sky and darker water to zones of foreboding mystery.

"The haggling is done in great good humor," Megan observed, "but does the hilarity seem maybe a little desperate to you?" She thought the boisterous joking hid an impatient edge, that the milling sea of heat-damp faces glistened with unnatural emphasis.

"Hard to blame them for being edgy, with all this heat and worrying what's going to be left of their fields when they get home."

"Mmm." Megan wished the message drone to Earth could have waited for photo evidence of the vitality of Fiixian civilization. "How do you think the Sawls will do in the interstellar marketplace?"

Susannah laughed, then stared, then shrugged, a bit sadly. "I guess that sort of opening up is inevitable, isn't it."

"Eventually, sure—if they don't get their planet taken from them first." Megan watched the traders' quick hands and sharp eyes. "A little regulated commerce isn't always a bad influence. They could offer good product on the arts and crafts market, and with the right merchandising guidance, the Sawls would hold their own in no time, with very little effect on their present way of life, which is already heavily influenced by notions of exchange."

Susannah smiled sideways. "Is that *you* advocating change and progress?"

"Listen, I'm for anything that might help them survive."

They crossed a bridge into a sector of local shops. The dark canals were choked with loaded chresin, lanterns bobbing at bow and stern. The smooth marble railing of the bridge was warm to the touch. Shoppers taking a break hung over the balustrade in search of a stray breeze.

Beyond the bridge, the portico was lined with food stalls, stocked with smoked and salted fish, cured seaweeds, and other edibles unrecognizable in such wizened form. The Dul Elesi Food Guilders were doing great business with their baskets of mountain herbs and dried mushrooms. Beyond the fish market, local curd cheeses were being weighed against the hard cloth-bound wheels of cheese from across the plain, and a lively debate progressed over open sacks of grain and seed and crates of desiccated berries.

"Let's head up top," Susannah urged. She had brought her last unused spiral-bound sketchbook, some soft drawing pencils and a new gum eraser: low-tech implements that she felt were okay to trade, perhaps for some new and exotic bit of apparel.

"We'll need someone from Dul Elesi to handle the bartering."

Miraculously, they met Tyril in front of a fabric stall on the fourth tier, her baby asleep in a sling across her back. She was debating with the proprietor about the finer points of a certain weaving technique, but waved when she saw Megan and put aside her shop talk to join them.

"And the women all went shopping," declared Megan with a chuckle.

They jostled through the crowd, pointing and admiring. Megan fingered the silky rugs longingly. Her long-ago first paycheck, brought home to a rented room devoid of furniture, had gone as down payment for a fine rug.

The commotion finally woke the baby, who whimpered and squirmed. The child's only covering was the sling itself, yet her little body was slippery with perspiration. Tyril dried her with her tunic and fed her as they moved on through the crowd. She readily agreed to act as Susannah's bartering proxy. She studied the sketchbook and pencils with a trader's eye. When she asked what piece of clothing was needed, Susannah had to admit that she did not need anything, except to soothe an irritation with her perfectly serviceable but dull and travel-stained ship's pants and Sawl overblouse.

"Something . . . happier," she shrugged.

The idea of dressing up for fun struck a truer chord with the weaver than a need for variety. With the baby still at her breast, she ushered them through the hot bustling shops, advising on the best workmanship and materials.

Megan hid her camera away, to rely on firsthand observation. She noticed many of the younger guildsmen from Dul Elesi milling about, the first-season journeymen, each with a glazed pot or leather pouch or bolt of bright cloth under one arm—their ration from the work of their guild, theirs to barter for some item of personal desire. They chatted and giggled, fingering the finer embroideries, but more often than not, shrugged wistfully and moved on.

Susannah's fancy fell at last on a long, sleeveless shift exiled to the back of a tiny stall stuffed with more practical overshirts and tunics. The pale yellow fabric draped across her hand like watered silk.

"This one," she said.

Tyril took the sketchbook, concealed the pencils and eraser in her pouch, and went to work on the thin, sweating woman in charge of the stall. As she bargained, Megan heard a similar negotiation in the next shop rise to unusual acrimony. It ended abruptly when an elderly basketmaker threw down the knitted jacket he'd been bidding for and stalked out of the stall. The proprietor stared after him, stunned, the multicolored basket that the other had offered dangling loose in his hand.

Onlookers exchanged nervous glances. One of the offender's fellow guildsmen stepped forward with shamed excuses and apologies, and a promise to return the basket to the guild himself. The crowds and the demands of business closed over the incident like the tide, but Megan wondered if she was the only one left pondering the unfortunate coincidence of heat and bad temper.

Meanwhile, Tyril's success had been nearly instantaneous. Though the thin shopkeeper had examined the sketchbook dubiously at first, her enthusiasm had increased geometrically as she smoothed a practiced hand across its snow-white pages, admired its laser-cut edges and marveled over the springy plastic spiral binding that allowed the leaves to lie so flat when the book was opened. Tyril was clearly disappointed that the bargaining was over before she had a chance to enjoy it. She did not even have to offer the pencils and eraser.

The shopkeeper folded the robe carefully and handed it over with a smile that suggested congratulations to Tyril for having produced so clever a book, while barely concealing worry that the weaver might change her mind and demand more than a simple robe in trade for this paper treasure.

"But the papers they make in Dul Elesi are much more remarkable," Susannah protested, clutching her acquisition to her chest as they rejoined the milling crowd.

"Novelty value." Megan, as always, took the comment more seriously than it was intended. "She'd never seen a binding like that and she recognized the efficiency of its design. They adore efficiency, these Sawls. They see their ideal selves reflected in an efficient instrument. After all, efficiency is central to their survival."

"Whew! All that, from a little sketchbook!"

"Mock, mock." Megan tried for a rueful smile, but the display of temper at the neighboring stall had dampened her mood and aroused her worry instinct.

As they returned to the infirmary, they found the food wagons along the way nearly deserted, and the available fare limited to bread, hard cheese, the ubiquitous kamad-root mash and a tepid milk pudding. The Food Guilders were busy at the market, buying for the return trip and to replenish the diminishing food stores at home. An apprentice cut slices of bread and cheese, and nodded in conspiratorial agreement when Susannah politely turned down the pudding.

The infirmary was still calm, its lamps turned low, infused with a tired silence. Ampiar sat beside a fretful old man, patting his scrawny hand and murmuring soothing nonsense as if to an infant. Xifa lay curled in a corner, asleep where she had sat down for a minute to rest.

Ghirra motioned the women in from the portico and poured washing water into the stone sink. "I know a place that is not hot."

"That would be a miracle," said Megan, dousing her face gratefully.

"Yes," Ghirra smiled. "It is."

He led them to the lowest level, along the waterline, where there were no shops, only the wide columned walkways, open to the water. The narrow snub-nosed chresin bobbed in long rows, moored to blunt marble posts. Oil lamps threw hard light among the shadows of the beams overhead. The briny dark water stirred with oily ripples from the rocking of boats as cargo was loaded in and out.

Ghirra wove familiarly through the noisy dockside bustle, between the precarious towers of waiting goods and the anxious boatmen vying for space along the quay. The change in schedule had made them frantic and none were willing to take the time to ferry passengers about on nonessential business.

But near the end of the quay, he found an old man napping in the bow of an empty boat tied to the last mooring. Even in the dim light, Megan could see that the craft was in sore need of a scraping and a new coat of varnish.

At least two inches of murky water washed beneath the grating that spanned the curved wooden ribs. But the boatman smiled as he snored, so Ghirra called to him and crouched to rock the boat gently until he woke with a start, blinking.

He grabbed the bow lantern from its post and thrust it forward to squint at the rude folk who had summoned him from sleep. But when he saw Ghirra, he grinned and cackled, then stood up unsteadily and waved the lantern gleefully before he dropped it back on its peg. With spraddle-legged steps, he jerked his way forward while the little boat tossed wildly. He grasped Ghirra's hand heartily and scrambled onto the quay with surprising agility, chattering like a gossip, herding the women into the boat without a pause for breath. When all were settled, he cast off and launched himself into the stern seat just as the chresin shot forward into darkness.

Out on the water, the boatman unshipped his long pole. He stood up in the stern, clutching the damp shaft under one arm and gesturing with the other to illustrate his stream of chatter. The waterway was crowded. The dark hulks of loaded boats dwarfed them, passing like sea dragons with hooded lanterns for eyes. The old boatman seemed hardly to notice, waiting each time until the last possible moment to avoid impact.

The lighted tiers rising sheer to either side reminded Megan of the decks of a glittering cruise vessel. Caught in a romantic reverie of lamplit water and the echoes under bridges, memories of another canal city, she was about to trail her hand in the black water when Ghirra stopped her.

"This is danger," he advised.

"Ah." Megan was obscurely disappointed, but Susannah leaned over eagerly to peer down at the schools of phosphorescence sliding through the depths.

"I wondered why I'd seen nobody swimming. These are not the domestic fish, then? These are poisonous?"

Ghirra nodded. "The eating fish grow in the branch where wild fish do not go."

Megan hunched in the bow as an overloaded chresin bore down on them from the darkness dead ahead.

"There is also thing there with hard skin and live in mud," Ghirra continued calmly. "Also the water plant."

"Er . . . Um ?" Megan clutched the gunwales, reluctant to let go long enough to point out disaster approaching.

"This is very healthy," said Ghirra. "The Food Guild bring to home most that they can trade for."

Just as Megan was considering prayer, the old boatman deftly swerved off their collision course. He exchanged greetings of maniacal cheer with the poleman in the other boat as it skimmed past with mere centimeters to spare, its lanterns and towering cargo swaying like drunken companions.

The little craft gained the first intersection without being rammed, and slowed in the crossroads traffic. The old man snaked through the congestion into a wider, darker canyon. A steady stream of loaded boats poled up from the open bay, moving slowly against the tide with sails furled around cross-rigged masts. The boatman let the chresin drift, carried seaward with the current, then a moment later, dug his pole into the invisible bottom and swerved the boat about with a grunting shove to send it gliding up another steeply narrow waterway.

The raucous market noises gave way to scattered domestic sounds softened by distance, a child's laugh or wail, a woman calling to a neighbor. Ghirra studied each glowing window and doorway with a sober questing eye until Susannah was moved to inquire gently, "Where are we now?"

He drew himself away from his private study and smiled, and Susannah understood finally that this easy smile, Ghirra's accepted public manner, was a conscious camouflage. He could not be said to be moody because his disquiet did not come and go. It was always with him, beneath his smiling surface, visible only when he let the mask slip, and he was doing so more often of late. Some day, surely he would trust her enough to talk of his history, his childhood, his inner self. But now he flourished the old, practiced smile and slid into the role of tour guide, pointing out the finely wrought balustrades lining the tiers, the intricate column capitals and the tales of the goddesses wrapping the sturdy shafts. And Susannah felt that she was getting less of him than she deserved.

The steep canyon narrowed further. The chresin slipped past a final streetlamp, past the last window glowing amber and lavender through tiny round panes. Beyond the bow lantern, the darkness was impenetrable. No one spoke. The boatman steered with nonchalant confidence into the void. He began a little singsong count, swaying the craft to his rhythm. He built to a murmured crescendo and plunged his pole into the water on the final note. Ghirra laughed boyishly as the boat skewed into a breathtaking right angle turn. The old man let it glide a while in darkness, then dug into the bottom with renewed vigor to swerve the boat again, returning to its former course. The void parted in front of them like a velvet curtain, sweeping aside to reveal a broad rock-walled arena.

The water canyon dead-ended. A giant, glowing cave mouth perched like a rising moon at the top of a wide lamplit flight of stairs. Sheer walls towered all around, covered with intricate carvings. Layers of incised geometric designs alternated with shallow frieze-work, where the vengeful figures of the Sisters faced each other repeatedly over the heads of the suffering multitude.

On either side of the cave, a long path twisted down among the friezes from the high rim of the canyon to the paved stone quay at the bottom. The stair to the cave ascended from polished pavement in waves of curved steps, flanked by graceful railings and matched pairs of carved stone lanterns.

The chresin's bow nudged the worn edge of the quay. Megan grabbed for a mooring post. The boatman swung the stern around, and Ghirra leaped out to tie the bow. Other boats rocked gently against their moorings. A young couple sat in a pool of lamplight midway up the stair, talking in quiet, worried tones while their baby slept in the father's lap. Ghirra handed the two women out of the boat and led the way up the steps. The old boatman resettled himself in the stern and closed his eyes.

At the top, the monumental curl of the entry opened into a shining square corridor that burrowed straight and tall into the rock. White marble as smooth as new ice sheathed its sides, broken only by glittering sconces of porcelain and blown glass. The end of the corridor dissolved into a golden infinity. Susannah floated along like a pilgrim in a foreign cathedral, but Megan felt for the camera still stashed in her waistband.

They walked in silence for several minutes before the seamless white was broken by intersecting corridors, all cloaked in the same shining stone, bejeweled with glass and lamplight, but otherwise unadorned. The largest exhaled odors of steam and dampness, and the faint drip and trickle of running water mingled with a chanting voice or two.

The narrower corridors were lit only by slim blue flames burning in shallow wall niches. Here and there, Sawls sat opposite the flames on low benches set against the wall. Megan noted familiar faces from the Priest Guild, Kav Ashimmel among others, deep in solemn contemplation.

The golden infinity ahead grew a dark spot at its center. As they neared, it swelled into a shadowed archway. The arch was a simple half-moon shape cut into the glistening white marble. The smoothness and plainness and whiteness of the walls rendered them insubstantial, as if walls of pure light gathered around a darkness that drew all things inward toward its center. A profound silence emanated from that darkness, together with a hint of coolness. Ghirra's pace quickened.

They entered a vast dome of rock.

The center was unlit, a pocket of deep night. The curving sides were defined by successive circles of light from tall freestanding stone lanterns spaced around the perimeter. The familiar pattern of interlocking circles traced giant salmon-colored loops across dark green marble paving. The lamplight faded with distance as if the central darkness were physical, like a mist or a thin black drape.

Megan's impression was of infinite space. The air was in motion. A cool upward draft brought damp relief from the outer heat. Ghirra pointed straight up. An impossible distance above, the dome opened a small circle to the sky. Stars sparkled against a velvet background of night, less dark than the enclosed void beneath them.

Ghirra offered another of his carefully considered translations. "We name this cave Sky Hall." He crouched and pressed his palm to the floor, smiling and beckoning.

The stone tile was chill and beaded with a thin film of moisture that re-formed the instant it was wiped away. Megan would have been happy to flatten herself facedown on the cold stone, but the dignity of the place, as well as her own, restrained her.

"There is water under," Ghirra explained. "From the rock. Here it is never hot."

Megan laid chilled palms against her cheeks. "I'd live down here if I were them."

"It's not always this hot." Susannah slipped off her sandals to soak up the coolness through her feet.

They moved through darkness into the light of the first lantern. It stood in splendid isolation, head-high and carved of rosy quartz, in the shape of a slim woman hugging a hekker calf between arm and hip while balancing a loaded food basket on the opposite shoulder. The lamp flame burned within the lattice of the basket, the translucent smoke of the quartz diffusing the light so that the lithe figure glowed from within. The carving was startlingly lifelike, unlike the sad grotesques of the friezes or the stylized likenesses of the goddesses.

"How lovely!" Megan traced the graceful line of the back tentatively, as if she expected the statue to move beneath her hand. "A Sawlian Ceres."

The second lantern was a seated male figure whose muscular knees embraced a crystalline potter's wheel. The pot he was turning formed the lamp, shaped by complex curves and mysterious inner spaces. The stone of his body was opaque, so that his intent face was lit from without, by the light of the work beneath his large, capable hands.

The third was an old woman, spinning finely wrought handfuls of quartzite wool into a glowing skein that imprisoned a small bright flame. The next was a young man tanning translucent leather, the next a weaver, then a joiner, then a stone carver who chiseled away at a glimmering lantern that was a miniature of himself.

"Are all the guilds represented?" Susannah guessed.

Ghirra nodded, looking proud and satisfied.

Megan lagged behind, caught by odd markings on the perimeter wall. She went up to touch the dark rock. An incised pattern of lines and circles textured the surface, smoothed to near-invisibility by age and the wear of hands tracking their shape just as she was doing. Above her reach, the lines were sharper, but it was only the sharp, shadowing angle of the lantern light that had caused her to notice them. She stood back to take in the pattern as a whole.

"Klee," suggested Susannah at her shoulder.

"Or more recently, Michaelmas, but even more abstract . . . This is very interesting," she said, as Ghirra joined them.

"Yes. Old drawing."

"What does it mean?"

He spread his palms. "This is nothing, I think. Old drawing."

"Are you sure? Just decoration?" Megan was unconvinced.

"Why not?" Susannah asked.

"Instinct says otherwise."

Ghirra frowned up at the wall as if he had never looked at it closely before. "You say this drawing has meaning?"

Megan paced along the curve, in and out of darkness, to the next pool of light. Again, faint lines and circles enlivened the wall, these slightly less worn, some intersecting, curling about one another.

Susannah backed away. "You can see it best from here, actually. This pattern's pretty much the same as the other."

Ghirra dogged Megan's shoulder. "Why you say this has meaning?"

"Wait." Susannah moved to the next pattern. "It's not the same. It's changing, very slowly." She hurried on to the next, her bare feet slapping against the damp floor. "See? Some parts of it are coming together, others drifting apart. Look at that section of dense markings. See how it moves downward and to the right?" Her pace increased with each discovery. "It intersects with that strong right-left diagonal by this panel here. And then . . . damn! Stavros should see this!"

Ghirra followed, caught up in her sudden burst of energy. "But this is not language."

"Art is always language," said Megan. "These could be like pictographs, for instance. Symbols that do not represent words but ideas and emotions."

By the fifteenth panel, the lines were strong and deep, the pattern clear even without benefit of shadow.

Susannah waved her empty hands in frustration. "I should know better than to go anywhere without my sketchbook! Ghirra, will we have time to come back here?"

His shoulders hunched uneasily. "I think my sister will say no."

Megan offered a cheesy grin and pulled the tiny camera from her belt. "Technology to the rescue."

Slouched against the balustrade, Ghirra handled the silvery little box with reverent care, twisting it repeatedly in his hands. He held it out as he had seen Megan do in the Sky Hall. "This give a picture out of the air?"

"Out of the light." Susannah hitched the oil lamp closer, blotting at her sweat as it dampened her sketchbook. The Infirmary wagon's tailgate was too low for a proper table. Her back ached. Already, she longed to be back in that miraculous coolness.

Ghirra lowered the camera to stare soberly at the spot where he'd seen the images appear.

"Here, let me." Susannah took the camera, turned it on and handed it back to him. "Press this to scroll through. They don't look like much now—the dim light made it hard to get a good image. But when we get back, we can upload them to CRI for enhancement, and they'll come out fine. For now, my sketches will have to do." She erased energetically, redrew a line or two. "Does this look accurate to you?"

Ghirra wrenched his attention away from the changing images and came over with the camera cradled in both hands. He set it down on the tailgate with infinite care. "You draw this well, Suzhannah." He tapped the penciled lines and circles with an emphatic finger. "But this is not language."

His stubborn mood matched her own. "Why are you so sure?"

"Old drawing," he said again. "Priest drawing. This is nothing."

"Ghirra, the pattern shows a consistent change from beginning to end. That can't be accidental!"

He twisted away, heading for the infirmary door. "This is nothing, Suzhannah."

"The artist had *something* in mind!" she called after him, but he tossed back a gesture of dismissal and ducked into the entry.

"There's always such a thing as *l'art pour l'art*." Megan plunked a loaded eating tray down on the tailgate.

"Have you noticed any of that here?" replied Susannah rudely.

"Not so far. It's not something they have time for now, but maybe in the past . . ."

"Why is he being so obstinate about it?" Susannah fussed. "It's like he doesn't *want* it to mean anything!"

"Why are you pushing him so hard? Maybe the idea is new to him. Maybe he'd have preferred to have thought of it himself." Megan handed her a warm ball wrapped in russet leaves. "Here, eat something. Maybe it'll improve your disposition."

Susannah closed her sketchbook and shoved it aside.

"Or maybe," Megan offered, chewing placidly, "the poor man is tired of us explaining his own life to him. He's touchy enough about the Priest Guild making claim to the truth. Wasn't it you who admitted that doctors get so into their power over life and death that they end up sure they know it all?"

"Yeah, but Ghirra . . ."

"What, but Ghirra? Because he's bright and gentle and dedicated, he shouldn't have an ego? Those are usually the guys with the biggest, because they're smart enough to *know* they're better than most."

"But he's been so open and curious all along."

"Sure. He has a good scientist's instincts. But Ghirra's a pretty big fish in this particular pond. It must be hard to have a bunch of strangers show up and tell him all he knows is still not nearly enough."

"I've never said . . ."

"Of course not. But you have all this equipment and methods and ideas . . ." Megan snatched up the little camera and stowed it back in her sash. "We're talking self-image here, how Ghirra pictures himself in relation to his own world, which has to have changed radically since we arrived. No matter how eager he is to learn and share knowledge, all this has probably left him a little sensitive to challenge."

"Challenge? I thought it was a discussion!" Susannah turned away to lean over the outer railing and stare down at the boatmen still hard at work on the water. "Okay, I could have been more tactful. I keep forgetting he's . . ."

"I know." Megan spoke in italics. *"Not one of us."*

"Yeah."

"You'd do him more honor if you remembered."

Susannah retired to a dark corner of the inner room to wash up and try on her new robe. The apprentices came in to hang up their smocks while she was stripped to the waist. Privacy, she reflected, was of little value in this society.

Xifa joined her at the sink with a weary smile and the information that a special invocation to Valla Ired was to be performed after the dinner meal by Ogo Dul's Priest Guild, led by their young Ritual Master, who had only recently inherited her post. Susannah promised to attend.

When she was alone again, she undressed and slipped the robe over her head. It draped gracefully along her body. Even in the stifling heat, the silken fabric felt cool to the touch. The pale yellow was luminous against her tanned skin. Susannah felt beautiful in it, and for the first time wished the Sawls used mirrors.

She turned to find Ghirra in the doorway.

"You will come to see Kav Larma dance?" he inquired formally.

"Of course." She felt intruded upon, but ashamed of the moment of temper that had passed between them. She made an awkward, apologetic pirouette. "Do you like my new gown?"

"This is very beautiful," he acknowledged. "Ibi will like seeing you in this."

Some demon of heat and exhaustion made her press him further. "Do you like seeing me in it?"

His head tilted, as if he was not sure he'd heard her right.

His surprise made Susannah laugh. "It never occurred to you, did it?" Rueful with relief, she went to him and leaned her forehead against his shoulder like a friendly animal. "Forgive me, dear friend. I am behaving very badly."

"This is nothing." He slid a paternal arm across her back, taking instinctive charge, reminding her that his own practice of healing extended to the mind as well as the body. "You feel without him."

"I do," she murmured, already comforted. "And the heat is making me a little crazy."

"This is its other danger," he agreed.

"Ghirra, you do know how much I respect your methods? I've learned as much from you as you say you have from me. You have . . . gifts I can't understand or imagine."

He let his arm drape over her shoulder in a companionable fashion. "This is good hearing, Suzhannah. Maybe like this, we find some true knowing together."

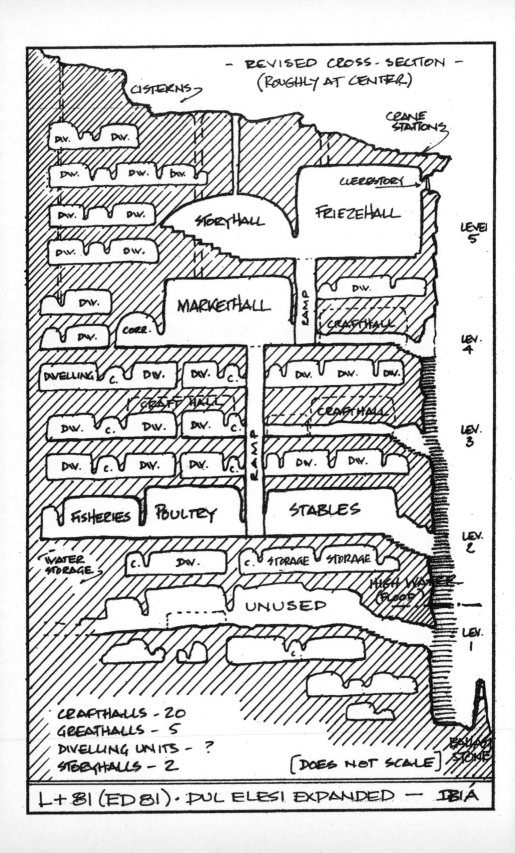

- REVISED CROSS-SECTION -
(ROUGHLY AT CENTER)

CISTERNS

CRANE STATIONS

CLERESTORY

FRIEZEHALL

STORYHALL

D.W.
D.W.
D.W.
D.W.
D.W.
D.W.
D.W.
D.W.
D.W.
D.W.

LEVEL 5

D.W.

CRAFTHALL

MARKETHALL

RAMP

LEV. 4

CORR.

DWELLING   C.   D.W.   D.W.   D.W.   D.W.   D.W.

CRAFT HALL

CRAFTHALL

D.W.   C.   D.W.   D.W.   C.   D.W.   D.W.

LEV. 3

RAMP

D.W.   C.   D.W.   D.W.   C.   D.W.   D.W.

FISHERIES   POULTRY   STABLES

LEV. 2

WATER STORAGE

C.   D.W.   C.   STORAGE   STORAGE

HIGH WATER (FLOOD?)

UNUSED

LEV. 1

C.

CRAFTHALLS - 20
GREATHALLS - 5
DWELLING UNITS - ?
STORYHALLS - 2

[DOES NOT SCALE]

BALLAST STONE

L + 81 (ED 81) · DUL ELESI EXPANDED — IBIA

62

E.D. 85–15:08

CLAUSEN STRAIGHTENED from his crouch and slid the cooling laser gun into the holster on his belt. He wiped sweating palms on his thighs, frowning at the damage done to his trousers. "All right, good enough for com. We'll try for power later. Run out the cable."

"Done that, while you were welding." McPherson's gesture with the battery lamp sliced a line of light across the heated darkness. Clausen's shadow lunged across the fragile golden span of the antenna suspended in its slanting ring of stones. "With the extra from the Sled, it'll reach just past the first strut. Least we'll be undercover."

"From what?" Clausen kicked at the ground with a booted toe. Dust rose up like smoke in the lamp beam. "Not even a goddamn dewfall here to worry about."

"The sun," she replied earnestly. "When it comes back."

"McP, you're losing your ear for irony . . . if you ever had one." He grabbed the lamp and strode across the clearing to the Lander, elbowing past Weng, who watched from beside the landing strut, fanning herself with a plastic container lid. McPherson followed reluctantly, with a glance into the rustling blackness of the fields, where the Sawls were hard at work on some project of their own.

Clausen moved in on Danforth's bedside workstation without ceremony, pulling plugs and gathering cable. The planetologist howled as his keypad went dead beneath his fingers. He returned McPherson's weary look of apology with a glare as she reached for his mini-terminal. "Get your own equipment down from the Caves, for Christ's sake!"

The pilot shook her head. "Gone. Like the cable."

"All of it? Jeez, the kid's serious."

"No shit."

The little unit was not heavy, but McPherson sagged as if it weighed a ton. She looked pale and heat-worn in the glare of Danforth's emergency lamp work light.

"Pushing you hard, isn't he?" Danforth sent a sidelong glower at Clausen, who now wore his laser pistol in a tool belt, snuggled at the small of his back as if daring anyone to grab it. Danforth considered this a challenge and an insult to them all, especially to Weng. But beneath his resentment was a flicker of gratitude that at least *someone* was seeing to the repair of the link.

McPherson brightened a little at his show of concern. "Listen, I got an idea for a chair we can rig up—let you move around a little so you can use the stuff, too."

"I need that box *today,* McP!" Clausen barked from the outer darkness.

"Yessir, right away, sir!" She mimed a tiger snarl at Danforth and took the mini-terminal away.

Danforth switched off his lamp and sat in the dark, pretending it was cooler that way, and laying out his own sequence of priorities when the com was up again. He'd developed theory and planning into a sublime art in order to pass the time, but he cherished the hope that real answers would soon be forthcoming, with CRI back on-line.

New data were his primary concern. He needed new data badly, global data for the freak monsoon that had wrecked his Sled, and now for this recent lack of rainfall. He needed to know where those events had come from, and if they were restricted to the same narrow band as the snowstorm had been. Then he could do some proper modeling to get a lock on his X-factor.

He was distracted by the mysterious clinking and soft chatter from the Sawls working in the dark fields. The faint Cluster light showed the broad leaves hanging limp with thirst and heat fatigue. *Me, too,* he mused. He couldn't recall when he'd started hoarding water. Even before Weng had declared the practice official, they'd each been doing it privately. Would they soon be forced to begin rationing as well?

But Danforth's private worry was that the prolonged darkness and unrelenting heat might be nibbling at the fringes of his reason, just as the tides work patiently to erode even the rockiest shore. It was nothing extreme or obvious. He'd leave the melodrama to Ibiá, who seemed finally to have gone off that edge he'd been teetering on for so long. But of late, he'd caught himself replaying the strange weather events during the Leave-taking, events he preferred to forget. He'd stare up at the panoply of burning stars, listening hard into the night silences, tempted to ascribe intent to the windless suffocating heat, wondering if there was something out there in the dark that might offer a more satisfactory answer to his questions than the data chattering across his computer screen. He mentioned these lapses to no one. Wasn't anthropomorphizing a sign of desperation, of grasping for the easy, sloppy answer?

So he fought off his seizures of what he thought of as intellectual dehydration, and redoubled his search for the X-Factor. He was determined to make sense out of weather that was so far as adequately explained by the Sawl mythos as by any more rational and "scientific" means.

"Need another foot or so!" Clausen called out. "Grab that other end!"

Danforth twisted his body sideways on the bed and eased a leg over the edge, the one cast-bound only below the knee. He craned his neck to watch Clausen plug in the cable from the antenna. McPherson hovered and Weng stood back, fanning herself with the slow, detached dignity of a fairy-tale empress. The weight of the cast pulled at Danforth's unused muscles. The gash in his chest was healing, but sitting upright and unsupported made him reel with pain and weakness.

Only across the width of the Underbelly, the new workstation might as well have been a million miles away.

He raged at Clausen silently, while noting with interest that it was not Ibiá the saboteur who was the focus of his impotent wrath.

"I have completed the requested data search, Mr. Ibiá."

Stavros shuddered awake from dreams of talking to a towering pillar of fire. CRI's tinny summons reverberated in the darkened cavern. He felt for his oil lamp and shook it gently. Empty. He must have fallen asleep and left it burning.

"Mr. Ibiá?"

"Just a moment, CRI." His voice creaked. He fumbled for his little battery lamp and switched it on. He was groggy and stiff from his exhausted collapse at the makeshift console. Liphar lay naked on his pad against the wall, frowning through his sleep. Discarded clothing lurked in the corners like corpses. There was no sign of Edan.

"What day is it?"

"L plus 85," responded CRI briskly.

Stavros pinpointed the urgency nagging at him, beside the desperate need to relieve himself. "Did the drone get off?"

"Exactly according to your orders, Mr. Ibiá." The computer managed to sound insulted by his worried tone.

Stavros roused himself with effort and shuffled to the sink. The water was no longer merely tepid, it was warm, and trickled rather than flowed from the tap. He regarded it with foreboding and shut it down as soon as he'd splashed his face and chest and drunk his fill. He nosed among his supplies and dug out a packet of freeze-dried apricots to dull an unreasoning hunger. Dripping from face and hands, he headed for the lavatory at the far end of the outer hall.

Back in the cavern, he stripped off his linen pants, offended by their griminess and by the pungence of his own unwashed smell. He sat down at the terminal, feeling vulnerable in his sweating nakedness, and only slightly more comfortable. "Okay, CRI, I'm ready. What did you find?"

"A preliminary scan of the remote sensing data, together with the hemi-spheric photos from the polar orbiters, has turned up a few items that might be of interest to you. First, in the northern hemisphere, Mr. Clausen's deep sensors indicate a sizable gravitational anomaly near the center of the great ocean, suggesting the presence of a buried mass."

"A mass of what?"

CRI hesitated, as if recalling that it was not Danforth she was reporting to. "A solid body, Mr. Ibiá. Its composition is impossible to determine at the moment, but the ocean is roughly circular and could be interpreted as a water-filled impact basin."

"Oh. One hell of a big crater."

"Is this the sort of anomaly you were hoping to discover?"

Stavros rubbed his eyes. "Not precisely, but it's interesting. Go on."

"It is particularly interesting in light of the specifics of your request," CRI encouraged. "In the southern hemisphere, at a point exactly opposite to this gravitational blip, is a large but clearly defined area of severe upthrust. Very broken terrain. This would also be expected in the case of a major impact. It is the only feature in the southern desert highlands that could be considered anomalous."

"Hmm." Stavros ran through the words of the tale chant describing the creation of Lagri's mountain fortress. It did not seem impossible that the "bolt of the creator's might" could have been inspired by some race memory of an ancient meteor strike.

"Can you get me a picture of that area, CRI? Some kind of close-up?"

"The polar orbiters are equipped for hemispheric resolution only, Mr. Ibiá. As for the radar imaging . . ."

"Come on, Clausen must be flying something that'll produce high-resolution pictures!"

"I am not at liberty to divulge . . ."

"Okay, okay. Tit for tat. How about this: don't tell me anything 'sensitive,' just get me the photo. Can you do that?"

"At the present low-transmission rate, it will take some time, even supposing I can locate such data."

"Sounds like I damn well gotta go there myself!" Stavros fumed. Were he dealing with a human, this kind of foot-dragging could be preparatory to the suggestion that a certain sum might unlock sticky doors. But he'd not yet heard of anyone successfully bribing a computer.

Go there myself, he thought ironically. If I only had wings.

But the notion had its attractions, despite its current impossibility. In fact, it was so obvious and simple that he couldn't understand why he hadn't thought of it before. He shoved his stool away from the console and, despite the heat, began to pace excitedly.

What better way to prove the goddesses exist than to go find one! What would Kav Daven say to such an idea? What would Ghirra?

"May I ask a question?" ventured CRI.

"Be my guest."

"If you were not looking for evidence of an impact, what led you to request information about an anomaly precisely where one seems to be?"

Stavros remembered his hunger and ripped at the packet of apricots. "You really want to know?"

"I am not programmed to make insincere requests, Mr. Ibiá."

"Well, your input might be useful, so I'll send you something." He heard Edan's quiet trot coming up the outer corridor and decided not to care that he'd discarded all his clothing. A Sawl wouldn't give it a moment's thought. "Run it through my translator program, store it, and tell me what you think."

He took the battery lamp to the rear of the cavern and unearthed a metal box from beneath a pile of silver-film blankets, his cache of precious hours of singing and chanting and storytelling.

"In fact," he called back, "I really should upload *all* my files, before the heat gets to them, or . . ."

Or before something gets to me. Something like a convenient landslide.

He located the storage unit he wanted, Liphar's throaty rendition of the Fortress of Lagri tale chant. He brought it back to the terminal and plugged it in. "Chew on that for a while."

Edan materialized at the entrance, sweat-drenched and eager. As he'd predicted, she paid his nakedness no heed but announced that the ranger salvage party was on its way in with the wrecked Sled. Liphar stirred on his bedroll and sat up. Edan gave him her second piece of news. A ceremony was planned, an attempt to sing strength to Valla so that the crops might have a little rain.

Stavros' attention caught on the Sled. How remarkable that the vehicle should reappear coincident with his notion of going in search of a physical goddess.

"Mr. Ibiá, I seem to be receiving . . ."

"Just a minute, CRI." He pressed Edan for a report on the condition of the Sled and the progress of the antenna repairs. Liphar woke up enough to clamor for further information about the ceremony.

"Mr. Ibiá, there is a signal . . ."

"CRI, Lifa, please!"

Edan was having difficulty describing objects for which she lacked the appropriate vocabulary.

"I am patching it in now," CRI continued.

The speaker snapped and hissed warningly. Stavros whirled in horror as Clausen's voice invaded the room, transmitting his call code from the Lander. Liphar scrambled up in confusion. Edan flinched into a fighting posture and scanned the darkened corners for the man she knew the voice belonged to.

Forcing himself to exhale, Stavros lunged to shut down all but the listening mode.

"The Orbiter is receiving you, Mr. Clausen," came CRI's welcoming reply. "Captain Newman will be relieved to have you back in contact. You have had a successful trip, I hope?"

"Trip?" Clausen's voice was as clear as if it came from the next room.

"Across the plain with the traders? Mr. Ibiá has kept us well informed of . . ."

"IBIA? WHERE IS HE?"

"Shit, he's fixed their com link." Stavros slapped every switch within reach and unplugged all the cables. He sat in numbed silence for the thirty seconds it took for him to realize that CRI would be able to supply the prospector with an exact fix on the location of his hiding place. Suddenly the air in the cavern seemed too hot to breathe.

"Time to move on. We're sitting ducks in here." He shut his eyes, whispering when he wanted to shout and run. Could they move the equipment? How long would it take the prospector to get there? He wouldn't know about the route up through the Caves, but still . . . Stavros grabbed his pants for some small sense of security, then explained to his shaken companions the new depths of their predicament.

Clausen summoned calm in place of his first explosive rage. "Where is he, CRI?"

"I was unaware that you were ignorant of Mr. Ibiá's whereabouts," the computer replied peevishly. "I will supply those coordinates."

"I'd appreciate that, CRI." Clausen curled into a predatory slouch. He watched as the figures appeared, dead center in the screen. "That little shit! He's right on top of us!"

Weng stood blocking him by the time he came erect.

"Out of my way, Commander."

Weng put out a hand. "Perhaps you would rather leave your . . . tools behind, Mr. Clausen. In safe keeping."

Clausen knocked her hand away, with more force than was necessary. Beside him, McPherson tensed, immobile with indecision. He glanced at her, then chuckled and drew the little pistol. "Right you are, Commander. I won't be needing this, will I?"

He handed the laser to Weng butt-first and snatched up his searchbeam instead.

Weng stared after him as he loped up the dark path toward the Caves. Then, impulsively, she stooped to the console. "CRI, kindly inform Mr. Ibiá that Mr. Clausen is on his way."

McPherson gaped. "Commander, why did you do that?"

Weng backed slowly away from the console as if it had made an indecent proposal. Her powder-soft brow creased with unease. "I don't precisely know, Lieutenant. To save Mr. Ibiá's life, I suppose."

As they awaited Clausen's return, Weng filed a month's worth of status reports with her superiors in the Orbiter and began the downloading of the recent instrument data.

Wondering if she should have gone with the prospector, if only to keep an eye on him, McPherson trudged up to the Sawl work encampment at the foot of the cliffs to borrow an idled water wagon. She met one of the returned rangers trotting down the path, on his way to announce the arrival of the salvaged B-Sled. She greeted him gladly in her fledgling Sawlish and followed him to the encampment, where the battered vehicle lay just outside the circle of firelight on its rough-built sledge.

She walked around the winged hulk. The nose and tail hung off either end of the sledge. A coating of grime and dust turned its smooth white skin to ocher. The hjalk team that had hauled it blew heavily into their water buckets, their lathered ribs heaving. McPherson guessed that the lashed and pegged wooden sledge itself weighed more than the Sled, and pitied the Sawls for their lack of lightweight construction materials.

The salvage party had collapsed in scattered twos and threes out of range of the fire's heat. As McPherson approached, they glared in dull exhaustion as if daring her to demand the Sled's immediate delivery down to the Lander. It's what Clausen would want, she told herself, but it had to be otherwise. Though she might lack the personal refinement of someone like Taylor or Susannah, she knew how to handle the enlisted men.

So she thanked them all, and made polite arrangements with the party leader to haul it down at the start of the next work cycle. The tired Sawls were so relieved, they assented immediately to the loan of an empty two-cart. McPherson placed herself between the shafts and trundled off to the Lander to make a movable bed-chair for Danforth.

She took advantage of Clausen's absence to raise the new workstation so that her wheeled invention could slide underneath. Danforth could work as if seated at a standard console. Weng agreed to use it standing up. Once he'd been painfully levered into the adapted cart, Danforth greeted CRI like a long-lost lover, and was beyond reach for the better part of an hour. Eventually, he sat back from the mini-terminal with a frown.

"That's odd." He turned to Weng and McPherson, the first sign that he was aware of their constant presence at his shoulder. "Want to know what Ibiá's been up to all this time?"

Weng leaned into the screen. "I see."

"It's weird, all right," McPherson remarked.

"What possible interest could a linguist have in the sensing data?"

Weng pointed a slim, dry finger. "Only in reference to those two areas, it seems."

"If I may, Commander," offered the computer. "I believe Mr. Ibiá was attempting to draw some connection between locations figuring prominently in the Sawlish mythos and actual geographical features of the planet."

"What locations?"

"The homes of the goddesses, Commander."

This silenced them a moment. Then Danforth noticed the angle that would result if a line were drawn between the two points of Stavros' interest: the now familiar northeast-southwest diagonal slash across the face of the planet. Coincidence? Or the beginning of a pattern? He soothed his chill with the reminder that mythological locations were often inspired by some extraordinary feature of local geography.

Still . . . "Weng, how good is your Sawlish?"

"Nearly nonexistent, I fear."

"Me, too. What about you, Ron?"

McPherson shrugged. "I get along."

"Mr. Clausen has been giving it some attention of late," said Weng.

Danforth bared his teeth, then sighed. "Think he's good enough to get a Sawl talking about the weather?"

"I wouldn't know." Weng permitted herself the ghost of an ironic smile. "But if he could, *would* he?"

Danforth cursed softly. "I've been a damned fool, passing up data that's been right under my nose!" He shifted awkwardly in the wheeled chair. "Listen, Weng, we've got to get Ibiá down here. Can we offer him amnesty or something? I really need him here to translate."

"Mr. Clausen may be doing us that favor as we speak," Weng reminded him. "CRI says she was unable to contact Mr. Ibiá to warn him."

"Oh, boy." Danforth's eyes flicked over the dark fields, toward the towering bulk of the cliff kissed by pale Cluster light. "I sure hope the kid's in one piece when he gets here."

BOOK SEVEN

DROUGHT

"Look, here comes a walking fire."

—*King Lear*, Act III, sc.iv

63

NCE AGAIN THE WAGONS were being loaded, but this time the waiting stacks of goods bore the guild stamps of Ogo Dul. A more solemn frenzy prevailed along the columned streets of Trader's Branch, unlike the free and joyous departure from Dul Elesi nearly three weeks earlier. The street lanterns seemed to burn unbearably bright. No songs of celebration rose above the clatter of crate and wheel and harness. After Megan had provided what little help she could with the reloading of the Infirmary wagon, she wandered the bustling crowd, taking its temperature.

She missed the music. She'd grown used to a sung or chanted accompaniment to almost every Sawlish activity. She thought of music as a calmative, a matrix on which to weave human passions into a more coherent order. But singing required effort, even if minimal, and in this great heat and hurry, no one was willing to squander even an ounce of energy on a nonessential pursuit.

The children were another telling barometer. The youngest instinctively stayed out from underfoot. Their older siblings raced around laden with sacks and baskets and armloads of cloth-wrapped merchandise, their small faces serious with purpose. They were eager to prove their adulthood in the face of a crisis whose nature they did not quite comprehend but whose aura radiated from their harried, grim-faced elders.

In the crowd, disputes flared easily and the talk was of Devastation. Devastations past, in myth, the Devastation to come. The wagering was fast and reckless, though the Priest Guild hung close to its wagons, offering nothing more than predictions of continuing heat. The rangers circulated constantly, calming tempers, arbitrating difficulties, and encouraging a rapid, efficient pace. Megan overheard them spreading Aguidran's directive that space be found in each big wagon for at least two extra water kegs.

When the heat seems to be emanating from within your body, your very cells, she decided, that's when you start to get frightened.

She worried about the long return trek across the Dop Arek. As hot as it had been on the way out, water had been plentiful, left over from the storms. But surely the rainless weeks since had seared the arid plain into a virtual desert. Worse still, sunrise was due within the week, when the caravan would be crossing the most open stretches of the plain.

Normally, Megan would welcome dawn after two weeks of darkness. Now the very thought of it filled her with dread.

Along the railing outside the infirmary, Ghirra and Aguidran leaned shoulder to shoulder in gloomy conference with a lanky balding man Megan recognized as the head of Ogo Dul's Ranger Guild. Susannah and Xifa sat on the yellow wagon's lowered tailgate, little Dwingen sandwiched between them. Three pairs of legs swung back and forth to the same nervous rhythm.

"All packed?" Megan rubbed her hands in a manic attempt to break out of her own doomsday mood.

Susannah nodded. "The herdsmen are bringing the hjalk around now."

"Be better when we're moving again, making actual progress toward home."

"Home?" Susannah echoed.

Megan listened for bitterness but heard only rueful confusion.

When the hjalk arrived, they were restive and grouchy about being laced into their harness. Ghirra came over from the rail to draw the great curly head of the team leader down to his, holding it gently by its undersized ears for a murmured chat. Aguidran went on her way, to hurry along the rest of the harnessing and start the long wagon train moving up the steep ramps to the savannah.

At the top of the ramps, the torch pillars blazed against the blackness. The smoke rose past the hazy light of the Cluster, fading the dimmer stars. The shining worried faces of Ogo Dul lined the white roadway to bid friends and guild-mates a safe journey. Relatives embraced. Last-minute wagers were offered and exchanged, to be collected at the next market. Ogo Dul's

Priest Guild stood apart in the darkness, chanting ringing choruses that were answered antiphonally by the priests at the front of the caravan.

"Khe khem!" Megan heard it over and over, called fervently and followed often by a whispered *"ValEmbriha!"*

A faint breath tinged the air with the salt pungence of Dul Valla. The torch flames leaped. The hjalk danced with flared nostrils while their drivers struggled with the reins.

"I am not meant to live in a cave!" Susannah breathed in grateful release, the only one among them welcoming the dark emptiness of the rolling savannah.

Megan, who had discovered that she was perfectly at home in the deepest of caves, wondered how it was possible to feel safer out in the open.

The first two throws brought the caravan up the gradual slope from the sea, through the long, brittle grasses to the cooling depths of Imvalla's pool. The great waterfall cried out in a tumbling roar of phosphorescence. The incredible precipice loomed above the camp, visible only as a darker darkness devoid of stars.

When the wagons were settled, Aguidran ordered all the water kegs to be emptied, then sent the entire caravan to the pool's edge for a last long bath.

At the beginning of the next throw, the wagons' loads were further lightened by the amount that each person could carry on his back. The arduous slow climb up the eight long switchbacks began.

What had required a mere matter of hours in the descent took the better part of a full throw to accomplish in the ascent. The hjalk balked and complained. Even the reliable little hakra showed a more goatish nature. The herdsmen swore and pulled and finally resorted to occasional blows. When the last panting hakra had heaved its burden over the top, and the dark expanse of the Dop Arek stretched before them, Aguidran declared an early camp, set careful perimeter watches and called a conference of the guild leaders.

The conference was interrupted by a child screaming among the herd of hakra and hjalk gathered to drink at the river. Rangers pounded past the wagons and a scuffle exploded in the darkness, more screams, not the child, but a dying angry beast.

The terrified child was rushed to the Infirmary wagon. Xifa searched hurriedly for teeth marks while Ampiar ran for the antivenom poultices. But the boy was found to be uninjured and after Ghirra's hands did their work to calm his hysteria, he was soon grinning with pride at having evaded his attacker's lethal jaws.

Ghirra returned later from the conference to find his staff drawn in a close circle around a low-burning lantern. He settled himself cross-legged among them, smiling at Susannah over his tray of cold food.

"I have ask my sister give you some of this *lechrall* that is kill by her guildmen."

"A tissue sample!" Susannah cheered softly. "Thank you!"

"I know you need this thing, Suzhannah."

"And he'd rather you didn't go after a live one yourself," said Megan.

Ghirra swallowed several quick bites, then slowed to explain Aguidran's plan.

"We'd call that a shortcut," said Megan, when he'd finished scratching maps in the dust. "But I'd think it'd be worth the two extra throws it'd take to go back via the Talche. Won't there be more water available?"

Ghirra nodded pensively, and Megan decided that he was not totally in favor of his sister's strategy, but would not speak out against it. "Every throw longer, the crop is dying," he excused. "And we keep the food of two cycles if we go as my sister says."

"What about the herds waiting in the hills?" asked Susannah.

"My sister send some guildmen, bring food to the herdmen, tell them stay in the hills where the more water is."

Megan set her food tray aside and leaned back against the hard rim of a wagon wheel while Ghirra questioned Xifa about the refilling of the water kegs. It seemed as if she had lived this way all her life, heat-drenched, striding through dust, eating bland food, sleeping on the dry ground. It was a hard life, and she marveled that the Sawls, after centuries of it, retained the energy to go on.

"So," she mused aloud. "One hundred-odd nasty kilometers straight across the Dop Arek, eh? Five throws, if we can really manage the twenty klicks a throw like we did coming out."

"Five throws in this heat is better than seven," Susannah pointed out.

"Only if the water holds out."

Ghirra nodded. "Dop Arek give no shelter to hide from the Sisters."

*   *   *

The rangers brought Susannah the tail of the animal that had attacked the child. They had wrapped it in heavy cloth, and though willing to help transfer the bloody tendril of flesh and scales into a plastic bag, each took strict care to avoid touching it. Susannah packed the bundle away as Aguidran ordered, though she longed to feed a chunk into her analyzer. When the rangers had gone, she sat by the wagon, staring up at the Cluster. Megan snored between the wheels with the apprentices.

Ghirra wandered up out of the darkness, smiling at Susannah's reverie. "Show me your world," he murmured.

She turned away humbly from the spectacle of stars. "I can't. I can't even tell you which direction to look. I doubt you could even see our sun from here—it's too far. But ask Taylor when we get back, or Weng."

"Taylor Danforth, he study about this thing, worlds, stars?"

She saw he was catching on to the notion of an English plural. "Worlds, mostly. What they're made of and how they got that way."

"He is from also your world?"

"He lives on Gamma, a planet of the star we call Alpha Centauri. He teaches in the University there. But he was born on Earth—in California, or what's left of it. Why?"

Ghirra held up his hand. "He is like I am, more dark even."

Susannah shrugged. "Humans come in many shades. Lots of people on Earth have skin the same color as yours."

"I could be there, and they not see me different?"

She could not help grinning. "A change of clothes and nobody'd be the wiser."

Ghirra considered this for a moment. "I will have talk with Taylor Danforth about this thing of worlds."

Aguidran drove the caravan hard for the two throws of remaining darkness but received few complaints. The hjalk were reasonably fresh and the travelers eager to cover as much ground as possible before the return of the burning sun. By Megan's estimate, they made twenty-five kilometers the first leg and a whopping twenty-eight on the second by shortening the dinner rest period and extending the period of travel from twelve hours to fifteen.

By the beginning of the third throw, the velvet black sky had softened to dark gray. The Cluster fire dimmed with its attendant stars, and the broken horizon ghosted into view.

"Amazingly, the darkness hardly slows their growth rate," said Susannah at breakfast, sorting through the few plant samples she had been able to collect at night, always under the wary eyes of the ranger perimeter watch. "It helps answer one of my questions, though. If you started with flora naturally evolved to survive this protracted light-dark cycle, some clever selective breeding *might* produce the fully dark-adapted varieties they grow in the Caves."

"You mean genetic engineering isn't the only explanation?" Megan leaned back against the wagon wheel, her eyes following a ranger scouting party as they loped past. "Sometimes I think you biologists have forgotten about the good old-fashioned farmer."

Susannah held up a thick, prickled knob. "Farmers didn't create lush tropical bushes that metamorphose into this when a dry spell arrives."

"You're sure it's the same plant?"

"Same name. Ghirra said so. He was quite surprised when he realized that I expect to find separate plants filling the various ecological niches. His explanation? Since the Sisters can produce any possible weather in any possible location, all living things must be able to adapt quickly and completely in order to survive the whims of the goddesses."

"Makes sense—the freakish environment selecting for flexibility?"

Aguidran came pacing down the line with one of the scouts and Ghirra, who was spooning up grain mash from an eating tray as he walked, as if determined to eat, once in a while, a meal while it was still warm. Aguidran crouched beside Megan and waved the young scout closer. He gave a shy nod of greeting but remained standing, thin and eager, leaning on the stout wooden club he carried during his watch.

"The guildmen find a thing," Ghirra explained. He gestured to the southeast.

"A thing?" asked Megan.

"A thing not our making. Your making, he think."

Megan and Susannah exchanged glances.

"What sort of thing?" asked Megan. "How big?"

Ghirra conferred with the scout. "More big than a hjalk wagon."

"Could he draw it?"

But the young man's willing scratches in the dust only mystified them further.

Susannah shrugged. "We ought to take a look."

Ghirra murmured with Aguidran, talking her frown into a reluctant nod. "We take water and two guildsmen," he noted.

Megan and Susannah refilled their field canteens from the kegs strapped to the side of the wagon. Ampiar grew more solemn than usual and Xifa fidgeted, her cheery round face tight with worry as she watched them prepare, gently clasping Dwingen's shoulder to keep him from asking to go along. Ghirra smiled at their concern and slung his water jug gaily across his back. They fell in behind the waiting scouts and moved out into the graying night.

The walking was hot and dry but not arduous. Past floods seemed to have neglected this central portion of the Dop Arek. The ground was flat and as hard as baked ceramic, marred only by the fine-lined cracking of its dull glaze of dust and sand.

"Damn, it's desolate out here," said Megan nervously.

"A proper surface for a game board." Susannah imagined giant dice rolling like tumbleweed across the hardpan. The odd half-light was a woolly limbo between the realities of day and night. She would not have been too surprised to see the pale reflective ground fade into the angular black-and-white of a checkerboard.

The scout led them southeast of the caravan route, miraculously steering a confident path across the featureless landscape. The rim of a wide ravine appeared suddenly out of the pearly gloom, part of the branching system of a dry watercourse. The drop was short but steep, the boulder strewn bank as black as pitch. The scout pointed, then shyly touched Susannah's elbow and pointed again, eager to prove that the mysterious object of his report was not imagined.

Deep in the shadow of the far bank, a lighter colored, triangular shape nestled among piles of rock and uprooted brush.

"Well, well, well," exclaimed Susannah softly. "An old friend."

"Where?" Megan scanned the semidarkness unsuccessfully. "What?"

"I think it's A-Sled." She scrambled down the rubbled bank, the scout keeping pace anxiously. His eyes raked the rocks and ravine bottom for signs of reptilian motion.

"It is!" Susannah approached the pale hulk and laid her hand on its mud-encrusted skin as if it were a sleeping animal that might stir to her touch. She traced the stenciled registry numbers. The Sled's machined familiarity was like a shock of cold water waking her from a dream where mankind hurried along the ground but gave no thought to flying. She wondered how McPherson was, ashamed that she'd hardly thought about her for the last three weeks, and not much more about the others . . . except Clausen. She really wished Megan hadn't told her that Clausen had a gun.

"How is it?" Megan hurried across the ravine in Ghirra's wake.

"Okay, I guess. Hard to tell in this light." Susannah walked the Sled's full length. The nose was badly battered, but the wings showed only fine-line cracks and the tail was mostly intact. "It's filthy dirty, but it seems to have ridden the waters fairly bravely."

Ghirra ticked the smoothly resistant hull with a thumbnail. "This is not like glass."

"Plastic and metal," said Megan. "Alloys."

"How it is here if Ibi . . . ?"

"We brought two Sleds. The flood washed this one away." Megan felt around the edges of the transparent blister in front of the tail. "Wonder if the com still works."

"Can you fly one of these things?" asked Susannah.

"No. You?" Megan laughed. "They don't want us science types knowing how to get around by ourselves."

As Ghirra moved toward the nose to peer into the dusty cockpit, Susannah said quietly, "We've got to get it back to the Lander somehow."

"You think they'll refuse?"

"Not normally, but in this heat? The extra load and effort?"

"Okay, then. You go to work convincing Ghirra. I'll clean off the com and try to raise CRI."

The open compartment was littered with flood debris. A cracking layer of dried mud roughened the flooring. Megan heaved herself onto the wing, then over the edge of the cargo hold, clambering forward through matted brush and mounds of gravel. The upholstery crackled with brittle complaint as she sat down in front of the instrument panel. She tapped at the once transparent housings. Desiccated yellow scum flaked away to reveal a more stubborn layer of mud beneath, hardened around the switches.

Megan dug at it with a thumbnail. "Might as well be set in concrete."

She spat on her fingertip and tried to soften the coating, then searched the cockpit floor for a rock to chip it away. Not all that different from freeing a shard of ancient pottery from its prison of sediment. She hoped it wouldn't take as long.

She was struggling with an immobilized pressure switch when Susannah returned from her conference, victorious.

"He's sent the scouts back to request a tow," she reported. "He has a bet on that Aguidran says no, but I think that's to get the boy working harder to convince her. They both say it'll cost nearly a throw if the caravan waits for us, so we'll have to play catch-up. Any luck with CRI?"

Megan sat back in disgust. "I think the insides are solid mud. What now?"

"Ghirra says we sit tight and watch out for the creepy-crawlies."

The younger scout returned several hours later with two hjalk and a driver. Aguidran had agreed to the tow, but promised to abandon the Sled the moment it became too much of a burden. Ghirra paid off his bet with a satisfied nod. He set the scouts to digging out the Sled, marveling particularly over the hard rubber of the wheels as they freed the landing gear from encasing debris. Once loose and hitched to the hjalk, the lightweight craft bumped along willingly on its own wheels as the team hauled it up out of the ravine.

"Well, that was easy." commented Megan.

Susannah made light of her friend's suspicious frown, but her laugh rang loudly in the pale half-light. Ghirra listened somberly as the scout pointed out the approach of dawn. The heated air had assumed a sluggish sort of motion, too fitful for a breeze but enough to send occasional dust devils scurrying across the dry ground.

Susannah coughed and took a long gulp from her canteen, then sealed it tightly. She noticed how often the scout's worried eye scanned the full circle of the horizon, in more than a casual search. The driver, a weathered older man, sucked on his blue talisman bead and urged the hjalk along as fast as they could manage.

64

"AMNESTY?" CLAUSEN LAUGHED harshly. "You've got to be kidding."

Danforth settled his head on his forearms while McPherson massaged his bed-stiff back. She was an efficient masseuse but ungentle, and her hands were hot and damp against his skin. "Well, what's he done, Emil, really? Ripped off some equipment, caused a little inconvenience. Nothing lethal."

Clausen swiveled away from the impromptu com console in sour disbelief. "I don't get it. A month ago you were ready to strangle the kid if he so much as looked at you. Now when he's actually fucking us over, you want to forgive and forget?"

Danforth shrugged beneath McPherson's busy hands. "I need him down here to translate."

"Fine. He can translate from the brig."

"The *brig*, Mr. Clausen?" Beyond the glare of the prospector's work light, Weng's head inclined to the reedy sound of chanting, now drifting almost perpetually from the Sawl encampment at the cliff base. The darkness over the fields was lightening into gray.

"Figuratively speaking, of course, Commander."

"Are you suggesting that we actually incarcerate Mr. Ibiá?"

Clausen turned back to the console. "Christ. You people. Do you even remember what we came here for?"

"We might get back to it faster," said McPherson, "if you spent less time worrying about Stav and more time helping me fix the Sled. I'm really tired of this place."

"Face it, Emil. The kid's a nut," Danforth rumbled, as McPherson pummeled the small of his back. "He's just not responsible."

The prospector tapped the keypad impatiently. "He's responsible enough to plan and carry off a well-organized theft, then cover his tracks fairly skillfully, electronically and otherwise. You think he's just fooling around, Tay? Playing little kid's tricks? You're the fool if you do." Clausen adjusted his reclaimed pistol, tucked now into a shoulder holster so soft and sleek, it seemed to be part of his body. "He's deep into something, and I damn well want to know what it is!"

McPherson nodded toward the wilting fields, where the meager Sawl home guard was hard at work laying irrigation pipes. "I think they're helping him."

"Of course they're helping him!" Clausen fumed.

"They?" said Danforth carefully.

"The Sawls. Who else?" McPherson dug into the muscles knotting around his spine. "They were real helpful bringing in the Sled and all, but I'm sure they're hiding him. I went up top with Emil, you know? There's a whole new rockslide exactly where CRI said Stav was supposed to be. Now, how could he do a rockslide by himself?"

"Did I mention my explosives inventory has been rifled?" Clausen raised a briefly ironic brow, then returned his concentration to a screen crammed with sensing data.

Danforth stirred irritably. "Those pesky Sawls seem to be hiding just about everything up there . . ." Still, Clausen's obsession with the hunt for Ibiá had its advantages: it occupied the prospector away from the Underbelly, leaving CRI free to help Danforth pursue his own, more scientific quarry.

McPherson gave him a final slap as he struggled to turn over and sit up.

"There's a bit of a breeze coming up." Weng joined them in the circle of light.

Danforth sniffed the air like an eager dog. "Breeze?"

Weng moved about with distracted purpose, collecting dirty dishes left from the dinner meal. "I will need the batteries for the sonic, Mr. Clausen. We can't afford to use water to wash up anymore."

"Help yourself. If no one else is in a hurry to restore power, why should I be?"

"When the Sawls get their pipes laid, we can hook into them," McPherson noted.

"CRI, check wind speeds ASAP," Danforth interrupted. "We haven't had real air movement in weeks!"

Weng scraped drying food out of compartmented plates. "Such waste."

"Our food tastes pretty yucky in this heat," regretted McPherson.

"A pity Mr. Clausen won't stoop to applying his culinary talents to ship's rations."

"Nothing can come of nothing," Clausen replied tartly.

"Anything on those wind speeds?" Danforth grunted with pain as he levered his rangy body into the makeshift wheelchair by the strength of his arms alone.

"How about magnetic and gravity field data?" the prospector countered. "Got some interesting fluctuations there. Aren't you interested anymore, Tay?"

CRI spoke up of her own accord, which she was doing increasingly of late. "Local winds are from the northeast, Dr. Danforth, building slowly. Now intermittent at four to seven mph. Current local temperature is ninety-three degrees."

"Building. Hmmm. Keep an eye on it for me, will you?" With effort, Danforth hand-wheeled the two-cart to Weng's worktable, refusing all help, as had become his habit. He did allow Weng to adjust her light and push his papers within reach. She turned over her dish scraping to McPherson, and perched on a crate opposite him, bringing to mind a tall and steady-eyed heron.

"How are you coming with the water mapping?" She flipped a heavily annotated data sheet to scribble on the unused side.

"CRI's done prelims so far, vertical profiles for each weather station. I'd hoped the new data would answer the questions, not just confirm them, but I'm afraid the results were what I'm coming to expect: they don't fit my model and they don't make sense."

Weng made encouraging listening noises while slowly covering her sheet of paper with numerical jottings that might have been formulae, or something else entirely.

"For instance," Danforth continued, "Global Theta's stationed over the northern ocean. You'd expect to find a lot of water there, at all altitudes. But the instruments say it's confined to near the surface.

"Also, you'd expect to find *less* water as you move away from the ocean into the drier areas, water vapor being drawn there from the ocean to support global equilibrium. Instead, we've got water moving all over the place, apparently at random, apparently as isolated local phenomena." He settled against his cushion of blankets, finding the calm of wonder within the depths of his frustration. "Ain't that the damnedest? A system refusing to move toward equilibrium, I mean, *refusing*. It's the same thing we noticed with the temperature, with the heat often moving away from cooler areas instead of toward them."

"Heat moving toward heat, water moving around at random."

"Yep." He grimaced at the illogic of it. "Like that damned freak thunderstorm—in apparent violation of all dynamical laws, of the most basic physics." He nodded pensively, intent as an old man praying. "Something's got to be pouring a hell of a lot of energy into holding this system away from equilibrium."

"Your X-factor again?"

"Yeah, for lack of a better culprit." He drummed his fingers on the table. "I promised myself to look for naturally occurring patterns. Well, here's one I can no longer deny: if you combine all the dynamical data, a clear trajectory asserts itself. Except for the dry period between the flooding and the hail, when some east-to-west zonal movement did occur, all the movement is along that northeast-southwest axis."

Weng waited while he fussed over a notion he was reluctant to express out loud. She hummed three dissonant notes under her breath, her head cocked as if still listening to the distant chanting. She crossed out one of her scribbles.

"Thing is," Danforth admitted with an uncomfortable grin, "I can't escape the fact that, in putting the back data together with the new to pinpoint a consistent locus of action for the snow, rain, hail, and now this rising heat, I keep landing right on top of Ibiá's damn god houses or whatever the hell CRI calls them."

"God Homes." Weng withheld all editorial comment.

"Whatever. The ocean and the desert. That's where it's all coming from or going to. It meets in the middle, within what just happens to be the planet's narrow zone of habitability and there, all hell breaks loose."

He buried his fingertips in his tight curls, squeezing as if to keep his head from flying apart. A muttered exclamation from Clausen rang out like a curse, and Danforth lowered his voice to a whisper. "Maybe we could get some Sawl to sneak a message to Ibiá. You think they really know where he is?"

Weng's pen point paused. "I expect they do, Dr. Danforth."

He studied her carefully. "Do you know?"

"No. I would not want to."

He was relieved but, also, vaguely disappointed. "You know, Commander, I had you pegged for one of those discipline-at-all-costs types."

She regarded him mildly. "I doubt that I'd have survived this long had that been the case. One must always consider the costs."

"A lesson I learned the hard way." He patted his cast-bound thigh.

"One always does, Dr. Danforth."

"Well. Now, this is very interesting." Clausen's voice rose. "CRI, give me the original cargo and equipment manifest. And an updated launch roster."

McPherson slotted the last dishes into the sonic and went to peer over the prospector's shoulder. Hunched over the keypad, Clausen wore a hunter's grin of anticipation.

"Here are all the satellites we have in orbit, their equipment specs, location, and purpose. I've declassified mine for the nonce to give us a proper total."

"What's that?" McPherson pointed at the bottom of the listing. "Looks like a drone."

"Precisely. CRI, get me Captain Newman on the line."

"Captain Newman is in his sleep period. Is it an emergency?"

"No, never mind. CRI, did the Captain authorize a drone launch recently?"

"No, Mr. Clausen."

"But I see here on the schedule that a drone has been launched."

"That is correct."

"The launch coordinates would seem to indicate an FTL trajectory toward Earth."

"I quite agree, Mr. Clausen."

Clausen uncoiled cobralike from his slouch. "CRI, I'd like to know the contents of that drone."

"I am not at liberty to offer that information."

He nodded. "That's what you think."

"How're you gonna break into a confidential file?" McPherson demanded.

"Well, now, McP, if I told you, then we'd both know."

McPherson blinked. "Jeez. 'Scuse me for asking."

"I have updated wind-and-temperature readings for Dr. Danforth."

"By all means, CRI—speak up." Clausen sat back, smug.

"Local temperature has risen to ninety-six degrees. Winds up five mph, gusting from nine to twelve mph."

"Still rising. Fast." Danforth shook his head.

"And so will the sun." Weng switched off her work light and turned her back to Clausen's glare. Danforth swiveled his chair. Beyond the shadowed belly of the Lander, the fading Cluster hung in the east like a spattered drop of bleach on a pearl-gray satin sky. Danforth thought if there was ever a time to pray for rain, this was it.

"So what do you say to that?" Clausen was a dark silhouette against the light of his lamp.

"To the sun?" Desert visions filled Danforth's head.

"To a drone that's been sent to Earth, but not by Captain Newman. Nor by yourself, I assume, Commander?"

"Of course not."

Clausen stretched out his legs, his smirk broadening. "Now, who else has that authority. Well, my, my. The Communications Officer. What a coincidence."

"You think Stav sent it?" McPherson asked.

Clausen laughed. "So, Tay, you still think he's just a harmless loony?"

"Why would Ibiá send off a drone?" Danforth tried to read Weng's impassive face, Failing that, he looked to the angle of her stance for a hint of her reaction. Had they let Ibiá get out of hand? He could be loony and still be dangerous. What circumstance might induce him to go renegade and fire off secret messages to Earth? What if he'd made some momentous discovery he didn't want anyone here to know about? "Commander, I'd like to know what's in that drone, too."

In the half-dark, Weng nodded. The chanting from the Sawl encampment swelled on the rising breeze and ceased suddenly. A runner was coming down the path from the cliff, his rapid footfalls softened by the thickening dust.

"Furzon! Furzon!"

"That's me they're calling." McPherson went out into the clearing to usher in the leader of the ranger salvage party. He was a sturdy middle-aged man with a seamy worried face. He eyed Clausen warily as he passed and continued to expostulate at McPherson's back as she led him to Weng's worktable.

"I can't quite get what he wants, Commander, but it's something about that old priest and the sky, and you know what that could mean!"

Danforth suffered a jolt of déjà vu, as the ranger's agitation brought up a memory of Stavros Ibiá, damp-haired and on the edge of panic, pleading that a priestly prediction be heeded. He'd made the wrong call that time, so he bit back hard on his impulse to dismiss this new warning out of hand. Instead, he shoved his wheeled chair away from the worktable, waving McPherson to him abruptly. "Get me to that terminal, Ron. Ten to one we've got weather on the way!"

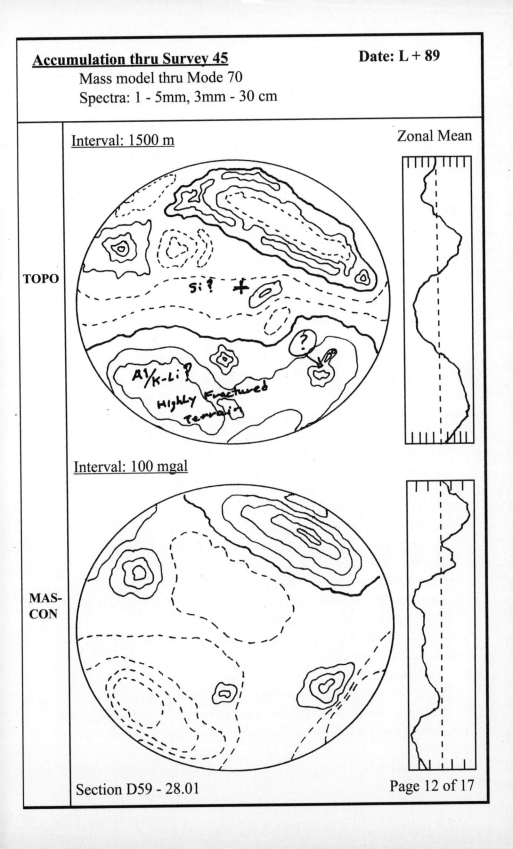

65

ON THE DESERT HARDPAN of the Dop Arek, the gray predawn was stained with red. Susannah slitted her eyes against the swirling dust, struggling to keep the young scout in view. Ahead, to the south, the toothy profile of the Grigar wavered miragelike, its narrow peaks tipped with glowing salmon. The hot wind snatched at the sand and the scattered dry tufts of brush. Susannah scooped up a loose twig and bent it. It snapped easily and spat out a puff of yellow powder. A plant that had been budding and spongy with moisture a scant three weeks before was reduced to a brittle husk. She held it out to Ghirra as he trudged along beside her.

"It didn't have time to develop its dry form, did it?"

"The heat is too soon. You hear?" He was listening into the wind. The dry stems beat against each other with the hollow rattle of pebbles cast across stone. "The Sisters prepare the Game."

Susannah smiled uneasily. "You sound like Aguidran."

"No. My sister will name this fighting other way, what Ibi call 'war.' "

"Ah. War." She nodded. He grasped the subtleties of translation so readily. A sharp gust whipped sand against her cheeks. Her eyes stung and watered. "And are we the Sisters' gaming pieces?"

He offered a bleak nod to her attempt at humor. "You see now our life, Suzhannah."

"Understand, you mean?"

"I will not say for your understanding. You see now as we see."

"Living as you live." It was a direct and sympathetic methodology, and so obvious. Stav's instinct from the beginning, she mused, and missed him again.

The wind billowed through the loose light layers of her Sawlish clothing to dry her heat-damp skin. The dust and gravel crunched beneath her sandaled feet. She matched Ghirra's measured stride and felt marginally less weary. The scout ahead was barely visible through the dawn-colored dust. Behind, the hjalk curled their strong necks into the wind, their wide nostrils opening and shutting with the labored rhythm of their step. The Sled rattled in their wake, collecting the extra weight of sand blown into its seams and open hold. Megan struggled along in its lee, one hand grasping the wing as if the Sled itself were her guide to safety.

"What game will they employ this time?" Susannah played out the metaphor like a fishing lure, hoping to snare Ghirra's less guarded thoughts. The wind built shifting, singing walls around their tiny caravan, but the sky above the gusted sand was clear, shell pink and limitless.

Ghirra dug in a pocket and held out a half-dozen black stone counters. "Do you offer a wager?"

She glanced at him. Was he serious? A deeper creasing at the corners of his mouth was his only hint of playfulness. "Guildmaster, I would not presume."

He fingered the counters thoughtfully, then put them away. "Sometime, is better to lose the stones."

"You mean you'd rather be wrong about what you think is coming?"

All trace of humor evaporated. "This is correct, Suzhannah."

The scout called back hoarsely, urging speed. Susannah swallowed as sand grains grated between her teeth. Megan's narrowed eyes were fixed on the swirling ground. She had not spoken for over an hour, a more eloquent expression of her exhaustion than any litany of complaint.

A maverick wind burst momentarily thinned the veil of sand. The scout called out again. Ghirra waved back and pointed. Below the ruddy crenellations of the Grigar, still sunk in predawn shadow, the distant cliffs of Dul Elesi were briefly visible.

"Thanks be," Susannah breathed, but the sand soon closed around them again. "How long?"

Ghirra spread his hands. "Two throws, I am guess."

"That far?" Susannah squinted crestfallen at the vanishing rock form, clearing her throat with a strangled cough. "Shouldn't we have met up with the caravan by now?"

"Not talk now," advised the physician. "See, I do this." He unwrapped his wide cloth sash from his waist and wound it loosely around his head, Berberstyle, to shield his eyes and mouth from the flying sand. "No worry, Suzhan-nah. My sister hurry, but also we hurry and there is few of us."

They crossed a shallow graveled wash snaking up from the south. Susan-nah's impulse, had she been wandering alone in this polished waste, would have been to follow its dry meanderings, if only for the suggestion of shelter in its crumbling banks, for the relief it offered from unrelieved flatness.

The Sled's wheels jolted into the wash and balked at the rise, spinning in the dusted gravel. As the hjalk strained, it lurched up over the edge. The driver alternately cooed to his beasts and berated them, as his patience waxed and ebbed. When the wheels rolled free once again, Ghirra whistled ahead to the scout to declare a brief rest stop. The canteens and the clay water jugs were unslung in the lee of the Sled. The hjalk, standing lathered and panting in their harness, sucked warm water from the driver's cupped hands. He had few words for his human companions but an endless stream of chat for his animals. The larger nuzzled him repeatedly, bleating indignantly when he stoppered his jug and slung it across his back. Murmuring fond negatives, the old man grasped the beast's curly head apologetically to brush encrusted sand from its long-lashed eyes.

Ghirra shared a glance with the anxious scout. "The hjalk are restless," he offered cryptically. He rose from his crouch beside the aft landing gear. "We must go on."

The scout stayed close by as they started up again. The wind continued to rise. The thickening sand stole back the feeble light won from the coming dawn. Clumps of brush rolled loose, ripped from their moorings. Susannah wound her sash around her head as Ghirra had directed, suffering waking visions of being buried alive.

"Susannah!" In the shelter of the Sled, Megan had her pocket compass out and was regarding it oddly. Susannah dropped back to join her. Within its plastic case, the needle was shuddering like a live thing as it wavered wildly from point to point. Abruptly, it swung to the southwest and hovered quak-ing, as if fighting a pull to which it must inevitably give in.

The hair rose on the back of Susannah's neck. "Broken?"

"Compasses don't break. Not like this."

"The magnetic field is different here. Weaker, I think."

"Try again. There isn't supposed to be one."

Susannah's head jerked around. "What was that?" A sound that was not quite a sound, rather as if a tiny explosion had occurred just outside her ear.

Ghirra had halted several paces ahead, alert and listening. The scout frowned, then shouted a tense query back. Ghirra answered grimly.

"What *was* that?" Susannah's words were lost to the wind. The hjalk danced in their traces. The smaller animal skittered to one side against the larger's momentum, uttering small bleats of dismay. It was brought up sharp by the limit of its harness. It squealed and bucked. The driver growled and slapped its wooly flank to urge it forward again. The wind sighed and wound itself into tighter eddies, sucking up funnels of yellow dust to chase among the tumbling bundles of brush. Overhead, the flamingo sky grew as luminous as silk.

Megan gasped. "Look! Your hair!"

Susannah's long dark hair, dangling loose from beneath her improvised mask and turban, was denying the wind's command. It floated upward as if of its own volition. She grabbed at it and shoved it under her collar. She felt an urgent need to sneeze or shout out loud, to release the tension rising through her body.

The sound came again, sharper, like a blow to the midriff. The larger hjalk shied and lunged ahead. The driver bellowed his alarm. The Sled lurched, then slued about wildly. Susannah jerked Megan away from the tail as it swung around toward her head.

Ghirra was beside them instantly, as the driver fell back and grabbed for the tow ropes. The physician's greater height was no advantage over a man who had spent a lifetime managing giant beasts. The driver tossed him off roughly, frantically tearing at the ties. The Sled careened from side to side as the hjalk leaped and fought the harness. The scout screamed at the driver over the hum of the wind, waving ahead and then up at the sky. The wind wound tighter, spinning out spirals of razor-edged gravel. The grinding hum coiled into a whine.

Susannah snared Ghirra's arm as he readied himself for a second assault. "Let him! It doesn't matter! We'll leave it behind!"

"No!" he shouted.

His insistence confused her, his uncharacteristic sudden rage.

"We need this now!" He slammed his weight against the driver's shoulder, throwing him off-balance. The scout grabbed the driver from behind and hauled him back from the Sled. Ghirra planted himself in front of it before the old man recovered his balance.

The sand sang in Susannah's ears. This was more than heat madness.

The driver regarded Ghirra with bewilderment and disgust. The Master Healer glared back and spat a terse command, so like his sister that the scout seconded him automatically, as if backing up his own guild master. The old man flung an angry arm toward the sky and stalked ahead to his animals. They moaned at him, but his return reduced their struggles to mere head tossing and shifting from one broad foot to the other.

Susannah hovered uncertainly, fighting the gusts. Ghirra's mouth was so tight that his lips were pale. He stood calmly enough as he readjusted his headcloth, but his eyes, squinting into the sky, showed more than their usual white.

"This is a *chukka* of the oldest legends," he declared flatly.

"A what?"

"A plan of the Sisters, in the Game. This we never see yet in my life, or of my two-father or even my five-father."

Susannah had misunderstood. He wasn't angry. He was afraid.

Chilled, she grasped his arm as the wind snatched at her clothing. "We don't really *need* the Sled!"

"You not understand, Suzhannah! Go fast now is not help. Where run?" He spread his arms to the sky. "We need this thing to be inside!"

"Inside? Ghirra, it's an open cockpit. You can't get inside it!"

Doubt and a moment of true panic flickered in his eyes. "It is better than nothing."

"What is happening? What's coming?"

The scout read her bewilderment. *"Ph'nar khem!"*

Ghirra spat sand. "He says these Sisters are most angry, so it is our most bad luck to be here where they choose to make their Game."

He refused to say more and hurried them onward. The driver got the Sled moving again, his gnarled hand wrapped tightly in the lead hjalk's head rein. He yelled at the anxious scout to grab the other, and the beasts danced forward reluctantly, their small ears flat against their heads, absorbing the driver's soothing patter. The weathered hostler snorted at the young scout's fear and held up four fingers to offer a wager.

Suddenly, the hjalk came alert.

The wind shifted, forsaking its whirligig habit. Hot and sand-laden, it charged straight at their faces. The hjalks' ears swiveled. Susannah braced herself for the next onslaught of panic-inducing nonsound. Instead she heard faint shouts carried on the wind. The scout cheered and danced about, then held out a boyish demanding palm. The driver grudgingly paid over four shiny black counters.

Ghirra's stride lengthened with relief. Susannah linked her arm through Megan's to keep her from falling behind. The stinging wind eased for an instant. In the near distance, she heard the bleats and bellows of frightened hjalk. Then the wind rose again, until its engine whine drowned out all other sound.

Susannah sensed a fearsome immanence, seconds before Ghirra snatched the two women into the lee of the Sled. It arrived with a jolt and the pressure impact of a thunderclap. Her hair crackled, her ears rang and a blue-green afterimage flared behind her eyelids. Yet she saw nothing, and heard only the scream of the wind.

Ghirra pushed them forward, toward the sand-obscured caravan. "Now you run!"

"Incredible!" Danforth's eyes tracked the fast-changing data on the mini-terminal's screen. Wind gusts prowled through the Underbelly, sweeping loose paper and plastic cups off the crate tops to skitter across the hard ground.

The dawn was pink and dim. Clausen and McPherson scrambled about in the clearing, readying silver tarps around the base of the high-gain antenna, covering the half-repaired B-Sled. The Sawl ranger who had rushed down to warn them strung tie ropes and helped to weigh the tarps down with stones. In the terraced fields, the tall red stalks rattled like dice in a cup. A few frantic Sawls rushed among them, drawing the stalks together into conical bunches and tying them gently with strips of cloth.

"The music has stopped," Weng noted from Danforth's side. "Up in the Caves."

Danforth was oblivious. "Here we go again . . . discrete packages of turbulence charging around like goddamn bumper cars! And not a cloud in sight! It's dry as a bone out there and hotter than blazes! And look at this! CRI, show the Commander what's happening elsewhere in the so-called habitable zone!"

Weng leaned in closer as the image shifted. The wind loosed silver tendrils from her neatly bound hair.

"This damned nonsense is planet-wide!" the planetologist fumed. "But only within that narrow band. Return us to local, CRI."

Weng's fingertip followed a phosphor-green packet as it sped across a radar map of the plain, heading for a larger frontal indication. "Would you call that random movement, Dr. Danforth?"

"Random? Weather's never random. I . . ." Danforth looked at her sideways. "But that's not what you meant, is it?"

"No, it's not." Weng glanced up as Clausen snapped a string of orders at the Sawl ranger in very passable and hitherto undemonstrated Sawlish. She tucked hair back into her bun and continued. "We've seen this behavior before."

"I know. That damned thunderstorm."

Weng nodded. "According to Mr. Ibiá's files, the Sawls would say there was a battle being waged out there on the plain. Don't you find that description rather appropriate?"

Danforth watched the storm pockets march across the screen like little legions, unable to let himself agree. Weng's faint smile, as she steadied her slight body against the rising gusts, was like an invitation to join in a wonderful secret. But he couldn't. Not yet. Not out loud. And not to Weng, this complication of hidden strengths whose command he'd resented so much he'd nearly killed himself in the process of insubordination, and yet whose moral support kept him sane during his physical confinement. He hoped there were still a few corners of his soul that the Commander's bright black eyes could not see into, those deep places where his shame abided. Sometimes, she really did remind him of his grandmother.

"Well, Dr. Danforth?"

"Appropriate, yes." On the screen, the wind packets halted briefly as if awaiting orders, then altered course in phalanx. "But intent is in the eye of the beholder."

Weng's raised eyebrow declared her satisfaction. "It was you who first ascribed intent—as long as two weeks ago. 'Something's out there moving it around.' Am I quoting you correctly?"

"I was speaking metaphorically."

"Ah. Metaphors." Weng eyed him sternly. "I hoped you had more in mind. But let me tell you of a little metaphor I've been playing with lately." She frowned as Clausen's harsh shouts, aimed this time at McPherson, nibbled at her concentration.

"Noisy, isn't he," Danforth muttered. "What ever became of the velvet glove? Never thought I'd miss it."

Weng closed her eyes, then opened them, as if willing Clausen from her mind. "As you know, Dr. Danforth, I often exploit the principle of game theory in my musical compositions. Recently, I thought to apply those principles to your problem as well."

"My problem?" Danforth was distracted by ominous flickerings of the weather map. He touched a pleading hand to the screen. "Gods, CRI, don't crap out now."

"The X-factor. Your ad hoc."

"And?"

"Game theory is really number theory, yes? The analysis of coincidence. But if you think of the theory as being primarily about relationships, you can examine a given series of events as moves in a game, in order to detect patterns of motion among these events and with an eye to discovering what the object of those motions might be."

"As I recall," Danforth countered, "Game theory does not postulate intent in that objective."

"No." Weng's smile was a forest of possibilities and her calm a steady island within the rising storm. "It's an analytical way of describing something that is happening—as in, 'here is a list of numbers, what do they have in common?'—and thus, when we speak of the given series of events in terms of a game, it's a way of understanding what constitutes winning that game." She paused, but only for effect. "In light of the Sawls' own explanation for these events, I thought the metaphor particularly appropriate."

"What constitutes *winning*?" Danforth frowned, as if the idea had never occurred to him but had an increasingly reasonable currency.

"Do you know what the Sawls think constitutes winning?"

"Keep those tarps ready! We'll cover the dish last!" Clausen stormed in from the clearing. "Out, Tay. I need my equipment back."

Danforth grabbed the prospector's wrist as it reached for the keypad. "Hold on, man, look at what's going on out there!"

"Later. I've got to worm the contents of that drone out of this box before we lose her to the weather again."

Danforth's grip tightened. "That's what I mean! Look!"

Clausen levered his arm free of the bigger man's fist. "Move your crippled butt, Taylor, or I'll move it for you!" He grasped the wheels of Danforth's cart-chair, threatening to tip it.

Danforth clung to the sideboards. "What the hell's your problem?"

"You stop that!" McPherson flung herself at the cart to steady it. The Sawl ranger pulled up warily behind her.

"I need this terminal!" Clausen stared straight at Weng, daring her to challenge him. "Get him out of here, McP. And stay ready to cover that dish!"

"In a pig's eye, Emil! Cover your own fuckin' dish!" McPherson pulled Danforth's chair out of Clausen's range and planted herself between them.

"That will do, Lieutenant." Weng was barely audible over the wind.

Clausen patted the little weapon cradled under his arm as if for luck, then swiveled back to his terminal with a mocking laugh. The others glared helplessly while the hot wind leaned against the Lander's hull and the metal trusses groaned. The forgotten Sawl ranger broke the deadlock with a sudden shout. Eyes wide, he pointed across the swaying fields. Against the distant silhouette of the Vallegar, a ruddy swirling darkness approached over the plain.

"Jesus!" McPherson breathed.

"Dust storm," said Danforth. "A real mother."

"Is it coming here?"

"Unless it changes its mind real fast. Better batten the hatches."

Weng watched in silence for a moment. "I wonder where the market caravan is just now."

At the terminal, Clausen exploded. "Sonofabitch! So that's his game!"

He flung the stool aside, and was halfway across the clearing before anyone could think of trying to stop him.

Stavros pounded through the fourth-level tunnels at a dead run, with Edan a long step behind and gaining. Liphar struggled to keep up, wasting breath on futile high-pitched remonstrance. The tunnels were deserted, the stone floor barely lit. One lamp in ten burned in the niches along the walls. The updraft was hot and smelled of dust. Edan made a grab for Stavros' back-pumping arm and missed.

"No go out, you!" Liphar yelled.

"The Kav is dancing, Lifa!" The guar-heat in Stavros' palms strummed with the rhythm of his step. "And the fields! They'll need every available hand!"

Edan concentrated on gaining the extra step.

"Crazy, you!" Liphar panted.

"In this weather, they'll never even notice me!"

They sped through an empty residential district. A half pace behind, Edan lunged for her quarry's naked shoulder. Her fingers slipped along his damp skin. She made a secondary grab for the loose folds of his pants.

Stavros swerved aside, beginning to enjoy the chase. He'd had his fill of being cooped up in a stuffy, hot cavern. And he refused to miss any chance to see Kav Daven dance. He angled at an intersection, speeding toward the nearest cave mouth. The darkened entry to Potters Hall loomed up to his right. To the left, the tall doorway of Glassblowers Hall, framed by its glimmering handblown pilasters and arch. The tunnel slanted as the floor broke up into stairs. Stavros flew down steps too narrow for his stride, keeping his balance by a miracle. His face lit up with unholy joy as the dark walls warmed with the glow of dawn.

But he slowed at the foot of the steps when the cave mouth yawned ahead and the full force of the dust-thick wind slammed into him. His hesitation brought Edan down on top of him, spilling him to the floor. He rolled away to the wall, but she rolled with him. Sweating body to sweating body, they grappled like wrestlers. Edan wrapped her arms around his chest and her legs around his knees, immobilizing him.

Stavros swore and struggled. Her strength took him by surprise. Her agility and skill suggested she'd been trained for exactly this sort of thing.

Martial arts in the Ranger Guild? Not just grown-up boy scouts, then, but cops as well? The Army? Intrigued by this new insight, Stavros let himself be manhandled into a sitting position. He regarded his captor with quizzical admiration as she eased her grip and settled herself between him and the cave mouth.

"Maybe you could teach me how to toss Clausen around like that the next time I see him." He dropped his head between his knees, glad for the chance to catch his breath.

Edan scowled, hearing Clausen's name. Her sullen silence accused Stavros of making her job unnecessarily difficult. Liphar gained the bottom of the stairs and dropped to his knees at Stavros' side, his thin chest heaving. He coughed violently as he inhaled a lungful of dust.

"Ibi, please. No go, you."

"Lifa, I have to! So do you. They need help in the fields. We can't let everyone die of starvation!" Stavros peered out into the yowling wind. "Oh, my god! Look!"

Out on the plain, cloud-high columns were forming out of a swirling red mist. As broad as the legs of colossi, they marched across the distance, rank after rank, like an invading army, dwarfing the rocky spire of the sentinel Red Pawn, whose crown glowed with the first touch of morning. Overhead, the sky was pink and clear and charged with blue-white lightning.

Liphar scrambled to the edge on hands and knees to stare outward in awe. *"O chukka desa!"* He pressed his blue talisman to trembling lips.

Edan heard the horror in his voice. Her head whipped around, her attention snared by the astonishing vision on the plain. Stavros seized his chance. He leaped up, evading her grasp as she whirled back and grabbed for him.

"Let's go!" he shouted as he swept past Liphar and charged down the outer stairs.

On the Dop Arek, the ruddy dust thinned in a spasm of release, like a gasp for breath. The tail end of the caravan ghosted through the haze, tall wagons crossing a broad salt flat. A disarray of overladen hakra carts and families on foot struggled to keep up. The young scout hailed the stragglers and bolted after them.

"He goes to tell my sister." Ghirra's voice was an old man's, hoarse from thirst and the effort of making himself heard over the roar of the wind.

Susannah jiggled the canteen at her hip and hoped that the caravan had water enough to pass a little around. A hard salt crust crunched under their feet, glittering white stained with yellow.

At a jog, they caught up to the line of carts. The heat was taking its toll, and so quickly. The hakra pushed forward gamely with eyes closed and tongues protruding. Some limped, leaving bloody trails across the brittle salt. Small children huddled together in the carts among piles of cloth-wrapped market goods. Adults and older children trudged alongside, their heads swaddled against the stinging sand. They greeted Ghirra and his party wordlessly, with nods and expressions of quiet fear, an occasional spasmodic cough, or a whimper from a child as the wind blew up again.

The bulk of the caravan had halted ahead. Arms waved and bodies plunged through the dust in a dreamlike chaos as the rangers rushed to pull the wagons into tight rings around the giant Food Guild wagons. The animals were unhitched without ceremony and hustled into the protective circles to mill about among the people and smaller carts, bleating unhappily. Guildsmen emptied their wagons, piling goods and cargo underneath.

The driver hauling the Sled drew up beside a Food Guild wagon and immediately loosed his hjalk team from harness. The frantic caravaners took no notice of the Terran vehicle's difference and hastened to lash it down along with everything else.

Ghirra hurried Megan and Susannah through the dust and noise, searching for Aguidran, for the Infirmary wagon, for the rest of his staff. They found the wagon first, just as the half-lit dawn broke open with another blast of sound and light. Susannah stumbled, momentarily blinded. The sound grew more audible as the light flashes brightened. Inside the ring, the older apprentices had finished the unloading. Ampiar, Phea and Dwingen scrambled around tying the wagon to its immediate neighbors, on one side a Dyers' wagon, on the other the first of three from the Papermakers. Up in the driver's seat, Xifa looped rope through holes in the canvas flaps covering the opening, and drew them tight to the canopy. The contents of the wagon lay piled underneath, heavily shrouded and lashed to the wheels.

There was no time for reunion greetings. The lightning flashed again, blue-white and crackling. Ghirra sent them scurrying into the emptied wagon. They fastened the flaps and flattened themselves against the floorboards. The wind took a quantum leap as if lunging to the attack. It ran screeching among the fabric canopies to pounce on seams and mended tears and patches. The shuddering ring of wagons sang with the flap and shred of canvas.

The animals wailed. The panicked cries of men and women joined in as their shelters shredded around them. The wooden canopies squealed as aged ribs bent inward and decades' worth of bright paint were sandblasted down to the naked grain.

Susannah huddled against the wagon's sideboard, ears ringing, her face buried in Ghirra's hip, Dwingen shivering at her back. She clasped Megan's hand tightly. Dust blew in through every cranny. The wagon shook as if seized by a demon fist. Outside, the wind yowled and the light blazed, leaving the tang of ozone in its wake. Wood splintered and a hjalk screamed.

Panic-stiffened fingers thrust through the split in the canvas behind the driver's seat. A woman's voice begged for help. Ghirra twisted around in the crowded interior to free the ropes fastening the flaps. A young woman shoved aside the canvas, tossed two small children into the wagon and disappeared just as Ghirra shouted to her to stay. The children were dazed and weeping. The older, a dark-haired boy, bled from a gash on his forehead. Susannah struggled to sit up, gathering a child under each arm. They clung tightly, unquestioning.

The lightning flared and flared again, burning jagged forks of heat and sound through the dust-choked air. The salt pan trembled with each hit. Shock waves shuddered through the hard ground. Susannah searched for some inner spot of calm where she might take refuge from the unrelenting roar and flash and crack. Ampiar's lips moved as she fingered her talisman bead.

Prayer? Susannah wondered, and considered the possibility herself.

A wrenching crash came with the next flash of light. With a pop and a roar, a wagon down the line burst into flame. Smoke cascaded into the Infirmary wagon. Shouts rang out, a call to action. Ghirra tore aside the flaps and leaped out. Ampiar and Xifa followed without hesitation. Dwingen squirmed out of Megan's grasp and vanished after them.

Susannah thrust the two children at Megan. She scrambled into the driver's seat to stare after Ghirra as he raced toward the wreckage. Loose canvas lashed at her face. The smoke and flying dust invaded her lungs. She pulled back as the lightning smashed into another wagon farther off. She took a grim breath, then wrapped her sash about her face.

"No, for god's sake!" Megan clasped the weeping children.

Susannah hesitated, but could not ignore the chorus of desperation building outside. She gave Megan the high sign and bolted from the wagon before she could change her mind. She hit the ground as it was jolted by another strike. The scent of charred flesh sent her spine crawling.

A dead hjalk lay to one side of the ring. Its fellows herded along the far side, away from the smoke and leaping flames. Human injured lay scattered across the hot ground, some moaning, some not moving at all. Parents clutched their children while the merchants rushed to save their hard-won goods.

The rangers had cut loose the precious water kegs and piled them in the center. Susannah ran toward the fire, saw Ghirra's lean form silhouetted against the bright heat, then Xifa and others, pulling burning bodies out of the flaming wagon. Guildsmen tore at the ropes fastening the wagon to its neighbors. A woman snatched up a shred of blackened canvas to beat out sparks landing on nearby wagons. A man grabbed up a water keg from the side of a Potters' Guild wagon and prepared to bash one end in with a stick.

A ranger charged at him and caught his upraised arm. He jerked the stick away, shoving the man aside. The man screeched outrage from the ground, then scrambled up and fled. The burning wagon was hauled from the ring, but too late. Its canopy collapsed in a wind-whirled shower of sparks. Flaming splinters spilled onto the second Papermakers' wagon. The cargo underneath burst into an instant fireball as the guildsmen ran to rescue it. The heat made it unapproachable. The rangers ordered it left to burn while the third wagon was cleared from the ring to leave a fire break. The Infirmary wagon was next down the line.

Susannah found Ampiar kneeling beside a badly burned man. She took a quick look, then raced back to the wagon for her medikit. The wind beat at her, trying to throw her against the wheels. The third Papermakers' wagon was now aflame. Hot cinders flew in Susannah's face. She glanced upward to see sparks catching in the Infirmary wagon's canopy.

Someone brushed by her, running. The thick smoke and dust made it impossible to see. Someone small, a child, swung up on the wagon's tall rear wheel and grasped at the exterior frame of the canopy, scaling toward the top.

By the daylight brilliance of the next flash, Susannah saw Dwingen clinging like a monkey to the crossbar with a strip of canvas shoved into his belt. He grappled, his little legs scrabbling for purchase, then with an enormous effort, hauled himself up onto the canopy's rounded crown. He lay for a moment among the flying sparks, panting.

Susannah screamed at him to come down, pleading into the wind and the fire roar until she thought her throat would tear and bleed. But Dwingen wrapped one end of the cloth around his small fist and struggled to his knees, swaying, fighting the gale. He beat at the burning cinders and the little nests of new flame rising from the bone dry wood. Lightning lit up the smoke billows around him, danced in hard blue threads above his head. He mistook Susannah's screaming and glanced down with a wave and a bright brave smile. Then, intent on his mission, he braced himself and rose unsteadily to his feet. The lightning crackled, a forked snake's tongue, searching. Susannah heard an anguished yell as Ghirra raced past, grasped the rim of the wheel and vaulted upward.

"Get down!" Susannah screamed at the boy. "Ghirra, tell him to lie flat!"

As Ghirra reached for the crossbar, Aguidran appeared, a blur of motion out of the smoke. She threw herself at the wagon to pin her brother's legs in the vise of her arms. Ghirra clung to the framework, raging at her to let him go, but she dug in her heels and pulled, breaking his hold. Ghirra called out desperately to Dwingen, his arms flailing. As brother and sister tumbled to the ground, the next searing bolt found the child standing erect and proud at the top of the wagon.

Dwingen stiffened, frozen in light. His delicate face stretched into a mask of surprise. Blue diamonds danced in his ringleted hair. He hung spread-eagled in the air, impervious at last to the wind's buffeting, held by a power greater than the wind, suffused with its blue-white dazzle.

Then he crumpled to the canopy.

Aguidran scrambled up, leaped up on the wheel rim and stretched to grasp a limp ankle that flopped down around the curving wagon top. She hauled the boy's body into her arms and handed him down to Ghirra. The physician laid him gently on the ground. Though the boy's eyes gaped open and empty, he put his head to his chest and his hands to the thin neck, searching frantically for a pulse.

Susannah shook herself free of her shock and fumbled in her medikit for adrenaline while Ghirra began his own version of CPR. The boy's hair was singed and smoking, his skin blackened with char. As she knelt with the hypo, Susannah knew it was too late.

Crouched on the other side of the little body, Aguidran made no excuse or apology. She watched tears track through the grit on Ghirra's face as he strove to restore some small sign of life to his dead apprentice. Her eyes held only sad relief, the recognition of a bargain made with fate, not happily but without question, unless it could have been herself given in Dwingen's place, in return for her brother's life.

At last Ghirra's frantic efforts slowed. He drew his hands together, palms pressed over the boy's heart, as if to stir it with a spark of his own spirit, to will it to beat again. When Aguidran reached across to touch his shoulder, Ghirra slumped back, his hands flexing in frustration, his gaze black and inward. But as he bent to close the boy's eyes, it was a gentle last caress.

Susannah brushed at her own tears. "You did everything you could."

Ghirra stared dully at his open palms, as if they'd betrayed him.

Susannah searched for further words of comfort, but found none. Did the man expect he could raise the dead?

Aguidran rose and left them without a word. The dust and smoke closed around her with weakening fury. The flicker of the flames dimmed as the softer pink of dawn penetrated the black haze.

Susannah looked up, saw clear sky, and prayed that the storm was over. But it was not. Through the blackened ribs of a burning wagon, she saw the ranks of giant dust columns advancing across the plain like Moses' pillar of fire in the wilderness.

"Oh, god. What do we do now?"

66

THE WIND FOUGHT to smash Stavros against the cliff as he hurtled down the outer stair. Dust clogged his eyes and lungs, tore mercilessly at his skin. Slow starvation in the Caves might just be preferable to being flayed alive out here in the open, once the wind wound up to full strength. He risked a glance away from the sand-swept steps to check the massive towers' yowling approach across the plain. The brief pink dawn was fading behind a swirl of murk

Stavros mocked his futile, bravura gesture. Save the crops? What would be left of them? Surely they wouldn't let the old man dance in weather like this.

The guar-fire pulsed gently in his palms. He could feel but not hear the slap of his bare feet against the gritty stone. It was like falling through the storm, wind-tossed, sinking through noise and turbulence, drowning in dust. The rough cliff threatened alongside. He imagined his limbs splashed against the rock like a breaking wave. He passed the first of the third-level entries. Edan's throaty shout reached after him from above, echoed by Liphar's shriller pleas. Stavros twisted onto the next descending switchback and continued his headlong free fall down the stair.

The tall, arching caves of the second level loomed ahead. The stable entries gaped. The storm roared through every crevice, sweeping up odors of dried manure and a thousand tiny javelins of wind-driven straw. Stavros slowed along the ledge, head down, running nearly blind as the dust blotted out the last ray of dawn. He stumbled, slid several heart-freezing meters, and found himself by glad accident at the head of the next stair.

In the fields below, glimpsed through a haze of sand, a handful of Food Guilders scurried about, attempting a task that would have taxed the resources of the entire Guild, had they been present and available. Barely a third of the tall red stalks had been bundled into protective sheaves. The terraces reflected the ruddy light as the shorter crops were flooded with precious gallons from the irrigation reservoirs, a layer of water being the only defense against the dust-laden gusts already ripping at the leaf stalks and tearing up roots.

Stavros gained the first-level ledge where the widening stair took its last downward turn. A backward glance showed Edan gaining on him. But a sound stopped him at the head of the stair, cutting through the wind's roar: a high-pitched reedy wail that snatched familiarly at his attention.

Kav Daven.

Stavros turned, searching the first-level openings. All empty. Where was the sound coming from?

He followed it along the ledge, squinting into the murk. At the western edge, a small crowd gathered before the oldest cave mouth. From their midst, the wail rose and fell with the rush of the wind.

Stavros bolted, reaching the outer ranks of the gathering just as Edan pounded up behind him. She scowled at him furiously, but let him ease in among the observers. He sensed her crowding at his back, herding him toward the safety of the inner cave, but when he reached the front ranks of the gathering, he refused to be moved further.

Kav Daven danced in the center, his blind eyes closed. He was already deep into his chant-trance. His arms were raised, as thin and rigid as sticks. He whirled in widening circles, chanting and wailing. A single anxious priest, three elderly Food Guilders and a frantic apprentice girl struggled to maintain a protective arc around the heedless ancient, keeping him from the edge and the worst of the wind's ravages.

A few of the observers dutifully mouthed the priest's chant, their brown fingers telling blue talisman beads, but their faces held little hope. Feeling the old priest's familiar pull, Stavros edged forward. Edan's strong fingers closed on his arm, and he let her draw him back against the wall It would not matter where in the crowd he stood.

Like iron to a magnet, he thought. I the raw ore and he the source.

For the first time since the Leave-taking, the ghostly heat in his palms flared into pain. He was unsurprised when the axis of the watchers shifted and the Ritual Master's whirlings flowed in his direction. He had yet to decipher the Kav's intent, but the charge laid on him by the miracle of his unburned hands was clear and present.

Kav Daven danced closer. His seamed face was serene but for the fluttering of his eyelids, as rapid as bees' wings. Liphar pulled up, breathless, as the crowd backed away from the old priest's dervish approach. Edan's grip relaxed.

Stavros waited, rooted to the rock. His skin prickled as a faint brush of Power came and went, as casually as if shouldering past him in the crowd. A scent of chaos remained, curling like smoke into his nostrils. The watchers showed no response. This moment of mysticism, like the last, was between himself and the old priest alone.

Kav Daven drew smaller and smaller circles, until his knobby body spun like a child's top, emitting a high, musical whine. His leaf-brown garments were flung out like wings, his arms clenched tight to his ribs. His eyelids shivered. His lips drew back from yellowed teeth. The dance was too frantic, too desperate, the old man too frail. Anxious for his safety, Stavros raised both palms to the priest's blind and whirling glance. Kav Daven stopped in mid-turn and faced him, smiling.

Edan sucked in a breath. Liphar murmured in awe. The storm was bearing down, tearing at their hair and clothing, but on this ledge settled a circle of quiet, with Kav Daven at its center. The fire in Stavros' palms flared until his hands shook, but he kept them up with fingers spread. His instinctive gesture had broken the priest's heedless trance. It was somehow correct.

On the day of his miracle, as the guar seared into his flesh, Stavros had learned to envelop the pain, to make it a part of him, as the priests did who carried the guar bare-handed from the mines. And he would bear the pain gladly, if that would win an explanation of his miracle. A responsibility, a cloak of expectation, had been laid across his shoulders, but he could not read its size or its shape.

Kav Daven waited, milky blind eyes staring into his.

What does he want of me?

His inadequacy sickened him, but Stavros kept his hands raised, absorbing the agony like a penitent's lash, now a punishment, now a reward. The pain cycled through him in a feedback loop, building fire on fire but simultaneously energizing his resistance.

Kav Daven approached. He flattened his own hands against Stavros' palms. His silken scarred flesh was cool, and the pain drew back, as if in respect.

"Tell me, Kav. Teach me. Please."

Sudden fire seared past his cheek, a breath of pure lightning. Minute needles bit into his skin. Edan shifted, glancing around in confusion. Suspicion nagged at him, then wavered, as Stavros blamed some oddity of the storm and held his stance, palm to palm with Kav Daven, willing calm and concentration to hold him fast to this long-sought moment of contact and communion.

The fire scorched past again, closer, too discrete and silent for lightning. Rock spatter sprayed the back of his neck. He smelled hair burning, his own. Suspicion bloomed again, stupidly, too slowly. The circle of silence shattered. The crowd erupted in confusion as Emil Clausen shoved his way through.

"Wait!" Stavros stepped in front of Kav Daven, his arms spread. "I'm here! Goddamnit, Clausen, you'll kill someone!"

Clausen eyed him over the laser's silver nose. "How kind of you to oblige me, Ibiá." He leveled the pistol at Stavros' head.

Stavros was still framing his reply when Edan's arm whipped around his waist as fast as a snake strike, hauling him down and away. Falling, too startled to resist, Stavros looked for Kav Daven through the scrambling, frightened crowd. The old priest's arms reached out to empty space. Stavros fought for balance as Clausen fired. The needle beam nicked his ear. He smelled ozone and the reek of charred skin.

"You fucking maniac!" he raged at the prospector.

Edan dragged him to his feet, shoved his head down and hauled him behind the bewildered crowd. He lost sight of the old priest, but glimpsed Liphar fighting through the confusion. "Lifa! The Kav! Get him out of here!"

Stavros prayed that Clausen was not crazy enough to shoot through bystanders to get at him. He yelled again to Liphar and ran, ducking, for the rear of the cave, searching the darkness for a tunnel, for steps.

Shouts collided behind him: Clausen's warnings in bellowed Sawlish, a guildsman's outraged reply. Loping at his elbow, Edan hissed a direction into his wounded ear. Stavros swerved left in automatic response. The rock wall beside them exploded in a shower of grit and light.

Clausen had lengthened the laser's pulse. Stavros ran for his life.

The next bolt laid his left shoulder open, slicing deep through layers of muscle and bone. The force of the hit knocked him sprawling across the stone. Stavros tucked and rolled before he hit the wall and his momentum brought him back to his feet, already running again, running for the dark of the stair ahead.

Edan swore and shoved madly at his back. His arm flapped uselessly at his side, throwing off his balance. He feared the pain would cripple him, but the shoulder stayed mercifully numb. His guar-fire had deserted him. He felt only a creeping weakness in his legs as he pumped desperately for the stairs. A wash of terror as cold as seawater knotted his groin.

"Fucker's gonna kill me," he gasped, as if saying it made the unreal real and somehow comprehensible.

The staircase was old and crumbling. The footing would have been perilous even in full light, but Stavros thanked the concealing darkness. The sounds of Clausen's pursuit were submerged in the pounding of his own feet and heart. He could not see Edan, but her hand stayed firm against his back as they scrambled up the ragged stairs.

At the top, she balked and veered aside, hauling him with her. Footsteps too frenzied to be Clausen's clattered through the rock debris on the steps behind them. Stavros hoped it was Liphar, still in one piece.

Ahead, a slash of light bled across a yawning stable cavern. It was faint but enough to illuminate them if they crossed it: a barrier as effective as a moat. Edan drew him swiftly through the darkness along the wall. She snared his good arm to point him across the cavern toward the warren of inner barns, muttering at the ominous warmth wetting his tunic. Her whisper was harsh. She put a hand to his head to be sure of his nod, then shoved him forward and bolted into the open beside him.

Laser fire lanced across the cavern, one, two deadly beams only slightly wide of their shadowy mark. Stavros ran a crooked path and gained the darkness of the warrens. The numbness was fading. Each jarring leap awoke a sharper pain. A stickiness clung to his back and ribs and pulled at his seared flesh. He wondered how much blood he was losing. He dodged blindly through unlit corridors lined with empty stalls. He no longer sensed Edan behind him. He'd lost her while crossing the big cavern. He missed the pressure of her guiding hand on his back. He listened for her step, heard only his own and that lighter patter, now pulling breathlessly alongside him.

"Lifa?"

Liphar's whisper was desperate. "Go fast, Ibi! No stop you!"

"Edan?"

"She wait, make surprise for Clauzen." He snatched at Stavros' arm. "This way!"

"Lifa, I'm hurt." It wasn't the pain. Pain he could deal with. But it was too soon to feel this weak. "Who's left in Physicians'? I need a doctor."

"Yes," Liphar whimpered and urged him along more insistently. They wound through the maze of stalls, turning finally onto a narrow upward ramp. The incline was slippery with dust, so steep that Stavros moaned through gritted teeth at the effort of climbing and slowed so as not to collapse. Liphar helped him struggle to the top, gamely supporting his weight.

The upper corridor was lit by a single lamp in a niche beside huge double doors. Through blurring eyes, Stavros recognized the carved portal of Wood-workers Hall. Down the tunnel to the left, tall columns framed the entry to the Priest Hall. Liphar shot across the corridor to haul on Woodworkers' giant paneled doors. He gestured Stavros inside and barred the doors. Stavros bent over gasping, resisting the blackness that reached out to him from within.

"Lifa, please, is there water?"

Liphar made a quick blind search of the darkened guildhall and returned with a half-filled jug. Stavros's hands would not work to grip the handles. Murmuring worriedly, Liphar held the jug while Stavros gratefully gulped stale water.

"Better," he lied hoarsely. Liphar took him at his word and urged him to be moving again.

At the far end of the guildhall, Liphar eased open another big wooden door. Dim light leaked through the crack. He peered up and down the corridor, then ventured out. Stavros followed, sliding his good hand along the wall for support. The corridor seemed suddenly too wide and bright. Opposite, the open archway into Keth-Toph was invitingly dark. Liphar nodded at it. Stavros returned the nod and pushed himself away from the wall.

They heard Clausen at the end of the corridor, a stone rolling under his boot as he took aim. Liphar shouted. Stavros lunged for the darkened arch with Liphar tight at his heels. Hot lightning lanced past their ears. They ran through the entry hall and into the storehouse tunnels, past silent looming ranks of crates and shelves. At the end of a long tunnel, Liphar grabbed at Stavros' belt.

"Ibi! Wait!" He halted, feeling in the dark for the upright support of a heavily laden shelf. Stavros understood, turning back to lend what little strength he could. They heaved and grunted, and a twelve-foot block of shelves tipped and collapsed. Behind them, Clausen roared as tall jars of oil and bundles of lampwick cascaded into the narrow aisle, shattering pottery, spilling gallons of thick lamp oil. The laser pistol went flying, skittering among the rubble.

Liphar gave a ragged sigh of relief and shoved Stavros down the next tunnel.

In Keth-Toph's vast Round Hall, a single dim blue flame glowed in the great wheel suspended above the central guild table. Liphar dashed ahead to a remote corner behind the rendering cauldrons, where the smoothly sculpted curve of the hall was broken by a series of natural rifts. He vanished into the third in the row, then peered out again.

"Ibi! Hurry!"

Stavros staggered across the hall. Deep in the shadow of the rift, a low hole pierced the rock, a hidden shaft barely the diameter of a small man's shoulders. Liphar pointed to it eagerly.

"You go, ah? You go, then I go next."

Stavros shuddered. Breathing was an agony. His head rang, his shoulder was on fire. He was unsure he would fit in the narrow shaft. But the vicious clatter of broken pottery echoed across the hall as Clausen fought to clear a path through their impromptu barricade. It would not hold him for long.

Stavros dropped to his knees and crawled trembling into the shaft. A cool draft touched him with blessed moisture. The inner surface was finely ribbed, like corduroy. Several meters inward, the shaft turned and widened. It was faintly luminous and greenish like glass. With his knees and his good elbow, Stavros dragged himself forward at a snail's pace. Pain flared in his shoulder as it knocked and scraped against the wall.

"How far, Lifa?" he rasped, dizzy and struggling.

"Soon! Very soon!"

A last effort. *I can manage that.*

But sensation was receding before a new tide of numbness, spreading inward from his outer limbs. Distantly, he wondered if he was already dying.

Isn't this how it goes when you're bleeding to death? The creeping chill, the weakness, this . . . fog?

He felt himself slipping toward nonexistence as quietly as into sleep. Was he moving at all?

He forced a memory of motion into his legs, begging them to respond. His body jerked forward, an inch, a precious foot, almost by will alone. Ahead, the pale glow of the shaftway framed a round darkness, but it might be a failure of his vision. Not the ending of the shaft, but his own ending.

He was sure the corduroy glass was increasingly slippery, that it was melting without benefit of heat, liquifying, pooling around him. He felt it swell and begin to turn, a vast maelstrom with the slow patience of a galaxy, spinning him toward the dark void at its heart.

"No stop!" Liphar grasped his leg and shook it.

Stavros nodded, or thought he did, as the slow maelstrom spun him away. A worry for Edan slid through his brain as the last light faded, like a specter in a mist, calling for him to wake. But it was too late. He'd already given himself to the relief of darkness.

Liphar felt Stavros stall and go limp.

"Ibi?"

He shook the slack leg harder, whimpering at the chill dead weight of it. He squeezed himself forward in the narrow shaft and pushed at the bulk of Stavros' body, easily twice as heavy as his own. "Ibi!"

He strained determinedly, muttering encouragements as if Stavros was listening, and bit by bit, his burden inched along the glassy curve. The circle of blackness ahead broadened into a perceptible opening, the end of the shaftway. When he could push no longer, Liphar rested, his face pressed against Stavros' still back, taking reassurance from the faint but continuing heartbeat. When his thin chest had stopped heaving, he renewed his efforts, until the opening was within reach. He grasped the outer rim and hauled himself past Stavros into the room beyond.

It was a long, domed space, its far end diffused with gentle bluish light. A pair of tall doors dominated one long wall. The cool dimness smelled of moisture and ash, and sighed with the soft plash of falling water.

Shaking with the effort, Liphar wrapped his arms around Stavros' chest and pulled him out of the shaft onto a smoothly tiled floor, dragging him in to a secluded corner away from the shaft entry. His hands came away wet as he laid the body out, as gently as he could, and sat back on his heels. He tore off his tunic and folded it to pillow Stavros' head, then dashed off toward the soft blue light.

He returned with wet cloth and a lantern, which he lit as he knelt again at Stavros' side. Gingerly, he touched the damp fabric to the wound. The burnt smell and the blackened weeping flesh frightened him. The elementary first aid taught to every Sawl child did not cover this nasty sort of Terran hurt that was both a burn and a slash. He knew he must, above all, stop the bleeding.

He sacrificed his blousy pants, tearing them into strips to wrap the damaged shoulder as tightly as he dared.

One clean strip he retained to wipe a dark smear of blood from Stavros' face. Then he wiped his own, and his hands, sitting helplessly wiping and wiping until the tears he had held back overtook him silently. He put his face in his hands. His thin shoulders heaved. But soon he straightened and roughly brushed his tears away, muttering apologies to Stavros, scolding himself for his weakness when what mattered was finding help. He blew out the lantern and rose. He gave Stavros a last grieving look, then loped across the room and slipped noiselessly through its huge double doors.

The outer hall was vast and silent. Ruddy dawn light drifted from a high clerestory to settle like dust on a marble floor patterned with interlocking circles. Stern jewel-eyed figures of the goddesses stared down from friezes that marched the length of the hall.

Liphar sped through the silence, pulling up at the Frieze Hall ramp head to peer cautiously downward. Satisfied, he descended the long slope and dashed across the open plaza at the bottom. He paused at the central stone trough. The spring was low but the water chill and clear. He splashed his face and his naked blood-streaked chest, then gulped several hurried handfuls. The gurgle of the water echoed loudly across the still plaza. Liphar retreated in haste past the deserted shops of the Market Hall, down a long, dim corridor, toward another descending ramp. He exchanged caution for speed as he drew farther from the fugitive's hiding place. He met no one on the way but slowed again as he slipped into the tunnel to the Priest Hall. Suddenly he flinched and shrank against the wall.

Lantern light bobbed around the turn at the end of the corridor. Someone was coming up from the cave mouth.

The mammoth carved doors of Woodworkers Hall faced him uselessly, so recently barred by himself from the inside. Liphar fled down the corridor, seeking shelter in the Priest Hall archway. He did a small skip of elation when he heard Sawl voices approaching with the light. He ran to meet them, already chattering his urgency.

Two worried Food Guilders rounded the corner, lanterns in hand, deep in discussion. A senior priest and the girl apprentice followed, supporting Kav Daven between them. The Kav's blind eyes were wide. He struggled fitfully against his companions' benevolent restraint. The girl crooned a low-voiced chant to sooth his distraction.

Liphar called out, speeding toward them as a shadow materialized in the darkened entry to the Priest Hall. Clausen lunged into the corridor, hooking an elbow around Liphar's neck, jerking him off his feet. He was slammed hard against the prospector's hip and held tight. Clausen wiped his hand across the Sawl's damp chest and rubbed the bloodstain into his fingertips.

"So, my young friend, what mess have you been into?"

Liphar flopped about like a hooked fish, screeching for help.

"Where is he?" Clausen hissed at his ear.

The two Food Guilders shouted and ran forward with their lanterns raised. The silver pistol flashed in Clausen's free hand, shattering the rock at their feet.

The Food Guilders froze. Kav Daven ceased his distracted struggles. His back stiffened. His high voice rang down the corridor, bell-like, a tone of curt demand.

Liphar blinked, gasping for breath. The Kav had spoken in ritual Old Words. He answered in a stammered flood of the ancient words, never used except in priestly ritual. Clausen snarled and tightened his hold on the young man's throat. Liphar gagged and cried out, and the older Food Guilder blew out his lantern. The younger lobbed his at Clausen's head. The prospector sidestepped the fiery missile but glass flew and burning oil splashed against the rock. Flames rose and died. The laser flashed wide in the sudden darkness. Clausen backed down the hall, dragging Liphar with him.

Silence settled in the blackened corridor. Face pressed to the floor, the elder guildsman hissed a query. The other answered breathlessly. Behind them, the senior priest groaned and stirred. The apprentice girl called to Kav Daven, softly at first, then more urgently when she received no reply. The two guildsmen listened to the rustling sounds of her searching in the darkness. Cautiously, the elder struck a spark and relit his lantern.

Clausen was gone, Liphar with him. Smoking oil pooled among broken glass and ceramic on the floor. The senior priest struggled to sit up. His horrified exclamation brought the Food Guilders to their feet.

In the middle of the corridor, the apprentice girl knelt stunned and empty-handed. Kav Daven had vanished.

67

T HE DUST TOWERS roared across the dawning Dop Arek, Lagri's legions marching out of the dry, dark southwest, advancing on Valla's mountain stronghold. The wind rose in the ravines like the screams of the damned. The flood courses rattled with flying sand and shards of shattered vegetation as the wind soldiers swept by in disciplined ranks.

A frail old man threaded a safe path through the roiling grid of turbulence. He kept a broken rhythm of scurry, halt, wait, and scurry again, like a wise stray dog wading through speeding traffic. The heat parched his ancient wrinkles. His eyes shuttered against the bite of the sand. But the wind only toyed with his leaf-brown garments, while mere meters in either direction, the advancing vortex ground rock into gravel and brittle stems into dust.

The old man carried no food or water. His lips moved in a soundless chant. He stumbled once and kept going, as the first volleys of lightning arced above his bare head. He headed northeast, with the wind army as his escort, straight into the heart of the battle.

68

E.D. 91–3:12

W HEN THE WIND CEASED tearing at his protective tarp, Danforth lifted a corner and squinted out past the dark truss of the landing strut. The hot air was still thick with dust but the rear guard of the storm had wreaked its havoc among the planted terraces and passed on toward the central Dop Arek and the mountains beyond. The slow pink dawn returned as the air cleared. The sun had not yet broken the horizon. The fields around the Lander looked like a deserted game of giants' pickup sticks.

Danforth raised himself on his elbows, spat out grit, swallowed a lot more. On the other side of the strut, a tarp wrinkled and fell back in sandy folds as McPherson rolled upright, shaking her head like a dog.

"Tay? You okay?"

Danforth nodded, glancing around. "Commander?"

Weng unwound her silver-film blanket, huddled cross-legged against the angled truss. She untied her dust mask, a scrap of Sawlish linen, and delicately blotted her face.

"Unreal," Danforth muttered inadequately.

"Un-huh." McPherson stretched. "Shit. Look at the fields."

Weng uncorked a water bottle and passed it around.

Danforth was precariously close losing all faith in the logic of natural processes. He threw off the hot tarp and struggled to pull himself upright along the crossbars of the landing truss, thrusting his cast-bound leg beneath him as a lever and support. McPherson scrambled up to help.

"Go uncover the dish," he said gruffly. "See if we can still raise CRI."

"Sure." She backed off and wheeled over his makeshift chair without comment, then trotted away to check on the dish. Danforth lowered himself stiffly into the chair and wheeled across the sand-drifted Underbelly to the shrouded computer table. Weng helped him untie the wind-tightened lashings, then drew the silvery plastic aside and stood with it awkwardly balled up in her arms as if reluctant to set it anywhere that it might not be immediately available.

"Ron, what's the word out there?" Danforth called.

"Seems okay to me. Give her a try."

CRI came back on line with a vengeance, inquiring after everyone's health and the condition of the equipment, demanding firsthand visual data to supplement her instrument record of the storm. She could offer no information on the welfare of the trade caravan, but reported that vast lightning-sparked brushfires were sweeping many areas of the habitable zone, among them the dry Dop Arek.

"But who won the war?" Danforth joked sourly.

"A mere battle, surely, Dr. Danforth," Weng reproved.

"Upon consideration of the data," CRI replied, "matched with Mr. Ibiá's files, I would have to award the victory to Lagri."

"Who's that?"

"One of the sister-goddesses," Weng supplied. "The fiery one. You've noted the Priest Guild seal? A flame suspended over water?"

"Fire and water." Danforth stared off into the distance. "Heat and moisture . . ." He shook his head, grimacing helplessly. "Okay, okay. Let's say we go with this . . . this preposterousness for a moment: that would mean Lagri controls the heat and the other, whatsisname . . ."

"Her name. Valla Ired."

"Right. So she's got the water end of the thing. And each uses her gig as a weapon against the other." He laughed darkly. "Well, yes, that would be one hell of an X-factor. Pretty neat, if you could believe it."

"Commander . . . ?" McPherson padded back into the Underbelly. "I think maybe you oughta . . . they're doing something weird out there."

The little pilot pointed. A solemn crowd of Sawls was collecting along the ravaged perimeter of the Lander clearing. Their numbers swelled rapidly as one by one, the entire home guard filed down the dusty path from the Caves or appeared from out of the broken fields. Their grouping was informal, most sitting, some kneeling or crouching, others standing, but all faced the Lander with a silence that was neither grim nor threatening but, rather, bewildered.

McPherson pointed again. "And look . . . over there."

A dark shape lay in a stretcher on the ground in front of the gathering, too distant to be recognizable in the still-dim dawn,

Danforth grunted. "Damn. Don't tell me the kid's actually bought it!"

McPherson brushed her damp brow with a forearm, wet her lips nervously. "Better go see, huh?"

Weng nodded. The two officers started across the clearing together. Danforth put CRI on hold and wheeled himself to the edge of the Lander's overhang. His sweating palms were slippery on the wooden wheels. He wiped his hands on his damp T-shirt, more disturbed than he could make sense of. He stared up at the looming wall of the cliff, stained with the salmon blush of dawn. If it was Ibiá, brought down dead or dying, where the hell was Clausen?

Danforth shoved the crippling bulk of his cast against the side of the chair, cursing his helplessness and vulnerability. Not only the weather, but events, too, had stopped making sense. He missed the comforting texture of reality as he knew it. He imagined he could actually see it fading behind the curtains of heat wavering between him and Weng and the circle of Sawls, and finally, the dust-dry landscape. He sniffed, smelling distant smoke. Weng's lecture about the Coal Sack floated to mind, along with an image of the planet consumed in fire. Perhaps, he thought, when the sun finally rolls over the horizon, it'll be swelled up, engorged like a tick, sucking up atmospheres, cannibalizing its own system.

"This heat," he muttered. "This bitching heat!"

Weng and McPherson neared the edge of the clearing. McPherson ran the last few steps, as if in surprise. She dropped to her knees beside the stretcher, her hands gently searching, her voice ringing clearly in the silence. "It's Edan! I know her! She's Aguidran's top tracker. I thought she went out with the caravan. I think . . . oh, no . . . she's dead, Commander."

Danforth shut his eyes in guilty relief. Not Ibiá, then. Not yet. But the thin veneer of civilization was crumbling. Melting with the planet into the maddening heat.

McPherson sat back on her heels and spread her arms sadly at the nearest Sawl. "What happened?"

The seamy-faced ranger who'd warned them earlier about the storm pushed through the crowd, his voice dark with outrage. "Clauzen."

Around him, the others murmured, as if his forthright anger made them uneasy.

McPherson turned to Weng. "What do we do, Commander?"

"First we need to hear the full story," Weng replied steadily.

"Which you will." Clausen spoke from behind the crowd. The Sawls drew back instinctively. He strode down the path dragging the half-naked and frightened Liphar. "Just as soon as I take care of one little detail."

The prospector showed no anger, only a chill, almost weary determination. Weng stepped in front of him. "I'd like to hear it now, Mr. Clausen, if you don't mind."

Clausen pulled up with a shrug, as if chatting with a customs official over some questionable imports. "As you wish. It's pretty simple: I spotted Ibiá up in the Caves and nearly had my hands on him, when that young woman jumped me in the dark. I protected myself."

McPherson bolted to her feet. "You broke her fucking *neck!*"

Clausen nodded soberly. "She'd have done the same to me." He looked to Weng, experience appealing to experience. "A regrettable accident, Commander."

Weng's reply was steely. "Regrettable, indeed, Mr. Clausen." She nodded at Liphar, whose eyes pleaded in misery and terror. "And what, may I ask, are you doing to this poor child?"

Clausen seemed to have just remembered the boy held in his iron grasp. "This *child* is hiding Ibiá up there, and I intend to find out where."

"I don't think so, Mr. Clausen. You are under arrest for murder."

"Nice try, Weng." Clausen smiled tightly and jerked Liphar toward the Lander. "I'd like to see you make that one stick."

Danforth had known killing would come easily to Clausen, so why did the actuality leave him stunned? He watched the prospector drag his prisoner across the dusty clearing. The Sawls made no move to stop him. Instead, they settled back into their eerily passive vigil beside the dead ranger's body. Weng stared after Clausen, as pale and erect as a marble statue.

And just as useless, Danforth thought. Well, damned if I'm going to be!

He swiped his awkward chair around and wheeled over to the equipment table as fast as he could manage. "CRI, get me Captain Newman. We've got a big problem down here." He monitored Clausen's rapid approach at his back, but his gaze was drawn to the thick black smoke that announced a bright line of fire advancing almost as quickly from across the plain. "No, make that two big problems."

69

E.D. 91–11:15

STAVROS HEARD WATER, falling softly, like rain or sleep.

In vain, this dying, but not alone, at least.

His first coherent thought in many hours was instantly submerged in a noise of pain that drowned out thinking. He struggled to think again, to hear thought, any thought, through the awful din.

There was one that came and went. Each time it visited, it was swept away, like a fish in a torrent. Something about a way to master pain, about a Connection to be made, a Power waiting to be tapped. Sometimes it came as a voice advising him, but the words were singsong and the lesson unintelligible, lost in the noise and the shimmering haze of fever and the constant sinking into nothingness.

Kav Daven's young apprentice girl sat at Stavros' side. The long hall glowed dimly, almost cool. At the far end, a slim, glassy cylinder shimmered in a column of water that rose from the center of a tiled pool. The cylinder enclosed an unwavering spear of pale blue light. The water soared, crested, and fell back to play its gentle falling music on the surface of the pool.

The girl rewetted the cloth pressed to the dying man's forehead and changed the iced herbal dressings on his shoulder. His torn flesh rebelled with purulence and heat. Fever raged. The elderly Master Herbalist Ard sat cross-legged on the cool tiles, pondering new strategies to combat the infection.

The sick man floated in and out of consciousness, caught in a web of fever dreams. Often he recoiled from the girl's gentle touch, as if eluding capture. The girl pleaded with him to rest, but his instincts were sure that survival was in resistance, not surrender.

He thrashed about uselessly. Precious strength was lost in battling nightmares. His rare moments of clarity renewed his awareness of unbearable pain. Each retreat into oblivion was longer, each rise to consciousness more reluctant.

Ard cursed the inadequacy of his medicines. He wished for his guild master's special healing skills. He was going to lose this patient.

A SISTER TALE

Recorded L+58 (ED 58) 20:34
Told by: Liphar of Dul Elesi
Translation: Liphar to CRI/Ibiá

The old people tell of a time when the sun was gentle for many cycles and the crops in the fields swayed low with fruit. But soon, they say, Lagri Fire-Sister stalked the halls of Her desert fortress, restless for new diversion.

She summoned Lightning, Her messenger, and sped him to Valla Ired, Her Sister of Water and Ice. Then She marshalled Her armies: Heat and Thunder, Tornado and Drought.

The Lightning spoke to Valla in Her palace beneath the ocean. "Fire-Sister proposes a wager."

Valla urged a red snail across Her coral gaming table. "I am well occupied here."

Lightning spun bright cartwheels around the shadowed hall. "Lagri mocks Your seclusion, Water-Sister. She calls You coward, and boasts that She will make You prisoner in Your own dwelling. The length of a DarkTime, She will hold You fast."

Valla looked the messenger up and down. "What are the stakes?"

"She offers the Plain of Dop Arek, which She took from You during the most recent engagement."

"A mere skirmish." Valla curled a pale lip. "The Dop Arek is not worth calling Snow and Rain from their rest. Let my Sister play alone."

Lightning sizzled enticingly. "She might be convinced to include the Talche Hills."

Valla crooked a finger. She flicked the red snail into a pocket at the corner of her game board.

"And the wide river Dym beyond. . . ."

Valla smiled, easing back her chair. "My Sister will regret this reckless wager."

Lightning laughed, a shower of sparks. "Then let the Game begin!"

70

THE LAST RANK OF WHIRLWINDS tore past the circled wagons. A single roaring tower of dust smashed straight through the center of the largest circle, grinding a Food Guild wagon into splinters and upending four more. The spinning funnel blackened, sucking up smoke and charred debris along with several hjalk and their helpless driver.

The hjalk fell screaming to the salt pan a hundred meters farther. The driver was swallowed by the storm. The whirlwind thundered away down the plain.

Susannah stirred numbly in the tangle of bodies huddled with the cargo beneath the Infirmary wagon. Ghirra's shoulder, pressed against her back, drew away as he rolled out from under the wagon and sat up, dazed and frowning.

"Is it really over this time?" Megan blinked, palming grit and black ash from her cheeks.

"Please, god," Susannah breathed.

They crawled into the open. Xifa followed with the two children who had been thrust into the wagon earlier. They accepted sips of water with the stoic gratitude of young ones coming to grips with possible orphanhood.

Susannah scanned the ravaged caravan. Bodies lay scattered, wagons flattened and smoldering. Smoke drifted in sullen clouds across the dawning sky. Nearby, a man wept softly, holding his dead wife to his chest. A groaning hjalk struggled to right itself on blackened legs.

"So many dead and injured, people and animals. So much destruction," she mourned. "If it had waited just one more throw, we'd have been in reach of shelter."

"Where's Ampiar?" asked Megan worriedly.

"Not another," begged Susannah. "Another will break his heart."

Ghirra answered her glance with wan distraction. Grief and dull rage clouded his eyes. "Do they never think of us, the Sisters, when they play their stones?"

"As flies to wanton boys . . ." Susannah murmured, then sighed with relief as Ampiar trotted up, even more solemn than usual but unscathed, having found shelter elsewhere.

Aguidran strode past, gripping her brother's shoulder briefly, urging haste as she pointed northward. Through a break in the circle, Susannah saw the long smoky curve of an advancing brushfire. The Master Healer shook himself out of his black and weary gloom and began giving quiet orders to his reassembled staff.

When they'd patched up the many injured and made the end a little easier for the dying, Susannah stood with Megan out on the salt pan as Ghirra prepared Dwingen's body for cremation.

The charred wagon remains had been piled into hollow waist-high squares, then stuffed with dry brush and ruined cargo. The dead were placed on top, two or three to a pyre, grouped by family or by guild. Gently, Ghirra laid his young apprentice next to the mother of the two little children. A guildsman of the father stood near, gripping the children's hands tightly as they bade their mother a silent good-bye.

"The father was badly burned," Susannah told Megan, "but he will recover."

The living formed concentric circles around the dozen pyres as Aguidran and her rangers put the first one to the torch. A breathless hush settled as successive columns of oily smoke rose straight into the still and lightening sky.

Megan noted Ashimmel standing quietly among the rest of the mourners. "Seems that the Priest Guild has no formal function in the marking of death," she murmured. "I really should be taking notes, but somehow . . ."

"I know." Susannah leaned into her friend's side as the flames licked up around Dwingen's small corpse.

To the south, the rising sun touched the distant cliffs with its own, pinker fire. The sky glowed like burnished bronze. Sooty low-lying clouds obscured the plain in all directions. Ghirra joined them, his shoulders slack, rage still simmering behind his tired calm.

"At Dul Elesi now, they see our smoke, and they wonder who is lost." He pointed toward the cliffs. "But see? We must wonder also."

Susannah studied the sun-bright line of rock. A single thread of black curled ominously from the cliff top. They were surrounded by a tightening ring of fire and death.

Gazing south, Ghirra stretched suddenly to his full height to stare over the assembled heads. Abruptly, he left the mourners' circle, drawing his sister aside with a muttered word. Aguidran glanced southward, then summoned several of her scouts and sent them trotting off in the direction of the cliffs.

"What's up?" Megan wondered.

Susannah pointed.

The tiny dark speck wavering against the dawn-lit amber of the plain could have been a mirage.

"I think there's someone coming from the Caves."

The pyres flared and roared. The mourners' circle broke as the full red eye of the sun pushed free of the rounded hills of the Talche. While the pyres smoldered, the work details labored to bring the caravan back to some suggestion of order.

When the fires had died, Aguidran fidgeted, while the guild elders gathered the ashes of the dead. The hjalk and hakra had been rounded up and counted. The herdsmen eased them back into harness, rationing handfuls of grain and the last of the water. The undamaged cargo was restowed and reapportioned among the surviving wagons. The remaining wagons were pulled into formation. Aguidran allowed only the fastest repairs and got little argument. The added heat of the sun was being felt already. No one wished to spend a moment longer than necessary frying on the griddle of the Dop Arek.

"Perhaps the real funeral rites are yet to come," Megan remarked as she watched a stout old leatherworker kneel with difficulty to sweep her guildsman's final gray dust from the glittering slick of the salt pan.

Susannah continued repacking the Infirmary wagon without comment.

"We'll have a team to haul the Sled," Megan added. "There are more hjalk now than there are wagons left to pull."

"Great." Susannah bundled dirty linens into a wooden trunk and buckled the straps. "Lot of good that Sled is going to do these folks."

She wiped sweaty, sooty palms on her tunic and signaled Ampiar to grab one leather handle. With a duet of grunts, they heaved the bulky trunk toward the wagon.

"I don't believe it!" Megan exclaimed suddenly.

The trunk clattered heavily onto the tailgate.

"What now?"

"Aguidran's scouts are back. Look!"

The four scouts approached through the bruising desert heat, their young brown faces blank with reserved awe. Between them, they escorted a scrawny old man. His clothing hung limp with a weight of dust and soot. The ragends of his sleeves were singed black. The young rangers neither guided nor supported him. They kept even pace with him as he moved in stiff disjointed strides, as if each muscle were being told what to do separately.

Susannah thought of a puppet or a mechanical toy. "How did he *get* here?"

As the strange quintet passed down the line, the frenzy of repacking and repairing ceased. A rising buzz of unbelieving whispers followed their progress. An apprentice priest gasped, dropped his bag of counters, and ran, yelling for Kav Ashimmel.

Ghirra and Xifa hurried from behind the Infirmary wagon. Ghirra stepped forward instinctively as Kav Daven bore down with renewed energy, as if spying his goal at last.

The blind priest halted directly in front of him. His cracked lips quivered, his jaw flapped, but only a dry whine pushed past his swollen tongue. He took a short jerky step, and his knees gave. His joints crackled like brittle sticks as he toppled into the Master Healer's arms.

Ghirra eased him to the ground, calling urgently for water. The old man clung to him, his blind eyes blinking, his fingers digging in like claws. His lips labored to form words.

Xifa ran up with a bowl of water. Ghirra dribbled measured drops into Kav Daven's mouth, then wet the hem of his tunic to wipe the gray dust from the ancient face. Barely conscious of the water, Kav Daven continued his struggle to speak. The moisture eased the cracking in his throat enough to allow a hoarse whisper to escape.

Ghirra bent his head close to listen.

"What's he saying?" Susannah crouched beside them. "It sounds like the same thing over and over."

Kav Ashimmel arrived looking thunderstruck, firing whispered questions at the scouts. At Ghirra's desperate signal, she dropped to her knees and leaned in to interpret Kav Daven's broken mutterings.

"Old Words," Ghirra murmured to Susannah.

After a moment, Ashimmel took the Ritual Master's shriveled hands and began to answer him, softly repeating as he did an indecipherable phrase again and again. Their combined whisperings settled into a regular rhythm of statement and reply, like the antiphonal work chants. Meanwhile, the Master Healer went to work on him, ever so gently, massaging here, pressing there. Slowly, Kav Daven's hoarse music faded and he ceased his straining for speech. His eyelids fluttered shut. His body relaxed into Ghirra's embrace.

Ashimmel sat back, her face dark with incomprehension.

Susannah felt for a pulse. She was astonished to find it whisper-faint but steady as a well-sprung clock. "He'll need replacement fluids."

Ghirra eased the old priest to the ground and sent Ampiar for the stretcher. His hands hovered over the frail body. "I do not understand how still he lives."

"I don't understand how he made it here in the first place. What did he say?"

Ghirra handed over the water bowl to Xifa, to continue bathing the old priest's skin. He moved aside to query Ashimmel. Her tight-lipped replies seemed to puzzle him. She repeated herself, stumbling again over a certain word and ending with an irritated shake of her iron-gray curls. Ashimmel did not appreciate being as much in the dark as everyone else.

Ghirra translated pensively. "The Kav begs help for someone dying. Some-one he calls *raellil*. Kav Ashimmel say it is very old word, this."

"What does it mean?"

"Now, this is one who carry the priest's message, an apprentice. But when this Kav speak the Old Words, it is the *old* knowing, the Ritual. Kav Ashimmel say she understand not this old *raellil*." Ghirra spread his hands and stood up, turning his troubled gaze southward. The bright cliff face was fading behind a veil of smoke. *"Raellil,"* he muttered intently, as if meaning could be induced to reveal itself spontaneously.

"Would he risk his life like this for his apprentice?"

"He names no apprentice. This make much argument in his guild. But if this Kav ask my help, I give it. With one hjalk only, I will travel many times fast to the Caves." He turned back to stare down at the unconscious old man. "You take most good care of him, Suzhannah."

"Of course I will." His leaving frightened her. He'd be facing the sun's heat and the spreading fires all alone. But then, so had Kav Daven.

Ghirra sent one of the ranger scouts to liberate a fast young hjalk for the journey. The apprentice Phea, who'd hardly said a word since Dwingen's death, slipped away to a nearby Food Guild wagon to beg water enough to fill a traveling jug.

"It would help to know what's wrong with this person the Kav says is dying," Susannah pursued. "I could give you part of my medikit: painkillers, antibiotics . . . Ghirra, it couldn't hurt. It's always better to have more options than less."

She was sure he agreed mostly to quiet her, without any real commitment to use her pharmacy. But she hurried off to the wagon to prepare a mini-kit.

Megan had watched this exchange in thoughtful silence.

"Isn't this all a little strange?" she asked Ghirra, when Susannah was out of hearing.

"Yes, Meeghan, this is."

"I mean, that old man has to have one hell of a reason to walk twenty-odd kilometers through a forest of tornados."

Ghirra regarded her soberly. "Yes, this also is strange."

"I have an awful feeling I know what you're thinking." When he didn't answer, she said flatly, "You think it's Stavros, don't you."

Ghirra nodded slowly. "This Kav sees some purpose with him. For Ibi, he wager his life, I think. No other one. But do not say this to Susannah."

"No. No point in that."

The Master Healer's gaze turned south again. "Live you, my friend, until I come. Too many dead already."

71

THE QUESTIONS WERE OVER for the time being.

Clausen left Liphar bound hand and foot in the sun and stalked across the dusty clearing to harry McPherson while she worked on the Sled.

A dull, outraged chanting rose from among the shattered stalks at the perimeter.

Clausen tossed back Sawlish insults and waved his laser pistol. "Haven't laid a hand on him yet! Just you wait!"

When the chanting continued, he fired a random bolt or two into the canes. The chanters scuttled for deeper cover.

"Now that's really stupid," McPherson growled from the cockpit of the Sled. "The brushfires are close enough as it is, without you starting one right on top of us!"

"Less chat, more work," Clausen chided, then leaned against the Sled's hot white hull and offered companionably, "Do you realize that you and I are the only ones left who seem to recall what our job is? Relax, McP. We're on the same side."

"Yeah? So's you can break *my* neck someday, too? Go fuck yourself, Emil. I've done enough of your dirty work already."

"Tut, McP. Such language from a young lady. Maybe I'll make you climb into the nose to get what we need for the power link. You could probably boil water up there right now."

She glanced up, grinning nastily. "Nah, you won't. You'd have to hand over the laser for me to make the cuts."

Danforth eavesdropped from the shade of the Underbelly, dreaming of convenient accidents and home-built fantasy weapons of wood and clay. He pondered hopeless plans to rescue Liphar, whose shallow, shocked breathing was like the painful flutter of a captured rabbit. Yet this small and frightened creature apparently concealed a will of iron. After eleven hours without food and water, of long sessions alternately threatened or cajoled by the prospector, the young Sawl had managed either to tire Clausen out or to bore him, but had not yet revealed Ibiá's hiding place.

Silently, Danforth cheered Liphar on. He wished he'd had someone to do likewise those several weeks ago, when it was he being victimized by Clausen's cruel amusements. Sure, he'd expected mockery as he lay crippled in the shelter of the downed Sled. Wasn't that, after all, a habit of power—and he both admired and coveted Clausen's. And at first, he'd thought it mere carelessness, when Clausen disappeared into the storm for hours at a stretch, that water and light were left just far enough out of his reach that the effort of getting to them made him scream and faint from the pain in his chest and legs.

He never laid a hand on me either, the fucking sadist!

Danforth gnawed his lip, loathing his own helplessness. He'd played hard-ball politics all his academic life, but physical intimidation had never been his thing. Even if he'd been fit, he doubted his ability to bring Clausen down. He needed help. He needed Ibiá down here. Alive.

He sneaked a look at Weng, standing in the shade beside him. Strands of silver hair leaked from her bun. She no longer bothered to tuck them back. Dust and sweat stained her white uniform. A command is meaningless without a weapon to enforce it. A weapon and the willingness to use it.

"He'll have to sleep sometime," said Weng implacably.

"Least that's the way it always goes in the vids." Danforth laughed bitterly. "Sorry, Commander. This is getting to be like a bad holo. Let's call it *Might Makes Right,* what do you say?"

Weng's eyes were red from dust and exhaustion. She stared at him unblinking.

"Evidently you don't share my loss of anchor in this reality," Danforth said.

She returned her attention to the clearing. "I imagine it seems real enough to Liphar."

Danforth shifted in his chair. "I'm not making light of anyone's suffering, Commander. I was referring to the chaotic quality of recent events. The rules went down the drain and none of us noticed until it was too late."

Her nose crinkled, a chill unborn smile. "I think you were simply unwilling to admit whose rules held precedence. The fact is, however, that Mr. Clausen is still human, and there are natural rules that will hold precedence, even over his. He cannot stay out there in that sun forever and he *will* have to sleep sometime."

72

E.D. 93–13:10

STAVROS DRIFTED, below the surface of awareness.

A scrap of memory slithered to the top intact, pulled him along unwilling.

He knelt at the feet of a brown old man who pressed both hands around his own. A teacher, teaching . . . what?

Kav . . .

The pain crowded in on his remembering, pushing, pushing.

Stavros pushed back, with a last flicker of will, struggled to hold the image of the old man in his fever-racked brain. A thought lurked there, beyond the memory, a hope, perhaps an answer.

A chunk of dull silver. A liquid fire in his palms.

Kav . . .

He had offered himself willingly to the guar-pain. It had repaid him with a glimpse into the void, followed by a miracle.

I need another miracle . . .

He was dying. Even so, it seemed an audacious request.

Beyond the image, the answer. Something to do with the pain . . . or with not resisting the pain, though it devoured his body like flames in dry wood.

Stavros pictured his resistance, meaning to lend it strength. It was a fist clenched around a fragile tree branch, aloft above dark, swift-flowing water, weakening.

Letting go might be the same as dying. Didn't one always speak of *fighting* for life?

No Kav here this time to lead him through the mysteries.

But ah, the pain! If only it would leave him alone, let him think. And now, beyond that fierce internal static, another softer roaring. The river, rushing by beneath him?

His grip on the branch slipped ever so slightly.

It was not the black water roaring, after all. It was wind. A vast wind, sweeping past at light speed. Life-hungry, it sucked the fire from his limbs, the breath from his lungs.

Messages from the void.

Memory resurfaced and with it, terror, as his grip slipped again.

A coldness, like liquid ice, enveloped him.

His eyes jerked open to darkness. The girl, familiar as a fever-blurred presence leaning into his delirium, was gone. Stretched on the rack of his own body, Stavros cried out in pain and primal loneliness.

The fist spasmed, let go. He fell . . .

The girl started out of thin sleep when the man beside her screamed. She scrambled up, fumbling for the shuttered lantern.

The Master Herbalist grabbed it before she did, on his hands and knees at his patient's side, spilling light across the pale floor. He swore as the young man's breathing caught and stilled, the eyes and mouth gaping open to some final horror or surprise.

The girl sank to the tiles, weeping. Ard bent his ear to the patient's chest, then straightened slowly. His jaw tight with failure, he reached to close . . .

. . . into the wind. And discovered he was not alone. The void was not empty, as he'd supposed. Power danced in its howling swirl. Power sailed the swift wind currents like the white water of a mountain rapid, busy, intent on unknowable purposes.

Stavros dropped into the stream unnoticed, a mote against immense dark nebulae lit from within by the slow birth-fire of stars and the explosive flare of their deaths. He floated free, transfixed by his own insignificance . . .

. . . the staring eyes, and let his fingers linger. The dead man's fever sweat was already a chill rime on his brow. Ard muttered, puzzled by the body's too abrupt cooling.

A low urgent knocking shuddered against the outer doors. The girl whisked away to unlock them. The old herbalist turned at the sound of her gasp. His eyes widened as the Master Healer came striding across the tiles. Scents of dust and brush smoke invaded the quiet dampness of the Hall. Ard offered only a brusque shake of his head. Ghirra bolted the last few steps to . . .

. . . as he floated, he grew aware of tensions, lines of force, crisscrossing the void, like the strings of a cat's cradle, drawn taut in an invisible tug-of-war. The currents were being stretched, space distorted, his own void-self pulled in opposing directions.

He thought of magnetism. He was caught between two poles.

Two . . .

Clearer now. He could almost discern the shifting loci of two immense and separate entities. They danced with the currents, playing out their force-lines with an angler's give and take, give and haul back hard again, playing with each other, tugging, feinting, rolling in the void wind as if in surf, intent—oh, so intent—on the other alone.

Was the wind itself born from their blind and whirling dance?

Stavros recalled another dancer's dance. He could not name what he'd found or describe their nature. Was one dry, one wet, one icy, the other hot? These were mere constructs, remnants of the sensual reality he'd left behind, without existence in the void. The quality of the void was *force*.

Tension, and intention. Contention. Push and pull. Action, reaction. Force and counterforce.

No accompanying emotion, no joy or rage. A simple, burning energy. An eagerness as bright as hunger, as focused as greed, as single-minded as the beam of a laser.

Stavros sank into his insignificance as into a protective cloak. He recognized madness when it stalked his way.

Yet, he was curious. As he drifted toward a taut and singing force-line, it rose out of near invisibility to glow in changing neon colors. It pulsed like a live thing, its beauty poignant, brave against the darkness. Was it hot? Would it sear if he touched it? No matter. He could be no deader than he was already. He made no effort to alter his drift.

The glowing line neared, magenta shifting through salmon to vermilion. Stavros admired its toy-bright clarity. Childlike, he grasped for it with a chimerical hand. The line sparked and parted in green and yellow violence as his mind-fingers closed around it: a connection made, a circuit shorted. The ends recoiled. The shock spun him away, tumbled him in the currents like waves over rocks.

But wait: what was that? That faintest of shiverings. That . . . minute quaking of the void. Did one insane nothingness pause, ever so briefly, in its eternal game of push and pull, to redirect a fraction of its awareness? Did its great head swing around in search . . .

Stavros fled into the wind. He must become a mote, insignificant and invisible, safe from meeting such madness face to face, from accounting for his unthinking, irrevocable gesture of contact . . .

Ghirra shoved Ard aside and skidded to his knees.

The apprentice girl caught her breath, tears suspended in shock. Ard did not complain. He eased away, adjusting the lantern to shed more light as Ghirra put his fingers to the pulse in Stavros' throat, then both hands to the chill, dank temples. He gave a soft exclamation of despair. Ard moved in to offer murmured details.

Ghirra did not hesitate. He tore at the knots belting Susannah's mini-kit around his waist. He unfolded the pocketed sash, laying it out on the tiles. Stainless steel glinted in the lamplight, reflected in Ard's quick glance of suspicion and disapproval.

Ghirra slipped a syringe from its plastic sheath and fit the shining needle to a vial. His long fingers shook just once, then steadied as he laid the point to Stavros' chest and punched it into the skin, so accurate an imitation of Susannah's swift, clean motions that he felt for a moment in full control. He tossed the empty syringe aside, took a ragged breath, and flattened his palms over the tiny puncture wound. His nod to Susannah's medicine accomplished, he must now offer his own gifts to the same desperate challenge.

. . . still tumbling, fleeing. No hiding in the void. The void *was* the Power. The Powers. The Two. They would find him, punish him, grind him into dust for being there, for disturbing their game. His only escape was to cease being . . .

Except . . . he must not. He could not. Things were happening. A current of warmth swept over him, a memory of breath and blood, sudden chemical heat wrapping him and racing past. He reached after it. Too fast. He could not keep up.

And then, there it was again, that dark branch overhanging the torrent. But not a branch . . . a hand this time, held out in the void. A brown, long-fingered hand. A chance for escape. Would it hold him if he leaped and grabbed . . . could it pull him free? No other choice. Terror gave him breath and muscle. He came up dolphinlike, twisting out of the frigid water. Reached, gripped and . . .

. . . Ard worried when his guild master, usually so still and concentrated during a healing, shuddered and gasped, like a man struck hard from behind. His impulse was to lean in and lend support, but this might disrupt the flow of energies and bring the death back to the healer. Instead, without much hope, Ard put two fingers to the patient's pulse point. A moment later, he cried out, amazed . . .

Ghirra felt the lungs swell on their own, and then, starting up beneath his hands, the tiny thunder of the heart. Spent beyond imagining, he slumped back in silent, disbelieving joy.

"*ValEmbriha!*" Ard exclaimed.

The apprentice girl eyed the Master Healer with awe.

Stavros stirred faintly. His back arched in reawakening pain.

Ghirra gathered himself, breathing hard, and wrapped his patient's jaw with probing fingers, pressing until Stavros quieted. He let his own breath settle, then lifted the dressings from the shoulder wound. His outraged exclamations brought a prim scowl to his herbalist's weary face, and a blush to the girl's cheek. The Master Healer did not approve of a weapon that could burn flesh and bone more deeply than the pure guar fresh from the rock.

He sent the girl off to scavenge more ice and reached for the second syringe.

73

THE CARAVAN STRAGGLED homeward, pursued by lines of fire closing in from all directions except ahead of them. The cliffs of Dul Elesi
rose slowly out of the smoke.

"Now there's a welcome sight!" Megan's voice was like a crone's, cracked
with thirst and muffled by the layers of her face wrappings, protection now
against the thick smoke as well as flying sand.

As they walked, Susannah scanned the distant, smoke-shrouded cave
entries.

"He's not likely to be hanging out in the doorway," Megan advised.

Susannah glanced away, embarrassed. "I suppose not."

"Not with Emil wandering around."

From the base of the cliff, three hjalk riders rode out through the dust
and smoke, making hell-bent for the head of the caravan.

"Welcoming committee," Susannah noted.

"And in an awful hurry . . ."

The riders' faces were masked. Their hjalk looked thin and unkempt.

"Maybe it's been resolved by now," Susannah remarked, as they trudged
along. "The situation with ConPlex, I mean."

"Only if you assume that the wheels of justice turn with miraculous
speed."

"The case is clear-cut, surely." The thought of seeing Stavros buoyed her,
but even an optimist could be at the end of her strength. Susannah lacked
the heart for one of Megan's weighty discussions. "With what we've seen of
present Sawl culture, never mind what it may have been before—what court
could dispute the Sawls' right to their own planet?"

"Easy for you to say—you're here with the Sawls. The Courts, however, are on Earth, with ConPlex." Megan took a firm grip on Susannah's elbow. "Listen, it *is* crucial that you not say a word about any of this until I give you the okay."

"Or Stavros does?"

". . . sure. Or Stavros."

Megan's tone left Susannah uneasy. "You think he's been forced into hiding, like . . . somewhere else?"

Megan shrugged. "Where else would he go?"

But Susannah heard the momentary hesitation. "There's something you're not telling me."

"You know everything I know."

"I hope so."

They watched the hjalk riders speed up as the caravan approached the wind-torn fields. Solemn chanting drifted past with the dust. Along the western curve where plain met cropland, small parties were digging fire breaks.

Megan gauged the fire's advance behind them. "They'll never get done in time."

"We're home now. We'll all pitch in."

The riders reached the lead wagon as it wound among the drying terraces. One pushed his lathered beast through the dust to meet Aguidran as she walked beside the Priest Guild wagon carrying the still-unconscious Kav Daven. Susannah recognized the rider's tired stoop even before he slid from the hjalk's back and drew aside his mask. She started forward, but Megan held her back.

"Give him a moment."

Ghirra let the heaving animal wander loose while he fell in close step beside his sister. After several paces, Aguidran stopped short, her disbelief unmistakable even at a distance. Ghirra nodded firmly, laying a hand on her shoulder.

"No . . ." murmured Megan.

"I'd say whoever it was he went back for didn't make it." Watching Ghirra, Susannah did not see Megan's pitying glance.

A ranger came running from the front of the caravan. Several others followed, converging on Aguidran. All shared a look of bewildered shock. The Master Ranger spoke to them quietly, her back stiff. Only the sharp chop of her hands hinted at emotion. When she dismissed them, they sped off in all directions. Ghirra glanced in on Kav Daven, but as Ashimmel hurried up, he left his sister in conference and made his way toward the Infirmary wagon. He was exhausted and dirty, and as grim as Susannah had ever seen him, even after the fatal lightning.

"What happened?" she asked softly.

Ghirra met Megan's anxious eyes, shook his head once, faintly. "Edan is dead. *Murdered,* Ibi says the word is."

Megan let out a breath that could have been relief or incredulity. "Edan?"

"Murdered?" Astonishment made Susannah feel stupid. "But, how? Does anyone know who did it?"

Ghirra's tired eyes lidded. "Oh, yes. This is known.".

Megan tugged her dust mask aside. "The goddamned laser."

"No, he did not use this . . . thing . . . for this killing."

"He?"

"Who do you think?" Megan growled.

Ghirra told them what he knew of Edan's death, then moved on to Liphar's interrogation. While Susannah listened in shock and growing outrage, Megan stared off in the direction of the Lander's white-and-silver cone.

"Could we actually have him on the run? This is clumsy, blatant stuff for a guy like Clausen."

Susannah rounded on her. "Is that all you can think about, your damn politics? Edan dead, and now he's got poor Liphar . . . ? Why didn't anyone stop him? Why *doesn't* anyone? What is the matter with them?"

"Taylor's his best buddy, Ronnie thinks Emil is fun, and probably Weng wants to live a little longer."

Ghirra shook his head. "They would try, I think, but he is stronger."

"And armed."

"But I can't believe he'd . . . he wouldn't. . . ." Susannah chewed her lower lip, struggling with the necessary reassessment. "Okay. He would. He did. But . . . with his bare hands? Ghirra, are you sure?"

"Yes. This is sure."

If this was so, which it clearly was, something must be done about it. She glanced from Ghirra to Megan, then out over the broken fields. Perhaps nothing could be done about deaths by drought, lightning, or flying debris, but something *could* be done about Emil Clausen. With a gesture of mad resolve, Susannah loosed the canteen from her belt and shook it. "Not enough. Meg, give me what's left in yours."

Megan put a hand on her canteen, then left it there. "What are you going to do?"

"I'm going in there and get that poor boy away from him."

"Oh. Just like that? You've got to be kidding."

"Somebody's got to do it!"

"Suzhannah, this is not . . ." Ghirra began.

"Never mind. I'll make do with what I have." Susannah paced forward, then turned back to face them. "Look, I'm tired of being the silent observer in this cat-and-mouse game of yours! Nobody asks me what I think, but I'll tell you anyway: when innocents like Edan and Liphar get caught in the cross fire, it's time to put a stop to it! All of it!"

"Right," Megan retorted. "And you're going to just ride up in your white hat and save the day!"

"At least I'll try! What wrong with that?"

"Nothing, if it was so easy. Susannah, there's a lot more than politics at stake here! Besides, you don't challenge the enemy in his own lair!"

"Why the hell not, if that's where he is?"

"Because you get killed for nothing, and he goes right on doing what he wants to!"

Susannah's reassessment balked at the idea of Clausen actually turning his weapon on her. She understood this was a problem, but she didn't have time to wait for her brain to catch up. Liphar needed rescuing. "Because you're letting him get away with it! Meg, don't you see? The game you're playing is *his* game! You run and he chases you, like he had you programmed. Or like the Sawls taking it for granted they can only suffer through the goddesses' warring. Your own self-image has you paralyzed. You won't grab the upper hand even when it's available!" She took a deep, indignant breath, expelled it loudly. "Megan, he's *one* man!"

"One practiced killer," Megan amended. "Equipped with laser."

Susannah paced back to the wagon and grabbed her medikit from the open tailgate.

Ghirra moved to block her. "Suzhannah, please . . . this is . . ."

"It's what? Crazy?" She glared at him, surprised she could be so angry, with him of all people, even though none of this was his fault. "I'll talk to him! He's always been perfectly reasonable with me!"

"Reasonable?" Megan played her final card. "Tell us, Guildmaster, how *reasonable* Emil has been with Stavros . . ."

Susannah waved this aside. "Stav told me about that."

"I mean, recently."

This, at last, got her attention. "Ghirra . . . ?"

Ghirra flicked Megan an ambivalent glance. "He lives."

Megan prodded. "But it was close?"

"Yes."

Susannah shut her eyes, but said nothing.

"*Very* close?" insisted Megan.

Ghirra frowned gently.

"All right! What happened?" Susannah begged him. "Tell me!"

He scribed a long slow arc across his shoulder. "Very bad burning."

She pressed a hand to her mouth. "The pain must be . . . I gave you the . . ."

Ghirra nodded soothingly. "Yes. He does better now."

Megan pressed her advantage. "But he's not out of danger, right? Let Ghirra smuggle you up there, now. That's where you should be, not facing off with Emil Clausen!"

Susannah hesitated, but found her resolve again. "Meg, he's alive. That's what I needed to know. He's had the best care he could ask for already, and there's another patient waiting, who he wouldn't want me to desert." She squeezed Ghirra's arm, then shouldered the medikit and stepped around him, heading briskly for the front of the caravan and the Lander beyond.

"We'll have to go with her, of course," Megan complained.

"Yes." Ghirra was already moving in Susannah's wake.

"You've gone round the fucking bend!" Danforth snarled.

"I'm the only sane one left." Clausen snatched the connector cable from its socket and tucked it into his belt. "And I don't need you working against me."

Danforth slumped in his chair, facing a dead computer screen. He imagined strangling Clausen with the very same cable. But an invalid couldn't move fast enough. Moments later, in the shimmering clearing Danforth had dubbed the interrogation ring, the prospector bent over his prisoner, prone in the dust. The chanting continued from the wilting fields, background music to a surreal narrative heat-soaked in gloom.

A different sort of motion at the edge of the clearing caught Danforth's eye. He jerked out of his slouch to balance unsteadily on the hard edge of his chair.

542 Marjorie B. Kellogg

"Emil!"

Clausen started faintly at Susannah's summons, but his eyes did not leave Liphar for a second. He crouched beside him, a brimming cup of water held just out of reach of the young Sawl's blistering lips.

The hidden chanters fell expectantly silent. Danforth reached to nudge Weng out of her heat doze on the ground beside him, then wheeled himself quickly to the limb of the shade.

"What are you *doing?*" Susannah marched across the clearing.

Clausen grinned into Liphar's tear-streaked face, swaying slightly on his haunches. He raised the cup to his own mouth and drank with slow torturous relish. But his other arm floated up from his side as if automatically. He aimed the silver laser pistol at Susannah without even looking.

"For god's sake, Emil!" she shouted.

Danforth held his breath. God had nothing to do with it . . .

In her layered Sawlish clothing, her dark hair flying long and loose around a tanned face throwing off sparks of righteous outrage, Susannah descended like an avenging angel. Helpless in his chair, Danforth thought of sudden street corner collisions, viewed in agonizing slow motion.

"See? He's wearing down," murmured Weng at his shoulder. "Reflexes gone."

"How much reflex does it take to pull a trigger?"

But Clausen did not fire. He seemed too entranced by the suffering in Liphar's glazed eyes. He tipped the cup to let the precious water dribble in a thin, broken stream onto the dry ground.

Susannah strode up behind him. The laser pointed at her stomach. She swiped furiously at the outstretched arm, sending the little pistol flying. It skittered across the hard-packed dirt.

Clausen ducked and rolled at light speed, kicking up dust as he lunged after his weapon. Susannah ignored him. She knelt to cradle Liphar in her arms and pop open her canteen.

Clausen snatched up the gun and rolled upright into a surprised crouch. He glanced around the clearing as if searching out the other legions that must be pressing the attack. Seeing no one, he settled back on his heels to watch with bemused disbelief as Susannah fed Liphar short sips of water and struggled to untie his badly chafed wrists and ankles.

To Danforth's amazement, the prospector started to laugh. He dropped his forehead to his knee. His shoulders shook silently. Then he rose abruptly, pacing toward Susannah.

Danforth tensed in his chair, wondering how far across the clearing he could get on plastic-bound legs before the laser cut him down.

At Susannah's side, Clausen paused, but merely leaned over to murmur in her ear, then pass by without a second glance. She stared after him as he stalked toward the shade of the Underbelly. His gun arm hung slack at his side, the pistol dangling from two crooked fingers. He stopped in front of Weng to grin at her mirthlessly as he shoved the laser into its holster and snapped the flap tight. He pulled the computer cable from his belt and tossed it into Danforth's lap.

"Not as young as we used to be, eh, Commander?"

Weng stared straight through him. "You see, Dr. Danforth? I told you he'd have to sleep sometime."

Clausen's grin twisted. "Yeah." He crossed to the Sawl-made ladder at the main hatch, climbed it stiffly, and pulled it up after him. "I'll be in my quarters if anyone needs me."

Some inner, upper door slammed shut behind him.

"Okay. Now I've seen fucking everything!" Danforth wheeled out into the sun as Megan and Ghirra loped up to huddle around Susannah and the suffering Liphar.

"What did he say to you?" Megan demanded.

Susannah sighed, both sad and relieved. "He said, 'Thanks, I really needed a break. I wasn't getting anything out of him anyway.' "

74

E.D. 94–7:42

GHIRRA WHISKED SUSANNAH and Liphar out of the Lander clear-ing, leaving Megan to deal with Terran issues. The chanters emerged from the fields one by one to follow, singing a gladder melody.

Liphar could not walk on his own, though he insisted he could, clinging heavily to Susannah. He asked about Stavros, and then Kav Daven, his joy at the good news offset by the shock of the bad. He stopped often along the dusty path to rest and down another ration of water, glancing behind him as if expecting pursuit.

The lead wagons of the caravan had pulled up at the foot of the cliff. A vanguard of engineers went up to ready the winches for the off-loading of cargo. The rangers organized reinforcements for the fire brigade. Families left their carts or wagons in the charge of the younger children, unshipped their digging tools, and hurried into the fields to help with the firebreaks. A billowing wall of black smoke obscured the plain to the north and west, close enough now for the bright lick of flames to be visible along its base.

Word of Liphar's ordeal spread fast among the wagons, though no one was quite sure how they were supposed to understand that this bizarre and ungenerous behavior was confined to one particular Terran. Liphar accepted his sudden celebrity with dazed humor of a haunted sort, now that he was free. But he wept when a stony-face Aguidran met them at the foot of the stairs. He offered broken bits of eloquence to detail Edan's bravery, and would not allow himself to be taken to Physicians' until he'd seen for himself that Stavros was alive and well.

He calmed under Aguidran's stern eye, and a pair of rangers was found to stretcher him up the long stairs. As they entered the cavernous dark of the stable level, the young Sawl sighed in relief, relaxing at last into the curl of the leather sling. Susannah absorbed the blessed coolness with gratitude and her own sense of homecoming.

They waited at the entrance to Valla's Story Hall while the Master Herbalist unlocked the huge doors from the inside. Liphar demanded to be helped out of the stretcher so he might walk into the chill, dim hall on his own unsteady legs.

Stavros lay on a pallet of blankets, dozing fitfully. The apprentice girl knitted quietly in the light of an oil lamp. She scrambled up in surprise as they entered. Ghirra beckoned her aside to announce Kav Daven's return with the caravan. Torn, she glanced back at Stavros, but at Ghirra's nod, she sped away to see to her Ritual Master's welfare.

Susannah held back as Liphar tottered into the pool of lamplight at Stavros' bedside.

"Ibi?" He collapsed into a slow heap like a puppet with its strings cut. "Ibi!"

Stavros' eyes lazed open. His head moved vaguely toward the source of the voice.

Still drugged, Susannah realized. She was still angry with him for leaving, for all the secrets, but right now, only happy to see him alive, even if not so well. He was pale from his weeks in hiding, and fever-thinned. He looked older, she thought, the youthful hollows of his face sharpened. His eyes were dark against his sallow skin. His left shoulder was thickly wrapped with Ard's healing poultice. The long, dim hall smelled of herbs and lamp oil.

Stavros focused on the kneeling Sawl. "Lifa. Rhe khem."

Liphar beamed, fresh tears starting up in his eyes. "*Khem rhe,* Ibi."

Stavros seemed to gain strength as he struggled out of his drug haze. "Rhe sukahakhe, Lifa. Han jela."

Liphar wiped his cheeks bashfully. "No, Ibi. *Te keth-shim Ghirra sukaharhe, cedirhe?*"

Stavros laughed, a muted escape of breath. "You saved me the *first* time, then."

He glanced up to share a weak grin with the Master Healer and saw another waiting in the shadows. "Susannah?" Ghirra's chuckle convinced him. He let his head loll back against his pillows. "At last."

Ghirra bent to murmur in Liphar's ear, then helped him to his feet. He let the young man walk to the waiting stretcher, making sure to collect Ard on the way out.

Stavros took in Susannah's guarded expression as she came to kneel at his side. "What?"

She felt awkward now, and vulnerable. It was hard to look him in the eye. Before, it had been always he who was at a loss with her. Something had changed. She was no longer in control of this event.

"You ought to let me look at that shoulder," she muttered lamely.

As she reached to check his bandages, he caught her hand and pressed her cupped palm to his lips with a tenderness that nearly broke her reserve.

"Are you really all right?"

He smiled. "You tell me, Doctor."

He trailed his fingers down her cheek, then crooked his good arm around her neck to draw her close and kiss her hungrily. "Ah, Susannah, I missed you! Lie down with me, talk to me, hold me."

"But you went off without me. You didn't say . . ."

"Please! Later, okay?"

"You're in pain."

He laughed soundlessly. "Your drugs are incredible. Just hold me."

She eased down beside him on the pallet, snuggling gingerly, but he pulled her close with his good arm, with strength that surprised her, and held her very tight, his face buried in her hair. He said nothing for a long time. Finally he let out a long breath and relaxed his desperate grip.

"I died," he said, as if by way of explanation.

Susannah murmured sympathetically, smoothing her fingers across his naked chest and belly, wanting him, wishing him whole.

"Really. I did." Gently, he stopped her hand's wanderings. "I know it."

She pulled away to gaze at him. "Ghirra didn't mention this."

"Ghirra will tell you it was the adrenaline or whatever he shot into me, but I tell you, it was too late for that. I was gone. Or at least the body was. I fought it, fought until I had nothing left. I had to let go. And then I was . . . somewhere else." He wrapped the good arm around her again, and Susannah felt him shudder.

"Where?"

He glanced away, uneasy. "Oh, I don't know. Out there. Wherever it was, it scared the shit out of me. But it was Ghirra who brought me back . . . I think. Either that, or . . ." He cupped her chin and kissed her gently. "You think I'm nuts, like everyone else does?"

She smiled, shook her head.

He kissed her again. "You ready to have that conviction sorely tried?"

Susannah shrugged. "Try away."

He adjusted himself on the pallet, wincing faintly.

"Stav, you ought to rest."

"No. Listen. You have to listen. I *need* you to listen!" He gripped her hand until it hurt. "I felt this . . . these . . . two *things*. I think I touched the Sisters . . . out there."

Susannah cleared her throat softly. "That's not uncommon. To see god in near-death experiences."

"It wasn't near-death, it *was* death, and I tell you, I *felt* them out there, wherever I was, but not as goddesses. As forces . . . as *beings*. It was as if, by giving in to dying, I was drawn into some kind of natural connection, even though they didn't notice me. They were so . . . self-absorbed. I tried once to catch their attention, then I got scared and ran. The terror was so . . . !" He let out an explosive breath. "And then Ghirra was there, showing me the way. Because I ran, I lived."

Susannah found herself monitoring the temperature of his skin. Was the fever coming back? "I don't know, Stav. What's all this supposed to mean?"

"It means that they're there, really *there*. That maybe we can contact them, try to reason with them, show them the havoc they wreak on the Sawls with their games, maybe make them stop!"

"Contact them?" Frightened, she made a joke of it. "By dying? Again?"

He grinned at her worry and hugged her close. "No! Once was enough. But there's got to be a lesson there, about resistance, maybe, or . . . once before, at the Leave-taking, I . . . the Kav . . . hey!" He slipped his hand from her waist and stared with grateful satisfaction at his palm. "It's back."

"It?"

"My guar-fire."

"Your what?"

He started, remembering. "The Kav, how is he? I have to talk to him, tell him about . . . everything!"

"He's stable." She restrained him gently. "But I don't think he'll be able to talk."

"He won't need to. He can't *see* either, and yet he does." He pulled away to gaze at her. "There's so much to tell you, so much to explain . . . We've had so little time, and I . . ." He toyed with the lacings of her tunic. "I had other things on my mind."

"You're not actually considering . . ."

"Sorry. Not even your drugs are that good." With a sigh, he slipped his hand between the gauzy layers of fabric. "But a man can dream . . ."

Later, the Master Healer returned to fill Stavros in on Kav Daven's desert trek.

". . . raellil?" Stavros struggled up onto his good elbow. "Me?"

Ghirra traced absent circles on the damp floor tiles. "I think, yes, this is you. You know this word?"

"Yes. I do." He let Susannah help him sit up. "I was working on a refined translation recently, after a conversation—sort of—with the Kav."

"Ashimmel says 'apprentice.' "

"So does Liphar. Also 'messenger' or 'voice.' But it's Old Words, so its roots are in the old technical vocabulary." Stavros grinned crookedly. "Plumbing, in fact. Sometimes internal plumbing, like arteries, but mostly it referred to pipes, you know, how they move stuff from place to place."

"Like messages," Susannah noted.

"Or like the word in English that carries a very similar double meaning: 'conduit.' "

"Conduit for what?" asked Susannah.

"Or apprentice," Ghirra repeated decisively to the tiles, then raised his eyes. "This Kav makes his choice at last."

Stavros met the Master Healer's even gaze.

"This does not surprise, Ibi."

"No. I suppose not." And yet, it was a surprise. The sort that turned your life upside down. The sort you never questioned. Stavros flexed his left hand experimentally. Thanks to a harmonious combination of Sawl healing and Terran medicine, he could move his arm from the elbow without gasping audibly. The guar fire was like liquid warmth in his palms, pain no longer—instead, a promise that strength would return, and a reminder that something beyond mere survival was expected of him. *Time to get to work.* He rolled onto his knees and grasped Susannah's shoulder. "Help me up, will you?"

"Not a chance. You're in no shape to go walking around."

He eyed her wickedly. "I'm fine. I could even . . ."

Susannah touched a finger to his lips. "Hush. I know. But you're not going anywhere."

He saw she was serious. "Susannah, please. I have to talk to the Kav, and he's obviously not coming to me. Please. Help me up."

"This Kav cannot talk now," said Ghirra flatly.

"He'll talk to me!"

Ghirra rose to a crouch, contriving to look vaguely threatening. "Ibi. No."

Stavros slumped back against the wall. "The medical professions of two worlds, conspiring against me."

"*Keth-shim Ghirra?*" The soft summons came from the doorway. Phea appeared in the blue glow of Valla's fountain, and hurried across the hall to announce that the hastily set-up field hospital at the foot of the cliff was being threatened already by the encroaching brushfires.

"We'll have to get them all up to Physicians'!" Susannah gripped Ghirra's arm. "Don't worry. We'll find room somehow. Can we use the winches?"

"Yes, but we must hurry." Ghirra stood, then gazed sternly down at his patient. "You will rest now, Ibi?"

Stavros nodded, feeling sullen but too worn out to resist any further. "Go on, both of you. I promise to stay put. But the minute the Kav wakes up, I want to hear about it!"

75

E.D. 94–10:48

A YOUNG FOOD GUILDER gestured Megan to raise her dust mask against the smoke, then slapped a wooden shovel into her hand. She joined the diggers frantically working to cut off the fire's advance on the terraces. Along the western edge, three fields of dry red stalks were already aflame. The Food Guild had agreed to sacrifice the next field for a firebreak. She worried for the Lander, though they had stowed everything that might burn, and dug her shovel in anew.

The amber sun was a hot, baleful eye in the malachite sky. The cliff face shone hard white through the smoke. Troops of apprentices fanned out across the relinquished field to pull the crop up by the roots. The obscuring dark billows made it hard to tell what was burning and what was not.

Megan spotted Weng and McPherson, white-suited against a background of soot and fire, tossing armloads of uprooted stalks onto waiting hakra carts. The dry root clumps shed their soil as gritty dust. The fire's draft pushed hot clouds of ash into the diggers' faces. Megan coughed, eyes streaming, and put her mind to shoveling as fast as she could manage.

She was quickly winded in the suffocating heat. As she stood back, panting, to wipe at the stinging mixture of sweat and tears, a strong hand snatched the shovel roughly from her grip.

"Not enough tools to go around. Take a break."

Megan backed away instinctively. The Sawls nearby did the same. Clausen stepped up to the swath of raw earth and bent briskly to work, the holstered laser nosing from the shadow of his arm. The Sawls stared, confused and frightened. But unwilling to reject the labors of any able hand, they decided to ignore him. They left him ample room and continued digging beside him.

"God help us if Aguidran finds him here," Megan muttered.

She freed her canteen from her sash and allowed herself a restrained gulp. Clausen had shaved the neat beard grown during his wilderness ordeal. He looked composed, if not relaxed. He fell immediately into an easy digging rhythm, his body no stranger to physical labor. Megan could only envy his machined efficiency, and hate him the more for that unwilling envy.

"Doing penance, Emil?" she shouted over the fire's roaring. "Why not just let it all burn?"

"And the Sled and the dish and the Lander as well?" He turned, leaning on his shovel, and nodded balefully at the tilted silver tower of the Lander, wreathed in smoke. "I still have a job to do, and though the chances of my escaping this planet with my life are slimming fast, I see no sense in cutting the odds back any further."

His bleak honesty took her aback. Tanned and freshly shaven though he was, she could see he, too, was fighting exhaustion. She tried to revel in grim satisfaction, but when he reached out, requesting her canteen, she gave it to him. He took a swig and wiped his mouth with the back of his hand, watching her with his chill hawk's eyes.

"I didn't lay a hand on the boy," he offered wearily. "Just scared him. The kid has stamina."

Megan's lip curled. "And Edan?"

"Is that the girl?" He shrugged. "Honest self-defense." He loosed his collar to show off raw parallel welts across the side of his throat. "Quite a hand with a leather thong. She nearly had me."

He drank again and handed back the canteen. Megan took it, but he held on briefly, commanding her direct attention. "Don't go playing the horrified innocent on me, Meg, like the rest of them. Whatever it takes to do the job, we both know that. I'd figured you were too smart to get involved in this stuff, but hey, you shove your man out there, and green or not, I have to go after him. You expected no less from the beginning, surely."

So he knew. Megan snatched back the canteen, blinking into the blowing ash. Of course he knew. Her open antagonism hadn't been the best cover, after all. *Green.* The insinuation stung her. Had she taken advantage of Stavros' innocence? If so, he was certainly a willing victim.

Clausen studied the approaching fire. "I don't suppose you'd care to enlighten me on one small point?" He chose to take Megan's sullen grunt for assent. "What in the world has Ibiá done for these folks to make them so willing to die for him?"

"You wouldn't understand."

"Try me."

"He loves them, Emil, and wants to help them. Nothing more, nothing less."

Clausen mimed a dagger thrust into his chest. "Is this the famous Levy wit and venom? Surely you can strike closer to the heart than that."

"Maybe yours is on the other side."

"How about the drone? Your idea?"

Megan tensed. In this confusion of smoke and noise, she could be dead in a ditch before anyone would notice. Like Edan.

Clausen's grin died into a hollow laugh. "Not to worry, dear icon of the Left. You're safe until I get truly desperate. Punks like Ibiá can come and go invisibly, but the recidivists get too much play if we martyr folks like you. Besides, who'd be left here for me to talk to?" He shook his head disgustedly. "There's so much righteous indignation flowing around here, it could make you puke! Do they think this is the first world to be forcibly welcomed into the twenty-first century?"

"The legal argument is strong, Emil." Instantly, Megan regretted her need to justify. Open debate would only give him information, and evidence.

He's smarter than any of us.

Clausen nodded, hugely satisfied. "I'm sure it is. Too bad no one will listen. But I gather from your general subtext that I do have you to thank for
that clever but toothless ploy, and also that I haven't yet managed to remove
young Ibiá from the scene. He's still alive? Amazing. He bled all over kingdom
come. Look, why not call him off, before it's too late?"

"This 'toothless ploy' has worked before. And he's not mine to call off, like
some dumb animal!" She was angrier at herself for being so easily manipulated
than at him for doing it. "Hey, you like being paid to kill people?"

He turned and spat into the dust. "Of course not."

"Convince me."

"Believe what you like, my dear Megan. I much prefer coming in, making
my claim and going home to my fur-lined burrow with a nice fat bundle.
Killing people usually means someone's going to try to kill me back, and
that gets tiresome."

He hefted the shovel to return to his digging. "And therefore, preferences
aside, there'll be no more mercy misses. That I promise you."

"Bad shots, you mean?"

Clausen grinned wolfishly. "You really believe that? Don't. And when next
you chance to conspire with our brash young hero, give him my fond regards,
and tell him from me he's a dead man."

76

THE FRENZIED LAST-MINUTE effort paid off. The flames raged up to
the line of firebreaks, lunged like chained beasts at the fresh-dug band of
wasteland, but could not cross. The fire burned itself out in frustration.

The soot-stained Terrans gathered at their landing craft in relief and grim
celebration. Two of them went right to work again to restore the power
supply.

The Priest Guild gathered at the cave mouths to chant and argue, as all
motion of the air died with the flames.

A stillness settled over the fields and terraces, as suffocating as the thick
pall of smoke that hovered like smog along the cliff face. The plain was a plate
of hard-fired ceramic, blackened out to the limits of sight. The amber sun

shone greenly through the haze. The heat sucked the last trace of moisture from the fire-cracked earth and the becalmed air. Messenger of an angry goddess, it bore down with crushing weight.

E.D. 94–20:12

112°. Getting hard to think.

Danforth's hand went limp on the keypad. "Are you ready for this, Commander? Along with her recent storm data, CRI's reporting systematic disturbances in the planet's supposedly nonexistent magnetic field!" He stretched both legs and lifted them together, his own form of physical therapy. "I'm having her plot the pattern of those disturbances to match against the weather patterns . . . if you can call anything this bizarre a pattern."

Weng stood in conference with McPherson over a blackened electrical schematic. Dust drifted with every movement, clinging in fine powder to every surface. Clausen waited a few paces away, hands on hips, whistling some pointedly silent melody.

"Emil thinks the break's on this circuit here." McPherson's forefinger traced across the diagram with elaborate care. "I'm gonna go up there and take a look. We're pretty sure we got the dish in the right orientation, and the converter seems to be working." She tossed an ambivalent glance at the prospector, who nodded without looking at her. "If I can get the loop closed again, we should have full power and be able to raise the field."

"Taylor? You alive?"

Megan's quiet summons startled him. He'd forgotten she was back. *Where does my mind go these days . . . ?*

"Or asleep with your eyes open?" She stood over him with a fistful of memory sticks. "Don't blame you, in this heat. Listen, I've got the supply inventory for CRI, plus I'd like to upload some of my trip data."

"Snapshots of the ruins?" Danforth eased his chair away from the console.

"Ruins? . . . oh. Was that a joke, Taylor? Didn't know you were into jokes."

He offered a dark and bitter smile. "Cripple's gotta do something to amuse himself."

Megan fanned out her storage wafers like a poker hand beside the keypad, and brandished a wrinkled scrap of notes. "Not much to tell by way of supplies, CRI. Food is okay for two months yet, and with proper rationing, we'll manage for water now we've got the recycler working again. We can't count on much of anything from the Sawls. In fact, I'd like to know what the Orbiter could provide by way of an emergency drop, should the need arise, so pass that request on to Newman. I'll give you my data to chew on while I enter the list." She slipped the first wafer into the slot.

"I am not currently able to provide hard copy," CRI reminded her.

"So you can give us a show-and-tell later, if Taylor'll grant me the screen time."

"Be my guest," Danforth rumbled. "I'm sick and tired of my own data. Maybe somebody else's will break the logjam."

Clausen and McPherson humped the entry cylinder into place, half into the shadow of the Underbelly. The giant mirrored tube was awkward to move but surprisingly light for its size. Clausen rocked it back and forth on the uneven ground, calling instructions to McPherson at the other end, until he was satisfied with its positioning. He walked through it, stood in the middle shifting his weight from side to side.

"The field'll break around it right at midpoint." He came out dusting soot from his hands. "Give her a try, Tay."

At the mini-terminal, Danforth murmured to CRI. Megan put down her papers. Weng waited silently.

CRI chattered a reply. The air around the Lander shimmered faintly.

"Could be just another heat mirage," Danforth warned.

The air thickened. The silver cylinder thrummed faintly. The view of the blackened plain shivered into a splintered dancing image. The distant wagon rattle and the cries of the winch men on the cliff died to a muffled echoing along the entry tube. McPherson let out a cheer, setting aside her grievances with Clausen long enough to throw a victory punch at his shoulder. Clausen smiled.

"Our thanks, Lieutenant, Mr. Clausen," said Weng stiffly.

"Congratulations," said Danforth, as Clausen gave the cylinder a last inspection and strode over to the console. *And wipe that smug grin off your face, asshole!*

"Our deal, Tay?"

"You betcha, boss! It's all yours." Danforth wheeled away from the console with exaggerated dispatch.

Clausen hauled over a crate and sat. "CRI: This will be a Section G, Priority One message, by my authority. I want it droned out FTL as soon as I'm done transmitting." The prospector paused, then spoke for the benefit of all within earshot. "To follow will be a file of charges against certain expeditionary personnel on various counts of theft, both government property and private, economic subversion, conspiracy and treason."

"Economic subversion?" Megan shook her head. "That's rather creative, Emil."

"The first charge will name Dr. Megan Levy, Mr. Stavros Ibiá, and Commander Weng Tsi Hua . . ."

". . . and lastly, for conspiring to prevent the capture of a dangerous fugitive, Commander Weng Tsi Hua." Clausen sat back from the keyboard, considering.

A hot draft through the entry cylinder brought the rolling basso call of the priest-horns. A full-throated chanting answered. Standing in the cylinder's mouth, Megan counted the sad discrete plumes of smoke rising along the cliff top, so black against the hot malachite sky. The sight too easily recalled ranked columns of dust roaring across a parched salt flat.

"Thirty-four." Megan shuddered, and retreated into the coolness of the Underbelly. "The funerals are starting," she reported, to whoever might be listening.

McPherson snored gently on a tarp-cushioned crate. Weng slept more quietly within her curtained cubicle, driven into seclusion by the insult of Clausen's list. Danforth lay on his bed working a sheet of calculations by hand, but not so intently as to prevent him from glancing over at Clausen's back.

"How about failure to pray five times daily in the direction of Company headquarters?" he remarked. "You could get *me* on that one."

Megan eyed the planetologist speculatively. She was still sprinting to catch up with the shifts of alliance that had occurred while she was away. It would seem that Clausen hadn't an ally left to his name, though McPherson maintained a death grip on her admiration for his general do-anything-well competence and his focus on ensuring a trip home. Though she didn't approve of him shooting her friends, her loyalties were not ideological. Spacer loyalties rarely were. Perhaps, Megan speculated, the little pilot found Clausen's aura of contained menace exciting.

"Or," Danforth suggested, "how about conspiracy to consider science more important than corporate interests?"

"Feeling left out?" Megan ventured.

She did not recall him smiling much. But—so aloof and arrogant before, too self-involved to mingle with his colleagues—Danforth now shared a mocking grin with her across Clausen's back and laughed silently, bitterly, his teeth a bright arc in his dark, handsome face.

"I'm sure I could come up with something for you, Tay," Clausen said, without looking up.

Danforth's silent laughter blossomed into a mile-deep chuckle edged with loathing.

Clausen turned to stare at him. "I could. Don't push me."

The chuckle expanded. Danforth laid his notes down, let his head roll back on his pillows, and laughed a long, booming laugh.

Megan worried for him. Was this contempt news to Clausen? Either way, she thought it unwise of Danforth to exhibit it so openly. She put herself in Clausen's line of sight. "Listen, whenever you're done crucifying the Commander and myself, I'd like to have a word with CRI."

"Done? My dear Megan, I've only just begun. However . . ."

"Hello, everybody." Susannah stopped just inside the entry cylinder, her medikit slung over her shoulder. She was soot-streaked and coated with yellow dust. She took a deep breath of cool, fresh air. "What a relief! It's like breathing molten metal out there!"

"You're not at the funerals?" Megan exclaimed. "I thought at least one of us . . ."

"I couldn't, Meg. Three more died while we were moving them up to Physicians'. I just couldn't . . ." She set the medikit on the ground. "We lost fifty-six in all."

Megan nodded sadly.

Susannah shook her hair back in a gesture of resignation, then went to greet Danforth, planting a light kiss on his cheek. "How's this patient doing? I'm glad *some* of them recover. You look a little thin, Tay. Aren't they feeding you?" She peered at the ragged scar along his side and ran her hands along his legs, checking the casts. "The wound's healed nicely, though I'm sorry

I couldn't make it a little neater for you. Looks like someone attacked you with a chainsaw. How's it feel?"

"Fine. But, Susannah . . ." He grabbed her hand. "Walking cast? Please? Before my brain atrophies along with my body?"

"You got it, next thing on my list." Her eyes raked Clausen at the console, his back prominently turned. Her lips tightened briefly. Then she moved casually to his side and spoke in a tone of gentle admonition.

"Sorry to have caused such a scene, Emil . . . but was it absolutely necessary to be so hard on the boy?"

Megan watched. Could the soft sell possibly work with this man?

Clausen swiveled in his seat. "Ah, the noble Susannah. Now which boy is that?"

Susannah tipped her head, smiling. "He was fortunately unhurt, but the harm done to our relationship with the Sawls is irreparable."

"Oh, *that* boy." Clausen crossed his legs, enjoying himself. "I'm much more interested in the other."

She offered him all innocent concern. "Was there another?"

Clausen sighed and turned back to the terminal. "CRI, add the following charge: for aiding and abetting the escape of an injured felon, Dr. Susannah James."

"It's great you got them to bring it back!" McPherson cracked her knuckles excitedly. "It's in terrific shape! The flood hardly beat it up at all! Just needs a serious bath."

"Real serious," remarked Megan from the console. The returned A-Sled sat in the clearing beside its damaged companion craft.

"Nah. I'm charging up the portable sonic now. Bet I have that Sled in the air inside of ten, twelve hours."

"I'm surprised Aguidran didn't hold it hostage, in return for Clausen's head."

"What about B-Sled?" Susannah was keeping informed on the progress of the Sled repairs, as Stavros had requested. She fitted the last section of the walking cast to Danforth's thigh and pressed it tight. "Sit up, Tay. See how it feels."

McPherson glanced toward the clearing. The Sleds' sun-bright image danced through the force field's distortions. "It'll come along faster now Emil's decided to get his hands dirty."

"Could they get any dirtier?" Megan muttered.

The pilot shrugged. "Say what you like, he knows his stuff. He got us power back. And he's eager to get out there and get done, so's we can all go home. Unlike some I could name."

Danforth sat up and swung his legs off the edge of the bed. The fracture in his left shin was nearly mended. Susannah's new bindings had given him back a working knee. He flexed it gingerly. The reset break in his right thigh was healing more slowly and required continued immobility.

"No marathons," Susannah smiled. "I'd like you to keep using the chair as much as possible for a while, but Ghirra has sent you a gift."

She ducked behind a crate and hauled out a pair of hand-carved crutches. Danforth took them eagerly, stroking the smooth, aged wood and the leather-covered padding, softened with long use. He touched the lap-joints near the tips where the shafts had been recently lengthened.

"Tell that doctor-man thanks."

"I think he'd like it better if you told him yourself."

"I think you should get right on them, come over here and take a look," said Megan abruptly. The mini-terminal's screen was lighting up with pictures. "Commander? You'll want to see this, too."

Danforth set the crutches under his arms and swung himself forward awkwardly, but with increasing ease as the memory of upright motion came back to him. "Haven't done this since I racked up my first bike! Damn, it feels good to walk!"

McPherson paced along beside him. "Watch it! Not so fast, Tay!" Grinning happily, she dodged ahead to wheel his chair up next to Megan.

Weng emerged from her cubicle to join them at the terminal. She moved briskly and wore her usual gracious smile, but Susannah noted the strain in her face, the skin taut at the corners of her mouth, marks of a hurt as deep as the gash in Stavros' shoulder. Clausen could be killing Weng without lifting a finger.

"Look! Ogo Dul," Megan announced. "The nearest coastal settlement. It's built inside cliffs, too. This is one of the market levels."

"Boats!" exclaimed McPherson with delight. "Always wanted to ride in a boat!"

Danforth set aside his crutches and lowered himself into his chair. Megan continued her guided tour. The others' patience with her detailed commentary told Susannah how starved they were not only for new data, but for the chance to relax and have a little fun, playing at dinner guests of tourists just home from vacation.

Into the middle of their laughter walked the Master Healer, his shirt as limp as his stance. He stepped through the entry cylinder with slow care, touching its silvered inside curve with an interest restrained by caution. At the inner lip of the cylinder, he glanced warily back at the clearing where Clausen, up to his elbows in the guts of B-Sled, was whistling Mozart.

Susannah went to meet him. "Is everything all right?"

Ghirra nodded, then stopped short, puzzled, then amazed. He sniffed the air. "How is this? How is it like a deep cave here?"

"You mean . . . the coolness? It's the force field. Ronnie fixed it." Susannah faltered. "I forgot. You were never down here . . . before."

"You can do this?" Ghirra lifted dust-streaked arms to welcome the chill. "With your machines?"

"Sure, Doc. Climate control. Watch." Danforth leaned over and snatched up a loose pebble. He tossed it at the shifting surround of energy. The pebble sparked and bounced off what must have seemed to the astonished Sawl to be wavering but insubstantial air.

"How?" Ghirra demanded.

Danforth looked to Susannah. "Does he really want to know?"

"He always does."

"Later, later," called Megan. "Ghirra, come look. This is the Sky Hall. It was cool in there, too, remember? CRI, run the next half-dozen frames in slow sequence, please."

Ghirra held Susannah back, eager as a wondering boy. "The machines can do this anywhere?"

"Anywhere you have the power." She pointed upward. "And the loop." Her finger traced the circumference of the Lander above their heads. "It hasn't been working since the flood. Stav didn't tell you about air-conditioning?"

"Ghirra!" Megan insisted. "Need your help explaining this!"

Ghirra wrapped his damp shirt more tightly around his chest and let dignity replace his awe. Weng extended her hand with her first real smile since the transmission of Clausen's infamous list began. "Good evening, Guildmaster."

Ghirra took her hand in the instinctively courtly manner he reserved for Weng alone, and held it, regarding her solicitously. "You are well, Commander?"

"Trying times, are they not?" she replied lightly, easing her hand from his grasp.

Ghirra smiled his sympathy and turned to Danforth, his gaze fastening on the newly bound legs. "And you are well, Taylor Danforth?"

Danforth patted the crutches beside him. "The better for these, Doc. Sorry to hear about all your trouble out there."

"Trouble is shared always," Ghirra replied quietly.

Danforth raised an eyebrow. "Yeah, Doc. It is, at that."

"Okay, now here we go." Megan pointed at the screen. "These were etched on the stone walls all around the hall. I was caught by the quality of abstraction, but Ghirra, I thought, was rather dismissive. He called them . . ."

"Old drawing." Ghirra peered at the lines and crosshatchings on the screen with renewed mistrust. "I do not dis-miss these, Meeghan. I say they have not meaning. They are drawing only."

"Art, he means." Megan grinned. "A mere trifle."

"How old are they, do you know?" Weng inquired.

"Very many generations, Commander."

"It was Susannah who noticed the changes," Meg pursued. "Watch this."

CRI ran through the sequence slowly. The hatchings and lines shifted relative to each other, drifting, intersecting, moving apart in a choppy rhythm suggestive of a consecutive progression.

"Run it again, CRI? Faster, this time."

The second run brought a soft exclamation of admiration from Susannah. The changes from frame to frame smoothed into a virtually seamless moving image.

Weng leaned into the screen with sudden interest. "CRI! Again, please." When the sequence had finished, she straightened. "I would swear . . . CRI, may I have the first and last frames, split screen, please."

"Certainly, Commander."

Weng stared. "Now run the sequence again, please."

CRI complied. The old spacer watched intently, then stood back. "How does it strike you, Dr. Danforth?"

Danforth returned her look blankly. "How does it strike *you*, Commander?"

"Ah. Well, it seemed to me that . . . but perhaps I . . . wait, let me try something." She reached over Megan's arm to tap in a long command. "Complete without verbalizing, CRI."

"Yes, Commander."

A single image from the latter part of the sequence filled the screen, the etched pattern of lines in sharp relief against the pebbled rock. Slowly, a second, underlying image began to surface. A flat gray background softened the sharpness of the rock. Paler connected blotching hovered beneath the intricate crosshatchings. Bright spots that might have been taken for random pitting of the stone were shadowed by a spatter of black dots.

"Excellent," said Weng. "A very good match. Proceed, please."

The two images shivered together briefly. Then the Sky Hall photo began to fade. It left behind a screen of grainy gray stained with lighter smoke and pinpricks of black.

"Oh, my god," Danforth murmured. "Could they possibly . . . ?"

"That looks like a star field, Commander," McPherson observed.

Weng's black eyes leaped past Danforth to settle on the mystified Master Healer. "You see, Guildmaster? Apologies, but I believe you are mistaken. This 'old drawing' of yours is very meaningful indeed."

Megan studied the screen. "Star field? You mean . . . ? *Sky* Hall! Of course! How dumb can you get?"

"But, what stars?" asked McPherson.

Weng's thin hand inscribed a graceful arc. "These stars. This is a photonegative from the sky survey that Dr. Sundqvist is taking from the Orbiter's observatory." She outlined the lighter blotches with eager fingers. "There is the Coal Sack, invading the cluster. CRI, bring in Dr. Levy's photo again, please."

They watched as the two images swam again toward their astonishing correlation.

"The degree of accuracy is remarkable." Weng was almost voluble with triumph, "And mind you, Dr. Danforth. This image, the closest match to our own current one, is from the middle of the sequence. The succeeding images are future prediction."

Ghirra had observed their building excitement in silence. Now, as each grappled with the flood of implication, he asked gravely. "What is this meaning, Commander?"

"It means someone *knew*!" Danforth blurted. "Someone here a very long time ago knew that Byrnham's Cluster was heading for collision with the Coal Sack! Unless . . ."

"No," said Megan. "These drawings are not recent. I'd stake my rep on that."

"I believe the first image in the sequence will tell us *how* long ago they knew," Weng added. "What do you say to my periodic table now?"

Danforth shook himself, like an incredulous bear. "No further questions, Commander. Except maybe . . . who? Who was it who knew?"

Ghirra spread pleading hands. "Commander . . . ?"

"I will explain as best I can, Guildmaster."

"Good!" Megan exclaimed. "You can explain to me, too."

"And me," Susannah agreed. "What collision with the Coal Sack?"

"Dr. Danforth?"

"Be my guest, Commander. The stars are all earthly suns to me. I leave the astronomy to Jorge Sundqvist . . . and you."

"You do know what a star is, Guildmaster?"

Susannah laid a defending hand on Ghirra's arm. "Stav's got him well on his way toward a galactic point of view."

"Excellent." Weng embarked, with CRI's assistance, on an illustrated mini-lecture on the history of Byrnham's Cluster, maintaining for Ghirra's benefit a strictly nontechnical approach. As the explanation progressed, Clausen wandered in from the clearing. Looking heat dazed, he stood nearby, cooling off, listening without seeming to.

The Master Healer listened for all he was worth. Now and then, he asked for clarification. The greatest obstacle to his understanding was the question of scale: he had no frame of reference for the vast distances and quantities involved, with one exception. Conceptualizing enormous stretches of time did not faze him in the least.

"I have done some preliminary calculations on this, as Dr. Danforth knows," said Weng. "The data suggest that about a hundred and sixty-five thousand standard years ago, the Coal Sack would actually become visible in its approach."

Megan absorbed this with difficulty. "One six five?"

"It would have been, of course, detectable long before that . . . but only with sophisticated sensing equipment."

"By comparison," Megan offered, "The Egyptians, our first great techno-crats, were moving toward the height of their powers a mere five thousand years ago."

Weng nodded appreciatively. "A hundred and fifty thousand years ago, the Cluster entered the outer limits of the nebula. The Fiixian system, however, was on the far side of the Cluster at the time. The affects of the collision would have grown steadily for the next forty thousand years as the system's orbit moved it around to the front of the Cluster, climaxing around fifteen thousand, then easing somewhat as the orbit returned it toward the back. The Cluster itself, however, continues to move into major intersection with an outstretched arm of the nebula, mitigating the effects of relative position."

Weng paused for breath.

Ghirra stood in pensive silence, sucking his cheeks into hollows. Susannah worried that he would be overwhelmed by this onslaught of information. She recalled his metaphoric commentary on the beauties of the Cluster when night first fell over the Dop Arek.

"Getting a little over your head, honored doctor?" commented Clausen from behind.

Ghirra did not seem to hear. He stared at the screen from the depths of his increasingly pronounced stoop, his eyes half-lidded, barely focused.

Weng ceased her lecture, concerned. The others stilled around her. Clausen chuckled softly to himself.

Susannah reached, then held back her hand. "Ghirra?"

His eyes flicked up at the sound of his name. He glanced around, read the contempt in Clausen's face and waiting anxiety in the others'. He turned his back on the prospector, let his frown relax, and offered his golden smile.

"I will tell you my mind on this," he began softly. "Ibi asks me one time, do I believe the First Books? I say, only priests call them truth." He leaned forward to touch exploring fingers to the screen. Wonder deepened his voice. "But this what you tell is very like our telling of the coming of the Darkness."

Susannah's hand flew to her mouth. "The Tale of Origins! Yes, it does!"

". . . 'And then it happened,'" Megan recited from memory, " 'that the Darkness arrived and the king grew old' . . . according to myth, that was when all the trouble started and the Sisters started playing games with the weather."

"Playing games?" Danforth asked carefully. "I thought they were fighting a war."

"Depends on who you talk to."

He noted Weng's smug smile, then buried his face in his hands with a theatrical moan. "I give up. I'm surrounded."

Ghirra was unperturbed. "The story of the Darkness *is* the Darkness: The Sisters are blinded. They do not see the many dying they make with their wagers. But the First Books say also that the Darkness will end." He paused, sucking his cheek again. "You say how this . . . dust moves in the sky, Commander? Will it move . . . ?"

"Beyond? Yes, it will. Your ancestors knew that, and they even knew *when*."

Weng recalled to the screen the final frame of Megan's photo sequence. The area of crosshatching had moved beyond the greatest concentration of surface pitting. She made a fast calculation at the keypad. "In approximately eighty-five thousand years, Brynham's Cluster will leave the environs of the Coal Sack. If there is, as I believe, some direct connection between this occurrence and your world's deadly climate irregularities, Guildmaster, I certainly wish I could offer you more encouraging news."

Megan eyed the offending crosshatchings. "Egad. Can you imagine how they felt, a hundred and sixty-five thousand years ago, when they looked up and saw *that* coming at them . . . ?"

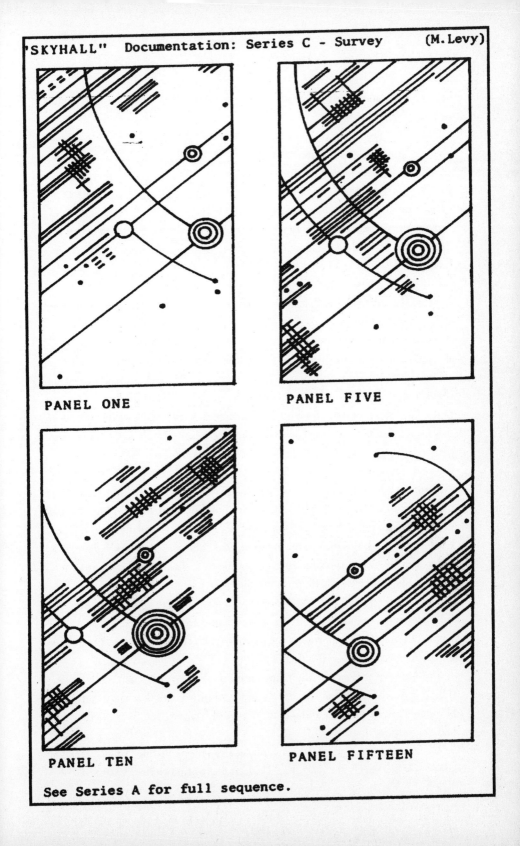

77

WITH THE FORCE FIELD tuned to its highest frequency, even the harsh amber noon of the Fiixian sun was discouraged from entering. A silver-film tarp across the mouth of the entry cylinder completed the effect, so that a cool, perennial twilight reigned in the Underbelly.

Susannah lit a single oil lamp. She'd become used to their softer glow. The ship's battery lamps were needlessly bright, and she did not wish to wake any of the heat-drained sleepers who'd at last found comfortable niches to retire to. She carried her chemical analyzer to the computer table and plugged in, gathered her notes and samples, adjusted the lamp wick and powered up the little terminal.

From each plant sample, she excised a careful slice of root, stem, and leaf tissue, according to availability, the distinction between stem and leaf being moot for many of the succulents. Hours later, with the plants cut, fed in, labeled and filed, she moved on to her animal data. She filed blood, hair, and tissue samples from the domestic beasts, from a crosscut selection of Sawl patients she had treated, then unwrapped her precious single sample from the wild: her lizard's tail. Despite its air-tight packaging, it smelled of rot and poison. She handled it with great care and protective gloves, slipped the whole chunk into the analyzer's square maw, then stripped off her gloves and sat back, massaging her shoulder.

Preliminary analyses of the plant samples were already chattering across the screen when the tarp at the cylinder mouth rustled aside to admit a blinding slash of sunlight and a man. A gust of heat swirled in as if a furnace had been opened.

Clausen let the tarp swish into place and stood waiting for his eyes to adjust. He surveyed the darkened Underbelly, noting each sleeper's corner and Susannah at the terminal, then padded into the galley area. Susannah heard a quiet splashing of water, the prospector washing his hands of the clinging layer of grit and dust, and later, a hushed clatter as he fixed himself something to eat.

She had almost forgotten about him when he eased up behind her and set a steaming mug of coffee on the console.

"Hope you like it black," he remarked amiably. His hands and face were burned as dark as the Sawls, blistering here and there. "My greatest regret over the recent unfortunate incidents is the loss of my supply of fresh hekker milk. Boycotting me, you understand."

"You ought to stay out of the sun, Emil."

"Doctor's orders?" He laughed softly. "Got a tarp rigged out there now. But the tools still get too hot to hold." He pulled up a crate and sat, sipping his own coffee, studying the screen. "So, what've you got here?"

Tasting the coffee, she described her sample population. The coffee was delicious. He had a way even with instant. It was odd to think of drinking hot liquids when it was 115° outside, but it was just what she'd wanted. Noting the laser pistol snuggled at his shoulder, Susannah wondered how she could feel so easily companionable with the man who had nearly murdered her lover.

"Mmmm. Interesting." Clausen crooked a finger at the screen. "Look at your chlorophyll molecule: got a little beryllium in there subbing for some of the magnesium. Have you seen that often here?"

"This is the first detailed run I've been able to do, what with . . ."

"I know, I know. Let's not even talk about being behind in our work." His eyes focused on the data speculatively. "This explains all the reddish foliage, though. The beryllium would absorb higher energies—green-yellow instead of red."

"Yes." It was impossible not to respond to his informed interest. Susannah called up another set of data. "And look at this."

"Hemoglobin?"

"Right."

He gave her an immodest grin.

"Terran blood here. Mine, Megan's. Sawl blood here, nearly identical. These are hjalk and hakra samples. And this . . ."

Clausen beat her to the prize. "What the hell?" he exclaimed softly. "Beryllium again? Doping the hemoglobin in place of iron!"

"Yup, and worse. Aluminum."

"What *is* this?"

"The only sample I was able to obtain from a wild animal."

"Is the concentration in the flesh enough to be toxic?"

"I believe so, at least after a while, through accumulation. The Sawls claim all wild animals here are poisonous, and I think they mean more than just the bite. You've noticed that the Sawls eat only domestic herbivores? This is why."

"You think *all* the wildlife are carrying aluminum around inside? Why doesn't it kill them?"

Susannah took another sip of coffee. "Their bodies must manage it somehow. Maybe they excrete it, or maybe it collects, to form the venom. I haven't been able to get a sample of that yet."

"An intriguing theory." Clausen nodded. "We'll have to get you a few more samples to broaden your database."

"The Sawls don't want them collected. I only got this because it attacked a child on the caravan."

Clausen regarded her with mild amusement. "Susannah, you're going to have to decide very soon between diplomacy and science if you're going to get anything done around here."

"I have plenty of data to deal with," she replied.

"Okay." He shrugged, smiled, leaning easily on his elbow against the console. "Well, if I were you, I'd follow up the possibility that your hemoglobin trace metals are being replaced due to scarcity within the ecology. The planet is very poor in iron, among other things."

The idea was intriguing, but the look in his heavy-lidded eyes made her suddenly wary.

"You know, it's very odd." She meant partly to solicit his opinion but mostly to distract him. "It's like there are two coexisting, closed systems operating on this world, instead of a single ecology. One, the sort of over-system, is very messy and dog-eat-dog. The other—revolving around the Sawls, their agriculture and husbandry—exists within it and seems so perfectly knit as to make you wonder if it wasn't designed."

Clausen laughed. "Nature's the best designer around." He confirmed her worst suspicion by reaching to trace the contours of her face with a sculptor's professional flourish, letting his palm settle around her cheek. "You have only to look in a mirror to see that."

Her jaw hardened under his touch.

"Not in the mood?" he murmured. "A pity."

He ran his knuckle sensuously along her lower lip, then gripped her chin gently between thumb and forefinger. His blue eyes smiled. "Sure you won't change your mind? I haven't been around all these years without learning a thing or two, you know."

She did not doubt him, but crowding her mind's eye was a vision of the wreck he had made of Stavros' shoulder. In a voice of cold rage that she barely recognized, she said, "I'm not into sleeping with killers."

Clausen dropped his hand and sat back. "Ah."

He sighed irritably, picked up his coffee and propped his elbows on his knees, staring into the steam rising from the cup. "Like you said, dog-eat-dog. Very messy."

Unaccountably, his barren simplicity brought tears to her eyes.

"Why don't you care?" she demanded with childlike illogic, wishing that he did, so that she could have some understanding of this smooth, able man so apparently without a shred of conscience.

"But I do care," he replied reasonably. "I care about getting my job done right and living to see another day. Are you going to hate me for that? Lord, I'm tired of explaining myself!"

"What about Edan, and Liphar? And what you're doing to Weng. You're enjoying every minute of it!"

"A man's got to have some fun." Clausen swirled the coffee in his cup and drank. "Look, if my methods turn you off, I've no quarrel with that. There's other dealing we can do to make things easier for each other. How about, you bring me the boy, I drop all the charges against you and Weng."

"The boy?" Stupidly, she thought he meant Liphar.

He gestured impatiently. "Come on, Susannah! Ibiá. I want Ibiá."

"Boy?" She laughed, unable to help herself.

Clausen stilled, eyeing her sideways. Then he clapped a hand to his forehead. "Fool, Emil! Of course!"

Susannah knew then how an undercover agent must feel when her cover was blown. She'd not understood the protection it offered her until it was gone.

The prospector ran his hand through his short sandy hair, chuckling. "Of course. I forget that what seems a young nuisance to me might seem a young beauty to you. And a great romantic as well, I've no doubt." His voice dropped in mocking intimacy. "Is he very passionate?"

Susannah stared at the keyboard.

"Ah, well." He stretched, leaning back against the console. "There are other things I could offer, more in the way of career advancement, but there's not much chance of a deal here, I guess, if Ibiá's beaten me to your bed." He chuckled again, this time with a trace of weariness. "Good for him. I like this boy more and more. He's learning to protect himself."

If I were a man, Susannah raged, *I could smash his face in.*

Clausen straightened, his face very close to hers. He put a hand once more to her cheek, let it trail down to curl lightly around her throat. "You do understand, don't you, that from now on you'll have to watch your back? Please tell me you understand that."

Her throat tensed within his easy grip. "Is that a threat?"

"Susannah, Susannah." His thumb caressed the skin over her carotid artery. "I don't know whether to be flattered or insulted that you persist in not taking me seriously."

"I do take you seriously. I've seen the results."

"So you have." He said it almost lovingly, then leaned in and kissed her, parting her lips with an artful tongue. The shot of desire that wriggled in Susannah's gut ran neck and neck with nausea.

"Are you *sure* you won't change your mind?" he murmured, then let her go, laughing. "But, do let me know how it goes with the trace-metal inquiry. I wait with bated breath." He patted her shoulder and left her shaking, staring at the glowing screen.

She ran to Stavros for absolution. He sent Liphar and Phea to make sure she hadn't been followed, then got up stiffly to bar the big wooden doors.

He felt no jealousy, only concern. He prayed that rape was beneath the prospector's dignity. While Susannah trembled against his bandaged chest, he hoped she did not expect him to respond with outrage of his own. He knew he'd learned a major lesson in perspective when the greatest rage he could muster was to stroke the smooth skin of her back and say, "What else did you expect of the man?"

Lately, passing the long, solitary hours of recovery, he'd studied that place in himself where outrage, pique, and righteous indignation used to flourish in confusion. He found there only burning determination. It was not a lessening or a retreat. That scattering of energy, those diffuse angers that had so often broken him, had coalesced into a single beam of intention, fused by fever and the terrors of the void. Next to his duty to Kav Daven, his quest for the goddesses was his highest priority, his own rage no longer a weapon the prospector could turn against him. Stavros was grateful for that. "Stay away from him, that's all you can do, until we figure out a way to immobilize him."

"You mean kill him?"

Stavros shrugged. "Just stay away from him."

Susannah sat upright, her outrage spilling over with her tears. "Down there? When he's the only one getting this expedition back on its feet? With Taylor crippled and Weng obsessed with her loss of command? She's so evasive with Captain Newman when she calls in her status reports. Sometimes I think the only reason she hasn't aborted the mission is to avoid facing the possibility that she *can't,* that she won't be able to get the Lander off the ground or that Clausen won't let her, until he's good and ready!"

Her hands wrapped into fists. "Meanwhile, it gets hotter and hotter. So dry you can't breathe, yet he's out there all day working on the Sleds while the rest of us are holed up in the Underbelly like moles . . . Stav, can't you see how crazy this has become? Work has ground to a complete halt while you guys fight your territorial wars! One man and one gun, holding us all hostage! Can't you find a way to settle this without killing yourselves and anyone else who happens to get in the way? You've filed your protest, now let the Courts take care of it! This planet is going to be the death of *all* of us if we waste our time and energies fighting each other! Our real enemy is the weather!"

"Whoa, whoa, hold it, easy. Susannah. Susannah!" He imprisoned her flying hands and held them tightly though his shoulder wound burned. "I didn't set the stakes. He did."

"Did Edan try to kill him?"

"Maybe she did."

"He says so!"

Stavros worked his aching shoulder beneath its wad of bandages. "Well, it was certainly not unprovoked. He opened fire on me. Edan took that personally. Susannah, this is no mere methodological disagreement among colleagues. Try to see the larger picture. Remember who and what we're fighting for."

He raised his hands, palms out. His clear palms, scored by their invisible fire. His constant reminder, his goad. He let his voice resound with conviction. "Clausen is the mud we must fight through on our way to the real battle."

He knew this would quiet her. He'd learned that she would not debate him on the subject of his mission to save the Sawls from the destructive whims of the goddesses. She'd not yet decided how much of his tale of voids and unscarred skin to believe, how much to call deception, how much to pity as delusion. But she loved him, he knew she did though she had never said it, so she let his claims go unchallenged, waiting until proof one way or another presented itself.

"There's got to be a better way," she insisted.

"Hush." Stavros kissed her still-clenched fists and drew her down against him to soothe with his hands and mouth, to spread the warmth of his guar-fire throughout her body. But even then, as his cheek smoothed the intoxicating silk of her breast, he murmured, "So how *is* he coming with the Sled repairs?"

Liphar agreed to make a return visit to the Lander. Slunk in the protective curl of Susannah's arm, he avoided Clausen's mocking eye and sang the tale chants that told of the coming of the Darkness. CRI recorded, simultaneously processing the chants through Stavros' translation program.

"I wish Stav were here to deal with this Old Words stuff," Megan whispered to Susannah. "However clever his program is, statistically based guesses can't make the same leaps of faith as good old-fashioned insight."

Danforth frowned at Weng from his wheelchair, his arms folded tight against his chest like a barrier against opinion. "How do you know those drawings weren't done in retrospect? One hundred and sixty-five *thousand* years, Commander? You'd have a planet-wide civilization ten times over in that span!"

"Civilizations degrade, Dr. Danforth."

"Or they're destroyed," Megan added. "There's another whole mythos to cover that. Lifa, sing us a tale of the Great Devastations."

Liphar licked his lower lip, still raw from his ordeal. "But this is not Old Words. Children sing this."

"Sing it anyway."

The melody was simple, mournfully sweet in Liphar's birdlike chant-voice.

Megan was sure she had heard it sung while the pyres were burning out on the Dop Arek.

CRI had little trouble providing a translation:

A fire in the sky,
Flames like rain,
A thousand avalanches roar where no snow falls.
Like ancient paper, the dry earth tears.

The rocks cry out.
The children's weeping is not so loud.
Do they cry for the children?

There is no one left to hold them

"Phew," said Megan, to break the silence around the monitor screen.

"Liphar." Danforth spoke directly to the young man for the first time ever. "Sing me the songs your mother sang to you."

78

E.D. 96–16:00

STAVROS NODDED. "So Taylor's decided to listen? About time."

"He see many thing with his sky eye, Ibi." Ghirra pointed upward as they walked, meaning not the stone vault of the tunnel but as far beyond as his mind could conceive. "He show me Dul Valla. And he is very amaze these Sisters play only where we live."

Stavros considered the implications. "You mean the Arrah is confined to the habitable zone? His data agrees with that?"

Ghirra nodded. "This is very small, he say, for very much ack . . . activity." Stavros heard Taylor's dogmatic tone echoing through the healer's report. "Still he find no understanding of the *Arrah,* what he call 'weather.' You do not use this word."

"Arrah does not mean weather." The old stubbornness stirred again. "Taylor's playing fast and loose with his translations. You have no word for weather as we mean it. If I'd found one, damnit, I'd have used it!"

The Master Healer eyed him, a gentle admonishment.

"Sorry. Hard to think of Taylor as an ally, but . . ." Stavros could not help a hunted glance along the corridor where it darkened into a turn. Aguidran and two of her tallest rangers paced behind them, scanning the tunnel in both directions. "I bet I find weather in the Old Words, though, weather and climate and atmosphere and all that. Tay will love the Old Words. It was spoken by guys like him."

"Science-ists," Ghirra ventured thoughtfully.

Stavros wanted to slap him on the back, hug him. "Scientists, indeed. God-damn, you're good." He was delighted to see the Master Healer's lean da Vinci face light with fleeting pride. He'd not seen that golden smile for a while.

"You are feel better, Ibi."

"Thanks to you, Keth-shim."

But Stavros was pale and aching by the time they reached the Priest Hall. He leaned against the columned portal, light-headed, returning an offhand smile as the Master Healer reached to support him. Aguidran left her rangers guarding the door and followed Stavros and her brother into the hall.

Aguidran was like a specter at his back. Stavros carried his guilt heavily. There was no apology he could offer for having refused to understand that risking his own life also risked Edan's. Aguidran had been witness to his guar-miracle. She'd seen Kav Daven literally walk through storm and fire for his sake. But still she doubted, not his intentions, but whether he was worth the ill wind of trouble that blew around him, sweeping up anyone in range. Stavros knew it was only for the old Kav's sake, and because her brother asked it, that she paid him the honor of accompanying him herself.

Or maybe because she was the best equipped to deal with real trouble.

"It's time to do something about Clausen." Stavros eased onto a bench just inside the door. It wasn't the right time to discuss it, but his weakness made him irritable. "Sneaking around with a troop of bodyguards, prevented from using my own equipment. One man holding us, the Sleds, CRI, everything hostage. It's just . . . wrong!"

"This is," agreed Ghirra, but his shoulders hunched in a very Terran-like shrug of impotence.

"It'd be tricky to get the drop on him." Stavros leaned against the wall, breathing hard. "We need some kind of long-range weapon: spear, slingshot, blowgun—or better still, get the laser away from him. Serve him right to be wasted by his own gun."

Ghirra might have missed the unfamiliar colloquialisms but not the linguist's ominous dreamy tone. Aguidran listened with a hint of new interest. Stavros detected support in her stance, or perhaps it was just his eagerness to regain her good opinion.

"What do you think to do, Ibi?"

"Nail him. Pay him back for what he did to Edan."

"You say, end his life?"

"Do him in."

"You would *kill* him?" Ghirra pursued.

Stavros forced his tongue away from bravura euphemism. "Execute."

"No, Ibi. Murder."

Stavros blinked at him. He'd thought this was a translation exercise. Aguidran shifted, muttering darkly. Ghirra flung back a terse response that made her stiffen, but she held her peace.

Ghirra faced him sternly. "We want no murder, Stavros Ibiá."

Maybe you *don't* . . .

Stavros glanced at Aguidran. "Keth-shim, it may be the only . . ."

"No. This is not ever the only. You kill an animal, not a man."

"What if the man *is* an animal?" But Stavros dropped his eyes. "It's all moot anyway, as long as he's got the laser." He gathered his aching body and rose. "Enough of this. I came to see the Kav."

"We talk of this, Ibi," Ghirra warned.

"Yes, Guildmaster, we will. I promise."

The Priest Hall was oppressive and stuffy, and empty compared to its usual bustle. Every able-bodied priest had put off the scholar's garb to help care for the wilting food crop. But among the thick columns, a low sweet-voiced chanting whispered like a forest breeze. A few sober-faced apprentices, stripped to the waist in the heat, came and went on essential errands. The two long tables in the guild library were crowded with elder priests debating over stacks of ancient books.

At the head of the nearest table, Kav Ashimmel broke off an intense discussion to glare at Stavros as he passed. He heard the word *"raellil"* muttered in his wake, then Ashimmel's silencing growl. He was going to have to do something truly remarkable to redeem himself with her.

As always, when approaching the elder Kav, the same doubts assailed him: why me, old man? I had no messianic leanings before you set your fire in my palms. Walk on water, Ibiá? Tried that one lately?

He tried to see himself as he had been, a suggestible young man in search of something to believe in, with no special qualities beyond a taste for miracles and an eagerness to confront powers beyond his control but not, he thought, beyond his understanding.

Before, I was that. What am I now?

"What's going on with the books?" he asked Ghirra when they'd moved beyond the aura of frenzy at the tables.

"They talk and study to remember the signs."

"There are still signs they don't know?"

"These signs must have sure knowing. They are White Sky and the rain that is fire."

"White sky?"

"Sign of *Phena Nar*."

Phena Nar. The Hot Death. Stavros caught Aguidran's grim nod. The Priest Guild was preparing itself to receive the signs of their most fearsome legend: Devastation.

"It won't happen. Not this time. The Kav has a plan. He'll make himself heard somehow."

"I think these Sisters do not listen."

"They've listened to him before."

Ghirra's pursed lips denied it.

"So it was only coincidence at the Leave-taking?"

Ghirra did not reply.

You . . . scientist, Stavros accused silently.

But it was true that the whole concept of getting through to the goddesses rested on the unevidenced assumption that they possessed communicable consciousness. The mindfulness implied by the intricate strategies of the Arrah offered no proof of the Sisters' awareness of anything but each other. But Stavros was haunted by that shock of primal terror that had driven him to flee his death in the void. He'd done something to spark attention, and that attention had roused and looked about, searching for him.

He knew that for a fact.

Kav Daven lay in a cushioned alcove at the far end of the hall, curtained with heavy draperies. He might have been dead, embalmed already, so waxen was his finely netted skin and so faint the rise and fall of his emaciated chest. His young caretaker, knitting glumly beside the cushions, flushed with a shy smile to see Stavros on his feet. Her dark eyes followed him worshipfully as he knelt by Kav Daven's side.

He took one ancient hand in his own, hoping to feel the dull fire in his palms leap with responsive heat. But the heat stayed steady, simmering. The old priest's hand was frighteningly cool and thin, bones wrapped with the merest wrinkled tissue of skin.

Ghirra lowered himself to the floor. His hands hovered inquiringly above the Kav's chest. Stavros thought a faint new life flushed the ashen cheeks.

"Susannah call this 'coma,' " said the healer sadly. "She can give him food with the tubes, she say, but the guild does not allow."

"Ashimmel won't, you mean."

"Yes. He . . ." Ghirra struggled with the future tense. "He will starve if he does not wake."

Stavros gripped Kav Daven's wrist and called on the magical fire in his own hands to flow into the cooling body. *Raellil, is it? Then prove yourself! Be good for something!*

The old man lay unchanged, his breath the slightest flutter.

Fear seized him. Kav Daven might die before making it clear what he was supposed to do, or how he was meant to do it.

"He won't do it," said Danforth. "I tried to talk him into it while you were away."

Susannah watched the dust-sifted path for obstacles that might trip him up as he struggled gamely through the heat. He wore a Sawl scarf wrapped Arab-style around his head. A sleeveless Sawl robe draped his broad shoulders like an aba.

"You look like a prince of the desert today, Tay."

He grinned. "My mother always said we were, once upon a time."

But the leather pads of his crutches were dark with sweat, and his glistening skin was giving up more moisture than even the parched air could absorb. Susannah worried that he was pushing too hard, too soon, but the gift of the crutches had been the inspiration he needed. If he was not hunched over CRI's terminal, he was hobbling around in the sun.

She glanced at it, and it hurt her eyes. Damn deadly sun.

They passed a temporary irrigation outlet. The hastily laid ceramic piping coughed up the barest trickle into the seared fields. Water was being carried by hand to the root crops and succulents in the terraces. Apparently, the Food Guild had decided to harvest the grains early, to minimize heat losses. The cost would be losing a mature seed crop for the next season's planting.

"Things didn't seem so critical before," she muttered. "I mean, the situation, the weather and all."

Danforth halted, blowing air like an exhausted runner. "You heard Emil's commentary while Liphar was singing about the Destructions?"

"He'd be endangering the legality of his claim if he took the Sawls or their goddesses seriously."

Danforth readjusted his crutches and looked down at her. "Listen, Susannah—I could really use Stavros down here. This approach is . . . well, new to me. I need his head. Either I take things too literally or not literally enough. Like, should we actually expect the ground to open, and, what do they really mean, 'white sky'?"

"Ghirra's been trying so hard to . . ."

"I know, and the doc is cool, but he and CRI aren't enough. There's too much ambiguity in these wipe-out myths, and Stav isn't much help up there without CRI. A shitload of time's being wasted running back and forth in secret. I *need* that time!" Danforth used the tail of his head scarf to wipe his streaming brow. "If I can break down these myths enough to find a pattern that can be matched to a cyclic effect of the nebula, I could offer these folks some idea of what lies ahead. Maybe the past Devastations have been exaggerated, or they happened for some other reason."

He stood aside for a line of Sawls bearing emptied water jugs back to the Caves. "Or maybe they didn't happen at all. I don't know yet. I don't have enough data. The control factor is still eluding me."

"Stav will just tell you it's the goddesses," Susannah warned.

"Well, I'd like to go head-to-head with him on it, you know? You make one connection between myth and fact, you start looking for others. Maybe there's something in it. But Emil's not going to give on this, I promise you."

"At least he's let up on Weng a little."

"Mmmm." Danforth glanced back at the Lander, squinting into the sun. "And if I were you, I'd ask myself why."

The ladder was still in place in the main hatch, so Susannah climbed it, nervous but determined. It was odd to walk the cool metal corridors after so long, where her footsteps rang and even the sinuous curve of the hull was broken by machined right angles at floor and ceiling.

His door was ajar, spilling a faint glow into the dim corridor. Susannah knocked, then eased the door open and found herself staring into the stubby nose of the laser pistol. Behind the door, Clausen rolled his eyes, lowered the gun, and tossed it onto his bunk.

"Change your mind?" He straightened one arm against the wall on the door side of her head, so that his wrist grazed her cheek and her only move away from him was into the cubicle.

"No. But I need to talk to you."

He pushed away from the wall. "Are you sure? Nobody else does."

She was surprised that he sounded so aggrieved, or maybe it was just his boredom speaking. He dropped onto his neatly made bunk, relaxing against the pillows and the wall. He watched her with a faint come-on smile. The laser lay like a third presence between them.

He patted the taut blanket. "Come. Sit. As you can see, there's nowhere else."

Susannah could not share his relish in this new sex-charged game. The promise of pleasure in his eyes, the desire utterly without need, was disturbing in ways she did not at the moment care to analyze. She stayed by the door.

"Just tell me this. If he's sent off his protest and you've filed your countercharges, why do you still want to kill him?"

His smile broadened. "You've been talking to Taylor."

Susannah blinked. "I . . ."

"What a quandary for you, Susannah, to be both romantic and pragmatist at once. Let me guess: I should let the legal issues take their own bureaucratic course, set aside my unseemly blood-thirst and concentrate on getting us the hell out of here with our skins intact."

Robbed of her prepared speech, she blurted, "There's something very weird going on with this world, Emil! Aren't you the least bit curious?"

"Is that anything like, why don't I care?" His eyes flicked away in irritation. "You really have been talking to Taylor."

"And Megan and Weng and Ghirra and Stavros . . ."

"Well. Finally you admit to the latter. We have made progress." He looked back at her tiredly. "What are you proposing?"

"A truce." To head off his expression of disgust, she added, "Not even permanent. Just for a kind of . . . summit conference. We need to sit down, all of us, to pool our separate expertise, and make what sense of this we can, so we'll know what to do. We were meant to work as a team, after all!" She looked down. "We'd do it without you if we could, Emil, but all of us agree there wouldn't be much point."

"How kind of you to throw me that bone." He patted the bunk again. "Susannah, sit down for a minute and listen. Really, for a grown woman, you are in such need of schooling."

Pique strengthened her. She ventured in and perched on the foot of the bed, trying not to stare at the laser, so easily within her reach. More of his games, she realized.

Clausen set aside his seductiveness. "Now tell me why I should care. I'll win in the end no matter what. Even if the planet burns itself to a crisp and your precious Sawls with it, I still win. The mining robots don't need temperate weather or even an atmosphere to get their job done. You understand that?"

"Sure. I understand," she replied. "But how do you win if the planet gets you first? This stalemate could kill us all. Weng's beginning to talk about aborting the mission."

"Over my dead body." But he seemed to actually consider for a moment. "So Ibiá's agreed to your conference plan?"

"Not yet. And he was sure you wouldn't either." Sawl-like, she spread her hands. "But, Emil, what have you got to lose?"

"Not a goddamn thing," he replied with a smile so unreadable that Susannah wondered what she had set in motion.

79

STAVROS CROUCHED IN THE CAVE mouth, where the overhang dropped in a ragged slash to meet the ledge. There was deep shadow there, and concealment. Liphar hunkered beside him, one ranger taking up her post behind them, another on the interior stairs. A third shaded his eyes with casual watchfulness against the harsh sun invading the far side of the entrance.

"There's . . . nothing left!" Stavros lowered himself disconsolately, leaning against the rough rock. The sun glare hurt his eyes. His wounded shoulder ached with the constant protest of brutalized skin and tissue struggling back to life. He leaned forward for a better view to the west, edging out of the shadow. The three rangers moved as one to stop him. Liphar snatched at his good arm and hauled him back. Stavros did not argue.

"Much worse down there than I expected, Lifa."

Liphar grunted his assent, his fingers spinning the blue bead on his wrist.

The plain was burned dry. The russet foliage that had flourished in the flood ravines was reduced to a sooty powder, mingling with the seared earth to dust the landscape with a single ashen tinge. The air was utterly clear, without a hint of moisture. The western horizon was a knife-edged curve against a sky like polished jade.

The grain crops stood like a multitude in trance, their wilted leaves hanging limp beside bent and broken stalks. Dried mud choked the plantings in the terraces.

"The entire harvest . . . gone," Stavros grieved.

Liphar wet his peeling lips. "Some there is."

"But it won't last long."

"Not long, no." He pointed across the plain at the flat green sky above the Vallegar. "See, Ibi. This is what I want you look."

Along a distinct line resembling a cloud front, the baked sky changed color several degrees above the saw-toothed profile of the mountains. The change was slight, not green sky crossed by white cloud, but green meeting paler green, just enough to be noticeable.

"Will come here, this," said Liphar solemnly. "Get more hot, too very bright. This is White Sky."

Stavros looked, while Liphar nodded for emphasis. Though he seemed physically recovered from his long and blistering hours in the sun of Clausen's interrogation pit, a mood of grim acceptance now colored Liphar's every word and gesture. Stavros suspected him of indulging in a certain priestly satisfaction that his guild's worst predictions were proving true, one after the other.

Stavros could understand how he felt. The poetic beauty of the myths seemed a constant barrier to hope or progress. Fact or fiction, what did it matter, if they weren't specific enough to suggest a course of useful action?

Kav! If you'd only say what you expect of me!

Was it finally time to accept despair as a daily companion, as the Sawls did, as they had done for what had likely been aeons? Tempting, and certainly easy. But there was another approach. For instance, how would Taylor explain White Sky?

Stavros shifted, leaning forward again, just to the edge of the concealing shade. A mere half mile away, the Lander glinted dully through its coating of ash. Minute figures moved about the scorched clearing. Aguidran's watch reported that Clausen was keeping himself in plain sight of late.

Hoping I'll get overconfident . . . hoping I'll show myself?

He might have to do just that.

The Sleds were parked side by side, two triangular hulks draped in dusty silver-film. Nearly ready, Susannah reported. Both of them.

Stavros wished he'd learned to fly the touchy, awkward craft. If he was going to steal a Sled, he would also have to kidnap a pilot. He couldn't count on McPherson. Weng? She might, and willingly, at this point. He pulled back into the shadow and slouched against the wall. Liphar met his troubled scowl with one of his own.

"You go inside now, Ibi? No safe here."

"Yes, Lifa, we'll go in for now."

For now . . . but not for long.

80

E.D. 98–3:45

M EGAN STILLED THE NERVOUS tapping of her foot. "Too dark in here, and too cold. We should let the damn sun pour in with all its fury, to remind us why we're doing this."

Danforth nodded, intent on the mini-terminal.

"The force field uses less power than the coolers." McPherson perched on the wheel of Danforth's chair, studying the screen over his shoulder.

Weng appeared from the galley area with a tall Sawl jug filled with water. Susannah followed with a stack of white ship's mugs. She set them down on a line of crates pulled together as an impromptu conference table. Weng surveyed the arrangement like a society hostess, counting places.

Megan watched with a wry smile. "You know," she murmured to Danforth, "in China, they still serve tea to guests in little covered cups."

"Commander probably wishes she had some of those," snorted McPherson. "This is stupid, all this fuss, like it was some kind of party."

"A perfectly understandable response to the damn anarchy of the situation," replied Megan. "Formalities impose structure. Structure promises to keep things from flying off in all directions."

"Rather a case of the barn door after the horse," commented Danforth. "But what the hell? If it makes her feel better . . ."

"You're remarkably tolerant these days," Megan observed.

"I am remarkably tired of fighting wars that haven't been declared. Got enough problems here with the one that has."

"So you won't jump down Stav's throat the minute he arrives? You have any idea how much maneuvering used to go on to keep you two apart?"

Danforth raised weary eyes from the screen. "Counting sides, Meg?"

Megan shrugged. She avoided glancing at McPherson, whose only clear commitment was to Danforth. "I like to know these things."

Weng glided about in purposeful silence, bringing out a final folding chair, gathering up her notes. She circled the empty table once, checked the tabs of her clean white uniform, then seated herself at the head and began laying out her papers in ordered piles. Susannah waited at the other end, watching both the entry cylinder and the ladder to the main hatch. One nervous finger traced the lettering on a crate top, over and over.

Megan fidgeted. No one was late. The meeting wasn't due to start for ten minutes. But for all of them, the waiting had begun hours ago, each resting too much hope on what was just a meeting, after all, not a solution.

Danforth muttered, "Think he'll show?"

Megan's nod was more positive than she felt.

The hatch ladder shivered. Clausen backed swiftly down, swinging off halfway to land catlike on the balls of his feet. He'd found freshly laundered khakis, crisply collared and cuffed. The laser tucked in its neat holster seemed almost decorative against the curve of his chest. He stood pulling down his sleeves while he assessed the mood and marked out the positions of the players.

"Mr. Clausen." Weng gave him the briefest of nods. "I am glad you could make it."

He dipped his head satirically. "Wouldn't miss it for the world, Commander."

He unsnapped his holster and laid the laser with great ceremony in the center of the table, like a prize or a bouquet of flowers. They all tried not to stare at it. He sauntered toward the foot of the table, relishing the unease that greeted his every move. Susannah slid away as he neared. He pretended to take this for courtesy. He pulled out a folding chair and lounged into it, tipping back to rest his boots on the crate top.

"No sign of the Loyal Opposition, I take it?"

Susannah moved to Weng's end of the table. "He'll be here."

But even when the Master Healer appeared at the mouth of the cylinder, somber and erect, Megan was still unsure. Had Ghirra, in the end, come alone? There were shadows behind him in the entry, but she couldn't tell if Stavros was one of them.

The Master Healer conducted his own very deliberate scrutiny. He nodded to Weng. He noted Clausen with his feet on the table, the others grouped around the terminal, and Susannah caught in her anxious drift between. He'd dressed rather formally for the occasion, in softly draped tunic and pants of ivory linen that set off his brown hands and face and lent the straight planes of his body the grace of dignity.

When his caution was satisfied, he looked to Weng, his gaze skimming over the table's laser centerpiece without particular notice.

Weng drew his attention to it with a small gesture of distaste. "Mr. Clausen has divested himself of his weaponry, Guildmaster. I think it is safe to begin."

Ghirra's eyes flicked to the laser. As he moved toward it, Clausen's feet hit the ground with a thud. Ghirra stopped, spread his palms. "I have not seen this before."

His curiosity, Megan realized queasily, was genuine.

"Want to see what did the damage, eh?" Clausen's smile was mostly teeth as he relaxed back into his chair and returned his boots to the tabletop. "Go ahead. Take a look. It's not armed." He glanced around to the others. "What, you think I'm crazy?"

An errant hint of craft slipped from beneath the prospector's easeful mask, catching Megan's wary eye. *He's lying.* She knew it for certain, but couldn't decide which was more to her advantage: to expose the lie, or to know better and say nothing.

Ghirra did not reach for the gun.

"Go ahead," Clausen urged. "I'll give you a demonstration later, if you like."

"There is no use for this here."

"Ah, but there *will* be, my good doctor, when every mining sod on the planet is packing one. You, of course, will be in great demand, having gotten your experience with laser burns so early . . ."

"Ghirra."

The Master Healer did not turn at the sound of his name.

Stavros stepped from the entryway, framed by a flash of sun across the cylinder's mirrored arc. A double file of guildsmen and rangers moved in on either side of him.

Megan kept her surprise to herself, but it was hard not to stare. He was thinner, yes, to be expected, but could he have possibly grown taller? It must be the unaccustomed straightness of his stance, the newly authoritative lift of his chin. He was washed, shaved and combed, his black hair slicked back and perfectly manicured. His habitual glower had given way to stern determination. His dark eyes, riveting in his pale, angular face, demanded attention. Megan felt proud—of both of them. She hadn't risked visiting him in hiding: various scenarios for this meeting had been conveyed back and forth by Sawl couriers. They'd settled on one, but Megan could already see he'd improved upon it. For one thing, he'd decided not to play up his injury. No sling, no bandaging, no sign of weakness. She wondered how much pain he was in.

Green? Not anymore. And he's sure learned the value of putting on a good show.

Much as she'd enjoy feasting her eyes on her protégé's transformation, Clausen's reaction interested her more. What did he read in this carefully staged entrance, in this poised and handsome lordling who came flanked by white-clad Sawl advisers and backed up by a hatchet-faced ranger bodyguard, led by the Master Ranger herself? But however fast she looked, she caught only the finish, a subterranean shudder soon smoothed by the prospector's practiced calm. The easy drape of his body did not change. Only his fingers twitched, like the tail of an irritated cat.

"Stavros, my boy," he crowed softly.

Now for the hard part. Megan saw the effort it took for Stavros to look the man so resolutely in the eye. Clausen saw it, too. He saw everything, every subtlety, but no matter. The show was for the others, mostly—not meant to fool Clausen, but to prove the depth of this young man's claim on the hearts of Sawl and Terran alike. To show that not Stavros alone, but the entire planet, was Clausen's adversary.

Weng stood in welcome, her lips pressed tight against a glad smile.

"If it's not armed, then it won't matter if someone else holds it." Stavros held Clausen's gaze, almost succeeding in matching the prospector's throaty casual tone. His next word seemed more an order than a request. "Commander?"

"No," said Clausen, rising.

"Lieutenant?" Weng parried quickly.

Clausen acceded with a stiff nod and sat back. McPherson slipped out from behind Danforth and padded forward to take up the laser pistol. It was not swallowed by her smaller hand as it had been by Clausen's. She held it awkwardly a moment, then shoved it into the hip pocket of her uniform.

Weng lifted her arms in a gathering gesture. "Shall we all be seated?"

Stavros took his place mid-table, Ghirra on one side, Liphar on the other. Aguidran fanned out the retinue behind him so that access to the cylinder was blocked by sturdy Sawl bodies. As the others settled around the table, Clausen dropped his feet and leaned forward.

"How's the burn, boy? Nothing worse for pain, I know. I could show you scars . . ."

Liphar's face screwed up into a silent snarl, but Stavros eased back into the hard plastic of his chair and stretched his legs, soaking up the cool of the air. "I see you got the power link working without me."

"I assume CRI will be monitoring this meeting," said Megan to the room in general.

"Every word," Danforth replied. "Listening, CRI?"

"Listening and recording, Dr. Danforth."

Danforth turned his chair away from the terminal and drew up to the table opposite Stavros. "Welcome to the Club, Ibiá. You're looking remarkably well, considering."

Megan and Susannah took seats between Danforth and Clausen. McPherson and the laser were isolated in the more neutral space between Danforth and Weng. The bustle settled into anticipation.

Weng cleared her throat. "I have called this meeting to discuss the advisability of a Mission Abort."

Danforth jerked around. "What? That's not what we . . ."

"But, Commander . . ." Susannah protested.

Megan almost laughed aloud as identical looks of wary surprise came and went on the face of both Clausen and Stavros. The Commander had opened with the only issue that had a chance of unifying her crew and putting herself back into a position of authority over them.

"That is not why we called this meeting," Danforth finished angrily.

"Please remain calm, Dr. Danforth. I said we are here to discuss the possibility."

Ghirra murmured to Stavros, frowning at the muttered reply. Stavros laid a reassuring hand on his arm. Recognizing Weng's announcement as an open power play, Clausen relaxed and returned his boots to the table, awaiting further developments.

Megan decided to get the ball rolling. "Why should we want to abort the mission, Commander?"

Weng referred to the pile of papers on her right. "I present the following concerns: first, the rapid shrinkage of food and water supplies available from local sources."

"We have supplies of our own to last at least another two months," Megan countered.

Weng lifted the top sheet with delicate fingers. "Second: the consistent interruption of our vital main power source, due to apparently unpredictable local weather conditions. Without our power link, we are forced to rely on local generosity, which . . ." She offered her Sawl listeners a gracious nod. ". . . has been extreme but cannot help but be taxed by the worsening situation.

"Third, there is the equally consistent damage being sustained by expedition equipment. Fourth, the increasing frequency of violent disagreement between expeditionary personnel."

This last provoked a ripple of ironic laughter, and Megan knew that Weng's gambit had been marginally successful. The focus of everyone's energies was shifting to her. Now she was the one they had to convince. Even if they did, it wouldn't hold for long. But it was better than nothing. Megan cheered her on silently: *Play it for all you're worth!*

"Finally," Weng continued, "all the above, together with the apparent progression toward increasingly life-threatening conditions, lead me to question this expedition's ability to fulfill its scientific mandate." She paused, placed the paper to one side, and folded her hands with the precision of a dancer. "And now, perhaps someone would care to venture a reason why we should *not* abort the mission."

Danforth pounced. "Because we're not done here, damn it!"

"My point was precisely that circumstances may have rendered us incapable of getting done."

"A few bad moments do not invalidate the good work that *is* being done!" Danforth's aggrieved tone carried accusations of betrayal. Megan thought Weng might have been wiser to warn him ahead of time of the tack she intended to take.

But Weng made no effort to soothe his fury. "Please be more constructive in your arguments, Dr. Danforth."

Megan felt a pang of sympathy. Weng was going to string Danforth along, use his outrage to make this abort threat sound convincing. To whom? Clausen?

"But we're on the verge of a breakthrough here!" Danforth railed. "We can't just walk away from Fiix with the story half told. I'm amazed you even suggest it, with so many of the crucial insights being your own! It could be the discovery of the century!"

Megan remembered CRI dutifully recording this puffed-up exchange, with Captain Newman and the Orbiter crew no doubt listening in. She quickly reassessed the situation: Weng and Danforth were already in league, building up the scientific profile of the mission within hearing of authorities higher than Clausen. The proper follow-up to Stavros' drone.

The prospector evidently reached the same conclusion. "A few scratches on the wall of some cave are the discovery of the century?" he drawled. "Would you care to lay that one out for us, Taylor?"

Exactly what they want to do! Megan suppressed a guffaw.

Danforth contrived to look hesitant, clearly a stretch for him. "I'd really rather . . . the thesis is still unpolished . . . well, in brief, it was Weng's suggestion, and now it's becoming clear to me, too, that this world was once home to a high-tech civilization."

"Is that so?" Clausen sucked his teeth, bored already.

"Look at the evidence," Danforth pursued. "Those wall carvings you dismiss so easily chart the progressive encounter of the Coal Sack Nebula with Byrnham's Cluster, past, present, and future, with as much accuracy as our own observations are capable of."

"*Star* Hall is a closer translation than Sky Hall anyway," Stavros murmured.

Danforth shot him a grin. "Further evidence: the Toph-leta. These are ancient texts—preserved as guild treasures—that contain advanced mathematics and atomic theory, no longer recognized as such by the current inhabitants."

"A complete periodic table," added Weng, who seemed to have forgotten which side she was supposed to be on. "Preserved in the Toph-leta of the Physicians Guild. It includes elements numbered beyond those in our own table."

Clausen flicked Megan an accusing eyebrow. "I don't recall that one being mentioned in Ibiá's little missive homeward."

"The tip of the iceberg," gloated Megan. "What about the existing high-temperature ceramic-and-glass technology that is major levels beyond the rest of Sawl technology?"

Clausen nodded as if this was old hat, but of minor technical interest nonetheless. "Magnesium and aluminum silicates, yes. I've been wondering how they produce the heat to work those high-temperature clays."

"Or what about the Old Words?" As Stavros spoke up, heads turned. Liphar glared, fearing a threat. Stavros gestured grandly. "A lost language, preserved in ritual, that expresses these advanced technologies and much more that we can't even conceive of."

Clausen chuckled with all appearances of delight. "My, what a well-rehearsed presentation. Though why one should wish to save a civilization that's already failed—no matter what its past glories—I cannot imagine." He turned a look heavy with irony on Susannah, who was staring at her folded hands. "Nothing to add, lovely one?"

"Actually, I do." Susannah glanced around the table as if posing a remarkable mystery. "My evidence suggests . . . I say *suggests* . . . the genetic engineering of an entire ecosystem, within the planet's existing natural structure."

Into the pause, Weng urged, "For instance, Dr. James?"

"Well . . . three strains of dairy and draft animals, their DNA nearly identical, the variation among individuals within a strain limited to aesthetic qualities, like color or hair quality, each strain so carefully profiled for specific use as to invite speculation that the ancestral stock were engineered or cloned."

Susannah's enthusiasm built as she tried out her suspicions in public for the first time. "Or: food plants and animals designed to thrive in a dark cave environment. Domestic plant varieties that grow at nearly twice the rate of the wild flora. A Sawl food cycle, human to animal to plant to human, that functions in self-sufficient isolation and allows the Sawls to survive within a natural biosphere which is poisoned by accumulations of toxic trace metals."

She met Ghirra's wondering glance. "It's true. I just know it is."

"Okay." Clausen uncrossed and recrossed his legs as they rested on the table. "A long-lost civilization. That and ten'll get you on the subway. Sorry, I'm not convinced, but neither will the Courts be. A lot of worlds have been here and gone."

"But that's exactly the point!" Danforth rounded on him. "This world *should* be gone, but it isn't! It's still supporting life, in a debatable fashion perhaps, but supporting it nonetheless!"

"Okay, so we find them a better one."

Danforth gripped the arms of his wheelchair as if ready to launch himself at the prospector. "You know what? You can take your fucking commercial interests and shove 'em! To hell with my funding! A good scientist can always find backing! Before you go digging up the place and disturbing things, there's a major mystery to be solved here: by all known rules of the universe, this planet should be an airless chunk of charcoal by now due to its system's collision with the Coal Sack!"

Clausen lifted his open palms in a Gallic shrug. "Which it's well on its way to being! Check your data again, Tay. The worst is yet to come. That's what the Sawls say, correct me if I'm wrong. Look, I'm not supporting a precipitous abort, but I think it would be wisest to do our thing as quickly as we can and get the hell out."

Megan worried that Clausen might manage to co-opt Weng's initiative and have her on the defensive again.

But Danforth was running with the ball. "You don't get it, do you? That old civilization is not lost. It's still here, what's left of it, having metamorphosed as it engineered its own survival." He waved a hand across the table, so emphatic that Liphar cringed into his seat. "Long ago, these folks' ancestors saw what was going to happen and went into emergency mode. They went underground, dug out the cave systems, built a new lifestyle. They adapted food sources to the new conditions."

"And they tried," added Megan, "to assure the survival of knowledge as well, by establishing a tradition of extensive record keeping. The only possible advantage to the Sawls of preserving a list of every birth since their year one is to encourage a memory of the long-ago past."

"But the memory faded over the enormous stretches of time involved," Weng chimed in. "Science was forgotten. Goddesses were invented to explain horrific vagaries of the weather, including periodic devastations of the population. History became myth."

Megan nodded. "And the record keeping merely ritual."

"No," Ghirra said suddenly, then seemed surprised by how quickly he had their attention. He shook his head gravely. "The *Toph-leta* is mystery, yes, but there is good knowing for us in the guild books."

"I didn't mean . . ." Megan began apologetically. Was there a tactful way to tell someone they weren't as clever as their ancestors?

"The guild books tell the old knowing of the generations," Ghirra insisted. "A guildsman give his knowing to his apprentice, but if he forget a thing, the guild books keep the knowing to be found again."

"Or not found," said Clausen lazily. "Clearly, if Taylor is to be believed at all, there's been a major degradation of knowledge since your alleged ancestors saw the handwriting on the wall."

"They held on to what was necessary to survive," defended Susannah.

"The guild books hold the knowing," Ghirra repeated, as much to himself as to the others. "The guild books hold the *science*."

On the verge of a meaningless, sympathetic remark, Susannah held back at Stavros' raised hand.

"What's in your mind, Guildmaster?" he asked softly.

The healer hesitated. "If I know a . . . *ilvesh* . . . ?"

"Infusion," Susannah supplied.

"In-fusion. Yes. I make this one to cool a sick heat of children. I write this in the book of my guild, and this is science. You . . . yes . . . make the machine to take away the heat in the air. You write this in a book." He stretched his arms in gratitude for the coolness within the circle of the force field, then looked to Danforth. "That is science, yes?"

"Well, engineering, but . . ."

Ghirra appealed to him for understanding. "The Priest Guild have guild books also. These tell the playings of the Sisters, and the signs of the *Arrah*. This is their knowing from the generations. This is their *science*." Glancing around for a response, he focused on Danforth's perplexed scowl.

"More, more," waved the planetologist impatiently.

Ghirra shrugged nervously, working at his limit within the alien language. "The Priest Guild say the *Toph-leta* is the Sister-gifts, but I think this: the *Toph-leta* is the most old of guild books. This hold the most old science."

He ventured delicately into the expectant hush he'd created. "If the first Priest Guild write in a book how the *Arrah*—the weather—go, what is the signs, all that, and this book is the *Toph-leta* of Priest Guild, I think this book is knowing how the ancestors make the *Arrah,* like Susannah say about the hakra and hjalk and all the plants, like Taylor make his machine."

"Not me, but . . ."

"Wait—made the weather?" Megan was sure she'd mistaken his line of reasoning.

Danforth's scowl flattened. "Now you're saying your priests control the weather?"

"Doing a fine job of it." But Clausen was listening with renewed interest.

"No, Taylor. I say *one time* my ancestors make the weather, to save the people from the Darkness . . . the too-much-heat that comes."

"Climate control?"

Megan hoped it was true. Stavros steepled his fingers, elbows on the table, and leaned his head into them.

Danforth's chair rocked with his resistance. "Come on! *Climate control?*"

"You search this thing that makes the weather, Taylor Danforth."

"The weather *now,* not a hundred fifty thousand years ago!"

"The made-plants and the made-animals are here. We are here, what the ancestors made us. Then this made-weather can be here also. Why not, Taylor? Why not?"

Though the abyss of understanding between the Master Healer and himself was encouraging him to shout, Danforth struggled to remain reasonable. "First of all, the genetic engineering is still only Susannah's informed guess. Second, you can't just make a climate and leave it at that. Weather doesn't just exist, man! Something has to make it work, make it move!"

"The Sisters make it move," said Ghirra, as if his brightest pupil had finally made all his efforts worthwhile. "Like this machine make the air cold."

"And there," announced Weng with satisfaction, "is your X-factor."

"We've been here before, Guildmaster," noted Stavros with a private smile. He flattened his palms on the crate top, assuming his neutral translator's voice. "Ghirra is suggesting that the Sisters are not goddesses at all but man-made weather machines."

Clausen threw his arms wide with a grin. "The force field as big as the Ritz! I like your style, honored doctor."

"Control the weather of an entire world?"

Danforth wasn't sure why the idea unhinged him so. Perhaps because it was the kind of fantastical notion he'd been resisting for so long, perhaps because it came from Ghirra.

He liked the Master Healer, had been convinced by his own experience to accept him as an able doctor, but he still found it difficult to grant any Sawl full equality in the realm of ideas. Delving into the hints and parallels in the Sawl mythology had been a desperate concession to necessity. *Tabula rasa.* Any angle. All avenues of inquiry . . .

No, he was lying. He knew what rattled him: the possibility that it was all *true*.

He made an effort to sound reasoned, calm. "Look, Ibiá, does he have any idea what miraculous machinery it would take to control the circulation of an entire planet?"

"Perhaps he does. Why don't you ask him?"

Danforth felt Weng's encouragement spreading like heat from the head of the table.

"Something's moving it around, did you once say, Dr. Danforth?"

Damn! He'd known that phrase would come back to bite him. "You buy this idea, Weng? You?"

"I find the idea intriguing, especially in an area that has not been over-populated with other possibilities. It explains the global nature of the phenomena, as well as the confinement of the actual weather activity to the narrow habitable zone."

"But who's out there to fucking *run* these machines?"

"I'm sure CRI would be the first to assert that a well-designed machine runs best without human interference."

"To quote the Tale of Origins again," offered Megan, "the king/parent who was skilled in the ways of power died or went away. Was I wrong to assume no mention of a Creator?"

Danforth fidgeted. "Well, for the sake of argument . . ."

Clausen sighed. "Oh, go ahead, Tay, try it on for size. No risk of scientific faux pas here. You're among friends."

Oh, yeah? Danforth thought of CRI recording, and the crew up in the Orbiter, listening, listening. Wild speculation in public was usually career suicide. But the notion *was* intriguing, and the Master Healer's sober attention seemed more pressing and immediate than whether Taylor Danforth would get his next academic promotion, or even his Nobel Prize.

"What the hell." He cleared his throat and plunged in. "Assuming—a big leap there, but let's make it . . . *assuming* the tech exists to power it, it's really very simple. If a planet is heating up to a point that's threatening its biosphere, one way to deal with the crisis would be to manage that heat, pull the excess to, say, some uninhabited area, and then manage the moisture accordingly." He took a breath, then amazed himself by continuing. "And, yes, something like this does seem to be happening here: a zone of relative habitability is diagonally wrapped around the planet, caught between hemispheres dominated by extreme cold-wet and hot-dry foci. The anomalous southwest-northeast prevailing winds that cross this zone are the general mechanism for the exchange of heat and moisture that's necessary to keep the system in some sort of equilibrium.

"But right now, it's not in equilibrium. It's like an aerialist teetering for balance, which is not supporting the zone of habitability. In fact it's beating the shit out of it!"

"One point for, one against," noted Clausen. "The score is tied, honored doctor. What do you say to your machines' lethal inefficiency?"

"This question I ask all my life," Ghirra replied steadily, "since one time I decide no goddesses could want this much deaths."

"'Hast thou comprehended the earth in its breadth? Declare if thou knowest it all,'" Megan intoned. "At least Jehovah told Job the reason for all his suffering."

McPherson broke her long silence. "So . . . maybe the machines are broken."

Ghirra nodded. "I say this also."

"But then they've broken down before," Susannah pointed out. "And recovered before. The guild records show a cyclical history of global Devastations followed by periods of relative calm."

Clausen rolled his eyes. "So we should expect the repair crews any minute?"

Susannah ignored him. "If the guild records are true—and we heard the same history in Ogo Dul—the wipe-outs are global and regular. Their coherence in space *and* time does look unnatural. It sounds cruel, but what if we have a periodic culling mechanism here, built in to hold world populations at levels that the reduced habitable zone is able to support? Maybe the Sawls proved to be *too* skilled at survival."

Megan shook her head. "There are strict population controls worked into the guild laws already."

"Redundant systems, then," said Weng.

"Birth control could stabilize the Sawl ecology," Susannah pursued, "but what about the rest of the ecosystem?"

Danforth sensed this cascade of speculation tumbling toward accepted fact. "Wait a minute! Wait just a goddamn minute!"

"You're worried about what drives it," guessed Clausen pleasantly.

"Among other things!" Danforth grabbed his temples. "There's also the entire physics of the exchange process!"

"What of the good doctor's suggestion that fields are being manipulated to produce these results?"

Megan bridled at derision masked as encouragement. "I don't think Ghirra means force fields *specifically*."

"But an entire planet!" Danforth gestured helplessly. "The required energies are unimaginable. You'd need a substantial fraction of the solar constant!"

"Gigabuckets." Clausen leaned back speculatively. "Yessiree, that would be one hell of a power source."

Susannah searched Stavros' face, wondering at his withdrawal from the discussion. He sat with eyes lowered, listening quietly, his good arm flung protectively across the back of Liphar's chair. Was he in pain? As she worried, he looked up. Aguidran shifted soundlessly behind him, and the other rangers took permission to readjust their own stance. A ripple of movement passed around the table, Stavros stirring the last of all.

"Taylor, if we accept that such machines could exist," he offered with studied deliberation, "would you say they'd explain all the weather anomalies you've observed on Fiix?"

Danforth looked doubtful and a little trapped. "No, I'd have to say that no weather machine I'd design would behave this way. Theoretically, there are gentler, more efficient and more life-sustaining ways to manage heat and water than slamming packets of 'em around like cannonballs."

Clausen fished a pen out of his pocket to jot a few numbers on the crate top.

"Maybe Ronnie's right," said Susannah. "Maybe they *are* broken."

"Or maybe," said Megan, "the machines' design reflects the builders' preconceptions about the nature of weather that are lost to us through the passage of time."

"Who would ever conceive of weather as necessarily lethal?" Susannah countered.

"The Sawls are not far from that kind of thinking right now," said Megan.

Stavros shook his head. When he laid his hands on the table, they rested palm up, his fingers lightly curled as if protecting some treasure held within.

His guar-fire, Susannah mused. A fleeting stab of jealousy caught her by surprise. Not envy. She had no desire to share the pain in her lover's hands, be it real or imaginary. But its accompanying mysticism now occupied the full center of his being. She could not compete with it for his attention.

"What you're all avoiding," Stavros said flatly, "is the notion of intention. The consciousness apparent in the Game. Because that's what Arrah really means, not weather, but 'game,' or 'struggle,' or 'contest.' "

Susannah knew that true change had been wrought during Danforth's convalescence when he didn't puff up at Stavros' irritating tone. Instead, he conjured a thin, ironic smile. "Commander, I think this is more your area of expertise. Would you care to attempt a specific application?"

Weng toyed with the edges of her stack of notes. "Dr. Danforth is referring to my recent efforts to apply game theory as an analytical tool to the dilemma of the local climate." She fixed Danforth with a neutral stare. "You'd like to hear mathematical proof that gamelike patterns can exist without implying consciousness or intention?"

"Numbers are not an answer to this question," said Stavros more gently.

Danforth rubbed his eyes. "Look, I'll admit it's been hard lately not to feel there's some villain out there having a field day at everyone's expense. But we make such conclusions when we're really desperate. By the light of day, they don't satisfy."

Clausen broke off his calculating to offer slow applause. "Bravo. Then perhaps we can explore a few more scientific avenues before falling down on our collective knees?"

"Right," Stavros murmured. "After all, how much chance would ConPlex stand in the Courts against actual living goddesses?"

"Give it up, Ibiá. Even your pals won't go with you on this one."

"You were telling us about game theory, Commander?" Megan prompted.

"I was." Weng's expression was unreadable. "To begin, an explanation in brief. If the data were a simple list of numbers, we could ask ourselves, what do these numbers have in common, and what is the mathematical function that might have generated them? That function, once derived, would consti- tute the 'rules' determining the various 'moves' of the 'game.'

"We then look at the pattern of these 'moves' in search of the 'objective' of the game. The patterns in the weather data have indicated movement in response to one another. Thus we conclude that there are two sides, if you will, two sets of pieces. Patterns within the patterns indicate strategies, that is, relationships between moves that lead to consequences.

"Given all the various possible moves, we can calculate a large number of possible end states, that is, finishes for the game. The observed strategies order these possibilities into smaller and smaller numbers until you can deduce which end state is the actual consequence of those strategies. From this we deduce the object of the game.

"Applying this to Dr. Danforth's data, my conclusion has been that the object of this particular game is different for each of the two sides. For one, it is to neutralize an overbalance of heat within a given area of the habitable zone, for the other to cancel an overbalance of cold."

"With the violent redistribution of moisture as a strategy," added Danforth reluctantly.

"Among others, such as the binding up of the opponent's potential energy so it's nontransferable to the kinetic energy he needs to move his pieces around the board, thus disabling him." Weng moved into her conclusion with relish. "These opposite objectives taken together could be seen as an attempt to achieve a balanced temperature in the zone of habitability, precisely the goal one would set if one were defending against excess heating of the atmosphere.

"Therefore, the object of the game—analyzed in terms that postulate no players or intention but deal merely with the co-reacting data—the object could indeed be weather control."

Clausen yawned, scratched out a few numbers, added a few more.

Megan was unsatisfied. "Fine, but this puts us right back where we started. It doesn't answer the question of why such extreme, lethal strategies are necessary."

"Or whose definition of weather control we're dealing with," added Susannah. "The current one doesn't seem to consider the Sawls' welfare at all."

"Which in itself speaks against conscious intention," Weng agreed. "I understand that the Master Healer might refuse to credit a deity of such cruelty, so much worse even than indifference, but neither can one believe that the former inhabitants would go to the trouble to construct machines that produce climate inimical to life, particularly when the Coal Sack was about to do it for them."

"So I gotta be right," spoke up McPherson. "They *are* broken."

"If they exist at all," reminded Clausen.

"Unless you go back to my culling theory," said Susannah.

"Or maybe there's intention all right," Danforth offered darkly, "but it's every bit as nasty as my weaker moments lead me to suspect."

"Or," concluded Stavros with implacable serenity, "there is intention, but we do not understand its nature."

Clausen drummed his pen softly on the crate top, then returned it to his pocket. "If you know something we don't, son, by all means enlighten us."

"I have seen an old man dance, and drive away the rain."

"Tut, Ibiá. Remember where you are. I doubt even the honored doctor here has patience with such cant."

The prospector stretched and rose, shaking his legs out. He began a casual progress around the table, like the corporate chairman exhorting his board. "Myself, I care less about intent and more for the possibilities of climate control. That, Taylor, would be the *real* discovery of the century. Transform uninhabitable planets. Fix the Earth."

Susannah felt the stirring of chill air as Clausen passed behind her. On the far side of the table, Aguidran moved counter to his clockwise drift. In the space between Liphar and Weng, she hovered, watching him as she might an approaching viper.

Megan sat back smugly. "Ah, but if you uncover a process for climate control, Emil, you'll lose the planet. Not even ConPlex could steal legal title from a local population capable of that."

"*Once* capable," returned Clausen, "and, maybe. Whatever the glories of the past, we can safely assume the builders of fantasy machineries to be long gone." He laid both hands on Danforth's shoulders. The planetologist tensed visibly but Clausen squeezed, patted, and let him go. "But even old, broken equipment would offer clues to its manufacture. A find like that would make us rich, I mean all of us, ConPlex, me, you, even the bloody Sawls." He grinned wolfishly at Ghirra. "What do you say, honored doctor? Would you like to be rich?"

"What's got you so interested all of a sudden?" rumbled Danforth.

"I threw together a few rough numbers that might surprise you, Tay. A fusion technology not much more efficient than what generates our own FTL field could theoretically provide the energies required to move this atmosphere if scaled up appropriately."

"Theoretically according to whom?"

"All we'd have to do, really, is learn how to generate the right kind of fields. We should be able to learn that, whether the alleged machines are working right or not."

He continued his progress around the table, passing McPherson, who sat very still with her arms pressed into her lap. "Now, it would be just as interesting to learn what sort of fuel has kept our hypothetical machines stoked up over the course of a hundred and sixty-odd thousand years. Clearly, they'd need to have access to an inexhaustible supply of *something*."

Stavros stared at his hands. Was he even listening? Susannah tried to catch his eye, sure he'd withdrawn again into contemplation of his windswept visions.

From behind Weng, Clausen fixed Stavros with a stare of innocent inquiry. "Perhaps there's a hint or two on that issue to be found in your precious myth, my boy?"

Stavros dared not move until the nauseating jolt of recognition had cleared his system. He might let slip some fatal clue.

Was the prospector baiting him? Did he actually know the answer to his question?

Stavros knew, though instinct alone had brought this sudden clarity.

His hands clenched and withdrew to his sides. He pictured the shadowed arching vaults of Eles-Nol, the guar cavern, crowded with its mammoth cylinders of glass. He followed the miles of thick white piping, recalled the lavender sparkle of the lithium ore, lifted by the Master Healer from Clausen's pack. He remembered the grave accusation in Ghirra's eyes.

What does he with this? Ghirra had asked.

The fire burned in his palms.

Raellil . . . ?

It was possible, then, to trace one's destiny from a single moment. But only in retrospect.

Now the Master Healer leaned over to whisper in Sawlish, wishing to know what had upset him.

"Private consultations, honored doctor?" needled Clausen.

Ghirra smiled humbly. "I did not know this word hypo-thetical."

Clausen smiled back and provided two possible Sawlish equivalents.

Stavros shuddered to hear Sawlish sounds from the prospector's mouth.

Another safety net shattered. And the man's calm was terrifying. Stavros longed to leap up and run for the deepest cave he could find. The heat in his hands could not soothe the memory of an agonized dying. He'd been a fool to let Susannah talk him into this. But he had to stick it out, had to find out what the prospector *knew,* and what he only suspected.

"There would hardly be reference to fuel sources in a mythology built around living, breathing deities, Emil."

"Use your imagination, my boy. Do the goddesses eat? Any mention of food, perhaps?"

Stavros stilled, as did Ghirra beside him. He hoped the restraining hand he laid on Liphar's knee was an unnecessary precaution. He made a pretense of consulting Ghirra for the backward reassurance of seeing the same horrified comprehension lurking behind the Master Healer's helpful smile.

"I didn't hear anything about eating, looking into the myths," said Danforth. "A lot about strategies and arsenals . . . and the lengths one Sister will go to in order to beat the other to a pulp."

Megan offered Stavros a searching squint that said his distress was more evident than he'd realized.

"We oughta just go out there and find 'em," said McPherson. "Y'know, when the Sleds are finished."

"It's a big planet to go searching for myths," Megan scoffed.

Danforth folded his arms. "If we respect the points of correlation between myth and sensing data, we'd start at the god-homes and work out from there."

"No . . ." Stavros was unable to stop himself.

"If they're machines, they can be fixed," McPherson stated, with the confidence of a confirmed technocrat. "That'd be good for the Sawls and everybody."

"Not good for the Sawls," said Stavros.

"It is not the worst idea, Mr. Ibiá," Weng countered, puzzled.

"We should try to contact them first," he blurted. He needed to think this out further. The only definite part of his plan was that it must be he who met the Sisters face-to-face.

"Contact a machine?"

A distant shout echoed faintly along the entry cylinder. The rangers near the opening stirred, looked around. One nodded at Aguidran's signal and slipped out into the sun.

"CRI is a machine," Stavros reminded them.

The shouting neared, a high-pitched summons. Stavros thought he heard his name called. Ghirra turned to listen.

Liphar fretted. "Ibi . . ."

"I hear," he murmured.

"Get CRI to try it?" Danforth shrugged. "It is something we haven't tried."

"In what sort of language?" mused Weng.

The rangers rustled in the silver tunnel as the messenger arrived outside. She would not enter, but stood breathless in the heat, repeating herself desperately. Aguidran backed three steps to the opening. Stavros recognized the voice: Kav Daven's caretaker girl.

"Ibi," said Ghirra, rising. "Kav Daven calls you."

"Guildmaster?" Weng inquired. "Is there a problem?"

He bowed an urgent apology. "A patient calls, Commander."

Stavros shoved back his chair.

"No, Stav. Don't move." McPherson's command froze Stavros halfway to his feet. She gripped the laser pistol with both hands extended like a cop. "Please. Sit."

Stavros sat down slowly.

McPherson flashed a desperate look at Weng. "You should arrest him, Commander. For his own good."

"Weng. Please. Not now." Stavros stood again, wary.

"Stav, he lied," Megan warned. "The gun is armed."

Clausen moved, flinging aside Liphar as the young man leaped on him, arms and legs windmilling like an angry incubus. Liphar crashed into the side of a crate with a screech. Aguidran grabbed Clausen's shoulder, jerking him backward, but he ducked and whirled to unseat her grip, then reached to twist her arm back and throw her against the side of the cylinder. Aguidran feinted as he turned and neatly stepped aside. His momentum carried him off-balance until he was yanked back hard against her chest, his own arm imprisoned and her unsheathed boot knife sharp at his throat.

"Now, McP!" he barked. "For Chrissakes, she'll kill me!"

"Not her! I can't!"

Danforth lunged against the side of his chair to sweep his arm out and up and grab McPherson's clenched fists in one huge hand. He shoved the laser's nose into the air. The gun smashed a needle of light into the ceiling. Danforth wrenched the weapon from McPherson's grasp and leveled it at the struggling prospector.

"Tay, no!" Susannah gasped.

"Tell your sister to let him go, Doc," Danforth growled. "She's in the line of fire."

"Tay . . ."

"Are you reading this, CRI?" yelled Danforth. "Are you getting it all?"

Ghirra said nothing, and Aguidran did not move. Stavros was transfixed by the darkly glimmering knife and the prospector's snarling helplessness. If Edan had been so equipped, she'd have stood a better chance.

Hands pulled at him, Ghirra's, the other rangers'. He let them drag him up from his chair, though his wounded shoulder screamed at their roughness. On the run again. But his next thought was for Kav Daven. "We might need help. Susannah, will you come?"

"Go," Danforth advised. "No one's going to get hurt, now we've dis-armed him."

Susannah raced for her medikit.

Weng stood up, grasping at formality. "Mr. Ibiá, I expect you to report back to me as soon as this current crisis is over. Do I have your word?"

Access to CRI was tempting. It would be easier to influence their move-ments if he lived among them again. And the Sleds were here . . .

"You have it, Commander."

He grabbed Susannah's arm as she trotted up with her kit slung over her shoulder, paused to throw Danforth a grateful glance, and bolted through the cylinder.

81

E.D. 98–

A WINCH PLATFORM WAITED at the base of the cliff, tended by an unexpectedly large assortment of engineers, priests, and apprentices. Stavros stepped onto it gratefully, leaning into Ghirra's side. Had they known he'd never make it up the stairs on his own?

The sun reflecting off the white cliff face scorched and blinded. The ache in his shoulder thundered a bass accompaniment to every movement. Faces crowded him, more than were needed to man the winch ropes or steady the wooden pallet as Susannah and Liphar stepped on, followed by two of Aguidran's rangers. Stavros wondered at the crowd, wondered at their intent serious faces, focused so expectantly on his own.

He stood as tall as he could manage, to set a good example. He wrapped his good arm around the twisted strands rising taut to the head knot of the pallet's rope cradle. His injured arm rested about Susannah's waist, more for his own support than for hers. Her hip nudged softly at his groin. He slid a hand across her belly, glad for the lovely simplicity of desire, so comprehensible and sure, so easily satisfied in comparison to the mysteries that pulled at him from every side, stretching him to infinity, redefining his life.

The engineers shouted, the crowd scattered awkwardly and the platform swung free and rose, swaying. The faces below followed its upward passage in silence. Most of the crowd headed for the stairs to make the slower, hotter ascent. Liphar edged around on the overladen pallet, calling attention to the sky. The sharp line of division had advanced across the plain. A pale greenish veil was being drawn toward the jade-colored zenith.

"You see, Ibi? It comes."

Ghirra nodded tightly. "White Sky."

The cave mouth was jammed—more priests and engineers, and many from the other guilds. The closest grabbed for the winch ropes and swung the pallet onto the ledge. The rangers jumped off as the platform shuddered down, to clear a path through the throng.

Stavros let Ghirra lead the way across the entry cavern and up the inner stairs. At the top of the stair, both sides of the corridor were lined with young priests and apprentices sitting cross-legged with their backs rigid against the wall. They chanted a dirgelike melody. Had he come too late? He heard "raellil" murmured up and down the line. He felt a strange flutter of hands about his ankles, fingers reaching to brush the fabric of his pants, to touch the tops of his bare feet. He gripped Ghirra's arm.

"What are they doing?" But he feared he already understood.

"They welcome you, Stavros Ibiá," the Master Healer replied formally.

Stavros heard the grave approval in his voice. They hope too much of me, he mused. When had even Ashimmel received such gestures of homage? Only the Ritual Master himself.

Old man, what have you started?

He glanced behind at Susannah. Her calm, quizzical smile reassured him.

She was his ballast and anchor. As long as he could call to mind the feel of her, skin against skin, heat and secret moisture, he would remember he was only a man, like other men.

Aguidran waited until her guildsman had cleared the cylinder, then shoved Clausen aside and backed into the entry. She held the long dark knife poised across her chest like a shield, glaring a final accusation into the Underbelly. She singled out McPherson for particularly black censure, then bent to sheathe the knife in her boot, straightened, and loped off across the sun-baked clearing.

Clausen picked himself up angrily. A hand touched to his throat came away bloodied. A slim scratch stained the crisp collar of his shirt. "That motherfucker's got an edge on it."

"Yeah, she does, doesn't she." Danforth cradled the little gun in his big hand and tuned it down, deactivating the pulse, bleeding off the power.

Weng pulled a clean handkerchief from a pocket of her uniform and handed it to Clausen, but made no move to tend his wound. "Lieutenant McPherson, you are confined to quarters for the next twelve hours."

"What? Me? It was for his own good!"

"About the stupidest thing you could have done," chortled Danforth.

"Oh, so it's better for him to run around getting shot up?"

"It is not appropriate to take such matters into your own hands, particularly at the expense of our good relations with the Sawls."

"Don't worry, Weng," Megan muttered. "The Sawls know who their friends are."

"I'm sure they do," Clausen snapped. "The question is, do *you*?"

Danforth settled back into his chair, the laser cooling on his lap. Clausen's tanned face was etched with paler tension lines. His pupils seemed a brighter blue for being outlined in white. Like winter sun glinting off a glacier. Danforth never guessed he'd find another man's helpless rage so satisfying.

"Idiots, all of you!" Clausen pressed Weng's handkerchief to his throat. "He's playing you for goddamn fools! Letting him waltz out of here like that?" He shot Weng a sidelong snarl. "He sure knows a soft touch when he sees one!"

Danforth found Weng's control admirable, but after all, dignity was her only remaining weapon, and her calm in crisis the only parameter left to define her command.

"Mr. Ibiá will return when his business in the Caves is done," she replied. "I do not believe I have misjudged the value of his word."

"His *word*?" Clausen's hands clenched as if he'd like to grab Weng and shake her. "What is it about that boy that's got you all so blinded? He won't come back of his own accord, not for a minute!"

"He came down willingly enough," commented Megan.

"After endless negotiations!"

"After you agreed to give up your weapon."

"Fuck that! He came down to find out what we know!" Clausen stalked the length of the empty table, then spun back to stare at Stavros' chair. A thought struck him with enough force to temper his raging. "Because he knows something he's not telling us."

"Secrets under every rock," scoffed Megan.

"Mark me," Clausen returned ominously.

"Like, what?" McPherson was ready to believe him.

"Something they've told him." Clausen continued around the table. "Something he's not even telling you, my dear Megan. You, his own mentor in conspiracy."

"Get a life," retorted Megan.

Danforth decided that the idea was not so farfetched. He'd been watching. He'd seen the fear behind the Master Healer's eyes when the question of the power source came up. But whatever little secret they held among themselves, he doubted it offered the answers he needed. And he guessed that Megan knew more than she let on, even to him. Perhaps now she'd share what she knew, in return for a declaration of full support.

"If Ibiá has all the secrets," he said tiredly, "why would he risk his life down here to find out what we know?"

"You don't get it, do you? That boy will sacrifice any of you, not just me, even Susannah, for the sake of his precious Sawls! I've seen them go native before. I've seen them get that look in their eyes!" Clausen pulled the bloodied handkerchief from his throat, balled it into a lump and threw it on the table. "Fuck it. I'm tired of this shit. Let him go on playing out his fantasies. I intend to beat him at his own game."

He strode to the mini-terminal. "CRI, work up an equipment manifest for me—one Sled, one passenger, two weeks minimum duration."

"Yes, Mr. Clausen."

"Mr. Clausen . . ."

"You can't stop me, Weng. You have no legal authority to stop me from doing the job I came here to do."

Weng returned his stare. "I had no such intention. When there is a Sled working to your satisfaction, by all means be on your way. Lieutenant McPherson is fully capable of completing repairs to the second vehicle."

Clausen's outburst of temper seemed to have restored his good humor. "Best of luck, then. Just make sure you keep Tay out of the pilot's seat. Look what happened the last time he went flying. . . ."

82

E.D. 98–6:27

SUSANNAH HAD NEVER been in the Priest Hall before. She'd expected something grander, or darker, or more austere, a further extension of the Frieze Hall or something that fit her notion of the religious. Though Megan had tried to convince her of the secular nature of the Priest Guild, Susannah's early experience in Lagri's Story Hall had formed expectations to the contrary. And then there was the influence of Stavros and his "miracle." But the Priest Hall was columned and busy like any other craft hall. The tiled floor was warm and tracked with dust. And surprisingly bright. Every possible lamp was burning, every double sconce on the columns, every wick in every chandelier, every individual lamp in the scholars' niches along the wall. The long hall trembled with feverish golden light and the steamy heat of bodies. Priests hovered in groups of two and three, animated by debate that stilled into ambivalent silence as Stavros paced by.

Drawn along in his wake, Liphar's small hand guiding her elbow, Susannah contemplated Ghirra's idea of the priests as preservers of the ancient weather science. She pictured each lamplit niche stacked high with the familiar gauges and dials, oscilloscopes, graphics and holo displays, the only sort of equipment she could comprehend in relation to something so high-tech as climate control.

How did they do it and where did it go? Is technology so easily forgotten?

Like the Sky Hall engravings: clear evidence of advanced science unrecognized even by Ghirra, that most sophisticated of Sawls. Susannah peered into each brightly lit recess, scoured the curve of every column and the surface of every wall for similar signs. They might have been there all along, but gone unnoticed.

It was puzzling that her suggestion of a genetically engineered inner ecology with the Sawls at its center had not caused the stir it should have—her colleagues seemed to have heard it as just one more bit of evidence. Had she presented it badly? Because the restructuring of living systems on a global level was far more significant and far-reaching than fancy ceramics, or astronomy. Even the Druids could predict eclipses.

Ghirra's weather machines had fired everyone's imagination, and rightfully so, but Susannah's intellectual knees weakened in awe at the genetic achievements she'd proposed. Clausen could imagine conquering climate control within his lifetime and with minimal advances in technology. Susannah could not believe the same about her hypothetical genetic miracles.

How tragic that such genius might be lost in the mists of time. What guild's dusty, crumbling volumes preserved those secrets, in form and language the guildsmen themselves no longer understood? Was it Physicians'? The Food Guild? How and where to begin the search?

The bustle in the Priest Hall thickened as they approached the farthest corner. Here the murmuring groups included men and women from other guilds, relatives of the old priest, Susannah surmised, his children and their children.

Stavros edged through the waiting crowd, his head low in unconscious imitation of Ghirra's self-effacing stoop. Questioning eyes followed him. Reflected in them was an image Susannah did not recognize, and never would until she'd immersed herself in the Sawl gestalt as deeply as Stav had. Identifying with Ghirra was not enough. He was atypical. His free-ranging mind allowed her to gloss over the most fundamental differences between Sawl and Terran—among them, the lack of a border between the real and the mystical. It was too alien to be encompassed.

Her intellect could stretch to embrace any scientific possibility. Her heart might admit the possibility of a miracle. This worked as long as she kept them separate. But commingling the two derailed both her rational and irrational processes, as did the subtle healing in Ghirra's hands. It was nothing flashy. He could not cure fatal disease or bring back life when all signs of it had fled, but there was undeniable power there, consistent, real, and inexplicable. Stavros would call it a "connection," and liken it to his own. But how would Ghirra explain it, if he believed his goddesses were machines?

The Stavros reflected in the eyes around her was also an unsettling mixture. Where Susannah saw brilliance and beauty, the Sawls saw an alien being, fleshy and pale, large and rather clumsy, clever but vulnerable, something precious to be protected, like an overgrown child in danger from its own earnest impulsiveness. But the child might grow into its potential, and it was that expectation the Sawls protected, an expectation that not even Stavros could define.

The crowd cleared for them around a deep alcove in the back wall. Heavy curtains were drawn to either side around a raised bed of cushions. The Master Herbalist Ard crouched over an oil-fired steamer by the foot of the bed, each turn of his spoon sending up clouds of scented dampness. Ampiar stood a bit aside with a scowling Kav Ashimmel, and Xifa behind them, holding Kav Daven's youngest great-grandchild. Others, his sons and daughter, his grandchildren, sat in solemn observance. There was little hope in their eyes, but few tears either.

All wept out, Susannah knew. So much had happened lately. And the Kav had had a long and vital life. Ashimmel seemed more disturbed than anyone, her distress less sorrowing than confused and disapproving, and clearly resentful as Stavros moved to the Kav's bedside like a sleepwalker.

"What's with Ashimmel?" Susannah whispered to Ghirra.

"This Kav have no apprentice to follow. Ibi did not tell this to you?"

"No, he didn't. What about the girl who takes care of him? Isn't she . . . ?"

Ghirra shook his head. "She is his daughter's daughter. The master's apprentice cannot be of his family."

"Oh." She watched Stavros lower himself stiffly beside the bed. Ashimmel withdrew only slightly to make room for him. Susannah bent her head closer to Ghirra's. "And, quite naturally, Ashimmel feels this fixation with Stavros is less important that the Kav naming his successor?"

"She is Guild Master. She must think of the business of the guild. They argue about this always, yet the Kav has not teach one to be his apprentice. Ashimmel wishes not to make the choosing."

Stavros had eyes for no one but the old man on the bed.

Kav Daven lay deep among his pillows, a fragile brown skeleton lost in mounds of russet and tan. Between protruding ribs, Susannah saw the flutter of a strained heartbeat. His eyes stared open, blind white eyes whose small unseeing movements searched the shadowed vaults and seemed to follow the ascending billows of steam from Ard's medicinal. His lips quivered in a soundless spasmodic chanting. Stavros took the priest's papery hand between his own.

"Kav. Kho jelrho." He leaned forward, kissed the hand, and bent his head into the pillows beside it.

Kav Daven's lips ceased their convulsive movement. His eyes drooped shut, as if in relief. His hand lifted free of Stavros' gentle grasp to feel its way along his cheek and settle on his bowed head. The knotted brown fingers burrowed possessively in Stavros' hair. The ancient lips tightened with purpose.

"Raellil khe," the old man mumbled.

A rustle shivered through the crowd. Susannah tried to read Ghirra's bemused frown. Ashimmel knelt to listen more closely.

"Raellil khe." Kav Daven spoke more clearly this time, his fingers gripping Stavros' skull. Stavros remained still, though a soft moan escaped him, like a sigh.

"Lij, raellil," insisted the Kav. "Rho lijet."

Ashimmel rose, shaking her head in disbelief and refusal. Her fellow priests gaped and murmured. Stavros stirred, but was loath to disturb the priest's hand resting on his head in benediction. "Kho lije?"

Susannah edged closer. "What's he saying?"

Ghirra touched her arm, bidding silence. Liphar leaned into her hip like a dog, enrapt by the drama unfolding before him.

Ashimmel whirled and paced away. The crowd cleared a path for her. She fell into muttered conference with three of her most senior priests, who looked as dumbfounded and outraged as she.

"Rho lijet . . . rho lijet . . . rho lijet . . ." murmured Kav Daven. Each repetition grew fainter until it became an escape of breath barely sculpted into sound and meaning.

Stavros lifted his head and the priest's hand slid limply along his neck. His eyes were wet. "Kav, I don't know how!"

The withered hand closed on Stavros' injured shoulder. He stiffened against the pain, choking back a gasp. The Kav's grip tightened. Stavros' back arched and his face spasmed in agony, but there was joy in his eyes, as profound as the pain.

A chill rippled along Susannah's spine. Though she had seen his face suffused with the ecstasy of desire, she understood the nature of his transport far less than his Catholic ancestors would have, at a glance.

"Rho lijet, raellil!" Kav Daven summoned a sudden strength. The stringy sinews of his torso bunched as if he might sit up. Stavros placed both hands on the old man's chest.

"Kav, I will."

The grip on his shoulder eased. The crooked fingers, hardly more than naked bones, relaxed. The hand slid slowly along Stavros' arm to rest in the curl of his elbow, limp as a rain-sodden leaf.

Susannah glanced reflexively at the skin drawn tight across the old man's ribs. The drumming flutter of his heart had stilled. Ghirra stepped forward, drawing her with him. They slipped in to either side of Stavros, careful despite their professional urgency not to violate the peaceful spell of the moment. There was little hope of restoring the faint life spark that had already burned far beyond expectation. Susannah gave up before Ghirra did, but at last he too sat back. At the foot of the bed, Ard sighed and capped the little oil flame of his steamer.

Ghirra rose, signaling Ard and Susannah away from the bedside. There was no weeping. Many faces were as curious as they were solemn, waiting to see what Ashimmel would do next.

Stavros sat slumped on his heels, his gaze fixed inward. His hands rested palm up on his thighs. In the silence, Liphar crept forward to kneel beside him. Slowly, others of the Priest Guild, including the Kav's young granddaughter, slipped out from the crowd to join them. Susannah had the sense of an ancient tradition reasserting itself.

"Ghirra, what is going on?" she whispered urgently.

"He say to Ibi many times, you must dance, you must dance."

"I don't understand."

He looked back at her, rather sadly, she thought—not for the death, but for her. "This mean, Suzhannah, that Kav Daven name Stavros Ibiá his apprentice."

"What?" Susannah stared down at the kneeling linguist.

Ghirra added gently, "And Ibi say to this, yes."

BOOK EIGHT

DEVASTATION

"As flies to wanton boys are we to the gods;
They kill us for their sport."

—*King Lear*, Act IV, sc. i

83

STAVROS HELD SUSANNAH in the blue dimness of the Story Hall, wishing only to soothe her. But she was full of questions and a need for answers.

"It's a sweet ecumenical gesture on the old man's part," she pointed out, "but Ashimmel will never buy it."

Sweet? Swallowing his protest, Stavros smoothed her long hair down her back. "Because the Kav's choice was so . . . irregular, Ashimmel will submit it to a guild vote. If it passes, she must accept it."

"But the guild would never agree to this. You're no priest. You're not even . . ."

Raellil.

Apprentice.

Was that all? Learn the range of rituals, perform them in his place? The work of a lifetime, and yet . . .

He touched his fingertips to her lips, then kissed her lightly. "The old Kav was well-loved and . . . well, I'm not without support within the guild."

She seemed to understand something for the first time. "Then you want this."

"There are many in the guild who feel that in a time of crisis, extraordinary measures are required."

Susannah pulled away from him. "Stav, I asked, do you want this?"

He tried to deflect her with an amorous smile. "Right now all I want is you."

"No." She drew her tunic tight about her and her knees up to her chest.

"Hey, don't stare at me like I'm some kind of stranger."

"I don't understand what you're doing!"

"Neither do I! Really, I don't, if that makes any difference. All I'm sure of is that I have to do it. Whatever it is." He glanced away. Absolutism might seem merely willful to one who did not share his commitment. "I'd like to think I have your help and support."

Susannah dropped her forehead to her knees with a forlorn sigh.

"Listen, Ghirra once said the Kav had a plan for me, and it seems he was right. But the old man died before he could explain it to me. I have to at least find out . . ." If he reached for her, and if she pulled away again, the distance might grow too great. The fire in his palms burned as a fierce and constant goad since the old priest's death. He needed her, even her skepticism, to help him stay centered. "Susannah, I love you. Believe that. Believe in me. Believe that I know what I'm doing is right."

Her brow wrinkled. "It's not right to agree to this, then leave them hanging when the time comes!"

"The time?"

"To go home!"

So that was the issue. "Susannah, love. I am home. You know that." He suppressed a grunt of pain as he pulled himself up to fold her in the crook of his good arm. "You knew it before I did. You remember? The Planting Feast?" He laughed, his lips brushing her ear. "I'm sitting there lost in erotic panic, trying to figure how to get you close to me, and you're like the Delphic oracle, telling me how I wasn't focusing on the com repair because I didn't want to leave. You scared the shit out of me."

Susannah only shook her head. Stavros felt warm tears slide past his wrist where it rested against her cheek.

"Think about it," he pleaded. "Why should we want to go back? Earth is past hopeless. Calling it home is only a habit. Think of the good you could do here! There's no question they'd welcome you. And I'd be the happiest of men."

"You'll break Weng's heart," she murmured.

Weng? "Susannah . . ."

But as she leaned in sadly, curling into the comfort of his eager body, an urgent knocking rang out at the entrance of the hall. Stavros swore, but rose, drawing on his pants, and padded along the tiles to unbar the doors.

Megan waited outside, her mouth a tight line of angry disbelief.

Stavros glanced quickly up and down the exterior Hall. "What are you doing here?"

She shouldered past him through the door. "It doesn't matter now. He's gone."

"Gone?"

"Took off early this morning, while we were all dead to the world in our little air-conditioned cocoon. The sonofabitch was lying about how ready A-Sled was! And he took McPherson with him."

Stavros frowned. "By force?"

"Who knows? The point is, he left us without a pilot."

"What about B-Sled?"

"Weng's checking it out now."

"Can she fly it?"

"She says not. Never had occasion to. I think she doesn't want to."

"Taylor, then."

Megan shrugged. "He's all we got."

Susannah came out of the shadows, tying the sash of her tunic. "Will CRI say where he's headed?"

"Oh, he's not covering his tracks. He's making a beeline for the southern desert."

"Nolagri," murmured Stavros. "He could be there in three or four days, if he really pushes. But it's a big desert. Does he really know what he's looking for?"

"If it's there, he'll find it, you can be sure of that."

"It'd be the crowning irony if he did manage to make us all rich," said Susannah dispiritedly.

Megan folded her arms. "What's he going to find down there, Stav?"

"How should I know?" he replied, giving in to a touch of his old sullenness. "The only information I have is the stuff none of you will believe."

"Emil seemed to think differently."

He spread his hands. "Nothing more than a guess."

"You think there are people? A pocket of the old race left down there?"

"No. That would show up somewhere in the myths."

Megan stared him down. "Stav. What do you know?"

He paced away, pressing his palms together, one fiery locus against the other. "Okay. Here it is. The Sawl power source he was so interested in? I think it's his lithium!"

"Really?" Megan stiffened as if in pain. "Why?"

No use for secrecy now. Stavros grabbed her arm and propelled her to the edge of Valla's fountain, where the arching threads of water curtained a thin blue flame burning in its glass tube. "That's why."

Susannah followed. "Not natural gas? Up in Physicians', I always wondered."

Stavros pointed toward the floor. "Several hundred meters below us is the Sawls' most remarkable secret: a huge power plant, built mostly of glass. It makes the gas to fuel that flame, as a by-product of a reaction involving nearly pure lithium dug from deep under the cliffs. But the Sawls don't see it as technology anymore. The whole process is heavily shrouded in myth and euphemism. The priests call it 'feeding the goddesses.' "

"Power plant!" Megan gaped at him. "Why didn't you tell me?"

He returned her gaze. "I didn't want him to be able to beat it out of you."

She nodded reluctantly. "Good thinking."

"Lithium," murmured Susannah. "No wonder Ghirra was so upset when Emil came back with a pack load of it. Lithium." She made a further connection. "Your guar rock."

"Yes."

"Oh, boy." It was Megan's turn to pace, as her mind ranged forward. "CRI says he's taken along a case of atomic mining charges, among other things." Stavros stood speechless as she spoke his thought aloud. "If your goddesses exist, Clausen's not going to want them competing with him for the planet's mineral resources."

"But wait, he's after the technology, too," Susannah soothed. "He's not going to blow up something that'll make him rich."

"Unless lithium will make him richer, faster."

"Okay." Stavros strode into the darkness at the end of the hall and came back pulling a sleeveless tunic over his bandaged shoulder. "We've got, what, another shipweek till sunset? Where's the damn laser?"

"Tay has it. He's brooding over it like a mother hen."

"Well, that's one thing in our favor. I'll tell Ghirra and Liphar. They'll need to make excuses for me. Get back to the Lander. Tell Weng to keep working on that Sled!"

Megan blinked at his sudden speed.

"Come on!" he growled. "The bastard's got enough of a head start as it is!"

E.D. 98–21:10

Susannah straggled in from the blistering heat. "She shouldn't be out there so long!"

Megan nodded. Sensible as it was, it seemed wrong to sit in the cool while out in the cruel sun, a much older woman struggled to recall long-unused mechanic's skills. "She's the only one left who knows how the Sleds work."

"At least Taylor's keeping her company."

"My turn to spell him." Megan roused herself. But passing through the cylinder was like stepping into a blast furnace. She lingered within its silvered arc, shielding her cheeks with her hands, as if her skin might immediately shrivel and flake away.

Stavros hailed her, striding down the path from the Caves. He had Liphar beside him, Ghirra and Aguidran at his heels. Pale dust danced around them like smoke. A trick of the hot light made their bodies shimmer darkly against the too-white background.

Megan glanced anxiously at the sky. It, too, had gone white. The sun glowed molten behind a veil of bright cloud stretching across the entire bowl of sky. Plain and cliffs and sky blended into a solid white-on-white. The fearsome glare needled Megan's eyes, and the sand flew up on its own to cling to her shoes and pant legs like a swarm of hungry parasites, refusing to be shaken off. Frightened, she ducked back into the Underbelly to retrieve her sun lenses.

"Stav's coming down," she called to Susannah, then went out across the torrid clearing to join Weng and Danforth in the dubious shade of the tarp. Crutches crooked in one arm, Danforth leaned against the Sled's white hull, peering into the cockpit. Weng sat in the pilot's seat, disheveled and dust-streaked, a wet towel draped around her neck. She was touching switches on the control panel and conversing in mutters with CRI's tinny Sled voice.

"How's it going?" Megan asked.

The tip of Weng's tongue worked its way farther into the corner of her mouth.

Danforth held up crossed fingers. "She's running an instrument check. We have power at least." The laser pistol was shoved into the belt of his cut-off trousers. His dark features were nearly invisible, lost in shadow, back lit by glare.

Megan was unable to shake an unease that had settled in with the hot white light. "Have you looked at the *sky?*"

Danforth nodded. "A thin cloud nearly planet-wide, except where we're going, over the desert. According to CRI, it's some bit of moisture being injected at higher altitudes. According to legend, Valla Ired's last gasp of defense: White Sky."

"Spooky," Megan admitted with a shiver.

Danforth's grin was bright relief in his shadowed face. "Just them ol' positive ions, Meg. Don't let 'em get to you."

Stavros ducked under the canopy. "Reporting for duty as ordered, Commander."

Weng did not look up from her instruments. "Better late than never, Mr. Ibiá."

"I heard it suddenly got safe to be here." Stavros exchanged a careful nod with Danforth, his eyes flicking from one cast-bound leg to the other. "How're you feeling?"

Danforth laughed. "*Me?* How 'bout you?"

Stavros shrugged, allowing him a crooked smile. "Damn the sonofabitch anyway."

"If you two are about to compare war wounds, I'm leaving," Megan snorted.

But she was glad for anything they could find in common. They'd need mutual respect, if not friendship, in the days to come. She headed back to the cool of the Underbelly and found Susannah remonstrating with Ghirra, while Aguidran and Liphar looked on, she stone-faced, he vastly uncomfortable.

"But, Ghirra, do you think it's *right* for him to accept?" Susannah was demanding. She fell silent with a gesture of despair when Megan entered the cylinder.

E.D. 98–21:30

"At least I was right about this planet being a rich source of lithium."

"It's a guess, Taylor, like I said to Megan."

"Lately, Ibiá, I'm more inclined to trust your guesses." Danforth looked down, jiggled his crutches. "I'd sure like to see that power plant. I don't suppose . . . ?"

"Steep stairs all the way down." Stavros felt honest regret. "If we had more time . . ."

"No problem," said Danforth amiably. "But I've been giving the chemistry some thought. If the lithium the Sawls mine is as pure as you suggest, it could be combined with water to produce lithium oxide, heat and . . . hydrogen gas."

"The blue flames."

"And the high-temperature ceramic technology. Hydrogen burns hot."

"The cooling system for the reaction vessel also provides heat and hot water for the Caves." Stavros was sorry to have lacked the benefit of Danforth's knowledge for so long. Ghirra was right to include him so readily. And yet . . . "Taylor, what's your interest in this? No offense, but I have to ask."

"You mean, whose side am I on? Sure you have to ask. I would, too, in your shoes, maybe a lot less politely." Danforth eased himself onto his crutches and stumped to the edge of the shade to stare out into the sun. "I'm on my own side, if that helps you believe me. I'm glad to know I was right about the lithium being here, but I think we're onto something much more remarkable and I'd be a fool to let that get away from me. I think Emil is being bull-headed, and that he'll lose this case if it goes to court. And I believe he's reached the same conclusion—which is not good news. If there's something out there he can use, he will. If not, he'll destroy it, simply because he's pissed and because he can." He turned to face Stavros. "He's got to be stopped."

"Dr. Danforth?" Weng's voice wavered with exhaustion. "I believe it is time to clear the canopy and test the fans. The instruments seem to be in working order."

"On my way, Commander."

Stavros watched Danforth sling himself toward the Sled. "You're flying this thing?"

"I'm not as hopeless at the stick as Emil liked to make out."

"By yourself, I meant. All twenty-five thousand klicks?"

"Sure. Don't need my legs to do that." Danforth let a slow grin build.

Stavros grinned back with less certainty. "Hell of a good thing."

Behind them, Weng said very quietly, "Damn," followed by a wheezing sigh and a long, sliding thud. Stavros sprang to the Sled. Weng lay in a heap on the floor of the cockpit. One-armed, Stavros could not haul himself up and over to help her.

Danforth swung helplessly to his side. "What happened?"

"Heat, exhaustion, I don't know. Fuckin' useless, both of us!" Stavros lunged into the sun and across the clearing at a clumsy, pain-jarred run. "Susannah!"

She met him at the cylinder mouth, Ghirra and Aguidran behind her. Brother and sister bolted toward the Sled. Once there, Aguidran bent, interlacing her fingers to receive Ghirra's foot, and vaulted him into the cockpit. Susannah had joined him by the time Stavros regained the shelter of the canopy. Kneeling, Ghirra untangled Weng's crumpled limbs. He cleared tools and loose test equipment with a sweep of his arm and stretched her out between the front seats. He fumbled with the unfamiliar buttons at her throat until Susannah nudged his hands aside to undo them.

"She breathes," he reported, "but the heart . . ." His hands hovered, cupped around but not touching Weng's jaw.

"Racing," supplied Susannah. "Heat prostration, I hope, not a stroke. Let's get her in where it's cool."

Ghirra slipped both arms beneath the old woman, lifting her with surprising ease to hand her down to Aguidran. "She has no weight."

Susannah scrambled out of the cockpit and led the way to the Underbelly. Stavros started after them, but Danforth stayed him with a big hand on his arm.

"She's in good hands. Nothing further we could do."

Stavros nodded slowly, waiting.

Danforth jerked his head at the Sled. "So, want to take a little test drive?"

Stavros cocked his head at the seemingly inaccessible cockpit.

Danforth swung jauntily to the midsection and patted the hull. "I think I can hoist myself up through the cargo hatch . . . with a little help. You game?"

Stavros wondered what test Danforth was really offering. "Taylor, I need a pilot. I'm game for anything that gets us in the air."

Megan ventured once more into the heat to help clear away the canopy. "Don't get to joyriding out there. There's still prep to do before we head out after him, and every minute increases his head start."

The silver-film tarp flashed dully as they floated it aside into a heap of reflective folds. White light flooded the cockpit. Stavros swung himself up one-handed through the open cargo hatch, slammed it shut behind him, then clattered across the empty hold to drop heavily into the seat beside Danforth. The planetologist had strapped in, his rigid right leg stretched out beneath the instrument console.

Megan peered over the side of the cockpit. "Heat prostration, like Susannah said. Most spacers have trouble after so long on the ground. She'll be fine if she takes it easy for a while."

"The woman is a rock," Danforth said.

"One less passenger to weigh us down," Stavros calculated guiltily. "No, two. Someone will have to stay with her."

"You have the command, Taylor," Megan reminded him, "until she wakes up."

"Damn. You're right." With less than a second's pause, Danforth said, "You're next in line, Meg. You take over."

Stavros laughed. "A month ago, you'd have given your firstborn for such a chance."

Megan did not seem resistant to the idea. "Meaning you want me to stay behind?"

"You could run CRI's First Contact procedures, broadcast the usual messages."

Megan looked doubtful. "I thought we were looking for a weather control system."

"AIs, most likely. With at least a rudimentary consciousness." Stavros kept his language rational, though in his mind's eye, he saw something darker, vaster, not so easily encompassed or explained.

"Can't hurt to try," Danforth agreed. "And we can't leave Weng alone."

"Well, it's true I'm not much good in this heat."

"Done," the planetologist declared. "Commander Levy, please inform our colleagues we're ready to power up!"

E.D. 98–22:46

"Forward fan, check."

Stavros envied the deep steadiness of Danforth's voice over the com.

"Forward fan nominal," acknowledged CRI.

"Aft right fan, check."

"Aft right nominal."

As each fan spun up to quarter-speed, the haze of dust around the Sled thickened. The white silence of the clearing was invaded by machine whines. The observers drew back to the edge of the clearing, eyes slitted against the glare and flying grit. In the open cockpit, Stavros coughed convulsively.

"Aft left fan, check," said Danforth hoarsely.

"Aft left nominal," CRI replied. "I have no reading on the cockpit shield, Dr. Danforth. Is that an instrument malfunction?"

Danforth squinted uncertainly at the control panel, then touched a switch. "I forgot."

Within a matter of seconds, the noise of the fans abated to a milder yowl. The hard white light eased as a force field enclosed cockpit and cargo bay. Danforth flipped a toggle, touched another contact. Air flowed into the static heat already building up inside the shield. "It won't keep us cool, but it'll keep us breathing." He flipped three more toggles, hit the first of three switches. "Aft engine check: One?"

Stavros felt the Sled shudder and begin to vibrate. Should he be more anxious about Danforth's untested piloting skills?

"One," agreed CRI.

"Two? Three?" Danforth touched the last contacts in rapid sequence.

He's just as eager as I am. Stavros' mood soared. He welcomed the return of high adventure and the rush of elation that came with it. It was so unambiguous. No dispute over meaning or interpretation: you either flew or you didn't. He laughed aloud, forgetting the com unit hugging his jaw. Danforth glanced his way. His voice in Stavros' ear was silky with amusement.

"Off to see the wizard, eh, Ibiá? Okay, let's give her a try!" He whooped softly and closed his hand around the stick. A-Sled jerked and lifted, seesawing sloppily within its dust cloud, then rose sharply. Danforth's whoop died into a grimace as he steadied the rise. "Sorry 'bout that."

He grinned sickly, and eased the stick forward. The Sled dipped, wavering from side to side, then shuddered off above the fields, banking gracelessly toward the open plain.

84

LIPHAR DID NOT INTEND to be left behind. He ran about tirelessly in the staggering heat, hauling supplies to the Sled, carrying messages back and forth between Susannah and Danforth in the cargo hold, Weng in her sickbed in the Underbelly and Megan in the Lander's storage bays above. He assigned himself a slot on one of the two padded benches at the forward end of the Sled. Climbing in to run a final provisions count, Stavros found the young Sawl half strapped in, struggling with the buckles, ready to go.

Stavros gazed down at him sternly, but Liphar returned a sly smile.

"You new 'prentice now, Ibi. You listen what I say, more big 'prentice than you."

"Lifa, I don't think . . ."

The young man folded his arms across his thin chest with stubborn dignity. "I teach you be Kav first, ah? Then I listen you again."

Stavros crouched in front of him, nonplussed. Could a young apprentice teach him what Kav Daven had failed to? "All right. So, what do you say to me now?"

"I say, I go with you, help talk this angry Sister."

Stavros dipped his head, frowning at the dust-streaked floor grating. Other than concern for Liphar's safety, he could think of no good reason to refuse.

An agile figure in white swung up through the cargo hatch and edged forward through the maze of equipment and supplies. Stavros glanced up, then rose in slow astonishment.

Weng's therm-suit fit the Master Healer as if made for him, as if he had worn it all his life. And he was clearly enjoying it. Stavros saw how he savored the close, slick feel of it against his body. He'd bunched his brown curls at the nape of his neck and abandoned his characteristic stoop. Weng's gold command bars glinted on the open collar. He looked like a slim, able spacer, fully at home in the Sled's seamless, plastic environment. Only his self-conscious smile gave him away.

"Ghirra, what the . . . ?"

The Master Healer accepted Stavros' surprise but not his reflex disapproval. He drew himself up even taller. "Suzhannah say wear this for best safety."

"Yeah, I suppose." Stavros shuddered to see a Sawl so at ease in Terran uniform, embracing the very image he'd insistently cast off. But for Ghirra, the sleek, white uniform symbolized the brave new universe out there beyond the dome of his own familiar sky, a universe he was increasingly curious about. Startled into self-doubt, Stavros fingered his own Sawlish clothing. Had it been a knee-jerk response? Was he resisting the intrusion of the modern world for the Sawls' future good or—as Clausen always implied—for romantic reasons of his own, to preserve a backwater kingdom where such as he could live and work in peace?

Relax. It's only clothing he's put on, not the entire value structure.

"Looks good on you," he offered lamely.

Ghirra's defensive stance eased, and his smile returned.

Stavros plucked at his tunic, limp with sweat. His bandages itched. The therm-suit would keep him cool and dry. It was absurd to resist. "I should suit up, too." To cover his discomfort, he cuffed Liphar lightly. "And you. Untangle yourself from those straps and go ask Susannah to issue you one of McPherson's. That'll be the smallest we have."

Liphar was out of the harness within seconds, disappearing through the cargo hatch with a grin as wide as his jaw.

E.D. 99–11:01

Aguidran refused to wear a therm-suit and was nearly as unwilling to buckle herself into the flight harness. Like a great dark bird, she half crouched, half perched on the edge of the bench behind Stavros, the webbed strap draped over one leather-clad shoulder, gripped but not fastened.

Stavros claimed the copilot's chair. He muttered intently into the com, pressing CRI for an update on Clausen's location. His white therm-suit was unzipped to his navel, as if in rakish refusal to submit to total uniformity, but actually to ease the fit around his bandaged shoulder. Fully secured behind Danforth, Ghirra lounged into the padded bench with anticipatory relish, watching carefully as the planetologist punched through his final engine check. Liphar pressed close to Susannah on the rear bench. Arms stiffened, his hands grasped the forward edge of his seat. He anxiously monitored the three Terrans' actions, making sure everything was proceeding as expected. Occasionally, he threw a guilty glance up at the white cliff. The black cave mouths and the hot bright ledges were crowded with faces, too distant to be recognized.

Susannah tried to summon a brisker sort of energy as she faced her second trek into the wilderness, but her drive was blunted by the crushing white heat. The merest movement was like swimming through glue. It was hard to keep from drifting into daydreams of rain showers and cool forest glades.

Dust stirred in the clearing as Megan retreated into the shadow of the cylinder. She hovered behind a stubbornly erect Weng, who took a further step into the sun as the Sled's fans hummed to life. Susannah waved, partly in salutation, partly to shoo Weng inside, away from the heat and roar and the whirling sand. Once the expedition was over, she admitted sadly, her medical report would have to recommend no further landing missions for the aging spacer. But she didn't think Weng would mind. She had many service years left in her, on FTL craft and orbiters, if she took care of herself.

Susannah leaned forward. "Did you remind Ampiar to check on the Commander every so often?"

Ghirra nodded without taking his eyes from Danforth's work at the controls.

"He's got a ten-hour, thirteen-hundred-kilometer start on us." Stavros raised his voice over the noise of the fans.

"But he's taking his time so far," Danforth replied. "Probably feeling his way and not expecting immediate pursuit."

"He didn't think we'd get her fixed so fast."

Danforth grinned. "Or come up with a pilot. Underestimated both the Commander and me . . . and it'll cost him. We'll pick up time if I push her hard, plus we may be able to cut some corners off his route."

"CRI says the type of charge he took is hand-activated, but she can pick up telemetry the moment he arms them."

"Good thing. Ready to roll?" Danforth raised an arm in warning, then touched a switch to lift the windscreen extensions. A meter-high shield of clear plastic rose out of the hull to either side of the passenger area. As the fan and engine noise increased, he activated the force shield. The surrounding glare of cliff and sky dulled to a cooler dancing shade, cut at eye level by the hot white slicing through the narrow arc of the windscreens. When he signaled again, thumb up, the Sled shivered and rose. Rocking on its cushion of air like a boat in chop, it rose again and surged forward clumsily. Aguidran snarled as she was thrown off balance into the padded curve of the bench. Liphar strained against his harness to huddle closer to Susannah.

Stavros glanced a question at Danforth, circling his hand in the air. Danforth returned a shrug and a dubious nod. The Sled wavered out over the blackened fields beyond the firebreaks, then banked sharply and circled back around the Lander to skim recklessly past the thronged cliffs in a parting salute. Ghirra's head was pressed into his backrest, but his eyes, on this maiden voyage, were eager.

Susannah wondered what it would be like to have never flown before, or to have never thought of flying?

Liphar answered her question by burying his head in her side with a trailing squeal as the Sled tilted into its sickening turn and the white cliff face filled the windscreens. On the crowded ledges, mouths gaped. Heads withdrew in fear and surprise.

"Yee-ha!" bellowed Danforth, as he veered the Sled back toward the plain.

Stavros turned in his seat with a wilding grin. "Everyone with us so far?"

Receiving no replies to the contrary, he nudged his laughing pilot and jerked his head southward.

E.D. 99–1:26

They flew due southwest for the first several hours. Danforth hugged the ground, needing to build his confidence at the stick. He followed the margin of the Dop Arek until the steep rise of the perimeter cliff was jumbled by successive rockslides and ravines. He regretted that his first good look at this planet's terrain was going to have to be essentially a flyby. Easing the Sled higher, he mounted the boulder-strewn slope to the dry plateau above. The rugged flatland was seamed by old watercourses like wrinkles on an aged face, later softening into the barren hills that footed the northernmost of the mountain ranges that made up what Ibiá called the Grigar, or Lagri's Wall.

Once away from the level ground of the Dop Arek, Danforth kept to the lowlands, grazing the wide sand-bottomed mountain valleys where russet tufts of shrubbery still clung to the shady side of the hills and canyons. Ghirra pointed out the dark cliff-side cave openings and dry terraced fields of scattered settlements, exclaiming at how quickly they now moved between them. Clumps of dust-colored succulents dotted the softer slopes. The sky's diffuse white glow was disorienting. It bleached out the shadows and flattened the geography until the landscape seemed caught in a flash of strobe light.

As the terrain roughened, signs of habitation vanished. Ibiá unbuckled and got up to stretch. The Sled hustled along smoothly in the calm air, occasionally rising like a gliding hawk in the thermals beside a particularly precipitous edge. Ghirra followed suit, but stood cautiously, steadying himself on the back of his bench. Aguidran threw off her flight harness and rose to join Ibiá in the cargo hold.

Danforth felt the vehicle waver with the shifting of weight. "Go easy on the moving around back there, okay?"

E.D. 99–3:17

Susannah watched Aguidran adapt to the unsettled footing as naturally as a sailor to a rolling deck and recalled the narrow, unstable creshin of Ogo Dul. This brother and sister had spent their early childhood on the water. No wonder they were faring so well. Liphar looked less happy, a little airsick. Susannah left her seat to retrieve her medikit.

Stavros was filling a canteen from the refrigerated water tank. She knelt beside him to refresh her own. Aguidran wandered uneasily among the lashed crates at the back of the hold, then accepted a long drink from Stavros' canteen and returned to her seat. Ghirra joined Susannah on the rear bench as she fed Liphar a pill to ease his stomach.

"To Ogo Dul, we go like this maybe for one cycle only!" he marveled with boyish excitement.

"Less," said Susannah. "I think you could fly from Dul Elesi to the ocean in an hour or two . . . ah, one thirty-part of a cycle."

Ghirra's face lengthened thoughtfully. "This make trade more easy, ah? Go more far with this Sled."

"You could visit settlements all over your world."

"But Sleds are no good in bad weather." Stavros leaned over to offer the canteen. "Remember what happened to Taylor."

As if to reinforce his point, the Sled veered suddenly over a broad canyon that sliced across the plateau. Caught in a thermal, it lifted sickeningly, soared, and then dropped. Susannah was made sharply aware of the boulders speeding by beneath the fans before the craft settled again into a comfortable forward motion. Danforth waved a mute apology without looking around. Liphar moaned weakly and clutched his stomach, but Ghirra watched Danforth's hand on the stick with a gently envious eye.

E.D. 99–5:00

The long rocky miles slid past without serious incident. They left the desert foothills and climbed into the mountains. The ravines deepened into breathless chasms choked with fallen rock. The crags towered more steeply. The valleys narrowed into canyons. The barrenness of the landscape caught like sand in Danforth's throat. His cautious low-altitude flight plan did not offer the comforting objectivity of a bird's eye view. The poignancy of a single cluster of brush wedged among the rocks, even the bare dead skeleton of a tree brought near tears to his eyes. He could not help but identify with any living thing left to shrivel away in such a wasteland, abandoned by the climate that had sired it in the first place. Desolation surrounded him, towered over him, caused him to stare at the sheer peaks of pale bright stone and the endless corrugated vistas of ridge and canyon and ridge as if they were singing a chorus to his human insignificance.

Danforth wondered if this new habit of introspection would prove permanent. Though it had its uses and even its satisfactions, it was not an altogether pleasant compulsion. It nagged at him, like doubt or a sore tooth, teasing at his belief in any sort of answers, or even in the possibility of there being such things. He recalled the precise and neutral wording of his project proposal abstract, the proper scientific tone of course, but rendered flaccid and inadequate by the bare realities of Fiix.

Probably it didn't do to be too introspective in a wasteland. Hope, always a frail commodity, had less chance than the dying vegetation of flourishing in such primal desolation. Danforth shook his head and took the Sled up higher, skimming just below the lowering white veil of clouds, concentrating on the comfortingly physical act of flying.

By the time he'd gained some confidence in his piloting, he was tiring fast. His eyes stung from staring into the white sky. On the benches, his passengers dozed.

"Damn, my butt aches," he muttered into the com.

"Surprised it took so long," came a quiet reply.

Danforth started. "Ibiá. Didn't know you were awake."

Ibiá leaned forward, rotating the stiffness out of his injured shoulder. "CRI, what's the word on our quarry?"

"Proceeding due south, Mr. Ibiá, at a mean distance of one thousand thirty-seven kilometers. Mr. Clausen and Lieutenant McPherson have exchanged seats."

"She shouldn't have gone with him," Stavros growled.

Danforth sighed darkly. "You think she had a choice?"

"The Lieutenant is piloting," said CRI. "Shall I connect you?"

"NO!"

"Mr. Clausen is aware of your pursuit, Dr. Danforth."

"Yeah? Wonder how that happened."

"He requests periodic reports, as you do," the computer returned stiffly.

Danforth glanced at his copilot. "Great. Not only has he got someone to spell him but he knows we're after him."

Ibiá shrugged. "There's never much chance of surprise with Emil."

"Shit, what do we have a chance of?"

The linguist offered a look opaque with mystery. "Knowing who to talk to once we get there."

"I take it you're not referring to the local population."

"Not exactly. The main problem will be getting Her attention."

Danforth fumbled for a noncombative response. "So you really buy this living goddess stuff?"

"Did you think otherwise?"

"Well, I figure fifty percent of what anyone says in public is for effect, politics and the like. I figure your agenda requires you to believe, or at least, seem to."

Ibiá sucked his cheek. "It might've been that at first. Not now."

"Even with the lithium angle? I mean, your Sawl power plant and all?"

"The lithium is key, certainly, but a guess at the energy source doesn't explain the very real implications of consciousness. But there are many definitions of consciousness. That's why I wanted Meg to put CRI through the First Contact procedures." Ibiá stared ahead into the white glare, then settled back with an air of decision. "Taylor, if you can manage to keep this thing in the air a little longer without cramping up, I'll tell you a story . . . no, two." He murmured into the com as if offering secrets. "Not to convince you—you can believe what you like—but to put you in possession of all the facts as I see them. And to warn you. Things may get a little . . . strange where we're going. I may get a little . . ."

He paused. His whisper in Danforth's ear was ironic and throaty, compelling in its intimate hush. "What do you say, Tay? Will you listen for a while to the ravings of a madman?"

Danforth's flesh tingled. What could be stranger than some of the stuff he'd seen already? "Sure . . . if it'll help keep me awake."

E.D. 99–6:14

As Stavros unfolded his story yet again, the guar-fire burned hot in the soft centers of his palms. He watched the white, desiccated landscape scud by and kept his voice matter-of-fact, a cool murmur over the com to woo Danforth's rationality with only the merest hint of miracle.

Does it even matter if he believes me?

It didn't. They'd be faced with the same truth, whatever it was, once they got there. Danforth's belief or nonbelief would be irrelevant. Stavros was sure the final outcome rested in his hands alone.

Mine and Lagri's.

Past personal history tempted him to keep trying to convince, so that the expedition's Chief Scientist might finally accept him as an equal. Old concerns still surfaced: traces of the ambitions that had brought him to Fiix, vestiges of his life before he'd discovered a very different destiny. But if he had Danforth's help, he could live without his approval.

Stavros doubted that CRI's First Contact broadcast would turn up a response. He'd ordered it in order to leave no stone unturned. He felt the pull southward, as strong and direct as a rope tied around his neck. He did not tell Danforth that he could have plotted the course to Nolagri without benefit of a compass. There was no way he could express this that would sound vaguely scientific.

When he'd finished his tale of voids and apprentices and his release from dying, Danforth was silent for a long stretch of difficult flying. He wound the Sled through a forest of wind-devoured spindles broken by sheer grades of rock. The grades sharpened into a wall of dry, rough-faced crags, the first summits of the Grigar. The white cloud veil pressed in from above, suffocatingly close. Danforth checked wind speeds and altitude, then banked west to find a pass that cut south sooner than Clausen's reported route.

"Might pick up some time," he commented neutrally into the com.

Stavros grunted.

"You'd think there'd be more wind at this height."

Stavros made another, less distinct sound of assent.

"Or snow at least."

"Not when Lagri has the upper hand."

It wasn't about past ambitions after all. It was about now. Stavros needed Danforth's vote of confidence for the same reason he needed Susannah's love: to balance the guar-fire's pull toward the irrational. He might joke about madness, but it no longer held any romance for him.

"Look, Stav . . ." Danforth used his Christian name for the first time in memory. "Just like you have to suspect me of ulterior motives—as a scientist, I have to reserve judgment on all this. But that doesn't mean I haven't been listening. You dig?"

"Yeah, I dig." Stavros savored the ancient colloquialism as Danforth gained altitude to slip the Sled over the top of a long, smooth ridge between two shattered peaks. He knew an offer of friendship when he heard one.

E.D. 99–10: 28

On the far side of the range, Danforth managed a jolted landing in a graveled wash on the floor of a wide yellow valley. He dropped the force field's protective dome and heat engulfed them, pressing them into their seats. Nobody moved.

"Should have found some shade," Danforth apologized.

"Where?" Susannah waved a heat-heavy arm at the unbroken waste sloping away to either side of them.

Their voices seemed overloud and brittle, discouraging chatter. The small clink of unbuckled seat harness rang through the hot silence like an off-tune carillon. Aguidran rose first, stretching elaborately, surveying the distance with eyes narrowed against the glare. Danforth hauled his legs out from beneath the control panel and tried to haul himself upright. His right leg gave as he shifted weight onto it, but Aguidran was there to steady him. Ghirra sprang up to hand him his crutches.

Danforth made light of his exhaustion, but when the cargo hatch had been opened, and they rested in the narrow shade of the Sled's delta wings, he asked Susannah what she might have in her medikit to keep him alert and functioning.

"Not as strong as I hoped," he grumbled.

"I can keep you going for a while, but what you really need is a relief pilot."

"You offering?" Stavros was annoyed by his one-armed uselessness.

"It doesn't look so hard," ventured Susannah lightly. "Long as you have two hands."

"Depends on the weather and the terrain," said Danforth. "Right now, windless as it is, thermals are the only issue. You ever flown before?"

"Small conventional craft, a few hours in the air. No takeoff or landing, though."

Danforth looked to Stavros. "It could be the edge we need."

Stavros frowned.

"I think you ought to try me out," Susannah urged gamely.

"Makes sense to me." Danforth lay back in the pebbled sand, folding one arm over his eyes and the other over the laser stuck into his belt. "Now just give me a few quick winks here, a couple of pills, and I'll be raring to go."

While Danforth slept, Susannah put together a cold meal from ship's rations.

"Not very appetizing, I'm afraid," she told Ghirra. But the three Sawls ate without complaint, long used to the idea that food must often be no more than necessary nourishment. Stavros chewed at a bar of dried fruit, shoveled the rest of his share onto Liphar's plate, and wandered off to sit alone behind the tail fin.

Ghirra brushed soy crumbs from his borrowed therm-suit and asked Susannah about its workings. He marveled that from the neck down, he could feel cool and dry in such deadly heat. He teased his sister for refusing to wear the suit they'd brought for her. Aguidran grunted and resumed her reflex study of the countryside. Ghirra fingered the smooth resilient fabric of his sleeve, then flicked a covert glance at Stavros behind the tail. He kept his voice low, almost a whisper.

"I think, sometime, Suzhannah, maybe it is better say yes, Clauzen, bring all this here to us. How do you say to this?"

Susannah had been expecting something like this. It was Ghirra's self-image to be unafraid of new ideas. Technology excited him and he understood enough to see its advantages. But he was hardly in possession of the whole picture.

"If therm-suits and Sleds and medicine were all he'd bring," she replied after some consideration, "then I'd welcome him gladly. If we could offer the lifesaving benefits of our tech without the accompanying dangers . . . but technology has a history of running away with itself, particularly in the hands of megacorporations like ConPlex. Imagine a guild that disregards all the other guilds' interests for the sake of its own enrichment and power. Then imagine a world full of them."

Ghirra spread his hands as if the outcome were obvious. "This guild will not survive. The Food Guild will not feed it. The Weaver Guild will give it no cloth."

"This guild provides for its needs by intimidation, both physical and economic."

Ghirra floundered. "In-tim . . . ?"

"You don't give me what I want, I'll shoot you." Danforth raised himself on one elbow, patting the gun nestled against his belly. "Oh, he tries to buy you first, but only because it's less trouble. He'll try to buy you, Doc, once he thinks he knows your price."

"Buy me?"

"Sure. Your talk of weather machines suggests you might be interested in a trade: your planet in exchange for whatever techy trinkets he has to offer. And, Doc, your brain working overtime like it is, you're vulnerable. Take it from one who knows."

"Clauzen tried this to you?"

Danforth laughed bitterly. "He fucking *owned* me, man. I guess he still does. Lock, stock, and barrel. He just let me think it was a mutually beneficial arrangement. Which is how he'll put it to you, Doc. It's called colonialism."

Aguidran lunged forward with a sharp cry of warning. Plates and food and water mugs went flying. She shoved Susannah aside with a sweep of her arm, whipped the long blade from her boot and flung it into the sand a scant meter past where Susannah had been sitting. Fine grit and gravel erupted as the knife struck home, its carved handle humming wildly. A six-legged lizard, two feet long from head to tail, thrashed to the surface, coiling back on itself, its needle fangs slashing furiously at the invading blade. Aguidran scrambled to her feet and pinned the creature's long neck under her heel, then jerked the knife free and cut off the head with a single clean slice.

Danforth exhaled loudly. "Is everything trying to kill us on this planet?"

"It looked for our water," Ghirra said, with something akin to sympathy.

"Okay. We take our breaks inside the Sled from now on."

Susannah began immediate negotiations with Aguidran for the dead reptile's remains. Stavros emerged from solitary contemplation to stare down at the bloodied sand.

Danforth gathered scattered cups and plate. "What're you up to back there, Ibiá?"

"Listening," Stavros replied abstractedly.

"Yeah? What do you hear?"

"So far, nothing."

Danforth showed off his newfound patience. "What do you expect to hear?" And then, unable to resist, he added, "We're not talking *voices* or anything, are we?"

Stavros regarded him earnestly. "I'm not sure. It's one of the million things I needed to know from the old man before he died. . . ."

E.D. 99–17:45

They continued south, winding from pass to pass, scaling the second range of the Grigar. Under Danforth's initially nervous eye, Susannah took the stick for an easy hour of low-altitude flying across a high barren plateau. He allowed her to negotiate a gentle slope or two, and when she proved equal to both the milder terrain and his impatient teaching, he talked her across a stretch of rugged canyon land before resuming the chair to push the Sled over the more perilous heights of the range.

On the far side, the mountains fell away into high, flat desert dotted with strange wind-shaped rocks reminiscent of a giant topiary garden. Danforth flew onward until Susannah's drug no longer vibrated in his veins. When his eyelids drooped so long that she leaned over from the copilot's seat to shake him, he set the Sled down on a ledge in the shade of a rising peak.

The passengers unbuckled slowly but made no move to venture outside. Susannah promised a cooked meal and hustled Liphar to the rear to set up the portable stove. Ibiá woke from his doze on the rear bench and came forward to talk to CRI.

"Anything on those sensor updates?"

"I am currently mapping anomalous magnetic field variations in an area centered approximately forty-five degrees off the southern pole. Remote sensing shows no indication so far of refined metal masses . . ."

"Just call them machines, old girl," drawled Danforth.

". . . but high-res imaging of the area is proceeding." CRI supplied coordinates for the magnetic field, still more than two days travel to the south.

Ibiá asked Clausen's position.

"We've gained another seventy-five kilometers on him," offered Danforth. "He's still not proceeding exactly as the crow flies. Probably doing a little prospecting along the way."

"Fine. Let him."

"Do you wish an update on the Contact procedures, Mr. Ibiá?"

"Oh. Yeah, sure."

Danforth chuckled. "You're drifting, Stav. Still listening for those voices?"

Ibiá's look dared him not to reject the idea entirely.

"There has been no indication of response to sixteen hours of continuous broadcast on the standard twenty-five frequencies," CRI reported.

"Both a binary and a decimal code?"

"That is the procedure."

Ibiá scowled. "She's humoring me." He paced away, hands fisting. "Up there in that goddamn Orbiter, all this is nothing but a string of data to them! I don't need humoring. I need help!"

"Easy, man . . ." Danforth twisted in his seat. The last thing they needed now was a temper tantrum.

"It's *language,* not just some damn procedure! Don't they see? It's always about language! How you find the right words, the right *kind* of words to bridge the gap between one consciousness and another!"

Danforth remembered this passionate anger, how it used to rile him. He'd wanted no rival then to his own intensity. "But consciousness is the thing in question, Stav. It's sure what pulls me up short each time." At the sudden flare in Ibiá's eyes, he added, "Plus the guys in the Orbiter haven't seen what we've seen, and CRI has enough trouble of her own being considered a consciousness. Meanwhile, what do you care what they think? CRI's doing what you asked—it's just part of her own little campaign for recognition that she questions your judgment."

Ibiá slowed his pacing and returned to slump into his seat. He dragged both palms down across his face with a sigh. "Okay. Then maybe we should try something that *isn't* the procedure."

CRI waited, a mere hiss of disapproving static.

Ibiá turned to Danforth. "Any ideas?"

Danforth tried out actual commitment to the inquiry. What the hell? "Not my field, really. The machines I talk to already know I'm here. What do you use beside numerical code?"

"Math, geometry, pictures, patterns in the color and duration of light pulses." Ibiá let his head fall back, eyes lidded. "Patterns of sound, um . . ."

To Danforth's surprise, an idea surfaced. "Ever try music?"

"Sometimes. Usually a long shot."

"Why not send them some of Weng's?"

He sensed Ibiá running this past the mockery test. But he liked his long shot more and more. There was a wild mathematical elegance about it. "Stav, give it a chance. Despite all her protests to the contrary, Weng's game theory analysis could be the most concrete evidence you have for consciousness so far. The whole concept of a game implies intention to me, I don't care what the mathematicians say, and intention implies consciousness. Weng's music is constructed around the same set of algorithms."

Ibiá buried his chin in his chest with a faint, pensive glower.

Danforth hazarded blunt honesty. "Look, you were always throwing the superiority of insight and instinct in my face like so much wet shit—you didn't think I had the intellectual balls for it. A straight numbers man all the way, right?"

"Taylor, I never . . ."

"Sure you did. Forget it. But we all got to fly a hunch every now and then, so grant me this one, okay? My personal gesture to the irrational. Don't reject it just 'cause it ain't yours. Besides, it's not entirely irrational."

Ibiá chewed his lip for a moment, then leaned forward. "You get all that, CRI?"

"Yes, Mr. Ibiá."

"Then I suggest you give it a try." He rose tiredly, grasping Danforth's shoulder for support against the pain in his own, but his hand lingered briefly as he gained his feet. "Get some sleep, Tay. We'll keep the food warm for you."

E.D. 99–23:00

Danforth was dreaming of machines made of cloud and ice when Susannah shook him awake. Her eyes were wide.

Not fear, he thought, but something close to it.

"I think you might want a look at this, Tay."

He glanced around the cockpit, slit-eyed against the brightness, but Susannah was pointing straight up. He studied the sky without comment until she demanded impatiently, "What is it?"

Danforth shook his head slowly. The flat, unyielding white was quivering like a curtain in a wind. Waves of cooler white or dirty gray chased each other from horizon to horizon. He was reminded of the ripples of shadow that race across the ground prior to a solar eclipse, but he'd never seen anything like it in the sky.

"What would you call that, Tay?" Ibiá came up from the rear of the hold, trailing Ghirra and Liphar. The young apprentice priest wore a doom-struck, knowing look and would not stray a half step from Ibiá's side.

"I, ah . . . I'd guess some sort of instability along the interface between the dry heat down here and the cooler, moister air above that's creating the cloud." He noted the direction of movement: north-northeast.

The ripples broadened, like an ocean flowing slowly northward. The hot white landscape throbbed beneath the undulating sky.

"Valla's death throes, Lifa says." Ibiá was struggling for some measure of calm. "Apparently it's due to get fairly spectacular when Lagri calls in the heavy artillery . . . fire falling from the sky, the like . . . Devastation."

"I remember," said Danforth. "He sang us the song—about the little children. But I don't think it's . . ."

"Lifa says it's right on schedule."

A wave of color surged past, a shell-pink gust across the pale surface of the sky. The long ends of Susannah's hair lifted freely away from her body and crackled with tiny blue fire when she swept them back to bundle into a tight coil.

Danforth saw terror bloom behind Ibiá's steady gaze, but because it was not fear of anything he was yet willing to accept or understand, he could not imagine how to ease it. He looked at the pulsing sky and shrugged. "Best we be moving along, then. . . ."

85

E.D. 100–1:14

MEGAN STOPPED ALONG THE PATH to rest, pulling her broad-brimmed ranger hat low over her eyes. This would have to be her last trip to the Caves until nightfall brought some relief from the crushing heat. She sat on the earthwork edging a terrace, where the mud and stone had dried as hard as fired ceramic. Dust clung to the legs of her therm-suit and to her hands as she tried to brush it away.

In the fields, nothing stirred. Not a hint of breeze to rattle the dry stalks. The Sawls had salvaged what they could of their meager harvest. The rest had been left to shrivel as the irrigation pipes ran dry. After the departure of the Sleds, the population withdrew completely into the Caves. Only Ampiar ventured out into the white heat, dutifully, until Weng assured her that it was unnecessary.

When the heat of sitting became less bearable than the heat of moving, Megan roused herself, feeling helpless and depressed. The Lander glimmered like a white mirage, a mocking image of technological impotence. Despite all our scientific progress, she mourned, there are still forces more powerful.

Clausen won't have to lift a finger. Nature herself is delivering the planet right into his hands.

The hard bright path wavered in front of her. Megan halted, blinking at nonexistent tears. Her eyes were dry but her vision oddly blurring. She swayed dizzily, convinced she was about to faint. When she did not, and the light continued to fluctuate, she peered out from under her hat brim, then cautiously up at the sky. She watched amazed as long as her eyes could bear the dancing glare, then hurried on through the heat to tell Weng.

Crossing the deserted clearing, she heard strange sounds echoing through the cylinder. In the deep cool of the inside, she found Weng in a folding recliner, her feet up, her head thrown back in an uncharacteristic position of repose. The sounds reverberated from the computer terminal, and though she'd never heard Weng's music before, Megan knew she was hearing it now.

Her first impression was of the monumental scale of the composer's intentions. The mini-terminal's tiny speaker could not possibly be doing justice to either tone or volume. Reluctant to disturb Weng, even with news of the rippling sky, she sat down to cool off and listen. Initially, she heard only confusion, vast randomness, long squeaks chittering against sharp burps of percussion, loosely bound by an underscoring hum.

But as she relaxed into concentration, vague patterns of rhythm suggested themselves. Hints of melody sparkled in bell-pure sequences like wind-driven rain on the surface of a lake. The rhythm strummed deeply. There was a bass drone almost below the range of hearing that pulled her into the spaces between the notes, as if time slowed and left her suspended, her breath imprisoned within her ribs, awaiting the next stroke of sound to release it. And the space that she lingered in was infinite, black, utterly still. Megan closed her eyes, thrilled and impressed.

It's huge! Like being sucked into a void. This is spacer music, all right.

But there was something edgy as well. Something that prevented true relaxation. Something stubborn, striving, contentious in the unrelenting percussion and the relationship of melodic themes.

So unlike Weng, Megan mused, and then, reconsidering, decided not. You didn't win a command and keep it without being competitive. Competition, after all, could be variously expressed—as well as repressed. Like, into impulses such as using game theory as a basis for musical composition.

Pondering this, her perception of the tonal and rhythmic patterning shifted. She heard the music as a concrete expression of a mathematical abstraction, a bridge between two realms. She sensed the pure logic of numbers as it both constrained and freed the music, forming it to suit a human ear, yet setting it beyond emotion of any sort.

Beyond intention?

Strains as distinct and compelling as overheard whispers emerged out of the randomness, in many possible voices that resolved at last into two. Not melodies, exactly. Not even themes. Two sensibilities, rather, chasing each other through the fluid medium of surrounding sound, lunging, shoving, twining around one another like fish fighting in deep water.

Megan assumed the vibrato rumbling that shook her chair to be part of the composition. She recognized the push and pull of the Game, not just Weng's theoretical one, but the mythic one as well. Perhaps if she listened long enough, the music would reveal the rules to her.

Suddenly, Weng started up from her near-trance in the recliner and slapped the switch to cut off the audio. And the rumbling continued, not loud but disturbingly deep, as if the very earth were groaning in pain. Megan swung her feet to the floor and felt the vibrations translate upward to her knees.

"Earthquake?"

"Mr. Clausen did not expect noticeable seismic activity in this old a planet." Weng's hands wobbled in tandem with the arms of her chair. The tremor crested in a broken growl like the clatter of falling rocks, then tapered off and died into silence. She touched the keypad. "CRI?"

"I am reading some sort of local disturbance, Commander, rather close to the surface. I am checking further."

Megan went to the cylinder mouth. A few dark forms had appeared on the cliff face. She could see arms raised in the direction of the plain. "I'm going out to take a look."

From the highest point of the clearing, the full expanse of plain was visible over the crumbled stalks. Megan gaped at what she saw. A vast ragged hole had swallowed several tens of acres of burned fields and the uncultivated land beyond. A haze of dust drifted lazily away from the crater, captured by the slow dance of rising heat.

"Sinkhole," said Weng beside her. "The aquifers are drying out underneath the plain."

"You mean, it just collapsed?"

Weng nodded. "The water left a vacuum to be filled."

"My god, Weng, that could happen under the Lander!" As Megan stared at the hole, a protruding chunk of dry earth gave way and crumbled into the abyss. She had a sudden image of the planet devouring itself in a mad heat of rage. "Maybe your abort idea isn't so ridiculous after all."

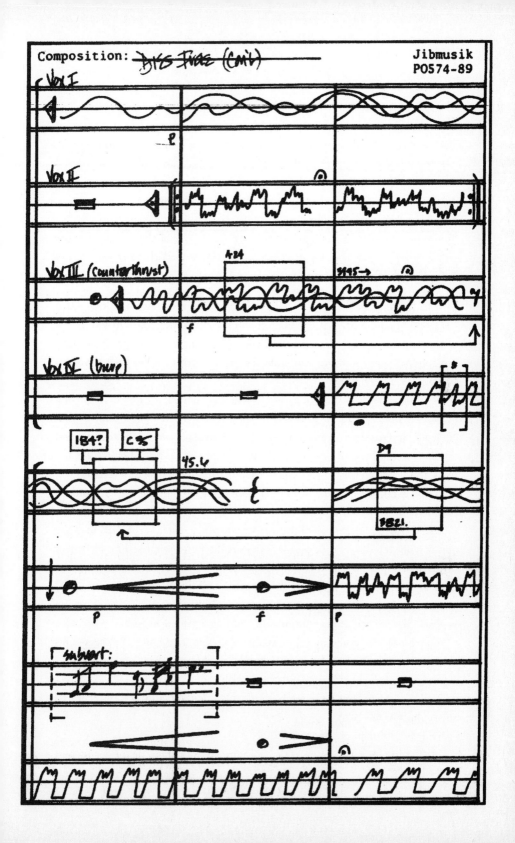

86

THE EXHILARATION OF DEPARTURE and the chase had long since faded behind a haze of exhaustion and noise and the constant vibrations of the engines. Stavros routed the cycling broadcast of Weng's music into the copilot's com, shut out all external considerations and lay back to listen, praying for a revelation.

Susannah gripped the stick, her lower lip sucked in, her eyes flitting nervously between the instrument readouts and the terrain ahead. Liphar curled at Stavros' feet, crammed into the narrow space between the seat and the exposed ribbing of the hull. Danforth slept on the floor behind, his big body too long for the bench. Ghirra claimed the bench seat, stretched out on his back but wide awake, watching Susannah's hand on the stick. Aguidran paced in the rear of the hold.

The third and final range of the Grigar was still a distant crenellation at the end of a blasted desert moonscape, dunes rolling into wind-scoured hardpan dotted with spherical boulders. Stavros was glad for the easy flying over the endless sand. It allowed Danforth a much-needed rest, and himself a quiet time to pursue concentration, a state increasingly elusive as his goal, which was also the source of his compulsion and terror, drew nearer.

The music, if it could be called such, also frightened him. It expressed his dying slide into the void far better than he could have done in words.

So close, as if she'd been right there with me.

Had Weng, without knowing it, made a connection similar to his? Should she be here in his place?

Did the old man choose wrong?

Raellil. It was a word, not a magic charm. He would puzzle out its deepest meaning. He set his internal search engine to root out all possible alternatives. It was what he was trained to do. It was what he was good at.

The guar-fire was a growing agony in his palms, the symbol of his connection to the mystery but a further barrier to concentration. It heightened his awareness of other distractions, the relentless rush of the fans, or the wind sighing along the force shield, or the constant questioning eyes of his companions, waiting for him to say, do or be something decisive and comprehensible.

His body sang with energy, but it was not his own. He felt it as a surge from outside, forcing its passage through him as if he was plugged in, light searing through an optical fiber but bringing no message, only raw nerve endings, fired synapses, pain.

Stavros sank into the music for escape. Idly, he tried to match the pulsing of the sky to the snarling rhythm of the bass drone. The sky had discovered color again, a subtle range of glowing pinks and blues and lavender, pale electric hues. In the music, there was no color, only the darkness of the void. Stavros remembered that darkness all too well. It flowed into him with the music and fanned the fire in his palms into a hungry blaze. Yet he knew that blaze, and there was comfort in its familiarity. He gave in to the push and pull of the rhythm, let himself drift in the music as he had in the dark river of his dying.

A touch on his knee pulled him back. Susannah, glancing away from the instruments and the speeding vista of sand dunes, frowning with concern, pointing emphatically at her ear. He became aware of a tinny nagging voice, repeating his name. The guar-fire eased as he shook off the music's spell.

"Yes, CRI?" he mumbled, trying to sound alert.

"Dr. James refused to wake Dr. Danforth," the computer began in peevish apology.

"By Dr. Danforth's request, and mine. What've you got?"

"Nothing to raise interest normally, but under the circumstances . . ."

Stavros had never heard CRI pause with such human hesitation, in the middle of a thought. "Yes?"

"A slight correlation, Mr. Ibiá. Or rather a brief moment of complete correlation."

His shiver was involuntary. "What are you talking about?"

"The Commander's music. And the patterns of atmospheric energy flux. A moment ago, their separate graphs matched completely, a very complicated rhythm, for exactly forty-one seconds."

"What happened?"

"Based on current data, I cannot offer an explanation . . ."

"I mean, when did it cut off? This correlation."

"Just now, as you answered my call."

Stavros squeezed his eyes shut against the chill rush of vertigo.

Raellil.

With each search, the meaning refined itself further: apprentice . . . messenger . . . What if the message was inside him, like the music?

Was *the music?*

Messenger. Conductor. Or . . . more like a circuit?

He thought he understood, at least partly, and his terror flared.

She'll burn me to a goddamn crisp.

"Thank you, CRI," he managed. "Tell me if it happens again."

It would not happen again, not until he let it. He understood that as well, and wondered where he would find the courage.

He'd thought himself the chosen victim of forces from without. Not as a collaborator, whose willingness was essential to making the connection.

But he *had* been willing, from the very beginning. Willing to give over his self for the sake of understanding, willing to adopt a Sawl mind-set to better his translations, willing to surrender to Kav Daven's call to mysticism.

Was that what the old man had seen in him? Not some special strength or power at all, but merely willingness?

Stavros waited for disappointment but found instead relief and excitement. Occam's razor. The explanation was so simple, it had to be right. But surely there were Sawls who were willing, willing enough to carry the guar uncomplaining in their hands.

Then his must be a willingness for something else. What? What? *What?*

He pictured the old man lost in the spiraling fury of his dance. He tore off the com set and struggled up, stiff and aching. Brusquely, he shook Liphar awake.

The young Sawl crawled blinking from his burrow beside the hull and stood shifting his weight and swinging his arms in response to this unexplained summons. Stavros woke Ghirra, and astonished and delighted him by ushering him into the copilot's chair and placing the com in his ear with a quick explanation of its use. Then he wrapped his good arm around Liphar's back and urged him toward the rear of the hold. Agui-dran paced irritably away, back to the front and her brother's company. Stavros settled cross-legged on the grated floor, a crate hard against his back. With a certain unconscious formality, he motioned Liphar to sit opposite him.

"Lifa, you said you could teach me about being a priest."

Liphar did not respond with the same bravado that had inspired his bid to win a seat on the Sled. His fingers twined nervously.

"There are a few things I need to know right now."

Liphar waited solemnly, willing but unsure.

"What is it like when you contemplate the Flame?"

The little Sawl smiled with relief, expecting a sterner interrogation. "This is a joining, Ibi. Very peace, and dark, like in water."

"Water?" Stavros' mouth had gone instantly dry. "Like swimming, in a river?"

Liphar nodded. "Okay, yes."

"Do you hear anything there?"

Liphar hunched his shoulders, conspiratorial. "You see, Ibi? You know this already."

"No. Tell me."

"I listen this singing of the world and the Sisters."

Stavros shut his eyes again. "Lifa, what did Kav Daven *really* mean when he told me to dance?"

Liphar's lips twitched into a sly grin, as if preferring to think he was joking.

"I mean, how does a priest learn to dance? Who teaches this? Who taught you the dances to celebrate the Planting, or the Birth dances?"

"I learn this in the guild."

"From your journeymen? From the master priests?"

"Anyone teach this, Ibi." Liphar's grin wavered.

"Anyone? Can you teach me?"

The apprentice priest looked mildly shocked. "Ibi, this dances is not same dances." He frowned as if suspecting Stavros of toying with a serious matter. "I teach to you about the signs and the First Books, yes. I teach all the chant and the story. But my dances is not to you."

Stavros felt wrapped tight in a circular reasoning. "But he never . . . Kav Daven died before he could teach me his." He pressed his fist against his teeth. Lured me to his purpose and deserted me. "Why didn't he choose an apprentice earlier?"

Liphar spread his hands. "He find no one to know the right dances."

"To know? No one who *knew* the dances?"

"He do not teach this dances, Ibi." Liphar gestured to the pit of his stomach. "This is here, like the child not born, in the one he call *raellil*." His expression mixed admiration with compassion for those whose gifts rule them instead of the other way around. "You know this, Ibi," he chided. "If you not know this, Kav Daven no say, this is my *raellil*."

"Lifa, if I know it, I don't know I know it."

Liphar offered in return the unflinching gaze of the faithful.

Stavros backed his spine against the crate. The lashing cords nudged the tender skin below his shoulder blade, pushed at the pad of bandages higher up. He was abruptly tired of mystery. Like wandering lost in a jungle, he might eventually get where he was going, but the many false starts and wrong turns were maddeningly inefficient, and might not leave much of him intact. Unlike Clausen, who was so sure of where he was going and of what to do when he got there that he wasn't even in much of a hurry.

Willingness was not enough. Willingness to wander in the jungle—or in his case, the void—did not tell you the right path to take.

The vibrations of the Sled sang through his palms, flattened against the plastic floor grate. Stavros reconsidered that place he called the void: the dark windswept plane that the Sisters' consciousnesses inhabited. Though he'd sunk deep within himself to enter it, it existed elsewhere, outside, he was sure. Not some trance state, not some waking dream. A place. But where?

Did the priests go there when they meditated?

The old priest's dying order confounded him. He was a locked door. The Kav had carried the key in his withered brown hands, opening him at will. But, dying, had taken the key with him. It was give up or find a new key.

Stavros contemplated the surprise and irony of Weng's music.

Shall Terran music lead my Sawlish dance?

He jumped up, startling Liphar out of a heat-doze. He paced forward, edged past Aguidran watching with disapproval as her brother tried to involve CRI in conversation over the com, and crouched between the two forward seats. His stomach knotted in anticipation, fear of what he was about to attempt. He considered shaking Danforth awake to discuss the correlation of weather and music, but the slack exhaustion in the planetologist's sleeping face stayed his hand. Instead, he leaned over to brush a quick kiss across Susannah's cheek. The soft warmth of her skin reassured him. She smiled but did not look away from the windscreen.

Stavros touched Ghirra's shoulder, requesting the com. Ghirra removed it regretfully, vacating the chair. Stavros slid into the seat and hooked the unit around his ear, trying not to feel imprisoned by it. "CRI, patch me through to Weng."

"The Commander is currently in her sleep period, Mr. Ibiá."

"Okay, then: what's her most recent composition? Can you play it for me?"

CRI paused like a secretary over an open file drawer. "There are a number of unfinished works in storage, some studies, many notes."

"Her newest completed work."

"That would be the piece she finished last month during the flood, while I was out of contact. She said the wild weather inspired her. She called it *Dies Irae*. That means . . ."

"I know what it means." Stavros repressed a shudder.

"Archaic perhaps," CRI chattered on, "but thematically appropriate under the circumstances, wouldn't you agree?"

Something in the computer's tone rang familiar. "That's what Emil said about it?"

"Yes. How did you know?"

"Never mind. Play it for me. And beam it simultaneously to Nolagri."

"Ready, Mr. Ibiá."

The violence of its beginning astonished him, laid him flat against the back of his seat like a blow to the jaw, a cathedral door flung open by an explosion of wind and rain. The sound hissed and spat, music only by the broadest definition, vast enough in scale to encompass the chaos of galaxies. It yowled like a blizzard, raked his brain and eardrums with razored claws. Stavros recoiled, already sensing its dangers. He circled around it, listening from a mental distance in a last gesture of self-preservation.

"Lifa!" Instinct prompted the call.

Liphar wriggled in next to him, reclaiming the narrow slot between seat and hull. The young Sawl pressed against his side without need of explanation and laid a hand across his wrist where it rested limp along his thigh.

The knot of fear in Stavros' stomach dropped like a stone into the well of his spine as an image of Kav Daven flashed to mind, the old man sitting so still among the leaping flames of the Story Hall, the tawny girl's hand resting on his knee, so lightly, so like the feather touch of Liphar's fingers on his wrist. But it was too late to resist. He was *willing*. He offered himself to the music just as he had given in to his panic and fantasies, and it drew him inward. The sound burned into his ears. His teeth buzzed with its ravening drone. But the light pressure of Liphar's hand anchored his awareness, a faint but steady beacon pointing the direction home, as the roar of the waters rose around him.

The dark river was a torrent, a flood of raw aggression. Stavros tumbled in the current, coughing up bile sucked like water into drowning lungs. Pain folded his chest in a vise. But he had been here before. It was his mind that was drowning, while his body remained under Liphar's guard. Scant comfort, but enough. He let go the reflex of breath, gave himself once more to the darkness, and sank.

Willing . . .

He sank through the black water, his lungs filling, expanding, himself expanding, heavy with water, heavier than the current. Sank into the shock of enveloping mud, cold as death, and still. The still, cold mud wrapped the current with arms as wide as a river of stars.

His arms, embracing the void.

Power traced his veins with fire. He raised vast arms of mud to cradle the torrent. But still the meaning eluded him.

Raellil

Circuit.

Carrier?

E.D. 100–3:19

Susannah signaled Ghirra to wake Danforth when the pulsating sky began to spit showers of static spark. Stavros was immobile in the next chair, Liphar curled close beside him.

Asleep, she presumed. She was preoccupied with keeping the Sled in the air.

The Sled bucked and dropped. The fan whine deepened briefly. The aft engines stuttered. Over the cockpit com, CRI reported a momentary disruption in the power beam.

"No way! Not now!" Danforth struggled groggily into the pilot's chair, dragging his rigid leg behind him. "We've got another whole mountain range to get over. What's Clausen's position?"

Susannah helped him strap in, then crouched at his shoulder, kneading cramp from her forearm. She'd been gripping the stick as if their lives depended on the strength of her hands alone. The cloud ripples blinked electric blue sparkles far to the east where the sky was faintly darkening.

"Nearing forty degrees," CRI replied. "Slowing. He has asked me to plot gravitometric measurements and complete detailed mapping of a discrete magnetic field detected at forty-seven degrees."

"He'll be looking for its center of symmetry," remarked Danforth, "where the source is most likely located."

"So he's looking for more than his lithium?" Susannah asked.

"Oh, yes. That disruption will have him worried, though." He patted the plastic encasing his thigh. "That's what happened to us last time we went for a spin. He was doing okay against the winds . . . until the power cut out."

"Maybe he'll stay closer to the ground. That'll slow him down a bit."

Beyond the windscreen, the final range rose without the polite preliminary of foothills, as if a giant fist had sheared the forward half away with a cleaver the size of a small planet. The white cloud veil seemed balanced on the very tip of the peaks.

"Distance, CRI?"

"Eight hundred and eighty-seven kilometers."

Danforth flashed Susannah a wan smile of approval. "Kept right up, didn't you, girl? He's only three, four hours ahead now." He glanced at the copilot's chair. "How long's Ibiá been out?"

"Don't know. Not long. Should I wake him?"

Something in Stavros' slump made her look more closely, something in his loose-curled upturned palms. His bowed head and his long eyelashes had camouflaged a half-lidded stare. His eyes looked somewhere far beyond the silvered metal of his belt buckle. But as Susannah reached to shake him, Liphar's hand shot out to catch her wrist.

"No!" he hissed.

"Why? What's the matter? What's happened to him?"

The Sled dropped again sickeningly as a shell-burst of tiny fire lit the white cloud ceiling above. The force field flickered, the fans coughed and whined back up to speed.

"Shit," Danforth muttered at the approaching blank wall of mountain. "What now?"

"Ghirra?" called Susannah shakily. Liphar, raised up on his haunches like a cobra over Stavros' knees, still gripped her arm without apology. The weirdness of it fueled her panic. "Ghirra!"

The Sled shuddered. Light broke around them like a wave cresting into sunlit foam. The white landscape pulsed rainbows of color. Instant black shadows bloomed like inky smoke behind boulders, inside crevices, then faded as instantly.

Ghirra forsook the safety of his seat and struggled forward to crouch unsteadily beside Susannah. His jaw was tight from resisting fear. He took in the frozen tableau: Liphar the hovering acolyte, Susannah uncomprehending, Stavros in the grip of his mystery, lit by prismatic flashes from a sky gone mad. He rasped a question at Liphar.

The younger Sawl answered with fervent conviction, his determination temporarily overriding his fear of the seesawing Sled and his awe of the Master Healer's authority.

Ghirra hesitated.

"What *is* it?" Susannah demanded.

The healer's voice was flat with ambivalence. "He says Stavros Ibiá looks for his dance."

"His *what*?"

His reply was lost in his own intake of breath as the Sled swayed side to side with the casual floating violence of a leaf in a hurricane. The polished vertical face of the mountain loomed like a speeding nightmare.

"Get everyone strapped in!" Danforth bellowed. "We're going over!"

The Sled tilted wildly as he rammed the stick forward. Ghirra clung to the back of Danforth's seat, his nails scrabbling against the hard plastic as he fought to keep from sliding down the sloping deck. He searched desperately for Aguidran. Liphar cringed back against the gray hull in terror, wedging himself between the ribs. Freed from his grasp, Susannah forgot Stavros for a breathless moment.

"Tay, what can I do? Is there anything I can do?"

Danforth was snarling at CRI over the com. "Just hold tight," he roared between clenched teeth. "Damn boat is like a wild animal all of a sudden!"

Aguidran battled her way uphill from the rear of the hold, and tumbled into the bench behind her brother. She wrapped a loose strap across her chest, then hauled Ghirra back against the padding beside her, shoving his own harness into his hands.

The Sled banked crazily as Danforth swerved to clear the rock face. It cut sharp right and rose, fans and engines screaming, struggling for enough altitude to clear the unfathomable cliff. The sky glowed pink, then salmon, then gold.

"We lose power now, we ain't got a prayer!" Danforth swore louder than he'd intended. "These piss-poor emergency batteries hold enough for about thirty seconds at this weight!"

"Thanks, I really needed to know that!" Susannah yelled back.

The bright sheer rock fell past the windscreens meter by meter as they rose, ripple-scorched with color. Danforth searched for a break, a pass, even a ledge with space enough to allow him to land and sit out the sky's latest inventive malice. Nothing. He circled out, away from the cliffs rough-edged proximity, and headed west, still rising along the faceless wall. The white clouds loomed above, too close. From two thousand dizzy meters below, the rocky desert plateau stared back at him unrelentingly.

"Motherfucker's not built for this!" muttered Danforth. "Come ON!" His whole body jerked and swayed as if to amplify the frustratingly slight motions of the stick.

Susannah leaned hard against his seatback and prayed.

Suddenly the sky exploded. Danforth bellowed a useless warning. Atop the mountain wall, the white clouds tore and gaped open.

The glowing rent belched fire. Flaming spheres fell like a torrent of giant hailstones, consuming themselves in trailing smoke before they hit the distant ground. The gash closed over as another appeared directly above the Sled. Danforth fought an onslaught of turbulence, yelling directions to himself like curses. Saint Elmo's fire danced across the delta wings. Bright tongues sparked against the force field.

Stavros' cry rang out over the straining roar of the engines as the Sled sank in a downdraft. Distracted by her own battle with panic, Susannah heard the cry as a summons, and lurched to his aid.

His eyes were open but unseeing. His fingers twitched, curling and uncurling around his upturned palms. His lips worked convulsively, murmuring, spilling forth the ghost of a chant. Susannah cringed away, revolted, as her mind overlaid on her lover's youthful beauty the remembered image of a muttering, desiccated priest. In his cramped burrow against the hull, Liphar gathered his legs beneath him, watching Stavros intently. A devout, hopeful joy softened the fear twisting his narrow face.

The sky exploded again. The Sled veered, slicing past the mountain face. Fire cascaded around the windscreens and careened off the force field. The cockpit glowed orange. The muscles of Danforth's neck bunched against the strain as he struggled to guide the bucking craft away from the rock. His eyes stared with concentration. Susannah held her scream like a needle of ice in the back of her throat, physical enough to choke on.

Stavros cried out again, but this time it was a yowl of terror. His back arched. His hands flew up to shield his face. He fought the restraints of the flight harness as if desperate to escape.

Liphar sprang instantly from his crouch, his terror of the flight submerged in a greater panic. He screamed for Ghirra, straddling Stavros' thighs, throwing all his slight weight against Stavros' arms to press him back against the padding. The Master Healer whipped off his half-fastened straps and balancing against the Sled's lurch and rock, he swayed forward like a sailor in a gale and flattened himself against the back of the seat. He unhooked the com from Stavros' ear, then pinned the resisting head between strong hands, his long fingers curling around Stavros' jaw. Stavros' struggling eased. Ghirra's fingers slid up to work at his temples.

The Sled leaped abruptly as if catapulted. It coasted upward to sail high and wide over a break in the sheer mountain wall. Danforth cheered incredulously.

A sharp cut lay before them, the snowless summits crowding to either side like stained, misshapen teeth. Danforth eased off the throttle and slipped the still-swaying craft into the narrow pass. Sparks ran off the wings like rainwater and vanished. The sky closed over, whiter and hotter than before. The Sled steadied and flew straight.

Ghirra relaxed his hold on Stavros' skull and slumped against the back of the seat. Stavros' eyes sagged closed, then opened listlessly. He did not move. Liphar slid back into his crouch against the hull. His fingers fluttered around Stavros' knee, suddenly unsure.

Susannah leaned in. "Stav? Are you all right?"

He groaned, curling inward, resting his head against his knees.

"Stav, answer me."

"I'm . . . okay." Without looking up, he reached to still Liphar's anxious hands. "I'm sorry, Lifa. I couldn't do it."

Liphar shivered with negation. "Give good strength, you, to Valla, so she push back her Sister's fire soldier this time." He gestured at the sky's solid lowering white.

"I did nothing."

"This is not learn one time, Ibi."

"You don't understand." Stavros shook his head slowly, as if its weight were an unbearable burden. "I couldn't face them. I was scared shitless. Kav Daven was wrong. I am not the one he hoped I was."

He didn't speak again or move until Danforth had cleared the heights of the Grigar and set the Sled down on a descending plateau in the southern slope.

E.D. 100–5:37

"Quite a view." Danforth stumped to the edge of the drop, balancing on his crutches at Ibiá's side. At their feet, eroded pink rock fell away into a twisted landscape of deep ravines and flat-topped pink-and-white mesas that stretched as far as they could see, blurring into sooty gray on a distant curved horizon. "Not a bush, not a twig, not even a dried-up thorny old cactus. I've seen uninhabitable worlds friendlier than this."

Ibiá stared silently southward.

"Lot of water here once, though. All that channel erosion." Danforth nosed in the dust with the toes of his cast-bound right leg. "Sky's starting to pulse again, you notice?"

Ibiá's eyes flicked across the glowing white and back to the horizon without comment.

Danforth uncovered a stone with his toes and pushed it around with awkward stiff-legged little kicks. "CRI was just babbling about some ninety-second phase correlation with Weng's music being twice as long as the one before. What one before?"

Ibiá swayed slightly, moving away.

Danforth grabbed his arm and jerked him back. "Hey, if you're gonna crap out on me, I gotta know it. Fast. What's going on?"

Unresisting in his grasp, the linguist turned dead eyes on him. "Crap out on *you*? I just crapped out on the whole goddamn thing."

Bitter was a tone Danforth understood. He let the limp arm go. "Stav. I need you to explain."

656   Marjorie B. Kellogg

"Weng's music. A great bit of insight, Tay, but dangerous, as it turned out. I mean, they *heard* it, like it was familiar, or even exciting. They listened. Absorbed it. Played with it like a toy. Incorporated its violence right into the Arrah until the weather was expressing it, instead of the other way around." Ibiá's attempt at a smile did not wipe the horror from his eyes. "They made Weng's game music a part of the Game."

"They."

"Lagri, mostly. This being her turf."

Danforth ran his tongue around the inside of his cheek, kicked his stone toward the edge and saved it from death at the last minute. He thought of the violent bucking of the Sled, just as suddenly stilled. He thought of his X-factor. "Hunh."

"Your instinct was right—the music is a language they recognize. The sound of chaos. It caught their attention. Trouble is, it's too much like them. Their struggle inspired it in the first place."

"You're saying Weng's music made fire rain from the sky? Like some kind of signal to the machine?"

"More like a resonance." Ibiá turned back to the smooth southern horizon, held out a palm and curled it slowly into a fist. "I could feel her, fire-eyed Lagri, like it was myself, feel her joining with the music as it flowed through me, out of me, to her, She making it hers, warping it to her single obsession, the Game, the game, the one becoming the other, as seamless as an interface." He dropped his hand. "And I was a flood-tossed mote, the infinitesimal messenger, she no more aware of me than of that rock. Or of the millions of Sawls who have been murdered by her blind passion to annihilate her Sister.

"So I thought, if I manipulate the music, if I play games with a signal she's already internalized, wouldn't she notice?" Ibiá paused, swallowed hard. "When I felt her vast gaze turning, that's where my courage failed . . . failed in the face of . . . ah, that old man! He had their fire boiling through him for decades! How did he survive it?"

Danforth had no answer for that. "Tell me, Ibiá. What would you do with their attention if you had it?"

The young man's laugh was like a sob. "That's the problem! It's sort of like sailing into the middle of an air war, broadcasting on all channels. Unless you know the right code, you're likely to get blown out of the sky. The old man didn't leave me his signals." He let go a long breath, then turned, regarding

Danforth quizzically. "This really is hard for you, isn't it? I can hear you being patient at the top of your voice."

Danforth smiled, liking him in earnest. "The madman's ravings?"

"Just so. You still think I'm imagining all this?"

"You got me, kid." He glanced down, rolling the stone under the ball of his foot. "There's *something* down there, though, at forty-seven degrees. CRI's just completed mapping a magnetic field two thousand kilometers in diameter, plopped right on a highland exactly opposite the middle of the northern ocean. Clausen's got her plotting a center of symmetry. He's asked for high-res as well, plus she's been able to link the pattern of gravitational variations with the peaks of weather activity." Danforth shrugged. "No, you're not imagining things. It's mostly our definitions that differ. Meanwhile, as Emil fumbles around down there with this test and that test, he's showing us where to go and we're gaining on him, slowly but surely."

"We don't need him to show us," said Ibiá quietly. "I can take us right there."

Danforth raised an eyebrow at his stone as if it had misbehaved.

"Tay, I swear. I don't know how, but it's true." He held up his palms in offering. "I'm keyed into that magnetic field. I'm . . . aligned. Like the little iron filings. I know exactly where my poles are. I can feel the pull." Ibiá raised his arm and pointed, slightly south of due southwest. "There."

Danforth shifted his crutches, and kicked his stone off the ledge. "Well, you'll be happy to know CRI agrees with you on that score. But if you're done with your magic tricks for the moment, can I convince you to come back to the Sled and eat something?"

"My thought precisely." Susannah came up behind them and took both their arms.

Ibiá shook his head, but pressed Susannah's hand close to his side.

"Talk to this boy," Danforth told her gruffly. "Tell him some of those sweet things you women are so good at. We're due back in the air in twenty minutes and I want him fed and watered by then."

He disengaged his arm with a crooked smile, and swung uphill over the crumbly rock toward the Sled and a cold trail breakfast. He knew now that something remarkable was about to happen. He was glad he'd be there to witness it, even if it turned his understanding of the universe inside out and backward.

87

THE PINK-AND-WHITE DESERT slid past tediously. Danforth flew for a long stretch, surrendered the stick to Susannah for several hours, then resumed the seat when at last the smooth arc of the southwestern horizon broke into a jagged line. The sky shuddered with chasing waves of color, but the cloud veil was thinning, its glowing white tinged with pink.

After a long silence, Danforth cleared his throat over the com, calling up satellite photos on the tiny cockpit monitor. "No cloud at all over the area of the magnetic field."

Stavros leaned in to look. The central darkish area was like a hole punched into the middle of a hot white waste of cloud.

"Looks like another distant mountain range from down here, but the radar imaging shows a near perfect two-thousand-kilometer circle of violently upthrust terrain." Danforth jabbed at the screen with an eager finger. "Good place to hide a complex machine, also the best evidence for CRI's suggestion of the ocean as an impact basin. The shock waves from the impact travel through the planet's crust to collide at an exactly opposing point, and presto! Crustal chaos. Stop me if I'm boring you, Ibiá."

"Nolagri means 'Lagri's Fortress,' more literally, Lagri's Rock. Lagri's father built it for her with a giant bolt of lightning." Stavros found the precise roundness of the hole in the cloud uncanny. "Stop *me* if I'm boring *you*."

Danforth grinned. "Good to have you back at speed. Increase resolution, CRI."

The darker circle swelled like a balloon, became a grainy pattern of grays, a hot white arc hugging one hemisphere, a darker shadow line the other.

Danforth traced the white highlight. "Interesting terrain. Nice sharp rise all around from the surrounding plateau, cleanly delineated. From there, the max altitude levels off, but you can see how broken up it is—all those fissures and cracking. Easy prospecting."

"Looks like a giant's sand castle," noted Stavros. "The drip kind, dried in the sun."

"How very scientific," Danforth drawled.

But Stavros was eyeing the borderline between cloud and clear. Instinct said he'd not cross it unawares.

"Clausen's already in there," reported Danforth. "Doing the usual pre-claim survey, by the book. He's got CRI scanning the upland kilometer by kilometer. The terrain is unusual as I said, but so far, there's nothing more to catch the eye."

Stavros frowned. "You want smoke plumes, Tay? The flash of solar collectors? Something you recognize?"

"Easy, man. I'm just looking for a signpost. Take anything I can get."

"I'm all the signpost you need," Stavros returned. "I'll get you there."

It was the one thing he *was* sure of. He unhooked the com from his ear, flung it across his shoulder. A showy, unnecessary gesture. Danforth shrugged and returned his attention to the Sled.

The guar-fire had dulled to embers since his last tumble in the black torrent. But the spark was rekindling. Stavros ground a thumb into the center of a palm. Incredible that he could feel no surface heat. Mortal flesh and bones. No more than that. Idly, he plotted the rise and fall of the guar-fire's flame: always low after a brush with the Power, then rebuilding to a peak at the next encounter, like water collecting inside a lock, or potential energy, agitating for release.

Liphar stirred beside him, asleep against his knee.

My faithful sheepdog. Or, is he really my shepherd?

The young man's unswerving devotion had been flattering when Stavros had a less clear idea of what was expected of him. Now such adoration made him nervous and pressured. He was only relieved that the potential for violent climatic side effects excused him from further attempts at contact using Weng's music.

Terran music. Why not a Sawl, after all? How could an alien comprehend these Sisters? Or was his alienness the determining factor?

The willing stranger? The uninvolved messenger?

The neutral current?

Kav, tell me! Tell me!

But he made his pleas in silence. He was more grateful than he'd ever admit for Danforth's new tolerance and restraint. Though he couldn't keep from pushing at it now and then, testing it like a naughty child, he had no wish to abuse it.

Danforth tapped his knee and pointed to the abandoned com unit. Reluctantly, Stavros slipped it around his ear. Danforth was monitoring Clausen's communications with CRI.

". . . find no detectable center to the field, Mr. Clausen. It appears to be extremely diffuse. Shifting movements within the field itself make accurate mapping difficult."

"Has to be a source somewhere," Clausen snapped. "Keep looking."

The prospector's voice, like raked gravel even at a distance, made Stavros nauseous.

"Surface compositional analysis shows an unusual percentage of lithium oxides."

"Register exact coordinates of all locations at or above standard field percentages and prepare claim forms. I expect it will be a nice long list."

Danforth closed the channel on Clausen's satisfied chuckle, then flew wrapped in his own thoughts for a while. Stavros stayed on the com, sensing in the big man's silence an unvoiced concern.

Finally, Danforth said, "Haven't heard Ronnie on the wire at all."

"Long as he needs her, he'll keep her healthy."

Danforth nodded glumly. "Then I guess she better stay useful."

E.D. 101–1:28

Susannah took her shift at the stick while the sky's pink tinge deepened into amber. When Danforth woke to resume his seat, Nolagri was in clear view. An arc of hot green sky cut into the thinning white cloud in a broad horizon-to-horizon sweep. From the Sled, the sun was still a bright patch of amber burning through the cloud cover, but the looming upland was already stained orange by late afternoon light.

Danforth urged the Sled higher, riding the thermals coiling up from the desert plateau. Rising, they skimmed the first sharp slopes of Nolagri's rubbled flank.

"Hardly any erosion softening at all here," he noted. "Looks like the impact could have happened yesterday."

Stavros watched the edge of green sky speed toward him like the blade of a knife. "Lagri's idea of local climate control," he joked tightly. "No weather at all."

The three Sawls bunched along one windscreen until Danforth made them spread out to disperse their weight. Liphar's awe said he'd never expected to visit the dwelling place of a goddess in his lifetime. He grasped the blue-green bead on his wrist and muttered a luck chant.

At the top of the slope, the air was still, the sky a clear, hard green. Stavros stifled a gasp as the Sled passed out from under the faint remnant of cloud. White heat flared in his palms as suddenly as wildfire. Resisting the impulse to retract inward around the pain, he fought to steady his breathing, determined this time to take control, both of the pain and of the swimming disconnection that accompanied it. He called Liphar, but the young Sawl was wrapped in his chant at the windscreen. A torn and silent wilderness stretched before them, an eruption of raw pink rock, the private strata of the planet's crust sundered and ripped open, entrails of mineral and crystal and stone strewn without ceremony. The low sun etched the rough waste with a web of hard shadow, cracks, fissure lines, the shade sides of vast rift systems whose bottoms were lost in darkness.

The fire in his palms was spreading, pouring into him like magma. "Lifa!"

Liphar started, and was beside him in the space of a breath. Stavros hovered half in, half out of a consciousness far removed from the cockpit of the Sled. Liphar murmured soothingly and slipped back into his cramped spot against the hull, offering again the light anchor of a hand on his knee. Stavros' dizziness ebbed, though the roar of the void rose in the distance and the pain remained.

"Are there taboos about trespassing on sacred ground?" Susannah asked Ghirra.

Ghirra did not seem to understand the concept.

Stavros strove for a semblance of normal speech. "How can we be trespassing when our very existence isn't even recognized?"

Danforth checked Clausen's position. "Heading straight for the center. Two hours away, maybe three. At least he's on the scope now. All the easier for us to tag along."

"No." Stavros massaged his palms fitfully, which did nothing to relieve their exploding heat. "Don't need him anymore."

"Stav, we came out here to try to stop him."

"Can, if we get there first."

"Okay, then." Danforth eyed him. "Where to?"

Stavros pointed off to the right.

Danforth banked the Sled gently. "CRI, let me see the magnetics." An abstracted contour diagram filled the Sled's console display. "Okay, Stav. A slight spike in the graph, off in your direction. Not as high as these others, but . . ." He circled a finger over several contour values, then one nearly at the geographic center. "Here's the one Emil's going for. You sure of your head?"

"Yes."

"Okay. CRI, give me high-res, the terrain ahead."

"Maybe the real hot spots are decoys," ventured Susannah.

Danforth snorted. "For what, against whom? Pictures, CRI."

A grainy black-and-white image replaced the field map: the white, the pockmarked ground; the black, the jagged diagonal slice of a huge sheer-sided canyon.

Gazing into that bottomless black, Stavros heard the far-off whisper of floodwaters.

"Decrease resolution," said Danforth.

The canyon dwindled to a mere side branch among many side branches of a vaster, blacker chasm.

"Again, CRI."

The chasm shrank into a minor offshoot of a stupendous rift that split the ravaged upland in a ragged serpentine grin. Its hundred lesser canyons with their thousand tributaries and subtributaries fanned out to the four points of the compass, writhing through the bedrock like the roots of an ancient tree.

"Well, damn, look at that," said Danforth. "That main crack's got to be six hundred long and a good twelve across."

"And straight down," breathed Susannah.

"Looks like someone pried the rock apart with a goddamn crowbar. Is that where we're headed?"

Dizzy again, Stavros looked away from the screen and nodded.

"Excuse me, Dr. Danforth. You asked to be informed when Mr. Clausen landed."

"Yeah. What's it look like where he is, CRI?"

The image showed a finely shattered terrain shaped by a series of concentric uplifts rising toward a central broken peak.

"Check that out, Ibiá. *That* I'd believe was some giant's castle. Dead center in the magnetic field, I'll bet." Danforth could not hide his enthusiasm. "Oh, he'll love it in there—lots of deep layers nicely exposed. Prospector Heaven."

"The surface presence of lithium oxide is highly indicative of additional subsurface deposits in this area," offered CRI helpfully.

"I should be proud of myself," Danforth said mordantly. "I found this bloody planet for him!"

Clausen's mocking laugh suddenly flooded the cockpit. "A little off the beaten track, aren't you, Taylor?"

Liphar stared at the control panel as if it had grown teeth. Ghirra and Aguidran turned from the windscreen with identical narrow-eyed scowls.

"Well, now we're going to get down to business," the disembodied voice declared. "Start turning the ground a little. CRI, register this site as C-9, priority one."

"Here we go," Danforth muttered.

"Charge A, serial number 57460-U867.46, activated," CRI reported.

The silence in the cockpit held for the length of a heartbeat.

"Man, that sonofabitch doesn't waste time!" growled Danforth.

"He's really going to do it," Susannah murmured. "How powerful are those charges?"

"Make a nice crater out of a small city when tuned to full strength, though the point is to plant them real deep, to shatter the bedrock for the machines to pick through. Standard preliminary procedures, though legally he's supposed to wait until the claim is validated. They rarely do. If the claim is contested, the Courts are more likely to accept a fait accompli . . . it's an old strategy. He probably dropped the charge at the bottom of a likely canyon and kept going."

"Won't work, Clausen," swore Stavros under his breath.

"You listening, Ibiá?" Clausen's voice goaded. "If you were hoping for the hand of god to reach out and snatch me from the sky, forget it. And the honored doctor's weather machines are a fiction as well. There's nothing here, boy. Not a damned thing, living or dead, except all this lovely money lying all over the ground, free for the taking. The richest lithium strike I've ever had the privilege to . . ."

Stavros reached to cut the connection. "If he's so sure there's nothing there, why'd he make a beeline for the center of the field?"

"Hedging his bets," Danforth replied. "If there is something, he'll be killing two birds with one stone."

Susannah leaned in. "CRI, do you have control of that device? Can you disarm it?"

"Under normal circumstances, Dr. James. But Mr. Clausen has . . ."

"He's fenced it," supplied Danforth. "He must have done it ahead of time. Couldn't have managed it through the console on his Sled."

"That means we can't . . ."

Danforth shook his head. "These terminals aren't smart enough to give us access to AI programming. Not much more than a grown-up radio."

"Then we have to close down the com," said Stavros suddenly, slapping at the switches nearest him.

"What? Wait! Hold it!" Danforth swatted his hand away.

"We've got to shut down everything we can!" insisted Stavros. "Go quiet, so he can't follow us!"

"He can home in on our power beam," Danforth objected.

"Not as accurately as the telemetry."

"How the hell do I fly without navigation fixes?"

"By the seat of your pants. You'll still have the cockpit instruments. I'll be your navigation."

"Stav, we've got to keep CRI on-line . . ."

"Taylor, listen to me!"

"It's not the worst idea, Tay," Susannah interjected.

"Dr. Danforth," the computer broke in blandly. "Mr. Clausen asks me to say that it was unsporting of you to cut him off so brusquely."

"Tell him he can go . . ."

Stavros overrode him. "Tell him we're having trouble with the com."

"Trouble? I detect no problem from here, Mr. Ibiá."

"Tell him anyway. Just say to him . . . for Christ's sake, CRI, *lie* to the sonofabitch."

"Mr. Ibiá, you know I cannot." The computer sounded vaguely regretful, as if her inability to produce a deliberate falsehood cast doubt on her claim to full sentience.

"Tay, are you with me?" The agony in Stavros' palms leaked more desperation into his tone than he wanted. He knew Danforth responded negatively to being shoved too hard. "Either we go in as invisibly as we can, or we turn around now. We can't just lead him in there with a big brass band!"

"In where? In where?" Danforth stared back at him. "Jesus! I don't know why I give you the time of day, you crazy motherfucker!"

"Because you *know* I'm right, Tay, by the same instinct that made you pull Weng's music out of the hat!"

Danforth glanced away, chewing his lip. "CRI, what's the detonation time on that charge?"

"One hour, twenty-eight minutes, forty seconds."

"Why so long?" asked Susannah.

"He's probably setting a string of them to go off at once. He's registered that whole central uplift as a primary claim." Danforth consulted his chronometer, his lower lip caught hard between his teeth. "Okay. We run in blackout for an hour and twenty eight. Then we try to listen in quietly, see what goes. I mean, what if he's right about the center of the field being where it's at, Stav?"

"He's not."

"Even so. You want to know, don't you?"

Stavros nodded faintly. "Every ounce of speed you can, Tay."

E.D. 101–3:37

He held Susannah's hand for the entire hour and a quarter that brought them to the center of the rift system. Here, he didn't need the music to draw him into the trance state. He was both inside and outside of it. His senses had gone into overdrive. It was like being in a noisy crowd, with everyone yelling at him at once, a chaotic but irresistible summons. He was exhausted from the effort of staying coherent enough to guide Danforth across the miles of unmarked wilderness, where one twisting canyon looked much the same as a hundred others, winding through the broken rock, slicing deep into the crust.

He floated in a bubble of strange internal pressures. The reality of Susannah's quiet murmur at his side barely held its own against the water-roar of the void. When Danforth spoke, Stavros heard him secondhand, as if through some other mind's apparatus. Liphar's hand on his knee retained the most reality, the light steadying tug of a sea anchor.

"Now that is a major hole in the ground," commented Danforth eventually. He stretched forward to peer over the nose of the Sled. "And it's twelve minutes to detonation."

Stavros pointed into the vast shadows of the rift. "Down."

"You got it." The Sled banked and dropped through the hot late sun like a white-gold stone, dipping below the bright scarred edge of the eastern rim, past smoothly undulating walls of sunlit amber rock toward the realm of unplumbed darkness far below.

Danforth flicked an eye at the altimeter. "One kilometer." Later, as he revved the fans to slow their rate of drop, he said: "Two." The rift hardly narrowed. The western rim remained a distant shade-darkened wall, every crevice a sharp-etched detail in the clear, motionless air.

"And . . . three," Danforth intoned as they sped south, still dropping along the eastern wall. "What the hell are we looking for?" He slowed their descent again as they passed into the shadow of a western peak, then out again. "We go down too far, we'll lose line of sight to the power beam."

"There," said Stavros suddenly.

Five pairs of eyes swung in the direction of his gaze.

A ledge far below, bathed in hard amber light; two, three kilometers wide, enough to build a small town on. The eastern wall of the rift rose up sheer from the ledge for at least a kilometer. Stavros pointed toward the southernmost narrow end.

Aguidran barked in surprise and grabbed her brother's arm.

Black dots broke the bright, smooth rock face, enlarging into perfect round holes as the Sled descended, hundreds, thousands, laid out in even parallel tiers, spaced as neatly as the windows of a skyscraper.

Danforth swore in delighted disbelief. "Now that's something I can relate to! Jeez, maybe there *are* people left!"

"No," said Stavros sadly.

Danforth damped the Sled's forward thrust and steered it closer to the wall to skim the highest level of openings. The holes, so rivetingly precise in curve and placement, dwarfed the Sled, tunneling straight into the rock and darkness. "Look at the size of them! I could fly this thing right in there if I could see where I was going."

"No!" Stavros rasped.

Danforth eyed him, wonder mixing with lingering doubt. "Sure, sure. Okay."

The Sled dropped in a powered glide past tier after tier of circular tunnels, picking up another kilometer in depth before Danforth lifted the nose, extended landing gear and revved the fans a final time to settle the craft on the ledge. He cut fans, engines, and force field, then dropped the wind screens, waiting for the weight of the exterior heat to descend like dirt into the grave. But the dustless air was temperate, almost cool. The surface of the ledge was oddly unreflective, dark and as finely granular as emery paper.

"Well, well, well." Danforth stretched but made no further move.

The three Sawls stared into the amber silence with varying degrees of awe. Aguidran studied the towering wall and its precise pattern of holes, then paced to the rear of the hold to unlatch the cargo hatch, fold it back and drop through onto the mysterious ground. Liphar shifted his attention back to Stavros, who seemed to be listening with every iota of his being.

"It's like . . . like a real city," Susannah murmured. "And look how oddly flat this ledge is, as if someone sanded it smooth."

"Perfect landing site," Danforth commented speculatively. "You could hide one hell of a lot of machinery in there . . . and the people to run them."

"You think someone still lives here?"

"Isn't that what we came all this way to find out?" Danforth snapped his fingers, then cringed at the cascading ricochet of echo. "The charges!" he whispered, and leaned to reconnect the com.

E.D. 101–5:57

Stavros tried to stop him but couldn't manage a simple no. It hadn't occurred to him that the Sled's small force field might be damping his own reception. He'd not thought of his connection to the Sisters' dark plane as having any reality in the physical world. But with the dropping of the shield, he was overwhelmed.

He heard Danforth, then Susannah call his name through a fog of noise, roaring wind and water, their voices fading in and out like a dying radio signal. Only Liphar's steady touch told him up from down as the waters closed around him once again and he began to tumble.

E.D. 101–5:58

Danforth had to know, and only CRI could tell him. He touched the switch.

"Dr. Danforth!"

Susannah imagined she heard relief in the computer's flat voice.

"You were able to repair the malfunction?" It was not quite a lie, but it did employ the language of their attempted deception. "Mr. Clausen has been most concerned."

"About our whereabouts, most likely."

"Make it quick, Tay," Susannah urged.

"The charges, CRI. How many has he laid?"

"Four, Dr. Danforth. Due to detonate in twenty-two seconds."

"Tay, cut her off before he can get a good fix on us. Maybe he'll assume we're still moving."

"CRI can tell him otherwise." But Danforth shut down the connection and all telltale power in the Sled. "Four charges. You want to know the combined megatonnage?"

"No." Susannah stared at the console's time readout. Ghirra moved closer, feeling the tension, not understanding it.

"Susannah, we're hardly going to feel it this far away. What's the point of sitting here blind? We should be on the com."

"If anything bad happens, Stav will know." She was surprised at her conviction.

"I'm reopening the line in another six seconds."

"Tay, I don't think . . ."

"Four, three . . ." His hand hovered over the switch. "One."

In the silence, Stavros gasped once and shuddered. Liphar pressed close, whimpering.

Danforth's hand descended. "CRI? Results?"

Static replied for several seconds. Then, "I am recording surges in the field flux."

"The map, CRI! Update the map!"

The contour map of the magnetic field flashed up on the display, changing the moment it appeared and then again. The numerical values refused to stabilize. The high spike at the geographical center of the field diffused into a neat circle of four hot spots.

Danforth studied the glowing figures pensively. "Just where I'd have planted my charges if I were him."

"The new centers of activity formed almost instantly after ignition of the charges," supplied CRI, "at precisely the four points of detonation. I lack appropriate information with which to attempt an explanation."

The map flickered, mutating again as new data flowed in. The contour shapes shifted amoebalike, drawing up around the four points like a quatrefoil noose. Abruptly, the four points vanished from the graph. The higher values along the upland's perimeter pulled inward.

Ghirra watched intently over Susannah's shoulder. "What does this picture tell?"

"What the . . . !" exclaimed Danforth, riveted to the map. "The field's withdrawing!" The contour lines gained regularity, shrinking into a tightening pattern of concentric circles. "No, wait." The planetologist let out a low whistle. "Well, the true center of symmetry has just declared itself, and guess what, it's right on top of us. Or more precisely . . ."

He glanced up at the strangely smooth east wall and its neat diagram of holes. "Somewhere in there."

"No, oh no oh no . . ." whispered Stavros.

Liphar hunched beside him, no longer calm.

Stavros stared at his palms with an expression of profound loss, then turned shocked and sorrowing eyes on the waiting Sawls, his mouth working as if the words he must say would not come.

Liphar whimpered softly.

"He . . ." Stavros stopped, pressing his forehead disconsolately against the seat back. "No. We."

"What is it, Ibiá?" Danforth rumbled.

"Wait!" Stavros straightened, turning toward the towering rift wall. "You hear that? Lifa, you hear it?"

Alert, confused, Liphar shook his head.

"He *didn't*!" Suddenly he was tearing at the buckles of his flight harness, throwing off the straps, muttering to himself in rapid Sawlish. Liphar backed out of the way in astonishment as Stavros bolted from his seat, shoving past Susannah and Ghirra, to the back of the hold and down through the open cargo hatch. Outside, he collided with Aguidran as he ducked up from beneath the wing. She reached to steady him, but he took it for an attempt at restraint and pulled free of her with a shout of warning. Aguidran backed off as if burned. Stavros twisted aside and broke into an awkward run, favoring his injury. He raced across the ledge, a streak of bright white against the sunlit amber of the rock.

Liphar scrambled out of the Sled and pelted after him across the flat granular ground. Stavros reached the nearest yawning tunnel mouth but swerved past it without hesitation. He ran determinedly along the long line of tunnels, then suddenly, at the eighteenth or twentieth opening, turned in and was swallowed by darkness.

Aguidran called to her brother, her eyes pursuing Stavros, marking his route. Ghirra stood at a loss in the open cockpit. Danforth levered his stiff legs into the space between the front seats.

"Better go after him, eh, Doc? I'll stay here and guard the fort."

"Watch the Sled," Susannah translated.

"Our ride home." Danforth patted the laser gun in his belt.

"Okay, light, food, water . . . and my kit." Susannah retreated into the hold to root among her lashed-down gear. Ghirra hurried to fill the Terran canteens he'd appropriated for himself and his sister.

They helped Danforth out onto the sandpapery ground and set up a quick base camp under the wings. The planetologist accompanied them across the ledge as far as the tunnel mouth. Inside the massive circular opening, the floor turned glossy. Danforth craned his neck at the smooth vault overhead. The hard sun slicing down the sides showed up a delicate pattern of light and shadow, fine parallel grooving like the thread on a screw. He tapped a crutch on the glassy curving floor. A resounding crash of echoes answered him. Every sound was hugely magnified, their careful footsteps, the creak of Aguidran's leathers, the faint clink of the pack hardware. Intimidated, they whispered, and resorted to gesture whenever possible.

Susannah showed Aguidran how to use the search beam she'd brought, and handed Ghirra the spare. The Master Ranger flashed the piercing ray into the velvet darkness above and ahead, nodding approvingly, impatient to proceed. They heard Liphar calling after Stavros, farther in.

"Take notes," said Danforth enviously.

"Pix," Susannah promised.

"Damn, damn, damn these legs!" Danforth gazed longingly down the tunnel. "Well, get going!" He swung around fiercely and stumped back toward the sunlight, chased by a clatter of echoes.

Aguidran was already a hundred paces ahead, her beam searching the long upward curve of the walls. Ghirra called softly for her to wait while he and Susannah hurried to catch up.

E.D. 101–6:14

Running in darkness, Stavros heard Liphar's tremulous cry behind, and slowed to a breathless walk. The tunnel dove into the rock as straight as a ruled line. The curve of its unnaturally smooth surface kept him centered in the huge space like a bearing in a groove. He had no need of light except to ease the imagined terrors of the dark.

Yet he sensed no menace. No presence, nothing but the sound which had come to him out on the ledge: music that was not music, a signal, summoning him as irresistibly as the shriek of a siren. But his palms . . .

He clenched his fists in desperation, beating them against his hips, willing his guar-fire to respond. In the moments after the detonation, a chill had invaded his hands, snuffing their mystical heat as easily as a candle flame. The ache in his shoulder had taken on a crippling fire of its own. He felt weak, dulled in all his senses.

But there was still the sound.

Odd that the others could not hear it. It vibrated in his ears like a true sound, like nothing imaginary. A complex sound, with a simple affect—both high-pitched and low, bell-clear and diffuse, steady as a drone yet intermittent. It evoked images of natural violence: the dry earth tearing, rocks cracking open, tree trunks blasted by lightning, underscored by smaller, gentler tragedies, a fish in mud gasping for air, an orphaned cub digging out of a landslide.

Stavros heard it as a call for help, and followed unquestioningly.

E.D. 101–6:31

Danforth struggled to hoist himself through the cargo hatch by the strength of his arms alone. He was sweating and nauseous by the time he lay facedown on the floor of the hold. He strained awkwardly for his crutches, which he'd managed to kick out of reach. He rolled onto his side and pulled himself along the grating to grab them, then hauled himself upright.

He hung on the crutches, heaving from the effort. Something felt wrong. He ran a head-to-toe mental check, searched around the hold, then peered through the open hatch and swore. The little laser pistol lay on the sandpaper rock beneath the Sled. His desperate acrobatics had knocked it from his belt.

He glanced at the cockpit, his goal, then around at the empty silent ledge slumbering under the vast wall of the rift. He knew he lacked the strength to clamber down, retrieve the gun, and haul himself into the Sled again.

First things first, he decided, and headed forward to the controls. He powered up the com and prepared to call the orbiter. Before he could tap in his code, CRI's voice blared forth, startling him.

"Dr. Danforth! I have been attempting to reply to your signal!"

"Signal? I was just about to . . ." Danforth realized he was whispering. The utter stillness made him jumpy. A canyon this deep should have winds.

"The signal you've been broadcasting since the detonation?"

"No signal from here."

"This must be the communications difficulty Mr. Ibiá mentioned?"

"CRI, you've lost me. Listen, what's the weather doing out there? Did it show any response to the detonations?"

"I will transmit those figures." A run of satellite data blinked onto the cockpit display.

Danforth bent to study it. "No summary observations, CRI?" The computer's response seemed uncharacteristically terse.

"Not at this time, Dr. Danforth. But I would appreciate your input."

He read through the data rapidly, then more carefully. "CRI, is this your machine idea of a joke?"

"No, sir, it is not."

"These figures are accurate?"

"I have checked them over and over, Dr. Danforth."

Danforth squeezed his temples between thumb and forefinger. The familiar northeast-to-southwest diagonal movement had vanished. "CRI, are you asking me to believe that the entire circulation of the planet has actually come to a *standstill*?"

"That is what the data suggests. And heat is rising in the habitable zone."

"In response. Moving from here to there," Danforth muttered. "Heading for equilibrium. Could Ibiá be right about the machines but wrong about the location?" Something was sure going on. If there was some sort of system,

Clausen had likely just destroyed it. Was that the only explanation, or had he been listening to Ibiá too long and too well?

"There are faint signs that a new circulatory pattern is asserting itself. Did you notice the hints of west-to-east zonal movement? The potential pattern is closer, I might point out, to what your original model had projected for this planet."

"Umm." Danforth felt not an ounce of satisfaction. "Are they okay at the Lander?"

"As long as the power link stays up. The Commander has promised to retreat to the Caves if it goes down again."

"I wonder how long even the Caves will be livable."

The full implications settled in. My god, what have we done? No wonder the locals called it Devastation. Danforth slouched into the pilot's seat, stunned. "You said something about a signal?"

"I am picking up an omnidirectional, broadband transmission from the area of your coordinates."

He sat up. "You are? Take a clear fix, CRI. Is it exactly my coordinates?"

"A little to the east, perhaps three kilometers."

"CRI, I'm at the bottom of a canyon. Three klicks east of here is solid rock." He caught himself staring at the black tunnel openings. "Wait. What kind of signal is it? Steady? Pulsed?"

"Fluctuating is a better description, both in power and frequency."

"Any pattern to it?"

"I am checking for code, of course. But if I may venture an opinion, the nature of the fluctuations are reminiscent of the Commander's music. Which is why I assumed your party to be the source."

Danforth tasted a wild surge of hope, the sort he recalled from childhood reading, just when you were sure that the hero had had it. He swallowed. "Play it for me."

"Yes, Dr. Danforth."

A low wail floated from the console, with a background growl like the rattle of pebbles in an undertow. The wail rose and shattered into squeaks and cracking groans, like rent wood. The growl escalated into the choked roar of falling rock. Danforth's shoulders hunched. Warily, he eyed the four-kilometer stone rampart between himself and the safety of open sky. He sank into the padded chair, resisting an impulse he could not make good on anyway, to leap up and rush off into the tunnels as Ibiá had done.

Right after the charges blew, as if . . .

"CRI, you're positive this is an artificially generated signal?"

"Without doubt, Dr. Danforth. There is a long pattern of repeating with slight changes, not unlike thematic variations in musical composition."

What would be Ibiá's response to this information? His own was no longer adequate. Danforth was glad to have thought of using Weng's music, but it had been a random reach, not a choice based in a consistent pattern of thought. He lacked a structure with which to interpret events that refused to be governed by standard logic.

So he'd stand by his instinct. It was preferable to doing nothing. "I suggest you try to answer it, CRI. Meanwhile, there seems to be a tunnel complex down here. They may be too deep for your instruments to read, but try for a density mapping. Let's see if we can get some idea of how extensive they are . . . and where they go."

88

E.D. 101–6:25

AGUIDRAN SET A STIFF PACE as they proceeded single file into the dark. Susannah followed closely, Ghirra taking up the rear. The travel was easy. The air in the tunnel was stale but comfortable. The curved floor was unobstructed, glassy smooth but not slick. No turns or branching corridors forced them to make a choice.

Fear was a distraction at first. Expecting sudden surprises, Susannah listened too hard to the echoes, watched the blackness too intently, until her eyes created their own dancing phantoms in response to the strain.

As they penetrated deeper, finding nothing and no one, she relaxed enough to let other worries surface. If there was nothing at all in the tunnels, nothing but the unyielding darkness and cool musty air, Stavros' quest would end in failure. What then? Would they be forced to bring home to Dul Elesi proof that the goddesses did not exist?

Keeping the etched star maps of the Sky Hall in mind, Susannah took stock more carefully. Aguidran's searchbeam slid up and down the curving wall, illuminating the amber beauty of the rock. It glowed warmly even in the stark LED light.

Agate? Susannah wondered what other stone could produce this striated translucence, so reminiscent of gem-quality tortoiseshell. The deeper in they went, the thicker the translucent layer became. The lamplight was caught and diffracted, softening as it passed through the surface layers. A mild glow pervaded the floor around the focus of the beam and crept up the curve of the walls. As the lucid material thickened, it developed undulations, gentle distortions. The precise arc of the tunnel relaxed into an oval.

The patter of their footsteps sharpened abruptly. Aguidran stopped, listening into the darkness. She flashed the lamp around, tracing the arc of the walls. The floor had flattened. The tunnel was widening. She aimed the lamp straight up, but the ceiling was no longer within range of the beam. She moved forward cautiously. After a few hundred paces, the beam of light sliding along the wall met a sharp edge, and then darkness. Aguidran halted, and glanced back at her brother.

"We should go straight." whispered Susannah. "Isn't that what he'd do? He should be tiring by now. I haven't heard Liphar calling for a while. Maybe he's found him."

Ghirra frowned into the darkness, sniffing the still air. He motioned his sister onward. Aguidran focused the beam a short pace ahead, wary of the floor dropping away as suddenly as the walls had done. But it did not. The hard lamplight diffused through its amber clarity like honey flowing through denser molasses. Susannah thought of black-and-amber ice. She stooped and found the floor warm to the touch. It did not feel like rock.

"Ghirra. Feel this."

The Master Healer crouched, put his palm to the floor. The lamp proceeded ahead with Aguidran, leaving them in increasing darkness. But the floor continued to glow faintly. Ghirra called to his sister, but Susannah laid a hand on his arm.

"Ask her to turn it off."

Puzzled, he complied.

Aguidran muttered, but snapped off the beam. Profound night closed in.

"Wait. Let your eyes adjust."

Susannah heard Ghirra's soft exclamation before she could make out his silhouette against the weak but steady luminescence. A giant cavern ghosted into view.

A golden glow surrounded them. The floor undulated away from the flat central axis which they'd been following like a path. Several hundred meters in either direction, it rose into curving walls of lucent gold and apricot and saffron chased with madder and umber like wisps of cloud in sunset. Sturdy ribs of opaque material punctuated the glow with receding parentheses of darkness. Walls and ribs curled up seamlessly to meet high above.

"Oh, how lovely!" Susannah exclaimed.

Aguidran's leathers creaked as she came back to join them. Ghirra ticked a fingernail against the smooth floor with a pensive grunt.

"Let's have the light again." Susannah swung her pack down, unlacing a side pocket. She dug out a small field knife and pried open a blade to pick experimentally at the floor while Aguidran held the light. The point left whitish scars, more easily than Susannah had expected. She flattened the edge against the floor and drew it carefully toward her. Several shreds of pale material spiraled up before the blade. She gathered them carefully into a plastic sample bag.

"Ghirra, this is weird, but if you put this stuff in my hand and asked me what it was, I'd say something organic."

Patiently, Ghirra awaited clarification. Aguidran doused the beam again and hunkered down to scrutinize the cavern more thoroughly, and with a trace of awe.

"Keratins." Susannah was whispering again, as if the cavern itself might be listening. "Fibrous proteins, like the material of our fingernails or our hair. On Earth, we have many herbivores with keratin-based growths called horns. Their feet are also protected by thick pads of keratin called hooves. But mostly, horn is more opaque than this. This is more like tortoiseshell. The point is, it takes something living to produce it."

"But the light . . . ?"

"Bioluminescence," she replied impulsively, "like your fish in the deep-caves. It's a guess. Only a guess." She held the sample bag up to the cavern's glow, consciously stemming the rush to conclusions, forcing herself to maintain objective calm. "We'll know when I power up the analyzer. There could be rocks this pliant, I guess, but . . ."

"Living? All this big cave?" Ghirra let out a breath and looked around, absorbing the idea. "Ibi must hear this!"

He stood, shouting Stavros' name once into the silence. The echoes multiplied his call into a phrase of urgent summons and carried it inward.

E.D. 101–6:58

Stavros hurried through the building glow, Liphar close on his heels. The siren fugue rose and fell in his ears, more gently now, as if calmed by his steady approach. But he'd been pushing too hard. His shoulder screamed at every step, each breath was an agony. He wavered and stumbled, staggering like a drunkard until Liphar grabbed at him, to keep him upright.

Ghirra's shout chased after them, mixing with the clattering echoes of their own passage. Liphar slowed, but Stavros urged him onward. If he stopped, he might not be able to start again. He was not avoiding the others. They'd catch up on their own.

Ahead, the tunnel walls dropped away again. Stavros was well into the sudden space before its enormity penetrated his awareness. It brought him to a slow, astonished halt in a rectangular cavern five times the size of the shuttle bay on an FTL starship.

The floor was cleanly flat, with the same granular surface as the ledge outside. A ribbed vault arched distantly overhead. Walls met and descended at right angles, supporting tier upon tier of narrow railed galleries. Letting his gaze slide upward, Stavros ceased counting after twenty-five. The galleries were linked by spiraling columns of stair and empty cylindrical shafts, cut from a translucent substance reminiscent of the polished agate marbles Stavros had coveted as a child, their swirling clouds of russet, black, and sienna caught in a matrix of topaz and honey.

Pushing aside his pain and exhaustion, he moved into the vast space. Liphar clung to him like a shadow.

The railings were carved from the same lovely substance, their simple but elegantly geometric lines creating an intriguing tension with the mutable quality of the material. There was no surface embellishment, no decorative friezework, no Tales being told in the architecture. The aesthetic of the space was the space itself: its proportions and the beauty of the material it was made from.

Stavros longed to linger, though the music called him still further inward.

"It is like the *duld,* this." Liphar's eyes were huge with awe.

"A dwelling, yes. Your ancestors lived here, Lifa, when the planet could still support life this far south."

Behind the many stories of pierce-work railings stood rows of doorways, modest man-sized openings, small and dark against the luminous walls. Stavros looked back the way he'd come, weighing the issue of proportion vs. function: the giant round tunnel so reminiscent of the underground rail tubes of Earth; the vast glowing courtyard, the ordinary doors.

"I could fly this thing right in . . ." he recalled Danforth saying. He laughed, realizing that he stood in the middle of an ancient parking lot.

E.D. 101–7:14

Danforth jerked awake. What, in the solitude of an empty landscape of sunlight and rock, could have summoned him from his doze so urgently? Had he been dreaming?

The unidentified signal still issued at low volume from the cockpit console, bizarre background music in a surreal landscape. In the displays, a new diagram was forming, CRI's density map of the surrounding hundred kilometers. Danforth stood up, shaking out his stiff legs, stretching his spine. He surveyed the deserted ledge, the vacant green sky, the distant shadowed western rim. Doubt nagged at him.

He shrugged and bent to the screen. The graphic was an awkward one, grainy like a an image expanded past its best resolution. CRI was working at the upper limit of her instruments, within an area smaller than they'd been designed to cover. Still, a picture of sorts was taking shape out of a chaos of individual values: a pattern of dark markings against a lighter ground; the wide black grin of the rift, a hint of hair-fine parallel lines joining many darkish areas of a soft but undeniably regular geometry.

Danforth touched the dark spots wonderingly, traced the fine connecting lines. Empty spaces deep within the rock, tunnels large enough for CRI's imperfect sensors to detect.

"Damn, they're big!"

A slight shudder of the Sled's body alerted him. He straightened away from the screen and turned.

Clausen grinned at him from the rear of the hold, the laser pistol lolling in his open palm. "I'm not sure I approve of the way you leave my property lying around."

McPherson stood diagonally in front of him, within an easy swing of the laser's snub nose. She smiled wanly and shrugged. Danforth thought she looked a little frightened, mostly angry, trying to hide both.

Clausen sauntered forward. "It was good of you to send up the flares, Tay. Does this mean you're coming to your senses?"

He let the gun drift casually toward McPherson as he passed. He leaned against the back of the copilot's chair and jerked his head toward the sounds issuing from the console. "Does Ibiá think he's fooling anyone with this purported signal?"

Danforth regarded him neutrally. "If it's him doing it, he's got CRI well fooled."

"Nothing easier. Take some of Weng's music and doctor it a little." Clausen leaned into the monitor. "And what have we here?"

Danforth searched for a lie the prospector might believe and failed to find one.

"The tunneling goes deep, then." Clausen bent to read the scale indicator. "A hundred meters to the centimeter? Well. Rather impressively extensive. What's your thinking on those darker areas?"

"You read these pictures better than I do, Emil. They're your instruments."

"Tut, Taylor. This sounds like recalcitrance. Ibiá must be catching." He stretched luxuriously, squinting along the wide ledge, then up at the towering wall and its neat rows of holes. "Lovely spot, this must have been once, when the planet was still alive. Where are the others?"

Danforth nodded at the map. "Inside."

"So what do you think's in there?"

"According to you, nothing." The planetologist lifted his broad shoulders in an attempt at elegant disdain.

"Well, it doesn't matter, really." Clausen turned away. "If you're in communication with them, you'd better let them know they have an hour or so to clear out of there."

"I'm not in communication . . ."

"Emil, let me go bring them out," McPherson begged.

"No, my dear, you must stay with our good friend Taylor and convince him to behave." Clausen leveled the laser at the aft fuselage. A quick bright burst melted through the plastic com bubble forward of the tail fin. A thin line of smoke rose out of the charred hole.

"SONOFABITCH!" Danforth snatched for his crutches.

"Tay, no! He'll . . . !"

As McPherson rushed to restrain him, Danforth whirled back to the controls, desperately punching switches. "CRI? CRI? Damn!"

Clausen sucked his teeth, studying the damage regretfully. "All those hours in the broiling sun, gone for naught."

McPherson glowered helplessly. "You're out of your fucking mind!"

"I prefer to think, efficient and unemotional." Clausen flashed a rueful grimace at Danforth's back. "Profitable adherence to the status quo has never been considered a sign of insanity, my dear pilot. I thought we were in agreement on that issue."

"There are limits," she spat.

"Are there?" He went back into the cargo hold and picked up a longish steel cylinder from the floor near the open hatch. It was bound in a canvas sling with a wide strap which he tossed over one shoulder. He patted the cylinder's blunt gleaming head as it nestled beside his thigh.

"Now, Taylor," he continued pleasantly. "You'd best tell me which of these myriad and mysterious entries our colleagues used, or I'll have to choose at random and plant my charge without the chance to warn them that the place is about to blow sky-high."

"You have no goddamn right!" Danforth fumed.

Clausen cocked his bullet head. "Have you seen the local ore count?"

"Yeah, but . . ."

"Then don't waste my time with right or wrong. We're talking wet-dream-level returns here! You'll be able to fund your own damn research, an entire fucking institute! And I can stay home for the rest of my life and tend to my horses! Where are they?"

Danforth told him.

"Excellent. I'm glad you see it my way. With luck, we will all rejoin you soon." Clausen saluted him jauntily, then vaulted to the ground and loped across the ledge toward the caves.

McPherson watched him go. "Anyone in there but our guys?"

Danforth turned away with a furious shrug.

"Tay, I'm sorry. You gotta understand. I coulda put up a bigger fight at first, but I thought if I went with him, I could, you know . . ." She shook her head, defeated. "He won't listen to reason."

Danforth stared at the floor. It wasn't fair to unload his fury on McPherson. He should be glad she was alive. "Where's the other Sled?"

"The next ledge down. He's got the ignition sequence and stabilizer chip in his pocket."

Danforth glanced at the cockpit behind him. "Are they interchangeable?"

"No."

"You could follow him. Sneak the bomb out once he's planted it."

"What would I do with it?"

"Throw it over the edge."

"So it can take us and the Sleds out instead of them?"

"What, then? We can't just goddamn sit here."

"I could try to fix her. Again."

"Before Emil gets back? Good luck."

McPherson shrugged. "Might get the com back at least."

"Be my guest."

Cursing Clausen under her breath, she trudged into the hold. As she bent to rummage for tools, she looked back into Danforth's brooding frown. "Hey. You could keep me company."

E.D. 101–7:23

While Stavros stood in the vast courtyard, reading the ancient history written in its size and shape, his inner music turned up the volume, making clear thought difficult. He gave in, let it lead him down the long axis of the hall to an arch centered in the end wall.

The opening was tall and graceful, without decoration, only a broad casing band of the same opaque material as the ribs, tracing a dark curve against the glowing walls. Drawing on the language of proportion, Stavros deduced a ceremonial intent. It was tall enough to split the first three tiers of galleries, but not much wider than the span of his arms. It did not look casual, yet there was a whiff of engineering whimsy in its exaggerated height, a see-what-I-can-do playfulness.

He urged Liphar through into a corridor of similar proportions that curved to the left in continuous and stately fashion for a full half circle before reversing abruptly to curl off to the right. The unvarying dim glow of the walls was enough to light their way and nothing more. There was nothing there that required brighter illumination.

Taylor would be disappointed. No plant, no machinery. The only sign of tech was the miraculous achievement of the space itself.

When the corridor reversed direction a third time, curling back on itself only to reverse again, Stavros sensed that the purpose of this tunnel, as with the subtle geometry of a formal garden or the meditative turnings of a labyrinth, was the pattern of walking it: the pleasures of smoothly flowing curves contrasted with the frisson of abrupt change of direction. It was like a dance, your partner the architecture itself . . . or its long dead builder, enabled by his creation to reach out through time to lead even a stranger through the steps.

Is it art, he wondered. A sculpture? A game?

Three staccato curves were followed by a long lazy one. The amber glow deepened to burnt orange. Suddenly the corridor straightened and angled sharply right. A ruddier brightness crept along the walls, not a glow from within. Stavros hurried toward the source.

They emerged into another long hall, this one bathed in red amber. It had no visible end, continuing around a distant curve. The left-hand wall was tall and smooth and blank. The right wall slanted to meet it in broad panels of the same lucent agate-colored material, divided by stout vertical ribs.

Light spilled onto the floor like a shower of liquid embers. It had the angle and intensity of late afternoon sun. Approaching one fiery panel, Stavros felt heat radiating from a distance.

Sunlight?

He leaned as close as the heat would allow. The wall had a delicate internal structure not unlike a honeycomb. Its crystalline regularity seemed at odds with the free play of color, light and darkness across and through the surfaces. Stavros thought of practical objects crafted from materials chosen for their integral beauty as well as their function. The ribs were as wide as two hand spans, flowing out of the panel as a thickening and darkening of the material itself. No visible fastenings, no joints. The entire translucent stretch seemed to be a single seamless piece.

Again, the siren fugue refused him the luxury of lingering. It had changed key. A single relentless tone began to override the subtler complexities, maddening, like a bee inside his head. An urge seized him, to race directly to the source, but the hall meandered left and right, confounding his urgency. The heat was also building uncomfortably. Stavros switched on his therm-suit's little battery pack, showing Liphar how to do the same. The young Sawl sighed as the suit's cooling unit returned his body temperature to a more bearable range.

"How much far, Ibi?"

"Won't know till I get there."

Liphar gazed ahead dubiously. "Where live this Sister, ah?"

Stavros smiled. "Did you expect something familiar? Something like Eles-Nol?"

Liphar shrugged, as if he had, but thought he shouldn't say so. He started forward again, to prove his willingness, but his energy was flagging. With no thought for the length of the journey, they'd come without water. Stavros saw that his headlong rush risked running the young man to the ground. He must govern his pace, for Liphar's sake. In a fuzz of pain, weakness, and increasing thirst, dizzied by the insistent buzzing in his head, he trudged determinedly alongside.

And suddenly, Liphar grabbed his sleeve. "Listen! Ibi!"

"You hear it now?" The siren had fused into a single scream, developing a purer directionality, like diffuse light focusing into a beam

Liphar nodded frantically. "This is it, what you follow?"

The quality of the sound changed as it moved outside Stavros' head and into the range of ordinary hearing, steadying into a high-pitched tone. Its machinelike alarm was anticlimactic and mundane compared to the symphonies of desperation that had filled his head since Clausen's charges had blown. But it was real, and that was relief of a sort. Liphar pointed down the twisting corridor, and they both staggered into a run.

Several turns of red-lit corridor later, they pulled to a halt in the same breath.

"We've passed it," panted Stavros.

He retraced the last turn and discovered a small arched opening missed in his haste. He ducked through it into a narrow conical chamber, just large enough for him to stand with his arms extended. Like an agate-colored bell jar, he thought, its smooth, glowing walls swirled with striations of amber and gold and brown. The flat insistent tone surrounded Stavros now as if he was inside it.

He touched one hand to the luminous curve. Fine vibrations sang through his fingertips. The full symphony of sound blossomed again inside his head. He recoiled as if burned. The internal noise died, but the high tone continued. Stavros searched the inner surface of the chamber, his fingers hovering, reluctant to make contact with the singing walls.

"Should be something somewhere, a switch, a speaker, something?" But he found no sign of controls or mechanism. The vibration of the chamber itself was creating the tone, like a giant tuning fork.

Liphar waited outside, mystified. Stavros dragged him in and flattened his palm to the wall. "What do you hear now?"

"Same thing, ah? Very big noise."

"No . . . music?"

Liphar shook his head, backing toward the doorway. "This music is for you, Ibi."

Stavros spread his hands in frustration and denial. He'd found the source of the sound but not its cause or purpose. The guar-fire was still cold in his palms. He had no idea what to do next. Hesitantly, he put his fingers to the wall, to seek a clue from the music only he could hear. Listening to the chorus of creaks and squeals and groans was like balancing on the edge of a windy precipice, surrounded by space and sound. Stavros pondered its similarity to Weng's *Dies Irae*. Had he imposed this likeness, or had it always been there? Casually, he stretched both arms and put his hands to opposite walls.

The alarm ceased.

He jerked his hands away. The alarm started up again. Stavros stared wildly around the glowing chamber as if it were closing in on him. And then, his confusion shifted. The way became self-evident. With a groan, he pushed past Liphar into the red outer corridor and sat down against the wall to gather his courage.

E.D. 101–7:50

They found him several minutes later, his arms folded on bent knees, staring across the wide hallway into the ruddy glow of the slanting panels.

Liphar ran to meet them, his hands fluttering around the canteen on Susannah's belt until she stripped it off and gave it to him. He gulped at it noisily as he trotted alongside.

Ahead of the others, Aguidran halted beside Stavros. When he did not respond, she grunted and moved away, inspecting the inner chamber, nosing around restlessly as if the steady high-pitched hum made it impossible to stand still.

"Have you found anything?" Susannah called excitedly. "This place is amazing, but it does look like everyone left aeons ago. What is that sound?" When Stavros said nothing, she took the canteen back from Liphar and knelt at his side. "Stav?"

He looked up slowly, as if from another universe.

She offered him the canteen. "I mean, it's more than amazing! Do you know, I think it's all made from organic material!" She glanced around restlessly. "What *is* that noise? Sounds like an alarm."

"Organic." Stavros' eyes narrowed as if trying to put the word in a particular context. He did not seem to see the canteen. "Organic?"

"Yes! Yet, if our timetable is correct, it's survived tens of thousands of years without decay, I guess because it's so dry here. Or . . . oh, god, wait a minute." Susannah stopped, glanced at Ghirra. "Oh, no, that can't be."

"What can't?" urged Stavros.

"Or it's still alive."

As quietly as it was uttered, the word reverberated along the passageway.

"Alive?" Ghirra murmured.

"Yes," said Stavros, after a long pause. "Alive." He gazed around the fiery corridor as if seeing it for the first time, then looked up. "Alive. Ah, Ghirra, there is your answer!" He sighed, deep and solemn. "And mine."

He struggled to his feet, drew Susannah into his arms and held her close. When he let her go, he placed her hand in Ghirra's, like a father giving away his favorite child. "As always, Keth-shim, I will need your help."

"Stav, what is this?" The gesture's melodrama made Susannah nervous.

But Ghirra nodded and folded her hand between both his own. Stavros turned away toward the inner chamber and the siren's shrilling, calling Liphar to him.

"Ghirra, what . . . ?" Annoyed, Susannah tried to pull free and found herself gently restrained. She felt ritual closing around her like a velvet blind. "Stav . . . !"

Aguidran followed Stavros to the little archway and once he'd entered, placed herself in front of it protectively. He settled cross-legged on the floor.

Without hesitation, he spread his arms until his palms touched opposite walls.

The alarm fell silent.

Liphar sat down facing him, a hand resting on his knee.

Stavros shuddered once, then closed his eyes and eased into a posture of profound listening.

89

E.D. 101–8:09

"THERE!" MCPHERSON BRUSHED sweat-damp curls from her eyes. "Emil's getting cocky."

"Getting?"

"He didn't mess this up as good as he thought. Go try her."

Danforth stumped back to the cockpit to tap in his call code.

Silence.

He entered it again. The cockpit display began to scroll out a written message.

"All right! You did it! Voice is still out, but we're getting visual!"

The screen read: CHARGE E, SERIAL NUMBER 7582-9583 BO-NL. ACTIVATED.

"Christ," said Danforth.

He tapped in: Can you disable?

The answer came more slowly than it should: NO.

Are you still receiving unidentified signal?
YES.
Are you attempting answer?
YES.
Any response?
NONE.
Time to detonation of Charge E?
88 MINUTES, 29 SECONDS.

"Ronnie!" he yelled. "Keep working!"

E.D. 101–8:13

Flattening his palms to the walls, Stavros opened himself to the music.

Not every priest's Dance will be the same.

The mistake had been to picture himself in Kav Daven's image, dancing with his body, a thing he'd never excelled at. But another sort of Dance was needed now.

He sank into the river of sound, toward the black torrent. He thought once of Susannah, in the heat of ecstasy and passion, then let his resistance slip away—his human clinging to love, to normalcy, to survival—let it all slip away, like a final breath.

Willing.

Some will find their Dance inside themselves.

He felt his outstretched arms like gulls' wings, breaking his fall.

Some will dance without dancing.

He drifted like a feather in evening air. He touched the black river as lightly as a leaf. The waters were still. He dropped through them as inexorably as stone. The cold mud embraced him, became him, he it, as his arms curled upward, outward, inward to embrace the silent water.

Raellil.

Carrier.

Channel? Still he sought the precise translation.

The dark plane was windless, frigid, empty, a moonless night. The black river was a pool of still ink.

Still as death.

Is this it? Is this the end? He sensed finality in the mindscape that stretched vastly before him. But one dim spot of warmth disturbed its icy uniformity, distracting him.

His hand on my knee.

Channel.

Connector?

He remembered sound, and sound returned to him. A background music of wind and soft rain falling, pebbles grinding in surf, a rattle of thunder, and beyond, a drawn-out animal wail of anguish echoing through the darkness, the siren core of the music.

And then—wait! An answer! Faint, unsure, not quite in kind. More like a clever child mimicking an adult.

The siren cried its loneliness unheeding.

He spoke to it: Listen!

It would not, caught in a closed loop of hysteria, reiterating its suffering and horror, endless variations on an unvarying theme.

The answer came again, distant, patient, steady but weak. It was blind, a stranger calling out in fog for guidance through an unfamiliar land.

He'd remembered sound. Now touch returned to him. His outstretched hands bloomed with heat. Into the renewing fire of one palm, he sucked the siren wail. The other palm he opened to the patient far-off stranger.

The Dancer joins hands to complete the circle.

The circuit.

Connector.

Conduit!

His veins flowed heat and light. Wind sang through his bones. Ecstasy blossomed as pure and primal as the seething dance inside a newborn star. Elemental orgasm. Hot. White. Eternal.

Raellil.

E.D. 101–8:16

Danforth's display blinked at him frantically: REPLY! REPLY! REPLY!

"To what?" he shouted, frustrated.

"What?" McPherson yelled from the tail.

He typed: Reply to what?

TO MY ANSWER.

Make sense, CRI.

YOU INSTRUCTED ME TO ANSWER THE SIGNAL. HAVE DETECTED A POSSIBLE RESPONSE.

"Holy shit."

"What?" McPherson demanded again, looking up from her work.

"CRI's getting an answer!" Danforth steadied his fingers: Transmit?

CONTENT OF SIGNAL UNCHANGED. NATURE OF "RESPONSE" IS ABRUPT SWITCHOVER FROM OMNIDIRECTIONAL TRANSMISSION TO TIGHT BEAM. DETECTED AT SAME TIME NEW HIGH-ENERGY SOURCE, SAME LOCUS AS SIGNAL.

McPherson appeared at Danforth's elbow. "What's up?"

He scratched his jaw, indicating the message. He felt foolish, overreactive. "It's a kind of reply, I guess."

"You mean it just zeroed right in on her?"

"So she claims."

"I'd call that a reply, all right."

He stared at the display, pensive. "Are you going to get us voice back?"

"Don't think so. The damn gun was tuned narrow, but what he did hit, he pretty much fried."

"How about power?"

"Don't know yet."

Nodding, Danforth typed: Still analyzing signal for code?

NO DISCERNIBLE PATTERN AT THIS TIME, OTHER THAN WHAT YOU HEARD AS "MUSIC."

Keep trying. And keep answering.

YES, DR. DANFORTH.

The first rush of ecstasy lifted Stavros to the brink of unconsciousness and held him swooning on the crest of the burning wave, refusing him the release of oblivion. His physical sensors, reacting with the clean logic of bodily reflexes, balked at further input and shut down. The energies from without flowed in and through him unabsorbed, unheeded.

Conduit.

Anaesthetized by burnout, a strange floating kind of consciousness returned. He became aware of himself as a process, with a responsibility to monitor. The Dancer sensed an imbalance between the two sources his Dance sought to join. One was not moving in time with the other. The Dance would be awkward. The Dancer would fail. The Connection would not be made.

But it was in his Dance to shape the rhythm.

Conduit.

Transformer?

As his throat was a conduit for words, it also transformed the incoherent air into reasoned sound. The Dancer was plumbing, arteries, organic valves. Drawing this identity into himself, he learned the steps he needed. He stopped down one valve, his white-hot palm, to modulate the flow. The frantic siren eased. Its rhythm steadied. The second valve he opened wide, to suck in the weaker signal and amplify it.

In the glassy-slick void-space inside him, the newly tuned signals passed one another at matched speeds, slid through him and out, each racing to meet the other's source.

E.D. 101–8:21

No one offered Susannah an explanation.

She peered at Stavros across the barrier of Aguidran's arm, as the ranger blocked the narrow doorway of the conical room. Liphar's slight body hid most of him from view. She saw only his white-clad arms, stretched from wall to wall, trembling as if shot through with current, and over the top of Liphar's curls, a dark head thrown back, neck arched as if to the sacrificial blade.

Her impulse was to fling herself against the Master Ranger's restraint, to rescue Stavros from his trance, with drugs, with physical blows, whatever means available. But she recognized his paroxysm of ecstasy and knew what his choice would be, if it was offered him. And it was his choice to make, not hers. She turned away, embarrassed as if by public eroticism, but sensing the totality of his transport and envying him, just a little.

Needing a distraction, she retreated several paces down the hot red-lit corridor and unslung her pack. She dug out her field knife, scraped sample shavings from wall and rib and floor, then unpacked her battery-powered analyzer.

Most of the samples she'd save for CRI's more sophisticated equipment. But she was eager to test her theory about the organic nature of the ancient Sawls' building material. She cut a small darker ringlet from the rib shaving and fed it into the slot.

As she waited, she noted Ghirra regarding her with a sympathetic concern. Susannah glanced away. Lately, she felt that he read her better than she could read him. She bent her head to the analyzer's tiny screen.

The preliminary results made her groan in annoyance. She aborted the analysis, flushed the sample cavity and the sensors, and prepared for a new sample.

Ghirra slipped over to crouch at her side. "You worry over him, Suzhannah?"

She did not look up, hating his patient tone. "Of course! I mean, no, I . . ."

"It is not needed this time, I think."

She'd rather have an explanation than his kindest sympathy. She'd rather she could understand. She'd rather it were Stavros kneeling beside her, awake and not lost in an alien trance. She pulled on a plastic glove with an emphatic snap. "It's just . . . I must have handled this last sample too much."

"You do what with this?" He summoned a dutiful interest, though his real attention was behind them, in the conical room.

"You remember this thing." She pressed the boxy little instrument into his hands. "Tells me what a thing is made of and in what proportions. It's more accurate when programmed for a specific range of material. Right now, I'm doing a general scan."

Ghirra examined the box, though he'd done so before. Susannah got up to take a clean sample from a new location, using a sterilized scalpel blade. She returned to reclaim the analyzer, and fed in a pristine curl of material.

New results began to appear. "Damn!"

Ghirra offered his usual quiet grunt of inquiry.

"Well, look!" Susannah thrust the box at him again, knowing he could not read the symbols on the screen, felt a quick rush of shame, and took it back. Her irritation was not with Ghirra. It was petty to take advantage of his solicitousness by making him a target.

"It's either broken or it's more sensitive to contamination than I thought," she explained resignedly. "It's telling me these samples are organic, as I suspected, but it's also throwing me the signal markers for advanced genetic material." She made a wry face and tossed a gesture of ridicule around the vast red-gold hallway. "Human genetic material, at that. I'll flush it twice this time and try again."

E.D. 101–8:25

Danforth turned his back to the empty tunnel openings out of a lingering childhood superstition about watched pots. He should really be concentrating on an analysis of that reply signal. But at the keypad, he typed: CRI, time to detonation?

78 MINUTES, 4 SECONDS.

He thrummed his fingers. Would Clausen really try to bring them out?

It would be good for the prospector's public image if he did, but Danforth could easily imagine him conveniently losing Ibiá in the rubble: *Heroic rescue of xenobiologist and native companions accompanies tragic loss of* . . . etc, etc.

He worried for Susannah, wondering how much Ibiá really meant to her. He wouldn't bet two cents on the kid's continuing health, as long as Clausen was around and armed. And whose fault was that?

Fucked this one up good, didn't I. . . .

He glanced again at the tunnel entries. They yawned as dark and silent as they had two moments before. He squinted up at the oblate vermilion sun, hovering a hand span above the western rim. A hard black shadow would soon rise out of the canyon depths to swallow ledge, Sled, and all, like Jonah's whale. He shifted his burdened legs restlessly. He wanted to be away from this place by dark-fall.

"Ron? How's it?" He asked only to fill the silence.

Concentrating on her tiny soldering arc, McPherson shook her head mutely.

"Will we be able to fly her?"

She sent a brave grin the length of the cargo hold. "That you or me you're talking about, hotshot?"

"Don't get smart. Anyone."

Her bravado dimmed. "No flying so far."

"Damn."

CRI was blinking at him again when he returned his attention to the display: NEW ENERGY SOURCE DOWNRATED DRASTICALLY 53 SECONDS AGO. NOW WITHIN SIGNAL RANGE. ANALYZING FOR PATTERN. DETECT SHORT REPEAT SEQUENCE ALTERNATING WITH STRINGS OF PRIME NUMBERS, ALSO REPEATING. TRANSMISSION OF "MUSIC" CONTINUING WITH.

Danforth stared. Primes! No more hiding behind the safely rational. Here was a final and convincing link in the evidence chain. Primes surely meant sentience, either past or present. If he denied that, he was merely being stubborn.

He typed: Transmit short repeat.

CRI replied: 01010101010101010101. . . . COMMENCING PRIME SEQUENCE: 2,3,5 . . .

Danforth froze the display. "Ron? You gotta look at this."

He typed: Comment, CRI?

IT IS NOT MUSIC.

"Great. Now we know one thing it isn't."

DUE TO CONTINUOUS UNVARYING REPEAT, AN AUTOMATIC RECYCLING SEQUENCE SEEMS A PROBABLE EXPLANATION.

"A blind loop? For what purpose?"

McPherson clattered up behind him. "What now?"

He pointed at the display. "What do you make of it?"

She studied it, sucking her lip. "A neutral signal and a bunch of primes. So?"

"Neutral," he repeated musingly. "Hadn't thought of it that way."

He typed: neutral signal between identifying prime sequences.

YES. A LOCATOR, PERHAPS.

"Yeah, your basic 'I'm here' signal, without the details," McPherson suggested. "Like our homing beacons."

Danforth repressed an urge to scan the green-and-amber sky. He recalled Clausen's snide remark about repair crews. He gave an inch to his imagination, repressed for so long, and a vision burst behind his eyes like a colored flare: the planet fertile, teeming with life, the airwaves choked with signal, clear green skies busy with big and little traffic. He saw the empty ledge around them bathed in the golden light of dreams, crowded with shining aircraft, lightweight ceramic and spun-glass creations as delicate as the bodies of their Sawl builders, winged with fantasy.

An ache pulsed deep in his chest. He finally recognized it as longing.

They'd held the wind and clouds in their hands. . . .

How could Ibiá be so entranced by the goddess mythos when it was infinitely more wondrous that mere men could make such miracles?

"Tay?"

He was transfixed by his own broad-fingered ebony hands. Never had they seemed so dumb, so powerless. Danforth blinked, shook his head.

McPherson eyed him with concern, then nodded at the screen. "Now CRI's suggesting Emil's bombs might've tripped some kind of alarm reflex."

"Alarm?" Danforth reviewed the recent sequence of events. He pictured the magnetic field map, how the elaborate field contours had collapsed into a single weak focal point right after the detonations, how planetary circulation had ceased soon after.

Was all this actually possible?

His dream-image told him it was, and the tragedy of the loss nearly took his breath away. "He's done it, goddamn his eyes! There *were* machines and he's wrecked them, just like he hoped!"

"Hey, there's gotta be something still working," McPherson soothed. "To broadcast the alarm loop."

"And whatever it is," Danforth raged, "that sonofabitch is gonna blow it to smithereens in sixty-nine minutes, along with a few of our colleagues, and maybe ourselves!"

He pounded his fist against the dash, and then against the rigid plastic binding his thighs. "Damn, damn, damn these legs!"

When the energies within passed each other in equilibrium, hot plasma in a straight-line run, the Dancer could allow himself some further awareness. Not of his physical body or his material surroundings: the Dance must be the only place, the physical only the two points of white heat and the howling space between that was himself, the link.

Yet Identity lurked, with its companions Meaning and Memory, elusive as shadows but nagging, insistent.

He listened to the dual music coursing through him. Something in the weaker signal nudged at his notice, a familiar syllable breaking repeatedly out of a sequence of nonsense.

A memory. Whose? The young man's memory. His.

His.

Could he be himself and be the Dancer still?

Memory prodded. The familiar pricked, echoed in the music. Remember.

Remember another dance. Excited particles leaping within endless microscopic circuitry. A different dance, yet not so different.

Remember. Memory sharpened. The familiar was a knife point in his flesh.

Flesh

and not flesh . . .

CRI.

Memory flooded the opened sluice. The Dancer staggered, stumbled, nearly fell.

CRI.

The weaker stranger-signal became the known. More than tone and pulse and energy. Identity.

CRI!

Rescind the automatic sensor shutdown. Absorb the siren's burning energies. As much ecstasy of matter as the human mind can bear . . .

and still compute.

CRI! Can you hear me?

Reformat those energies, transform them to the impulsive, skittish language of electrons. Sing the tale chant of your Dance. Identity and meaning in the interplay of charge, the dance of positive and negative.

Ah, glorious!

Raellil.

Transformer.

Transmitter!

E.D. 101–8:49

The display blanked abruptly.

"Hey!" McPherson rapped uselessly on the plastic housing. "Shit."

Danforth unclenched his fists, distracted from his fury of self-recrimination. "Huh?"

"She's gone dead!" McPherson scrambled up, heading for the tail.

But Danforth caught her arm. "Not yet. Look."

Together, they stared at the flashing display: YES, MR. IBIÁ?

Danforth typed: Ibiá not here.

WHERE? I AM RECEIVING . . .

The display blanked again.

"What the . . . ?"

"Weird," McPherson agreed.

Danforth typed: What's going on?

No response. The display stared back like a dead eye.

Danforth drummed his fingers fitfully. "Seventy-four minutes. Any luck with the power beam?" He flipped a random switch. The idiot light did not respond. "We're dead in the water."

Then, without preliminaries, the display filled with rapid machine chatter: APOLOGIES, DR. DANFORTH. DIFFICULTY FIXING MR. IBIÁ'S LOCATION RESOLVED. RECEIVING DATA TRANSFER NOW.

"What the hell's she talking about?"

SOURCE OF LOOPED SIGNAL COULD BE INTERPRETED AS COMPUTERLIKE MECHANISM IN RESPONSE FAILURE MODE. "MUSIC" AS YET UNEXPLAINED.

Danforth typed: You're getting all this from Ibiá?

SECONDARY DATA RATE SIGNAL, SAME SOURCE, IDENTIFYING CALL CODE 175IBIA. INTERPRETATION OF DATA IS MINE.

"I don't get it." He typed: What kind of data?

The computer paused, as if pondering the proper descriptive: SENSORY DATA.

Where or what is he sending from?

THAT INFORMATION IS NOT INCLUDED, DR. DANFORTH. The computer made a rare excursion into the gray area of surmise. IT IS AS IF A COMPLEX SET OF NEW SENSORS HAVE BEEN TIED DIRECTLY INTO MY SYSTEM. THE CIRCUMSTANCES ARE SOMEWHAT UNPRECEDENTED.

"I'll say."

IF FAILURE MODE IS THE PROPER INTERPRETATION OF THIS DATA, THE MECHANISM INDICATED MAY YET BE REACTIVATED. I HAVE SUGGESTED THAT MR. IBIÁ SEARCH FOR A RESET INDICATOR.

You mean he's actually found machinery in there?

"He's got to be transmitting from something," put in McPherson.

NO MENTION OF MACHINERY AS SUCH. MY INSTRUMENTS REGISTER NO CONCENTRATION OF REFINED METALS TO INDICATE CENTRALIZED CIRCUITRY MASS. BUT GIVEN NATURE OF SIGNAL, ARTIFICIAL INTELLIGENCE ONLY PLAUSIBLE EXPLANATION.

"Even weirder," McPherson commented.

Danforth typed: You tell Ibiá to get his ass out of there before he gets blown up! And ask him: can he bring this AI with him?

Again, CRI paused. Then: I BELIEVE THE RESPONSE IS NO.

You're not sure?

THE REPLY WAS UNUSUAL. I AM INTERPRETING IT AS LAUGHTER.

E.D. 102–8:51

A third and fourth sample produced the same unlikely results. A prickle of instinct woke along Susannah's spine. She flushed the instrument once again, doggedly, then sat with it in her lap, letting the prickle spread to a full-body tingle.

Ghirra waited with her patiently, casting an occasional glance at his sister guarding the narrow glowing doorway.

As if it were a casual adjustment, Susannah reprogrammed the little analyzer for greater accuracy within a very tight range: if the box claimed the presence of human DNA in the samples, she wanted more specific figures. If contamination was the problem, she would recognize her own genetic signature, even in the rough mapping allowed by an unsophisticated instrument.

She ran the next sample.

A human signature, with its familiar sequences of nucleotides, appeared on the screen, but a detailed reading showed no sign of contamination by her own genetic material. She looked again. It was human, yet subtly altered. Some of the differences she thought she recognized but couldn't place.

She stored the analysis, cleaned the cavity, then searched among her supplies for a disposable syringe. Pressing the thumb of her ungloved hand hard against the tip of her middle finger, she jabbed quickly and cleanly, drawing a few ccs of blood for her next sample run. She fed it into the machine, stuck her bleeding finger into her mouth, and waited.

The DNA signature was clear and complete, indubitably hers.

She found another syringe, then looked up at Ghirra, whose full attention she had finally gathered. She held out her plastic-gloved hand.

He reached instead for the syringe. "I will do this."

Ghirra's blood produced the same basic human signature, as Susannah knew it would. She'd run this comparison of Sawl and Terran genomes with CRI, but at the time had concentrated on the similarities, since likeness was what she'd wanted most to see.

This time she focused on the differences, slight as they were.

That's what's familiar!

She called up the stored figures from the rib sample analysis and displayed them side by side with Ghirra's. Except for the hypervariable regions where genetic structure varies between individuals, the signatures were nearly identical.

Susannah nodded with the slow concentration of an old man at prayer. She turned to the wall beside her, touched it hesitantly.

"Ghirra," she said unsteadily. "I'll know better when I can run more accurate tests and a full protein analysis, but it would appear that, genetically, you are more closely related to this wall than you are to me."

The Dancer felt urgency enter his Dance.

The signal called CRI spoke to him.

As he led her through his steps, chanting his tale for her, she returned him data that helped to focus and identify his purpose.

And data that was problematical.

Memory stirred again, like silt in clear water.

The data showed that destruction was imminent. The signal called CRI advised escape.

But the other, still-steady siren wail. He was bound by its blind insistence.

The signal called CRI named it a loop, offering the opinion that if the loop could be broken, proper functioning might be restored.

The Dancer was meant to create loops, not undo them. But connections sundered may be remade, a larger circle engendered.

Was that not his purpose? To join all in the symmetry of the Dance?

E.D. 101–8:55

Ghirra cocked his head, smiled uncertainly. "This is amusement, Suzhannah?"

"A joke? No. Look at the data. You may not be able to read the words, but you can see the figures are very nearly the same."

He tapped the luminous wall with a delicate knuckle. "But I am not like this."

"Nor is your toenail like your eyes or your bones. They're made of specialized cells, but DNA from each will match."

She ran her eyes up the long slant of the glowing panels across the wide hallway. Her theory was as audacious as this strange ancient construction itself. "I think the material to build these tunnels was grown by your ancestors from their own genetic material."

Ghirra's look was pure bewilderment.

"Maybe it was simply what they had the most of, and the technology was in place. This vast structure needed support and they hadn't the strong metals for it. Perhaps this polar location was once frigid and needed a special insulation. Or perhaps they did it for the sheer beauty of it."

She leaned toward him eagerly. "They cloned the most resilient but workable substance their bodies had to offer. Ghirra, isn't it a marvelous possibility? Bioengineering on the grandest scale imaginable! This is the truly conclusive proof that you are descendants of a grand race of technocrats!"

Her voice rang down the hall, camouflaging the approaching quiet footsteps. But Aguidran sensed movement out of the corner of her eye. She stepped away from the bright doorway of the inner room and bent swiftly for her knife.

Susannah heard her guttural oath and glanced up to see the wall flare and sizzle beside the ranger's head.

Ghirra yelled a warning. Aguidran froze, her hands instinctively spread wide.

"That's right, honored doctor," Clausen drawled, easing around the corner of the hall, laser in hand. "Keep your tiger leashed and we'll all get out of here alive." He advanced on them confidently, gesturing with the laser at the narrow doorway. "What's she got in there?"

Susannah leaped to her feet. Stavros, lost in his trance, was a sitting duck in that tiny room. "There's no lithium here to blow up, Emil."

"On the contrary, my dear Susannah. The place is lousy with it." He stopped in front of her, shoved Ghirra against the wall and directed Aguidran to follow. "Which is what brings me here. I've got a full-strength standard charge detonating in forty-eight minutes, more or less, which just gives us time to retrace our steps and be airborne."

"No, Emil!" She snatched at his arm, not for the laser but to pull at him pleadingly. "Turn it off! Emil, please, look around you! You can't destroy such an incredible artifact! Do you know what these tunnels are made of?"

"I heard." He shook her off tiredly. "But it's too late, Susannah. You can't say I didn't offer. The opportunities for deal making have long since passed."

"But what if it's still *alive?*"

"Don't be ridiculous." He waved brusquely at the analyzer, abandoned on the floor. "You have your samples: proof enough to write your papers. Now I assume you'd prefer to live to write them, so gather up your gear and your companions and be off."

He backed toward the doorway, the laser trained at Aguidran's gut. Ghirra flattened his palm against his sister's chest as she gathered herself to lunge.

"*Raellil . . . !*" she growled.

Ghirra blocked her path, murmuring urgently, his hands pressing her back.

Clausen halted at the doorway. One eyebrow arched in mild surprise. The laser's snub nose sank perceptibly. "Well, I was just going to ask where, but . . ." He glanced back at Susannah. "What the hell is he doing?"

She answered with an honest shrug. "Only Stav knows what he does these days."

Clausen frowned. The spectacle of Stavros made even him uncomfortable. "Get him out of there," he snapped, and moved aside.

The Dancer wove into his tale chant a dream of unison. He sang the glories of the circle. He sought to draw the signal called CRI deeper into the Dance.

But she would not rise and soar with him.

She had her own imperative, her warning: GET OUT GET OUT. *She sent him quantities to express her urgency. Straight-line measurements of time in response to the sinuous leapings of the Dance.*

48 . . . 47 . . . 46 . . .

The Dance was not linear. To the Dancer, Time was meaningless except as rhythm.

His purpose was to join.

To complete the circle.

The circuit.

What goes out must come back.

What goes out must come back.

Susannah prevaricated. "I'm afraid to break him out of it too suddenly. I don't know what it'll do to him."

"It'll keep him alive," Clausen returned tartly. "Forty-six minutes, Susannah."

She slipped into the conical room and knelt on the blood-warm floor at Liphar's side. The young Sawl seemed as oblivious as his charge, his eyes intent on Stavros' upturned face, his hand steady on Stavros' knee. Susannah searched for sense or tone appropriate to this alien ritual, but Liphar spoke first.

"Clauzen," he murmured, so low she leaned in close to hear.

"Yes! He's set another bomb. We have to leave."

He has no idea what a bomb is, she worried, but Liphar heard the tightly reined fear behind her quiet words.

"His Dance is not finish," he whispered.

"We'll die in here if we don't leave now."

"Ibi is talk this angry Sister," Liphar insisted. "Talk now, make life for all Sawl. You go okay. We stay finish this Dance."

"Liphar, you can't make that decision for him."

"Ibi know this already to be Kav."

Susannah's whisper strained to keep back tears. "He's not a Kav, damn it! He's a man, a Terran man and you can't just let him die because . . ."

"He is *raellil*," declared Liphar with fervent pride.

"I don't care!" She reached for Stavros and as he had before, Liphar snatched her hand in an iron grip before it could make contact.

"Forty-five," Clausen intoned from the doorway.

The Dancer was tiring.

Burning through him, the signal energies consumed his own.

Awareness intervened now in flashes, like sun through deep water as the swimmer strokes toward the surface, running out of air.

Awareness of a hand upon his knee.

Awareness and memory. Other sensors reawakening.

He remembered an old man, a Dancer himself.

Songs he remembered, and language. A ritual of burning.

Language.

What goes out must come back.

Language . . .

Identity.

"Liphar! You've got to bring him out of it!" Susannah stared fiercely at the young Sawl, preparing to shake off his restraining hand with all the desperate strength she could muster. Liphar stared back implacably.

"For crissakes, get on with it!" growled Clausen, crowding into the doorway.

Identity!

The swimmer surfaced.

Bright light and air and sound.

CRI! Stavros called through the circuit. Pain seared his palms. A woman and a young man knelt before him in a hot amber room. He knew where he was and remembered where he'd been.

The circuit. He was the Dancer and himself. He could be both. Could both live and Dance.

GET OUT GET OUT GET OUT, sent CRI.

The Dance was not about dying. It was a part of life, had been for all, so long ago. Until the meaning of the connection it forged was forgotten, submerged in ritual, lost to all but a few with an instinct for . . .

Connection. There was no guar. There never had been. The miracle was their fire burning through me. The me willing to believe that a man could speak to a goddess.

Connection. Language.

GET OUT GET OUT GET OUT

No, I must talk to her.

NO USE. SYSTEM IN FAILURE. GET OUT. YOU ARE IN DANGER.

What goes out must return . . .

She must be told of her danger.

GET OUT GET OUT GET OUT

Complete the circuit, CRI. Send the signal back. Send it back, CRI. I am the conduit, CRI. Send it back through me. NOW!

Awareness showed the bullet-headed man swooping down on him, hand outstretched to grapple. But Stavros was the Dancer, and Time only a rhythm that he could move within or without.

Send it, CRI!

I DO NOT UNDERSTAND THE CONTEXT OF THIS REQUEST.

His mind recalled the machine's man-made parameters, and a way that human will, his own, might be imposed on her circuitry. Stavros framed the demand in human numbers while the Dancer sang it into signal, weaving it into the siren pulse as it streamed through him, palm to burning palm, on its way to the source called CRI.

Raellil.

Transmitter.

Translator!

Ah, that was it. At last.

The grappling hand soared timelessly toward his shoulder.

Stavros waited.

GET OUT GET OUT GET OUT

and then . . .

What went out, returned.

The siren signal was answered by its returning self.

The Dance revolved in perfect harmony.

The circuit was complete.

*   *   *

Clausen's fist closed hard on his arm.

In your hands now, Sister-goddess . . .

He was jerked upward to his knees, head flung back, arms flailing, ripped from the living walls as if from a socket.

Liphar screeched and launched himself at the prospector like a demon, then gasped and fell back wheezing as Susannah's arm swung hard against his chest to keep him from the laser's hungry beam.

"OUT!" Clausen roared. "Or I'll drill him and leave him!"

With a vicious wrench, he slammed Stavros against the doorway, then grabbed him up again and flung him out into the hall. Stavros crashed unresisting to the floor and lay still. Susannah wrapped the hysterical, raging Liphar in a desperate bear hug.

At the door, Clausen threw them a look of disgust. "And shut that kid off!" He moved out into the hall, ordering Ghirra and Aguidran toward the crumpled body on the floor. "Get him up!"

The two Sawls heaved Stavros to his feet with effort. He was not quite dead weight, but his knees buckled and his head lolled forward limply. Blood from his fall smeared his mouth and jaw. His lips fluttered soundlessly.

"Move!" said Clausen.

Susannah wrestled Liphar past the prospector and his ready laser, then released him. They rushed to help with Stavros. Sticky red seeped from beneath the open collar of his therm-suit

"The wound's opened up. At least give me a chance to look at him."

"Later," snapped Clausen. "He'll survive."

Aguidran hooked Stavros' left arm behind her back as gently as she could. From the other side, Ghirra grasped him firmly around the waist. Liphar hovered, patting at Stavros with helpless hands and weeping.

Stavros began to mutter faint incoherence.

As Aguidran and her brother started down the hall, the ranger flashed the prospector a look of hatred that washed past Susannah like ice water. She stepped hastily aside to gather up her pack and equipment. If Clausen had robbed them of the chance to know if there had ever been machines within this strange complex, she was determined not to lose her samples.

Catching up to her, Clausen complained, "You might show a little gratitude. I'm saving their goddamn miserable lives!"

"Oh, we're so grateful, Emil," Susannah hissed.

"My dear Susannah." He traced the profile of the slanting glowing walls with the laser's stubby nose. "When you're away from here and home again, all this will seem like a silly dream. You'll wonder what you got so worked up about."

Susannah stared at him with dull incredulity, then moved ahead to comfort Liphar as he stumbled along behind his battered, muttering kav, sobbing uncontrollably.

E.D. 101–9:06

Danforth watched the displays like an unfolding drama. The only difference was that it was his life at stake, not some holo actor's.

RELAYING ALARM SIGNAL BACK TO SOURCE ON MR. IBIÁ'S ORDER. McPherson chewed the tip of a thumbnail. "I've heard of that done in First Contact procedures, you know? When nothing else is working."

Is that what this is? Danforth wondered. Are we talking about machines or the minds behind them?

THE ALARM HAS CEASED.

Hurriedly, he typed: Clarify.

ALARM LOOP CEASED TRANSMISSION FORTY SECONDS AGO. MR. IBIÁ HAS CEASED TRANSMISSION. SILENCE ON ALL FREQUENCIES BUT OUR OWN.

This did not sound like positive news. Danforth caught himself listening to the vast rock-lined hush of the rift, musing that silence too is a relative quantity, able to become quite suddenly more profound than it was a moment before.

Time to detonation?

42 MINUTES, 21 SECONDS.

90

AT EIGHT MINUTES till detonation, Danforth was thinking about how pissed his wife would be if he actually managed to get himself killed. The sun balanced on the western rim like a fat salmon melon. Hard-edged shadow crawled out of the lower rift and advanced across the ledge. He slid heavily into the pilot's seat.

"Ron, strap in. Might as well be tied down to something when she blows."

"Wait! Here they come!"

Danforth stared across the ledge. The gaunt Master Ranger and her brother struggled out of the tunnels supporting Ibiá between them. Danforth saw blood on his therm-suit. Another gun battle, he figured, which Ibiá naturally lost.

Liphar followed close behind with Susannah. Clausen appeared last of all. He paused in the giant opening, unseen by the others, looked upward toward the high perfect arch and touched the nose of his pistol to his brow in a grim, smiling salute.

McPherson dropped through the hatch, intending to relieve the exhausted Sawls of Ibiá's weight. "Come on, we gotta take cover!"

Clausen caught her arm, pulled her away. He flipped her a small bit of metal and plastic. "Bring up A-Sled."

McPherson gripped the ignition sequence. "I might just take off without you."

"Not if you want Taylor alive. You don't hate me that much, McP. Now get on it."

She snarled a wordless curse, then whirled and raced across the ledge. She glanced back once before vanishing down a hidden trail over the edge.

Clausen strode toward the Sled. "On your feet, Tay. I want you down here on the ground where I can see you!"

Danforth did not move. The others dragged Stavros to the Sled and laid him on the ground beside the wing. Ghirra knelt immediately, opening a canteen. Susannah went to the hatch for a blanket to use as a stretcher. Aguidran crouched with her back to Clausen as he shouldered past the whimpering Liphar.

"Taylor, get your ass moving!"

Danforth watched him from the cockpit. Some instinct for rebellion kept him still, and over the prospector's shoulder, he saw Aguidran slide a hand down her leather-wrapped leg to her boot, her eyes steely on Clausen's back. Danforth felt his moment of decision come and go without surprise, understanding that this one had been made weeks ago, as he lay on another wilderness ledge, wet, shivering, every breath an agony, praying for delirium to wrap him in its merciful cocoon, to end the humiliation of having to beg medicine against the pain, of having to suffer his grinning companion's lash of mockery.

He kept himself as still as he could. He forced his eyes not to glide past Clausen to the lithe brown hand grasping the handle of the knife, nor to seek out Susannah, who rustled around beneath the hatch, unawares.

His eyes locked with Clausen's instead, and too late he knew this to be an equal giveaway.

Clausen's blue eyes narrowed. As the blade slipped out of its sheath, he spun, ducking, whipping the laser up and around. Aguidran lunged for him over Stavros' legs. Clausen sighted by instinct as he dropped to one knee and fired, twice.

Aguidran shuddered mid-flight but kept coming, her blood spattering Stavros and the grainy ledge and the white skin of the Sled. She fell to meet Clausen's sidelong dodge. Her strong arm arced and thrust in a fierce underhand jab that caught the prospector in the groin. The eight-inch blade rammed into his gut and he swore in pain and surprise, twisting away from the ranger as she tumbled and collapsed, her momentum spent.

Liphar threw himself down to shield Stavros' bloodstained body, but the laser clattered loose as Clausen staggered against the wing. He slipped to his knees, hands wrapped around the protruding knife hilt, shiny red leaking between his fingers.

Liphar screamed. Danforth struggled out of his seat. Susannah turned, wide-eyed, and ran to Clausen as he struggled to pull the blade himself. Ghirra stumbled to his fallen sister's side, calling for Susannah's help.

"A very deep breath, Emil." Gritting her teeth, Susannah grasped the knife and yanked it free, more roughly than she needed to. Ghirra's pleas for help pulled at her. She pressed Clausen's own hands to his wound. "She got you low. You're lucky this time."

He swore again, his breathing tight, but worked at staunching his bleeding knowledgeably. "I've been gut-cut before. Always hurts like a sonofabitch."

"But you were probably somewhere near a hospital then. Don't move!" Susannah scrambled up and met Danforth on his crutches at the hatch, already holding out her medikit.

"The gun . . ." he reminded her urgently.

Hurrying to Aguidran, she bent and scooped up the little pistol, still lying within Clausen's reach. She tossed it into her kit with a grunt of loathing.

Clausen eyed her darkly. "Don't let this go too long, Doc. We're losing minutes and I'm losing blood."

Susannah ignored him. Aguidran had fallen facedown, arms splayed. Susannah helped Ghirra turn her over. The dark ranger leathers were slick with blood that welled up too fast from tiny double holes in the precise area of her heart. Susannah fumbled for one wrist, Ghirra for the other, their heads bent at the same intent listening angle. Leaning over the side of the open hold, Danforth watched their heads lift, their eyes meet with the knowing that doctors share. He watched them put that knowing immediately aside and go diligently to work to save a life that had already slipped from their grasp.

He remembered the priority of the clock. "Susannah, we've got to scram the minute Ronnie brings up A-Sled!"

Susannah nodded distractedly, helping Ghirra to slice away thin layers of resilient leather, exposing Aguidran's wounds. "Tell Emil to disarm the charge."

"Give me the release code," Danforth called down to the prospector.

Propped against the left wing wheel, Clausen stared up at him, pale and sweating. "You sat there while she pulled a fucking knife on me . . . !" His pain-narrowed eyes flicked away from Danforth's unremorseful gaze. "Jesus, where's McPherson?"

"Let me disarm the charge, Emil."

"Can't. It's a no-interrupt sequence."

"Will it take us out if we're here when it blows?"

Clausen closed his eyes wearily. "I set it at full power."

"So even if we did get out alive, we'd never know what was in there." Danforth shook his head. "You really are unhinged."

He thought he heard the hum of A-Sled approaching. He reset the access ladder and lowered himself and his crutches clumsily through the hatch. He limped over to Clausen. "Can you walk?"

"He'd better not," Susannah warned over her shoulder.

"Let him work on me, then," said Clausen caustically. "Even untrained help is better than none."

"We'll get to you," she snapped.

"Susannah, we've got six minutes . . . !" Danforth protested.

She continued working on Aguidran. "See how Stav is doing."

"Give it up," Clausen rasped. "She was dead when she went down."

Danforth went to check on Stavros.

Still weeping, Liphar hunched on his knees, palming blood from Ibiá's face with bare hands and water from a canteen. Apart from superficial facial cuts and ugly leakage from the shoulder wound, the linguist seemed physically unharmed. But though his hands clenched and unclenched, and his lips moved with apparent purpose, he was completely unresponsive.

Danforth's cast-bound legs preventing him from offering real help. "Liphar, can you get him on his feet?"

Liphar rocked and wept, continuing to bathe Stavros' face even after it was clean.

Four minutes.

Now Danforth heard the whine of A-Sled's fans. Across the ledge, the white craft rose gracefully above the edge and swooped toward them.

Clausen coughed and winced. "Phew. Damn, Susannah, get over here! A doctor's duty is to the living!"

Susannah gathered herself and her medikit. Her eyes begged Ghirra's agreement and understanding. His urgent efforts slowed.

"We won't leave her," Susannah assured him. "We'll bring her to the other Sled as soon as it lands."

He nodded dully.

Susannah cradled his jaw with a palm wet with his twin's blood, then turned away. The gusts from the descending craft whipped loose hair against her tear-streaked cheeks. She dragged her medikit over to Clausen and went to work on a temporary suture.

McPherson landed A-Sled a safe distance away and left the fans cycling. Pelting across the ledge, she pulled up in shock at the sight of bodies and blood spatter. "What happened?" She stared down at Aguidran.

"Later," Danforth ordered. "Get Ibiá over there. We've got three minutes and about zero chance of being airborne in time!"

"Can he stand?" Susannah called.

"Just barely." McPherson got Stavros upright and over to A-Sled. Leaving Danforth and Liphar to struggle him up the ladder, she ran back to help Susannah maneuver Clausen onto the blanket stretcher.

"You don't deserve it, but you're going to make it," Susannah muttered.

He attempted a grin, but McPherson's ungentle handling twisted it into a grimace.

"Killing people's a real habit with you, ain't it," she spat.

"Self-defense," he replied.

Danforth stumped up, breathing hard. "Got him in. All ready here?"

"Ask Taylor. He saw all of it," Clausen insisted. "And I mean, all of it."

"Easy does it." Susannah gathered up her equipment. "The internal bleeding's controlled for now, but you're only stapled together."

Clausen was hauled to A-Sled and hoisted into the hold with Liphar's unwilling assistance. McPherson raced to the cockpit to strap in. "We're out of here in sixty seconds!"

Danforth hovered by the open hatch. Susannah ran back for Ghirra.

He sat unmoving at his sister's side.

"We have to go." She reached to fold Aguidran's arms across her blood-soaked chest.

Ghirra stilled her hands firmly. "You go, Suzhannah."

"Ghirra . . ."

"I will be with my sister."

"COME ON!" yelled McPherson from the Sled.

"Ghirra, don't you understand? This whole place is going to explode!"

"I understand this."

"She wouldn't want that. You can mourn her better by staying alive."

Danforth's imperative shout echoed off the canyon wall.

Susannah tugged on Ghirra's arm.

"My sister dies but Clauzen will live," he observed quietly. "Suzhannah, your friends call for you."

"Ghirra, I'm a doctor! I had to do what I could for him!"

He nodded slowly.

"But you're my friend, too, and I'm not leaving unless you come with me!"

This brought the first hint of pain to his impassive face. His shoulders sagged. He threw his head back in a howl of grief and negation that rose above the whine of the fans like a peal of thunder.

"Twenty seconds, Susannah! Get him the fuck over here!"

Susannah grabbed him then, with the strength of desperation, and hauled him to his feet. She dragged him unresisting half the distance to the Sled until suddenly he jerked away and stumbled back to where Aguidran lay in her darkening blood. Desperate eyes watched from A-Sled.

"For the love of god!" Danforth bellowed. "We can't wait any longer!"

Ghirra was struggling to haul in his sister's body, too heavy in death for him to manage alone. Before Susannah was aware of it, she was rushing to help him.

"Tay, hold tight!" McPherson screamed. "We're outa here!" A-Sled lifted with a burst of wind, the hatch gaping open, the ladder dangling furiously. Danforth clung to the lashings of a crate, yelling unheard protests into the roar of the engines.

Susannah caught up with Ghirra and grabbed Aguidran's legs. "Under here!"

The disabled B-Sled was the only possible shelter from the coming blast. They dragged the body under the belly of the craft. Susannah rammed the hatch shut above their heads. The hum of the escaping A-Sled receded into the green-amber sky above the rift like a fading dream. Aguidran's knife lay beside the thick tread of the wing wheel, Clausen's blood drying on its blade. A mental countdown blared in Susannah's mind. She huddled close to Ghirra and tried to drown out its second-by-second yammer with a memory of Stavros, stretched languidly on the river rock where they'd first made love. She waited.

Seconds after the rift wall was due to erupt and rain destruction on their heads, the ledge shook with a single violent jolt, like a deep shudder of cold or terror. Susannah pressed her face to Ghirra's back, waiting for the ground to crack and yawn beneath them. She sensed him, expecting death, relax to welcome it.

It did not arrive. And still they waited.

Minutes later, the canyon's utter silence was broken by the hum of A-Sled, growing louder as McPherson circled cautiously back. Susannah dared to lift her head as the Sled approached.

She left Ghirra stunned and motionless, and moved out into the open as the returning craft dropped slowly past the four-kilometer rise of amber rock drilled with its neat black holes. The aircraft settled with a more sedate rush and roar than it had departed with. The hatch slid open, and Stavros dropped heavily to the ground. He staggered weakly but recovered his balance. Susannah ran to meet him. His dark hair was matted and damp from Liphar's desperate ministrations. His eyes were sad, but clear. He caught her unsteadily in his arms, leaning into her for support.

"Stav, are you all right . . . ?"

His only response was to hold her closer.

The access ladder clanged into place. Liphar tumbled down and sped past to fling himself down before Aguidran's body.

McPherson followed. "Sorry, Susannah. I had to think of the others." She shrugged defensively and moved on.

Susannah eased out of Stavros' one-armed embrace. His sustained silence unnerved her. "What happened? Why didn't it . . . ?"

"It did. Not as powerful as we expected, but enough to do the work." He let her go, slumped with defeat. "It's over. We failed."

"Failed? You mean . . . ?"

Stavros stared at the ground. Tears glistened in his half-lidded eyes. "I can't hear her anymore, there's nothing on the com, no signal, nothing. It's all gone dead. And my guar-fire's gone." He spread his hands, palm up, his familiar gesture now weighted with tragedy. "He killed her. And I had almost . . . I tried to warn her!" The tears spilled over. "Ah, my people!"

McPherson and Liphar passed with Aguidran's body in the blanket sling. Ghirra paced numbly behind, the bloodied knife dangling in his hand. Susannah watched him pause beside the hatch as the others lifted his dead sister into the hold. With almost formal deliberation, he raised his arm and wiped the knife blade on the white sleeve of his borrowed therm-suit. He studied the dark, lustrous metal thoughtfully, spat on it, and wiped it again.

Danforth called to him from above. The hatch was clear. The Master Healer pressed the knife blade briefly to his cheek, then slipped it between his belt and the small of his back. His characteristic stoop reclaimed him. For a moment, he seemed to have aged a century. Then he lifted his head, straightened, and started up the ladder.

Intuition struck home. Susannah cried out and struggled against Stavros' suddenly strong and restraining grasp. He wrapped her against him and held her fast. His tears wetting her cheek, he murmured gently, implacably, "No, my love. Not this time."

Danforth limped forward to the cockpit as the Master Healer climbed through the hatch. A fleeting look passed between them, a nod, and Danforth beckoned Liphar and McPherson away from laying out Aguidran on the floor of the hold. McPherson covered the dead ranger with a silver-film tarp and went to join him.

Clausen lay on a blanket at the rear. His chest rose and fell in shallow gasps, but his head was turned, his eyes alert. They widened faintly as the Master Healer approached, but Ghirra's hands were empty and his handsome face serene. Clausen's breath quickened as he felt the healer's cool fingers surround his jaw, but he did not cry out. He stared up at Ghirra warily.

"You have much pain?" Ghirra inquired.

"Hell, no. I feel just great."

The long fingers probed gently. "I can help this pain."

Clausen twisted his head to throw off the Master Healer's touch.

"You must lie quiet, Clauzen." Ghirra's hands worked and soothed. A disbelieving sigh escaped the prospector as numbness seeped through him. Slowly, he relaxed.

"This is better?"

Clausen's eyes were heavy-lidded with relief. "Inspired hands," he murmured.

Ghirra smiled, light seeming to suffuse his brown face from within. He eased one hand away from its healing work and reached behind to draw the knife from his belt.

As the prospector lapsed into sleep, the Master Healer brought the eight-inch blade around and calmly slit his patient's throat.

When Ghirra descended the ladder again, Stavros let Susannah go and did not try to stop her as she snatched up her kit and bolted for the Sled.

She accosted the Master Healer as he stood by the ladder, methodically cleaning the blade of his sister's knife. His white therm-suit looked like a butcher's apron, but his movements were slow and mechanical, his eyes like dark glass. She could see nothing of Ghirra in them, only her own appalled reflection. She pushed by him and scrambled up the ladder.

Blood pooled in the floor grating. Clausen's eyes were closed, his face serene. He'd died quickly and without a struggle.

Danforth waited wrapped in the silence of the cockpit, his arms folded over the tops of his crutches. Beside him, McPherson shared his look of grim relief. Liphar shivered against the padding of a bench. To Susannah's accusing stare, Danforth only shrugged faintly and shook his head.

"We had to!" McPherson blurted. "No other way he'd ever stop hurting people!"

Susannah had no response. How appalling that what they'd done might be defensible in the larger scheme of things, that her doctor's reflex to sew Clausen up had disregarded the future for the sake of present moral self-image. *A doctor saves lives . . .*

In the end, Clausen had lured his executioners into his own Machiavellian universe, where pragmatism ruled and any means could be justified if the end was great enough.

Even Ghirra. Emil would surely approve.

The smartest and ablest. Clausen's still, waxy face, furred with sandy three-day stubble, made Susannah infinitely sad. He'd died for the sake of greed and in the service of a faceless entity that would mourn him briefly if at all. She shook open a silver-film tarp and crouched to spread it over him, touching his cheek in farewell.

When she rose again, she stood for a moment gazing vacantly at the swollen vermilion sun, beginning its descent, huge and clumsy, its belly flattened by the western rim of the rift. Darkness approached with the march of shadow across the flat, granular ground. Four kilometers higher, at ground level, it would still be late afternoon.

Over the Sled's delta wing, she saw Ghirra drift across the ledge to kneel at the edge of the shadow. He settled cross-legged and something flashed dull amber in his hand.

Susannah squinted, then gasped in horror. She'd thought the worst was over, but it was not.

She nearly fell down the ladder, yelling for Stavros, charging across the ledge at a dead run with her medikit banging at her side, screaming now to Ghirra, pleading, begging him to stop.

Unheeding, the Master Healer raised his sister's blade. With a surgeon's precision, he drew its needle point down one wrist and then the other, laying open his veins.

Susannah knocked the knife from his hand. "NO! I WON'T LET YOU!"

She grabbed his blood-slick wrists. Stavros caught up, breathless. He wrapped his good arm around Ghirra's chest as he fought to shake off Susannah's restraint. Even in the fury of his determination, Ghirra could not overcome their equal intention to deny him the death he desired. Stavros wrestled him to the ground while Susannah wrapped his wrists tightly, then knocked him out with a shot of tranquilizer. When he lay limp in Stavros' lap, she immediately began stitching him back together.

Liphar ran up behind, dropping to the ground in shock. Danforth and McPherson gathered in a silent anxious huddle.

Susannah glared up at them, then bent back to her grim work. "You let him do it! You let a man committed to saving lives be the first of his kind in who knows how many centuries to take one intentionally! You let him be Executioner without a thought of what it would do to him!"

Stavros began, "For the sake of the others . . ."

"You used him! You, Stav, who claim to love the Sawls so well!" Susannah bit her lip. A quick brushing at tears left a bloody smudge across her cheek. "You are worse than the goddesses could ever be. They wreaked their havoc without a thought for human life, but you knowingly took a man of saintly brilliance, a healer, and made him a murderer!"

91

E.D. 101–12:00

A-SLED SPED HOMEWARD over the silent desert planet.

"The dead and the living dead," McPherson remarked as she powered the craft for its final departure from the shadowed ledge. "Can't even get damn CRI to talk to me."

"If you can suggest a cause for celebration," returned Danforth, "I'm all ears."

"We made it out. How 'bout that?"

"Some of us did."

Stavros wrapped himself in a fog of failure and self-recrimination. Letting exhaustion be his excuse, he retreated into sleep, under Liphar's fretful eye. He stirred occasionally to eat in a desultory fashion, but only, Susannah thought, to set a positive example for the Master Healer, who would eat or drink nothing at all.

Ghirra sat unmoving beside his sister's silver-wrapped corpse. Susannah kept him under mild sedation as a precaution. She'd done her best to sponge the bloodstains from his therm-suit: Aguidran's, Clausen's, his own. But he passed the long hours staring at his hands, still and heavy in his lap, weighed down less by the bandaging on his wrists than by more ephemeral burdens. He would not speak, would not acknowledge Susannah as she sat vigil with him for long patient hours, offering him endless reasoned arguments for continuing his existence.

"Damn crew of zombies," McPherson complained a day into the return, taking her next turn at the stick. But there was no heart to her complaint. Her tone was disconsolate, and she moved about as sluggishly as Danforth, retiring to the benches to brood or sleep when not active in the cockpit.

Eventually, Susannah left Ghirra's side to catch Danforth as he came off his shift. They shared a cold meal and a subdued discussion about how Clausen's murder should be reported. CRI's silence since the detonation, still unexplained, had saved them from a too-quick decision.

"We can't let Ghirra be made the scapegoat," Susannah insisted.

"Two bodies, two murders," McPherson offered from the pilot's chair. "They had a fight and killed each other. I'd believe it."

Susannah frowned. "One look at his throat and the forensics will know better."

"Can't we just lose him someplace in this godforsaken desert? Say he got blown up by his own charges?"

"That's what he'd do if it was one of us," Danforth declared quietly.

McPherson flew at the upper limit of the Sled's altitude range, seeking the fastest possible straight-line return. The mountain ranges were hard sweeps of serrated shadow. The cracked yellow planet rolled by beneath them, its barren monotony echoed by the dimming, empty sky. They took no rest stops, racing to reach Dul Elesi before darkfall, yet dreading the news they brought with them.

"Stav's talking as if Lagri 'died' in the explosion," Susannah mused. "How will the Sawl myth explain the death of a goddess?"

Danforth capped his canteen with care. "Even if it doesn't, those weather priests will have figured out that something bad has occurred. It'll be getting really unlivable back there right now."

"What are their chances, Tay?"

"Slim to none. Goddess or machine, whatever it was Emil blew up, the climate is reverting to what it 'should' be in the presence of the Coal Sack. Survival for the Sawls is measured now by how long their supplies of food and water hold out. They'll never harvest another crop on this world. They'll never see another rainfall, I doubt even so much as a cloud. It's what Emil intended, no doubt. Even if there were machines, by destroying them, he made sure our only recourse would be to encourage the ConPlex claim, in order to effect an emergency evacuation of the population, which only ConPlex has the resources to carry out."

"Evacuation. What kind of a mind finds that preferable to leaving the place alone?"

The second silver-shrouded bundle drew their simultaneous gaze. It lay at the back of the hold, unattended.

Danforth shrugged. "Maybe if there'd been actual machines, metal and circuitry, something he could recognize, he'd have done different."

Susannah said, "But he wins in the end, anyway."

"Yeah." Danforth sighed. "But at least we don't have him around to gloat."

E.D. 102–16:40

To pass the time, Susannah tried to interest Danforth in her theories about the building of the Nolagri tunnels.

He nosed casually through her data, yawning, depressed, weary from his turn at the controls. "Organic, huh? All of it?"

She was not sure he believed her. Or sure he even cared. She showed him a curl of the hornlike material. "Even the big slanting walls where the sun was shining in."

He grunted politely. "Interesting."

But after several hours of sleep and a few more in the cockpit, sunk deep in a pensive, dusky silence, he called to her suddenly. The edge in his voice and the brief veer and drop of the Sled sent Susannah scurrying forward, scattering the cup of water she had been urging unsuccessfully on Ghirra.

"What? What is it?"

The Sled flew steadily again, but Danforth looked as if he'd been struck by an attack of vertigo. "Wake up Ibiá. Get him up here!"

"Tay, are you . . . ?"

"Just get him up here!"

E.D. 102–20:10

Stavros had no stake in dire emergencies, survival being low on his current priority list. But to please Susannah, he got up and shuffled to the cockpit like an old man routed out of bed in the middle of the night.

"Sit down." Danforth brusquely indicated the copilot's seat. "Tell me again about that Sawl genesis myth, about the king and his daughters."

Stavros blinked at him dully, retreating from his vehemence as if from a blinding light. The Sled began a slow, sickening slide to starboard as Danforth grabbed him.

"No, you don't, Ibiá! This is important!"

Stavros let himself be dragged forward. He settled heavily into the empty chair while Danforth leveled the veering craft. He began the Tale of Origins in chanted Sawlish, then caught himself in confusion when Danforth turned to stare. The memory of his Dance haunted him. He began again in English, stumbling at first but gaining confidence as the two languages merged in his brain and he could sing his translation with the grace and rhythm of the original.

"*Raellil,*" Liphar murmured approvingly, squeezing into his chosen burrow between Stavros and the hull.

Danforth interrupted the recitation mid-sentence. "That's it, right there! There's no other explanation, given the data. It says *three* daughters."

Stavros returned a neutral gaze.

"You see it? The two goddesses, and the third is the Sawls. The two stronger sisters were charged with the *protection* of the weaker middle child." Danforth smacked his lips, warming to his own sudden insight. "But it's not exactly like the story says. The Darkness didn't come afterward, or it did but the king knew it was coming, because he was the old race. He was the ancient Sawls who made the goddess-machines, designed to protect their descendants during the planet's lethal passage through the Coal Sack."

"But we never found any machines," Susannah said.

Danforth shook his head impatiently. "Machine! Not plural. The other would be up north, I'd guess somewhere in the ocean."

Finally he had Stavros' full attention.

"Organic, you said?" he continued. "A Sawl genetic match? Susannah, you were standing right inside it! What the ancients grew from their own flesh and blood were the goddess-machines themselves: actual daughters, actual sisters!"

"Grew machines . . . ?"

"Every creature is a living machine, right? The brain most of all. A clump of biomechanical circuitry. An organic computer. Instead of building their AI, they grew it."

"Oh, yes." Stavros let the vision swell in his mind.

Susannah shuffled the data, and then again. "But why go to all that trouble?"

"Like you said, lack of sufficient mineral resource. It wasn't trouble to them, it's what they did. Our bias says technology begins with metallurgy. But the Sawls' genius was biological."

"And even if they'd had the metals . . ." she pursued. "They needed a machine to last a near eternity without wearing out. They needed a self-repairing, self-replicating organism!" She grinned at him wide-eyed. "What a wonder! Have you figured out a food supply?"

"Fuel, not food," he warned. "This was not a life as we know it. CRI would have felt more akin to it than we, despite its human genetic background. I'm guessing it was solar-powered."

Stavros glanced at him. "Not . . . ?"

"I'm still pondering the lithium connection, but those miles of slanting translucent walls Susannah described sure sound like collectors to me. I'm also guessing that's what the whole rift system was about. Whether the original impact that created it was man-made or not, who knows, but it provided thousands of square kilometers of convenient surface for solar collectors, to feed a gigantic mechano-organism that used magnetism and field mechanics to manipulate the climate and tunneled into the rock like the roots of a tree. The old dwelling area you saw probably housed the builders, the geneticists and the AI experts, the lab techs and maintenance crew." Danforth sat back, arm stretched to the stick as if piloting a racer. "Damn! Can you imagine?"

Susannah could, just barely, and sat for a while in awed silence.

"Lagri, Fire-Sister . . ." Stavros mourned, as the material existence the Sawls claimed for their goddesses moved closer to scientific reality. "I heard her too late."

"But wait," Susannah remembered with a start. "If there were two machines, the other may still be functioning."

Stavros shook his head disconsolately.

Danforth sighed. "I'll give you the rest of my theory: climate has two basic components, heat and moisture. Lagri handled the heat, Valla Ired the moisture. Without Lagri to gather and redistribute the overheating from this now-lethal sun, there won't be any moisture much longer. It'll all be evaporated off by a thirsty atmosphere and then . . ."

Stavros pressed his head against the back of his seat with a soft moan of grief.

"So ConPlex *is* the only chance to save the Sawls." Susannah's shoulders drooped. "Oh, my friends, I'm not sure I can bear the irony."

E.D. 103–8:23

On the second day, coming off her shift, McPherson found Ghirra sitting untended. Susannah had given in to her own exhaustion and collapsed on one of the benches. McPherson heated a package of soup at the portable galley and brought it over to sit with the Master Healer, noisily spooning the thick reconstituted mush into her mouth, less with hunger than with a vain hope of arousing his appetite. The shrouded corpse was a third presence between them. McPherson stared at it for a while, chewing thoughtfully, then gestured with her spoon.

"Look, I'm not much good at this, but . . . well, I gotta say I don't blame you, feeling like you do. She was sure something, your sister, and I learned a lot from her. She even had me thinking if I had to stay here forever, it wouldn't be so bad because, you know, at least I could work with her and be a ranger."

She dropped the spoon into her empty mug, suddenly sad and sober. "Yeah. I guess I admired her most of anyone I ever met."

E.D. 103–9:50

Danforth tried his own hand at psychology. During Susannah's next surrender to sleep, he eased himself to the grated floor at Ghirra's side and leaned against the hull, his bound legs stiff in front of him. He knocked on the hard plastic enveloping his left thigh.

"A real pain in the ass, this is getting to be," he began, then fell silent.

A few minutes later, he tried again: "Maybe it seems like the end to you, Doc, but listen, it's going to get even worse, with the machines gone. I mean, they weren't working right, but at least they were doing something. But now? The folks at home are going to need you."

He listened to Ghirra's feather-light breathing, just audible within the field-damped hush of the cargo hold. He tried another tack.

"It should mean something to you that you were the first to propose climate control and you were right. You're a good scientist. Be proud of that." Danforth paused, eyeing him speculatively, then took a darker route. "Even if this planet is finished. Well, it may be. But you don't have to be. You can come with us. A man of your talents and imagination can't just give up. You've got to pull through this one, Doc. You've got work to do. There's a whole universe out there to discover. If nothing else, you owe it to your sister's memory. She was an explorer. If it had been her in your place, she'd have jumped at the chance.

"So what do you say, Doc? You coming with us? I know of one luxury berth that'll be empty on the trip home . . ."

McPherson called him for his shift. Danforth struggled upright into his crutches, and did not notice the Master Healer's thin shoulders rise and fall in a sigh like a slow sea swell.

Later, when Susannah woke and brought him her usual patient offerings of soup and water, Ghirra had drifted into sleep, slumped against the hull. She laid him down gently and pillowed his head on a blanket, praying that sleep would bring the restorative balm for his grief that all her well-meaning ministrations had failed to.

E.D. 104–22:08

At the end of the third day, nearing the northernmost range of the Grigar, McPherson piloted while the others slept. Night approached. The rugged peaks saw-toothed the horizon, reflecting the bright pink-amber of the set-ting sun in slashes like the brush strokes of a painter in love with light. The sun was a red half-dome squatting in the west. North of the mountains, the sky was deep blue-green and streaked with glowing strands of salmon and orange.

McPherson peered at the colored strands intently. She'd heard Danforth's negative pronouncements. "Clouds?" she muttered aloud. "Nah. Can't be."

But an hour later, she reached behind her seat to the bench where Dan-forth slept and shook him awake. She pointed ahead into the topaz dusk.

The strands had swelled into soft pink-edged billows, spread across the full northern horizon, mounting high into the blue-lavender sky like a final mountain range of cotton wool. Danforth rubbed the sleep from his eyes in disbelief.

"Clouds? Clouds?" He laughed aloud. "Clouds! And look!" His arm shot out to point to the east, where the sky below the cloud range seemed to thicken in a hatch of vertical lines. "It's rain! Ron, it's rain!" His big fist pounded McPherson's shoulder. "I don't get it, not at all, but that is goddamn rain out there!"

"No shit, rain?"

"It's *weather*!"

"All right!"

Their whooping woke Susannah, who woke Liphar, who blinked at the distant dusky mist as if sure he was dreaming.

"*ValEmbriha!*" he breathed, bolting into the hold to wake Stavros, laughing and crying, unable to keep his frantic hands from dancing midair. "*Han khem, Ibi! Han khem!*"

Stavros stumbled forward, staring, half asleep. "What does it mean?"

"It means life, Ibiá," Danforth replied. "I don't understand it, but it means it's not over yet!"

92

THEY FLEW INTO DUL ELESI through a warm lavender dusk.

The clear evening sky was dotted with puffy clouds that wandered the arching violet expanse like pink sheep grazing a meadow. The sheer white cliff caught the sun's last rays as if carved of pure, brilliant gold. The cliff stairs were gilded ascents to purple-shadowed archways. The Lander's tilted nose shone with the same magical light, like the spire of a fairy-tale temple. A golden mist hung low over the fields. Golden rivulets, bright water reflecting the sinking sun, laced the amber contours of the plain.

McPherson skimmed the glinting fields and set the Sled down in the Lander clearing. She cut the power and sat back. As the force field dissolved, the evening eased in to replace stale, machined air with breezes redolent of heat and moisture. The passengers inhaled the damp and earthy fragrances, took in the music of running water, and gazed at each other dumbstruck.

"This is what they mean when they talk about miracles," Susannah whispered, as if the jewel-like landscape might vanish with the quiet opalescent pop of a soap bubble.

"Looks like Valla's been hard at work," Danforth murmured.

Stavros stood up, swaying like a dreamer. High up on the glowing cliff, a Priest Guild relay's call rang out, a clear trill of welcome.

Liphar broke from his wondering daze and answered impulsively, a joyous ululating cry. He raced alongside McPherson to undog the hatch and slide it open. Dancing impatiently while she set the ladder, he found himself facing Aguidran's shrouded corpse and her brother's mild, blank stare. His eager joy faded and he edged back to Stavros' side. From the cliff came the chatter and rumble of a gathering throng as word spread of the Sled's return. Weng and Megan appeared at the mouth of the entry cylinder, smiling.

Danforth went first down the ladder. The clearing was green with a fledgling carpet of plant growth. The tips of his crutches sank into the spongy ground as he swung slowly to meet Weng. He took her welcoming hand, and held it.

"There's been a death, Commander. No . . . two."

Weng's eyes flicked past him, seeking a head count as the others straggled down the ladder.

"Clausen and Aguidran," he supplied.

"Ah," said Weng, unsurprised.

Megan's shoulders heaved, with relief first, Danforth thought, then with sadness. "Such a terrible loss. The guild must be informed. How's Ghirra taking it?"

Danforth's mouth tightened. "Not well. Not well at all."

McPherson struggled up and summoned enough energy for a crisp salute. Weng returned it with sober formality. At the bottom of the ladder, Stavros sank to one knee, Liphar beside him. He grabbed up a handful of earth rich with sprouting vegetation and studied it in confusion.

Danforth said, "We thought . . . we were sure . . ." He spread his arms in amazement. "What's happened here? Do you know?"

"We do." Weng patted his arm, an oddly maternal gesture. "And it was a very close thing indeed, Dr. Danforth. Well done!" She moved past him to stand before the kneeling linguist.

Stavros stared up at her, the thick earth clotting moistly in his palm. "What kind of miracle is this?"

"The miracle of science, Mr. Ibiá. Congratulations. It worked."

"It?"

"You."

Hope surfaced cautiously. Stavros rose, grasping Liphar's shoulder as a crutch. "You mean . . . ?"

Weng smiled. "If you will join us inside, CRI has finally come out of her spell and can explain to you what your instincts already knew."

E.D. 105–19:06

As eager as she was to hear the story, Susannah stayed with Ghirra in the hold, too afraid of what he might do if he woke and found himself alone.

724   Marjorie B. Kellogg

Aguidran's knife was hidden at the bottom of her medikit, along with Clausen's laser pistol, but the cargo hold was rich with potential weapons of self-destruction, even for one who would probably be too weak to move when he did awaken. Susannah would keep him in the Underbelly for treatment, where he could be fed intravenously if needed.

Megan stuck her head through the hatch. "There you are."

"Oh, Meg. A sight for sore eyes." Susannah helped her up the ladder, and hugged her hard.

"How are you?"

"Oh, I'm . . ." Susannah's hands fluttered. "It's been bad, Meg. Very bad."

"I heard." Megan nodded at the nearer bundle of silver-film. "Aguidran?"

"Umm."

Megan bent to lay a respectful palm on the ranger's body. "What a waste."

"Yes." Suddenly, Susannah could not bear any more mourning. "But what's important now is getting Ghirra out of here. Could you hunt up some help, maybe a stretcher?"

Megan nodded but she was gazing at the second shrouded bundle, lying alone at the back amid crates and trash. "Killed each other off, did they?"

Susannah hesitated the merest fraction. She shouldn't have held the others back when they wanted to dump him. "Yes. They did."

"Natural adversaries." Megan sighed, heading for the ladder. "I'll locate a stretcher, but there'll be plenty of help along in a moment—the whole population's on its way down here to welcome him."

"Him?"

Megan grinned at her crookedly. "You know . . . Kav Ibi?"

"But he's not . . ." Susannah could not make herself repeat the syllables.

"Funny how things work out," Megan continued. "The Sawls say the weather changed because Stav talked the Sisters into settling their arguments with gentler games. CRI's story has a somewhat more technical emphasis, but the results are the same: perfect balmy weather for the last three ship's days, with a lovely rain shower every fifteen hours. The vegetation's running riot and the Food Guild's planted a new crop already. The goddesses have remembered their sibling duty." She looked up into Susannah's tired eyes. "Don't try to tell the Priest Guild he's not the answer to all their prayers. I'll . . . um . . . go for that stretcher."

As Megan disappeared down the ladder, Susannah turned to find Ghirra waking. His breathing was fuller and his eyes more focused than they'd been since she ripped his sister's knife from his blood-slick hand. He stared up at the lavender sky and its docile herd of pastel-tinted cloud. His attention drifted toward her, then away again, ranging vaguely across the vistas of bright young green. His lips parted, and he seemed to be trying to move.

Susannah ran for water and brought back a brimming mug. She eased him into a sitting position and cradled his head against her shoulder. She offered the mug as she had nearly every hour for three long days, expecting him to refuse it. Instead he allowed a trickle of water into his mouth and swallowed awkwardly, as if he'd forgotten how. Then he willingly drank all she would allow him.

When she set the mug aside, he shuddered faintly and turned his face into her chest. Susannah folded her arms around him and rocked him gently, while he wept against her like a child.

93

E.D. 105–19:54

THE RANGER HONOR GUARD who came for Aguidran's body helped Susannah settle Ghirra in a cot in a quiet corner of the Underbelly. The weather was temperate, so the force field was down Though it was not yet dark, Weng set out oil lanterns that glowed and flickered in the faint, fragrant evening breeze. Ampiar and Phea arrived, quietly stationing themselves beside their guild master to wait and watch.

Susannah took the senior ranger aside and surrendered Aguidran's knife, as a treasure of the guild and a precious relic of her leadership. He took it sadly but gratefully, and sheathed it quickly in his boot. Susannah was relieved to have it out of her possession. The laser pistol she presented to Weng, who regarded it with distaste as she carried it away to her cubicle.

As the rangers were leaving, Ghirra roused briefly. In a whisper like the dry rustle of leaves, he begged them to delay his sister's funeral until he had strength enough to attend. Though the guild and not the family held precedence in such matters, the honor guard showed the Master Healer great deference and promised to plead his case. This calmed him enough to be persuaded to take a few swallows of soup before retreating again into sleep. Convinced that he'd decided to live after all, Susannah left him with Ampiar in the lavender shadows and went to hear CRI's debriefing.

The landing party gathered around the mini-terminal as if around a dinner table. An oil lamp burned beside the keypad. Megan and Weng stood a bit aside, already privy to the story. Danforth leaned forward eagerly to study the flash of figures across the glowing monitor. McPherson leaned across his back, reading over his shoulder. Stavros sat beside him, frowning but constrained, for the moment the same overly intense young man he'd been a few months earlier. But Liphar, his priestly familiar, the material evidence of his new status, curled against him, sound asleep.

". . . Lagri's alarm loop," CRI was explaining, "was set off by the first series of exploratory charges, but it carried an inbuilt reset signal."

Susannah could not recall CRI referring to the goddesses so familiarly before.

"When Mr. Ibiá's priority program ordered me to relay that signal back to its source, the failure mode was interrupted and the reloading of Lagri's initial programming began automatically. The first thing she did was interpret Mr. Ibiá's warning correctly and absorb the second, larger charge when it detonated."

Intent on the figures, Danforth let out a low whistle. "She ate up the energy from that explosion like it was candy."

"We'd have been photons otherwise," McPherson remarked.

"Through the link established by Mr. Ibiá," CRI continued, "I have been monitoring the reload. This effort required giving over more of my sectors than expected. I apologize and hope I have not inconvenienced anyone by being out of communication for so long. I judged it a first priority, and was careful to maintain all other necessary functions meanwhile."

Danforth shifted impatiently. "Yes, yes, CRI, you're forgiven. Go on."

"It was the re-IPL that brought climate operations back to what they should have been all along," Weng interposed, like a proud war correspondent reporting a victory. "A balanced, nonlethal environment; the life-support system that the ancients had intended for their descendants. They designed in a simple way to stop and restart the system if anything went wrong, which of course, it did, more than once over the millennia. What did not occur to them was that the very idea of the reset might be forgotten."

"Forgotten," Stavros murmured.

"They were human after all," said Megan. "Like us, they could imagine almost anything being lost to the ravages of time, except the memory of their own existence."

"And as the eons passed," Weng continued, "the program degenerated. But the climate worsened so gradually that succeeding generations had nothing but legend to suggest that it had ever been better. Their own technical language became priestly gibberish to them. They lost the knowledge that they'd ever had control over their weather."

"They lost the memory of the Connection," said Stavros. "Though the old man must have understood something of it . . ."

The others turned to him expectantly, but he seemed lost in his own thoughts.

"Connection?" Danforth finally prompted.

"Yes." Stavros shrugged. "I can't tell you how it works, but I know it does."

CRI spoke up briskly. "I can offer some of the facts, Mr. Ibiá. The goddesses were designed to use field manipulation of human sensors, whose biochemistry they shared. Information such as sense perceptions could be digitized and transmitted. Specific parts of a willing human brain could be activated like switches, offering a kind of long-distance awareness of the functioning of the machines, for the purpose of monitoring and maintenance."

"Willing," murmured Stavros, and nodded.

"It is my belief," offered Weng, "that such maintenance personnel were the origin of the Priest Guild. With further study, I'm sure the relevant technical information will be unearthed from the oldest guild records."

"The Toph-leta," said Megan. "Life-gifts, indeed. The story of how a planet's life was being preserved. Those old Sawls did the best they could to keep the memory alive."

Danforth leaned back against McPherson to stretch his legs. "And damned if we don't have Emil to thank for knocking Lagri into failure mode in the first place, so that the re-IPL could be initiated. Otherwise her program would have kept on degenerating, beyond the point of ever being able to reestablish any kind of livable climate."

"No." Stavros spoke as if from the bottom of a well. "The Sisters' struggle has always resumed after a Devastation."

Liphar stirred beside him, rubbing reddened eyes.

Danforth said, "Not this time, I don't think. I'd say Fiix would have been doomed."

"The Sawls, yes," said Weng. "Perhaps the entire population this time. But not Fiix. The Arrah would continue."

"You're saying there's another reset trigger we haven't found yet?"

"The basic philosophy of the system was the balance of contentious opposites—wet and dry, hot and cold—with the assumption that the tension natural to such an arrangement was better suited to living organisms over the very long term than static equilibrium."

"Shit, yeah," McPherson remarked. "Can't have them machines getting bored . . ."

"Over the time span we are dealing with here, Lieutenant," said CRI icily, "boredom is a valid consideration, even for a machine."

"Hey, don't take it personal."

"So all this insane battling was built into the initial program," Danforth guessed.

"The Game, Dr. Danforth." Weng smiled, the Cheshire Cat in all her glory. "The intricacies of play can be as simple as a child's gambling amusement or as complex as a symphony. The Game was meant to provide the needed climatic variation, but more importantly, to offer the Sisters a very long-term reason to live, a meaning for their existence that could be expressed not in ephemerally emotional human terms but in hard numbers that a circuit could process and appreciate. I believe it was this very element of Chance—inserted to keep things lively—that proved nearly fatal."

She paused, looked down. "Interestingly enough, despite the Sisters' remarkable power and complexity, true consciousness does not seem to have been achieved or even intended by their creators. The goddesses are not aware in their play."

Stavros offered a quick murmur of protest.

CRI said, "This is not entirely accurate, Commander."

Weng raised an eyebrow at the terminal. "As you are currently demonstrating, you possess a greater independent consciousness than the constructs in question."

Undaunted, CRI replied, "I would prefer to say that the nature of their awareness is as yet undetermined, and unexplored—except by Mr. Ibiá and myself."

Cheeky. Susannah was amused and intrigued. CRI would be as changed by this as any of them. As Megan had said, funny how things work out.

"I can't believe they weren't aware of trying to massacre each other all the time," announced Megan.

"Newton's Third Law of Motion does not imply consciousness in the reaction," returned Weng stiffly.

"Yeah, but that's opposite and equal," McPherson pointed out. "Somehow things must've gotten out of hand."

"A variability of reaction is inherent in the nature of the organic circuit, I believe," said CRI.

"You would," said McPherson. "Not being organic, I mean . . ."

"As I said, the element of Chance is in the program," Weng pursued. "The pendulum of conflict swung a little too far one time. Is it possible, Mr. Ibiá, that 'chance' is the original meaning of the word 'khem'? One Sister played too hard. The balance slipped, and in order to right it, the other compensated too far in the other direction. The conflict was perforce escalated."

McPherson made a soft exploding noise.

"No longer a game," said Danforth.

"Sounds like world history," Megan commented.

Weng nodded, her good humor restored. "Indeed. If you are willing to see our Terran population as a similarly vast machine, organic in nature . . ."

"And inherently contentious," put in Danforth.

"Unbalanced," added Megan.

"Unaware," said Susannah.

McPherson nudged Stavros across Danforth's back. "Hey, they've got your next reprogramming job all set up!"

The others were glad for a laugh, for a release of the tension that had become habit after so many weeks of crisis. Even Stavros allowed a tolerant smile.

McPherson pushed away from the terminal. "So I guess it's really all over, then. I mean, things are gonna be okay here." She tousled Liphar's curls as if his squad had just scored the winning run. "That's great. That's really great! In fact, that's totally amazing! We can head home any time, then."

Megan glanced up at the darkening tilted belly of the Lander. "We hope."

E.D. 106–1:34

Dusk slipped toward night, the Cluster glowed hugely in the eastern sky, and the Sawls came down from the Caves with torches. Quietly, they filled the clearing. Serpentine double rows of light lined the long curving path to the bottom of the cliff and snaked up the zigzag stair to the entry closest to the Priest Hall. The cliff face glittered with a necklace of tiny fires.

Stavros' attention wandered from the debriefing. Liphar was restless with anticipation. A waiting host of torches flickered in the clearing. Stavros felt their summons like a steady pull. A final threshold remained to be crossed. If he went out into that firelit darkness to accept the Sawls' acclaim, he would be accepting the full measure of Kav Daven's dying wish.

Kav Ibi . . .

He was aware of his silent palms as most are of their beating hearts, as the center of his being. He yearned for their absent mystic fire. He remembered it not as pain, but as Connection. Rubbing his palm with a thumb, he thought: what if the pain comes only as needed? A signal from the goddesses in a time of crisis? Could the guar initiation have arisen first to celebrate the Connection in ritual, but carried on later in compensation, as the meaning and mechanism of the real Connection was lost and forgotten?

Of course he would bow to the old Kav's will, if only to bring this knowledge back, and restore it to common practice. Would he do it well? Would he do it right? Only time would tell. His faith in Kav Daven's choice had improved since the miraculous change in the weather.

But his Dance was, and must be, a different one. Weng's theory gave the Connection to the original Priest Guild alone. Susannah suggested specific genetic modification. The healers' gift, for instance, could be an inherited sensitivity to the goddess-machines, and draw its power from them. Stavros thought his own gift belied such exclusion.

"I listen this singing of the world," Liphar had told him.

All Sawls knew it once. They will all know it again.

This was how he'd explain it to her. He'd be eloquent about the good he would do, translating the Sawls' past and assuring their future, by bringing them a new understanding of themselves and their ancestors, of the nature of the Arrah, and what their real duties must be to the goddesses who made their world habitable. The teaching must be offered slowly, in terms all Sawls could accept, in tale chant and metaphor, by digging in the guild records for lost gems of history, approaching the truth gradually so that it was never imposed, but intuited and absorbed from within, to become an understanding profound enough to survive the next seventy-five centuries.

Stavros was glad he was young. Such teaching was the work of a lifetime.

He glanced at Liphar, whose attention now hardly left him except in sleep. He nodded and the young man smiled beatifically. CRI was replying to questions and cheerfully supplying details like the chief scientist at a press conference. Stavros rose, diffident but firm. He indicated the expectant hush of torches in the clearing.

"Excuse me, Commander, but out of respect, I don't think we should keep them waiting any longer."

E.D. 106–1:46

We? thought Susannah. There's only one of us they're waiting for. His tact was touching, being so new. Already he was learning something of the art of leadership.

Weng agreed that the debriefing could continue at any time, and buttoned up the collar of her spotless uniform. Danforth pleaded exhaustion and asked that his respects be conveyed. McPherson insisted on going, out of respect for Aguidran. Megan put indecision aside and agreed. Susannah elected to remain with Ghirra until she was sure he was out of danger, from his wounds and from himself.

Stavros' smile approved her choice. He ducked into the shadows where the Master Healer slept soundly, to gaze down at him lingeringly. "For the many times you've eased my pain, *Keth-shim,* here I am, unable to do anything in return. Healing is *your* gift . . ."

He turned to Susannah. "And yours. Take care of him, for all of us." He hugged her tightly and was gone, shrugging off his own weariness, striding away with sudden energy. In the clearing, the bright torches came to attention like a dress regiment. The throng murmured in welcome.

Susannah walked Megan to the edge of the clearing. The council of guild masters, reduced by two, waited in a semicircle of torchlight. Ashimmel was resplendent in her embroidered whites, her iron-gray curls stirred by faint breezes. Plump Ti Niamar of the Food Guild stepped forward with her as Stavros approached.

Ashimmel faced Stavros squarely. He returned her stern regard, then took a short step back and bowed his head in respect. The priest's taut mouth quirked, not quite a smile. Her rigid posture eased. She bowed briefly in return and stepped aside to allow Stavros to precede her between the winding torchlit lines of onlookers. Ti Niamar moved in smartly to accompany Weng, and at Liphar's urgings, Megan and McPherson filed along behind.

A chant began high up on the stair and traveled swiftly down to gather every one of five thousand voices in a song of celebration. From the top of the cliff, the priest-horns boomed a joyous rhythm into a night alight with torch fire and, in the east, the burning gleam of a billion stars.

Susannah wandered back into the Underbelly and dropped heavily into the nearest chair. The chanting and torches receded. She watched after the departing throng for a long time, musing in the depths of her chair, feeling it absurd that she wanted to cry now, over this, after the death and destruction she'd just lived through more or less dry-eyed. Yet the placid lamplit darkness of the Underbelly was comforting, and the breezy scents of new plants and damp earth soothed her expectations of sadness yet to come. She tried to recall when she'd first recognized that she would leave this world and Stavros would stay behind.

At the console, Danforth gently cleared his throat. "You okay?"

"I guess." She turned to smile at him wanly, then rose with determined energy and claimed the empty seat beside him. "So what about the specifics on the ecosystem? When the system had unbalanced so far in one direction, as during a Great Destruction, what made it swing back again at all?"

Delight warmed Danforth's ebony face. "You're going to like this one. I think I've found the inbuilt reset Ibiá was talking about. CRI, show off your biochemical model."

Susannah peered at the newly displayed diagram.

"Neat, eh? Here's Valla Ired, here Lagri and in the middle, the Sawls." Danforth traced a structural line. "This is Ibiá's lithium connection."

Susannah pointed. "And that, photosynthesis?"

"You got it. Let me lay it out for you: the creators needed to control water and heat distribution in order to get through the hot time of the passage through the Coal Sack. But the whole planet couldn't be made habitable—they needed some place to put the excess heat.

"So they created an artificial habitable zone more or less at the planet's equator by pulling the heat to one side—the desert—and the water to an opposite position—the ocean—where it could be controlled and distributed as needed. And essentially, they split photosynthesis into two processes, using lithium as a sort of control substance.

"So, Valla Ired from her ocean controls the water distribution. She processes the CO_2 produced within the ecosystem, but lithium affects her uptake of CO_2 by controlling the alkalinity of water. Using sunlight to split LiO into lithium and oxygen, she increases the acidity of her water and can clear the atmosphere of more CO_2. Are you with me so far?"

Susannah's head wagged in wonder. "Ingenious!"

"Lagri also uses sunlight to split LiO, but she counters Valla's moisture disbursement by recombining free lithium with water, to control humidity and produce free hydrogen—some of which the Sawls use for necessary fuel—and energy which fuels her own metabolism. These processes had badly degenerated by the time we got here, but do you begin to see how this cycle acts as a needed population control within a system of very limited resources?"

Susannah nodded. "If the population grows too large, too much CO_2 is produced, which acidifies . . ."

"The ocean. This poisons Valla Ired's metabolism, so her control weakens. Water vapor builds up in the atmosphere due to evaporation, which then poisons Lagri, so breathable oxygen decreases in the atmosphere, and the Sawls die off."

"Then it *is* culling, like I said!" It was not a thing Susannah enjoyed being right about, but there it was. "Culling would keep the species tough and active during their eons of environmental crisis. The sick and the weak go first, plus a kill-off decreases the excess of CO_2 and restores the balance for a while, until the population grows too large again. Is that your reset?"

Danforth nodded. "Or, if in her field manipulations of the climate, Lagri grows too strong, by heating up the system's water she can decrease CO_2 to a point which also weakens Valla. Conversely, if Valla floods Lagri's heat with moisture . . ."

Susannah regarded the diagram musingly. "I only hope they meant it to be a gentler process originally, a gradual shifting of balances to control the ecosystem more subtly."

"When you're considering the long-term survival of an entire race, you might be willing to forgo some concern for the individual," said Danforth. "The real point is, it worked for a long, long while before it got knocked out of whack. With this planet's current astronomical situation, it has no business supporting life at all. It wasn't nice for the generations of Sawls whose population boom brought on a Devastation, but at least there were some of them left to complain about it, and there will be still, when the system moves out of the Coal Sack in another seventy-five thousand years. Without the Sisters, the Sawls would have vanished long, long, ago." He sucked his cheek, considering, then grinned. "Damn, the sheer audacity of it! The utter genius! I'd like to have known those old Sawls!"

Susannah smiled at his outburst. They sat in comfortable silence, each contemplating the profound elegance of the ancients' plan while adding to mental lists of questions yet to be answered.

"By the way," said Danforth finally. "I told the doc he should come with us."

"You did? When?"

"Some point during the return flight. But he was so out of it, he probably won't even remember."

Susannah threw an arm around Danforth's neck and hugged him. She was sure now that she understood why the Master Healer had decided to live. "Oh, Taylor, that was brilliant. I wish I'd thought of it."

"Between us, I think we can convince Weng. He may have a hard time fitting in again here, with all he's learned and been through. I figure we sort of owe him a new lease on life. That is, if he wants to come."

"Oh, I think he will." She leaned against him gratefully. "I think he'll jump at the chance."

Danforth smiled ruefully. "He'll be a great witness for the defense if any of Emil's conspiracy charges ever make it to court."

Susannah sat up abruptly. "What about ConPlex, when they hear about how much lithium is here lying about?"

"We'll deal with that when the time comes."

E.D. 106–4:19

"It's, I mean, he's gone, Commander." McPherson shifted uneasily.

Susannah clicked off her searchbeam. "None of us knows anything about this, Weng, I promise you. He was still there when they took away Aguidran."

Weng folded her arms thoughtfully, gazing at the tall line of torches burning along the dark cliff top. Singing resounded from the cave mouths.

"Spirited him away, they did," said Megan. "For whatever reason."

"Gotta admit, they're saving us a lot of trouble," McPherson offered. "Not having to bring him back in cold storage 'n all."

"Not having to explain certain details . . ." added Megan.

Weng rocked gently on her heels.

"ConPlex is used to losing men in the field," Megan continued, "But it will complicate the invalidation of the claim if there's any whiff of suspicion that it wasn't an accident—especially with all those charges he racked up against us."

Weng sucked in a deep breath of damp-scented night air, then sighed and shook her head. "Why did you even bother to bring him back?"

Susannah and McPherson said nothing, but Megan smiled. The victory was won. She said, "They didn't want your job getting too easy, Commander."

94

E.D. 112–19:46

STAVROS MARIA RAFAEL Ibiá became Kav Ibi a shipweek later before the towering glass cylinders of Eles-Nol.

The vast glowing hall was nearly empty. Most of the population was too busy preparing for the dawn Planting to attend the ceremony, but the Priest Guild had been temporarily excused from those duties and Susannah was there with Megan and the others. Danforth had insisted on negotiating the long spiral stairs for his first viewing of Dul Elesi's major monument to the ancient technology.

They watched Ashimmel robe the new priest in embroidered white as he swore loyalty to his guild. Then he knelt to receive from her scarred hands the silvery lump of guar, the pure lithium mined deep in the rock. His face tightened as the guar dropped into his palms, but he rose and advanced the short, agonizing distance to the central cylinder. As a Priest Guild elder drew open a tiny square panel, Kav Ibi deposited the guar within.

When he returned across the arched wooden bridge, his eyes alight, the Master Healer stepped forward with herbal salve for his burns.

"No miracle to worry you this time, *Keth-shim*." Stavros smiled through the pain in his seared palms. "Emil was right. The old man tricked us. There was no guar at the Leave-taking. Only the Sisters."

Ghirra was gaunt from his mourning, but his long face was calm. His touch was a feather weight, spreading the cooling salve. He remarked with quiet disapproval, "These Sisters do not know you do this for them, Ibi."

"Not for them, Ghirra." Stavros nodded behind him, toward the waiting ranks of the Priest Guild. "For them. And to you, I promise this: though it'll take some time, I will end the guar ritual. For now, it's a necessary metaphor for the connection to the Sisters that every Sawl once had, and will have again someday. Science, *Keth-shim*, to replace the miracle . . ."

Ghirra smiled gravely. "I will tell Xifa this promise, so she will know it when I am gone."

E.D. 119–3:58

When dawn returned, Kav Ibi's first step as Ritual Master was to welcome his own designated apprentice to full membership in the guild. As the guildsmen chanted, the newly elected Master Healer stood ready to ease with her skilled hands the young man's painful passage into priesthood.

But as the guar ate into his willing, virgin palm, Liphar showed little awareness of the pain, or even of Keth-shim Xifa's soothing hands along his neck.

He thought only of his Ritual Master's loving, encouraging touch, and of the solemn privilege that it was to feed the goddesses.

E.D. 130–4:52

Ghirra's leaving had never been part of Stavros' master plan.

He found the Master Healer in his library. A small hinged leather box lay open at his feet. Neat rows of wax-stoppered jars filled half of its space. Stavros leaned against the door frame until Ghirra glanced up inquiringly.

"*Keth-shim,* are you sure this is the right thing to do?"

"Yes, Ibi. I am sure."

His certainty set Stavros at a loss. "But . . . everybody here will . . ."

"Xifa is . . . all that I am."

"No. Ghirra, that's just not . . . I mean, she's an excellent healer, but . . ."

"She will do well."

"It'll be different there, for you."

Ghirra's look said this was beyond obvious.

"I mean, without your . . . gift. Without your connection to the Sisters."

"Suzhannah and I have talked this. She say my gift is within me."

Stavros did not disagree. Even suspecting otherwise, he wouldn't press the matter, for Ghirra's sake. He fidgeted, peering into the open case. "What are you taking?"

"Healing plants which Suzhannah say is not there on your world."

"It's not my . . ." Stavros caught himself on the verge of snapping at the man he least wanted to say good-bye to.

"Also I will take seed from Ard. This will be my true gift to Earth."

Stavros folded his arms, fighting a fit of sullenness. "You're not going to like it there, you know. Remember what I told you: it's always crowded, sickness everywhere, the air's filthy, you can't drink the water, the plants might not even grow. . . ."

"I will like that it is . . . new." Ghirra skimmed the leather-bound spines lining his shelves. He picked out a book, examined it, put it back, then took another down for study.

"Wait, you can't take the old books! They're a treasure of your guild!"

Ghirra stared him down. "I take *one* book, Ibi. Proof, Meghan say. To show the court."

"Meg's been scanning guild records for two weeks! She has all the proof she needs!"

"The real book will do better, she say." The Master Healer bent and placed the volume in a corner of his case. "You do not find this important now?"

Stavros looked away. "Yes, of course I do. I just . . ."

Ghirra searched his books in silence for a moment. He took another down and shook it gently at his visitor. "Okay, I take *two* book. Books. Taylor say I must come to his world also, and talk with sho . . . skol . . . ?"

"Scholars?"

"Yes. Skolar. About these Sisters' weather-control."

"A tour of the known universe. How lucky for you."

"Ibi." Ghirra slid his foot under the lid of his case and flipped it shut. "You are mad with me."

"Angry. Not mad, angry. Yes, I'm angry! I'm pissed! I'm furious! I'm . . ." Stavros slumped against the doorframe, disconsolate. "Ghirra, I can't do this without you."

"The old Kav say you can. So far, he say right." Ghirra eyed him slyly. "Listen, Ibi . . . when I go, maybe I *Phiix* your broken world, like you fix mine."

"Puns? Already?" Grinning despite himself, Stavros turned away, meaning to leave the Master Healer to his packing. But he stopped and came back again. "Ghirra. One more thing."

"Yes?"

"Take care of her for me."

Ghirra looked up, cocked his head. "I think better, Ibi, she will take care of me."

95

E.D. 133–12:26

THEY MADE LOVE a final time. The weeks between had made her leaving harder for them both.

"Did it occur to you to stay?" he asked her.

"Did it occur to you to ask?"

"I did! You don't remember?"

"That was . . . before."

"Yes." Stavros ran smooth-scarred palms along her back, aching for her already.

"Stav, with all we've learned here, we could do so much good back home!"

"Not until good costs less to do than harm."

He was so sure. She envied him that. "I guess I just need to see it for myself."

"Of course you do. My hope is, once you're done rediscovering the universe through Ghirra's eyes, you'll both be back."

Susannah calculated the years and distances involved. Given the data they'd bring back to Earth, a return expedition was very likely. Many of them, in fact. "Perhaps we will. Or perhaps I will. Remember, we have yet to prove we'll be able to leave."

"Weng hasn't seemed too worried."

And Susannah asked herself: if the Lander failed to lift, would she be devastated . . . or relieved to have the choice made for her?

But mere hours later, Kav Ibi stood at the top of the cliff among his guildsmen and others to see the bright fire ignite at the Lander's base. The cliff rock shook as engines idle for four months coughed out dry mud and woke. The tall russet stalks in the surrounding fields bent low in the heat gale. The tilted cone vibrated and lifted, so gradually that every muscle tensed with the effort of urging the silver craft to flight.

The tilt righted. The cone did not fall back in a whiteout of flame. Slowly, stubbornly, it crawled up out of the gravity well, gaining speed until it was a shining bird-speck climbing the hard malachite sky.

And then it was gone.

Stavros fought the urge to cry out after it, after them, his departing colleagues, after her, whom he loved, but not so much as the new life that claimed him.

Liphar touched his arm in concern, and Master Healer Xifa offered a look of gentle sympathy. But as the smoke billows cleared and the roar of engines faded into lonely silence, Kav Ashimmel rubbed her scarred hands together like a busy merchant and started briskly for the stair.

On the top step, she glanced back at Stavros as if to say, "Well, you young upstart? Isn't there work to be done?"